MW00685849

The Mocklore Omnibus

Tansy Rayner Roberts

FableCroft Publishing

This edition published in 2016
by FableCroft Publishing

http://fablecroft.com.au

Cover design by Tania Walker
Design and layout by Tehani Wessely
Typeset in Sabon MT Pro and Handwriting – Dakota

National Library of Australia Cataloguing-in-Publication entry

Author: Roberts, Tansy Rayner, 1978- author.
Title: Splashdance Silver, Liquid Gold / Tansy Rayner Roberts.
ISBN: 9780994469038 (paperback)
9780994469045 (ebook)
Series: Roberts, Tansy Rayner, 1978- Mocklore chronicles ; bk. 1 & 2.
Dewey Number: A823.3

Also by Tansy Rayner Roberts...

The Mocklore Chronicles
Splashdance Silver
Liquid Gold
Ink Black Magic
Bounty

Love and Romanpunk
(2012, Twelfth Planet Press)
Roadkill/Siren Beat
(2009, Twelfth Planet Press
– with Rob Shearman)

The Creature Court trilogy
Power and Majesty
(2010, Harper Voyager)
The Shattered City
(2011, Harper Voyager)
Reign of Beasts
(2012, Harper Voyager)

Splashdance Silver

A Mocklore Book

Tansy Rayner Roberts

*For my beloved physicist, who made
me post the manuscript...
[1998]*

*...and declared it was time to bring
these books back again.
[2013]*

*For my daughters, who are both artists
and superheroes.*

CONTENTS

Chapter 1
With Snow Comes Beginnings

There are only three truly important questions in the universe. The first deals with why the sea is boiling hot and whether pigs have wings. The second is terrifyingly simple, concerning what true love really means, and why nearly true love is so much healthier for all concerned. The third most important question in the universe is about pirates.

In the little Empire of Mocklore, from the troublesome and hairy town of Axgaard to the scholarly and puddlesome Cluft, from the bleak, crime-ridden streets of Dreadnought to the gold-paved avenues of Zibria, from the enigmatic mysteries of the Troll Triangle to the blatant impossibilities of the Skullcaps, every now and again a Pirate of Note is born. No one knows why.

Anyone can be a pirate, of course. The most ordinary of farmboys can buy himself an eyepatch and run away to sea. But a Pirate of Note is always marked in some particular way. They might have a magnificently jutting brow, a surprising beard, or a third eye in the most unexpected of places. For instance, the daughter of Vicious Bigbeard Daggersharp had hair the colour of old blood and a birthmark shaped like a decapitated skeleton.

The third most truly important question in the universe is this: why is it so important that potential Pirates of Note be marked in such a melodramatic way? What would happen, what could happen if such a person ignored such a sign, and chose to avert that destiny? What if a Pirate of Note did not want to be a pirate?

-§-§-§-§-§-

In the Whet and Whistle Tavern and Grillhouse, the music started. It rose and fell and then rose again, just because it could. Then it faltered and went away. Half a dozen clumsily-carved harmonicas were cast aside. She hadn't arrived yet, and no one saw any point in making music until she was there.

Finally, the door scrunched open. They all looked up hopefully, but it was only the Captain of the Dreadnought Blackguards. He stood for a moment in the doorway, dripping melted snow on the floor. The Captain was a hunched man with weary eyes, sagging shoulders and a personality that only lasted for thirty seconds at a time. He said gloomily, "We've got a new Emperor."

"Ar," said Sparky the barman.

"It's a woman," added the Captain as he slouched on to his usual stool.

Sparky raised an eyebrow. "Ar?"

"I want a drink," said the Captain.

In the corner, an old man said, "The winds, they are a changing," but this was the sort of thing he always said, and no one took any notice.

-§-§-§-§-§-

The woman with hair the colour of old blood scurried through the first snow of winter and the damp streets of Dreadnought. She was late for work, and she had a suspicion that a pigseller had been following her for the last half hour. She stumbled on the slippery cobbles, and a familiar voice loomed up behind her. "Wanna buy a pig, lady?"

She lost her temper, good and proper. "I don't want a pig! I don't want to roast one for a dinner party, I don't want to tether one to my apple tree and keep it in my garden and I don't want to put one on a shelf to look at all day. I don't care if it does tricks, wears hats or sings a wonderful harmony! Will you leave me alone, you repulsive little merchant?"

"Only tryin' to do my job, miss," said the old man dejectedly. "There is a recession on, you know."

"You might sell more if you didn't stalk your customers!" snapped Kassa Daggersharp.

The pigseller's eyes lit up at this glimpse of encouragement. "Like to buy a rabbit, then?"

"Goodbye," said Kassa, turning on her heel and trying to keep her balance as she hurried along the slippery streets. The merchants were getting worse.

-§-§-§-§-§-

It wasn't much of a dungeon. The ceiling was not a very grisly shade of grey, there was no raw sewage trickling down the walls, and it was too well insulated for the screams of other prisoners to be heard.

Nevertheless, Aragon Silversword did not want to be there. He certainly deserved to be there—he was probably the only prisoner who was genuinely guilty of the exact crime he had been charged with, but that didn't make the accommodation any more appealing.

He had been waiting for three years. He was not waiting to be let out. That implied hope. He was just waiting. Waiting for the heavy hour chime of the palace to seep down to him. Waiting for his daily visit by one of the wardens, to bring him food and water (after spitting in it). Waiting to sleep so that he could wake up and start it all over again.

The door opened. Gordage stood there, a chicken bone hanging in the thick bristles of his beard. He was Aragon's least favourite warden. Gordage peered at the prisoner, trying to figure out what was wrong. "Why you on yer head?" he said finally.

Aragon was standing on his hands, his long legs folded up against the wall, so he chose not to shrug in reply. Instead, he broke one of his cardinal rules by actually speaking to a warden. "I thought I would try it for a month. Perhaps two. There's nothing like a new perspective on life. I imagine that chicken bone in your beard feels the same way."

Gordage grunted. "Come on, then."

That was not something Aragon had ever expected to hear from a warden. "I beg your pardon?"

"Yer being let out."

"Why?"

"New Emperor."

"The fourth this year," said Aragon acidly. "None of the others saw fit to release me."

"She wants to see yer," grunted Gordage.

Aragon's interest had been aroused. His legs unfolded. He pushed lightly off the floor with his hands, landed on his feet and stood up straight. "She?"

-§-§-§-§-§-

Ranulf Godrickskeyridge was the only man left who remained loyal to the last 'true' Emperor. Timregis the Puce had ruled Mocklore for fifty-five years before his champion, a scoundrel by the name of Silversword, had betrayed him and sent the Empire into confusion. Dozens of Emperors had succeeded him, not one of them lasting longer than three months. Nobody else in the city of Dreadnought or in the whole Mocklore Empire gave a purple ferret about Timregis. He had, after all, been a raving idiot. The recent chain of ineffectual Emperors had proven to the population of the city what they had always suspected: one Emperor is as bad as another, so you might as well let them get on with it.

But Ranulf was loyal. For some strange reason, Ranulf cared. Every time a new Emperor popped up, there was Ranulf with his revolutionary flag. Of course, his revolutions had never actually contributed to the downfall of any of the 'pretender' Emperors—most of them had either been executed, evicted for tax-evasion or had absconded from the Palace in the dead of night with a big bag of Imperial loot and a worried expression on their faces.

Ranulf Godrickskeyridge crept in through the window. This is not as easy a task as it sounds, as the window in question was fourteen floors up and the Imperial Palace had not yet installed drainpipes. He gripped his flag, closed his eyes and tumbled forward into the room shouting, "Death to the False Emperor who usurps the rightful power of the..."

The new Emperor reclined on a chaise longue of purple feathers. A silver headdress dripped down over her golden hair, and her long, lithe body was draped in soft silver silk.

She opened her eyes and spoke in a voice of honey and cinnamon. "Hello, there. Can I help you?"

Ranulf smiled weakly. "Wrong palace?" Very slowly, he began to edge back towards the window.

The golden woman raised a languid finger and pointed it in his direction. "Stop."

Ranulf froze to the floor. The idea of disobeying her was too painful to consider. She extended a perfect arm and touched a length of silk which spiralled from the ceiling. A melodious chime shimmered through the chamber.

A servant in black and white livery entered immediately, as if he had been hovering outside the door. "My Lady Emperor?"

The woman gestured at Ranulf with a flick of her perfect manicure. "Take him away and lock him in a barrel with as many tarantulas as you can find. At least a dozen, preferably twenty." And she smiled, a killer smile.

The servant bowed slowly, squaring his round shoulders. "As my Lady Emperor commands." He snapped his fingers at Ranulf, who followed him nervously out of the chamber.

The 38th Emperor of Mocklore smiled at the mirrored ceiling as she lay back on her purple feathered chaise longue. A thousand languid smiles reflected hers. "I could get used to this," she murmured.

The Empire was hers, and hers alone. She couldn't afford it, of course, but lack of finances had never bothered her before when making a major purchase.

-§-§-§-§-§-

Leonardes of Skullcap stretched his long, thick fingers against the desk. "I think we have a problem, Daggar."

Daggar, a seedy looking man who was either trying for a beard or was just bad at shaving, shifted uncomfortably. "Don't know what you mean, Chief."

Cold eyes burned into him from across the desk. "I think you should," said Leonardes.

"Oh, I do," said Daggar hastily, sensing danger. "Course I do. You're not happy, Chief. That's the problem."

"Indeed it is," said Leonardes. He stabbed a finger at the scroll before him. "Your file, Daggar. Petty theft, petty deals, petty profiteering. This is just not good enough."

"Well," said Daggar, swallowing hard, "I don't like to aim too high, Chief. It calls attention to yourself, and I know you don't like us to call attention to ourselves."

"What makes you think that?" said Leonardes mildly. "Attention reflects your success. You just don't like to stick your neck out, so you spend your time, our time, on petty crimes that promise little return. That is no way to be a successful profit-scoundrel, Daggar."

"In my experience, Chief, if you stick your neck out in this city, it gets bloody well chopped off..." Daggar paused bravely. The pause became longer and more dangerous until he added a hasty, "Sir."

Leonardes smiled. Nastily. "If I don't see something substantial on your file within one moon, I am going to have to assume that you have no wish to continue your service to the Profithood. And that means you shall have to be retired."

"Retired?" croaked Daggar, knowing full well that the only way you retired from the Profithood was by jumping into a deep lake with a gravestone chained to both legs.

"Retired," repeated Leonardes. "If you want the protection and rewards of the Profithood, then you will return something substantial. A theft, a deal, a scheme… some kind of profit. It is full moon tomorrow night, is it not? You have one moon from then, Daggar. That is all."

-§-§-§-§-§-

Cheerful noises were coming from the Whet and Whistle Tavern and Grill, now that she had arrived. She was a golden-eyed siren with blood-coloured hair, voluptuous in a costume of knotted silk. There was magic in her voice. She had even managed to cheer up the dismal Captain, who was watching her swinging hips with studied disinterest.

She began to dance now, turning her body upside down and inside out in rapid succession as she sang a fast, breezy song at the top of her extraordinary vocal range. And then the song changed.

The harmonica players, who were exhausted from trying to keep up with her, swapped their harmonica for a collection of old wooden flutes, squabbling only briefly over who got the one with the crack in the end.

The siren sang an ancient ballad which told the tragic story of two lovers, various melodramatic complications, a deep river and the ultimately predictable conclusion. Her dancing slowed, becoming languorous and curved. Her whole body grieved for the tragic lovers as her rich voice described their final poignant moments.

Even Bohoris the Boar Basher was weeping into his tankard by the final chorus.

It was then that a scrawny man smelling of sea-salt pushed his way into the tavern. He tramped across the floor until he got to the bar, and slammed a bulky package on to the counter. "I'm looking for Kassa Daggersharp."

There was silence. The flute wavered. Halfway between describing the grief of the various plant-life and furry animals along the riverside, the glorious voice halted. Everyone looked at the newcomer, waiting for what would come next.

"Never heard of her," said Sparky the barman flatly. He slapped a hand on the package. "I'll take care of this."

For a moment, it looked as if the messenger was going to argue. But he didn't need to. There was a rustle as the dancer climbed down from the makeshift stage and made her way around the tables. She stopped a few feet from the messenger and gazed at him flatly. "That would be for me, then," said Kassa Daggersharp, crown princess of pirates.

-§-§-§-§-§-

By the time Aragon was brought to the Imperial Receiving Room he had been bathed, shaved, scrubbed, garbed and scented with some peculiar perfume that a page had managed to dump into his bathwater before he could prevent it.

His new clothes came equipped with a dagger and a sword. Admittedly the sword was not a proper rapier, just an ornate knitting needle of the kind carried by courtiers. Nevertheless, it was sharp and in one piece. It was better than nothing. They had given him a dagger, too. If the new Emperor was as stupid as this suggested, things might not turn out too badly.

Aragon found himself pushed through a swinging sequined curtain into a room which had been tiled in ebony. "Aragon Silversword, former Knight of the Unmentionable Garment and Champion of the Mocklore Empire!" roared a little liveried servant with a huge voice. Aragon's eyebrow flickered in annoyance.

The chamber was empty. A huge circle of mirrored tiles lay in the centre of the floor, surrounded by the glossy ebony. Aragon moved forward. An emerald curtain at the back of the chamber slid aside to reveal a silken woman reclining upon a chaise longue of purple feathers.

"Lady Talle of Zibria, 38th Emperor of Mocklore and Holder of the Sacred Bauble of Chiantrio!" bellowed the servant.

The Lady Emperor acknowledged this with a slight movement of her half-lidded eyes. Aragon walked across the mirrored tiles, his new boots ringing sharply against the glass. Very deliberately, he looked the Lady Emperor up and down as if she were a kitchen wench.

Far from being affronted at his insolence, Lady Talle preened and stretched, enjoying his eyes on her. Then she tilted her head, and purred, "So you are the one."

"That's what they tell me," replied Aragon crisply.

"You betrayed your Emperor, throwing the Empire into chaos and confusion. Indirectly, you are responsible for the position I now hold."

"You're welcome," replied Aragon tonelessly.

She stood silently, moving around him as she spoke. "You intrigue me. I want you to be my Champion."

"I betrayed the last Emperor I championed," Aragon reminded her.

"I know," said Talle with a secret smile. "You will not betray me."

His eyes lit up. "Now, there's a challenge."

-§-§-§-§-§-

Kassa stepped towards the bar. A few serious drinkers slid their stools automatically aside to make room for her. She was that sort of person. Sparky the barman was suddenly very studiously polishing a glass. "You'll be leaving us, then."

"I expect so," said Kassa, toying with a bracelet. She wore a lot of jewellery. Necklaces, anklets, rings, spangles and bangles. Lobe-rings, toe-rings, beaded buttons. Anything that glittered. She eyed the package suspiciously. It was about the size of six large fists, and an awkward shape under the thick cloth binding. "Who sent it?"

Sparky grunted, and pushed the package in her direction. "Says on the back's from Vicious Bigbeard

Daggersharp of the *Dread Redhead*."

Kassa's expression changed and in one swift moment she grabbed the package, swept over to the door of the tavern, kicked it open and threw the package out into the snow. There was a heavy bang as the parcel exploded. Acrid smoke poured into the tavern, and she tugged the door shut to keep out the stench. "Sorry about that, Sparky. My darling daddy discovered troll thunderdust a few years back and now he uses it for everything. He shaves with it, salts his food with it, and unfortunately he seals his letters with it. He sent a load of his laundry to me a few months ago, and it ended up plastered all over the Skullcaps."

Sparky looked sidelong at her. "You're Bigbeard's daughter?"

"Don't spread it around."

Sparky then gave her the closest thing to a grin she had ever seen on his dismal, moon-shaped face. "So that's why his ship's called the *Dread Redhead*."

Kassa touched a hand to her suitably heroic blood-red hair. "Something like that. See you later, Sparky. I've got a package to scrape up from the pavement." She wrenched her overdress and cloak back on over her scanty stage costume before heading out into the night of early winter. It was bitter outside, with the promise of becoming even colder as the night dragged on. The bits of parcel that were scattered across the melted snow were black and soggy now, no longer hissing with thunderdust.

Amazingly, the contents of the package were still intact. It was a statue of some sort, still warm from the explosion. Kassa turned the piece over in her hands, slowly. She took careful notice of the hideously gaping mouth, the enlarged beaky nose and the large menacing eyes beneath a craggy brow, all meticulously carved in dull grey stone. It was a short, squat, rather repulsive gargoyle. Bigbeard's taste in objets d'art had obviously not improved over the years.

Wedged into the gargoyle's mouth was a lump of parchment. Kassa prised it out and unfolded it. There, scratched happily in a childish hand which clearly stated that it had better things to do than write letters, was a message from her father.

To: Mistress Kassa Daggersharp, probly in Dreadnought, Mocklore Empire etceterer, singin' and dancin' somewhere daft. From: Cap'n Vicious Bigbeard Daggersharp, Scourge of the Purple Seas, Master of the Dread Redhead *and Winner of the Violent and Truly Orrible Sea & Sword Olympics three years running.*

Wot ho, wench. If you is reading this, I am ded. Tarra then. See you in the underwurld. I'le be in the cave with the most rum in it. Enclsed is one gargole. Take care of it and DONT DROP IT YOU STUPID BINT. Doom lurks.

Now I am ded, you is the only proper Daggersharp left (except for Bloody Dangerous Pointybeard Daggersharp, Roaring Redbeard Daggersharp and Gormless Barechin Tim [hes your third cousin, legs removed] an they dont count cos theyr a load of girls blousies. It is your pirattical duty to get a gang together and wreak havoc. The silver I nicked from the Splashdance *will help you. Braided Bones will eksplain everything. Get our Mollys useless sprog to help you wif the crew. And shuvels.*

Yo ho ho, etc, Your Dad. [deceased]

PS: Dont marry a McHagrty or I will haunt you like the bastard I am.

Kassa shoved the parchment in a pocket and marched back into the tavern, ignoring them all as she headed for the stairs. Up in her cozy little attic room, she read the letter over again.

So that was that. It was time to stop playing around in taverns and take over the family business. It was time to trade in her sequins and silk for a sturdy sword and an eyepatch. It was time to grow up.

Kassa started throwing things at the wall. The pillows were first, followed by half her jewellery collection and an over-stuffed pink teddy bear which she usually hid under the bed. Then she dismantled the bed itself and threw the bits out the window without opening it first. Broken glass rained down upon the snowy ground outside.

Her collection of bawdy song-parchments from exotic locations was carefully shredded and strewn liberally over the floor.

The gargoyle was thrown at several walls, but she didn't even manage to dent the stupid nose.

Kassa had grown up believing that she was going to be a pirate—believing, in fact, that she already was one. But that had been a long time ago, before she had discovered that there was more to life than what could be seen from the prow of a ship.

There was another alternative, of course. No one could blame her if she rejected her father's career to follow her mother's original vocation. But Kassa didn't want to be a witch either. Witches were old and wrinkled, and spent their whole time muttering stupid spells. She knew from experience how dangerous that could be.

Kassa had seen enough magic and enough mayhem to last her a lifetime. She didn't want to follow either path. But now…

Frustratedly, she flung the last pillow at the jagged corner of the broken window. Goose feathers filled the air in a sudden, silent explosion. Kassa Daggersharp stood very still as the white feathers rained down upon her blood-red hair. "I suppose I owe him that much," she admitted to the empty room.

She shook her fist at the gargoyle, which lay accusingly on its side in a corner of the little room. "But I'm not promising anything!" she declared.

Feathers still drifted down from the ragged edges of the broken attic window. Kassa picked a few from her hair, and watched them flutter away into the night. "Bloody pirates," she muttered beneath her breath. "Just when you start taking them for granted, they get themselves killed."

"I remember you, Silversword," said the Lady Emperor, her silken skirts whispering as she circled around him. "You were the best man Timregis had. Brave, skilled, highly intelligent."

"Not loyal, though," noted Aragon.

"Oh, well you can't have everything." Lady Talle smiled like a cat with its claws into something small and furry. "I used to have a poster of you on my wall, you know. The mighty Champion of the Empire." She clicked her tongue. "People looked up to you, once upon a time. People believed in you."

"I'm sorry to disappoint you," said Aragon laconically.

"Oh, you didn't. Not at all. After all, a villain is much more interesting than a hero."

Aragon frowned. This woman seemed familiar, and he didn't know why. Then he remembered. "You!"

Talle frowned, and the tiniest of wrinkles marred her exquisite forehead. "Be careful, Silversword. Do not mistake my courtesy for favour. I can have you back in that cell in a thread of an instant."

He advanced on her, grey eyes gleaming. "I remember you now. One of Timregis' courtesans! Not even his favourite…"

"No," she said acidly. "But I was the most intelligent, Aragon. And the most powerful."

He laughed shortly. "You were a decoration, girl, a bauble on a shelf of ornaments. What makes you think you can run an Empire?"

A snarl flicked across Talle's perfect face. "I can be very, very popular," she hissed. "I have it all now, Silversword. I waited as useless Emperor after useless Emperor went by. None of them had a clue about how to organise things, they just sat back and enjoyed the view until the money ran out. It is my turn now. And I will hold the Empire just as I hold the Sacred Bauble. The city states will pay tribute to me!"

Aragon was intrigued. "It never occured to me that one could take over an Empire from the harem."

"It didn't occur to anyone. That's what made it so easy. Obviously you are not willing to work for me. I am sorry to have taken up so much of your time. I'm sure your cell will be just as you left it."

Aragon put out a hand, touching her wrist. His grey eyes were neutral, an expression very few people have ever fully mastered. "I did not say that I was not willing to negotiate, Talle."

She smiled slowly, a silken smile. "How benevolent of you. Let us discuss terms."

He touched her mouth briefly with a fingertip. "Not quite yet. I want you to tell me something first."

She regarded him, making no move to dislodge his finger. Then she spoke, "What do you want to know?"

His expression flickered only slightly. "What the hell is this Sacred Bauble you keep talking about?"

Lady Talle's eyes bubbled with laughter. "Oh, that. It was a gift from the late Emperor Timregis. Do you want to see?" She reached down into her bodice, and drew out a transparent ball the size of a small egg. It descended slowly from her fingertips, then bobbed up towards the ceiling and finally descended into her outstretched palm with the grace and speed of a drifting goose feather. Talle slipped it back into her bodice. "Perhaps someday I will tell you what it's for," she suggested slyly. "But for now, let me tell you the first task I have in mind for my Champion."

"She intends to keep the Empire in her bodice," said Aragon Silversword to himself. "An interesting metaphor."

Chapter 2
Braided Bones

Daggar Profit-scoundrel went home, a lukewarm sausage roll in one pocket and half a bottle of salt-whisky clanking under his jerkin. The snow was making his ears wet. He was whistling, more or less. Visions of the retirement scheme of the Profithood kept doing somersaults through his tortured imagination.

The trouble was, in order to pull off the kind of scam that might impress the indomitable Leonardes, Daggar was going to need contacts. Important contacts. Contacts on the cutting edge of criminal and/or merchant society. And he didn't have any. Not one. He didn't really get on with other profit-scoundrels, and the closest thing he had to a fence was the tavernkeeper down the street who would accept fob-watches in exchange for drinks, no questions asked. As very few people in Daggar's area could even afford to steal such a luxury item as a fob-watch, this wasn't a lot of use. Clockwork had been widely embraced by the upper echelon of Mocklore society, although everyone was mildly disconcerted by the fact that they didn't know how to make the damn stuff stop.

Daggar's lack of business contacts, however, was not quite as problematic as was the time-frame he had been given to work within. The local moon-cycle was not as reliable as those of other worlds...there were thirteen moons in a year, of course. Nothing could disturb that certainty. The problem was, the cycles of these moons were never of a regular length.

The shortest moon-cycle ever recorded had been four days from wax to wane and back again—the longest had been about twelve weeks. It was impossible to predict whether the moon-cycle Daggar had as a deadline would be on the longer or shorter side of the spectrum, but he knew in his heart of hearts that he was not going to get a long one.

Daggar's home was in the Skids, quite possibly the grubbiest collection of streets in any city, on any world, in any universe. His hovel was high quality for Skids accommodation, because there were so many rats living in the walls that it was almost guaranteed never to fall down.

He stopped attempting to whistle when he saw the bundle on the doorstep. It unfolded to reveal a familiar face, framed by blood-red hair. "I s'pose you want a drink," said Daggar grudgingly.

"I brought my own," said Kassa Daggersharp, producing a bottle of rum.

Daggar thought about it. "Better come in, then."

Theirs had always been a close family.

-§-§-§-§-§-

Daggar read the letter. "This makes sense to you, does it? Sounds to me like old Bigbeard was raving."

Kassa had given up looking for a glass in Daggar's dingy cupboards and was drinking the rum straight from the bottle. "It means Bigbeard is dead. And he wants me to take over the family business. Me."

Daggar looked slightly sick. "You mean piracy?"

"I am trained, you know," she reminded him. "I grew up on that bloody ship." She sniffed. "I was apprenticed."

"That was a long time ago," said Daggar darkly.

Kassa seemed to be trying to talk herself into the idea. "A girl's got to have a career," she said dubiously.

"I thought you liked singing and dancing."

Sitting on the floor, Kassa rested her head back against the wall. "I do," she sighed. "But piracy is in my blood. Yours, too."

"You'll know all about your blood if you starts playing pirate again," predicted Daggar gloomily. "It's a dangerous job."

"I've done it before, it wasn't so hard," Kassa said sleepily.

"Yeh," muttered Daggar darkly. "And I remember what happened when you did."

She shot an icy glare at him. "We weren't going to talk about that ever again, remember?"

"I'm a profit-scoundrel," he shot back at her. "I cheat."

She ignored him, chewing absently on a stray lock of hair. "It might be worth playing pirate to get my hands on the *Splashdance* silver. I wonder where I can find a crew."

"What's a splashdance?"

"It was a ship," she yawned. "Long ago."

Daggar's eyebrows shot up into his hairline. "That ship?"

"That ship."

"And the *Splashdance* silver is real silver. Money?" Dollar signs did not actually appear in Daggar's pupils, but they came close. His lazy brain was being kicked into overdrive.

"You catch on fast."

"Aye, when profit's involved." Daggar jumped to his feet. "Let's get cracking."

Kassa opened one eye. "Hmm?"

"Bigbeard said to grab his sister's useless sprog. That's me. Let's get digging for that nice shiny silver." With a percentage of the legendary treasure, Leonardes would have to be impressed. And Daggar would be a real profit-scoundrel at last!

"A few minor problems," Kassa reminded him. "We don't have a crew."

"There's me," he said in a hurt voice. "You can pick up some more followers later if yer really set on the idea. Anyway, a crew would just expect a share in our, in your silver. Let's go treasure hunting."

Kassa peered at him, trying to tell if he was serious. "Where do you intend to start looking?"

"You tell me," he said enthusiastically. "You understood the letter."

"The letter doesn't tell me where the *Splashdance* silver is," said Kassa patiently. "Only Bigbeard knows." She frowned, and corrected herself. "Knew."

Daggar plucked the letter out of her grasp and ran over it again. "What's this stuff about Braided Bones?"

"You must remember him. He was one of Bigbeard's crew. The tall one who scared you half to death."

"Means nothing," Daggar mumbled. "The letter says he can explain. So where do we find him, then?"

Kassa was leaning against the wall with her eyes closed. "This letter was set aside in case my father died suddenly. Obviously he has. The chances are very likely that the *Dread Redhead* went with him."

Daggar's face froze. "You don't mean…"

"It's a fair assumption that Braided Bones went down with the ship too. It's not likely I'll ever find that silver."

Daggar dropped to his knees in anguish. "Just kill me, Kassa!"

"Why is this so important to you?"

He smiled guiltily. "I'm in a little financial difficulty."

Kassa was instantly suspicious. "You want my silver."

"Course not," he protested. "I wouldn't do that to you. I just want some of yer silver."

"It doesn't matter either way. There is no silver to share out."

"Ey, don't say that. Don't even think it. I'm sure we can find it, somehow. Maybe we need a crew."

"What?" Kassa didn't sound pleased. "When did we become we? I haven't invited you yet, Daggar. You're cute but useless."

"I happen to be good at what I do," said Daggar in an injured tone of voice.

"If you were any good, you wouldn't live in a rathole like this."

"I like ratholes."

"Rats live in ratholes."

"Yer in a nasty mood."

"I've just realised that you're my only living relative. Do you have any idea how depressing that is?"

Daggar picked up the gargoyle, turning it over in his hands. "Maybe this has some clue."

"I doubt it. My father wasn't the most subtle of men. He's not the kind of pirate who leaves complex trails of evidence for people to follow. I'm surprised he bothered to send me a message at all. The gargoyle is probably just something he picked up somewhere."

"So why did he tell you not to drop it?"

"I don't know. Maybe he was worried I might stub my toe."

Daggar turned the statue over in his hands. "Could be important. Maybe it's valuable."

"Maybe it's magic and will turn into a djinni if you rub it," Kassa suggested, peering down the neck of her rum bottle.

"Hey, that would be worth a lot," said Daggar eagerly. "Maybe I should rub it."

"Rub it, don't rub it, it's all the same to me," said Kassa. "Does this rathole have a bed? I think I want to lie down."

Daggar solemnly rubbed the gargoyle, but nothing happened.

"Maybe it doesn't like being rubbed," suggested Kassa. "If some strange man came up and started rubbing up against me, I wouldn't suddenly get the urge to turn into anything."

Daggar put the statue down in disgust. "Why d'you suggest it, then?"

"Too much rum, and a perverse sense of humour."

He pulled her to her feet. "Let's get you to bed."

She leaned against him. "I am going to start feeling very sick, very soon."

"Do you want some water?"

She thought about it. "Yes."

Daggar leaned her against the wall and then rummaged in his cupboards. Miraculously, he came up with a water skin within the first few minutes of his search.

Kassa sipped and made a face. "That's horrible."

"I got it from a well in a good district," Daggar protested.

"Why is it unsalted?"

He looked at her in horror. "That's disgusting!"

"You drink salt-whisky, don't you?"

"Salt-whisky is an expression, Kassa. It means…cheap, bloody-awful whisky. Drinking seawater is just perverse."

She shrugged and handed the waterskin back. "Put some salt in it."

Daggar grudgingly added a few pinches of sea-salt to the water and then gave it back to Kassa. She drank greedily.

"That's really a horrible habit," he told her.

Kassa wiped her mouth. "Once a pirate, always a pirate."

"Remind me to find another family."

-§-§-§-§-§-

The next day dawned bright and clear. After a long lie-in and a late lunch, Kassa went forth into the marketplace, disgustingly cheerful. "Today we are going to start finding ourselves a crew," she announced brightly.

"Do we have to?"

"I'm going to need more than you, me and a garden gnome. Gargoyle. Whatever."

"Then can we go looking for the silver?"

"Can you please forget about the silver? This all has to be done in the correct order, and the silver is currently right at the bottom of the list."

"How can you be so cruel?"

"Talent," she replied crisply.

Kassa's search for a gang of loyal pirates was unsuccessful, mainly because she kept stopping at haberdashery stalls.

"Half a goose," said the merchant when she asked the price of a spool of gold thread.

"For this?" said Kassa in disbelief. "It's not worth a soup bone."

"That's real gold, that," said the merchant firmly.

"If it's real gold, why is the paint coming off on my fingers?"

"That's your problem," said the merchant, flatly refusing to haggle. "Half a goose."

"Have you heard the latest news, then?" said Daggar in his final attempt to catch Kassa's attention. "The new Emperor's a woman."

"There's always a gimmick," Kassa said dismissively.

"Oh, you heard about it?"

"Good luck to her, I say. What do you think of this blue?"

"It's blue, Kassa. There's not much more you can say about it. What about this crew, then?"

In the face of the coloured threads and the embroidery needles, Kassa seemed to have lost interest in the mission. "What do you expect me to do, buy mercenaries?"

"You can't really get away with stealing them, you know. They protest."

"A crew can't be bought. Don't you know anything? You have to acquire them gradually. They'll turn up, one at a time. When we least expect it."

Daggar was about to reply in the most sarcastic of tones, but he was interrupted by a lithe, dark blond man who leaped over the haberdashery stall, crashed headlong into Kassa and kept running into the crowd, scattering silk threads in his wake. A moment later, four Blackguards followed him, leaving a path of destruction behind them.

Kassa had a starstruck expression on her face. "Daggar, did you see who that was?"

"No idea," Daggar said disinterestedly. "You know I don't pay attention to the popular minstrels."

"That was no minstrel. It was Aragon Silversword."

"You sure?"

"Of course I'm sure." Her eyes were shining. "He's a legend, Daggar. I used to have a poster of him on my wall. So did all the girls."

"Must have been the influence of that posh finishin' school Bigbeard sent you to," Daggar grumbled. "I thought he was in prison."

"I would say that we just witnessed his escape, wouldn't you?"

"Why am I getting a nasty feeling that you want him in yer crew?"

"Come on," ordered Kassa, and hitching up her skirts, she began to run.

Against his better judgement, Daggar followed. "He's a traitor," he huffed as he tried to keep pace. "How can you trust our silver with a known traitor?"

"We don't have any silver."

"I'm not givin' up hope!"

Kassa halted suddenly, and Daggar took the opportunity to start breathing again. He was particularly disturbed by the distant sheen in Kassa's golden eyes. "Aragon Silversword betrayed an Emperor," she muttered softly to herself. "He will not betray a Daggersharp."

"Clean yer shoes, miss?" A small professional urchin had been hovering close to them for a while, his cleaning rag clutched hopefully at the ready.

"No thanks," said Kassa, scanning the marketplace for the fleeing prisoner. Spotting a Blackguard uniform, she started running again.

Daggar hurried after her. "Yer not serious. Aragon Silversword?"

"I'm thinking about it."

"Thinking's a dangerous habit."

"I know you've always thought so."

"Beware, songwitch!"

Kassa stopped so suddenly that Daggar crashed into her back. She turned, slowly. A haggard soothsayer stood motionless, daubed with white symbols and wrapped in ragged cloth, one cracked finger pointing unwaveringly in Kassa's direction.

"What did you call me?" whispered Kassa hoarsely.

"Songwitch!" snapped the old holy woman. "And so you are. Tonight the moon is full."

Kassa waited. "And?" she prompted finally.

The soothsayer sniffed. "Just beware, that's all." She spun on one heel, stamping back into the throng of people.

"Bad news," Daggar muttered in Kassa's ear. "Thirty years, and I've never once caught the attention of a soothsayer. Guess what—I'm still alive."

"It's all religious claptrap," said Kassa, but the customary note of assurance was lacking in her voice.

-§-§-§-§-§-

The Hidden Army didn't offically exist, which was why they had survived for so long. Mercenaries were illegal in the Mocklore Empire—warriors were expected to die for honour and duty rather than large amounts of ready cash. After all, money was an incentive not to die in the first place. The tribute-paying Lordlings of the city-states denied all knowledge of the Hidden Army of Mercenaries, especially when they were employing them. Many a besieged Lordling had suddenly produced a hundred extra 'reinforcements' overnight, all wearing local livery and looking suspiciously like they had been there the whole time.

The fact that no one seriously believed in the Hidden Army made it that much easier to hide.

Zelora Footcrusher been in the Hidden Army for twelve years, and already she was the deputy leader's assistant for K Division. She was expected to reach the rank of deputy leader any minute, but no one talked about that. Ambitious mercenaries were traditionally stepped on from a great height.

It was Zelora's afternoon off.

She managed to swim down to the third level of caverns before the pressure on the back of her throat told her she was running out of air. She relaxed and swam up to the surface, gasping deeply as she emerged. The full moon made vague patterns on the water, glittering like silver against the blue backdrop of the afternoon.

Some day she would find out the secret of the caverns.

But not now. There were two sieges scheduled for tomorrow, and she had much to prepare. Besides, there was also a personal matter she had to attend to. Zelora swam with easy strokes towards the shore.

-§-§-§-§-§-

When Kassa reached the alley, a full scale brawl was going on. Aragon Silversword was fending off four Blackguards with what looked like a jewelled knitting needle. The Blackguards all had curved swords (a fashion started by the last Emperor) and blankly menacing expressions.

Daggar hung back, hoping that Kassa would be content to watch the melée from afar. He kept hoping, right up to the moment when Kassa picked up a wooden garbage trough and hurled it into the alley. It struck Aragon Silversword in the face, knocking him to the ground.

The Blackguards looked in surprise at the wild-eyed woman who had just done their job for them.

Kassa raised her hands menacingly at them. “I am the Dread Redhead Songwitch of Bloody Creek! Leave this place, or I shall cast a thousand curses of blood and gore upon you!”

Daggar looked away, pretending not to know her.

The Blackguards did not seem to know what to do next. Their orders had been to leave Aragon Silversword in a battered but unbroken state. This being done, they left the area in an orderly fashion. Kassa smiled in satisfaction.

Daggar inspected Aragon Silversword. “I think he’s dead,” he announced.

-§-§-§-§-§-

It was getting dark when Kassa and Daggar got back to the Skids with Aragon Silversword’s body. “For the last time, he is not dead!”

"Oh, just resting, is he?"

"All right, he's unconscious. I accept that he is unconscious."

"Because you threw a garbage trough at him."

"I'm willing to acknowledge my mistakes."

"I just hope this isn't going to be the regular initiation for crew-members. I haven't received my near-fatal beating yet."

"Stop exaggerating."

They carried the body over the threshold of Daggar's hovel. "Ey," said Daggar, dropping Aragon's feet. "When we left this morning, was there a naked pirate on my kitchen table?"

"What?"

"A naked pirate on my kitchen table. I think he's dead too." Daggar had a nervous habit of seeing corpses everywhere when he felt his own life was endangered. In other words, when he was around Kassa.

Kassa dropped Aragon's limp shoulders and moved over to look at the body on the small kitchen table. It was a huge naked pirate, arms and legs everywhere, long black hair dragging on the floor. "I've got news for you, Daggar," she said grimly. "This corpse is snoring."

Kassa leaned over and seized the ear of the sleeping man. He awoke with a jerk, rolling off the table with a crash of rotted floorboards.

"Braided Bones," she snapped. "You can start by telling me how you managed to break into a profit-scoundrel's home. Then you can explain why my father is dead."

Chapter 3
The Art of Traitors

"Polite, Kassa," noted the large pirate in a placid voice. "Got that from Bigbeard."

Kassa's hands were on her hips, which only highlighted how much shorter she was than this oversized pirate. "Bigbeard is dead."

"Right." He rose, picking bits of floorboard off his skin. "Got to talk. Where's the sword?"

Distracted, Kassa's hands moved off her hips. "What do you mean?"

"Long pointy thing. Rubies."

"Dad's prime sword? Why should I have it?"

Braided Bones looked steadily at her for a moment. "Problem. Anything to drink?"

As he swallowed the last of Kassa's rum, the large naked pirate's eyes flicked towards the body on the floor. "Corpse?" he questioned.

"Kassa did it," said Daggar automatically. "Where's that gargoyle-shaped paperweight, then?" While Kassa had been buying embroidery threads, Daggar had lined up a buyer for the gargoyle, describing it as an ancient Zibrian artefact recently stolen from the Imperial Skirmish Museum. Wars in Mocklore were usually too small to be of any note, but most of the city-states were in a near constant state of skirmish.

Braided Bones laughed hollowly. "Haven't figured it out yet?" He paused, frowning at Daggar. "Aren't you..."

"Moll's useless sprog," Daggar confirmed, handing over a moth-eaten grey blanket. After all, Braided Bones was naked.

The huge black-haired pirate looked at the blanket and then tossed it over one shoulder. "Remember Bigbeard coming up with good insults about you. See if I can remember them later."

"What about the gargoyle, Bones?" Kassa reminded him.

"First things first," said the oversized pirate. "Bigbeard betrayed. Redhead's gone, crew too."

"Traitors," hissed Kassa. "I hate traitors."

Braided Bones took another swig. "That bastard Cooper."

"Reed?" spluttered Kassa. "How could he? He was just a cabin boy. An apprentice." She stared at Braided Bones, her golden eyes narrowing. "He was just an apprentice, wasn't he?"

"Apprentices inherit," said Braided Bones. "Reckon he got tired waiting."

"All right," said Kassa, sitting down on Daggar's only decent chair. "Tell me everything. I've been gone since Bigbeard sent me off to that bloody finishing school. What have I missed?"

"Cooper been Bigbeard's right hand for two years," said Braided Bones.

"I thought you were his right hand."

Braided Bones had the grace to look slightly embarrassed. "Not lately. Cursed."

"You're cursed?" said Daggar warily, keeping his distance.

Braided Bones ignored him. "Someone gave our position to Red Admirals. Caught by surprise. Then curse kicked in."

"What curse?" asked Kassa evenly.

The large pirate shrugged. "Turned into a gargoyle. Only human at full moon, see. Was fighting battle, then sun rose. Next I know, next full moon. Me on back of courier cart, heading to Dreadnought the long way round.

Heard Redhead sunk, all hands lost. Except one, hitched lift with Red Admirals."

"Reed Cooper," said Kassa grimly. "Remind me to kick his head in next time we meet."

"Won't need reminding," said Braided Bones. "Now we talk about sword."

There was a muffled thump from somewhere. "Expecting company?" Kassa asked their host.

"It could be the Lord Mayor come for afternoon tea," said Daggar. "But we don't have a Lord Mayor. Or a teapot, come to that. Shall I answer it, then?"

"It's your door."

Daggar slouched towards the door.

"Not door," said Braided Bones. "Corpse."

Daggar peered down at the body of Aragon Silversword. A leg twitched, involuntarily thumping against the wall. "I think he's still dead," he reported.

A hand lashed out, grabbing Daggar's throat and holding fast. Aragon Silversword's eyes opened as he tightened his grip. "Who are you?" he demanded. "Where am I? Who hit me? Please answer with speed and precision, I am not a patient man."

"Kak!" replied Daggar.

Aragon released him, and Daggar scrabbled back out of range. Aragon seemed to have no intention of moving off the floor. He looked intently at Daggar for a moment, and then his gaze flicked towards Kassa. "You threw something."

"I'm sorry about that," she said warily.

"Don't be," he said calmly. "Most people throw something at me sooner or later." He rose to his feet, his eyes holding hers. "Now we can be friends."

Kassa felt a little off-balance. "Perhaps we should introduce ourselves," she said uncertainly.

"Of course." He crossed the room towards her with rapid steps and took her hand in his. "You are Kassa Daggersharp," he informed her as he kissed her hand. "I'm very pleased to meet you."

"How do you know who I am?" she said in surprise.

Aragon gestured briefly to her companions. "A pirate, a profit-scoundrel." His eyes returned to her. "And blood-red hair. It was a lucky guess. You were a very memorable character, Mistress Daggersharp, when I was Champion of the Empire. Bigbeard's exceptional daughter." His tone grew disappointed. "I hear you are no longer a pirate."

"That may change," said Kassa. "Imminently."

"Then you will be looking for supporters," he said immediately. "A crew. You're wondering whether to trust me."

"How can you be so sure that you know what I'm thinking?"

A smile flickered across his face. "You're so obvious."

"The sword, Kassa," said Braided Bones urgently.

"What sword?" snapped Kassa, annoyed at the interruption. "Oh, that…why is it so important?" Another thought crossed her mind. "Braids, do you know where the silver is?"

"Sword knows," Braided Bones said insistently. "*Splashdance* location written on sword!"

Kassa was alarmed. "But I don't have the sword! It could be anywhere."

Daggar peered out of the grimy window. "S'dawn," he noted.

"I know," said Kassa in a different voice.

Daggar turned, to see that Braided Bones had vanished, and in his place was the small stone gargoyle. It was grimacing in a particularly repulsive way.

"An interesting phenomenon," commented Aragon Silversword.

Kassa looked very forlorn. "What do we do now?" she asked no one in particular.

-§-§-§-§-§-

It was a glistening sort of morning. Small birds were making fluttery attempts at warbling, but most of them gave up and went home to nurse head-colds. There had been no more snow, which left everything cold and wet and damp. Mocklore weather being what it was, the sun had come out and was trying to pretend that it was summer.

Three Imperial Ladies in Waiting lay on the hill behind the palace, bleaching their hair with the morning sun. It was the blondest of the three who first saw the man coming through the trees. She gestured to the others and they quickly sat up, artfully arranging their clothes to look fashionably disarrayed.

As the stranger came closer, they saw that he was terribly handsome in a brash, swaggering sort of way. He wore ripped velvet, and a black eyepatch which made him look awfully dramatic. He stopped a few feet from them. "Where would I find the Lady Emperor?"

"She won't see you," said the least blonde of the three.

The middling blonde giggled behind a hand. "Oh, I don't know," she said, openly admiring the muscles rippling through the torn shirt. "Maybe she will. If you ask nicely."

"What's your name, handsome?" the blondest asked boldly.

"Cooper," said the man.

"A barrel-maker," she squealed in disappointment, and the three dissolved into hysterical giggles.

Reed Cooper touched his forelock. "Good day, ladies." He sloped towards the Palace.

The blondes watched him go. "You know," said one after a moment, "I don't think he was a barrel-maker."

Another shifted slightly, spreading her hair out for the sun again. "How do you know?"

"I just don't think a barrel-maker would carry such a big shiny sword on his back."

-§-§-§-§-§-

Aragon Silversword had vanished into Daggar's grimy bathroom to clean the blood and garbage off his face.

His absence automatically made him the topic under discussion. "He's a traitor," insisted Daggar.

"Not lately," Kassa argued.

"He's been in a dungeon! There aren't that many opportunities for betrayal when yer only companions are rats, you know."

"You should know," she retorted. "Don't you believe people can change?"

A sly grin came over Daggar's face. "You fancy him, don't yer?"

"Don't be stupid," snapped Kassa, a slight flush betraying her cheeks. "I need all the help I can get if I'm going to find the silver. We both know you're useless, and Braided Bones is going to be a book-end for another month. Whom else do I have?"

"You could find someone more reliable," Daggar grumbled.

"I don't think so," she replied. "As long as we are useful to him, we can trust him."

Daggar looked at her as if she was crazy. "That's a clever piece of logic, then. Sounds like yer trying to convince yerself."

"Can I say something?" Aragon interrupted. He was standing in the inner doorway.

Kassa stared at him for a moment, wondering how much he had heard.

Aragon smiled thinly, giving nothing away. "I don't have a good track record for loyalty. And I do not imagine you would take kindly to being betrayed."

Kassa was mildly shaken by his abilty to predict what she was thinking. "So what surety can you offer me?' she said finally.

"I've played the traitor before, Mistress Daggersharp," he said coolly. "I didn't like the results."

"I'll give you a chance," Kassa said after a moment. She wasn't quite sure why. "But if you let me down, I'll kill you myself."

"I would expect nothing less," said Aragon Silversword.

-§-§-§-§-§-

The Lady Emperor did not even bother to open her eyes. "Do I know you?" she inquired disinterestedly.

"Reed Cooper, your Imperial Majesty," said the pirate with a measured bow. "We met at a garden party shortly before the Emperor Timregis was...disposed of. He was particularly insane that summer and had decided to give knighthoods to all the pirate kings. He changed his mind, of course, but they were invited to the garden party anyway. I came with Bigbeard's crew."

Talle's eyes opened slightly, although she was still pretending disinterest. "Oh," she murmured. "The cabin boy."

"You attempted to seduce me," Reed Cooper added.

Lady Talle's eyebrow lifted perfectly. "Attempted?"

"You were making your plans even then," he continued. "You were aware of the one thing a successful Emperor needs. Money, and lots of it. I happened to mention that Bigbeard had the *Splashdance* silver stashed away somewhere, and that the location was written on his prime sword." He smiled, showing perfect teeth. "You suggested to me that if you should ever rise to the exalted rank of Emperor, hypothetically of course, I should contrive to bring you the sword of Vicious Bigbeard Daggersharp. I believe you suggested that it would be worth my while to surrender such a prize."

Talle's eyes were fully open now. She batted her eyelashes slowly, suspiciously. "Bigbeard's ship was sunk months ago. I wasn't Emperor then."

Reed Cooper shared his killer grin with her. "I got tired of waiting. You would manage it eventually, I had no doubt of that, and when you did...I would have the sword ready and waiting for you. As it turned out, I didn't have long to wait."

The Lady Emperor sat up with a silvery rustle of silk. "You brought the sword? Where is it?"

Reed Cooper pulled the sword from the scabbard on his back, and handed it to her.

Talle's slender fingers slid lovingly over the eight rubies which sparkled on the hilt. "The key to the *Splashdance* silver," she murmured. "Once I have that wealth, I can get the Lordlings on my side. My Empire will be secured." Her probing fingertips found the catch beneath the seventh ruby, and something clicked. A small panel revolved slowly, revealing the hidden inscription in the hilt.

Talle's face changed. With icy blue eyes, she glared at Reed Cooper. "Is this some kind of joke? I warn you, I lost my sense of humour when I became Emperor. I can't afford it any more!"

"My Lady?" said Reed, confused.

She thrust the sword at him and pushed away, leaping blindly to her feet. The inscription was gibberish. Reed turned it over, trying to make sense of it. Even the alphabet was alien. "I don't know," he said finally. "I can't read it."

"Nobody could read it, you fool!" exclaimed Lady Talle ferociously. Her tone dropped to a dangerously calm level. "I think I'll have you boiled. And sliced."

"My Lady Emperor," he protested. "Kassa Daggersharp must be able to decipher it. The sword was meant for her. Bigbeard himself delivered it into my hands to give to Kassa, before he knew of my treachery."

"Oh, that's a good idea," said Lady Talle sarcastically. "Give the sword to Kassa Daggersharp!"

"Well, what else can we do?" Reed demanded.

She smiled dangerously. "We? Aren't you getting a little above yourself, Cooper?"

"I betrayed Bigbeard and destroyed his ship," retorted Reed. "By pirate law, that makes his booty mine. The *Splashdance* silver belongs to me by right of the sea."

"Rights?" said Lady Talle disbelievingly. "You are my subject, Cooper. You have no rights. You will serve me for as long as you live, and if you please me I shall reward you."

"Anything you say, my Lady Emperor," replied Reed Cooper obediently, but a little too smoothly. "I am sure that we can…accommodate each other."

"Besides," said Talle as she settled herself back on to her comfortable chaise longue. "I already have an agent working on Kassa Daggersharp. Soon we should have all her secrets and her silver."

Chapter 4
Get Me the Gargoyle

An extra-private of the Hidden Army of Mercenaries scuttled towards the latest headquarters, or at least towards where he thought they might be. He couldn't find them.

After half an hour of watching the hapless extra-private pitifully examine fern fronds for secret panels, the sentry on duty opened the trapdoor in the grass and let him in.

"Thanks," said the little soldier with great relief.

"No problem, soldier," said the sentry kindly. "Just send the usual blackmail fee to my quarters, and we'll say no more about it. Especially to those in command, wot?"

"What?" said the soldier, confused. "Message for deputy leader's assistant's assistant. Special message."

"Rainwiper?" said the sentry. "He's dead."

"Footcrusher," said the extra-private.

"Oh, her. She's not deputy leader's assistant's assistant no more, she was moved up to deputy leader's assistant the moon before last."

"Wasn't Chingritted Fingernails..."

"Yeah he was, but you know how fast promotions fly about when plague hits the camp." Suddenly the sentry frowned and peered at his clipboard again. "Hang on, I'm wrong. Telefonopolis died last week didn't he?"

"Did he?"

"That means Footcrusher is a deputy leader now. I should make a note of that somewhere..."

"Deputy leader Footcrusher, then. Of K Division. Special message. For her."

"Right," said the sentry, making a note on his clipboard. "In that case, you can bugger off."

"What?"

"Says here. She's besieging the Midden Plains. She's not here."

The little soldier took a deep breath. "Now, look..."

-§-§-§-§-§-

Kassa ran her finger over the newly-inked map. "Are you certain this is the exact layout of the palace?"

"Almost nothing is certain," said Aragon Silversword.

Daggar was looking worried. "One minute you're talking about treasure hunting, and the next you're planning to break into the palace," he said anxiously. "The palace. You know, the most heavily-guarded building anywhere."

"Look," said Kassa patiently. "Reed Cooper got the Red Admirals involved in this. That suggests an Emperor was involved. As there have been at least four in the last six months, we can't say for sure which Emperor it was, but the chances are likely that Bigbeard's sword is in the palace somewhere."

Daggar was pacing. "And why is he so keen to get back into the palace all of a sudden?" he demanded, waving a finger at Aragon. "I thought he just escaped from the Imperial dungeon."

"Oh, shut up, Daggar," snapped Kassa, losing patience with him. "Aragon is risking a lot to help us. You could try and be a little less hostile."

"I am risking nothing to help you," Aragon contradicted her calmly. "Your hairy friend here is right. It would be pointless for me to enter the palace less than twelve hours after escaping. I shall co-ordinate from a distance."

"Oh." Kassa looked crestfallen. This wasn't quite how she had imagined things. She glanced hopefully at Daggar.

"I don't suppose…"

"Oh, yes," he said sarcastically. "I could dress up as a washerwoman and smuggle you in under a pile of old socks. No thank you."

"I thought you wanted my silver," she flared at him.

"Even a profit-scoundrel doesn't commit suicide in the name of money," he retorted.

Kassa's face went very pale for a moment, and she sat down in a hurry. "So what's the plan?" she asked between clenched teeth.

Aragon almost smiled. "It's simple enough…"

-§-§-§-§-§-

Later, Daggar found Kassa sitting on an upturned water barrel outside his hovel. It was snowing, but she didn't seem to have noticed. "Quarter-penny for yer thoughts," he offered half-heartedly.

She glanced in his direction. "I thought a penny was the usual price."

"Buy cheap and sell high. That's the motto of the Profithood. One of them, anyway." Daggar looked more closely at Kassa, and grinned suddenly. "So what do you think of the plan, then?"

"I suppose there is a reason why this water barrel has a window in it," said Kassa quickly.

"There's a family of urchins living in it. Unless yer want to borrow a cup of sugar or you need something stolen in a hurry, it's best to leave 'em alone. I did notice you changin' the subject, by the way."

"The curtains are rather sweet," continued Kassa. "And the window box is rather a good idea. They could grow kitchen herbs in it, or tulips in spring…"

"It's a winner of a plan, isn't it?" Daggar pressed. "I 'specially like the way that it involves maximum risk for you, medium risk for me and no risk at all for His Nibs in there."

"It's a good plan," said Kassa staunchly, wanting to believe it. "A sound plan."

"Cobblers."

Kassa sighed, pushing herself to her feet. "You're right. It's a rotten plan."

Daggar looked relieved. "So yer starting to doubt the golden boy at last. Thank the imps for that!"

Kassa paced back and forth. "I want to trust him. I really do. When I was at school, he was held up as...well, a symbol of all that was chivalrous and decent. And after he killed the Emperor, he seemed even more dashing and romantic."

"Some school," commented Daggar, shuddering.

"After all, the Emperor was mad," Kassa went on. "And there's something very appealing about an anti-hero. I just wish...well, I wish he was a little more..."

"Heroic?" supplied Daggar. "Ruggedly handsome? Polite?"

"Tolerable," she conceded with a sigh. "I suppose three years in a dungeon could change anyone, but I can't shake the feeling that he was always this much of a cold-blooded bastard."

Daggar liked the sound of this. The sooner Aragon Silversword was out of their lives, the better. "Look at it this way, Chief—if we find the silver, yer know I won't steal more than my fair share 'cos I'm family and I'm terrified of you. Can you say that about yer precious Aragon Silversword?"

"You're right."

"I am?"

"Don't get used to it, it won't happen again. And don't call me Chief."

Daggar folded his arms, and tried to look decisive. "Well?"

"Right," said Kassa, and marched back into the hovel. But the speech she was planning just melted away when Aragon Silversword looked up at her with his clear grey eyes.

"You had something to say?" he inquired.

"Yes," she said awkwardly.

"You have a dilemma," Aragon observed. "You have begun to doubt my motives. Quite frankly, I'm surprised it took you this long. However, I am useful to you. You need a crew, and I am the only competent volunteer you have. I also know too many of your secrets, which you were foolish enough to share with me." He almost smiled. "It was very, very stupid to tell me about the silver before you knew if you could trust me or not. Now you have no choice."

"There is always a choice," said Kassa steadily.

"I don't think so," said Aragon Silversword. "You need me."

In the corner, Daggar rolled his eyes. This was not the way to handle Kassa.

"I don't need anyone!" she hissed. "Not you, not Daggar, and not that bloody gargoyle, although I might find some interesting new uses for it if you don't leave immediately."

Aragon looked almost surprised. "I beg your pardon?"

"Get out. Is that clear enough for you?"

"In very little time, you shall regret not having me on your side," he warned.

"I doubt it."

Not one for hesitation, Aragon Silversword stood up and walked out of the hovel. The door swung shut behind him, and the doorknob fell off. Kassa sat down. She breathed in. She breathed out. She breathed in again.

"So it's back to a crew of two," said Daggar cheerfully. "And old stony-features over there. Never mind. All the more silver for the both of us."

Kassa didn't say anything for a while, and when she spoke it was in a cold, calculating voice. "I'm going to get my sword, and find my silver, and pay for the best assassin in Mocklore to kill that son of a firedrake. I wouldn't want to sully my own hands with his blood."

"Plus you've never killed anybody."

"Oh, shut up."

-§-§-§-§-§-

It is never wise to annoy an executive mercenary, which can be a problem because the executive mercenaries usually get to be executive mercenaries by having a volatile temper and a knack for killing things.

It is especially not wise to annoy an executive mercenary if she is bigger than you. This is why the small extra-private was sitting on top of Zelora Footcrusher's wardrobe. He was hoping that this would constitute a subtle approach. Unfortunately for him, the fact that he was sitting on her wardrobe was about to annoy Zelora beyond all reason.

Some days, you just can't win.

"What in the Underworld are you doing in my quarters?" she demanded as she came in and spied him. "And speaking of the Underworld, how would you like the package tour?" This was a threat. She was taking evening classes to polish up her style.

The quarters of the Hidden Army were unique in that they were both underground and portable. It is not always easy to move tunnels and caves with their contents intact, especially while keeping a non-existent profile, but the Hidden Army had been doing it for decades. Top executives who retired from the chain of command almost always went into the removalist business.

"Message," squeaked the extra-private, trying not to sound nervous.

"What kind of message?" snapped Zelora.

"Special message."

Her eyes narrowed. "And?"

"Special message," repeated the little soldier. "For Zelora Footcrusher. Deputy leader," he added helpfully.

"Were you planning to tell me what the message is?"

"Okay," he said agreeably, and began to recite from memory. "Ship *Dread Redhead* sunk, all hands lost. After liberation from wreck, de gargoyle in possession of merchant Scrub Gorsespreader, known agent of V. Bigbeard Daggersharp. Gargoyle then passed on to Hucklebed de Messenger who delivered it to Kassa Daggersharp of Dreadnought, presumed daughter of de above, then living in Whet and Whistle Tavern and Grillhouse. Followed from there to slum hovel in Skids belonging to Daggar Profit-scoundrel, presumed brother of Profithood. Possible associations with Aragon Silversword, recently escaped from Imperial dungeon, presumed agent of Lady Emperor." He took a deep breath.

Zelora opened her mouth, and then closed it again. "Who gave you this message?" she demanded.

"Camelot," said the extra-private.

"Tell me why you're talking about gargoyles. I hired Camelot to locate Braided Bones."

"Same," said the little soldier laconically.

Zelora frowned. "What is?"

"Gargoyle. Braided Bones."

Zelora raised an eyebrow.

"Curse," added the extra-private helpfully. "Can I go now?"

-§-§-§-§-§-

Draped in coppery silk and dripping with emeralds, the Lady Emperor hissed at Aragon Silversword. "You will show your Emperor due respect!"

"I was busy when you summoned me," said Aragon shortly. "How do you expect me to keep the Daggersharp woman's trust if messengers from the palace keep dragging me away?"

"I heard you were found in a tavern, my lord," sneered Reed Cooper. "Has Mistress Kassa not even entrusted you with her address yet?"

Aragon studied this stranger briefly, and then deliberately turned his back on him. "My lady Emperor, why am I being interrogated by a handmaiden?"

"Handmaiden?" spluttered Reed furiously.

"Cooper is a loyal servant, Silversword," Lady Talle said smoothly. "You would do well to emulate him. He has brought me a great prize." She snapped her fingers, and Reed drew the prime sword of Vicious Bigbeard Daggersharp. The eight rubies in the hilt chose that moment to glitter.

"Interesting," said Aragon Silversword.

"That sword is the key to the location of the silver of the lost ship *Splashdance*," Lady Talle announced.

"I know," said Aragon absently. "Your lackey has done well. What do you need me to do?"

"What makes you think I need you at all?" purred Talle with a glitter in her eye.

"I'm not dead yet."

She accepted the point. "The message on the sword is written in a language that I cannot decipher. I believe Kassa Daggersharp can. I have put her name on my proscription list. A silver talent will go to the one who hands her in to me alive, or as close to that state as happens to be necessary. Your familiarity with her might make you more able to capture her than anyone else."

"I see," said Aragon coolly. "Until you have the *Splashdance* silver, you cannot afford to pay the reward. So you need Kassa to be captured by someone who is already working for you." He raised an eyebrow. "I didn't realise that the Imperial coffers were quite so low. Are any of your jewels real, or are they just coloured glass?"

Lady Talle smiled without amusement. "Fetch me that girl. If her crew get in the way, kill them."

"Her crew," said Aragon scornfully. "A deadbeat and a pirate. They should not pose much of a problem."

"A pirate?" interrupted Reed Cooper sharply.

"His name is Braided Bones, my Lady Emperor," Aragon continued, refusing to directly address the newcomer.

"That's impossible," scoffed Cooper. "Braided Bones is dead. He was turned to stone two years ago, when he insulted some mermaid's mother."

A faint smile flickered across Aragon's mouth. "He turns back into a human every full moon. Did your pirate king not tell you?"

Stunned by this information, Reed Cooper turned to Talle. "My Lady Emperor, if this is true then it changes everything. Bigbeard and Braided Bones shared secrets. He will know the code."

"I thought Bigbeard shared all his secrets with you, son of his heart," said Lady Talle with heavy irony.

"Evidently not," said Aragon. He did not smile, but managed to convey a certain degree of concealed smugness.

Talle regarded him thoughtfully. "Are you quite sure that Mistress Daggersharp trusts you, Silversword?"

"Of course she trusts me," Aragon replied, sincerity radiating from his voice. He had always been a confident liar.

Chapter 5
Lordlings and Ladybirds

It was morning, and Daggar was nowhere to be found. The front door of the hovel was propped open with the gargoyle as a door-stop. Wrapped in her cloak and some blankets, Kassa braved the slightly snowy day. She did not travel far, pausing by the upturned water barrel and rapping smartly on the window.

An urchin popped his head out through a neat little trapdoor in the top, yawning loudly.

"Like to earn a hot meal?" Kassa suggested.

The boy's eyes lit up. "Clean yer winders for yer, miss?"

"They're not my windows. I don't care who cleans them."

"Scrubyer chimney?"

"I don't have a chimney, thank you."

"Washyer windscreen?"

"I don't have a…" Kassa paused. "What's a windscreen?"

"Dunno," said the bright-eyed scruff. "Sound good though, dunnit? Watcha want me to do?"

"I need a thief."

His voice became shrill. "I never dun it! Ask anyone, they says I dun it, they's a liar."

"Oh, stop panicking," Kassa said crossly. "Are you going to help me or not?"

When Aragon Silversword dropped into the Palace kitchens to grab some breakfast, he was mildly surprised to find the Lady Emperor perched on one of the benches, licking her fingers as she finished off a delicate platter of tidbits. "You never cease to amaze me, Talle," he said, pulling up a stool. "I would have expected you to have your breakfast dragged up the fourteen flights of stairs to your bed by a team of butlers, accompanied by a fifteen-piece orchestra and a fine selection of mummers to entertain you while you eat."

Talle selected a honeyed walnut from her platter and popped it into her mouth. "I did that yesterday," she shrugged prettily. "It doesn't pay to be staid in this profession."

Aragon plucked a piece of sausage from the platter and chewed on it thoughtfully. "I don't understand you," he mused. "You are in a very precarious position until Dreadnought—not to mention the whole of Mocklore—accept you as Emperor. Why are you surrounding yourselves with traitors like Reed Cooper?"

"And you," she said pointedly, picking the poppyseeds of a tiny cake.

"And me," he agreed.

Lady Talle smiled distantly, her elegantly-nailed fingers picking the cake into individual crumbs. "I know where I stand with traitors, Silversword. I know how the mind of the traitor works. Men like you and Reed Cooper are predictable enough to make me feel comfortable, but dangerous enough to keep me on my toes." She sighed suddenly and pushed the platter in Aragon's direction, sliding to her feet with the grace of a peacock. "And now I simply must find someone to do my hair for me. The trouble with having so many servants is, I can never remember which ones do which tasks. I had a gardener mixing me cocktails yesterday." She paused, a calculating expression glittering in her ice-blue eyes. "You will capture Kassa Daggersharp for me, won't you?"

Aragon took a bite of seaweed confection. "It is in my best interest to do so, don't you think?"

The Lady Emperor smiled, a surprisingly genuine smile which suffused her whole body with a rosy glow. "Oh yes," she murmured. "I do."

-§-§-§-§-§-

The urchin looked uneasily around the interior of Daggar's hovel. "Bit cold here, innit?"

"You live in a barrel," Kassa reminded him.

"But's a warm barrel, yer know? Got any eats?"

Kassa waved a hand carelessly. "Look around. There might be something."

The urchin discovered a crust of bread and started gnawing on it enthusiastically.

"There is a woman who has something belonging to me," Kassa began. "I need someone unobtrusive to get into her residence and take it back."

"What rezzydents?" asked the urchin.

"The Palace," said Kassa crisply.

Still chewing, the boy's eyes widened. "An' this lady what's got the thing would be…"

"The Lady Emperor."

The urchin hurriedly stuffed the rest of the bread in his mouth. "Nice meetin' yer miss. G'bye."

Kassa snatched his sleeve as he made for the door. "Not so fast!"

Daggar burst into the room, eyes wild and waving a piece of parchment. "Chief, it's horrible!" he announced. "All bloody. We're going to be slaughtered in our beds!" He pulled up abruptly and peered intently at the boy Kassa was latched on to. "Who's that?"

Kassa looked down at the boy. "Oh. Who are you?"

"Grffn," said the boy, still chewing rapidly to finish the bread before she changed her mind and demanded it back.

"Griffin," repeated Kassa more distinctly. "Daggar, this is Griffin."

"Kassa, this is a proscription list," said Daggar, waving the parchment at her. "And you are the star attraction."

She snatched it from him, scanning the page quickly. "A silver talent as reward for my capture. Silver."

"Silver," agreed Daggar anxiously, hopping from foot to foot.

"I don't know who this upstart bint thinks she is," said Kassa slowly, "But she appears to be after my inheritance. Where would an emperor get a whole talent from? None of the Emperors since Timregis have had two beans to rub together."

"A talent is how much silver a man can carry without falling over backwards," Daggar reminded her impatiently. "That's a healthy incentive. Unhealthy in our case. Let's get going."

"I need to think," Kassa protested, her eyes glued to the parchment.

Daggar whipped the page away and cast it aside. His self-preservation skills had gone into overtime. "Thinking gets yerself killed, Chief. You need to run!"

Kassa considered her choices for half a second. "All right, we'll run." She grabbed the small sack which contained all her worldly possessions and shoved the gargoyle in, padding it well with her spare dress and embroidery threads.

"Where are we running to?" asked Daggar, scooping up his own worldly possessions (half a bottle of salt-whisky and a set of sharp knives) and tossing them into a pillowcase. The question was a mere formality, he knew that from was much more important than to when running away.

"Pick a forest, any forest," said Kassa. "I was getting tired of city life anyway."

"I wasn't," grumbled Daggar, but he knew better than to protest too much. If he didn't come up with his quota for the Profithood by the next full moon, he was finished in Dreadnought anyway.

Kassa looked back at Griffin the urchin who was casually stealing what morsels he could find in the back of Daggar's cupboards. "How would you like a hovel all of your own?"

"Oy!" protested Daggar.

The boy's face broke into a smile which almost sliced his face in half. "Ya couldn't pay me to live in a dump like this, miss," he said cheerfully. "I'm comin' wif you!"

"You're bloody not," said Kassa and Daggar in unison. It was the first time in a long while that they had agreed with each other.

-§-§-§-§-§-

Lord Rorey of Skullcap was just like the other Lordlings of the Mocklore Empire; mainly useless and horribly rich. He was a young man, but flabby from too much time indoors and not enough healthy food and exercise. He did get plenty of fresh sea air, although fresh was not necessarily the word to describe the fishy odour that wafted into his bedchamber whenever a servant opened the window in the mornings.

Skullcap was a seaport, walled off from everywhere by the treacherous range of mountains known, not unsurprisingly, as the Skullcaps. Every hazard known to anyone was located in those mountains and new ones were arriving every day, so most people came and went from the little seaport by boat.

"Hmm," said Lordling Rorey as he examined the messages that people kept sending to his office. "Pirates, eh?"

"Dead pirates, Lord," corrected his administrative assistant, a pretty girl who spent a lot of time painting her fingernails.

"Hmm," said Lordling Rorey. "Best kind, wot? Still, better do something about it. Any treasure?"

"No, Lord," said the administrative assistant, whose name was Dilys. "The wreck was empty except for basic supplies, a book of humorous hieroglyphs and a gargoyle which disappeared during the salvage."

"Hmm," said Lordling Rorey. "Still, better do something about it. Have the humorous hieroglyphs sent to my room. And get me my warlock. I have important matters to discuss with him. I'll be on the croquet field."

"I'll send him up to the roof, Lord," said Dilys efficiently. There was limited space in the busy little city and so the Lordling's abode was basically a two-up two-down in the middle of the High Street. The croquet field was on the roof, as was the cherry fountain, the rose arbor, the gazebo and the poisonous labyrinth which was presently full of a troupe of mummers.

"Hmm," said Lordling Rorey. "Yes, the roof. Of course the roof. Just send up my warlock, there's a good fellow."

-§-§-§-§-§-

The urchin scampered along, matching Kassa's long-legged walk easily, his fringe bouncing in the cold wind. "Who are you lot, anyways?" he piped up.

"We're pirates," said Kassa shortly.

That stopped him, but only for a moment. "Where's ya ship?"

"Foot-pirates," she corrected. "Look, you can't come with us. There are going to be untold dangers. Soldiers looking for us. Bandits. People trying to kill us!"

"Trolls," contributed Daggar gloomily.

"Trolls!" agreed Kassa.

The urchin considered this. "Coo."

Kassa sighed. Then she looked at his thin, pale arms. "Don't you have a cloak?"

"I'm a n'urchin," he said as if she was nuts. Kassa pulled a blanket out of her bag and handed it to him. Griffin looked at it for a moment and then handed it back. "Like I said. I'm—an—urchin."

And he ran ahead of her, barefoot, almost skipping on the thin layer of snow that covered the road out of Dreadnought.

Daggar just grunted, and pulled his scarf tighter.

From a distance, they looked like a close approximation of a family; nothing for anyone to take any particular notice of. Soon they would reach the multi-coloured forests of the Skullcaps where they could, if they chose, completely disappear.

At least, that was the plan.

-§-§-§-§-§-

Aragon's disguise was impeccable. He resembled nothing more than a hardened pirate, a seedy dark man with bright green eyes and a heart of gold. He was unrecognisable to anyone who knew him, particularly since the disguise made him four inches shorter.

He was too late. Daggar's hovel was deserted, and it was obvious they were not coming back. The proscription list lay on the floor, and Kassa's name was emblazoned across the top of the parchment.

"Damn," said Aragon Silversword with feeling. They were long gone. What was more, it would take him another three hours to rid himself of the stupid disguise.

If he was going to have any chance of finding them, he was going to have to think like Kassa Daggersharp. "If I were a madwoman on a rampage," he mused to himself, "where would I go?"

-§-§-§-§-§-

"So whassat then?" asked the tireless urchin.

"It's a tree," said Kassa shortly.

"Cor, reely? They look diff'rent close up. Gaps between 'em n'evrything."

"Have you never been outside the city?"

"Yah, once. Went on a n'urchin's excursh'n to that bit of dirt outside t' city wall. Dead neat it was. But nah trees." He gestured up at another tree. "Wassat, then?"

"It's another tree," said Kassa. "You get a lot of them in forests."

"But this one's blue. T' other one was pink wif yeller bits."

"Trees come in all colours around here."

"Why?"

They had been travelling through the forest for a while. The trees were coloured in various shades of blue, green, red and purple, covered only by a light scattering of snow. The colour scheme was due to the Glimmer, an event in the not-so-recent past which nobody liked to talk about, particularly Kassa.

"I don't want to talk about it," said Kassa.

"We don't talk to Kassa about multi-coloured trees," said Daggar, almost cheerfully. "She gets upset."

Kassa glared at him. "You keep your mouth shut."

"An' wassat?" The urchin was gesturing up at other tree.

"Griffin..." she warned, tiring of the game.

"Yuh, but wassat in the tree?"

Kassa looked up. A little silver light was weaving merrily around the branches of a purple she-oak, without any apparent purpose. "Actually, I'm not sure. Probably magic." Magic was never a surprise in Mocklore, and usually more trouble than it was worth.

"Dead neat," Griffin said solemnly. "Can we have grub yet?"

They stopped to eat under the tree with the sparkling silver light in it. Daggar kept looking up, as if the little light was twinkling at him personally.

Kassa dozed against the tree for a while, but jumped with a start when the silver light bounced gently against her nose. "Oh!" Daggar and Griffin seemed to have wandered off. She was all alone with a psychopathic light bulb.

She moved quickly, scrambling to her feet. As she turned around, she bumped nose to nose with a buxom blonde in a green dress with a very low-cut bodice. "Wotcha," said the stranger. Then she peered more closely at Kassa and grinned evilly. "Score! A songwitch!"

-§-§-§-§-§-

Service to one of the Lordlings was the best position a warlock could get. Fredgic hardly had to do any magic these days, except for card tricks to entertain at parties. To become a qualified warlock, you had to train at the Polyhedrotechnical for eight years, completing an Advanced Degree in Highly Improbable Arts. By the time of qualification, the resulting graduate tended to be both extremely well educated and heartily sick of magic. A job as court warlock was ideal, although qualifications (or, indeed, intelligence) was not a major requirement.

The Lordlings actually did a lot more about running the Empire than it was generally believed. Each of them was responsible for a city-state, which generally consisted of one major population centre and most of the boring bits that surrounded it. As Lordlings tended to inherit their posts rather than working to achieve them, the efficiency of the Empire largely depended on how good the Lordlings happened to be at picking staff. Lordling Rorey luckily had a very efficient administrative staff (Dilys and the tea-lady) which meant that he hardly had any work to do at all. Skullcap had very few skirmishes with other city-states, as it was too difficult to get past the mountains in order to attack. All in all, the Lordling's position (and that of his warlock) was very cushy indeed.

Fredgic's duties were quite simple. He had to listen when the Lordling talked about new regulations and laws he was imposing (but usually forgot about later), and he was sometimes called upon to play croquet. The rest of his time was his own, which was useful because Fredgic had a very time-consuming hobby. He collected exotic diseases.

"Hmm, yes," said the Lordling as his court warlock approached. "Freesia. There you are. These mallets are a bit short, don't you find?"

"That's because we ran out of flamingos, Lord," said Fredgic comfortingly. "We're on the pigeons now."

"Hmm," said Lordling Rorey, peering at the reproachful bird in his hand. "See what you mean. Have to do something about stapling some together. Or the rack, perhaps. That might help stretch 'em a bit. This just won't do."

"We have a new batch of flamingos due in next week, lord," Fredgic assured him, and then sneezed.

"Hmm," said the Lordling. "Poorly, are you?"

"I think it's Narachidnius Syndrome, Lord," said Fredgic proudly. "I expect my arms and legs to be dropping off at any minute. It's very rare, you know. Usually only apple trees infested with black willow-tongued spiders get it."

"Hmm," said the Lordling, not paying attention. "Well done, Freda. Now, I've got some very important business for you."

"You have, Lord?" sneezed Fredgic in surprise.

"Hmm, of course I have, by Juniper. It's those pirates. I won't have it."

"You want the pirates exterminated, Lord?"

"Hmm, good gravy, no! They're doing that themselves, don't you know? Brought in a shipwreck full of dead ones a while back. Just not good enough."

"It isn't?"

"Hmm, of course not. Use your loaf, man. There wasn't a single gold bullion to be seen. Pirates are supposed to have treasure. There just aren't enough, wot?"

"Not enough treasure, lord?"

"Hmm, not enough pirates! By Jelliwinks, it's just not good enough. I want you to get some for me to supervise personally. I'll soon whip 'em into shape. Have 'em raiding and pillaging and getting together a proper hoard. That's what piracy's all about!"

"You want me to find some pirates for you," said Fredgic carefully. This sounded too much like hard work.

"Hmm, wot?" said the Lordling, his attention now taken up by the pigeon in his hand, and how it could be turned into a working croquet mallet. "Hmm, yes, get on with it, man. Perhaps if I skewered several on a long stick. Hmm, you there! Jester! Fetch me a long stick!"

The pigeon looked distinctly unhappy with the situation.

-§-§-§-§-§-

"I'm not a songwitch," protested Kassa. "I'm not any kind of witch."

The buxom blonde pulled a face. "You think I don't know a witchy when I see one? Next you'll be telling me your mother was no witchy, and your grandmother, and your great grandmother!" She waggled an accusing finger. "You're keeping secrets, ladybird."

"I don't know what you're talking about," insisted Kassa, turning away.

But suddenly the blonde vanished from behind her and appeared in front of her. "Oh, no you don't, milady."

"Leave me alone!"

"Now, what kind of guardian sprite would I be if I did that?"

Kassa was taken aback. "But guardian sprites are supposed to guard witches..."

"Funny, that, isn't it," grinned the sprite. "Almost as if you were a real witch. See you soon, ladybird!" And she vanished.

It was only then, blinking herself awake, that Kassa realised she had been dreaming. A curious odour wafted past her nose. "What do I smell?" she muttered sleepily.

"Food bein' cooked," replied Daggar. "Thought you wouldn't recognise it."

"You mean you can cook?"

Daggar laughed in a rapid bark. "Do me a favour, Chief. It's the anklebiter."

"Griffin?" Kassa looked towards the fire, and saw her pet urchin solemnly stirring a stew in her little cauldron. "Oh. I knew there was a reason to bring him along."

After eating, they moved on. In the oak tree, a silver light flickered and suddenly a buxom blonde sprite was sitting on the high branch, watching the travellers depart. "So you think you're no songwitch?" she muttered smugly to herself. "We'll see about that, ladybird."

Chapter 6
Camelot

Goblins like dark, damp places. Small caves are best, but there are never enough small caves because there are so many goblins. So they all squish together, grumbling, muttering, sharing menacing silences and smelling like dirt.

From their holes in the ground (and the rocks and the trees), goblins watch the world. They can't see out, but that doesn't matter, because goblins can see in. Into every room, through every wall, over every mountain. Goblins don't need windows to watch the world.

At that moment, they were watching Kassa Daggersharp.

-§-§-§-§-§-

Kassa, concealed modestly behind a large bush, was changing her dress. Crossing rivers valiantly was one thing, but squishing around in wet clothes for the rest of the day was something else entirely. When she emerged, Griffin had a fire going. The urchin had developed a habit of lighting fires every time they stopped for more than five minutes.

With her hair still damp from the river they had fallen in, and with the promise of a cool evening hanging wetly in the air, Kassa was quite pleased to have the little lickering flames burning in the ring of stones.

"Night falls quickly when yer out in the landscape," noted Daggar gloomily.

"You don't like nature much, do you?" said Kassa.

"I got nothing against eating salad if it's put on me plate," said Daggar in a wounded voice. "Got no problem with trees and stuff outside either," he added in a muttered voice. "I just don't see why I have to be outside with them."

Griffin was cooking again.

"These mushrooms are very good," said Kassa, tasting from the cauldron. "What did you do to them?"

"Cooked 'em!' said the urchin proudly.

"See, Kassa," said Daggar knowingly. "It works with meat, too. You should try it sometime."

"I can cook," said Kassa. "I just choose not to. Anyway, I don't see you lifting a ladle, except to stuff more in your face."

"True enough," said Daggar cheerfully, holding his bowl out for seconds. "But then, I'm not a..." The word 'girl' froze on his lips.

Kassa's expression could only be described as dangerous. "Well?"

Daggar clamped his mouth shut and kept it shut for a long time.

-§-§-§-§-§-

The night got darker and colder. The moon rose, and Daggar was very depressed to notice how much it had waned. At this rate, it would be less than two weeks until the next full moon...and retirement.

They were camped by the slope which became the cliff which formed the first of the Skullcap Mountains. "We have to climb them?" said Daggar doubtfully.

"I imagine so," replied Kassa. "What's the matter? You wanted to run away from Dreadnought. I thought you would feel safer on the other side of the Skullcaps."

"I would love to be on the other side of the Skullcaps," said Daggar in a heartfelt tone. "But I'd rather get there without having to climb anything. Can't we go by the road?"

"Not if we don't want to be caught and executed," snapped Kassa. "Use your head."

The Skullcaps appeared menacing in the moonlight, which was their job. However, they also looked strangely alive. Dark caves made an intimidting pattern across the face of the closest rock formations. There hadn't been any caves there when they arrived.

"Lots of perils in the Skullcaps," said Daggar in a foreboding voice. "Goblins and those flaming sprites. Firebrands. Very nasty. And trolls, probably. You always get trolls in mountains. Blowing things up all over the place, and building trapdoors that lead nowhere but down. Big hairy whatsits with teeth. Predatory birds looking for munchies. And I know for a fact that half the Profithood visit the Skullcaps for their holidays, just to play with the passing bandits. Hermits too, up there. A menace, always muttering things and playing tricks. Willow wisps, those lights that lead you off cliffs. One of them bit me once, and I wasn't even in a forest, I was in a rose garden. And then there's the Hidden Army..."

Kassa had to stop him there. "Daggar, everyone knows that the Hidden Army have never existed. They're a myth. There is no such thing."

There was a sound almost exactly like a portable cave moving into range. Moments later, a crossbow bolt zizzed past, pinning a lock of Kassa's hair to a nearby tree.

"Don't move," said a ringing voice.

Kassa had already frozen still.

"Hah," said Daggar, unsurprised.

A woman stepped into the circle of pale firelight. "Footcrusher," she said crisply.

Since she was into descriptions, Daggar introduced himself helpfully as, "Coward."

The Footcrusher woman dismissed him with a sniff, and stepped towards Kassa. "You have something in your possession which belongs to me," she said in an unemotional but menacing voice. "I believe it is in the form of a gargoyle. Give it to me."

"No," said Kassa.

It was only then that the shadows moved, and Kassa became aware that she was not just facing one crossbow-wielding person.

There must have been nearly a hundred of them. She could feel their proximity, even if she couldn't see them all. She dimly remembered a moment from her childhood, when Bigbeard had given her some rare fatherly advice: "Never say you don't believe in fairies. Dozens of the little sods will turn up all over the place, and then you'll be sorry." The same, she imagined, applied to the Hidden Army of Mercenaries.

"May I rephrase my answer?" she requested politely.

-§-§-§-§-§-

Fredgic the warlock did not like trees. It was bad enough that they were such unhealthy creatures that even the smallest sapling had more exotic diseases than he could contract in a lifetime. He wouldn't object to that quite so much if they didn't keep going on about it. Being a warlock, Fredgic was exceptionally attuned to magic and exceptionally unattuned to nature. This meant that trees usually left him alone. But these trees, the Glimmered ones that hung around the Skullcaps, had more to do with magic than nature. Not that the two things are not exactly the same when you get right down to it.

In the aftermath of the Glimmer, a hideous magical catastrophe which had nothing to do with any warlock, no matter what anyone said, the trees of the Skullcaps had contracted the most exotic disease of all. Communication. And despite the fact that he was a mere warlock, Fredgic was still a magical human and therefore eligible for the forest to communicate with.

And communicate they did. They hummed. They tootled little songs at him. They shared fungus-in-law jokes. And because a warlock was the closest thing the Skullcap forest had to a tree surgeon, they confided all of their medicinal complaints to him.

Seething with jealousy as every purple alder, pink spiny-tipped hoak or gold-leaved swaxzleberry tree described its unusual dyspeptic bark rash or hacking acorn-grout, Fredgic stomped along a particularly hazardous ridge of the third Skullcap mountain. He didn't even bother to cough or sneeze, because his petty viruses were nothing to the luxurious unhealthiness of the trees. He had never felt so inadequate.

Of course, Fredgic could have vanished himself to the location of the nearest pirate band, but that would involve doing magic and he saw no reason to resort to such measures unless sorely provoked. He would rather put up with the dizzying heights of the deadly mountains, and the smugness of the trees.

Anyway, to capture a band of pirates he would have to be dastardly clever. Since he wasn't dastardly clever, he had decided to give himself lots of time to think up a plan.

Then, on the breeze that whistled through his woolly hat, he heard a word. Pirates…

-§-§-§-§-§-

"Pirates?" said Zelora Footcrusher, amused. She looked Daggar up and down sceptically. "Are you sure?"

Kassa bristled. "We are the Daggersharp Pirates."

"We are?" said Daggar, who had never been introduced to himself as such.

Zelora smiled, showing a mouthful of sharp little teeth. "Not the Daggersharp pirates of Vicious Bigbeard, the most fearsome Pirate King of the seventeen seas?"

"They're all dead," said Kassa shortly.

Zelora Footcrusher did not seem peturbed. "So they are," she said calmly.

Her second-in-command, a hairy young man called Singespitter, nudged her eagerly with his bony elbow. "You don't think they're Barechin Tim's gang of…"

"No, we are not!" said Kassa sharply. "We are a new crew of Daggersharp pirates. New and improved."

"We don't have a ship yet," Daggar added helpfully.

"Minor detail," snapped Kassa.

"So you're pirates?" said Zelora with a smirk. "All both of you."

"Two and a half," said Daggar. "We had an urchin, but we seem to have mislaid it."

Griffin emerged from behind an orange tree, holding a saucepan. "Sorry, Chief, but I didn't want the mushies to burn."

"Don't call me Chief," said Kassa automatically, feeling that she was fighting a losing battle.

"Who is this?" demanded Zelora scornfully.

The small urchin bowed neatly and doffed an imaginary hat. "Gracious lady, I am Griffin, son of Camelot."

Kassa frowned. Such lordly gentility was not what she'd come to expect from this particular brand of professional urchin.

"Not Baron Camelot of Eaglesbog, legendary knight of knights?" inquired Singespitter enthusiastically.

"My old dad, a Baron?" said Griffin disbelievingly. "I don't think so."

"Was he, then, Camelot the spy?" inquired Zelora in a cool, ringing voice. "We have never met, but he is currently in my employ."

Griffin grinned widely and lapsed back into urchin-speak. "My dad? Nah. He wuz Camelot the street-hawker." There was a brief pause, while Griffin replaced the imaginary cap on his head. "I'm Camelot the spy," he said modestly.

-§-§-§-§-§-

By Fredgic's calculations, the pirates were now in the cave below. And although he was not dastardly clever, his calculations were usually pretty close to being accurate. He hung suspended immediately above the cave, ready to swing in, capture the pirates with his clockwork net and have it away back to Skullcap where he would be met with praise, gifts and wild applause. He took a deep breath, sneezed twice, and counted slowly to three. "One, two, thr-ungh!"

It should have worked. It was a neat little plan which involved no magic whatsoever. It would have worked, if only the cave hadn't relocated itself during his count.

As a matter of fact, the cave had only moved about four tree-widths aside, but it was more than enough to squish Fredgic's plans. The warlock slammed face first into the rock-face and, whimpering uncontrollably, vanished himself back home to recuperate. So much for not using magic.

-§-§-§-§-§-

By the light of invisible campfires, the cave which contained Zelora Footcrusher and her prisoners slowly slid across the mountain.

"I feel sick," said Daggar helpfully.

Zelora ignored him, turning the gargoyle around in her hands. "So, Braided Bones," she murmured. "This is what you have been doing all these years."

Kassa was surprised. "You know who he is?"

Zelora ignored her as well. "Thank you, Agent Camelot. Your work is faultless."

Griffin looked pleased. "That's me. Urchin for hire. I do spying, political intrigue, publicity management and juggling at children's parties." He produced a small white card and handed it to her. "Recommend me to your friends."

"I told you not to go picking up stray kids," Daggar accused Kassa.

"When?" she challenged.

"I presume you found out all the necessary information about the gargoyle from these two," Zelora said to Griffin.

The urchin tried to look modest, digging the ground with his toe. "Well, I did delve a little."

"Good. Singespitter, take these two into the cave next door. If Agent Camelot doesn't have everything I want, I may wish to interrogate them."

"What if we don't want to go into the next cave?" protested Daggar as he and Kassa were pulled to their feet.

Zelora snarled, showing her teeth nastily. "Would you like me to demonstrate why I am called Footcrusher?"

Daggar smiled weakly. "I could say that I liked a woman with spirit, but you'd probably hit me, so I'll just go into the cave next door with Mangebiter, shall I?"

"That's Singespitter," corrected Singespitter in a tone which entirely failed to sound mean enough.

-§-§-§-§-§-

The K Division caves continued, rumbling slowly across the face of the mountain. Kassa could smell salt. She sniffed heartily at the air. "We're near the sea."

"I know," said Daggar glumly. The rock he was tied to was dangerously near the edge of the cave. "I think I'm going to throw up."

"Please don't."

The caves hiccupped violently, and stopped moving.

Daggar looked very green. "I wonder what they're going to do with us," he said dismally.

"They'll probably eat us."

"I wouldn't be surprised. Do you think they're after the treasure too?"

"If I didn't know better, I would say that you were more worried about the treasure than about us."

"Oh, I'm very worried about us," he assured her. "But if I don't prove myself profitable to the Profithood soon, I'm going to have a crack team of my dear colleagues hunting me down with murderous intent. Then is the time to be worrying about us. Well, me anyway." He peered out over the edge, and saw something which surprised him. "Speaking of traitors, lords and ladies..."

"Were we talking about traitors?" said Kassa tiredly

"We will be in a minute," Daggar predicted.

It was then that Aragon Silversword climbed into the cave. He stood silently for a moment, waiting for one of them to say something. They didn't. Finally, he spoke. "I don't suppose that either of you would care to be rescued?"

Chapter 7
The Earth Moves for Everyone

Fredgic the court warlock approached the Lordling's room cautiously. "Lord? Lord Rorey, are you there?"

A large figure leaped out in front of him. "Hahhaargh! Shiver your timbers, me blighties, hmm, and yo ho ho with rum balls and cream! Haharrggh!" Under the bright scarlet scarves, large purple trousers, four eye patches and two black hats, Fredgic could just recognise his Lordling.

"Hmmm," Lordling Rorey said thoughtfully, pausing to admire himself in the mirror. "Not bad, eh, Fruitcup?"

"Very flattering, Lord," said Fredgic, sniffling politely into a handkerchief.

"Hmm, all ready to start training my pirates," said the Lordling happily. "Where are they, then?"

"I have located a pirate crew, Lord," said Fredgic hastily. "But they appear to be travelling on dry land."

"Hmm, what a good idea," said the Lordling. "All the better to capture them, eh, Fructose? Are they in my dungeon yet?"

"You don't have a dungeon, Lord, you have a small wine cellar," corrected Fredgic.

"Hmm, better not put them in there, wot? The bounders will drink all my best claret. Just send them up to me, will you?"

"They are quite close by, in the Skullcap mountains," said Fredgic, hoping to gently dissuade the Lordling from ordering him to do anything about it.

Lordling Rorey peered at him. "Hmm, well, you had better go and fetch them, by Jellied Eels! They might escape."

"Perhaps one of your other retainers might be more suitable for this task, my Lord?" suggested Fredgic weakly.

"Hmm, but it's Cook's day off, don't you know?"

A tiny figure crept out of the shadows. It was a very small jester with spectacles and a large humorous hat. "If I might be so bold, Lord?" he squeaked. "I would very much like to accompany anyone going on such a mission. I have aspirations, you see, to be an epic-minstrel and to write songs about famous people who do mighty deeds, like yourself, Lord."

Lordling Rorey looked stunned. "Hmm, that's it, by gad! This is even better than the time I thought about putting a piece of bread inside two pieces of cheese for a comfortable snack. I shall go to capture the pirates myself! Marvellous, wot? You can come to write songs about me, jester, and you, Froogleberry, you can get my best golden carriage."

"We will be climbing mountains, Lord, perhaps a carriage is not quite suitable," said Fredgic weakly.

"Hmm, hitch it up to some mountain goats, then. Do I have to think of everything?"

"How many guards and warriors in the retinue, lord?" asked Fredgic hopefully, dimly aware that there was less than six in the whole city, and none were officially on the Lordling's payroll.

"Hmm, I don't want any of those fellows, use your brains, man! I want mummers, by gad. And jugglers, and people wearing humorous hats such as this little chap. Well done, little chap. What's your name?"

"Tippett, my Lord," said the little jester.

"Hmm," said Lordling Rorey. "Pack a suitcase, Tippett. Well, get moving, Fridgepick. We're going to capture some pirates!"

Mildly resentful that the Lordling had got the jester's name right first time, Fredgic went to arrange for a carriage. With mountain goats.

-§-§-§-§-§-

"So you want to turn pirate?" Kassa inquired.

"I didn't get much of a chance last time," said Aragon Silversword. And he smiled.

Kassa turned her head towards Daggar. "What do you think?"

"Why not?" said Daggar.

"I didn't think you trusted me," said Aragon.

"I don't," said Daggar. "But if she looks any further, we might end up with some real heroes in this crew, know what I mean? Anyway, right now I'm on the side of anyone who will untie me before that Footcrusher woman comes back."

Kassa thought for a moment, and then smiled generously at Aragon. "You may release us."

"Actually, I've been thinking about that," said Aragon Silversword. "I may have a more practical solution."

-§-§-§-§-§-

One of the blondest ladies-in-waiting tripped as she scurried through the door, the bubbles on her tray spilling all over Reed Cooper.

"Fetch more," commanded the unruffled Lady Emperor. The lady-in-waiting scuttled away again, blushing horribly.

Lady Talle was in her bath, and it was no ordinary bath. For a start, it was the size of an average town square. Once, in the time of earlier Emperors, this colossal sunken pool had been lined with solid gold. At some stage during the last few reigns, however, the gold had been stripped away and neatly replaced by half a million false marble tiles.

No one was quite sure how this had been achieved without anyone noticing anything suspicious, but a Profithood declaration of sheer audacity had been awarded to the unknown culprit.

The glittering soap bubbles which were protecting the Lady Emperor's semblance of modesty were being continuously replenished from the gardens, where they grew in abundance.

Reed scowled. After a pirate's life of danger and excitement, guarding the Imperial bath chamber lacked a certain something. Another lady-in-waiting squeezed past him, clutching a selection of fizzy drinks. Reed stopped scowling and began glaring openly.

The sacred bauble of Chiantrio was tied to a length of ribbon, and the Lady Emperor was amusing herself by batting it back and forth. "Something wrong, my precious pirate?" she cooed.

"I am a man of action!" exploded Reed. "I know Mistress Daggersharp, we practically grew up together. I should be the one to hunt her down."

"You are protecting my safety, Cooper," purred the Lady Emperor dangerously. "Is there any task more worthwhile?"

Reed leaned over the edge of the bath, thrusting his fists angrily against the delicate tiles. "You—can't—trust—Silversword," he grated.

"Oh?" said the Lady Emperor. "But I can trust you, of course." She seemed amused at the idea.

With a barely perceptible burble, the sacred bauble tugged impatiently at its ribbon. Lady Talle turned her attention to it. "Follow Aragon Silversword," she whispered. With a shrill "Yipppeeee," the bauble snapped its ribbon and went careering through the window, making a bauble-sized hole in the glass.

Lady Talle reclined again, floating lazily amongst the bubbles. "I suggest you follow it, Reed. The bauble will find Silversword instantly. Could you?"

In one swift moment, Reed Cooper vaulted out of the window, leaving a pirate-sized hole in the glass.

Lady Talle sank further in the bubbles, enjoying the cool breeze upon the back of her neck.

-§-§-§-§-§-

After a thorough briefing by her hired spy, Zelora Footcrusher ordered Singespitter to bring her the stupid-looking pirate. The prisoners were still tied to their individual rocks, glaring at each other.

"You," said Singespitter in a nearly menacing voice, advancing on Daggar. Surprisingly strong, he lifted the profit-scoundrel to his feet and dragged him away.

"Oy!" protested Daggar. "Yer could untie me from the rock first!"

When Daggar's muffled protests could no longer be heard, Aragon lowered himself back into the cave and released Kassa.

"Daggar won't like being a decoy," she warned him.

"He'll live. Probably."

She looked around. "Which way did they go?"

"Didn't you notice? You were in here at the time."

"I wasn't looking," she admitted. "Maybe we should split up. You take the tunnel on the left and I'll take the one on the right. One of us should find where they took the gargoyle."

"A remarkably sane plan," said Aragon. "You surprise me."

-§-§-§-§-§-

"So," said Daggar, settling himself comfortably on Zelora's sandstone cushions. "The Hidden Army, eh? I never met an executive mercenary before." He grinned. It was a grin that had softened a thousand hearts, opened a thousand purses and won a thousand hot meals from sympathetic farmer's wives. It had absolutely no effect on Zelora Footcrusher.

"I am the deputy leader responsible for K Division," she said in a clipped voice. "I am answerable only to the Hidden Leader."

"What does that mean?"

"Almost nothing. But let's talk about you."

He smiled hopefully, attempting to gaze into her eyes. "What would you like to know?"

"I want to know all about you," said Zelora. "And the gargoyle."

"Ey," he said offhandedly. "It's Kassa's gargoyle really. I were never formally introduced."

Zelora stood up. "Perhaps I should be speaking to her, then."

"I still know lots about it!" Daggar added hastily, remembering the role he had to play. "Ask me anything."

Zelora sat down again. "I want to know how you found the gargoyle, and what you know about where it has been for the last ten years."

Daggar was surprised. "He hasn't been a gargoyle that long!"

Zelora leaned forward. "Who hasn't?"

"You know," he said teasingly.

"Do I?"

"Sure, or you wouldn't be so keen to track him down." Daggar knotted his fingers together and stretched them behind his head. "Y'know, when yer eyes lose that nasty red glow of bloodlust, yer really quite easy on the eye."

Zelora frowned. "Is this some kind of attempt at charm?"

Daggar's grin widened. "Most women appreciate it."

"Oh, I doubt that."

-§-§-§-§-§-

All the tunnels were beginning to look the same. Kassa banged an angry fist against the blank wall beside her. "I hate the dark!"

"So why don't you shed some light on the subject, ladybird?" suggested a vaguely familiar voice.

A faint glow lit up the tunnel, and Kassa saw the buxom blonde sprite from the forest.

"What are you doing here?" she asked snappishly.

"I'm trying to help," said the sprite. "You're going the wrong way."

"What's it to you? You don't know anything, you're just a dream figment."

The sprite leaned against a wall. "Sleeping, are you?"

Kassa tried not to think about that. "Do I know you?"

"That depends," said the sprite. "Do you remember your christening?"

"I wasn't christened, I was witched," said Kassa crossly. "All my female relations got together and put a variety of interesting curses on me while submerging me in a cauldron full of unspeakable things."

"You do remember!" said the sprite happily.

"Of course not, I was a baby. I saw the crystal ball recording later."

"I was there!" insisted the sprite. "At the witching. I was the invisible one, third from the left, who was whispering advice in your mother's ear."

"I remember her swatting the air at some point," said Kassa doubtfully. "What has all this got to do with me?"

"It's simple," said the sprite. "I was your mother's guardian sprite, and when she ran away with that overgrown pirate, I got in terrible trouble for not looking after her properly. So now I'm your guardian sprite." She beamed at Kassa.

"Great," said Kassa. "I get a second-rate sprite. So now you've come to tell me that I'm going the wrong way, and you want to offer me directions."

"Absolutely," said the sprite.

Kassa waited. "Well?" she said finally.

"Wouldn't you rather reminisce?"

"No! I have a job to do."

The sprite made a face and pointed to a blank wall. "That way."

"But there isn't a tunnel that way," Kassa protested.

"There is, you know. It's about a quarter of a mile in that direction. There's just a lot of rock in the way."

Kassa put her hands on her hips, because she felt like it. "Look, sprite..."

"Summer Songstrel, at your service," the sprite said with vicious sweetness. "Since you ask."

"How am I supposed to reach the tunnel through a quarter of a mile of rock?"

"Can't you even do that much? Some songwitch."

"I am not a songwitch," Kassa said flatly. "I am not a witch of any kind."

"You know, I'm almost starting to believe you," said Summer Songstrel sadly. She sighed and waved her hands around for a while. The wall opened up, revealing a new tunnel. "Don't say I never do anything for you," she chided, and then vanished.

"Thank you," said Kassa to the empty air. And then she stepped cautiously into the sprite's tunnel, almost expecting that to vanish too.

-§-§-§-§-§-

The tunnel led downwards, along and downwards again. Aragon had counted eight hundred and eighty-three steps. From below, he saw a glimmer of light and heard a slow, bored voice.

"I'm sing-ing in the Brayne, not dan-cing in the Brayne, what a ve-ry dull feel-ing, I'm onnnnnn du-ty again..."

Aragon peered downwards to where the light was coming from. A gnome-like little man was sitting at a huge table made out of stone. Buttons and levers and strange flickering screens covered the surface of the table, all formed out of stones and pebbles and bits of bark.

A hollow, scratchy voice came out of one of the two stone tubes that hung down from the ceiling. "Hellooooo Bronkx. Hellllloooooo, Bronkx."

Grumbling, the gnome climbed up on his chair and shouted at the tube. "I'm busy! Go away!"

"Aww, come onnnnnn, Bronkx. It's importannnt."

"Whaddaya want?"

"Some pri-isonerrrrs escaaaaped from one of the entrannnnnce cavernnnnns."

"Whose bright idea was it to put prisoners there?" grumbled Bronkx. "No wonder they escaped."

"I think Footcrusher wanted them close byyyy!" the voice echoed.

The gnome went pale. "They were Footcrusher's prisoners and you let them escape? Are you crazy?"

"Sorrrryyyyyy," came the voice. "Send out an alerrrrrt to all the other guardddds."

"You mean Simon?"

"Whatevvveeerrrr," said the voice.

Bronkx stepped down from his chair. "Flaming idiots," he muttered, moving his chair until it was under the other stone tube. "Hey, Simon!"

"Whhaaaat," came a different voice.

"Keep an eye out for some escaped prisoners will ya?"

"I'm busssyyyyy," came the voice.

Bronkx climbed down again and sat on his chair. "Bleeding Hidden Army types. Who has to do all the work? Me, that's who." He tapped one of the stone controls on his table.

On the stairs, Aragon realised that behind him, the door had suddenly turned into a wall. He thought about this. The Brayne. The secret of the Hidden Army's relocating caves lay just below him. Aragon liked other people's secrets.

Aragon waited for a while, until a loud, growling noise came from below. The gnome was snoring.

Very quietly, Aragon stepped into the control cave. He leaned over the table, which was covered with moving diagrams and blinking runes. It would be impossible to know what they meant without proper instruction. He started looking for the manual.

-§-§-§-§-§-

Freshly bathed, swathed in an elegant white mouse-fur coat and wearing diamond rings on her toes, Lady Talle prepared to step into her carriage to follow Reed Cooper. Not that she didn't trust him, she just didn't trust him.

"Running away already, your Imperialness?" came a mocking voice.

Lady Talle turned, angry at the insolent tone. "How dare you..." She stopped.

Standing before her was a delegation. The most influential people of Dreadnought, except only herself, were gathered together with identical expressions of displeasure on their faces.

"On the other hand," said Lady Talle, her tone rapidly becoming inviting and relaxed. "How nice to meet you, gentlemen. Why don't you come inside for a quick café au lait?"

-§-§-§-§-§-

Aragon tossed the manual aside and tapped at the pebbles on the surface of the table, bringing up a diagram of Zelora Footcrusher's quarters. Simultaneously, he called up an image of where Kassa was. Even though he had known vaguely where she should have been, it had taken a while to locate her because she appeared to be walking through an area of solid rock. It wasn't so hard—after all, if a gnome could operate this damn fool system...

-§-§-§-§-§-

"This isn't getting us anywhere," snapped Zelora, standing up. "You're quite obviously not going to tell me anything."

Daggar's eyes had wandered to the gargoyle, so he was the first to notice when the stone shelf it was resting on vanished into a stone alcove that suddenly wasn't there anymore. "Ey!" he blurted out.

Zelora whirled around just in time to see the gargoyle vanish. She looked accusingly at Daggar who held up his hands hastily, protesting his innocence.

"I didn't do it! I wouldn't even know how!"

-§-§-§-§-§-

Kassa screamed as the floor beneath her exploded. She was pushed rapidly towards the ceiling which opened up to let her through. Fifty levels of tunnels or more later, she had completely run out of scream, and still the floor was spinning up through the centre of the mountain.

Behind her and around her, caves and tunnels changed shape. The whole cave complex was being turned upside down and inside out. It was pure chaos.

Finally Kassa was propelled out of the top of the mountain, tumbling out on to the silvery grass. "Bwlargh!" she said dizzily. As she leaned over to look inside the hole in the mountain, she saw something small and dark shooting up towards her.

The gargoyle burst out of the hole in the mountain, and all the layers of stone closed behind it as it flew towards the sky. Kassa stretched out her fingertips to catch it, but missed completely. It bounced on the grass, and lay still.

Before Kassa could get her breath back, a set of moving stone steps appeared out of the centre of the mountain, and Aragon Silversword arrived in a much more dignified manner.

"You're full of surprises," Kassa managed in a raspy voice, still sore from all the terrified screaming. She fished around for the gargoyle and held on to it tightly. "Where's Daggar?"

Aragon smiled, advancing on her. "Why would I care?"

"Shouldn't we rescue him?"

He kept advancing on her, his hand firmly curled around a small Hidden Army executive crossbow.

Kassa's head was still spinning crazily. She fought to get control over her thoughts. And then she remembered that he was a traitor. "Stay back," she insisted.

"Give me the gargoyle, my lady," he said warningly.

"I'll throw it over the cliff first," she threatened.

"You think I have forgotten that he is a friend of yours? Give it to me."

Alive was better than dead. Kassa handed the gargoyle over. "What do you want with it?"

"I have a customer. For both of you. Now turn around."

He tied her wrists tightly with the length of rope she had been using for a belt, and made her walk ahead of him. She did so, stumbling over the sharp rocks, trailing vines and hibernating furry animals which lay in her path. "There are a lot of hazards in the Skullcaps," she said hesitantly. "Especially at night."

"Oh, I know," said Aragon Silversword. "Firebrands and icesprites, trolls and trapdoors." He lowered his voice. "I even hear that some of the Profithood take their holidays here so they can play with the bandits."

"You were there when we were captured," realised Kassa. He must have been trailing them since Dreadnought.

"I have always been with you, my lady. Shadowing your every step. Those moving caves are quite ingenious. I'll have to sell their secret to someone someday."

She glared at her feet as she stumbled along. "I don't like you, Silversword."

"I know that," he replied. "But I won't hold it against you."

A few feet in front of them, a tree burst into flames. Light flooded everywhere, flashing gold and silver in their eyes. A throbbing beat seemed to be all around them. Ba-boom, ba-boom, ba-boo-boo-boom…

And then a male figure, swathed in orange flame, appeared before them. Heat resonated off him, and he swayed his burning hips crazily to the sound of the beat. He was wearing dark glasses.

They were surrounded by dancing flames. Some were jitterbugging, some were shimmying and some were doing the lambada.

"And this would be…" Aragon invited Kassa to explain.

"Firebrands," she said tiredly. "I hope you weren't in a hurry to get anywhere."

-§-§-§-§-§-

It was dark now. The mountain had stopped shaking. They were trapped in a small cave formed from a corner of Zelora's quarters and some spare boulders. There was no door. No way out. Very soon, there would be no fresh air to breathe.

"All right," said Daggar in the darkness. "I'm willing to believe that this is all Kassa's fault."

Zelora's breath was a hiss. "If we get out of this, I'm going to cut you into pieces small enough to feed to my pet termites!"

There was a long pause. And then, in the dark, Daggar grinned hopefully. "Do I sense that it's time to be charming again?"

Chapter 8
Playing With Fire

There were seven in the delegation.

First came Leonardes of Skullcap, large and imposing in his black ceremonial robes edged with thin gold coins. As Chief Scoundrel in the Profithood, he had precedence over all the other representatives. Plus he was bigger than most of them put together. He had single-handedly scared off at least a third of the pretender Emperors since Timregis, mostly by threats of heavy fines for tax evasion. Since there was no Dreadnought Lordling, the only people in the city who charged taxes were the Profithood themselves, and the Profithood took a very dim view of people who tried to avoid giving them money.

Standing next to Leonardes was the Captain of the Dreadnought Blackguards, looking as if he would rather be somewhere else.

Then there was the Red Admiral, a short, squat man with a large hat shaped like Pride of the Navy, the Imperial ship. The Navy only consisted of twelve men and a ship's parrot, all of whom held the title of Admiral, but Talle still needed their support. After all, they were the ones who had sunk Bigbeard Daggersharp's ship, and as far as she could tell, none of the profits had made their way to the Imperial coffers yet. Those Admirals were sneaky bastards.

Tamb Lint was the spokesman for the merchants and marketeers of Dreadnought. He had greasy hair and tended to start his sentences with "Geetchor horanges, cheap an' luvverly, gettem while they're hot..." Nevertheless, it was important not to underestimate him. With a single gesture, he could bring the city to an economic standstill.

Then there was the Chief Mummer, a small thin man with white face-paint and a rubber chicken, who was very highly regarded by all the entertainers, news-minstrels and creators of humorous hieroglyphs. If Talle didn't get this group on her side, she would be lampooned and sneered at throughout the Empire. She wanted positive propaganda, and for that she would have to be very enticing.

Present also was the Ambassador of Anglorachnis, the city just beyond the borders of the Mocklore Empire. He looked puffed up and important, but that was just because he was wearing purple. Ambassadors always wore purple. If Talle wanted to be taken at all seriously, his report would be crucial.

The seventh member of the party was elusive. He kept to the shadows, even in the bright chamber in which the Lady Emperor received her guests. He was so non-descript that Talle kept forgetting he was there. This could only be the Hidden Executive Leader of the Hidden Army of Mercenaries, which didn't exist, of course, but whom she might need the services of in the future...should she want anyone conquered, besieged or just generally frightened to death.

"May I ask the reason for this intrusion?" said the Lady Emperor asked, reverting to a voice of high and haughty royalty in a desperate bid to seize control of the meeting.

"We wished to pay our respects to the new Emperor of Mocklore," said Leonardes in his rich, dangerous voice. The thick fingers twisted and stretched as he spoke.

"I do not notice you behaving with particular respect," Lady Talle replied.

"Let's speak frankly," said the Anglorachnis Ambassador. "Mocklore is crumbling. This little Empire has become a colossal joke to everyone. No one cares who rules it anymore, especially those who live here. It is time that there was a stable Emperor. One likely to last more than a few months."

"And I need your support to do so," completed Talle in a chilly tone.

"Did we say that?" inquired Leonardes.

Talle shot a glare at the Anglorachnis Ambassdor which was cold enough to wither an indestructible artichoke. "What is your interest in these matters, Ambassador? I would think Anglorachnis might prefer Mocklore to be in chaos."

"To make it easier for us to invade?" said the Ambassador with amusement. "My Lady, your people are all either bandits, merchants or minstrels. Your crops are pathetic, it rains too much, and you have regular natural disasters. In the last moon alone, Mocklore was subjected to three earthquakes, a rain of lemmings, a wave of talking letterboxes and an exploding mountain which sprayed warm porridge all over the Midden Plains. And I hardly need mention the damage caused by that hideous Glimmer incident nearly a decade ago. You can keep your little island empire, we don't want it."

"So what do you want?' said Lady Talle suddenly. "What is your price for supporting me?"

"Are you offering to bribe us, your Imperial Highness?" suggested Leonardes of Skullcap. He sounded amused. "How much are you offering?"

"I have nothing," Lady Talle spat. "You must know that there is no money in the Imperial coffers. The rapid succession of failed Emperors have bled Mocklore dry. And until I prove myself to the Lordlings, I can expect no tribute from the city-states." She laughed hollowly. "I doubt if any of them are even aware that there is a new Emperor. And why would they care, if they did know?" She regarded them all, her voice immaculately calm. "After all, one Emperor is much the same as another. The only difference, gentlemen, is that I intend to stay. I will not be beaten by this damn Empire!"

There was a pause, and then Leonardes of Skullcap began to applaud, slowly. "Fine speech," he said with a quarter of a smile.

The Chief Mummer stepped forward and made a few shadow puppet gestures with his hands.

"He says that you can't buy the support of the Lordlings," translated the Captain of the Blackguards. "They all have more wealth than they know what to do with. You have to be more cunning to get their attention."

"So what do I do?" hissed Talle, finally admitting that she needed their advice.

"You enlist our support, my Lady Emperor," said Leonardes. "The Profit-scoundrels will support you unconditionally...provided that we are awarded ten per cent of any ill-gotten gains of which the treasury seizes control."

"Like pirate's treasure," Talle said coldly. "For instance."

Leonardes shrugged his massive shoulders, and smiled.

"We need new ships for the navy every year," said the Red Admiral firmly. "We will handle the recruiting of crews and captains ourselves, but we must have new ships. That is our price."

Lady Talle laughed. "What would you do with all those ships?"

"I would capture pirates, my Lady Emperor," said the Red Admiral without smiling. "And the navy would naturally take ten per cent of any treasure they provide for the Imperial treasury."

"Geetchor fresh honions," said Tamb Lint in his greasy voice. "H'and while you're h'at it, improve the h'economy. "No one's buying h'anything but the bare h'essentials to survive. The merchants are getting desperate. Some of 'em have started biting people, even."

"Reinstate the Blackguards," said the Captain of the Blackguards in a firm, dull voice. "I want paid jobs for real soldiers and guardsmen."

Lady Talle was bewildered. "But there are Blackguards everywhere. There are four guarding this chamber!"

The Captain shook his head very slowly.

"Then who..." demanded Lady Talle hoarsely.

The Chief Mummer stepped forward and made some more hand puppet signals.

"He wants his actors back," translated the Red Admiral. "There hasn't been a decent play in Dreadnought for more than three years, because the mummers get paid more to stand outside the Palace pretending to be tough." He made a face. "It was one of Timregis' last mad ideas, and no one got around to rescinding it."

"Are you telling me that for three years this city has been protected by mummers?" demanded Lady Talle shrilly.

"They're very good at it," said the Captain of the Blackguards dismally. "Most of 'em have fencing training, and a good ear for dialogue. But it's not the same. And to top it all off, there's all those ex-guards out there trying to scrape a living as minstrels. It's embarrassing, really."

Lady Talle sat back on her feathered cushions, trying to take it all in. "So I must send my current guards away to be mummers, and pull in all the second-rate minstrels to be guards. I must increase my navy so that they and the Profithood can be paid their percentages." She glared at the puffed-up purple Ambassador of Anglorachnis. "And what do you want, my lord? An amethyst carriage and six purple horses to match?"

"A state visit," said the Ambassador calmly. "An all-expenses-paid holiday for my Royal Family to see the best of Mocklore. And I want them impressed. Otherwise my pension is in jeopardy."

"And what will you all give me in return?" said Lady Talle faintly. "How can you repay me for these momentous tasks?"

"Oh, we'll help you accomplish them, my Lady Emperor," Leonardes assured her. "We are your liegemen now."

Leonardes smiled. They were all smiling. Lady Talle was not sure if she liked that.

The golden doors of the chamber swung open. "We have someone for you to meet, my Lady Emperor," announced the Chief Mummer suddenly in the voice of a circus ringleader. "A gesture of goodwill, if you will."

A very small man stepped into the chamber. When he removed his hat and bowed floridly, Lady Talle realised that he was not a very small man at all, but a mere boy.

"And this is supposed to solve my problems?" she demanded disdainfully. "He looks like a professional urchin."

"That is what Kassa Daggersharp thought, my Lady Emperor," said Griffin, son of Camelot. And he bowed again.

-§-§-§-§-§-

The prince of firebrands jiggled to the pounding beat. Jiga boom, jiga boom, jiga boom boom boom!

There were other, smaller firebrands around him, dancing and swaying and turning somersaults in the air. They were all moving to the beat which steadily grew louder. The music was all around them.

"I am Ferdee Firehazard Fiero, come dance with me, lady, don't say no," sang the prince of firebrands, swivelling his hips.

Kassa got the feeling that he was talking to her. "Nice to meet you, Ferdee Flame, but I'm all tied up, can't play your game," she replied.

"You've met these people before," Aragon noted darkly.

"On occasion," she whispered back.

Ferdee seemed pleased with Kassa's response. "Hey, come to the halls of Fiero, if you entertain us we might let you go," he offered.

The firebrands were all around them now. Escaping wouldn't be easy. Ferdee leaned forward, almost scorching Kassa's hair, and said in a leering voice. "So, what dooo you doooo?"

"I sing," she replied confidently. "And I dance."

Ferdee nodded once and looked at Aragon. "You?"

Aragon glanced down at his knitting-needle sword. "I can fence," he suggested warily.

"Whoop-de-whooo!" crowed Ferdee. "There's gonna be a show in Fire Town, so come on all, get down, get down!"

And then the mountain that they were standing on disappeared.

-§-§-§-§-§-

On the other side of the Skullcaps, with a clatter and a rattle, a gaudy little golden carriage was tugged up a sheer cliff by four mountain goats.

The creatures of the Skullcaps had a tendency to mutate. Skullcap ladybirds, for instance, were currently four feet long. They had also developed large tentacles with which they captured wildebeests and tickled them to death before peeling them, eating their insides and making attractive hats out of the remains. On the other hand, the squirrels of the Skullcaps had evolved into very effective chat show hosts. They spent their whole time jumping from talking tree to talking tree, asking each other about how they got their ears so bushy, and who had written the latest scandalous ballad about the peacocks down in the valley.

The belligerent Skullcap goats had decided right from the start that if they were going to mutate, then they would damn well decide what changes would be made. Hence the improved strength of the creatures, the fuller beards, the attractive gold plumage with silver spangles. Hence also their powerful suction-capped hooves, which allowed them to climb almost anywhere, and their built-in safety raft which, due to a miscalculation, was located somewhere in their spleen.

Music and laughter and juggling bears trickled out of the Lordling's carriage as it clattered upwards. Fredgic had an allergy to mutated goats with gold plumage and silver spangles. He sat in the bouncing carriage with a heavy heart, a runny nose, a droopy hat and a collection of clockwork nets.

-§-§-§-§-§-

They were underground, but these caverns were different to those of the Hidden Army. For a start, they were on fire. Flames flickered along every surface except the floor. The heat was stifling.

And there were stone seats everywhere, looking down to a wide stage. It was a cavernous theatre, lit from within by layers of flame. Even the seats had burning cushions.

A voice echoed sharply through the theatre of the firebrands. "Ferdiiiiinand Firebrand! Get here now!"

"It's the Mater," said Ferdee apologetically, taking off his dark glasses and hiding them in a fold of his flickering body. "See you later," he added, and vanished.

Aragon contemplated their situation. "What now?"

Kassa wasn't sure if he was addressing her or himself.

It was getting even hotter than hot. Ash rained down upon them. Kassa held her bound wrists against a flaming cushion, waited until her bindings caught alight and then pulled them apart, sending sizzling rope sparks everywhere.

Aragon turned his attention to his crossbow, which was gone. So was his rapier. And the gargoyle. "Shall we be allies until this crisis is past?" he suggested.

Kassa laughed scornfully. "Why should I help you, or even trust you?"

"Suit yourself."

A long, silent moment went by. "Have you noticed?" said Kassa after a while. "There aren't any doors."

And it was still getting hotter.

-§-§-§-§-§-

At least claustrophobia wasn't a problem. It was so dark that they couldn't see how small the space was. Daggar was trying vainly to create a relaxing atmosphere. "I spy with my little eye, something beginning with D."

"Shut your face before I pull it off," was Zelora Footcrusher's reply.

"Can't guess, can you?"

"Darkness."

"Your turn."

She shifted restlessly. "Why haven't they found us yet?"

"Maybe they're not looking."

There was a long pause.

"I could always flirt with you," Daggar suggested. "That would pass the time."

"No man would dare attempt to flirt with an executive mercenary of the Hidden Army without her written permission," said Zelora sharply. "There are punishments expressly designed for that sort of thing."

"You don't have a sense of humour, do yer," Daggar noted darkly.

Zelora's voice was as dry as bone. "I have never had occasion to find out."

-§-§-§-§-§-

"Tee-hee!" said the sacred bauble of Chiantrio.

Reed glared through his one good eye as only a pirate really can. He had been riding after the flying orb all night. It kept slowing down teasingly and then zooming away at top speed, giggling wildly.

Now it was hovering halfway up a steep cliff. Reed had been shouting at it for some time. "How am I supposed to get up there?"

The bauble giggled again.

"Excuse me, sirrah," said a rather wheezy voice behind him, "Are you a pirate?"

"I'm not giving autographs," snapped Reed, absorbed in trying to figure out how to scale the cliff.

Half a second later, a clockwork net grabbed hold of him and flung him into a tree. Reed gnarled and gnashed at the sniffling warlock whose trap it was. "I'm going to eat you alive, you little gonk," he snarled.

"How interesting," said Fredgic, considering all the diseases and viruses contained in an average person's stomach. "Do you happen to have any other pirate friends? Ideally, I'm supposed to be capturing a whole gang, but I suppose you'll do for a start. The Lordling will be ever so pleased. Over here, Lord! I've caught one, I've caught one!"

"Gnahhhhhh," growled Reed ferociously.

It was then that a curvaceous firebrand fluttered out of nowhere to blink winsomely at them. "Come one, come all!" she cried in a welcoming voice, "To the Firebrand Hall. A show, a show! Would you like to go?"

"No, thank you," said Fredgic grumpily. "I'm trying to capture this pirate, please don't interrupt. Over here, your Lordship!"

Reed thought fast. It was what he was best at. "I'll come to your show," he volunteered.

The firebrand girl clapped her hands, which fizzled. "Calloo, callay! Come, come this way!" she said delightedly.

And then she vanished. So did Reed, along with the clockwork net that Fredgic had spent hours setting up.

"Oh, bother," said Fredgic, too disgruntled even to sneeze.

"What ho, Flutedrip," called the Lordling as the carriage appeared from behind the rocks. "Well done, you. Where's my new pirate, then?"

-§-§-§-§-§-

The theatre slowly began to fill up. Firebrands of all sizes and all colours of flame popped in to their seats, chatting noisily, chewing lumps of coal and toasting marshmallows on each other.

The stage was not as far away as Kassa had first thought. It was just that the seats became smaller further down. Despite this courtesy, it seemed that the firebrands deliberately chose seats randomly so many of the large ones were perched on teeny chairs near the front, and many of the smallest ones were lost upon the larger chairs near the back. Many ignored the seats altogether and just hovered near the ceiling where the view was best.

Aragon and Kassa were not prepared to risk the flaming chairs, so they moved towards the stage where the heat was less intense. Hundreds of firebrands in one room provided more than adequate central heating.

Finally something began to happen. A golden light flooded the stage and a low voice declared, "Welcome to the Firebrand Show!"

Everyone clapped and cheered and threw balls of fire at the stage.

"This evening weeeee present the old favourites: Frio the Water Swallower!" Everyone cheered. "Also Fontze the Interior Decorator, Fieorella and the Froo-Froos, Fatricia's Flying Salamanders and Federick Fyne hosting your f-f-favourite game show: Blind Scorch!"

The audience went mad.

"Buuuuuut first," announced the voice. "Please give a warrrm welcome to our visiting acts: the most entertaining strangers of all time!"

"That would be us," muttered Aragon.

"Ladies and fire-hazards, we present: Kassa Daggersharp!"

Kassa looked up, and suddenly she was standing on the stage. The golden spotlight came from several yellow firebrands who hovered upside down from the curtain rail, almost blinding her.

There was no curtain. Even firebrands have some safety standards. Ferdee stood next to her in a tuxedo made from green flame. "Any props you need?" he asked, grinning toothsomely at the audience.

"Bells," said Kassa.

"How many?"

"How many can you get?"

Ferdee gestured, and hundreds of little silver bells swept across the floor in a wave.

Kassa eyed them critically. "That should do."

Ferdee vanished. Kassa removed her over-dress and petticoats, revealing her dance costume of knotted silk. She scooped up handfuls of bells, dropping them down her bodice, tucking them into hidden pockets and sliding them into her hems. Every movement she made caused a massive amount of jingling.

"Music!" she called out, and a slow, rhythmic beat filled the theatre. "Faster!" she commanded, and the music changed to a quick, pulsing beat. "House lights down," she commanded, and all of the firebrands in the audience dimmed their flame.

She paused for a handful of beats, listening to the wild pattern of the music. And then she began to dance.

It was a wild dance, of curves and high kicks. The bells flew into the air and Kassa juggled them, catching them on the tips of her toes or fingers and sliding them across her wriggling limbs. The bells had a beat of their own, but it matched the firebrand music closely. The tiny balls of jingling gold rippled down her back, circled around her waist, and slid down across her feet.

She stood on her hands and turned cartwheels and leaped, still dancing with perfect control, and the bells danced with her. She started to sing a bright, colourful song, and the bells sang with her. Even when the audience flared up with excitement, even when they threw balls of fire at her in appreciation, even when hot coals skidded across the stage, Kassa Daggersharp kept dancing.

And then she stopped. The music stopped. The last batch of airborne bells landed neatly into her cupped hands. Not a sound came from the audience. For a fraction of a second. And then they reacted.

With roars of delight, a huge wave of flame hurtled towards the stage. It was a wave of congratulations, but pure flame nonetheless.

"Help!" screamed Kassa, seeing imminent death at the hands of adoring fans.

The flame bounced harmlessly away. A small firebrand woman, as wide as she was tall, stood with her hands on her hips and a grim expression on her face. "Ferdinand Firebrand, what do you think you are doing?" she demanded.

"Aw, Mum, we're just showing our appreciation," Ferdee said shamefully, stepping forwards.

"By trying to kill the girl? That's not manners," Mrs Firebrand snapped. "Let her pick her prize and send her on her way."

"Okay," said Ferdee grudgingly. "Mistress Daggersharp, for participating in our show, you can pick a graaaaand prize!" He swept his arm around half-heartedly, only just failing to set fire to Kassa's already singed hair, and a wall of shelves opened up in the middle of the stage.

There were Ferdee dolls, fireworks, bags of flame treats, and bottles of fire water. Only three items on the shelves were not visibly made out of fire. Aragon Silversword's crossbow, Aragon Silversword's knitting needle rapier, and the small grey statue of a grimacing gargoyle.

Kassa considered her choice. "The flaming hair accessories are tempting, but I think I'll take the gargoyle," she said casually.

Below the stage, Aragon Silversword lunged forwards, but he was suddenly surrounded by big, muscular firebrands. "Not your turn on stage yet, sonny," they teased, spitting droplets of flame out of their mouths as they spoke.

Kassa smiled nicely down at Aragon and accepted her prize. "Free to go," said Ferdee generously, trying to ignore his mother's withering glare.

Suddenly, a man tangled in a net dropped out of nowhere, stopping several feet above the stage and hovering there.

"And now for our next act, the amaaaaazing Reed Cooper!" announced Ferdee. He leered at the wriggling net. "What's the act, Reedy, escapology?"

At the mention of Reed Cooper's name, Kassa whirled around, her eyes flashing vengefully. "What?" she shrieked, but she was already gone, vanished back to the mundane world.

Through the webbing of the clockwork net, Reed Cooper saw Aragon, and his single uncovered eye narrowed. "A duel to the death," he snarled.

"I accept," replied Aragon Silversword.

Chapter 9
Shopping With Ice

When the delegation had departed, Lady Talle turned to face her remaining visitor. She moved past him to the window seat, and perched there with her elegant knees tucked up to her chin. "Well, Agent Camelot? What can you do for me?"

"Call me Griffin," said the urchin. "Camelot is my spy name, but I'm not wearing that hat right now."

Talle blinked slowly, lowering her lashes and raising them again with perfect timing. "So if Camelot is a spy, what does Griffin do?"

"Have you ever heard of PR?" asked the urchin.

Lady Talle gave him a sideways smile. "Why don't you tell me?"

"I would be glad to," he said grandiosely. "My dear Lady Emperor, PR stands for Public Relations. To be more specific, it stands for the subtle art of propaganda." His smile became wider, and somehow more genuine. "I'm going to make you so famous that the people of Mocklore will not only want your pretty head on their coinage, they'll want you to personally open every concert, village school and supermarket from here to Axgaard and back!"

Talle frowned precisely. "What is a supermarket?"

"It doesn't matter," said Griffin dismissively. "The point is, you are going to be adored and worshipped beyond your wildest dreams. Just how popular would you like to be, Lady Talle?"

Talle's blue eyes flashed suddenly, aglow with her lust for success. "What have you got?"

-§-§-§-§-§-

The two men faced each other, balancing on the narrow bridge that swooped above the stage. Reed Cooper gripped the prime sword of the pirate Vicious Bigbeard Daggersharp. Aragon Silversword held a glorified knitting needle.

"Any additional props?" offered Ferdee Firebrand, still playing the role of Master of Ceremonies.

"A better sword would be good," suggested Aragon between gritted teeth. He didn't really expect a response, but the knitting needle was suddenly a proper rapier, balancing perfectly in his grasp. Tiny blue flames flickered along the edge of the blade. Aragon almost smiled. "That's more like it."

-§-§-§-§-§-

Kassa was still hot. She had no idea where the firebrands had put her, she knew only that she was back in the Skullcaps, and she desperately needed to cool off. Her hair was singed, her clothes were heavy with smoke and she was very, very thirsty.

The trees whispered that there was water further along the path. Kassa listened to them absently, and wandered on.

Sure enough, as the purple path curved a waterfall came into view. Kassa approached it cautiously, the gargoyle tucked under one arm. There was something strange about this particular waterfall. The water made no noise as it tumbled over the rocks and splashed into the wide pool beneath. Not a sound.

Not that she cared, really. She just wanted to wash the smell of fire out of her hair. She brushed one hand into the water, and recoiled at the heat of it. Moments later, she tried again and it was icy cold.

A sudden absence of noise bothered her for a moment. It was as if a twig had not snapped. Why should that disturb her? The next silence did not convey the gathering of tiny feet. Not at all.

Kassa tried to convince herself that she was being paranoid, but her argument lacked conviction. Feeling edgy, she started to turn around.

Many tiny hands pushed her in the small of the back, sending her sprawling into the water with a splash of resounding silence.

-§-§-§-§-§-

"Very interesting," commented Aragon. Slash, attack, guard, defend. "You don't fight like a pirate."

"You've fought many pirates?" sneered Reed Cooper.

"Ever hear of Evil Lackbeard Buttspike?" Guard, guard, parry, swipe.

Reed stepped out of range. "You fought Buttspike?"

"I killed him," said Aragon.

"That's interesting," said Reed dryly. Step, cut, parry, slide… "So did I."

"When would a cabin boy get a chance to kill a pirate like Lackbeard?" Jab, twist, thrust, dodge…

"Ever heard of Bigbeard Daggersharp's one golden rule?" smiled Reed tightly. Parry, parry, block left…

"Tell me," countered Aragon.

Reed's one good eye glittered. "Never hire a cabin boy who hasn't killed at least three Pirate Kings," he said with relish. Slash, cut, parry, don't fall off the bridge…

At this point, Aragon realised that he was going to have to do something special. The odds were against him. Reed Cooper was ten years younger and had been trained by Vicious Bigbeard himself, but he was also insufferably arrogant. Parry, slide, block, block, defend…

Aragon Silversword slid back out of range and bowed his head in defeat. Taken aback, Reed Cooper grinned wildly and lowered his sword in a mocking salute.

It was at this point that Aragon Silversword started fighting dirty.

-§-§-§-§-§-

Tiny, grabbing hands tangled in Kassa's hair and clothes, pulling her up until she exploded through the surface of the pool, gasping for air.

In the firebrand hall, she had been hot. Now she was cold. Very cold. The trees around her were bleached white, and there was ice everywhere. Kassa couldn't help thinking that she was on the other side of the waterfall.

For the second time that day, she found herself surrounded by a group of sprites. These were white and icy, regarding her with unfriendly expressions.

Clotted with spare magic since the days of the Glimmer, the Skullcaps were now the perfect habitat for sprites and magical creatures of all kinds. But to encounter both firebrands and icesprites in one day was more than unlucky.

Kassa knew about as much about icesprites as she had about firebrands…enough to know that there was no point looking forward to this encounter.

-§-§-§-§-§-

Aragon was on the attack now. He did not speak, he did not smile. His face remained calm, eyes flicking from left to right as his sword moved with practised swiftness. Just as Reed countered one of his particularly fine combinations, Aragon twisted the blade and shoved. Reed Cooper lost his balance and fell from the bridge. The prime sword of Captain Vicious Bigbeard Daggersharp fell with him, clattering harmlessly on to the stage.

Ferdee Firebrand bounced across to peer at Reed. "Alive!" he announced, and the audience cheered, throwing flame balls at the stage and each other. They preferred their entertainers to survive, because a clean-up crew was always selected from the audience. Dead bodies made nasty stains.

Aragon looked down from the bridge. The fall hadn't been too bad. Reed Cooper was already conscious, muttering something at Ferdee. All the better. Aragon wanted him to hear this. "I claim my opponent's weapon as my prize!" he announced, his eyes on the glittering rubies of Vicious Bigbeard Daggersharp's prime sword.

"Sorry," said Ferdee, not sounding particularly contrite. "Your opponent already claimed his own sword. Pick something else."

Aragon couldn't believe this. "But I won!" he protested.

"You both entertained us," said Ferdee, speaking slowly as if to a child. He waggled his sunglasses cheerfully. "You each pick a prize!"

Scowling, Aragon flicked the sword that he was carrying. "I'll take this, then." At least he would be armed.

"Cool!" exclaimed Ferdee. "See you later, crocogator!"

Aragon vanished. What nobody noticed was that the sacred bauble of Chiantrio, still dutifully following him at the Lady Emperor's request, vanished also.

Reed picked himself up, gripping the hilt of the prime sword firmly. And then he was also vanished back to the mundane world.

Not long after, a golden carriage appeared on the stage. While the Lordling, the mummers, the dancing bears and the mountain goats pranced around on stage, a small jester with spectacles and a humorous hat spoke very earnestly to Ferdee Firebrand and his mother for a long while, taking notes as he did so.

-§-§-§-§-§-

Aragon knew better than to keep to the path. He made his way through the purple undergrowth, keeping his eyes and ears open for anything. All he heard was a very quiet hum, surrounded by silence.

When he emerged from the trees, what he saw was Kassa. She stood hip-deep in the icy pool, her back to him, splashing slowly and silently around in the waterfall and humming a little song of no consequence. Her dress lay discarded in the pool, and she was only wearing the knots of silk which were her dancing costume. The wet silk was nearly transparent, but her long, tangled blood-coloured hair provided a semblance of modesty.

For a moment, Aragon thought her hair was white, but then he realised it was a trick of the light, a reflection of the ice-encrusted water.

Then he realised that her hair really was white. The woman turned around, and it wasn't Kassa after all. Her skin was as white as her hair, and she grimaced tenderly at him with small, sharp white teeth.

Aragon gripped his new sword, and the blue flames flared menacingly along the blade. The white woman looked at him in horror, and made a little yipping noise.

Freezing cold water drenched Aragon from above, extinguishing his sword. He looked up just in time to see hundreds of tiny icesprites leaping on top of him. They swarmed, binding him neatly with cords made from braided snow.

-§-§-§-§-§-

The icesprites' two prisoners were put in the same cell, a circular room made from bricks of ice. There were no windows, just a low crawling tunnel for a door. "Interesting," said Kassa, trying not to shiver obviously. "We just keep running into each other."

Aragon didn't want to talk about it.

The tunnel slid open and a little sprite poked her head in. "Do you have any money?" she asked. "Things to barter?"

"Some," said Kassa cagily.

The sprite glanced at Aragon. "You?"

"Probably," he said, glaring at the far wall.

"Right," said the sprite, and closed the tunnel again.

"Silversword," said Kassa after a while.

"What?" he replied harshly.

"I don't mean to be personal, but what is that thing behind your head?"

Aragon turned his head sharply, and the sacred bauble skipped around behind his ear so he couldn't see it.

Kassa lunged forward and grabbed hold of it. "This." The bauble wriggled and squeaked in protest.

"Oh, that," said Aragon in disgust. "The sacred bauble of Chiantrio. It's just a trinket. Cooper must have had it."

He had said too much.

Kassa was very quiet, turning the bauble over in her fingers. "I didn't think you had met," she said after a moment. "How do you know Reed Cooper?"

"Oh, we've met," said Aragon darkly. He chose not to say any more. He might need to get Kassa to trust him again, and that would never happen if she knew his employer was the Lady Emperor. "Keep it," he grunted.

Kassa looked down at the little bauble in her hand. "Thank you," she said in surprise. For no reason that she could think of, she put it in her bodice for safekeeping. The bauble burbled happily and went to sleep.

-§-§-§-§-§-

Daggar was dying. It occurred to him that if he killed Zelora there might be more fresh air for him and he would live a few minutes or hours more. It also occurred to him that Zelora would be better at killing, and so it was probably best not to put the idea into her head.

They had been trapped for hours now. Days? Every now and then they had heard a shifting of stone within the mountain, which meant that someone had control of the Brayne. There was still a glimmer of hope that they would be rescued before suffocating to death.

But the glimmer of hope shrunk into a glint and then vanished entirely. They were going to die.

Daggar wondered if this was better or worse than being terminated by the Profithood. Worse, he decided, because at least if the Profithood killed him he would be dying at the hands of his friends and comrades.

On the other hand, he was dying in the presence of a beautiful (if slightly homicidal) woman. There were worse ways to go, he mused in one of his more philosophical moments.

In between these snippets of being philosophical, Daggar had long bouts of mad panic. Zelora had had to knock him unconscious a few times to stop him shrieking hysterically in her ear. He still had the headaches.

Zelora seemed to be taking their impending death rather well. Perhaps she was accustomed to the concept.

Daggar was finally moving beyond both panic and philosophy. A strange feeling had come over him. He had a suspicion that it might be guilt. This bothered him for a while, as he had never experienced guilt before. That particular emotion was a liability for a profit-scoundrel. And yet he was pretty sure that what he wanted to do most was apologise.

"I'm sorry," he tried.

Zelora was caught off guard. "What did you say?"

"I was apologising. I think this might be my fault."

"Why?" she said suspiciously.

"I haven't worked that out yet. Maybe I helped Kassa trust Aragon long enough for him to rescue her, and I'm pretty sure that they're responsible for this imminent death of ours."

"Interesting," she said approvingly. "Without the artificial charm, you sound more like a real person."

"It doesn't happen very often."

Zelora might have been smiling in the darkness, but Daggar couldn't picture how that might look. He imagined her scowling in a friendly fashion instead. "I don't suppose you could pretend that you were not an executive mercenary in the Hidden Army for a minute?" he suggested hopefully.

"Why would I want to do that?"

"I was thinking about kissing you, and I don't want you to chop my head off."

Zelora Footcrusher was silent for a moment. "I don't think that would be a very good idea," she said finally.

Daggar retreated into glum silence. His momentary twinge of guilt had wandered away, and he decided it was time to start blaming Kassa again.

"On the other hand," said Zelora thoughtfully, "I could change my mind. Why don't you apologise again?"

"Oh, I'm past that stage," Daggar assured her. "I'm blaming Kassa now. It's her silver. I'm just in it for the greed. And to save my neck," he added, remembering. Then he started trying to work out how long it was before the next full moon, when the Profithood would come looking for him. He had a nasty suspicion that it wasn't very far away.

Zelora was silent for a while, and when she spoke again it was in an entirely different tone of voice. "What silver?"

It was then that there was a scraping noise from above, and the ceiling began to fall in on them.

-§-§-§-§-§-

After a few very chilly hours, Kassa and Aragon were led out of their igloo prison into the main square of a bustling icesprite market. They were fastened together by a chain which burned frostily into their wrists. All the icesprites gathered around to point and jeer and throw rotten ice cubes at the pair. Several of them were carrying large silver axes.

After some time a woman appeared before them. She was swathed in white frosted fur and her white hair was frozen into intricate icicles. She was obviously the icesprite leader because all of the icesprites chittered and curtseyed as she approached. She too was carrying a large silver axe.

To be frank, Aragon and Kassa both expected execution.

"I am told that you carry foreign money," the ice queen said, her voice crackling with cold. "And other valuable items."

"Possibly," said Kassa cautiously.

"You had better," crackled the ice queen.

"We do," said Aragon quickly. He was good at spotting avenues of survival, and right now it seemed like their survival depended on having money and items of value to barter.

"Well, then," said the ice queen dangerously. She swept a frosted arm around at the bustling market behind them. "Go shopping."

"Pardon?" said Kassa in a little voice.

"I said," said the ice queen in a voice of calculated menace, "Go shopping."

So they did.

-§-§-§-§-§-

The ceiling fell far enough to wallop Daggar lightly on the head before retreating upwards again at great speed. The walls were closing in now, but there was light from above.

"Sorry," a grumpy voice called down. "Was you wantin' to be rescued?"

Zelora Footcrusher stood up, and a dangerous expression took control of her face.

Daggar was suddenly glad that he hadn't been able to see her smile in the darkness. The concept was terrifying.

"Bronkx," said Zelora in a low voice which projected for miles. "If you do not get us out right now, you will have to find replacements for all of your body parts."

"Right you are, Deputy Leader Footcrusher, sir, miss," called the gnome humbly. A rope came spiralling down, and thus they were rescued.

"And now," said Zelora, once they were safely on top of the mountain (although Daggar did not feel very safe), "Tell me about this silver."

-§-§-§-§-§-

The K Division caves were a mess. Bathrooms were in kitchens, kitchens were in bedrooms, and most of the plumbing was all in the same tree, three mountains away.

No one wanted to risk living in the caves while the rescue and redecoration efforts continued, so they were all camping in tents on the surface. Because they were the Hidden Army, the tents were camouflaged to the point of invisibility. As evening fell they all sat invisibly around the invisible campfires, then tripped over each other's invisible tent-ropes and retired under collapsed (but invisible) canvas.

Daggar walked Zelora to her tent, which was disguised so well that nobody had even been able to trip over it. Until he opened his mouth, he had no idea what it was about to get him into. "Let me guess. For a man to enter a female executive mercenary's tent, the punishment is diabolical."

"Something like that," said Zelora contentedly.

Daggar tried not to think about what that punishment could be.

"Unless he is invited," Zelora continued.

Daggar was worried now. Was she really considering what he thought she might be considering?

Zelora hesitated by the flap of her tent, and then she half-smiled. It was not as scary as he had thought it would be. Apart from the slight fangs and and the red glint in her eyes, she was really quite...what was he thinking?

"Consider yourself invited," said Zelora Footcrusher.

Now Daggar was scared. And tempted. And worried. "You're only interested in the *Splashdance* silver," he accused.

Zelora's smile curled into a friendly snarl. "And what are you interested in, Daggar Profit-scoundrel? My army? Protection from all those little people who may wish to kill you?"

Daggar's brain kept ordering his feet to run away. The trouble was, another bit of his body kept telling his feet to stay just where they were. Or maybe to walk a little further forward... "That too," he admitted.

"Well then," she murmured with the contented purr of a vicious animal. "Perhaps we can come to some mutual agreement."

Daggar's feet promptly betrayed his brain. By the time he reached Zelora, he was convinced that this was a brilliant idea. The tent flap swung closed behind them both.

Chapter 10
Killing Time

On her way to her bed-chamber, the Lady Emperor had discovered the Imperial portrait parlour. She swept through the long hall in her lacy negligée and feathery dressing gown, critically examining the painted faces of Emperors long gone. She paused for quite a while in front of the portrait of Timregis.

The picture had been painted while Timregis was still reasonably young and unbloated, although his tendency to behave like a fruitcake had already manifested. His Imperial Majesty had posed in a suit of armour made entirely from sugarloaf, with a jewel-encrusted bucket of water perched haphazardly on his head. The inevitable had occurred, and the preliminary sketches had later been released as a very popular book of humorous hieroglyphs.

"You were insane, untalented and generally despised," the Lady Emperor said thoughtfully. "Your only talent was an unfaltering imagination. And you lasted longer than any of them."

The Emperor Timregis did not respond. Under the circumstances, Talle would have been quite disturbed if he had.

She moved on, past the long line of Emperors who had come between Timregis' reign and her own. Some of them had not been around long enough to have an official portrait painted, but some Palace bureaucrat had later arranged for the gaps to be filled in by an enterprising child with a set of crayons and an unlimited supply of goatskin parchment.

There were dozens of them. "Stupid, stupid men!" exclaimed Talle frustratedly. "You must have had some talent to make your way to the top in the first place, but not one of you managed to hold on to the seat of power. Well, I'll show you. I'm going to be around for a long time, so you just watch me at work. I'll show Mocklore what it means to have a strong leader again—what it means to have a woman in charge!"

The portraits of past Emperors stared impassively back at her.

Too incensed to go to bed now, Talle kicked off her furry slippers and went downstairs to see how Griffin the urchin was getting on with the propaganda drive.

-§-§-§-§-§-

The swampweeds were restless tonight. They rolled across the watery mud, grunting and grummoxing. Their mournful gurgles filled the air around the rocky path which rose out of the swamp.

The firebrands obviously had a perverse sense of humour. They had set Reed Cooper down in the middle of the only swamp in the Skullcaps. Having narrowly escaped the meaty mouths of the swampweeds and the gnashing gums of the riverwumps, Reed was now trudging muddily up a steep, rocky path.

He had lost the sacred bauble, but still had the prime sword of Bigbeard Daggersharp. And he still had his eyepatch, to remind himself that he was a pirate. There was nothing wrong with the eye underneath, but that wasn't the point. Pirates wore eyepatches, and Reed Cooper was nothing if not a pirate.

The first thing he noticed as he reached the top of the steep path was a large patch of nothing. Curious, Reed peered carefully at the space before him. The carefully concealed scent of charred meat studiously avoided his nostrils. Something was going on.

And then he saw them. Flickers of people making camp and cooking breakfast and bumping into each other. People who were very good at not being noticed.

Reed caught the sleeve of a flicker of a man who passed him. He almost expected his hand to pass through the man, but his fingers latched on to solid fabric. "Who are you?" the young pirate demanded.

Still flickering, the hidden man regarded him with horror. "You can see me?" he gasped.

"Of course I can see you," said Reed, irritated.

The man ran for it, plate armour clanking silently as he dived into a tent which seemed to be both a natural part of the scenery and not there at all.

Reed wrenched open the tent flap. "Who are you?" he demanded again.

"You can see my tent?" squealed the little man hysterically.

"Yes," snapped Reed. "Look, I need food, water. Who are you people?" Abruptly, the penny dropped. "Are you supposed to be the Hidden Army?"

A sudden sensation made Reed stand up straight and turn around slowly. Nobody was there. And then suddenly they were all standing there, a group of twenty or so, all armoured, all displeased with his presence.

The woman in the middle appeared to be some sort of commander. She regarded Reed disdainfully. "I am Footcrusher. What are you? Not another pirate!"

Reed sensed that this would be the moment to dazzle them with his true identity. "My name is Reed Cooper, of the pirate ship *Dread Redhead*," he announced haughtily. "I was second in command to the fearsome Pirate King, Vicious Bigbeard Daggersharp." He paused to allow them to gasp in awe. They didn't.

"Well, well, well," said the scruffy man beside the woman who called herself Footcrusher. "Reed Cooper." He smiled in a very nasty way. "You'd be the one what murdered my uncle Bigbeard."

-§-§-§-§-§-

After considering the options, the Hidden Army decided to throw him off a cliff. Reed Cooper protested, naturally. But the last thing the Hidden Army wanted was an Imperial spy in their midst.

Besides, it was Zelora's idea, and no one liked to argue with her.

"So," she murmured to Daggar as everyone milled around, trying to decide which cliff to throw Reed Cooper off. "You are related to the Daggersharp pirates."

"Most of them. Are you impressed?"

"Did you intend me to be impressed?"

Daggar grinned distantly. "I was under the impression that I'd already impressed you."

"Indeed?" murmured Zelora, not quite displeased.

Meanwhile, Reed prepared to die. The Hidden Army decided on the nearest cliff, a looming precipice which overlooked the point where the swamp met the river. The plan was that the river would neatly wash his body away.

Reed could not fault their logic.

To add insult to injury, the mercenaries had turned their Hidden ability up full blast, so Reed could not see any of them except for the scruffy nephew of Bigbeard. Daggar was smirking openly. "This will make Kassa's week," he said as they reached the cliff.

Reed could not see those who seized hold of him, and he could barely feel their hands as they heaved him off the cliff. In midair, rushing towards the bottomless swamp and the vicious river, he didn't feel anything.

The swampweeds welcomed him, dragging him beneath the mud and water, his body clamped tight in their meaty jaws.

-§-§-§-§-§-

Kassa haggled with an icesprite merchant.

"It'll cost you a goose, final offer," said the sprite.

Aragon followed close behind Kassa, speaking quietly but urgently to her. "Kassa, where is the gargoyle?"

She ignored him, speaking to the merchant. "I don't have a goose. I do have a chicken."

The merchant eyed her doubtfully. "You have a chicken? I don't see a chicken."

Kassa pulled a live, squawking chicken out of her bodice. The merchant was suitably impressed.

Aragon leaned closer. "They're obsessed with this market. They want us to barter everything we have. If the gargoyle is on your person, we'll lose it!" He couldn't see where she could possibly be concealing the gargoyle on her person, but he had thought the same about the chicken.

Kassa smiled mysteriously. "What makes you think the gargoyle is on my person?"

"All right," said the sprite-merchant after a moment. "One chicken and that ring on your little finger." He reached out for it, his white fingers tapering longer than they should have.

Kassa snatched her hand away. "Not my jewellery. I'm not bartering my jewellery away."

A hush descended over the ice market. All of the icesprites were looking accusingly at her, particularly those holding silver axes. After a pause, the lady sprite-merchant at the next stall brought out a tray and uncovered it, revealing a display of the most exquisite silvercraft. Finger-rings, toe-rings, lobe-rings, bracelets, necklaces and circlets sparkled mercilessly with perfect garnets, pearls, and sister-of-moonstone.

"On the other hand," said Kassa quickly, slipping off the ring from her littlest finger.

"Sold," said the sprite-merchant triumphantly, and the whole market applauded. "Would you like to try on your purchases, pretty lady?"

Kassa disappeared behind a screen of opaque glass, and Aragon found himself tugged by one arm. A little icesprite insisted he start shopping as well. Another one timidly pawed the iced firebrand sword which he held.Aragon slapped the sprite away. “I’m keeping that,” he growled.

The icesprites fell into a dangerous silence. The silver axes gleamed again. And then a sprite stepped forward, unsheathing a rapier which looked as if it was made of glass.

“Transparent silver-steel,” murmured the sprites knowledgeably.

Very slowly, Aragon took the sword. It was perfectly balanced. The ‘glass’ of the blade felt like good steel. Quality steel. He knew that he could fight better with this rapier than he had ever fought before. He wanted it. Badly.

They accepted the sword of the firebrands and the silver chain around his neck in exchange.

Kassa emerged from the changing cubicle. Aragon was so engrossed with his new purchase that he didn’t notice her until he caught a glimpse out of the corner of one eye. And then he stared openly.

The dress could have been floor-length or thigh-length for all he knew, because it was made of transparent gauze which was invisible unless folded or pleated. There were only two pleats in this dress. The gauze was adorned with hovering clasps, and the entire effect was that of a dozen silver butterflies perching absently on a naked body. The sacred bauble was nestled comfortably in this new bodice, which it approved of because it could now see out.

“What do you think?” Kassa inquired, looking straight at Aragon with her large golden eyes.

“You’ll get cold,” he replied.

Kassa smiled contentedly and shimmered into a coat of fur-lined dragon-scales. “Fireproof, too,” she said approvingly as she fastened her new silver belt. The dragon-scale coat fitted snugly to her body, with a plunging neckline and a swinging silver hem.

Eventually they had nothing left of their prior possessions, and Kassa was dripping with icesprite jewellery. She had also bartered her many concealed weapons for other, better concealed weapons. Aragon, scorning the icesprite fashions which Kassa had embraced wholeheartedly, eventually found a human-type outfit in grey and black which he agreed to trade his own clothes for.

They had spent their coins on icesprite food and novelties such as a solid ice candle snuffer. Kassa had also bought some silver needles and embroidery thread in various different shades of white. When Aragon had bought a crossbow which shot icebolts, Kassa eyed him warily but said nothing.

"Is all spent?" demanded the ice-queen, brandishing her large silver axe. "Have you nothing left to barter, swap or trade?"

"Nothing," replied Kassa and Aragon, ready to be let go.

"Are you sure?"

"Yes!" said Aragon impatiently.

The ice-queen smiled, revealing pearly white gums. "Good. Prepare the execution!"

-§-§-§-§-§-

It was dark in the swamp. Reed peered through the mud at his hosts. Two of the large, vegetable-shaped swampweeds waded through the muck, leading the way downwards. Through the mud they went, down into a giant cavern full of swamp creatures. The riverwumps ogled the newcomer with their big, runny eyes, and gnashed their gums expectantly. The marshgrugs wriggled and griggled along the walls of the cavern, hissing in an unfriendly manner.

Reed didn't question the fact that he could suddenly breathe swamp muck. In some perverse way he had expected it.

A swampweed in the corner was cooking, burbling away to itself as it added a few marshgrugs to the steaming cauldron. Reed was nudged into a sitting position on the floor of the cavern, and a lady riverwump with long nostril-lashes and a large amount of marshgrug goo painted on her gums brought Reed a hollowed-out swamp seed filled with the chef's soup.

Reed choked down a few mouthfuls for the sake of politeness. It tasted of mud, with a hint of fennel.

By now, the swamp creatures seemed to have accepted him as one of them. He wasn't sure that he liked this idea, considering they had no qualms about cooking each other, but there wasn't much he could do about it.

The swampweeds crowded around in a circle now, looking adoringly up at a larger swampweed who wore strings of hollowed-out swamp seeds and petrified marshgrugs around its neck. And then this High Priest of swampweeds, gathering in all of its mighty power, proceeded to raise the dead.

-§-§-§-§-§-

Kassa and Aragon lay side by side on a block of ice. The ice-queen stood over them, her silver axe gleaming. "Thank you for your contribution to our economy," she said sweetly, and the axe fell.

The sacred bauble of Chiantrio shot out in front of Kassa's throat, and it deflecting the blow. The axe glanced harmlessly aside. "Don't you know anything?" said Kassa in a voice colder than the ice around them. "You can't kill a pirate on dry land."

She didn't have a sword, or a knife. She only had a silver brooch with a long spiked pin. But it was enough. *All right, Summer Songstrel*, she said in her head. *If you're my guardian sprite, make yourself useful. I need fire.*

Do it yourself, came the reply of her guardian sprite.

Kassa burst into flames.

The icesprites flew back, terrified. The ice-queen did not move, but her eyes were frightened. Kassa sat up slowly and moved towards the frozen waterfall. Aragon followed her. It seemed like the thing to do. The ice began to thaw. Kassa scraped handfuls away with her burning sleeves. Aragon jabbed at the ice with his sword, and they broke their way through.

The waterfall flowed silently around them, extinguishing Kassa's flames. Behind the falling water the rocks froze again, sealing off the doorway. "Where are you?" Kassa demanded.

Summer Songstrel, the guardian sprite, was perched on an icy rock, dangling her feet in the air.

"Have you been in my head the whole time?" Kassa demanded.

"It's such a nice roomy place to visit," Summer smiled. "I suggest you start running, ladybird. They'll come after you." She vanished.

Kassa frowned. "What are you looking so smug about?"

"I thought you said you weren't a witch," said Aragon Silversword.

"I'm not," she retorted.

"Good," he said, drawing his icesprite sword. "Then you won't mind telling me where the gargoyle is."

Kassa said nothing, glaring at his chest.

Aragon moved forwards, the water lapping silently around his legs. His foot hit something under the water. He rolled his eyes and scooped the gargoyle out from its resting place. "Stupid," he said.

"I was being attacked at the time," said Kassa defensively. "I didn't have the leisure to hide it somewhere sophisticated. What do you want it for, anyway? I'm trying to protect it because the man it turns into every full moon is the same man who taught me how to carve toys and throw kitchen knives when I was a kid. What's your motive?"

"I told you," Aragon grated. "I have a buyer. For both of you." He levelled his new sword at her neck. "Get moving."

-§-§-§-§-§-

The sprites approached the wall cautiously. "Go after them!" commanded the ice-queen, brandishing her shiny silver axe in a menacing manner.

It was then that the gaudy golden carriage drawn by four mutated mountain goats plunged through the ice-wall. A small jester with spectacles and a large humorous hat climbed out. "Excuse me," he said politely. "I'm writing a ballad, you see. I believe you were recently visited by pirates. Could I ask you a few questions?"

"That depends," said the ice-queen, her silver eyebrows glittering. "Are any of you interested in…shopping?"

The Lordling poked his head out the window eagerly. "Did you say shopping? Do you have any humorous hats?"

-§-§-§-§-§-

Communication with the dead appeared to be the main source of entertainment for the creatures of the swamp. Reed was surrounded by phantoms of swampweeds, riverwumps and marshgrugs, as well as other swamp creatures long extinct. They seemed to be settling in for the evening.

And then there was a ghost who was not a creature of the swamp. It was a large man, a pirate with one baleful golden eye and a huge, thick black beard. He advanced on Reed, holding a ghostly facsimile of the sword strapped to Reed's back.

Something to say to me, Reed Cooper?" boomed Vicious Bigbeard Daggersharp, deceased. "Something to say?"

Reed could not think of anything to say. The best he could manage was a spluttered, "But you're dead!"

"So are you, matey," retorted the Pirate King. "Or had you forgotten yer at the bottom of a swampy river? Can't have a pirate dying in fresh water. Get out of there, boy!"

Reed was suddenly aware that he was choking. Choking on swamp muck.

"And another thing," muttered the pirate ghost as he started to fade. "Don't come around apologising when yer do finally kick the bucket. Last thing I want is you whingeing around me for eternity. Now I'm going back to the Underworld and my rum…"

-§-§-§-§-§-

Reed surfaced in the river that struggled through the swamp. The water tasted foul, but it was better than dying. He breathed in the swampy air and trod water for a few moments.

Glancing back, he had a nasty feeling that some clumps of mud in a distant corner of the swamp were waving goodbye.

Reed Cooper washed the swamp muck out of his mouth with the foul river water and then began swimming towards Dreadnought.

-§-§-§-§-§-

Aragon and Kassa were clambering up a steep ravine. Kassa's climb was made more difficult by the fact that her wrists were once more tied together, this time with invisible gauze.

"Be careful," Aragon snapped as she nearly fell.

"This isn't easy," she snarled in return.

"Said by a woman who can set fire to herself?"

"That wasn't me, it was that guardian sprite of mine," Kassa insisted. "And all she did was set fire to my coat. The dragon scales protected me from the flame. That's what dragon scales do." But it sounded unbelievable, even to her.

Aragon said nothing, careful of his footing on a ledge of firm dirt.

Slightly above him, Kassa missed a step and slid wildly. She screamed as she fell, a scream that was cut off with a gasp when Aragon's arm lashed out and grabbed hold of her sharply. She slammed against him, breathing hard. And then she looked up into his eyes. "I could thank you, but you wouldn't appreciate it."

"True," he said coldly.

She regarded him speculatively. They were dangerously close to each other. "Are you going to fall in love with me, Aragon Silversword?"

"I wasn't planning to."

"It's good to have these things clear from the start," she said approvingly. Then she kicked him in the crossbow, tearing the gauze which bound her wrists against a sharp rock as she did so.

The icebolt released and drilled crazily into the wall of the ravine. The crossbow went spiralling out over the long drop.

Aragon grabbed for his sword and slapped her with his other hand. Kassa stuck the long pin of her brooch into his upper arm. Aragon shoved her firmly against the wall of the ravine with his sword at her throat. She kicked him in the shins. He pressed the sword more firmly. A tiny smear of blood touched the transparent blade. Kassa tried to move away, but slid off the dirt ledge, falling backwards.

Aragon grabbed hold of her wrist and pulled her to safety again. They glared at each other.

From above, they heard a discreet cough. Daggar's head appeared, peering curiously down at them with a wide grin on his unshaven face. "Are we interrupting something?"

The head of Zelora Footcrusher appeared beside him. "I have an army behind me. We will pull you to safety if you will relinquish the gargoyle to me."

"Never!" screamed Kassa.

"Perhaps we can come to some arrangement," retorted Aragon, who carried the gargoyle in a sling over one shoulder.

The gargoyle was pulled up first. While Zelora examined it, Singespitter and another executive mercenary lowered ropes for Kassa and Aragon. Once they reached the top of the cliff, the mercenaries tied them up securely.

"Why?" Kassa demanded. "Why is everyone after the bloody gargoyle? He's just some old pirate. What possible interest could you have in Braided Bones, Zelora Footcrusher?"

Zelora's eyes did not change. She deliberately did not look at Daggar. "He is my husband," she said.

Chapter 11
Wise Fruitcakes

A blonde woman with a low neckline, a tall golden crown and a poutingly seductive smile beckoned enticingly at Reed Cooper. He examined the poster critically, reading it twice.

Some kind of festival was going on. Banners and garlands hung crookedly from every building. Small tribes of urchins were being trained to wave little flags on sticks and shout "Yay."

And then there were the posters. Most of them had pictures of Talle on them…or rather pictures of luscious blondes with crowns balanced on their perfect hair. The artists were being fairly free about details, mainly because none of them had actually seen the Lady Emperor. They had their orders from the Palace, however: make it sexy, make it glamorous.

The posters had slogans on them, for those citizens who could read. A popular one was "Our Lady Emperor needs U!" Others proclaimed, "The Best Emperor Yet!" The poster which had caught Reed's eye portrayed Lady Talle at her most beguiling, and announced, "Welcome to the Lady's Empire."

The posters all had a little note saying that the Lady Emperor's image had been used with the permission of Master Griffin, PR urchin. Reed had no idea what a prurchin was, but he didn't think he liked it.

-§-§-§-§-§-

No one was exactly sure where the Grand Hidden Mountain was, least of all the deputy leader in charge of K division. But Zelora and her prisoners had been summoned by the Hidden Executive Leader himself, so they didn't have much of a choice.

There was a door in the K division mountain complex which led directly to the Hidden Leader's abode. This was the good news. The bad news was that the innards of the mountain were still suffering from Aragon Silversword's handiwork, and the Hidden door was nowhere to be found.

Zelora decided to take the initiative. She called forth the carpet trainer and had him provide transportation for herself, Daggar, Kassa, Aragon, the gargoyle and a few sentries including Singespitter. It was a well known fact that flying carpets knew where everything was.

The carpets were a bit skittish and needed to be placated with a good rub down and a handful of chocolate dustballs before anyone could even think about riding them.

The Hidden Army were the only ones who had managed to capture some of the flying carpets from the highest peaks of the Skullcaps, where the wild creatures roamed. It was supposedly death to approach a wild carpet, but the Hidden Army had managed to break and tame some fine specimens.

There were three carpets. Zelora, Daggar and the stone gargoyle rode on the first. Kassa and the carpet trainer rode on the second. Aragon, who was not considered at all trustworthy, was bound by the wrists and strapped to the third carpet, guarded by Singespitter and another sentry named Brut.

"To the Grand Hidden Mountain," commanded the trainer, and the carpets rose into the sky, spiralling dizzily.

Kassa gripped the edge of her carpet firmly as the ground raced past below her. Behind, she could hear the sounds of Singespitter being violently ill from the turbulence.

On the first carpet, Daggar was silent.

"Are you sulking?" Zelora demanded.

"Why would I be sulking?"

"You're jealous," she accused.

"Me? Jealous of a badly carved house brick? I think not."

"My husband means nothing to me!"

"Hah," he said bitterly. "That's why you've been so casual about getting him back, ey?"

"I have been trying to trace him for thirteen years!" Zelora exclaimed. "I want revenge on the man who abandoned me for no good reason."

Daggar perked up slightly. "Is a wife's revenge anything like the punishment for kissing an executive mercenary without her permission?"

"Much worse," promised Zelora.

Daggar cheered up a bit.

The carpets swooped and dove towards an empty space in the middle of the Skullcaps. Suddenly they were inside the Grand Hidden Mountain. Momentarily confused, the carpets shuddered to a stop. A few gnomes with ladders came forward to help the visitors off their mounts.

"Why does the Hidden Army employ so many gnomes?" asked Kassa.

"Gnomes are suitably anti-social," said Zelora ominously. Zelora said most things ominously.

"The Leader wants to see you," said one gnome, grinning maliciously.

"Oo er," said the other gnome. "What you been up to, then? Eh, eh?"

"Anti-social," said Kassa grimly. "I can see why."

The gnomes led them to the library, where the Leader was to be found. Zelora peered into the musty room. "He's with someone else," she reported. "I think they're playing chess or something. We wouldn't want to disturb..."

"Leader says you're to go roight in," said one of the gnomes cheerfully. "You an' the scruffy one an' the pirate lady." He doffed his cap to Kassa. "How do, madam." Then he grinned toothlessly at the bound Aragon. "Said 'e was to be put in solitarrarry confineyment, eh, eh, eh?"

Aragon was dragged away with great dignity, and almost no kicking.

One of the gnomes knocked on the door and announced them in a very loud voice. "H'introducing 'er deputy leadership, Commander Zelora Footcrusher, de profit-scoundrel Daggar h'of Dreadnought h'and 'er piraticalness Mistress Kassa Daggersharp." He coughed grandly. "You can go in now."

The Hidden Leader was not the first thing they noticed about the room. He blended in so expertly with the walls that they barely saw him at all. But they did see his large companion, who flexed his large fingers as he studied the gameboard before him.

Daggar froze, sweat beading on his forehead. It was Leonardes of Skullcap.

The large Master of Profit did not pay any attention to the intruders. "Your turn, Kenneth," he said to the Hidden Leader.

The Leader glanced up at Zelora. "I hear you have come across some treasure, Footcrusher."

Zelora snapped to attention. "The location is still unknown, Hidden One. But we are in the process of locating it."

"The silver," said Kassa in a clear sharp voice, "when we find it, belongs to me."

"Indeed," said the Hidden Leader, amused.

"However, if you allow us to use the resources of K Division, we shall allow the Hidden Army a portion of the spoils," Kassa continued smoothly.

"How generous," said the Hidden Leader thoughtfully. "Yes, I believe we can do business. There is a gathering tonight which you shall all attend. Tomorrow you may return to the K division caves and resume your treasure hunting. I do not expect failure."

"Neither do I, Hidden One," said Kassa politely, trying to calculate how many shares of this silver she'd promised away so far. If the bounty consisted of one silver cake fork, she was going to be in trouble.

The Hidden Leader turned back to his game. "My turn, did you say, Leo?" He peered thoughtfully at the board. "Our wise women wish to have words with you, Mistress Daggersharp," he added as his guests tactfully withdrew.

"As you wish," replied Kassa, turning towards the door.

Daggar was the last of the three to leave, and as he sidled out he heard the menacing tones of Leonardes of Skullcap. "It is only a few days until full moon, Daggar. Make the most of them."

Outside, Kassa glared at Daggar. "What was that about?"

"Nothing, no one, don't know what you're talking about," gabbled Daggar. "I need a drink."

"Show us to our quarters," Zelora commanded a gnome.

As they were led away, the Hidden Executive Leader of the Hidden Army turned his attention to the gameboard before him. He tapped a finger thoughtfully against his chin. "I think it was Mistress Scarlett, in the Billiards Room, with the Pickaxe Handle..."

-§-§-§-§-§-

The Lady Emperor was exploring her new Palace again. The discovery of the portrait parlour had whetted Talle's appetite for exploration, and she felt that she deserved a little leisure time now. With a PR urchin organising her public image, Aragon Silversword hunting down Kassa Daggersharp and Reed Cooper hunting down Aragon Silversword, the *Splashdance* silver would soon be within her control and all would be well.

On the thirty-seventh floor, she discovered the menagerie. Strange and unusual creatures made funny noises at her from within their gilded cages. Talle saw four giant spiders, several monkeybirds with gold plumage, a talking tree, six sapient water lilies and a turf-accountant.

Then there was the cage at the end of the room which held a very old woman with stringy hair who peered intently at a crystal ball.

Lady Talle tapped lightly on the cage. "Who are you?"

"Shaddup," said the old woman.

"I am the Emperor of Mocklore!" declared Lady Talle, shocked by this insolence. "I could have you executed."

"I'm in a cage, lady, even the cleaning urchins could get me executed," muttered the old woman. "Now shove orf. I'm watchin' the Smug Family. Damien's about to tell Tallulah that her boyfriend Beelzibuck isn't really a warlock." She peered at the crystal ball again. "Bugger. Episode's over. I'll have to wait till tomorrow to find out what Jemima's life-threatening disease is. She's an elf by her second marriage, you know, and elves have a different disease for ev'ry day of the moon." She packed away the crystal ball and turned to her visitor. "Now whaddaya want?"

"A great more respect from you, for a start," commanded Lady Talle imperiously.

The old woman cackled. "Well, if you want that you'll have to go somewhere else, duckie. I'm a witch. We don't do respect."

"Can you see the future in that crystal?" asked Lady Talle, curious enough to drop her demanding tone.

"Heh, what use is the future?" said the witch dismissively. "Not here yet, is it, so it can't be up to much. Nah, the present's the thing to see. My li'l crystal is tuned to this field out in the middle of nowhere, right, and every day at half past five hours past noon these mummers an' minstrels all get together to do the Smug Family, right? There's Dave and Sharletta, an' their boys Damien and Hemlock, okay, and the girls next door, that's Lucrezia an' Tallulah and Mephistophelisa, an' then there's all the fey folk at the Healery, an' they all have perfect lives except for the occasional natural disaster. They've had two earthquakes this month, you know, and five weddings and twelve dead monks! It's just like real life."

"But can you see other things?" persisted Lady Talle. "Real things. Where people are, what they are doing."

"I don't know any real people," said the old, stringy witch in a bemused voice. "Just the Smug Family."

-§-§-§-§-§-

"Go on," said Summer Songstrel. "You know you want to."

"I can't think of anything I wouldn't rather do than visit some old gaggle of women," said Kassa stubbornly.

"How are you going to figure out how to be a witch if you don't meet other witches?" demanded the sprite, who had appeared uninvited in the chamber Kassa had been provided with.

Kassa glared icily. "I know all I need to know about being a witch."

"You admitted it!" cried Summer Songstrel in triumph. "Ha!"

"I know that I am not, never have been, and never will want to be one!" Kassa announced. "Please go away."

"It helped you escape the icesprites, didn't it?"

Kassa didn't say anything for a moment. "It won't happen again."

"Why not?" insisted the persistent sprite.

"Because I don't want it to happen!"

"Oh, rather be a pirate, would you?"

"Those aren't the only choices in life, you know."

"They're the only two you'll ever be offered, ladybird."

Against her better judgement, Kassa went to see the wise women.

-§-§-§-§-§-

The wise women of Hidden Mountain were a curious breed, renowned for their ability to bake fruitcakes, knit tea cozies and Know the Unknown. "Oooh, look," one of them squealed when Kassa was announced. "It's Nellisand's girl. Come here, child, I knew you when you were knee high to a ship's anchor."

"Ooh, it is, it is," agreed the others. "No doubt about it, absolutely, it's our Nellisand's little girl, and her a witch too, wouldn't she be proud? Oh, she would, she would."

One particularly wise woman took Kassa by the arm. "Just ignore this gaggle, dearie, you don't want to be swapping gossip and fruitcake with us all day. You go in and see Maitzi O, she's been waiting for you."

That set the gaggle off good and proper. "Oh, my, yes, Maitzi O, she'll know what to do, she's terribly good at this sort of thing, you can't do better than consulting Maitzi Orackle..."

Kassa left in a hurry, clattering down a flight of rocky steps. She emerged in a small cave draped with silken curtains and scented smoke. "Come in, sit down, I'll be with you in a minute," called a voice. "I'm just trying to pick up today's installment of the Smug Family."

A very old, very wrinkled gnome woman appeared, carrying a large crystal ball under one arm. "I missed the episode, see, because I was having a visitation of imps, and you've got to clean up after them right away or the smell lingers. I'm trying to tune this to half an hour ago. Ah, there we are." She put down the crystal. "I'll watch that later. Now, who are you?"

"Don't you know?" inquired Kassa. "Everyone else seems to."

The gnome woman peered at her, and then grunted. "Oh. You're the one whose mother ran off with that no-good pirate."

"My mother was a pirate herself," Kassa said indignantly.

"Second career," snapped the gnome woman. "I remember. Called herself Black Nell, as if Nellisand wasn't good enough for her. Drove her mother to distraction. I remember. Dyeing her hair," she added disapprovingly. "So now you come crawling to me, wanting to be a witch, eh?"

"I don't crawl to anyone," flared Kassa. "You summoned me. I don't want to be a witch. I don't even like magic!"

"Tough cookies," crowed the old gnome woman. "Destiny is destiny, and yours is to zap things. Be grateful."

"I'm an entertainer," said Kassa haughtily. "And possibly a pirate..."

"You're a witch, and you know it. Just like me."

Kassa gave in. "But you're so..." she said helplessly. "And I'm..."

The gnome woman cackled. "You don't have to be a withered old crone to practice witchcraft, girl. It just helps. I suppose you want that sword of yours back?"

Kassa leaned forward, intrigued. "You can do that?"

"I'm not going to," snorted Maitzi Orackle, the oldest and wisest of wise women. "You are."

Kassa was doubtful. "Don't I need some kind of certificate?"

"Would it make you feel better?"

"Not really."

"Then get on with it." The old wise woman deliberately turned her back and started watching the Smug Family.

Kassa closed her eyes. After a few minutes, she realised she had absolutely no idea where to start.

There was a throat-clearing sound from the direction of Maitzi O. "Sing if you must," she suggested grudgingly.

Songwitch, Kassa remembered.

Ten minutes later, the song exploded out of the mountain, informing the world that Kassa Daggersharp wanted her sword back. Never underestimate the speed of song.

-§-§-§-§-§-

Still caked with mud and swamp-slime, Reed Cooper found the Lady Emperor in the menagerie, arguing with a scruffy old woman in a cage.

"Why can't you show me Kassa Daggersharp?" Talle was demanding.

"Maybe it's none of your business," chortled the old woman, making faces through the bars of her cage.

"Now listen to me, old crone..."

"My Lady Emperor," gasped Reed Cooper.

Talle snapped her head towards him. "Back so soon? And without Aragon Silversword, I see."

"We were captured by firebrands," said the young pirate dismally. "They separated us. I couldn't find him again… he could be anywhere in the Skullcaps."

"My bauble?" inquired the Lady Emperor dangerously.

"It followed him," said Reed, still breathing quickly from his climb up thirty flights of stairs. "As you commanded…"

"You are a fool. What of Mistress Daggersharp? The gargoyle? Have you nothing to show for your effort?"

"I have information that Kassa is working with the Hidden Army," Reed said quickly. "A cousin of hers is with them now."

"The Hidden Army?" said Lady Talle, intrigued.

"With the assistance of the executive mercenaries she cannot help but find the silver!" Reed blurted.

Talle laughed in a mocking voice. She reached out and drew the prime sword of Bigbeard Daggersharp from the scabbard on Reed's back. "Without this? I don't think so. My PR urchin is working to secure the hearts and confidence of the city, and then the Empire. The tributes will come pouring in from the Lordlings and I will have no particular need of Mistress Daggersharp's treasure trove. She may have the means to decipher whatever is written on this sword, but I have the sword itself. I may not find the silver, but neither will she."

The Lady Emperor laughed again. It was a chilling sound, and Reed Cooper was glad he was supposed to be on her side.

Suddenly the air around the sword opened up. A brief snatch of song filled the space around them, and the sword was pulled through reality towards its rightful owner.

The old witch in the cage cackled hysterically.

Lady Talle's mouth became a very thin line. "Tune that damn crystal of yours to Aragon Silversword," she ordered. "Do it, or I will have you flogged."

The old witch shrugged and handed over the crystal. It showed an image of Aragon sitting on a stone bench, a white bandage on his arm and a bored expression on his face.

"I will speak to him," declared the Lady Emperor.

The old witch twiddled a knob on the underside of the crystal.

"Silversword," barked the Lady Emperor.

He glanced up, seemingly unsurprised at this method of communication. "Hello, Talle. How are you?"

"I presume you are still on my side," she hissed.

"Presume nothing," said Aragon blandly. "Only trust me."

"Allow the girl to lead you to the *Splashdance* silver," Lady Talle commanded in a shaky voice. "Once she has done so, kill her and bring the treasure to me."

Aragon's face did not change. "It will be a pleasure," he said coldly, settling back against the stone bench. Images in his mind of tangled dark red hair and deep golden eyes were swiftly banished in favour of wealthy, silver ambition.

-§-§-§-§-§-

"Not bad for a beginner," grunted Maitzi Orackle. "Well done."

"Um," said Kassa. "Should I fetch a doctor?"

"I'm a witch, I don't need no doctor!" snapped the wisest of wise women. "Now, if we can just figure a way to get this sword out of my arm—and out of the wall—we'll be in business."

Chapter 12
Splashdown

The Lady Emperor came before the crowd in the market square, smiling silkily. "My dear people," she pronounced with an attractive pout. "I have given bread to the poor and tax exemptions to the rich. I have installed new theatres, paved roads and visited the sick. What would you have me give to you next?"

One boy, too small even to be classified as an urchin, was pushed to the front of the crowd. He wiped his nose on his hand. "Please, miss."

Lady Talle leaned forward, and exactly half of the crowd craned to see down the front of her clinging gown. "What would you ask of me, my young soldier?"

"Please miss," sniffled the repulsive child. "Milk, miss."

"Milk," cried Lady Talle in a delighted voice. "Of course. Milk for the children! Free milk for all the children!"

Everyone cheered, except the milk-merchants.

"Chocolate milk!" added the boy hurriedly. "Wif bendy straws! An' sprinkles!" He was hauled away by an anxious parent. "An' doughnuts," his thin, reedy voice continued, fading into the distance. "An' a big truck! An' humorous hieroglyphs! An' biscuits an' cakes an' a thousand jellybaby sandwidges…"

Lady Talle moved away from the crowd with a smooth expression of satisfaction. She stepped into her velvety carriage and was drawn away towards the palace. "It is not enough, boy," she said through her soft smile.

Griffin looked worriedly confident. "Um," he said.

"What good is it if the news-minstrels inform the Lordlings that the peasants are happy? I need the nobles to be charmed, which means they must come here. Get them here, Griffin, to see me. To be stunned and overwhelmed by the gracious power of their new Emperor. Then let them pour their loyalty before me. Bring them to me, Griffin."

"Of course, my Lady Emperor," said Griffin with a bright smile. "Nothing could be less horribly difficult."

Lady Talle gave him a sharp look. "I presume there has been no word from Silversword as yet."

"No word, my Lady," Griffin acknowledged. He hesitated. "Are you sure that he is trustworthy?"

Talle's eyes were flinty. "Of course he is trustworthy. I would trust him with your life."

-§-§-§-§-§-

The Gathering Hall was an immense cavern with bright bunting and fairy lights looped all around the walls. A huge mirror ball hung in the centre of it all, reflecting light outwards in a thoroughly misleading way.

Kassa, with a recently-released Aragon trailing behind her, was stopped at the door by a woman with disturbingly black lips. "You will remove all weapons before entering," she pronounced. Many weapons, most flickering from hidden to visible, were already heaped by the entrance.

Aragon had no weapons because they had already been taken from him by the mercenaries.

Kassa removed two daggers and a long coil of sharp wire from her right boot and pulled eighteen glittering spikes out of her left boot. Then she peeled up the hem of her dragon-scale coat, revealing several tiny darts which she handled very carefully. From her belt she discarded two leather pouches full of sand, a pair of embroidery shears and a small mace. From her bodice, she produced a whip with metallic edging. A slender, icy knife had been braided under her hair.

Aragon watched this disarming process thoughtfully. Kassa looked up once and met his gaze. "I would not have been your prisoner long, Silversword. I did not need Daggar's pet army to rescue me."

"I believe you," he replied.

Having unloaded most of her concealed weapons, Kassa noticed that it was quite warm in the Gathering Hall, and she began to remove her dragon-scale coat.

Remembering the invisible gauze just in time, Aragon's hand grasped her shoulder firmly. "Trust me. Keep the coat on."

Kassa looked as if she was about to argue, until she too remembered what she was wearing under the coat. She gave him a twisted smile.

"That sword is a weapon, I believe," said the black-lipped woman.

"Tough," said Kassa, and she walked unmolested into the hall, grasping Bigbeard's sword firmly in one hand. Aragon followed her.

The music was loud and intrusive. Various executive mercenaries were dancing, drinking and brawling, in no particular order. Just as a flicker of interest in the music crossed Kassa's face, Daggar and Zelora appeared on either side of her and walked her into a corner of the room. "That sword," said Zelora crisply. "I believe it can tell you the location of the silver."

"Oh," said Kassa, shooting a dark look at Daggar. "You know about that, do you?"

Daggar eyed Aragon suspiciously. "What did yer bring him for?" he complained.

"It was him or a handbag," said Kassa breezily. "A girl can't go to a party without accessories. Isn't anyone going to offer me a drink?"

"Read the sword now," Zelora commanded, infuriated by this small talk.

Kassa gave her a long, cool stare. "I was planning two." The rubies in the hilt glittered menacingly. She found the hidden clasp and opened the secret compartment.

The message slid out, revealing the scratchy letters of a forgotten language. Kassa read it carefully, frowning.

"Well?" said Daggar greedily. "Where's our silver, then?"

"My silver," corrected Kassa absently. "And I have absolutely no idea where it is."

-§-§-§-§-§-

The goblins in these caves were just like any other. They squished together in the smallest holes, they smelled like dirt, they watched the interesting bits of the world when they chose to, particularly when the Smug Family was on. But these goblins differed from the rest of their kind in one respect. These goblins actually had a vague sort of purpose. They were guarding.

Every now and then these squirmy, dirty little creatures would come out of their holes to explore, stretch their legs, beat each other up or go for scampers. But mostly they came out of their holes to play with the silver.

-§-§-§-§-§-

Zelora Footcrusher remained quite calm under the circumstances. She took a deep breath and led them all to a little ante-cave full of empty buffet tables. Only then did she actually breathe out. A moment, later, she exploded. "You can't read it?"

"I didn't say that," said Kassa. "Of course I can read it. It's Old Troll. The most complicated and highly devious of dead dialects. Not even trolls know how that language works any more." She shook her head. "I really don't understand my father. He devotes ten years to learning an ancient long-lost language, and he still writes his letters in crayon."

"So if you can read it, what's the problem?" asked Daggar, sounding a bit desperate.

"Listen to this," said Kassa scornfully. "Where the strongest swimmer reaches, far beyond the hills and beaches, down into the goblin's space, hidden where the trolls give chase. Hah! It's a children's rhyme, or something equally stupid."

Zelora's eyes were distant for a moment. "It is gibberish," she said crisply, and then she stalked away at a steady, reasonable pace.

"She knows," said Kassa quietly. "Daggar, she knows something!"

When money was involved, Daggar could move surprisingly fast. He headed off Zelora's escape route. "We can do this the easy way," he said pleasantly. "Which means that you help us, and we give you a share of our silver."

"My silver," said Kassa firmly.

"Her silver," Daggar corrected himself without missing a beat. "Or we can do it the hard way, which means that no one gets happy. Which is it to be, Footcrusher?"

Zelora glared at all of them, her eyes glinting in a fetching shade of red. "You will relinquish your claims to the gargoyle?" she asked after a moment.

"You married him," said Kassa with a careless shrug. "We've got a few days until full moon. It's up to you what happens while he's in manform."

Zelora pondered in silence. "Very well," she said finally. "I will show you and Daggar what the riddle means, as long as you honour your deal with the Hidden Leader." She glared at Aragon. "But not him. This one is not to be trusted."

"Silversword comes," said Kassa in a hard voice.

Zelora looked surprised, but not as surprised as Aragon himself.

"Ey?" said Daggar in bewilderment. "Can I jump in here with the stupid question and ask why yer willing to give this blatant villain another chance?"

Kassa looked at Aragon and couldn't honestly think of a good reason. "Because," she said firmly.

A weakness, thought Aragon Silversword. *All the better to kill you with...*

-§-§-§-§-§-

It was evening. The moon was high, and swelling into fullness. The water swept gently against the shore, making contented little lapping noises. Too soon till full moon, thought Daggar. He had barely two days before the Profithood Retirement Scheme swung into action. Something else was worrying him. “How did Kassa get her hands on that sword?”

“She’s a witch,” said Aragon shortly. “Didn’t you know?”

There really wasn’t anything Daggar could say to that, so he just kept trudging across the damp sand.

“Here,” commanded Zelora Footcrusher.

Aragon dropped his armful of shovels and sat down, scowling. “Where is she?” There was little doubt as to which she he referred to.

High, black boots made neat imprints in the sand. Layers of silk shimmered. The bodice was tight-fitting, low-cut and black. Leather. The skirt flared out in a scarlet swish. She had found a large, wide-brimmed black hat from somewhere. Her dark red hair glowed eerily in the bright sunlight. With hands on hips, she surveyed the beach slowly.

Aragon Silversword, leaning comfortably against a large rock, watched Kassa from behind lidded eyes. “The costume change will help, will it?”

“Presentation is important,” she replied serenely.

“Would not a pointed hat be more appropriate?”

She turned blazing golden eyes in his direction. “I—am—not—a—witch!”

“Whatever you say,” Aragon replied with an almost-smile.

“So where do we dig?” grumbled Daggar, who didn’t like the idea of manual labour.

Zelora came as close to looking embarrassed as they had ever seen her. “Look,” she said finally, “I know this is where I explain this ancient legend to you, but I’m not going to do a faraway voice, all right?" After they shrugged and nodded, she continued. "Fine, then. They say that below this bay, many hidden underwater caves are contained within each other. It is said that if you swim down far enough, you can reach the seventh layer of caves, where there is air to breathe. It is also said that goblins guard the caves, and that trolls consider it their favourite hiding place."

"Who says all this?" said Daggar curiously.

Zelora lost her temper. "Look, I didn't have to tell you..."

Kassa snapped her fingers, ignoring them both. "Folklore! Why didn't I think of that?" She tossed her shovel to one side. "Let's go swimming."

"I don't swim," said Aragon immediately.

"Tough cookies," said Kassa Daggersharp. "We're going in."

-§-§-§-§-§-

The water rippled slightly, and then was still. The Cellar Sea is quite possibly the most placid ocean in the known universe. The tides are so mild as to be almost non-existent. Legend says that this is due to the Great Purple Kraken, who got tired of the noisy ocean life and did the magical equivalent of asking the neighbours to turn the radio down. Another legend claims that the water remains quiet at the express desire of Skeylles, the Fishy God who rules as Lord of the Underwater. Yet another legend claims that it is all because of the hedgehogs, but most people don't pay any attention to that sort of legend.

Suffice to say, the Cellar Sea remained calm and placid until Zelora Footcrusher burst out from under it, gasping lungfuls of air and sending violent ripples in every direction. One of these ripples eventually became a tidal wave which swallowed a whole fishing village, but that is another story.

"I have never been able to reach beyond the fourth level," said Zelora when she had her breath back. "It must be impossible!"

"Nothing's impossible when money's involved," said Kassa Daggersharp, standing waist deep in the water and peering down into its murky depths. She frowned suddenly. "Aragon, bring me my sword!"

Aragon was still sitting in the shade of the large rock. He opened one eye. "I don't swim," he said again.

"Well, bloody well wade!" Kassa yelled.

Very slowly, Aragon stood up, walking to where the water lapped the sand. With an expression of sheer distaste, he waded out to where Kassa stood, grasping the sword hilt lightly.

"You too," Kassa called.

Daggar, who had so far managed to stay dry, shuddered and bravely shouldered a shovel, rolled up his trouser legs and started squelching towards them. "Where are those mercenaries who were supposed to be helping us?"

"They're ready and waiting for your Mistress Daggersharp to deign to find a use for them," Zelora snapped. Daggar couldn't help noticing that she had been in a bad temper for a while now.

Kassa peered at the sword as Aragon handed it to her. "You know, I can think of lots of uses for some spare mercenaries now. Would you fetch them for me, there's a dear?"

Grumbling darkly, Zelora made her way towards the shore, splashing deliberately as she went.

"That got rid of her," said Kassa with some satisfaction. "No offence, Daggar, but I think this expedition will be more successful without any military intervention."

"What expedition?" asked Daggar suspiciously, but Kassa wasn't listening. Grasping her sword, she stared out at the obnoxiously calm sea.

"Now," she muttered to herself. "How would my father get down to an impossible underwater cave?" After a moment's contemplation, her eyes brightened and she snapped her fingers. "Of course! Mermaids!"

Daggar got as far as saying "Wha…" before thirteen pairs of slender hands grasped him by the legs, pulling him underwater at a frightening speed.

It was not a pleasant ride. Daggar refused to believe that he could breathe water, despite the obvious evidence that he was doing so. He hardly noticed the luscious water-sprites who were dragging him below, and paid no attention to the lovely tails which curled seductively around him, attempting to remove his clothes.

He was vaguely aware of Kassa waving her father's sword around in a threatening manner. The mermaids shrieked in burbles and twitters, trying to hide behind each other while keeping hold of their prisoners. Finally, as Kassa came dangerously close to slicing a piece of tail, the mermaids consulted with each other and flung the three humans down to the bottom of the ocean.

Daggar was no longer breathing water but sharp, dusty air. He had landed face-first in a cave full of sand. Coughing and spluttering, he realised that his clothes were not even wet. A moment later, Kassa, Aragon and the sword crashed in on top of him.

Kassa picked herself up, spitting out sand. "That would be right," she said scornfully. "He couldn't just dig a hole for his treasure like anyone else, ohhh no, he just had to bring sex into it."

Daggar's eyes were still wide and horrified. "Gah, gah, gahhghh," was all he could say for at least ten minutes.

Aragon's grey eyes were dazed. "Kassa," he said flatly, when he regained his poise. "Don't do that again. Not ever."

"Fine," Kassa agreed in a too-friendly voice. "You'll be making your own arrangements for transport home, then."

As they looked up through the layers of caves, they could see a ceiling of salt water, and a bevy of fish-tailed maidens blowing kisses at them.

"Interesting," was all that Kassa said.

"Gah, gah, gaggghhhgh," replied Daggar.

"So," said Aragon Silversword. "What do we do now?"

"We fight the goblins," said Kassa steadily, brandishing her sword.

"What goblins?" Daggar managed to choke out intelligibly, just as the swarm of vicious little goblins attacked them.

Chapter 13
The Mating Habits of Trolls

Screeching and twittering and smelling of dirt, the goblins swarmed from everywhere. There were hundreds of them, all small and knobbly and brown and making nasty noises. They swarmed over Kassa, pulling her hair and attempting to dive down her tight leather bodice. They swarmed up Aragon's legs, jeering and jabbing at him with long gnarled fingers. Daggar was still curled up in a protective ball, so he remained unmolested for the time being.

"Don't touch me, you wingless insects!" Kassa screamed angrily, prising them off her arms and slapping the intruding little paws away. "These are my caves!"

"Our caves, our caves," chorused a hundred unpleasant little voices, none of them quite in sync with the others.

Kassa leaped up on a rock, glaring down at the gibbering mass. "Where is my silver?" she demanded.

"Our silver, our silver," twittered the goblins.

Several leaped into her hair from above, and Kassa flailed at them, trying to pull them out. She kicked at several more, lost her balance and fell from the rock.

There were hundreds of goblins chittering below, trying to see up her skirt, and they almost certainly would have cushioned her fall if the ground had not at that moment opened up and swallowed her whole.

Aragon was surprised, which didn't happen very often.

Daggar crawled to his feet shakily, still clutching his shovel. "What I want to know, is why Bigbeard's dyin' wish was for us to bring shovels, if he didn't mean us to dig for the treasure."

Aragon took the shovel from Daggar and used it to bat away several goblins. They hit the cave walls with three thunks and a splat.

"Ey, lateral thinking," approved Daggar. "Where's Kassa, then?"

"She fell through a hole," said Aragon, gesturing to where Kassa had fallen through the hole.

Daggar peered at the ground, frowning. "I don't see any hole."

"There was one there a minute ago." For every half-dozen goblins Aragon squelched, a dozen more scampered up and pinched at him.

Daggar was examining the ground that had swallowed Kassa. "There's a trapdoor," he reported, opening it up and looking down into darkness. He prodded cautiously around with one hand. "It doesn't lead anywhere. Solid rock, unless I'm very much mistaken."

"We've lost her, then," said Aragon. "Careless of you."

They both sat down on the rock, ignoring the swarming goblins, and only occasionally bothering to bat them away.

"I suppose," said Daggar, very slowly, "the silver is ours now."

Aragon considered this. "What about your pointy-toothed lady friend?"

Daggar thought about Zelora for a moment. "Ey, what would she do with a fortune in silver? I'll spend her share."

Aragon looked at the ceiling reflectively. "So, you are willing to sacrifice your closest living relative and betray your lady for a potential fortune?"

"That sounds about right."

"I like the way you think. Of course, the silver may not even be here."

Daggar sniffed the air. "Oh, it's here, all right. I can smell it."

"I thought that was the goblins."

"No, I definitely caught a whiff of wealth for the taking. It must be close by."

"Much as I respect the skills of the Profithood," said Aragon dryly, "I would prefer some more tangible evidence."

Daggar stood up to stretch his legs, squelching half a dozen goblins as he did so. "C'mon, let's go find it, then. My neck's starting to feel endangered. Yer know how it is, professional death-threats an' all."

"I would have imagined you to be greatly experienced with people wanting you dead."

"Usually only family and friends. This is different. It's business."

"So it's agreed," said Aragon sharply, standing up. "We find the silver and split it in half."

"Agreed," Daggar nodded.

As they stepped towards the tunnel which was still pouring forth hundreds of goblins, an open trapdoor appeared beneath their feet and they both fell through.

They landed on a thick layer of dirt. Above them, the trapdoor swung shut with a clang of finality. A stone panel swung around to cover it. "On the other hand," said Daggar calmly. "We could try and rescue Kassa."

Aragon stood up and brushed himself off. "In the absence of a better plan…"

-§-§-§-§-§-

It wasn't that Kassa objected to falling from great heights. She was becoming quite resigned to such things. In this case, it was the soft landing that she objected to.

"Rgrunch!" said the large, hairy creature who had caught her in its arms. "Woman! Mine!"

"Of course," said Kassa dismally as she was carried off. "Trolls."

As everyone knows, trolls are a unique species. They are large, hairy, strong, usually violent and the creators of the most simplified legal system in existence. They have a very large vocabulary which they rarely use, preferring to simplify the world into five major categories: food, sex, hitting, games and shiny things. Anything else is deemed irrelevant. Their games consist mainly of putting trapdoors in inconvenient places and opening them at inconvenient times. Inconvenient, that is, for the victims.

-§-§-§-§-§-

"I know what you are thinking," said Aragon as they made their way along the rocky tunnel.

"Oh, do you?" challenged Daggar.

"You are thinking that one is such an easy number to divide by, and if I was dead, you could have all of the silver yourself."

"Ey," said Daggar guiltily. "Is that what I was thinking?"

"You're a profit-scoundrel."

"I'm also a coward."

"True. You won't actually get up the courage to try to kill me. But if it came to saving my life or not saving my life…"

"I would hide behind a rock until the question went away," admitted Daggar shamelessly.

"I expected no less." Aragon stopped walking. His eyes rotated upwards. "Trolls," he said. A ladder was fixed to the side of a vertical tunnel. It was decorated with modern trollish script which consisted of five crude pictograms, repeated over and over. Aragon gestured generously towards the ladder. "After you," he suggested.

-§-§-§-§-§-

Lady Talle floated gently on a flower-strewn ivory boat shaped like a swan. Her occasional explorations of the Imperial Palace had led her to discover an ornamental garden on the roof of the Library Tower. The swan-boats bobbed gently along on the surface of an exquisite boating pool decorated with water lilies and designer frogs. "Now," murmured the Lady Emperor, "Do you think I should go for the lace napkins or the pearl and magenta serviettes?"

Reed Cooper was poling the boat back and forth, a bored expression firmly fixed to his face. "It's a garden party isn't it?" he drawled. "Let them use leaves."

"That's hardly helpful," snapped Talle. A moment later, her eyes brightened. "Unless...pearl and magenta serviettes shaped like leaves! Perfect." She scribbled a few notes on the parchments which were piled up in front of her.

Reed barely restrained himself from grunting unintelligibly.

Talle glanced up sharply. "If you have a problem, Cooper, I suggest you vocalise it. I detest negative vibrations when I am planning parties."

"I didn't expect this," complained Reed. "You promised that if I gave you Bigbeard's sword, we would rule Mocklore together..."

Mentioning the sword was a mistake. Talle's blue eyes narrowed dangerously. "I do not recall promising you anything," she said icily. "I have no need of a consort, Reed."

"Then what use am I?" he burst out. "Why bother with me at all? You already have a champion—even if you haven't seen him for weeks. You've got that bloody urchin running around arranging your social calendar. What exactly do you need me for?"

"So that's it," said Talle softly. "You want a title."

"I want a role!" insisted Reed. "Otherwise, I might..." He hesitated at the warning expression on her face, but continued on bravely. He was a pirate, after all. "Otherwise I might take my services elsewhere."

"Oh, I wouldn't recommend that," said Talle mildly. "I doubt you would get very far. You're very right, Cooper. You do deserve a role in my administration. I intend to make Griffin my prime minister eventually and when Aragon Silversword returns with the silver, he shall be honoured as my Imperial Champion. But you...how does Ambassador sound?"

Reed froze. "Ambassador?"

"You would have to wear purple, of course, but that isn't a great sacrifice. And you would have to travel a great deal...perhaps even outside Mocklore on occasion."

Reed's throat was dry. "Will there be danger and excitement?" he managed to ask.

Talle's smile was indescribable. "Oh I should think so. Yes, I believe I can almost guarantee it."

-§-§-§-§-§-

"I hate trolls," muttered Daggar, staring upwards. "I hate trolls, I hate trolls!"

"You wait until you meet one," said Aragon cheerfully.

A huge, hairy paw reached down from behind them and picked up Daggar as if he were a spare gauntlet. Daggar screamed and gibbered as he was hauled into the arms of the monstrous creature.

Aragon watched with interest from a safe distance. "I think it's a female of the species," he commented.

Daggar's face froze in terror. "What's it going to do to me?" he demanded hoarsely.

"Use your imagination."

"Mmmmman!" growled the troll triumphantly, gazing into Daggar's terror-stricken face. She then turned towards Aragon. "Mmmmman!"

But Aragon had taken the opportunity to vanish.

The female troll had draped Daggar over her large shoulders and was striding through the tunnels at a bumpy pace. Daggar spoke rapidly, desperately trying to talk his way out of this. "You can't possibly find me attractive! I'm not nearly as hairy as you, I'm practically bald all over. And I'm too small. Really, don't you think it's time you settled down with a nice manly eight-foot troll and started raising monoliths? These inter-species relationships never really work out, you know... Oooof!"

This last bit was because the troll had dumped Daggar on the ground as if he was a sack of particularly thick-skinned potatoes.

It is traditional among trollish courtship rituals to impress a new mate with one's cave. The female troll waved a paw indignantly around. "Look," she growled.

"Oh," said Daggar, glancing around. His eye was caught by a puddle of silver coins in the corner. "Aren't they pretty?"

"Shiny things," said the troll proudly. Very few trolls had such an impressive hoard in their cave, but the pickings were good around here.

"Very nice," agreed Daggar. His eyes gleamed. "I don't suppose you know where there are any more shiny things, do you? Lots and lots, perhaps all buried somewhere?"

"Urgh!" agreed the troll, nodding furiously. "Close," she confided. "Big shiny hoard. But no go there." She shook her head with equal fervour.

"Why not?" asked Daggar.

"Yukky goblins," said the troll disgustedly. "Too many to eat. Too many to hit. Get everywhere. Pull hair. Hurts. Goblins yukky."

"Ey," said Daggar, looking disappointed. "I don't suppose you could tell me where it is, then?"

The troll had been thinking too hard. She wasn't used to such brain activity. Her massive brow furrowed. "There," she grunted, pointing vaguely down one of the tunnels that led away from her cave.

"Cheers," said Daggar, hurrying away.

After a moment, a plaintive call came from the direction of the troll. "Mate…"

"Not today, thank you!" Daggar called behind him.

He followed the twisting tunnel upwards, noting that the scuff marks from the troll's feet were old and dusted over. As the tunnel forked, he met Aragon coming the other way. "You again," he said bitterly.

"You escaped," said Aragon with polite interest. "Well done." He indicated the one path neither of them had tried. "This way?"

Daggar nodded grimly and they both turned down that tunnel. It opened out into a wide cave that had recently been redecorated with twigs, old leaves, straw, and general muck. A large pile of webby refuse clung to one corner of the cave. It was moving.

"Watch it," commanded Aragon sharply, drawing his slender, icy sword and moving cagily around the twitching heap.

Daggar stood behind Aragon, his eyes warily on the bundle. It looked like a kind of nest. The kind of nest a troll might make for a new mate? "Um, Aragon," he started to say.

Kassa exploded out of the bundle, dripping with gunk and scattering dead leaves in every direction. "They—put—me," she said indignantly, shaking with rage, "In—a—nest."

Daggar swallowed a snort of laughter.

"Are you ready to leave?" Aragon asked politely.

"A—nest," Kassa spluttered.

They helped her out of the bundle, picking twigs off her and wiping most of the gunk off the black leather and scarlet silk of her outfit.

"Right," said Aragon when she looked vaguely clean. "Which way shall we go?"

"I don't care," said Kassa, her eyes wild. "I want to go home to my tavern and drink something with bubbles in it."

"What's through this door?" asked Daggar. He had been looking at the door for some time. It was a real door, made out of wood with a hinge, a doorknob and everything. An odd thing to find in a cave. Now he pushed on it, peering through the crack as the door opened.

There was a very long pause. And then he closed the door behind him.

Neither Aragon or Kassa noticed him leaving. Kassa was still sputtering, and Aragon was watching her with quiet amusement. She caught a particular gleam in his grey eyes and rounded on him. "Are you laughing at me?"

"I wouldn't dare," he assured her.

She spat a mouthful of nestling grunge at him and stalked off down one of the tunnels.

Aragon chose a different tunnel.

-§-§-§-§-§-

Kassa was so infuriated that she walked straight into the ambush of goblins before noticing that she was surrounded. Hundreds of the little creatures pounced upon her, scratching and shrieking and smelling like dirt. "Oursilveroursilveroursilver!" they chorused wildly.

Kassa lost her temper completely. "That is enough!" she screamed, and her anger surged out of her in white-hot decibels.

The goblins fell to the ground, quivering and stunned.

Her face blazing, Kassa gestured at one goblin. "You! Up!"

The little goblin stood up shakily, his eyes glazing over. Kassa hummed a few notes and then gestured with her fingers. The hum wrapped itself around the goblin, pinning its arms to its sides. "Take me to the silver," she snapped, in no mood for arguments.

The bound goblin gazed pitifully up at her and then waddled off down the tunnel. Kassa followed, her eyes still burning with fury. Every now and then, she directed a sharp hum at the goblin's back, making him jump and whimper. "Your silver," she muttered in a grating voice. "It is my silver, my silver!"

And then she looked up, and her jaw dropped out of her mouth.

The huge cave before her was lined with silver. Silver dripped everywhere. Jewellery of all kinds: necklaces, chains, rings, bangles and baubles. There were silver clocks, silver platters, silver candelabras. And coins, of course. The old bags were close to rotting away, and silver coins spilt everywhere in puddles and piles.

And there in the midst of it all, Aragon Silversword was kneeling in awe.

"You beat me to it," said Kassa. Her voice echoed, seeming unnaturally loud in this temple of wealth.

Aragon's shoulders twitched, but he did not turn around. "Indeed I did," he said evenly.

Kassa moved past him, drinking in the sight of the glorious, glittering wealth. "Be careful," she cautioned absently. "Some of it might be cursed."

Aragon froze, stung by her casual tone. His eyes darted to his hand which gripped a glittering silver medallion, the chain looped innocently around his fingers. "What exactly do you mean by that?"

She turned as she spoke. "Well, don't touch anything until…" Her eyes widened as she saw her warning had come too late. "Oh."

Aragon opened his hand, dropping the medallion as if it were red hot. The chain snaked its way over his fingers as it fell.

There was a very long pause.

"How do you feel?" asked Kassa gently.

"Fine," he said aloud, his voice reflecting and rebounding loudly off every silver plate in the cave.

"Good," she said uncomfortably.

Aragon looked up, and met her gaze. "Good," he repeated.

He was still staring. "Why are you looking at me like that?" whispered Kassa, not feeling in control of the situation.

"I never noticed your eyes before," said Aragon quietly, getting to his feet. "How very gold they are. Like some sleek jungle creature."

"Are you all right?" Kassa thought that this time the question really needed to be asked, and in a desperately worried tone of voice.

Aragon smiled, and in the silver light it looked almost sincere. "Of course, my lady." He had called her that before, usually in mockery, but there was a different inflection now. A hand reached out and lightly touched her cheek. "My own sweet, beautiful lady."

Kassa's eyes glazed over in alarm. She looked down at the discarded medallion, which certainly looked as if it had a malignant curse upon it. Then she looked back up into the eyes of a lovelorn Aragon Silversword.

Chapter 14
Tender Moments Hurt the Ones You Love

The coldest man in the Mocklore Empire looked at Kassa with an earnest smile which would have melted a rock. It made her feel slightly sick. "Sit down for a moment," she said warily. "Maybe it will pass."

Aragon sat obediently on the cave floor. There was a long pause. He looked up at her expectantly.

Kassa produced a tiny, brown bottle from a hidden pocket. She had found it in the troll nest and recognised the symbol on the label, a troll skull with three daggers, an axe and a meat cleaver stuck into it, and red smoke pouring out of the eye holes. That could only mean troll brandy, a liquid which had melted more than a few human stomach linings in its time. It was a rarity this far south, and worth a small fortune. "Drink it," she commanded.

"As my lady requests," replied Aragon Silversword obediently. He took the bottle between his fingers and poured the thin trickle of liquid down his throat. He stood up and declared, "And now, my dearest, let me confess..." before his eyeballs rolled back into his head and he fell over backwards into a pile of silver toothpicks.

Kassa smiled.

There was a rummaging sound, and then Daggar emerged from behind a small mountain of cake forks. At least she assumed it was Daggar. She didn't know anyone else who would choose to wear an ankle-length robe of silver chain mail, a pair of silver boots, half a hundred silver armbands, four silver torcs, a large silver helm studded with silver, and a shiny silver umbrella hooked over one arm just because he could.

"What do you look like?" she demanded.

"I don't think I have ever been this happy," said Daggar in a stunned voice. "I'm even wearing silver underwear. Silver underwear!"

"I didn't want to know that."

He moved past her as if in a dream, absently stepping over the prone body of Aragon Silversword. "Wealth as far as the eye could see. I could buy an island. I could buy an island. An Empire! I could buy this Empire!"

"Have you looked up the recent statistics on local Emperors and assassinations?" asked Kassa dryly.

He looked a bit more subdued. "I didn't say I would, just that I could." He glanced down at the floor. "You've knocked him out again, I see. Does this imply a serious stage in your relationship?"

Kassa just glared.

Daggar moved slowly, like a mountain with very small feet. Very carefully, he plucked a slender silver plume from the top of a heap, and added it to his ensemble. Then, realising the abundance of buttonholes available with chain mail, he started adding plume after plume until he resembled a mechanical vulture. "I have a headache," he announced.

Kassa looked up at him, and her eyes narrowed suspiciously. "If you were anyone else, I would think that you had been cursed by the silver as well. Take off the helm."

Daggar started to protest, but Kassa raised an eyebrow at him and he grudgingly removed the helm. Coin after coin after coin spilled out, trickling into a large pile at his feet. He looked guilty.

Kassa just shook her head slowly, from side to side.

"I've always wondered how much silver a man could carry," he explained sheepishly. "And I always figured it would be twice as much for me."

-§-§-§-§-§-

This was the tavern where the Blackguards went. In old times, it had been a grim place with oppressive wallpaper and cheap beer that tasted of grit. The guards went there to sit and drink and commiserate with each other about what a rotten job it was, or to argue whether standing duty in the rain was actually better than protecting the body of the Emperor, who was mad as a tailor.

But not any more. There was only one real Blackguard left, and he tried to distance himself from the false ones as much as possible. The Sulky Pit had adapted to its new clientele, becoming Drinkies, an elegant wine bar which sold champagne cocktails, flat foreign beers, fizzy foreign water and small bits of protein on biscuits.

The Blackguards were relaxing.

"Did you see how I apprehended that cheese-thief?" said Nigellius. "I completely forgot my lines!"

"But it's dead easy, Nige," said Tarquin Suburbus. "They'll accept any old rubbish."

"I know, I know," said Nigellius, choking with laughter on a fishy biscuit. "But I couldn't think of anything, I swear! Even the old, 'Roight, mate, you're nicked' didn't even enter my head! Complete blank. In the end, I just thumped him around the head and dragged him off to the dungeon."

"I see," said Ginger Hurdleswitch thoughtfully. "So you found the thug character type easier to portray than the gruff, heart-of-gold copper."

"Well," said Nigellius cheerfully. "A change is as good as a holiday."

The door of Drinkies crashed open, and a small blackguard with curly hair and a dramatic scarf rushed up to them excitedly. "Look at this, boys!" He thrust a piece of parchment at them.

In honoure of ye Royale visit by our neighbours, the King and Quene of Anglorachnis, there shall be helde an Imperiale Garden Party at the Palace. Alle loyale servants of the Lady Emperore are invitede to take parte in the

Imperiale Playe Conteste for ye entertainmente of our Royale guests.

"A play contest," said Ginger slowly.

"We couldn't, could we?' said Nigellius. "Tarquin, do you still have that script you were working on?"

"It's not very good," said Tarquin Suburbus shyly.

"That depends," said Nigellius. "Are there guards in it?"

"No."

"I like it."

Playing the same kind of character lost its appeal after a while. Being a Blackguard might be steadier work than a Zibrian soap-opera, but a mummer's got to do what a mummer's got to do.

-§-§-§-§-§-

It was hours later when Aragon Silversword regained consciousness. Daggar was off somewhere, playing with the treasure. Kassa sat on a gnarled silver mushroom, pretending not to watch Aragon. "You're awake, then," she commented.

He touched a hand to his head, and regretted it. "Yes."

"Feel better, now? More yourself?"

"That depends. Was I always in this much pain?"

"You tell me." Kassa stood up and shook the creases out of her skirts. "Can I show you something?"

"If you wish." He got to his feet with the minimum of movement.

"It's through here," she said quietly, leading the way through a maze of piles of silver booty. Finally, she stopped.

Aragon looked around a heap of assorted silver gauntlets. After a moment, he saw the skeleton.

She was sitting demurely on a silver-embroidered armchair, her bones bleached white. Due to the laws of drama, the skull still had a full head of long, raven-black hair. A faded black leather eye patch was strung across the face, obscuring one eye-socket.

Kassa reached out and removed the piece of leather thoughtfully. "There was nothing wrong with her eye. There never is, for pirates. It is a tradition lost in the mists of time, which just means habit. No pirate ever thought of not wearing an eyepatch. It's like a witch's broomstick."

"I didn't think witches really rode on broomsticks," Aragon said absently.

"They don't, but it's the same sort of thing, do you see?"

"No."

"It's a symbol, Silversword. It means, here I am, look at me, this is who I am."

"You don't wear one."

"No, I don't, do I?" She blew dust off the old leather eyepatch and slipped it on, covering her left eye. "Perhaps I should."

"Who was she?" he asked, not able to take his gaze from the grinning skeleton in an old black dress which had probably once been tight and bustily revealing around the bodice.

"The captain of the *Splashdance*," said Kassa Daggersharp. "My mother."

Aragon paused, beause the situation required it. A thought crossed his mind. "But didn't your father—"

"Of course," said Kassa. "It was very romantic."

"He sank her ship?"

"Well, she was trying to sink his," said Kassa reasonably. "Fair's fair. That's the way pirate relationships work. Scupper or be scuppered." She frowned. "I was sent to school not long after that. Bigbeard didn't really know what to do with a teenage daughter, pirate or not."

Aragon sat down on a handy silver elephant. "I have something to tell you," he said quietly.

"If you like."

"I am an agent of the Lady Emperor."

Kassa moved away from him instantly, her uncovered golden eye flashing and her fingers automatically reaching for all handy weapons. The reflexes were still there, even if the weapons weren't. "What?"

"I am her champion, in fact. More or less."

The initial shock over, Kassa shook her head slowly. "I don't believe I didn't work it out long ago."

"I half thought you had," said Aragon mildly.

"Maybe I did," said Kassa. "Maybe I knew all along who this employer of yours had to be. I just didn't want to admit it. You've moved up in the world if you're being given the chance to betray Emperors again." She gazed evenly at him. "You were intending to betray her too, weren't you?"

"That was the plan," said Aragon Silversword. "I was supposed to insinuate myself into your trust until you found the silver, then kill you and take the silver to the Lady Emperor. Of course I did not intend to carry out that plan."

"Oh, you didn't?"

"I intended to kill you and take the silver for myself."

"I see."

"But how can I betray you now?"

Kassa froze. She stared at a point on the wall beyond him for a moment, and then she looked straight into his clear, grey eyes. "You're still bespelled, aren't you." It wasn't a question.

"Bespelled?" He seemed amused by the idea. "Enchanted, yes. Enchanted by your rosebud lips, your fiery grace, your one beautiful golden eye." He sank forward on one knee and took her hand, touching it to his lips. "Be mine."

"In what context?" asked Kassa dubiously.

He glanced up in surprise. "Marry me."

Kassa's response started out as a startled shriek, but somehow ended up as a hoarse, strangled whisper. "What?"

"Think about it," he urged. "Promise me you will think about it."

"Oh, I will," she promised. "I'll probably wake up screaming about it. Daggar, if you don't get here right now, I am going to cut off your inheritance and anything else I spot along the way!"

This was where the mummers went. It was a little café under an old theatre at the edge of the Skids. Coffee was cheap, and you could get a doughnut for a penny. It wouldn't be a very good doughnut, but it would always be exactly the same as the last one. Sometimes it was even the same one.

"Right," said Slasher Bearslapper. "That's the last time I play bloody Queen Mabcurse. I'm a laughing stock, I am."

"Dey throw you flowers at the end," said Grubby Thiefstrangler. "Dey never throws me flowers."

"That's cos you always play third thug from the left," said Brigadier Turpen. "And even that's not in your acting range."

"I always hit who I is told to," said Grubby defensively.

"Yeah," said Slasher. "No one wants to play the hero any more, cos you usually damage him by the second act. No one even wants to play understudy to the hero any more. Old Grimmm says he's gonna have to stop writing plays with heroes in 'em!"

Jack-the-Lad, the director's gofer, hovered uncertainly by their table. "Um," he said.

"Get us a doughnut, Jack," said Brigadier, and then wondered why. He didn't like doughnuts. Well, he had never met one yet that he liked enough to actually eat. Still, he reassured himself, a doughnut for a penny was a bargain.

"Um," said Jack-the-Lad.

"Spit it out, lad," said Slasher. "Not review time yet, is it?"

"Um, no," said Jack. "It's this notice. It was stuck on the theatre door."

"Well?" said Brigadier impatiently.

Jack read the message word by careful word, his eyes screwed up in concentration. "Um, Urgent Exclamation-mark For The Attention Of All Mummers Of Dreadnought Stop You Are Formally Requested To Allow Yourselves To Be Temporarily Drafted Into The Blackguards For The Duration Of The Anglorachnis Royal Visit Stop."

There was a long pause which was remarkably thoughtful considering the people involved.

"Still got your truncheons, lads?" asked Brigadier in a very quiet voice.

"Yar," said Slasher.

"Yup," said Grubby.

"Call the others together, mates," said Brigadier cheerfully. "I reckon it's time we did our civic duty."

-§-§-§-§-§-

Daggar emerged. He was whistling, although it was hard to see where there was a gap for the sound to come out. His silver helm was now swathed in two chunky veils of silver chain mail, topped off by a large crown-like object which glittered dangerously. He looked decidedly shorter and wider.

Kassa kept him between herself and Aragon. "I've made a decision," she said with surprising calm. She had been thinking about it ever since she had found her mother's skeleton, and particularly since she had put the eye-patch on. "I'm not taking any of the silver."

There was a small sound from Daggar that sounded like somebody swallowing frantically and realising how hard it is to swallow frantically while wearing three silver torcs and several chain-mail coifs.

"You see, I know my father regretted killing my mother," she went on. "Otherwise this silver would have been spent, not buried. I want it to stay that way."

"But he wanted you to have it!" protested Daggar wildly.

"No," said Kassa, "He didn't. He thought I might need it, and I don't think I do." She sighed. "Look, entertainers have to travel light, witches don't need money and pirates hoard their treasure in safe places. You have to admit that this is a pretty safe place. The silver will always be here if I need it."

"Balderdash," said the voice of a large, big-bearded shadow suddenly hovering over the silver cave.

"Shh," said another voice. A slender, ghostly arm hovered comfortingly in the direction of the big-bearded spirit.

"But she's getting it all wrong," he complained loudly.

"It doesn't matter," said the soft voice. "She's our daughter, and you know she'll make up her own mind. Now come back to bed..."

"Oh, stop looking so crestfallen, Daggar," said Kassa, putting him out of his misery. "You can take some. As much as you can carry, if that's what you want."

The small, sobbing heap of silver on the floor perked up slightly. His head lifted a little.

"And in case you think that's not a generous enough offer, I did notice a large silver wheelbarrow over there," she added with a smile.

Daggar shuffled off, grinning frantically under the layers of metal.

"You too," Kassa added to Aragon, her eyes expressionless. "If that's what you want."

"I don't want anything from you, my lady," Aragon assured her. "Only your kind regard."

"I'll hold you to that, later. Daggar, take your time! We're not leaving until I get Aragon cured!"

"But I don't want to be cured," said Aragon in a bemused voice. "I love you, and I will love you forever."

"If only it were true," said Kassa, and she almost laughed at herself. Almost.

Chapter 15
Ruthless Economies

Everything was starting to fall into place. Lady Talle practiced her reclining skills, her whole body relaxing languorously against the soft, velvety purple-feathered cushions which had been provided for this very purpose. Reclining, she believed, was a very important skill for an Emperor to excel at. She yawned and stretched and examined her fingernails. "Do we have real Blackguards for the Captain?"

"Arranged," said her PR urchin.

"Real actors for the Chief Mummer?"

"Check."

She pressed her luscious lips together. "What else did I have to do?"

"Improve the economy, provide a new ship for the navy and arrange for a Royal visit from Anglorachnis," said Griffin promptly.

"You make it sound so easy," she sighed. "Let's start with the Royal Visit. Have the Imperial invitations been sent?"

"By carrier vulture, my Lady Emperor." At her surprised glance, he added hastily, "They're very reliable. And, as an added bonus, they tend only to eat other people's messengers, usually of the human variety."

"And speaking of messengers…"

"Reed Cooper is on his way to meet the Royal party as your ambassador. He will escort them here by the scenic route. That means the road," he added helpfully.

There were many streets in Mocklore but only one road, a grandly sweeping highway which led from Dreadnought to the spindly bridge which connected them to the mainland. Of course, the road did not go straight to its destination. It had been designed with tourists in mind, and so it avoided most of the distasteful areas of the Empire, while getting worryingly close to some of the really interesting scenery.

"And have the shopkeepers been issued with instructions for making the Royal Visit souvenirs?"

"Yes, my Lady Emperor. And everyone who isn't a shopkeeper has been ordered to buy souvenirs on pain of horrible execution."

She smiled the satisfied smile of a panther, but without the dripping blood. "Good. That should please the merchants. Now, where will I find a ship to give the Navy as their first installment?"

-§-§-§-§-§-

Kassa passed a hand across Aragon's face, and murmured the crooning words of a lullaby. His eyelids gently closed and he drifted asleep. "Well," she said aloud. "At least I can do that much."

She concentrated. It had been so long since she had allowed any remotely witchy thoughts into her mind, and now she was desperately relying on them. Aragon's aura was easy to see—it was a dazed pink colour, glowing with enchantment. Kassa concentrated on banishing the pink, pushing it away in favour of the blue and grey colours which had previously been dominant in his aura.

Not that she had ever closely examined his aura. Of course not. She had just happened to notice.

The pink haze remained, with the persistence of melted fairy-floss. Kassa lost her temper. She was determined to get this spell removed before anyone found out about it. The only foolproof way to do that would be to kill him. Unfortunately, even though Kassa was trying her hardest to be a true pirate, she had witch's blood in her veins as well. And her grandmother had once solemnly told her that witches never kill. They just break things.

She would have to summon assistance. Swallowing her pride, she called out, "Summer! Summer Songstrel!" Nothing happened, for about ten seconds.

"He's a cutie, isn't he?"

Kassa whirled around. The buxom blonde sprite was perched comfortably on a pile of silver egg cups. Kassa made a face at her. "You can keep him if you like."

"Don't tempt me, ladybird." Summer hopped down from the pile and rolled up her sleeves. "Shall we get to work?"

Kassa pointed at the slumbering Aragon. "I need that spell taken off him."

Summer closed her eyes, probing the nature of the enchantment. She raised an eyebrow. "Are you certain?"

"Completely and utterly certain. I want that enchantment away, gone, finished, forgotten."

"I suppose you don't remember basic spell casting?"

"I never learned," Kassa admitted guiltily. "I don't know how to do all this magic stuff."

"You did all right at getting your sword back," grumbled the sprite. "And setting yourself on fire to escape the icesprites, and zapping the goblins..."

"Yes, but I don't know how I did it!" insisted Kassa impatiently. "I certainly don't know my limits. If I try anything on a human being, I might explode his head or something. I nearly killed Maitzi Orackle with that sword trick, remember. Can't you just..." She made a few vague gestures of the type that people who know nothing about the subject tend to assume to be mystical.

"I'm too easy on you," Summer grumbled. "You should get yourself properly trained." But she plucked a silvery-blonde hair from her head and rubbed it between her fingers, creating a fine powder. She clapped her hands and the powder rose in a puff of smoke, thinning out and swishing neatly into a nearby silver cauldron. "Just throw this in his face when you're ready."

"Will it work?"

"You doubt me? Of course it will work. You might regret taking that enchantment off, though. It could come in handy."

"Never," said Kassa emphatically.

Summer pursed her lips for a moment, thinking. "You're right. It's more fun when they fall in love with you naturally." Before Kassa could think up a suitably sarcastic response, the buxom sprite vanished in a puff of nothing in particular.

Kassa glared at the cauldron of silvery-white powder. Now she had a cure, her confidence was returning along with certain pirate-like thoughts to counter the witchy ones. She wasn't sure where the idea had come from, but she had a sudden urge to make the most of Aragon's curse. "Daggar!"

A silver blob broke free of the jungle of silver, swaying slightly. "Yur?"

"I need something. A ring. It should have been on my mother's skeleton. Silver and steel with a black seal on it, a spiral within a spiral."

Daggar looked guilty, even under the layers of silver armour.

Kassa held out a firm hand and Daggar dropped the ring into it. Kassa then nudged Aragon Silversword with her foot. "You. Wake up."

Aragon awoke and rolled to his knees in one smooth movement, clasping one of Kassa's hands to his lips. "My lady?"

Kassa showed him the ring. "Do you know what this is, Aragon Silversword? It is my mark. The mark of a witchblood pirate. If you give me your true-spoken word of allegiance, you shall bear this mark as a pledge to serve me until you die, or until I die, or until the world ends. Choose."

Aragon Silversword promptly ripped open his shirt and placed a hand over his heart. "Brand me here, my lady, for it will be the only pain I feel in loving you."

"We'll see," she muttered, thin-lipped. "Daggar, light a fire."

Daggar protested, shocked by this ruthless attitude. "Yer not really going to…" His voice faded away as Kassa looked at him, but he tried again, gallantly. "But he's not in his right mind…"

Kassa just kept looking at him, her single visible eye glinting with a certain golden ruthlessness. Daggar went to light a fire.

-§-§-§-§-§-

Lady Talle smiled slowly. "I think I will give the King of Anglorachnis a personal gift," she mused. "A token of our new friendship. Kassa Daggersharp's head on a spike should be more than suitable."

"But you don't have her head," pointed out Griffin. "Or any of her."

"Not yet," murmured the Lady Emperor. "But soon… my champion will end her life and bring her silver to me. Aragon Silversword will not fail the Empire."

Griffin regarded her skeptically, but said nothing. Lady Talle had not heard from her so-called champion in a long time. She would never admit, even to herself, that she was beginning to worry about his loyalty.

And she needed the silver. It was a matter of pride now. The King and Queen of Anglorachnis would not be impressed by an impoverished Empire. Lady Talle was relying entirely on the honesty of a man who had betrayed one Emperor already.

It was at this point that she, the ultimate image of grace and beauty, began chewing her nails.

-§-§-§-§-§-

Aragon Silversword awoke with a thudding pain in his chest. His mouth felt gritty, and he had that strange creeping feeling in the back of his head that you always get the next morning after something which you can't remember. He looked around, and saw that Kassa was wearing a black leather eyepatch. That did not bode well. "What happened?" seemed a more urgent question than "Where am I?" He attempted both, then sat back to wait for a result.

"Go on, Kassa," said Daggar. "Tell him what happened."

"You changed sides," she said shortly.

The pain in Aragon's chest increased as he sat up. "When did I do that? Why did I do that?"

"I imagine it seemed like a good idea at the time," she said succinctly.

Aragon looked down at himself, and noticed that he wasn't wearing a shirt. Then he saw the witchmark. A spiral within a spiral, burned into the flesh over his heart. It throbbed. Painfully.

Aragon knew what it was. When he was Imperial Champion, he had made it his business to poke his nose into every corner of the Empire. Even if he had been outside fashionable circles for two years, he knew the legends concerning the acceptance of a pirate's mark, particularly if that pirate was of witchblood as Pirate Kings and Queens often are. "What have you done to me?" he said hollowly. Under the circumstances, he felt it to be a reasonable question.

Kassa even sounded different. She was somehow more confident, more charismatic than she had ever been before. She was more powerful. "You swore allegiance to me with that mark," she informed him confidently. "You pledged your honour to me. And you are an honourable man, are you not, Aragon?"

"I'm a traitor," he muttered.

"Not any more," she said firmly. "You can not betray me. You are my liegeman now. You have no choice in the matter."

His grey eyes met hers. "Are you so sure about that?"

She whispered, "You are bound to the Daggersharp until you die, or I die, or the world ends."

"Well now," said Aragon darkly, "I'm not sure at the moment which of those I might prefer."

-§-§-§-§-§-

Queen Hwenhyfar of Anglorachnis was a pallid, ineffectual woman. This was largely as a result of too many hours indoors reading that particular genre of epic poetry known as 'bodice-rippers'. Due to an overly romantic nature, she tended to wear coronets of flowers and sway slightly.

Her husband, King Durraldo the Terribly Brave, was a hero-king and had seduced many foreign queens in his youth. It was for this reason that he knew the right sort of precautions to take about making sure his own wife stayed firmly un-seduced by anyone.

Firstly, he refused to let her have a champion of any kind as that sort were always lusting after pale, romantic ladies of royal blood. Secondly, he chose the Queen's bodyguards personally. They were all very able, healthy, smelly soldiers of over sixty. A white beard, sharp sword and body-odour problem almost guaranteed you a job in the Royal Household of Anglorachnis.

As an additional measure, a large collection of grim-faced priestesses and noblewomen had been selected as the Queen's ladies-in-waiting. They scared off all of her would-be seducers, including the King, most nights.

For her own part, the Queen was largely unimpressed with her husband, who was a full foot shorter than most heroes of epic romance claimed to be, and tended to lounge around the castle wearing smelly leathers instead of stately robes. Should a suitable candidate and opportunity come along, she was pretty well ripe for seduction.

The silver carriage of the Royal House of Anglorachnis left the glittering city and headed shakily towards the spidery bridge which was officially the border between the mainland and the Mocklore Empire. There were few people crossing the border that day, or any day, come to that. Every now and then one or two desperate refugees or escaped criminals would attempt to emigrate to Mocklore, but after a few days they usually emigrated back.

It was raining. The Queen sighed and sniffed into her hanky. The King shuffled about on the velvet seat and threw darts at a large target held by a nervous page. The Minister of Foreign Affairs slyly flicked through a scroll of erotic pictograms. The chief priestess-in-waiting carved her name in letters three inches deep in the side of the carriage with a wickedly curved holy dagger. Behind them, a hundred Spider-Knights marched in perfect formation, passing a bottle of troll brandy back and forth between them.

Halfway across the spindly bridge, the carriage jerked to a halt with a clatter. The King stuck his nose out to see what was happening, and the Queen peered out of the window on the other side. Ahead of them, a rider had come out of the fog. He rode a black winged thing which growled and nickered impatiently.

The rider dismounted and came forward, and the black winged thing behind him simply vanished, as if it was no longer needed. The man was tall, lean and dark with a black eye-patch and a long, ragged cloak. His doublet underneath the cloak was purple velvet, which the King noted with relief. This was obviously the Mocklorn ambassador.

The ambassador bowed suddenly, and his dark face was lit up by a wicked grin. The Queen sighed dreamily to herself. Then the ambassador walked forward, boots clicking, to greet the King. "My name is Reed Cooper," said he, in the smoothest of voices. "Please, allow me to escort your Majesty and your beautiful Queen to the city of Dreadnought." He flicked a politely smouldering glance in the direction of the Anglorachnid queen, who blushed all over.

Chapter 16
Ghosts and Epic-poetry

The silver ladder unfolded silently as Kassa read the label aloud. "Magic One Way Escape Route. Do not bend."

The ladder unfolded as far as the cave roof, and kept going. A tunnel opened up to let it through.

Aragon regarded it suspiciously. "Just where is this going to take us?"

"Out," said Kassa with a shrug. "It's this or the mermaids."

"Fine," he said abruptly, and started climbing.

Kassa reached out a hand to stop him. "Aragon, you're clanking."

He glared down at her, and opened one of the pouches on his belt, showing her that it was full of silver coins. Then he closed it again, very deliberately.

"So much for wanting nothing from me but my kind regard," said Kassa icily.

Aragon stared blankly back at her and then continued up the ladder, hand over hand through the tunnel until he was out of sight.

Kassa put a hand on Daggar's silver-reinforced shoulder. "This is a one-way ladder, remember. An exit, not an entrance. If you want to come back here, you'll need to go through the mermaids and the goblins and the trolls again."

"No fear," Daggar grinned. "I'm not greedy." He had hitched a long silvery rope to his barrow-load of treasure. "Just as much as I can carry, right?"

"Hmm," said Kassa doubtfully. She had strapped her sword to her back, and was wearing her mother's ring. The black leather eyepatch was still in place, and she had tied a shining silver thingummy around her neck. It was vaguely shaped like a boat.

Daggar's cheerful face creased slightly. "What is that thing? I thought you were leaving the silver here."

"Not this piece," said Kassa. "This piece comes with me. Are you ready or what?"

"Aye," said Daggar cheerfully. "Just in time for the full moon. I can hand over my ten percent to the Profithood, and retire to a sunny island somewhere."

"Full moon," said Kassa thoughtfully. "Doesn't that mean it's time for Braided Bones?"

"What does it matter?" said Daggar over his shoulder, starting to climb the vertical tunnel. "Makes no difference to us now, we've got the treasure."

"It might make a difference to your lady friend," Kassa pointed out.

Daggar looked slightly sick. "Let's just leave the area quickly, shall we? I don't want the Hidden Army coming after me for their pound of flesh." He practically leaped up the ladder. The rope harness around his waist tightened and the barrow-load began to lift slightly. After Daggar disappeared over the top, the silver wheelbarrow was hauled swiftly up by invisible hands.

A few pieces of silver were dislodged as the barrow tilted, and Kassa only just avoided being brained by a solid silver trinket box. Grumbling, she continued up the ladder, ignoring the fallen box as it crashed to the cave floor.

If she had looked more closely, things might have turned out differently. Engraved on the lid of the fallen box was a small inscription. All it said was 'Pan-dorah', which was Olde Trolle for 'Do Not Open on Pain of Glints'. The clasp had smashed when it hit the ground, and the lid was slightly ajar. Inside, something began to lurk.

-§-§-§-§-§-

The first thing Kassa noticed as she clambered out of the magic tunnel was that Daggar and Aragon were standing very still, surrounded by the Hidden Army. Singespitter was on his knees, pawing through Daggar's collection of silver goodies. Zelora Footcrusher had the stone gargoyle in a sling over one shoulder and Aragon's icesprite rapier in the other hand. She was looking vaguely cheerful.

Kassa tried to climb back down the ladder, but Zelora lunged forward just in time to catch a handful of dark red hair. She hauled Kassa bodily out of the tunnel, which chose this moment to vanish completely.

"You're not going anywhere," said Zelora Footcrusher.

It was nearing dusk. Soon it would be evening, and then dark. At some unpredictable stage between the two, the moon would rise. Did the full moon begin tonight or tomorrow night? Kassa couldn't remember. She glared at Aragon, remembering that he had been the first out of the tunnel. "You could have warned us we were being ambushed," she said darkly.

"I wasn't in the mood," replied Aragon in a chilly tone of voice. It was obviously going to be some time before he stopped being angry about the witchmark.

His animosity was likely to last for the rest of their lives. Or until the world ends, thought Kassa ruefully.

"March," snapped Footcrusher, and her men jostled the three captives into line.

As they marched onwards, Kassa noticed that there were no caves anywhere to be seen. The hills and mountains were bare. "They will be here," said Zelora in a sharp voice, as if she had heard Kassa's thought. "Soon."

The Hidden Army made camp. As the invisible campfire was laid, the sky began to darken. Somewhere beyond the cloudy greyness, the moon was beginning to rise.

"The moon, Kassa," said Daggar suddenly in a strangled voice. "My time's up. The Profithood…"

"Shut up," Kassa whispered fiercely. The invisible campfire gave off little warmth, but she was hot all over. Angry, and she didn't know why. *She would never again be denied her freedom, tied up like a dog...* These thoughts did not belong to her, although they sounded vaguely familiar. She knew only that she was going to have to escape.

The black clouds broke, and light filled the dark night sky. Daggar caught his breath in a strangled yelp. "It is the full moon!" he cried out.

"Be quiet," Kassa hissed. "There is more at stake now than your feeble life!" Daggar looked at her, his wide brown eyes mournfully hurt, and Kassa wondered what she had meant by that. She felt strange, and her throat itched with a prickly warmth. She looked down, and realised that the silver thingummy around her neck was glowing. She could not remember now why she had picked it up from the pile of surplus jewellery when she had been so determined not to take any silver away with her.

Somewhere beyond the invisible light of the campfire, Zelora Footcrusher screamed.

"Now," cried Kassa, not knowing what her brain had in mind. It was as if some force had taken over her mind and her body. She reached up and flung the silver thingummy away from her, away from the invisible campfire.

"Bloody hell!" squawked Daggar as the thingummy expanded with a pale light, forming a huge, a vast shape. It was a ship. A pirate ship. A witchy pirate ship. A shimmering ghost of a witchy pirate ship. And it hovered above the sandy grass, waiting for its Captain.

"Help Daggar get his silver aboard the *Splashdance*," snapped Kassa to Aragon, and when he hesitated she made a fist and held her ring close to his face. Its very proximity made the witchmark over his heart burn again, and he turned reluctantly to obey her command.

The Hidden Army could do nothing, as their leader had given no direct orders. Zelora Footcrusher currently stood helpless, bound by a torn sling to her recently-restored pirate husband. Braided Bones looked down at her placidly, wondering what all the fuss was about.

Aragon took this frozen moment as an opportunity to snatch his sword from Zelora's grasp.

Abruptly the shock wore off, and Zelora Footcrusher caught Braided Bones about the ear with a mighty blow. "Thirteen years!" she bellowed. "Thirteen stinking bloody years! Not even a farewell, just a note. Gone to Sea!"

Her left hook knocked him unconscious, and Braided Bones dropped like a felled tree. Because of the sling which still bound them together, Zelora fell with him. She struggled out of the tangled bindings angrily and continued to kick the unconscious body of her husband. She hadn't even noticed the loss of the sword.

Aragon and Daggar hefted the barrow-load of silver on to the deck of the ghostly ship and climbed aboard. Kassa was already there, looking strange, glowing in the pale light. "Are you planning to remove his curse too?" asked Aragon dryly. "It seems to be your specialty."

"I think their marriage might be more successful if I leave that curse right where it is," replied Kassa distantly.

"Good luck to them," said Daggar, almost wistfully, but mainly relieved. "I wonder which will kill the other first."

Zelora looked around now, seeing the ghost-ship for the first time. She began shouting orders.

"Go!" said Kassa desperately, and at her word the ghost of the *Splashdance* began to slide above the grass.

As they moved away, a little man with spectacles and a humorous hat emerged from the trees. He ran after the ship and grabbed on to a rope, desperately trying to hurl himself aboard. "You can't go without me!" he begged. "Please!" He managed to scramble over the side, dropping on to the deck.

Immediately, Aragon had a sword at the little man's throat. It was actually Bigbeard's sword, taken from Kassa when she wasn't looking, but he had no wish to put his own recently-restored sword to such a menial task.

"Who the hell are you?" demanded Kassa in an imperious, unpleasant voice which made Daggar squirm.

"Please," gasped the little man. "I've been looking for you for so long. I write ballads." And then, because his exertions had been all too much for him, he fainted.

-§-§-§-§-§-

Durraldo the Terribly Brave, King of Anglorachnis, would have been far more suited to a career in accounting or stamp collecting rather than kinging. But despite his natural inclinations towards golf and jigsaw puzzles, no one could say he had not tried to do his duty as a hero-king. He had travelled to distant lands, vanquished fearsome beasties (crocodiles, mostly), seduced foreign queens and discovered lost cities (which he promptly re-hid for tax reasons) before returning home to Anglorachnis and settling down with a queen of his own.

With all his wanderings and philanderings, King Durraldo the Terribly Brave had thus far managed to avoid Mocklore, or 'that blight over the spindly bridge' as it was known in Anglorachnis. On the other hand, a female Emperor was something of a novelty and his wife had jumped at the suggestion (by the long-suffering Anglorachnis Ambassador in Mocklore) of a royal visit.

As the King moved over on the velvety carriage seat to make room for the Mocklorn Ambassador chappie, he happened to notice that his wife was looking uncommonly bright-eyed and flushed today. Perhaps she was coming down with some form of plague, he mused to himself, mildly concerned.

After the King returned to gazing out the window, Reed Cooper smiled his killer smile at the hotly-blushing queen who nearly fainted with excitement. Cooper winked at her once and then settled back in his seat, feeling cheerful. This was much better. No more tedious hours playing maidservant or bath attendant—he was an Ambassador now. Travel, danger, excitement and a plentiful supply of beautiful women to make eyes at. It was almost as good as being a pirate again.

The King of Anglorachnis never imagined for a moment that there might be anything untoward going on between his wife and this Mocklorn fellow. Everyone knew that queens were always seduced by champions, never ambassadors.

-§-§-§-§-§-

A sudden bucket of cold water woke the little interloper, and Kassa repeated her question in an even scarier voice than she had used before. "Who the hell are you?" she demanded, pronouncing each word with venomous care.

The little man flinched at her words. I'm your, I'm your, I'm..." He got control of himself and took a big breath, puffing himself up importantly. "I'm your biographer," he said finally, pride oozing from him.

Daggar dissolved into a fit of laughter. Kassa stared at the trespasser with a flinty gaze. "Throw him overboard," she said crisply.

"Aye, captain," said Aragon absently, not moving from where he stood.

The little bespectacled man resembled a small furry animal caught in the headlights of a horseless carriage. "Don't do that, miladyship, I'm a jester, you see," he gabbled wildly, making noisy gestures with his hands as he spoke. "A jester. But ever since I was small, even smaller than I am now, I wanted to be an epic minstrel. I write poetry, you see. But you need heroes for that, and all the great living legends already have their own epic minstrels to sing of their mighty, yea, and terrible deeds." He took a deep breath.

"My father never had an epic minstrel," said Kassa thoughtfully.

"With respect, miladyship," said the little jester-poet. "Vicious Bigbeard Daggersharp had a bit of a reputation for eating epic minstrels, without salt even!"

"Rubbish," rebuked Kassa. "My father never ate anything unsalted." She frowned. "So what's your story?"

"My name's Tippett," said the little jester-poet belatedly. "Tippett. I worked for the Lordling of Skullcap, you see, because he was hunting pirates and I thought that would make a good epic. We've been following you for weeks!" he added brightly. "But Lord Rorey wasn't very heroic, and you all just sounded so interesting, that I decided to find you instead." He smiled, hopefully.

"So, little poet," said Kassa, her voice taking on a whole new dimension of dangerous tones. "You want to write my ballad. Just the one ballad, I presume."

"Actually, I was hoping for a trilogy," squeaked Tippett.

"Yes," said Kassa definitely. "Just the one ballad. Very well, you can stay with us and write my biography in verse, although I cannot guarantee heroics from any of us. There is one condition to this benevolence on my part."

Tippett swallowed, expecting something dire. "Mi-miladyship?"

She swung around, stabbing a finger in the direction of Aragon Silversword, who was deliberately not paying attention. "On no account, under any circumstances whatsoever, will you ever quote him!"

-§-§-§-§-§-

"So," said Griffin the PR urchin, making himself comfortable. "You trust Aragon Silversword implicitly, do you?"

"What of it?" said Talle angrily. Her once-perfect fingernails were now quite bitten and ragged, and she was rummaging through one of the old harem jewellery caskets in the hope of finding some fake nails to disguise her shame from the world.

"Mind if I ask why?"

Talle dumped the casket upside down, sending various strands of paste jewellery skidding crazily cross the floor. "Why what?" she demanded, scooping up a small bag and fidgeting with the knotted cord that held it closed.

"Why, when you are so canny about all the necessary details to keep your seat of power, do you insist on trusting someone who would as soon stab you in the back as look at you?"

The bag came undone, scattering pearly false fingernails over Talle's silken lap. She pawed through them greedily, picking out those of the right size. "Aragon Silversword will not let me down!"

"Sloppy thinking, your Ladyship," said Griffin chidingly. "You have to account for every possibility in this game, and I think it's time you started planning for the eventuality that he will let you down."

Lady Talle's eyes glittered venomously. "I want that silver, Griffin. I don't just need it to secure my position, I want it. I covet it as I have coveted nothing else before… except the Empire itself."

"Why do you want it so much?" Griffin countered. "So Aragon Silversword can prove his worth to you? So you can rub Kassa Daggersharp's face in your gain? Or just because you have a fascination for shiny things?"

"All of the above," snarled the Lady Emperor. "What are you, a therapist?"

"Only on weekends," said the versatile urchin.

-§-§-§-§-§-

The silver box lay smashed open on the cave floor. Inside the box, sinister things were beginning to happen. The occasional silvery tinkle or bright sparkle of light emanated from its murky depths.

The first goblin to find it started the panic. Before long, all of them knew about the terrible thing that had happened. With a burning desire to make themselves scarce, they all began to pack their little goblin possessions into little goblin suitcases with little goblin monogrammed initials on the top. Escape was foremost on their little goblin minds.

The evacuations had begun.

Chapter 17
Glimmer

The ghost-ship no longer glowed. It had completely faded into the background. Kassa and her crew were camping in the shadow of the Skullcaps, on a hill which would hopefully be free from portable caves. Below them they had a good view of the sea and the beach and the invisible camp of the Hidden Army.

Aragon took the first watch but Daggar, still hanging on to his barrow of silver, chose to stay awake rather than trust Aragon to guard his precious cargo. He stayed awake through Tippett's watch as well, and was only just beginning to yawn when Kassa awoke, a few hours past midnight.

Daggar had been feeling uneasy about Kassa since the silver caves. She was behaving very strangely all of a sudden, even for a daughter of Vicious Bigbeard Daggersharp. Perhaps that was it—Daggar had never in his life seen any similarity between Bigbeard and his daughter, who had always been the white sheep of the family. Until now.

"Kassa?" he said carefully.

"Hmm?"

"Why am I here?"

She regarded him with her single cold, unblinking golden eye. "Don't you think it's a little late at night to be asking philosophical questions?"

He growled to himself approvingly. This was more like the old Kassa. "Yer know what I mean. Why'd you get me involved in this at all? Running around playing pirates isn't my thing, and it's not like I'm useful to you."

Kassa laughed, not a familiar laugh but something much more sinister than was strictly necessary. "I know that, Daggar. Cute but useless. You always have been. But Bigbeard seemed to want you to help."

"I knew he never liked me," Daggar grumbled. There was a long silence, and he wondered why he was being so hesitant. Why should he be scared of her? This was his cousin, his baby cousin. When they had been children, he had pulled her hair and hidden her favourite knives. "Kassa," he said finally. "With all due respect, while yer always been selfish…" he paused.

"This is true," she agreed reasonably.

Emboldened by this result, he continued. "Scheming, manipulative, stubborn…"

"What's your point?"

He took a deep breath. "Well, you never been completely ruthless before. And now, ever since you put on that eyepatch, you been actin' different. What you did to Silversword…" He shook his head. "Yeah, he deserved it, but it wasn't like you at all. Yer beginnin' to resemble the scary side of the family."

Kassa looked at him sharply, but she was thinking about what he had said, turning the words over in her mind. "Ruthless," she said, very quietly, musing on something. She stood up abruptly, ripping off the black leather eyepatch. "I will not be manipulated!" she screamed to the full moon.

Aragon Silversword turned in his sleep, muttering something which did not sound particularly respectful. Kassa snapped something equally impolite in his direction and then stared back at the eyepatch, turning it over in her hands. "I've been provided with the crew, the ship, the eyepatch and the attitude to become a good little Pirate Queen. That seems rather convenient, don't you think?"

Daggar didn't say anything. Content that Kassa was now halfway sane and that he could trust her slightly more than the rest of her so-called crew, he had finally fallen asleep, one hand still protectively gripping the handle of his silver-laden wheelbarrow.

Kassa stayed awake, watching the stars and muttering to herself. This little scenario had been stage-managed by her father from the start. Since when had she wanted to be a pirate, anyway? She had outgrown all that years ago. The 'Dread Redhead' was not someone she wanted to be any more than she had wanted to be a witch. "I just wanted to sing and dance," she said aloud.

And then there was Aragon. She had no idea why she kept trying to bind him to her, giving him chance after chance to betray her and spit in her eye. She had always liked perverse challenges, but this was getting ridiculous.

The stars seemed to be moving. One fell, trailing a silver ribbon behind it as it streamed across the sky. Kassa realised to her surprise that it was getting larger, closer. It was coming straight towards her. But before she could jump to her feet and sound the alarm, she realised that it was not a star at all.

It was Summer Songstrel the guardian sprite, perched companionably on what might have been a piece of stellar matter, but resembled a bright silver rocking chair. "Here we are again!" she announced in a bright, cheery voice.

Kassa felt tired. This sprite was going to be part of the tug-of-war to decide her future, and she wanted none of it. "What do you want now?"

"Well, humph!" said the sprite good-naturedly. "What's got up your nose? If you're interested, Dame Kind sent me down here. She's the fairy sprite-mother, you know. Apparently she had a hunch that something nasty was about to happen, so I'm on standby. I don't know why, but we don't argue with the Dame." She stared closely at Kassa. "You look pale. Are you eating properly?"

"Probably not," said Kassa, but the sprite wasn't listening.

"Hmm," she said thoughtfully, peering at Daggar, and then at Aragon and Tippett, who were asleep on the ground. None of them had trusted the ghost-ship to stay solid while they slept. "All these lovely young men you have. Can I snuggle up with one?"

"Take your pick," said Kassa, not really caring.

Summer Songstrel made herself comfortable. "I don't suppose you want to have a long girly chat about your future, your love-life and the horrors of parental expectations, do you?"

"Not really," said Kassa.

"Fair enough. G'night."

-§-§-§-§-§-

In the early hours of the strange light before sunrise, Aragon awoke. A small blonde cuddly creature had tucked herself into the crook of his arm and was sleeping soundly with her head on his chest. She looked vaguely familar.

He became aware of Kassa looking at him from where she was standing over the campfire, burning breakfast. "I should have known you would never really love me," she said mockingly. "After all, why would you have any interest in a mortal woman when the alternative is so much more interesting."

The blonde bundle awoke and smiled sleepily at Aragon. He didn't smile back. "Excuse me madam," he said crisply. "Have we been introduced?"

"I'm Summer," she said with a cute yawn that entirely swallowed her dimpled face.

"Well, this is winter," he replied frostily. "Please remove yourself."

"Snooty," she noted delightedly. "I like it."

"Stop torturing the man, Summer," said Kassa from beside the fire. "I don't suppose you can cook?"

"I'm a sprite," sniffed Summer Songstrel. "I can do anything in the whole wide everything. I choose not to cook."

That sounded vaguely familiar, but Kassa chose not to acknowledge it. She stirred the bacon half-heartedly, charring it evenly all over.

When the others awoke, they all spurned the cremated bacon in favour of Tippett's food supplies, which consisted of bread, fruit and dried sausages in apparently amusing shapes.

"Where do we go from here?" asked Daggar gloomily, biting down on a tough piece of jerky shaped like a giant cockroach in a top hat.

The jester-poet whipped a spare scroll out hopefully, his pencil at the ready and his eyes fixed on Kassa for her response. Kassa was sitting on a rock and eating his last apple. "I don't know," she said, not sounding as if she was very interested in the subject.

"Well, you're all a bunch of gloomy gobstoppers, aren't you?" said Summer brightly.

Everyone wished she would go away.

Daggar yelped suddenly. "What are you doing?" he said wildly, as Aragon rummaged through the barrow of silver.

"Relax," said Aragon sharply. "I'm not stealing anything—yet. I thought I saw a silver spy-glass in here before."

"Feeling your age, Silversword?" asked Kassa sweetly. "The eyesight is usually the first to go..."

"What do yer mean, yet?" said Daggar suspiciously.

Aragon ignored them both. "Something appears to be happening down on the beach. It's too far away to see properly."

Everyone else immediately turned and peered down at the beach below them. Something was going on. Large brown stains were spreading outwards. It was as if rivers of mud were bursting free and flooding the sand.

"Goblins," said Kassa suddenly. "It's the goblins. Thousands of them, evacuating the underground caves. I don't know where they think they're going..."

"From," insisted Daggar, already beginning to gather his things together. "The important thing to ask is what are they running from? Because if they know something we don't, we should start running too. Just in case." He hauled himself and his barrow up into the ghost-ship. "Well? Let's go!"

The rest of the crew, not as well acquainted with the art of running away as Daggar, did not move an inch. Their eyes remained fixed upon the scene below. The light was changing, and the ocean was sparkling in the early greyness of the near-morning. A moment later, they realised why it was sparkling.

The dawn was coming, and something else too. Golden rosy light was spreading across the sky and the calm sea as the sun edged above the horizon. The caves beneath the beach exploded. Tiny bursts of light—silver and pink and blue and gold—shot out in spurts of magical energy. The magic streamed out with random precision, at least five minutes ahead of the sunrise.

"Glints," said Kassa Daggersharp in a voice of foreboding. Everyone shuddered, aware of what that meant. "Not again," Kassa whispered. "Oh no, not again."

The speed of morning was faster than the fragments of magic which had not seen the light of day in over a decade. The sunrise collided into the explosions of light and intensified into a column of magic which spiralled outwards in random patterns.

Magic burst around them all, screeching and glittering and glimmering for all it was worth. The goblins were nowhere to be seen—they were obviously good at hiding. But other creatures, helpless creatures were caught up in the magic explosion. Beetles and birds and stray sheep were part of the whirlwind now and as they were tangled into the twists of wild magic, they changed into strange things, horrible things, incomprehensible things.

"Did we do that?" said Kassa hoarsely.

"Just walk away," Aragon told her calmly. "No one can prove anything."

They did not panic, for the simple reason that the scene below them was entrancingly hypnotic. All they could do was watch. Tippett was scribbling notes frantically, his eyes glued to the colourful chaos below.

Summer Songstrel stood on the deck of the ghost-ship, her blonde hair tousled and a tight frown on her cherubic face. "It was the sprites who cleaned up the remnants of the Glimmer," she said darkly. "We couldn't save the Skullcaps, but we stopped the plague of magic spreading further than it had to. We caught all the glints and they were put in a safe place."

"A pirate's treasure trove," said Kassa quietly. "Safe as houses."

The light was blindingly silver, too bright to look at directly. It spread out behind them, over the Skullcaps. "It's bigger than last time," said Summer Songstrel ominously.

"I wish you hadn't said that," said Daggar. "Kassa!" he added urgently.

Kassa glanced at him. "Are you sure you want to be in the ghost-ship right now, Daggar? This is another Glimmer—it chews up magic and spits it out in another shape."

"I know," he growled. "I remember the last one. What are we going to do?"

"I don't know about you lot," said Summer Songstrel, "but I have a job to do." She produced a shiny silver mop and bucket out of nowhere, and flew off in the direction of the cataclysm.

-§-§-§-§-§-

The royal Anglorachnid carriage had spent the previous day trundling through the northern grunge of Upper Mocklore. This was a part of the Empire which most Mocklorns would not go anywhere near, it being regarded suspiciously as 'Foreign Parts'. The rickety road skirted around Axgaard, a city where the hairiest and loudest of warriors resided, spending most of their time head-butting each other and building ships with wheels. The day that they perfected these skills would be a bad day for Mocklore.

The hundred Spider-Knights still trailed behind the carriage, muttering about the grisly weather. It was snowing again and everything was covered with a layer of greyish sludge.

The royal party stopped for the night in a strange little tavern beyond Axgaard. The innkeeper had been warned (and paid) in advance, and came forward to welcome them with a red carpet, which he wore as a cloak. He bowed so low that his nose nearly touched the soggy ground. "Greetings to you, most noble of guests!" he fawned, providing hot wine and cold fingerbowls for the King and Queen of Anglorachnis, who spent most of their visit looking faintly startled.

Morning came, and with it a spectacular dawn. It was not just pink and gold, but purple, green, red, indigo and silver as well. Sparks bounced off the colours of the sky. Reed Cooper watched it from the tavern window. He had seen sunrises before—no pirate could really avoid them—but this was something very different. Hours later, after the King and Queen had breakfasted and made various vague compliments to their host, the sky was still multi-coloured, and the sun was nowhere in sight.

"Is something wrong?" the Queen asked him anxiously.

"I don't know," said Reed. "I hope not." It couldn't be. It was a blatant impossibility. Wasn't it?

There was no more rain or snow, which seemed to cheer up the visitors. The multi-coloured sky held their attention for quite a while, and Reed couldn't help wondering if it had been arranged by the Lady Emperor's PR urchin to make the royal visit more exciting. The alternative possibility was too nasty to imagine. What were the chances of something like the Glimmer happening all over again? He didn't want to think about it.

-§-§-§-§-§-

The magic was all around them now. Kassa's hair whipped around wildly as she tried to see a clear passage out of the chaos. She could see Daggar bent double over his wheelbarrow of silver, clutching on to it for dear life. She had a suspicion that Tippett was rummaging around for a quill to note down whatever decision she made. Aragon was standing very still, and she could tell that he was thinking over his options.

"I know what you are thinking," he said aloud.

"Tell me," she said, resenting his superior attitude. This was the old Aragon, all right.

"You are considering a most dangerous path."

"This is true," she replied.

"You want to take the risk of getting into this ghost-ship, or figment of imagination, or whatever you want to call it, and taking our chances," he said in a disgusted sort of voice.

"Do you have any better ideas?" she shouted above the wind, which was getting louder.

"Unfortunately not!" Aragon returned, although she could barely hear him above the roaring sound of condensed magic.

"Let's go!" Kassa screamed, grabbing hold of Tippett and scrambling towards the translucent ship. Daggar and Aragon clambered on to the deck ahead of her. A sudden gust of sparkling wind knocked Kassa off her feet, but she grabbed hold of a rope and managed to pull herself and Tippett over the side.

A sheep, caught up by the maelstrom, suddenly flew in their direction, thudding against the deck like a deadweight. "Lunch?" suggested Aragon.

"Certainly not!" snapped Kassa. She leaned over and looked carefully at the sheep. Its fleece had a faint green glow. As she watched, small buds sprouted from its back and unfurled into gloriously white albatross wings.

"Bloody Underworld," yelled Daggar, for the first time paying attention to something other than his treasure. "What is that?"

The sheep was now a lovely shade of emerald, and the wings were a bright, vibrant purple. "You know what the Glimmer did to the Skullcaps!" Kassa screamed. "Imagine that everywhere!"

"No, thank you!" he screamed in return.

They could see the sprites now. Firebrands in vibrant colours of orange, green and purple came flooding out of the Skullcaps, followed by the bright white icesprites. All were carrying glowing mops and buckets, or dustpans and brooms. The guardian sprites were there too, looking almost human apart from their abilities to fly and turn into puffs of air. The gnomes came also, carrying their buckets with a certain grim intensity despite their usual reluctance to be seen as part of the sprite family. The only ones not doing anything useful were the mermaids, who were just hanging around the shoreline to point and giggle at everyone else.

Down on the beach, the Hidden Army was no longer invisible. Many mercenaries were running around and panicking wildly. Others stood very still, watching the cataclysm in terror. There was little escape for any of them. Some were caught by entrails of the magic which either vanished them completely or changed them. If they were lucky, they escaped with only a minor alteration such as the colour of their hair, eyes or skin. Most were not that lucky.

Kassa stared in horror at the sheep in her lap. "Daggar, this is not a sheep," she said in a stunned voice. "It has a face."

"All sheep have faces," said Daggar dismissively, his anxious eyes on the mercenaries below. They were too far away for him to spot the one in particular that he was worried about.

"This face?" demanded Kassa, turning the sheep towards him. Daggar gulped. Tippett went green. Even Aragon looked slightly sick.

It was Singespitter, once the youngest, hairiest and most enthusiastic of executive mercenaries. Only his human face remained, white against the green fleece and purple wings of a Glimmered sheep. But the face, too, was changing. A moment later, it was the ordinary, placid face of a rather startled sheep. He bleated pitifully. Kassa hugged him to her, eyes wide. "We did this," she whispered. "We caused all this."

"You don't know that," said Aragon sharply. "Nobody can prove anything."

"Do you think this is a coincidence?" she screamed at him. "This came from the caves, Aragon, from Bigbeard's trove! We must have disturbed something! It is our fault!" She buried her face in the fleece of the mutated sheep. "It's my fault," she sobbed quietly. "It's happening again, and it's all my fault."

"Wild magic," said Tippett in a very small voice, shivering. He knew the old ballads. And the old ballads remembered the consequences of waking up wild magic. Ballads were a nasty thing to remember at a time like this, because they hardly ever had happy endings.

"Are we leaving yet?" demanded Aragon between clenched teeth.

"Which way do we go?" asked Kassa desperately. "It's all around us. Soon it will be everywhere."

"That way," said Daggar in a strangled voice, pointing straight ahead.

Everyone looked at him as if he were mad.

"What?" said Tippett in a very little voice.

"He is not serious," said Aragon flatly, not even considering the possibility that Daggar might have just made the only brave suggestion in his entire life.

"Why?" said Kassa incredulously.

"I know Zelora can look after herself," gabbled Daggar, the words coming too quickly. "But this is probably my fault, because I was the one who disturbed all the treasure, and I really don't want her to be turned into a purple sheep!"

"What do you think?" Kassa asked the others.

Aragon sighed. "It's inevitable, I suppose. It probably won't make very much difference in the end. It is likely to be just as dangerous to go in the opposite direction." But he didn't look very happy about it.

"You said there wouldn't be any heroics," said Tippett accusingly.

"I said that you could not expect heroics," said Kassa distantly. "But nothing is predictable where wild magic is concerned."

"Well," said the little jester-poet bravely, straightening his spectacles and looking around for his humorous hat. "I suppose every epic needs a dramatic climax."

"Forwards," agreed Kassa. And the ghost of the long-lost ship *Splashdance* went forth, sliding over the edge of the hill and gliding down gently towards the magic and the madness below.

Chapter 18
Plague

The whirling maelstrom of wild, old magic blustered across the beach, flinging bits and pieces of deadly glint in every direction. As Zelora Footcrusher knelt over her unconscious husband, a shard of glimmering magic crashed dangerously near them, sending up a cloud of sputtering sparks.

When a Glimmer is in full swing, the sunrise goes on forever and the sun is never seen. Because of this unnatural sky, Braided Bones had not returned to being a small, portable stone gargoyle. As an unconscious man, he was significantly harder to shift. No one in the Hidden Army was in any state to help Zelora move him. They were all running around like headless wildebeests, trying to save themselves.

The cloud of wild magic hissed, and spat out a ball of something silvery and nasty-smelling. Zelora threw herself out of the way and the nasty-smelling silver ball leaped with gleeful abandon upon the body of her husband. The wild magic did its random, viciously creative work. Braided Bones was Changed.

Zelora was not the sort of woman who ever got hysterical, but she came close to it as she watched the creature stand up. Braided Bones had grown to be eight feet tall, and was considerably more hideous than he had ever been as either gargoyle or man. He was halfway between the two now, and it was a very nasty combination. His face was grey and distorted, his talons were sharp and flexible. His skin stretched over a new, monstrous bone structure and his huge wings unfurled.

Just as Zelora was close to losing the plot entirely, the huge, hideous creature spoke in the voice of her husband. "Hit me now," he suggested in that familiar, placid way. "See what happens." And his gnarled grey face distorted into something very like the annoying grin she remembered so well.

-§-§-§-§-§-

The royal carriage trundled quickly along the winding road which circled neatly around the Midden Plains, an unpleasant place which would hold little interest for tourists. Queen Hwenhyfar sniffed suspiciously as the wind carried the scent of the Midden Plains into the carriage. It smelled like…well, like old porridge, although a queen should not be capable of recognising such an aroma.

Reed Cooper was worried. It was he who had encouraged the carriage to speed up as much as possible. The colours in the sky were ominous, and he knew better than anyone what dangers they might herald. To cover up his anxieties, he winked roguishly at the Anglorachnid queen.

Overcome by a sudden fit of blushing, Queen Hwenhyfar completely forgot about the unpleasant smell of the Midden Plains. She bent over the embroidered hankerchief she was working on and realised that she had spelt her name wrong in the stitches.

Unaware of his wife's embarrassment, as he was unaware of most things about his wife (despite his constant vigilance), the King made loud comments about the scenery being the blandest he had ever seen. Even the Teatime Mountain, an incredible structure which exactly resembed a giant teacup upside down on a saucer, failed to impress.

However, as the road swung towards Dreadnought, the King's mouth fell open. The grim priestess-in-waiting, who was taking her turn with the dartboard, dropped a dart and inadvertently trod on it, shattering it with her hob-nailed boots. The Foreign Minister looked up from his scroll of erotic pictograms, giggled once, and tried to hide under his seat.

The horizon was exploding with colour, bright light and sparkly objects. Reed stuck his head out of the carriage window. "As fast as you can," he ordered the driver. "We'll have to shelter at Cluft. Faster, man!"

He couldn't help wondering if Kassa Daggersharp had anything to do with it. It was her style, after all. Not that he had any reason to know what her style was anymore. Those days were firmly in the past. And now that they were on different sides, the past was becoming steadily further away.

-§-§-§-§-§-

"We're not really doing this, are we?" said Kassa, who had her eyes shut.

"Charge!" yelled Daggar, who was getting carried away.

The ghostly silver ship flew at a frightening speed towards the mess of magic and mercenaries. As it reached the beach, it bounced twice and lurched to one side. Singespitter the sheep made an alarming noise and tried to hide under Kassa's skirts. This would not have been quite so inconvenient had Tippett not been trying to do exactly the same thing.

Aragon Silversword stood upright beside the mast, very calm and very still. He was resolving to get off this ship of lunatics and emigrate to the mainland as soon as possible.

A swarm of glints broke away from the centre of the wild magic, punching right through the translucent sail and missing Daggar by inches. He yelled as a dozen silver coins from his hoard were converted into a swarm of rather nice-looking pink swans who took to the sky in elegant formation.

Several nasty-looking flying things with teeth descended on Kassa, and she slashed at them with her ruby-hilted sword, which chose that moment to be transformed into a long cast-iron poker with a twisted handle.

"I really don't think I'm going to forgive you for this, Daggar!" she screamed at the top of her voice, but her cousin was past caring. He had just seen Zelora Footcrusher in rapid flight from a hideous eight-foot gargoyle monster.

Daggar threw her what he thought was a long, coarse length of rope, but which was a rather sulky cobra by the time Zelora grasped hold of it. She hung on anyway, and allowed Daggar to pull her up into the boat.

A moment later, the monster hooked his talons over the edge of the ship. Kassa slammed her poker down over its knuckles, and the monster sucked them reproachfully. "Nice," he said sardonically.

Kassa pressed a hand to her mouth. "Braided Bones!"

"If you've quite finished hitting my husband," said Zelora snippishly, "Perhaps you would be kind enough to help him on board."

"I thought you were running away from him," said Daggar sheepishly.

"Yes, but then you've never been very perceptive, have you?" she replied, her eyes fixed determinedly on her eight-foot husband and his long grey talons.

Daggar went away to find a corner to sulk in, convinced that he had been hard done by.

Zelora only tore her eyes away from her husband once, and that was to remark that she thought Singespitter was much improved by being a green sheep with purple wings.

"I hate to be the bearer of unpleasant conversation topics," said Aragon Silversword, "But how were we planning to escape this beach after the heroic rescue attempt?"

Kassa glared at him, not having an answer immediately to hand. They were surrounded by the madness. The glints spread outwards, a destructive plague of random enchantments. The sprites were out in force, but even they were being changed into things now—pieces of fruit, assorted vegetables and sets of cutlery in unexpected colours fell out of the sky like autumn leaves, and in some cases it was hours before they would manage to turn themselves back.

This was why sprites were in charge of such clean-up operations as this. Humans rarely, if ever, could have glint-enchantments reversed.

Of course, not all of the sprites on the beach were around for humanitarian reasons. Many were busy squirrelling away pieces of the Glimmer for their personal use. By the time the day was over, the place would be crawling with witches and warlocks, all trying to salvage a bit of cheap magic-matter to play with.

There were also a few gods around, channelling the spare magic into forms that they could use. Just as the firebrands burned away the excess magic and the icesprites tried to freeze it to bite-sized bits, the gods used their own influences to counter the glints. The deity known affectionately as 'The Dark One', a greyish, long-nosed individual, had commandeered a whole corner of the beach and was transforming glints into a wall of shadow which he planned to piece together into a cloak.

"Not that way," said Kassa, dismissing possible escape routes.

The brunette goddess Amorata, patron of love elegies and negotiable affection, had headed off the maelstrom at the other end of the beach by encasing all the glints she could find in a rosy haze of spring fancies and lustful dreams. "Definitely not that way," said Aragon Silversword. He had experienced enough love enchantments to last him a lifetime. Even if he coudn't quite remember exactly what had happened in that cave, he was occasionally assaulted by embarrassing glimpses of memory.

Kassa sighed and looked upwards. A silvery green web arched across the multi-coloured sky like a fishing net, preventing all stray glints from venturing too high. It represented three deities far more dangerous than any down on the beach. "Aragon," she said tiredly, "Did I ever tell you that I didn't want to be a witch?"

"You may have mentioned it," he replied.

"And did I also happen to mention that I'm not that keen on piracy either?"

"I believe the subject came up once or twice."

"I think I may have to pick one over the other now. I don't think I can leave the decision for much longer."

"Explain," he said firmly, determined to be informed about the next risk she was planning to fling them headfirst into.

"There is a lot of magic going on here, and most of it is destructive," she replied, her eyes firmly fixed on the silvery-green web above them. "Our only escape route is to pick a sympathetic god, and they are the only ones with whom I have an appointment."

Aragon began to realise what she was talking about. "They," he said slowly, wondering if she could really be saying what she seemed to be saying.

"The Witches Web," said Kassa Daggersharp. "Destiny, Fate and the Other One. Three old women who have been debating my future for far too long. Shall we go and encourage them to make up their minds?"

"If we must," said Aragon Silversword. This was a better plan than he could have hoped from the daughter of a pirate king and a renegade witch. If it worked, of course. Any alternative was preferable to staying here, where people were being turned into farmyard animals.

"Oh, I think so," said Kassa Daggersharp, deciding suddenly that if she was going to face the Witches Web, she was not going without her crew, no matter what their preferences in the matter might be. "Upwards!' she called, and the ghost of the *Splashdance* began to rise, floating up in a lazy spiral towards the green web which was plastered across the multi-coloured sky.

It was quite a while before any of the others realised what was happening, and by that time it was almost completely too late.

-§-§-§-§-§-

Lady Talle, Emperor of Mocklore, slept late. She didn't open her lovely-lashed eyes until well into the afternoon. She then glided into her personal wardrobe and selected a perfect ensemble of silks and pearls, which she tossed carelessly on to her naked body.

She drifted down into her throne room, and went from there to the sunken bathroom where she ordered a light, refreshing brunch of pale poached sparrow eggs and glistening watercress soup.

Lady Talle was not in the habit of looking out of windows, and so she did not notice the abundance of unusual colours in the sky. No one told her of the rumours, fears and wild reports which were emanating from the coast. It was Griffin's day off, and no one else had the nerve to inform the Lady Emperor of such things.

So the Lady Emperor bathed for a few hours and returned to her luxurious bed in the comfortable knowledge that there was nothing very important to do today, and she deserved a nice rest.

-§-§-§-§-§-

The royal carriage rattled into the scholarly little town beyond the Midden Plains and the Teatime Mountain. The Lordling of Cluft hurried out to meet them. He was a shambling, bespectacled sort of fellow with a half-hearted grey beard and rather tweedy clothes with leather patches in the elbows and knees.

"Ah, there you are!" he said with some satisfaction as the carriage rolled to a halt. "Splendid. I'm the Vice-Chancellor. I do have another name, but I've momentarily forgotten it. Bertie. Yes, I'm fairly sure that it used to be Bertie. You may call me that, if it makes you feel better. Would you like to come into the library for tea and chocolate biscuits?"

Reed climbed up on a nearby park bench to take a good look at the horizon. "I think we'd better," he said hurriedly.

There were no chocolate biscuits in the large, sprawling library tower that squatted in the centre of the town. The teapot had gone cold as well, but Bertie, Vice-Chancellor of the largest educational institution in Mocklore and Lordling of the area immediately surrounding it, appeared very certain that someone called Mrs Miffins was going to appear at any minute and remedy both the biscuit and the tea situation. She failed to materialise.

The Queen of Anglorachnis sat up very straight on an unpleasantly green chair which wobbled slightly and oozed horse-hair stuffing all over the faded carpet. She smiled politely, trying not to make it obvious that she was peering at the ramshackle bookshelves in the hope that a new scroll of romantic epic might be displayed. Most of the books near her appeared to be about gardening.

King Durraldo had thoughtfully brought the dartboard and page inside and now challenged Vice-Chancellor Bertie to see which of them could miss the dartboard and hit the page in the most embarrassing places most often. Bertie became quite interested in this game, even if he did keep wandering away to pull the bell-rope (broken for several years) to summon Mrs Miffins.

The grim priestess-in-waiting stood sentry at the door to the library tower, her sturdy boots scuffing the elderly carpet as she marched back and forth. Mrs Miffins from downstairs had been attempting to bring a fresh tea-tray in for some time, but the priestess-in-waiting had thrown her bodily down the stairs twice, determined to fulfill her duties as bodyguard and chastity-supervisor for Queen Hwenhyfar.

The Queen, having given up searching the shelves for interesting books, was at this moment in silent ecstacy because she believed Reed Cooper was casually playing footsie with her under the coffee-table. As it happened, the constant nudges against her foot were the work of the Vice-Chancellor's tabby kitten, who was hoping someone might think to spill some milk or sugar cubes in a convenient place.

Reed Cooper, meanwhile, doing his best not to be recognised by the Vice-Chancellor who had been trying to place him. Every now and then he would turn around, frown thoughtfully, and say something like. "You weren't that lad who got expelled from the Department of Highly Improbable Arts for turning your gamesmaster into a banana were you? Splendid things, bananas." Or, "Weren't you that boy in the Lower School who had a scholarship for the Department of Certain Death but never came back from his work experience with those pirate chappies?" Reed denied both suggestions equally fervently, and tried to sit with his face away from the Vice-Chancellor as much as possible. This wasn't difficult, as he spent most of his time staring anxiously out of the library windows. The lights in the sky were getting bigger, brighter and more insidiously colourful.

The Foreign Minister was nowhere to be found, as he had wandered into a section of the library labelled 'X-tra curricular texts', and had his nose in the new centrefold edition of an encyclopedia of erotic hieroglyphs. He was busily engrossed in learning what the actress had really done to the bishop.

Mrs Miffins appeared on the window ledge, a tea-tray balanced in one hand and a stack of serviettes in the other. Determined not to allow the grim priestess-in-waiting to prevent her fulfilling her duty, she had shinned up the drainpipe and was now waving desperately at the Vice-Chancellor.

The grim priestess-in-waiting chose that moment to declare that her Majesty looked rather unhealthy. Queen Hwenhyfar was in fact blushing furiously because the tabby kitten had just jumped on to her lap and she was still convinced that it was Reed Cooper's foot. The priestess-in-waiting strode to the windows and flung them open with a flourish of satisfaction, saying something about the splendid benefits of fresh air.

Luckily for Mrs Miffins, there were some rather stout rhododendron bushes beneath the tower windows, and she remained relatively unharmed by the near-fatal fall. The chocolate digestives, however, were severely damaged. Mrs Miffins was rather cross at this, and most people in Cluft knew what happened when Mrs Miffins got rather cross.

"The sky is awfully colourful, isn't it?" ventured Queen Hwenhyfar, who always spoke about the weather in mixed company.

"Looks like rain," agreed Vice-Chancellor Bertie. "Fish, I expect."

"Does it rain fish often?" replied Hwenhyfar politely, but with a certain degree of trepidation.

"Oh, I think so," said Bertie in surprise, having never much thought about it before. "Once or twice a week, I suppose. Netted a splendid brace of lobster out of the gutters last week." He peered at the multi-coloured sky, which was still sparkling in various menacing hues. "You know what they say. Purple, green, yellow, indigo and red sky during the day, crops of fish are on their way. Should be trout tonight. Splendid, eh, Mavis?"

"Splendid," replied Mavis placidly.

No one paid much attention to Mavis. She appeared to be a fixture in the library, curled up in a woolly armchair with an expanse of pink knitting on her lap and the rest of the kittens snuggled up at her feet. Of middling-age with reddishbrown hair cut into an unfashionable bob and tortoise-shell glasses glued haphazardly to her face, she had a hot-water bottle under one arm, and a cold cup of cocoa beside her.

"And what do you do, Mavis?" asked Queen Hwenhyfar, aware in her dimly socially-conscious way that people who were not kings and queens actually did 'do' things.

"I'm the local goddess, dear," said Mavis pleasantly, her hands knitting and purling neatly. "Patron goddess of window-boxes, knitting, wet weather and learning curves. We all have rather a lot of duties since the decimalisation, you know. I'm probably goddess of quite a few other things I don't know about."

"Decimalisation?' said the Queen faintly.

"HO!" cried the King, who had just scored a direct hit on the page's left ear.

"Oh, yes," said Vice-Chancellor Bertie. "Didn't you hear about it? It was in all the news-scrolls. We had our gods decimalised a while ago…one of old Timregis' daft ideas. It worked out quite well, actually. We only have ten gods now, technically speaking. Of course, it meant that a lot of them had to cease to exist or retrain for other professions, but yes, it seems to have worked out rather well."

"I think I would like a cup of tea," said Hwenhyfar pallidly. She was becoming more and more anxious about this strange little Empire, and more and more positive that she did not want to be here. It was an odd sensation, for she had never been positive about anything before.

Then she caught sight of Reed Cooper anxiously pacing in front of the windows, and smiled to herself. Perhaps, after all, there were some rather good things about remaining in Mocklore…

Suddenly the door to the library tower burst open. Standing there was a grim figure in a suit of reinforced steel, a red bandanna tied around her forehead and a steaming pot of tea on a tray with biscuits and the best china cups. Mrs Miffins slammed a metal-clad arm into the stomach of the grim priestess-in-waiting and bopped her over the head with the tea-tray, admirably keeping the tray steady so that the heaped plate of chocolate digestives and the steamingly fat china teapot did not spill.

Mrs Miffins strode with pride across the library and set the tea-tray in front of Lordling Bertie, Vice-Chancellor of Cluft. She smiled a triumphant smile, bobbed a quick religious observance in the direction of the knitting Mavis and marched away, her armour clanking slightly.

"Ah," said Bertie in a cheerful sort of voice. "Here's our tea. Splendid."

Chapter 19
The Witches' Web

The decimalisation of Mocklore's religious structures had succeeded beyond all expectation. There were now only ten gods, although no one was quite sure what had happened to all the others. Each god was only allowed ten supernatural servants such as angels, imps, djinni, mutant spiders, etc. This was all fairly straightforward. Unfortunately, some of the gods had taken it all a bit too seriously—such as the case of the god who now refused to be known by anything other than Number Seven, and had enlisted endless humans in promoting his new image. Even the most fearsome of warlocks had to stifle a shudder when they heard, "Have you heard the glorious word of Number Seven?" drifting in through their letterboxes.

And then there was the Witches' Web. Technically, in this newfangled modern system, they counted as one god. The fact that there were three of them appeared to have gone unnoticed. There was Fate, a haggard old woman with a mean spirit, bitter heart and bad attitude. Then there was Destiny, who was known to be young and interesting-looking, as well as dangerous to know.

The Other One's name was only whispered in dark corners, lest she be summoned and do her vicious work. She was known to be calculating, manipulative and utterly unscrupulous when it came to using her powers. If the truth be told, the whole decimalisation thing had been a ruse to get rid of her, and it was only through assimilation with the Witches' Web that she had emerged unscathed. Strangely enough, she remained unaware of all plots to remove her from Mocklore's religious structure. It had never occurred to her that she was not the most popular and beloved of goddesses who ever let her sandal touch the earth. She worshipped the ground that she walked upon, so it just didn't occur to her that others might not feel the same way.

Her name, as it was whispered in the murkiest of corners, was Lady Luck. No one ever called her that to her face, perhaps because they feared it might give her ideas.

The ghost of the *Splashdance* swirled through layers of green cobweb, caught inexorably in the net of fate. At least, that was the plan. But every time Kassa gave the order to sail up into the Witches' Web, Daggar screamed a panicky countermand. The ghost-ship was annoyingly democratic, and remained on the cusp between one reality and another.

"Will you stop that?" snapped Kassa, getting seriously annoyed.

"No!" said Daggar wildly. "We are not going in there!"

"You didn't seem to mind us plunging headfirst into a Glimmer! Would you prefer to stay here until you get turned into a three-headed walrus?"

"Anything's better than calling ourselves to the attention of gods. Particularly those gods."

"Consider the alternative," said Kassa in a voice of dry ice. She gestured below them.

The beach was a dazzling spiral of fierce colours, devastating magic and supernatural creatures. Daggar gulped once, and closed his eyes. Kassa took this to be a sign of assent, and this time when she commanded the ship forward, he did not try to stop her. He squeezed his eyes even tighter shut.

"I don't suppose the rest of us have a say in this," demanded Zelora loudly.

"No," said Kassa Daggersharp. The ghost-ship plunged upwards, into the Witches' Web.

-§-§-§-§-§-

The Vice-Chancellor was busily trying to convince the Queen of Anglorachnis to sign up for some evening classes, while handing around the biscuits and pouring tea for everybody. Every time someone mentioned the storm brewing outside the library windows, he politely changed the subject.

The windows rattled, the roof shuddered and the occasional small tree flew past, smashing into some unfortunate undergraduate. A veritable hurricane was building up, and the sky was still daubed in unnatural colours.

"And we offer many splendid subjects here at the Polyhedrotechnical," chattered Bertie, handing a half-buttered chocolate digestive to Queen Hwenhyfar. "You know, if you did one evening class a week, you could complete your Bachelor of Nobility in only thirty-six years!"

The grim priestess-in-waiting was trying to close the windows against the raging storm outside. She heaved her weight against them, but was bowled off her feet by a sudden surge of powerful weather.

"Good gravy," said Bertie as she skidded crazily across the floor and fell into a waste-paper basket. "Are you all right, madam?"

Reed Cooper looked out of the open window, the wild wind plastering his black hair away from his face. "The sky is changing," he said.

"It's green," said Hwenhyfar in surprise. "No, silver. Goodness, what funny colours!"

A silver talon lurched out of the horizon and zapped an unfortunate undergraduate riding a bicycle. The young man turned into a startled looking lemon tree, then a small badger and finally a winged unicorn before dissolving completely into a puff of silver dust.

"She's done it," muttered Reed in a low, stunned voice. "She's done this, I know she has. She's done it again!"

Vice-Chancellor Bertie joined him at the window, speaking in a hushed voice so as not to alarm the other guests. "I assume you realise the import of these portents, young man?"

"Another Glimmer," said Reed Cooper flatly. "A cataclysmic plague of epic proportions, all over again."

"Well, obviously, dear boy. But better than that, it means I can finally finish that old thesis of mine. Such splendid luck!" The elderly Lordling peered at Reed from beneath his extraordinary eyebrows. "I don't suppose you can ride a bicycle?"

-§-§-§-§-§-

Colour bled out of the world. In black and white technicolour, the *Splashdance* ghosted between one reality and another, finally coming to rest in a small cave. The colours gradually seeped back, starting with an expanse of a damp sort of green which spread everywhere. There was grey in coils and lengths, spiralling out in too many directions. For no reason that anyone could immediately fathom, there was also a slight undertone of a very tasteful creamy beige.

In the middle of the cave, a woman sat at a desk, making a clattering sound as her fingers tapped rapidly on an old clockwork typewriter. She was a tall creature with perfect posture, neatly coiffeured blonde hair and expensive earrings. "Can I help you?" she inquired in a smooth, aristocratic voice.

Kassa clambered down from the deck, feeling ungraceful. This was probably because Tippett was still holding on to her leg. Aragon followed her, swinging down to ground level in a much more dignified fashion. Daggar peered once over the edge, decided that there was nothing immediately threatening in this scenario, and began scooping his hoard of silver into a large brown sack so he could carry it with him.

Zelora Footcrusher refused to even look, and only came down from the ship at all because Braided Bones showed no hesitation in jumping overboard, with Singespitter the winged sheep tossed carelessly over one shoulder.

Kassa realised what a sight they must all look. She coughed in an embarrassed way. "My name is Kassa Daggersharp, and..."

The aristocratic blonde glanced at her appointments diary, which was bound in the best blue leather. "Yes, Mistress Daggersharp, you have an appointment."

"I don't!" said Kassa automatically, before remembering where she was. "Oh. One of those appointments."

The aristocratic woman stood up, revealing her long legs and superior dress sense. She was clad in a long, sinuous dress of soft linen which clung to her contours in a shimmering pale colour.

Kassa was still wearing her 'pirate' outfit of black leather bodice and swirling red skirts, and she felt decidedly tawdry.

The woman glided towards a door which hovered unaided in the middle of the cave. "Fate will see you now," she said sweetly.

The door opened to reveal a swirling grey void. They all trooped through—Kassa, Tippett, Aragon, Daggar with his sack, Braided Bones with the sheep, and Zelora with a sulky expression. The door closed behind them.

Lady Luck smiled to herself, straightened her lovely pale dress, and went back to her typing.

-§-§-§-§-§-

Fate was not a nice person when you got to know her. But then, if a person spent her whole time deciding what would happen in other people's lives without having a life of her own, it was understandable that she might grow bitter. Fate was an old woman, grey-haired and stringy. If there was anything she hated more than sago pudding, it was attractive young women with their whole lives before them. It was for this reason that so many attractive young women were dealt rather nasty cards by Fate.

Kassa stepped through the doorway to find herself alone. Even Tippett's powerful grip on her leg had vanished into thin air. Grey fog surrounded her, seeming to go on forever. "Hello?" she called, hearing only a cackled echo in reply.

Something flashed towards her through the fog. It was a deck of elaborately illustrated fortune cards, swirling and shuffling themselves in mid air. "Pick a card," cackled a faraway voice. "Pick a card!"

Kassa chose one, plucking it out of the air and turning it over. "The Hanged Serpent," she said.

"Good choice," cackled the voice. "What do you want?"

"Passage through your realm," replied Kassa. "I want to get my crew to safety, away from the Glimmer."

"Which you caused," accused the faceless cackle.

"Possibly," Kassa admitted. "Will you help me?"

"Why should I?"

"I'm willing to offer a deal," Kassa called into the foggy void. "I keep being offered different destinies, and none of them seem to suit me. That must be very inconvenient for your paperwork. So I'll sort out the matter now, if you like."

"You don't want your destinies," cackled the cackle. "Yet you are willing to accept a single one, wholeheartedly?"

"If that's what it takes," agreed Kassa.

"Well," harumphed the voice, no longer a cackle. "If you want to talk about Destiny, you'd better go to her. I don't want you. Stop bothering me."

The grey fog abruptly dissipated, revealing a lush green garden stretching as far as the eye could see.

"Destiny," muttered Kassa. "Let's get this over with."

A sharp voice interrupted her. "Would it be too much to ask where we are?"

Aragon and the others were with her again, with Tippett's familiar grip once more attached to Kassa's leg. She looked down at him, and he blushed and let go.

"Can we leave yet?" asked Zelora impatiently.

"We only just got here," said Daggar, feeling contrary.

"I don't know what I ever saw in you," Zelora retorted crossly.

A laughing voice filled the air with birdsong and music.

"Destiny?" called Kassa, feeling silly.

"Of course," sang the voice. None of the others seemed to have heard it. They were all looking at Kassa as if she was mad. A glimmering, greenish ghost of a woman appeared before her eyes, and the others didn't see that either. "A choice," said the ghost woman. "You're here to choose."

"If I have to," agreed Kassa. "I never wanted to be a witch, although I do see the usefulness of it now. And I tried piracy to please my father, but I don't think I'm cut out for that line of work."

The green ghost giggled with bell-like mockery. "So which one will you select?" she sang, her ghoulish green hair whipping around her pale face fetchingly.

"Neither, if you please, my lady," said Kassa politely, "I don't think I'm cut out for either of them."

The green ghost roared now, angry and terrifying. "Refuse both my lovely destinies, will you? Ungrateful creature, I leave you in the hands of Lady Luck!" Kassa went pale. It was the most deadly of curses to be uttered by any deity.

The others had also heard the final words of Destiny, and they reacted suitably to this new threat.

"What have you done?" said Aragon Silversword hoarsely.

"Killed us all, I expect," Kassa replied.

Chapter 20
Sleeping with the Fishies

Queen Hwenhyfar watched in amazement as Reed Cooper and Vice-Chancellor Bertie mounted strange wheeled contraptions and took off towards the southern horizon, which was currently silver-green with unhealthy yellow blotches.

The wind from the south had brought the occasional gust of what Bertie had called 'progressional random hex-readings', and what Reed Cooper called 'those bastard glints'. In any case, the post-box was now an orange mulberry bush, a large section of street had been replaced with gingerbread and there was a bewildered-looking dragon where the Cluft Town Hall used to be.

Factions had immediately developed between the students, half of them insisting that the dragon be named the school's new mascot, and the other half remaining fiercely loyal to the current mascot, a marsupial mouse named Gerald.

The Vice-Chancellor and Reed Cooper were furiously bicycling towards the source of all this mad, wild magic. As Hwenhyfar watched them go, she wished fiercely that she was the sort of girl who could throw on a pair of trousers and join in their merry adventure. But she was a queen and a rather wet one at that, so she stayed where she was.

Reed Cooper had not ridden a bicycle since his student days, but he was beginning to get the hang of it again. He had discovered that it was like eating pickled herring;

you never forget how, but you wouldn't necessarily care to repeat the experience.

-§-§-§-§-§-

"Lady Luck," said Kassa in a stunned sort of voice. "I suppose it could be worse."

"How could it be worse?" demanded Daggar, so upset that he didn't even bother to call her 'chief'. "I s'pose we haven't actually offended her yet—that's something to look forward to, then."

"Does all this mean that you are no longer either a pirate or a witch?" asked Aragon, thinking of the allegiance-mark burned into his chest. If she renounced both her witchblood and her natural flair for piracy, Kassa's brand might become null and void.

"I don't know what it means, Aragon," she said snappishly. "I just said what it occurred to me to say at the time."

"Well, do us all a favour next time, and let me do the talking."

They were back on board the *Splashdance*, although none of them remembered getting there. The ghost-ship floated in a grey void, with nothing to see in any direction but greenish grey fog. All they could recall was the dreadful curse visited on them, specifically Kassa, by Destiny: "I leave you in the hands of Lady Luck."

"What are we going to do now?" asked Zelora Footcrusher angrily.

"I suppose we had better stop the Glimmer," said Kassa with a sigh.

They all turned to look at her, but only Aragon voiced their opinions on the matter. "What?"

"We caused it," she said reasonably.

"That's no reason to make it our business!" he returned.

She looked sidelong at him. "You're really quite a nasty person, aren't you, Aragon?"

"The nastiest," he growled. "What is your problem, woman? First you annoy the new Emperor to the point of near-assassination, then you provoke Destiny herself to throw you a deadly card, and now you want to go up against a tidal wave of raw magic?"

"I suppose it is practically suicidal," she considered, thinking the matter over. "My daddy would be so proud of me."

-§-§-§-§-§-

"Well, now," said Lady Luck, reclining in her soft office chair. She yawned contentedly and smiled her smooth, selfish smile. "A whole shipful of reprobates to deal with as I please. What shall I do with them?" She threw a pair of jade dice and her face lit up delightedly as the dice tumbled and clattered to a conclusion. "Snake-eyes," she said brightly, as if surprised.

-§-§-§-§-§-

"Down there," said Kassa, peering through grey-green fog.

Leaning over the edge of the ship, Daggar could just make out the multi-coloured glitters and minor explosions which marked the beach where the Glimmer was still wreaking havok. "But that's where we started from!" he wailed.

"We have to get this curse taken off us as soon as possible, correct?" said Kassa in a business-like tone.

"The curse which would not have occurred had we stayed where we were," said Aragon mildly.

"If you say anything else, Aragon, I will probably kill you," said Kassa. "That is who we want to visit." She stabbed a finger downwards to where a small man stood waist-deep in the sea, turning stray glints and zaps of wild magic into rather unimaginative fish.

"We don't want to visit him if he's another god," said Daggar immediately.

Kassa rolled her golden eyes tiredly. "Would you rather wait around to see what Lady Luck throws at us?"

As if she had been heard, a freak gust of wind caught a collection of glints and hurled them upwards. They tore through the ghost-ship like hot raisins through butter. The figurehead, which had previously been a wooden representation of a rosy-cheeked mermaid, was transformed into a rather surprised baby mammoth.

Several glints burst through the rigging, leaving trails of fluffy animals, rotten fruit and burnt custard in their wake. Daggar's silver wheelbarrow began dancing a merry jig as several glints ganged up on it. Daggar whimpered slightly and hung onto his sack for fear that the contents might be transformed into something cheap and worthless, like acorns.

Kassa tried to fend off the glints with her cast-iron poker, but it was suddenly transformed into a ruby-studded bronze umbrella which flapped frantically like an energetic butterfly stuck in strawberry jam.

The holes in the deck, the weight-change caused by the unfortunate arrival of the baby mammoth and the fact that the mast was now a small collection of rare tropical beetles had a drastic effect on the flying ability of the ghost-ship. "We're sinking!" screamed Daggar.

"Don't be ridiculous," snapped Kassa, half a minute before it became obvious that they really were sinking. The grey-green fog was above them, and they were plummeting towards the Cellar Sea at a worrying turn of speed.

Aragon Silversword was duelling with a moustached, sabre-wielding cactus which had once been his left boot. Braided Bones was wrestling with the deck itself, which bucked and reared like a flock of winged piglets. Zelora Footcrusher was surrounded by a nasty collection of hissing, spitting coils of rope. The anchor had already given her a nasty bite on the ankle.

Tippett the jester-poet had wedged himself between what remained of the mast and Singespitter the sheep. He was scribbling verse for all he was worth, his eyes fixed on the wild-haired, wild-eyed woman who was fending off a flock of rabid flying mice (previously the steering-manual for the *Splashdance*) with her flapping bronze umbrella.

Daggar yelled with something very like pain as two glints punctured his treasure sack, transforming its fabric into a shower of white rice. As the rice exploded and scattered around them all, so too did the pieces of silver. Daggar went down on his knees, scrabbling wildly, but most of the silver was lost overboard. Even the silver wheelbarrow fell through the cracks and was gone. Those glittering pieces which were not immediately transformed into winged creatures fell in a wide scatter across the Cellar Sea.

Aragon pierced the moustached cactus through the heart just as it turned into a large watermelon, trapping his arm up to the shoulder.

Zelora Footcrusher let out a yell of epic proportions as a glint brushed over her hair, turning it into something utterly repulsive.

Braided Bones bellowed as the thrashing deck finally booted him over the side, and into the sea with a large splash. A moment later, the *Splashdance* itself crashed into the water, sending a wave of spray over everyone.

Tippett made a shrill, unhappy sound as the last remaining glint turned his humorous hat into a pile of newborn kittens. They plopped into his lap, crumpling his poetry and attempting to claw milk out of his legs.

Kassa Daggersharp ignored all of this. She threw herself into the bow of the ship and screamed at the top of her voice, "SKEYLLES!" Too many moments passed without reply. Then, in desperation as she realised how much water was spurting up through the holes the glints had made in the side of her ship, Kassa seized hold of the ragged rigging with one hand and sang the single, clear note which would transform the ghost of the *Splashdance* back into a small glittery thing she could wear around her neck.

They all plunged into the icy brine with a colossal splash, most of them yelling curses at Kassa until their heads went under the water and they could curse her no longer.

-§-§-§-§-§-

Furiously bicycling along the only road in Mocklore, Reed Cooper kept his eyes on the sparkling, horrible horizon. There were just too many colours in the sky, and he could not help thinking that this Glimmer seemed much bigger than the last one.

"I suppose you're much too young to remember the first Glimmer, young man," said Vice-Chancellor Bertie in the cheerful, hearty voice of a professor who is out bicycling on a jolly adventure when he knows he should be marking exam papers.

Reed laughed hollowly at this. "Remember it? Of course I remember it. I was fourteen years old, and I was there when she caused the whole damn thing."

"Ah," said Bertie, slowing down his furious bicycling pace. "A witness. Splendid. May I quote you?"

"If you like," said Reed Cooper tiredly. "Do you think we could stop for a bit?"

"Certainly, certainly," said the Vice-Chancellor, bringing his elderly bicycle to a screeching halt and producing some promising-looking packages from the basket that dangled from his handlebars. "Cream tea?"

Reed Cooper accepted a squelchy chocolate eclair while Vice-Chancellor Bertie set some grass on fire to heat the kettle he had brought with him. "Now then, my boy," he said, producing a wax tablet and a wickedly sharp writing implement. "Why don't you begin at the beginning? You said it involved a girl?"

"Doesn't it always?" said Reed Cooper sardonically, but he told the story anyway.

-§-§-§-§-§-

Daggar awoke to find himself not actually drowning, but lying comfortably on a marble-tiled floor. He rolled over, spitting out seaweed, to see them all gathered around him, including a rather soggy Braided Bones.

"Could someone get my arm out of this watermelon?" requested Aragon, for he was still sunk up to his shoulder in the giant fruit, the tip of his sword showing through the other side.

Kassa examined the problem from all angles, and couldn't help laughing maniacally for a few minutes before attempting to break into the watermelon with her bronze umbrella. "Watch out for my arm," said Aragon crossly.

"I'm aiming for it as best I can," Kassa retorted.

Zelora Footcrusher, thoroughly miserable, had just realised that the repulsive things which her hair had been transformed into were undeniably long, hissy and fork-tongued. She was doing her absolute best not to shudder uncontrollably.

Tippett was moaning over his pages of poetry which had been thoroughly wetted, clawed and otherwise completely ruined.

It was quite a while before anyone thought to ask where they were, and when they did, it was Daggar. "Chief?" he said shakily, "Where the hell are we?" He had seen the skeletons lining the wall, not just fish skeletons but humans as well, and some in-between bones which could only belong to mermaids, or even scarier sea monsters.

Kassa was still busy trying to prise Aragon's arm out of the giant watermelon. "Haven't you worked it out yet?" was all she had time to say. "And don't call me Chief."

A huge, booming voice filled the marble-tiled hall. "Who Disturbs My Bone-Tiled Hall?"

Daggar realised to his horror that the tiles really were bone, highly polished and neatly segmented, but bone nonetheless.

"I should think it would be obvious who we were," said Kassa, not looking up as she scooped out a chunk of watermelon and tossed it aside. "Greetings, O Skeylles, Fishy Judge of the Underwater."

Daggar nearly swallowed his tongue.

A figure appeared in the huge, arched doorway. He was rather thin and insignificant-looking, despite his booming voice. "You Again, Kassa," he boomed sadly.

"Well, you could look pleased to see me," said Kassa in a mock-hurt voice. "Boys, meet my godfather. Literally godfather, I might add, although you'd worked that out for yourselves."

"You never cease to astound me," said Aragon dryly, wincing as Kassa hacked another chunk of watermelon away, narrowly missing his elbow.

"We Are Rather Busy At The Moment, You Know," said Skeylles, patron god of Skullcap, snatch-theft and most large bodies of water which were not actually puddles. "There Is A Glimmer On At The Moment. I Don't Have Time To Sit Around And Serve Tea To Visitors."

"I'll tell you a story," Kassa said enticingly.

Skeylles, the Fishy Judge, paused for barely a moment. "I Suppose One Less God Will Hardly Make A Difference To The Relief Effort," he said quickly.

"If I tell you a really good story," wheedled Kassa to the Lord of the Fishes, "Will you help us with Lady Luck?"

Skeylles laughed and boomed. "I Thought The Story Was A Bribe To Keep Me From Throwing You All Out. If You Want Me To Tangle With Milady, You're Going To Have To Do Better Than That."

"Deals later, story first," said Kassa.

The thin, unassuming figure of the Fishy Judge settled himself comfortably on his throne of kraken bone. "I Suppose It Would Be Too Much To Ask You To Do Something About This Glimmer?" he grumbled. "I Assume That This One Was Your Doing As Well."

"As well?" said Aragon sharply, shaking his arm free of the last globs of watermelon.

"As well?" hissed Zelora Footcrusher.

"Go on, Chief," said Daggar with a lopsided grin. "Why don't you tell them all about it?"

Kassa sighed a deep sigh. "Oh, well. I suppose it had better be that story, then."

"Oh, Good," said Skeylles comfortably, leaning back with a smug expression on his face. "I Like That Story."

"Don't all glare at me," said Kassa crossly. "What did you expect, 'Once upon a time?' It wasn't my fault then, either."

"Just tell the story, Kassa," said Aragon dangerously.

Chapter 21
Telling Tales

"There was a god," said Kassa, beginning the story at the beginning, as was the custom. "He wasn't a particularly bad god, but there was nothing very virtuous about him, either. He enjoyed a drink or two. More than two, to be honest."

"Binx," guessed Daggar immediately. The patron god of Dreadnought was rarely to be seen, but his especial patronage of strong drink, bad acting, people falling into gutters and other people selling crunchy things in a bag meant that his reputation almost always preceded him. Sometimes it completely surrounded him, pretending to be a pink elephant, but that was his own business.

"Who's telling this story?" snapped Kassa irritably. "Anyway, sometimes this god was a little worse for the drink, and when this happened he would lie in his favourite gutter and look up at the stars…"

-§-§-§-§-§-

"It's a story about a boy and a girl," said Reed, shamefaced. "You see, there was this Pirate King who had a daughter. Like most pirates, he didn't think much of her chances of succeeding him as King, so he brought in an urchin boy to raise as a pirate, just as he would have raised his daughter if she had been a boy. But the pirate king's wife was also a pirate, and she believed that girls could be pirate kings just as well as boys could, so she taught piracy to the daughter in secret…"

"When do we get to the Glimmer?" interrupted Vice-Chancellor Bertie, who was not an impatient man, but much preferred stories which featured his pet subject.

"Are you with me so far?" said Reed. "There's this boy and this girl…"

"Yes, yes," said the Vice-Chancellor tetchily. "I am a tenured professor, young man, and perfectly able to keep track of plot-threads. Proceed."

"Right. Well, one day, the pirate girl and the pirate boy decided that if they got married, then they could both become Pirate King, and everything would be all right." Reed coughed, looking more and more embarrassed as the story unfolded. "They were about fourteen years old or so, so it seemed logical at the time, okay? They didn't know how you went about being married, so they went to visit the goddess Amorata. She said that they weren't destined to get married, but she could possibly pull a few strings here and there if they did a favour for her…"

The Vice-Chancellor leaned forward eagerly, munching a mustard and potato-crisp sandwich and wiping his fingers on his leather elbow-patches. "Ho, now it gets interesting," he declared.

-§-§-§-§-§-

"Anyway," Kassa continued. "This god got it into his head that it would be a fine thing if he caught some stars to keep as pets. So he reached out his godly fist and took a handful of what he, in his inebriated state, thought were stars."

"Didn't his hand burn off?" asked Daggar eagerly, for he liked a good story, even if he had heard this one before. If Kassa was telling stories, they almost certainly wouldn't have to run away from anything for at least half an hour.

"Ssh," said Skeylles, Lord of the Underwater. "Let Her Tell The Story."

Kassa glared at them both. "Of course, they weren't really stars, for as modern philosophy tells us, the stars are reflections of our own sun, bouncing off the million shards of glass caused by the breaking of the ancient Moon Mirror, but that's another tale. What Binx—I mean, this anonymous god—got hold of was a handful of something much worse than stars. They were tiny silver things, glittering trinkets, barely large enough to cover His thumbnails. And He called them glints."

-§-§-§-§-§-

"But the favour," said Reed Cooper, "was something that two young pirate apprentices could never be expected to do. They had to hunt down this mad god who had been contaminated by this strange space-dust, and get the space-dust from him to give to Amorata, who liked shiny things. So they set off for Dreadnought, because this was where the mad god was to be found..."

The Vice-Chancellor was making notes on his napkin. "Ho," he said as he wrote furiously. "I'm assuming that this 'mad god' would be the habitually drunk patron of Dreadnought known as Binx?"

"Don't interrupt," said Reed Cooper, "We're just getting to the good bit."

-§-§-§-§-§-

"In time," said Kassa, "All this booze-fuddled god could think about was the glints. He just lay there, playing with them and staring at them, and doing little else. The other gods got jealous, and one particular goddess sent two, uh, young pirates to steal the glints for her."

"Young pirates, eh?" said Daggar insinuatingly.

"Pirates," she agreed.

"And who were these 'young pirates'?" asked Aragon.

Kassa looked flustered.

"Shut Up, All Of You," snarled Skeylles, the Fishy Judge. "If You Don't Let Her Tell This Story, I Will Turn You All Into Baby Dolphins."

Kassa grinned gratefully at him, until the Lord of the Fishies added, "And Yes, In Case You Are Interested, One Of The Young Pirates In Question Was Kassa Daggersharp."

Everyone else nodded knowingly at each other, but the smiles were wiped off their faces when Skeylles continued, "The Other One Was Reed Cooper."

###

Reed Cooper lay back on the pink and saffron striped grass and tucked his hands comfortably behind his head. "The stealing of the glints wasn't hard," he said. "Gods don't need to sleep, but one who spends most of his waking hours drinking hard liquor has to do a certain amount of sleeping off. We—they put the handful of glints into a special silver casket that Amorata had given them—us—them. And off they went. But it wasn't long before Binx awoke and gave the alarm, and then the chase was on."

###

"We ran through the night, taking turns to carry the precious box," said Kassa sulkily, hating to admit that she was a main character in this silly story. "And the servants of Binx followed us. He didn't have supernatural servants like most gods—he had a pack of trained warlocks. This was before the decimalisation, so he wasn't limited to ten. Close to a hundred men in pointy hats came flying after us, most of them sending firebolts and strange clockwork nets flying at us as we fled..."

"Into the Skullcap Mountains," said Aragon in a world-weary voice.

Kassa smacked his hand with a fish carcass she'd picked up from the floor. "Don't pretend you know what I'm going to say, Silversword. It's rude, pompous and utterly egotistic."

"I humbly apologise," he said courteously, making a small but florid bow in her direction.

"So you should," she retorted. "So the hundred warlocks gave chase, and the young pirates fled into the Skullcap Mountains, which were a great deal more normal in those days." She darted a quick glance at Aragon, daring him to look smug.

"There were few inhabitants of the mountains then," she continued. "A few sprites, the occasional hermit, but none of the grand communities you see these days. The Hidden Army were a lot better at hiding back then, and so the young pirates didn't meet them, either." Kassa grinned at Zelora, having added that last part just for her benefit, but the Deputy Leader of K Division was asleep on her husband's grotesque shoulder, the sulky expression still firmly fixed on her face and a nest of vipers writhing where her hair used to be.

"So they ran through the forests and climbed the mountains and found countless good places to hide," said Kassa. "But, warlocks being as over-qualified as they are, the pirates were always discovered, and had to flee again. The main problem was that they didn't have anywhere to go. Amorata is like the Dark One—she doesn't sponsor a city-state or a particular land mass. When they dared, the young pirates would call to her, but for some reason she couldn't hear them."

"I can guess why," said Daggar with a grin, but someone elbowed him in the ribs.

"And at last, on top of one of the largest of the Skullcap cliffs, the young thieves were surrounded," said Kassa. "And the boy suggested a method of summoning Amorata, but the girl would have none of it, and she threatened to throw the box over the cliff."

An old trick," smirked Aragon.

Kassa ignored him. "The warlocks advanced menacingly, and the girl..."

-§-§-§-§-§-

"As the warlocks closed in," said Reed Cooper, "The girl pirate—who was part witch, although she usually refused to admit it—somehow managed to open the box. It wasn't an earthly lock, so I can only assume she whispered some word of power. Anyway, the box was opened and the glints were released. It was sunrise, you see, and that seems to activate them. As soon as the glints were free, they all split into hundreds of pieces, each deadly and magical and all that. They bred like wildfire, and those that had finished breeding went on the attack. Have you ever visited the Skullcaps?"

"Once or twice, dear boy," said Vice-Chancellor Bertie. "For research purposes and scout camps, don't you know?"

"Well, somewhere up there is a grove of ordinary trees," said Reed Cooper. "They have ordinary brown trunks and ordinary green leaves, and the occasional ordinary starling makes a nest in one of them. These particular trees don't talk, don't dance and don't produce magic acorns. That is all that is left of Binx's Army of Hundred Warlocks. One glint did that. One." He stood up, stretching his legs. "So that's how the first Glimmer got started. I didn't think we would have to deal with another one."

"So," said the Vice-Chancellor, removing his spectacles and buffing them with his handkerchief. "You think this girlfriend of yours is responsible for this Glimmer too?"

"Undoubtedly," said Reed Cooper, fetching the bicycles while Bertie packed up the picnic. "Although she's not a girl any more, and I don't think I can count on her to be much of a friend. I killed her father recently, and it might be a long time before she accepts that I was just doing my job."

"Onwards," said Vice-Chancellor Bertie, hopping astride his elderly bicycle. "To Glimmers and glory, Cooper my lad. To Glimmers and glory!"

"Whatever," said Reed Cooper, and they set off down the road once more, towards the multi-coloured sky. It was evening now.

"That's it?" said Daggar in disbelief. "That's all the story we get?"

"There was more, of course," said Kassa with a shrug. "But that's not part of this story. I don't think any of us have time to sit around listening about the days of plague and horrible transmutation. After all, all we have to do is pop our heads outside—it's happening again.

"How did you open the box?" asked Tippett curiously.

Kassa looked slightly shamefaced. "If you must know, it was an accident. I dropped it, and the lid flew open."

"So you have now been responsible for two of these magical cataclysms?" said Aragon Silversword archly. "That's quite a record."

"We don't know which of us caused it this time," Kassa snapped, "You could just as easily have done it while you were mooning around in that love haze. Or, given that Amorata imprisoned the glints in a silver box, we don't have to look hard to find a culprit who might have disturbed it." She glared at Daggar, who entirely failed to look sheepish.

"Don't talk to me about silver," he moaned. "I've lost it all, remember? The haul of a lifetime, and it slipped through me fingers! The Profithood are going to eat me alive!"

Tippett glanced up from his parchments and asked, "Can we say it was Kassa who caused this Glimmer? It makes it more dramatically balanced, from the point of view of a ballad..."

"Who cares about ballads?" said Daggar gloomily. "I may as well stay down here now the silver's all gone. They're going to retire me! I hate water."

"Silver?" said the Lord of the Fishies with a frown on his little face. "Like That Shiny Shrapnel That Splashed Down Here A Few Hours Ago? You Can Have That Back If You Like, None Of Us Want It." He pulled back a seaweed curtain to reveal a hastily-stacked heap of silver, including the little wheelbarrow which had a purple and green winged sheep sitting proudly on top of it.

"Singespitter!" said Daggar cheerfully, looking around everywhere for a sack. "Good sheep. I think he's a tracker."

Skeylles loked at the strange creature. "That Isn't Right," he said with a frown, waggling his godly finger at the mutated sheep. Instantly, the purple and green hues faded into an ordinary off-white colour, and the wings retreated until they could not be seen. "Much Better," said Skeylles with satisfaction. No one had the heart to tell him that Singespitter was supposed to be a human. After all, he did make a very good sheep.

-§-§-§-§-§-

The ghost of the *Splashdance* emerged from the salty depths of the Cellar Sea, as unscathed as was nautically possible. The transluscent pirate galleon glided through the shallows of the water and up through the beach, heading towards a particular rosy glow which lit up the evening sky.

"Not another god," groaned Daggar.

"Not that one," said Aragon urgently.

"Don't worry," said Kassa. "You won't fall in love with her unless she wants you to."

"Oh, that makes all the difference," said Aragon sardonically.

The ghost of the *Splashdance* glided towards the sultry brunette goddess known (very affectionately) as Amorata. "Hail, my Lady," called Kassa politely.

The goddess, lying in a golden hammock as her winged servants captured stray glints and turned them into love spells, waved a lazy hand. "Greetings, travellers. It's young Kassa, isn't it? Where's that handsome pirate beau of yours?"

"We haven't spoken to each other since he killed my father," said Kassa. "I don't suppose you have any of those silver boxes left, do you?"

Amorata sighed prettily. "I wouldn't worry about the Glimmer, darling. We're diverting all the excess magic into the Midden Plains."

"What about the farmers?" asked Kassa in alarm.

"Well, they might get some interesting crops for a year or three," admitted the goddess. "They should be thanking us, really."

Kassa looked helpless. "But I wanted to..."

"Just walk away," advised Aragon. "It's not our problem."

"Listen to your handsome friend," agreed Amorata, settling back into her hammock. "I don't suppose you would like to trade him for anything?" she suggested with vague interest.

Kassa was far too impatient to get proper mileage out of that comment. "Can't you do anything to help us stop this?" she demanded.

"Sweetie, why would I want to?" replied Amorata. "All these pretty colours...I haven't had so much fun in Ice Ages!"

-§-§-§-§-§-

Griffin had returned to the Palace, and the Lady Emperor had finally been informed of the terrible news. "A Glimmer," she said in a stunned voice, swooning back on to her pillows.

"It would seem so," said Griffin.

"The last one nearly tore the Empire apart!"

"This one probably will. Most of the farms in the Middens have been evacuated, and the Skullcaps are close to exploding with the extra magic resonances. And as for the civil unrest caused by all this...well, it's no use telling the populace that the danger is over when they are already heading for the hills." He paused. "To be honest, most of the hills were hit worse than anywhere else, so heading for the hills is likely to make matters worse. Your Empire is about to fall apart, my lady."

"No, it shall not be!" said Lady Talle furiously. "What about me, what about my campaign?"

"The people are terrified about being turned into pink hedgehogs. They don't really give a rat's unmentionables about who might or might not be Emperor right now."

"Then make them care!" hissed Lady Talle. "That is your job, boy!"

"And how do you suggest that I do that?"

"We must make them forget about the devastation," said Lady Talle insistently. "We must do something magnificent, to make them think of higher things, grander things. To restore their faith in me!"

"Something to arouse patriotism and to reinforce an awe of royalty?" suggested Griffin slyly.

Lady Talle pounced on the note of enthusiasm in his voice. "You have an idea?"

"My Lady, I think I have the very thing," the urchin announced with a wicked grin. "How long do you think it has been since the people of Mocklore witnessed an Imperial tournament, with all the trimmings?"

Lady Talle closed her eyes in rapture. "Oh, yes," she breathed. "It would impress the Lordlings, appease the peasants, entertain our royal visitors and liven up my garden party! Not only that, but a tournament will be significant bait to bring the errant Sir Aragon Silversword out of the woodwork. It is about time I got my hands on him. Success and revenge, Griffin. Who could ask for more?"

-§-§-§-§-§-

Vice-Chancellor Bertie and Reed Cooper reached the top of a hill which looked down on the Glimmered beach. It had been easy enough to find the place; they had just followed a trail of anguished creatures which used to be trees.

"Ho," said Bertie approvingly, fishing his wax tablet and stylus out of his bicycle basket. "That's a Glimmer all right. Damned good specimen."

Anarchy of a particularly magical type reigned below. The multi-coloured griffins, dragons and ancient purple trolls outnumbered the people now, and the only survivors were those who had managed to hide behind the trees which hadn't been turned into blue ferrets.

And then, out of the middle of it all, a translucent pirate ship emerged, spinning wildly over the area of concentrated chaos.

"It's her!" said Reed Cooper, straightening his eyepatch. "Them," he added hurriedly, remembering that he still had scores to settle with Aragon Silversword and that mangy cousin of Kassa's who had thrown him off a cliff.

A woman, dark red hair flying in all directions, was steadily climbing the recently-repaired mast of the *Splashdance* ghost-ship. She was singing. High, bell-clear notes rose and descended in perfect harmony, altering the balance of reality.

"What does she think she's doing? said Reed Cooper in bemusement. "She's barely even a witch, and the greatest of warlocks wouldn't be able to…"

"Oh, clever girl!" interrupted Bertie the Vice-Chancellor. "Well done!" he added heartily. "That one's got quite a head on her shoulders. "Ho, fine shoulders, wot?"

"What?" said Reed, not quite listening.

"She's not trying to sing away the glints, dear boy," said Bertie. "Too sensible for that. She's doing a rain spell."

"How do you know?" asked Reed absently.

"I'll have you know that I have taken tutorials in Spell Recognition for thirty years," said the professor hotly. "And that's a rain spell, mark my words."

"But what good is a rain spell?" insisted Reed, who knew nothing of such things.

-§-§-§-§-§-

Aragon Silversword stood at the foot of the mast, wind biting into his face. "Kassa!" he yelled above the noise of the wind and bluster. "In the name of all that might possibly be merciful, what use is a bloody rain spell?"

Kassa sang one more resonant, perfectly sculpted note, and then she broke off to answer him in a single word. "Watch," she said serenely, her eyes fixed on the horizon. It was nearly evening, and the sky was no longer purple, green, yellow or anything else which it shouldn't be. It was grey, and getting greyer at a steady pace.

Chapter 22
Muddy Weather

It was raining, and there was nothing misty or romantic about this particular crop of sky-water. Rain dripped from the noses of statues, slid insidiously over the cities of Mocklore, and made nasty-smelling puddles in inconvenient places. But most important of all, it was raining over the Glimmered beach. Everything was wet, and getting wetter.

The sprites were all hiding, except for the icesprites and the mermaids who were literally in their element. Most of the gods had gone home to avoid the blattering, clattering streams of water in their faces and down their necks.

The Vice-Chancellor on the hill had rigged up a shelter from two bicycles and a torn raincoat, and was watching the scene below with keen interest.

Meanwhile, a wet figure, darkly plastered with rain, ran down towards the beach, waving black-clad arms at the ghost-ship which hovered above his head. None of the crew seemed to notice him, which was probably just as well.

Kassa Daggersharp clung to the mast of the *Splashdance*, thrown slightly off balance by the bronze umbrella which had been thrown up to her.

Most of the crew had sensibly gone below to wait out the rain comfortably. Daggar remained on deck, soaking wet and trying to figure out how to get his silver-laden wheelbarrow down the narrow ladder to the ship's hold.

Aragon Silversword was climbing the rigging, ignoring the streams of rain which blattered into his face and down his neck. When he reached Kassa's perch, he tried to look nonchalant. "I ask again," he said calmly. "Why a rain spell?"

"Can't you see?" she asked him, gesturing to the scene below them. "Watch carefully."

The beach was a mudslide now, full of screeching magic animals and the occasional terrified warlock. But there was no maelstrom of raw magic, no spare glints causing havoc. "Where is it all?" asked Aragon.

"Gone," said Kassa. "Most magic hates water, except the kind that thrives upon it. Some of the Glimmer will have gone underground, below the sand. The rest will have been washed out to sea."

"Is that wise?" said Aragon.

"Perhaps not, but it's better than letting it wipe out the Midden crops," said Kassa. "The salt in the sea will eliminate some of the magic, and I'm sure Skeylles can deal with the rest."

"Out of sight, out of mind," Aragon said cynically.

"What do you want me to do?" she demanded, her wet hair clinging to her face, neck and bodice. "I'm not a proper witch. I only had a clue about the rain spell because I used to stay with my grandmother during the holidays, and rain was the only thing she was any good at…"

"Why did you have to do anything?" he returned. "Why bother getting involved?"

Kassa turned towards him, close enough for him to taste the salt on her skin. "Guilt?" she suggested in an intimate tone.

"Ahoy, the ship!" called a voice from below.

Kassa froze, her skin as pale as ice. "I know that voice," she said, letting the bronze umbrella fall through her fingers to clatter on the deck below.

Aragon frowned. "It does sound familiar…"

"I need a sword," said Kassa frantically.

"You don't have a sword any more," Aragon reminded her. "You have an umbrella."

"I need your sword," she insisted, her hand darting to the scabbard on his belt.

Aragon moved away quickly, climbing down from the mast. "I'm not giving you my sword. You might damage someone."

"That's the plan," she said fiercely. "If you don't give me a sword, I'll just have to use my teeth. Down!" she commanded the ghost-ship, which immediately started to descend.

-§-§-§-§-§-

Reed Cooper watched the translucent galleon spiral towards him in the dim evening light. As it came close to the ground, he leaped into the darkness, his hands slamming in a vice-like grip over the edge of the ship. He began to haul himself aboard. Somehow, what with the blood rushing to his head and the drama of the moment, he had forgotten that Kassa was not going to be pleased to see him.

Sudden recall flooded into his brain as a bronze umbrella walloped him on the head, knocking him back into the muddy sand. A fierce figure in black and red skirts leaped on top of him, clawing and spitting at his eyes. "Bastard… traitor…murderer…" were three of the words he managed to recognise in the tirade that spewed forth out of Kassa Daggersharp's mouth.

He tried to talk some sense into her, but she filled his mouth with a handful of mud and continued screaming and sobbing at him while she raked the skin from his throat. Finally Reed gave up and punched her once in the stomach, using her surprise to roll away from her.

At a reasonable distance, he spat out the mud. "Kassa, you know the way pirate law works. Why do you think he took an apprentice on? There is only one way for an apprentice to graduate, and you know what it is as well as I do!"

The rain was doing little to wash the wet sand from Kassa's face and hair. She stepped shakily towards Reed in a trance-like state, but her lack of energy betrayed her and she sank to her knees in the swampy sand.

"It had to be one of us," Reed Cooper continued, still spitting mud out of his mouth after every second word. "Would you have preferred to do the honours yourself?"

Kassa looked up at him, her golden eyes wide, and then she said in a faraway voice, "What kind of pirate dies of old age?" She remembered her father saying those words time and time again as she grew up.

Reed Cooper began to walk away. He paused for a moment, aware of Aragon Silversword on the deck of the *Splashdance*, gazing icily in his direction. "I suppose you had better try to look after her!" Reed shouted up unenthusiastically. "She won't let me do it." He turned away, muttering under his breath, "I don't suppose she'll let you, either."

After he had disappeared over the hill, Kassa Daggersharp stood up. She wiped handfuls of wet sand from her face, hair and clothes. She trudged muddily over to the ship. Her 'crew' were all on deck now, and not one of them dared offer to help her as she clambered up to stand on the deck of the ghostly ship.

"What now?" asked Aragon Silversword eventually. The Glimmer had dissipated, leaving trails of horrors and destruction in its wake. The rain was beginning to ease, although such an amateur weather spell was likely to cause atmospheric trouble for weeks. Skeylles would probably never speak to Kassa again for polluting his ocean, and the terrible curse of Destiny was still in effect. They were in the hands of Lady Luck.

"I want a change of clothes, and then I want to sleep for a million years," said Kassa Daggersharp. "After that… well, we'll see."

-§-§-§-§-§-

Lady Talle, Emperor of Mocklore, absently stroked a white peacock which had wandered into her Imperial Receiving Room by accident. "What do we need for a tournament?" she inquired of her urchin.

Griffin chewed his pen. "Knights, usually. And ladies, of course. A bit of pomp and ceremony. Finger food, of course."

"There aren't any knights any more," Talle pointed out. "Not since Timregis…"

"True," agreed Griffin. Chivalric companies were traditionally dissolved upon the death of their patron, and none of the temporary Emperors had managed to pull even one company of knights together. "You might want to put that on your list of things to do."

"Hmm," said the Lady Emperor, distracted by her own troubled thoughts. The gossip minstrels were having a field day with the Glimmer. If even a quarter of the reports were true, Mocklore was in big trouble all over again. "Maybe I have bitten off more than I can chew…"

Griffin looked up in alarm. "Oh, no. You can't pull out now. I thought you had ambitions."

"Maybe the Anglorachnis Ambassador was right," Talle said frustratedly. "This is a dung-pit of an Empire. There is always going to be another Glimmer or an earthquake or a tidal wave of porridge. How can I rule over a constant disaster area?"

The urchin looked at her, very solemnly. "You wanted to rule, my Lady," he reminded her. "Can you think of another Empire that would let you anywhere near a position of power?"

Talle looked at him from beneath veiled eyelids. "So," she said softly. "We stage the tournament."

"Oh, yes," said Griffin the urchin. "We give the populace a hint of the days of chivalry and romance, only with better bathroom facilities and more glamorous costumes. They'll be eating out of your hand."

Partly reassured, Talle sat up and straightened her tiara. "I like the sound of that."

-§-§-§-§-§-

The proclamations spread throughout the land. The Lady Emperor had invited all the Lordlings, nobles and ex-knights in Mocklore to attend a spectacular tournament in the Palace gardens. This would coincide with the Royal Visit, bringing a certain air of chivalry and romance back to the Empire of Mocklore.

The news of the grand event even spread to the Skullcap forest, where a small band of outlaws were licking their wounds and swabbing the deck of their ship.

"A tournament," mused Aragon, liking the idea.

"You dare," said Kassa Daggersharp, brandishing her scrubbing brush dramatically and suspecting this to be a losing battle. "You just dare!"

Chapter 23
A Royal Reception

Where the Street of a Thousand Travellers crossed the Street of a Thousand Merchants, the Brewer's Pavilion stood. This was where you came for portents, poisons and pick-me-ups. Kassa Daggersharp was investing in a hex. She was also stocking up on poisons, just in case.

All witches end up buying pre-packaged spells sooner or later. Sometimes this is because they are trying to deal with something outside their speciality, or just for convenience. In Kassa's case, she still didn't trust herself to know what she was doing. After all, she was now in the hands of Lady Luck, so leaving things to chance was not a good plan.

"Here for the tournament, lassie?" asked Brewmistress Opia as she wrapped a sinister bundle of hazel twigs and black powder in brightly coloured tissue paper.

"That's right," said Kassa Daggersharp. "And I'm interested in an Advanced Enchantment, if you have any."

"Well, we're still waiting for the new shipment," said the Brewmistress doubtfully. "I can let you have an Insidious Incantation or two, but they've been on the shelf for a while..."

"Why don't you just let me have a Lucky Charm," said Kassa, winking twice.

"Oh," said the Brewmistress, returning the double wink. "A Lucky Charm, right." And she rummaged under the counter.

-§-§-§-§-§-

Against all expectations, the royal carriage of Anglorachnis finally trundled into Dreadnought, followed by the hundred Spider Knights and the Vice-Chancellor of Cluft who wobbled precariously on his battered bicycle. The royal party had made no comment when a bruised and muddied Reed Cooper had returned to collect them, although Queen Hwenhyfar longed to ask him where he had gained that interesting black eye.

Now all that was forgotten, because the Anglorachnids had just seen the city of Dreadnought for the first time. It was full of people. They had barely encountered a dozen natives in their trip south, and were certain now that this was because everyone was in Dreadnought. Crowds of people thronged through the streets, waving flags, selling things to each other, stealing things from each other and generally having a successful market day.

Souvenirs of the Royal Visit were everywhere, and more than one street vendor poked his head into the little carriage to offer some cheap mugs or colourful tea-towels at a discount price. Many of them were actually trying to see what the royal couple looked like so they could render a better approximation on their cheap mugs and colourful tea-towels, and charge twice as much for them as 'exclusives'.

The royal carriage made its way haltingly through the throng in the marketplace, and swept up to the front door of the Imperial Palace where the Lady Emperor was waiting to receive her guests.

Talle wore a trailing gown of gold silk trimmed with butterfly fur. Pearls literally dripped from her neckline, leaving a small trail of shiny puddles wherever she walked. She waved generously at the crowd, and some of them even stopped what they were doing to wave back at her.

The King and Queen of Anglorachnis alighted from the royal carriage. Hwenhyfar had tidied herself up at Cluft and was now garbed in a pale pink floaty high-waisted gown with blue velvet accessories and a tall, infinitely pointy hat from which wisps of silk fluttered.

The Lady Emperor was slightly taken aback. "Is she a witch?" she whispered to Griffin, the only one of her advisors who remained at her side.

"No, my Lady," he replied in a hushed voice. "I believe it is the current fashion in Anglorachnis."

"How odd," replied Lady Talle in a bemused voice. Her false smile became dangerously warm as she set eyes on the King of Anglorachnis.

As hero kings go, he was quite good-looking despite the lack of height. For this formal occasion he was wearing his best leathers complete with ermine trim. "Your Imperial Majesty," he said in an expansive voice, "We are most honoured to visit your splendid country! Empire," he added hastily.

"Do come in, I'm sure," said Lady Talle gracefully. "Ah, the Lord of Cluft," she added, as the little Vice-Chancellor on the bicycle drew level with the King and Queen. "How splendid. You received your invitation."

"Invitation?" said Bertie cheerfully. "No, I just barged in. The other Lordlings coming, are they? What-ho. Where can I park my bike?"

Lady Talle smiled as politely as a snake, her eyes now fixed on Reed Cooper, who was standing behind the foreign minister. "Ah, my wandering Ambassador," she cooed. "How nice. You must all come through to the withdrawing room for tea. We are having a garden party in the West Parlour this afternoon, and there is to be a marvellous theatrical performance for your entertainment. The tournament will commence tomorrow morning at Dawn."

-§-§-§-§-§-

Kassa found Aragon Silversword outside the Profithood offices. "Has he come out yet?" she called as she approached.

"Not yet," replied Aragon. "Kassa, I need a horse."

Kassa's lovely golden eyes narrowed visibly. "You are not going in the tourney tomorrow," she said darkly. "I absolutely forbid it."

"That's nice," he replied, "But I still need a horse, and as my esteemed liege lady and patroness, you are supposed to provide one for me."

"Blow it out your ear," she retorted.

Daggar emerged from the building, his silver barrow looking much less heavy, and a stunned expression fixed to his face.

"Well?" demanded Kassa urgently. "What happened? What did they do to you?"

"I've been made Profit-scoundrel of the Month," said Daggar in a faint voice. "They gave me a trophy."

"Astounding," said Aragon.

"Yeah," said Daggar, producing a small tin cup and turning it around thoughtfully. "Do you want to buy it?" he offered.

"Don't you ever think about anything except money?" demanded Kassa.

Daggar shrugged sadly. "What would be the point?"

"But did you talk to him?" Kassa persisted. "What did the Profitmaster or Head Scoundrel or whatever he's called say about the Lady Emperor?"

"Oh, that," said Daggar. "He likes her."

"What?" Kassa screeched. "But the Leaders of Dreadnought have never supported any of the temporary Emperors."

"They decided this one isn't going to be temporary," he shrugged.

Aragon leaned forward. "If I entered the tourney, I could get close enough to kill her," he suggested enticingly.

Kassa scoffed, turning on her heel and leading the way back towards the forest. "You think I'm going to let you anywhere near the Lady Emperor? You would just change sides again."

"Kassa!" said Aragon as if wounded by her accusation. "I thought you knew me by now. How can you think that I, a man of honour..."

"Don't you try that smarmy tone with me, Aragon Silversword," Kassa snapped, increasing her stride. "I know you too well. You will betray me the first chance you get."

"Well then," said Aragon reasonably. "Why postpone the inevitable? Let me go, Kassa. Give me back my freedom."

Kassa turned, and tapped him once on the chest. "No chance. I have my hand around your heart. Just try and sneak away, and see what happens."

Aragon had already attempted to escape three times that day, but had not been able to get very far. For some reason, which he knew had something to do with the witch mark on his chest, he could not deliberately move far from Kassa's side without her express permission. It was beginning to grate on his nerves.

They walked the rest of the way out of the city in silence, until they came to the bit of forest by the purple trees where they had parked the ghost-ship and the other half of the crew. Only Tippett remained, tied to a tree by his long, droopy jester shoes.

"What happened?" said Kassa in shock.

"They ran off with the ship," said Tippett piteously. "The Footcrusher lady and the big monster man. They tied me to this tree. I think my notebook fell in a puddle..."

"So that's that," said Aragon steadily. "No more ship."

Kassa seemed to be looking through the trees, far beyond the secluded little valley where they all stood. She opened her mouth and sang a single, blindingly perfect note. One hand scooped a brand new hazel twig from one of her many pouches, throwing it into the patch of expanding sound.

There was a glitter, and suddenly something silver was twisted around her fingers. Kassa fastened the silver thingummy around her throat without saying anything.

Eventually, she said, "There may be more to this witching than I thought." And then, "I will have to look into the possibilities." And then, "I hope they weren't flying too high when it came back to me."

"A homing ship?" said Daggar incredulously.

"Best kind," replied Aragon.

"Could someone untie me from this tree, please?" suggested Tippett.

Kassa smiled, an unpleasantly evil sort of smile. "Hang on, boys," she said. "I'm in the mood to wreak havoc."

-§-§-§-§-§-

It was a blindingly elegant garden party. Crustless sandwiches were served on silver salvers, scones were presented on intricate lace doilies, and the constant sound of chinking wine glasses filled the afternoon.

The West Parlour was a large garden enclosed within walls which had once been adorned with gilt and jewels, but had been picked clean over the years. Only the extraordinary murals depicting deeds of past Emperors remained, scrawled around the window frames in acrylic pictograms. A huge domed ceiling kept the rain away from the assembled guests and large red carpets had been spread out on the grass. The guest list was very select, consisting only of the Lordlings who officially ran the city-states of Mocklore, the bureaucratic and politically-minded fellows who really ran the city-states of Mocklore, and a handful of pretty fops and ladies-in-waiting to fill up the numbers, all hoping to be noticed by the gossip minstrels.

Leonardes of Skullcap was dancing with Queen Hwenhyfar, who blushed like an embarrassed radish. She had never had occasion to blush before visiting Mocklore, but now it appeared to have become a persistent character trait.

King Durraldo was gliding across the dance floor with the Lady Emperor, doing something halfway between a tango and a pavane.

Reed Cooper, his black eye sticking out like a sore thumb, was surrounded by three blonde ladies-in-waiting who giggled and swooned at everything he said, from, "Good afternoon, ladies," to, "Just go away, will you?"

Griffin son of Camelot was stationed at the door as bouncer and Chief Herald. "Baron Humpty of the Middens!" he called through cupped hands, as a pudgy Lordling with an extraordinary coloured moustache waddled into the Parlour, removing his cloak and hat. Wrinkling his nose at the distinctive odour of old porridge, Griffin put these items on the hat stand which was already groaning under the weight of a few dozen skink stoles, several ostrich-feathered hats and one bronze umbrella which Griffin could not remember putting there for the life of him.

"Humpty!" cried Vice-Chancellor Bertie from the buffet table. "Come over here, old man, get some bubbles into you! What a splendid moustache, how did you get it that colour?"

"Walked into a Glimmer, old chap," said Baron Humpty, twirling the colourful ends of his facial hair. "Still, mustn't grumble. It does look rather good, doesn't it?"

A little jester with spectacles and a brand-new humorous hat passed unnoticed through the crowd with a plate of aristocratic nibbles. A hand reached out from a curtained alcove and hauled him into the shadowy depths.

"I'm starving," said Daggar. "What did you bring us?"

"I fail to see the reason for crashing a party if we spend all the time hidden in here," said Aragon.

Kassa stood at the very edge of the alcove, craning her neck to get a look at the Lady Emperor, whom she had never actually seen. "You're the one who is most likely to be be recognised," she reminded him. "We're here for a quick look, and nothing more."

"They cut the crusts off!" announced Daggar in an injured voice. He was looking particularly smart tonight, in a velvety black surcote over white satin robes. The others were equally well-dressed because Kassa had insisted that Daggar sell a few items of silver for exchangeable currency. She herself was garbed in a swishingly fashionable emerald silk gown and a long black wig. Aragon, at her insistence, was disguised with a false beard and robes befitting a foreign nobleman. There was no need to disguise Tippett, as no one ever noticed an extra jester.

"Ey, let's move about," said Daggar. "He hasn't brought nearly enough sausage."

"Just a minute," said Kassa, finally spying the back of a golden head with a towering coronet perched on perfect hair. "Is that her? The infamous Lady Emperor?"

Aragon followed her gaze. "Oh, yes."

"She doesn't look anything special," said Kassa snippily, just as Griffin announced, "Lord Marmaduc, Sultan of Zibria," and the Lady Emperor turned her head towards her new guest.

Seeing the Lady Emperor's face for the first time, Kassa went very pale.

"You didn't eat one of them pickled eggs, did you?" said Daggar. "I knew they smelled funny..." Aragon's hand clamped over his mouth. He was busy watching Kassa, and wanted no interruptions.

"Marmie!" cried the Lady Emperor of Mocklore. She dropped the King of Anglorachnis like a hot brick and glided towards this new arrival with undignified haste.

"Toadface!" he replied with equal warmth, scooping her up in a tremendously familiar hug.

In the alcove, Aragon was not aware of Kassa's movement until she already had a firm grip on his throat. "Why," she said in a hoarse, half-strangled voice. "Did you fail to mention that Talle was the Lady Emperor?"

"You didn't know her name?" he managed to say as he struggled for breath. "Does it make a difference?"

Kassa released him and stalked out of the alcove with a snap of her heels.

Aragon rubbed his throat sorely. "Is there a problem?" he asked with supreme calm as Kassa pushed her way through the crowd.

"They were at school together," said Daggar grimly.

Aragon assimilated this knowledge. "Grab her," he said. "Before she—"

Chapter 24
Breaking Things

The sound of breaking glass filled the room. All the startled guests swiveled towards the source of noise. What they saw was so extraordinary that they just kept staring. Eventually, even Lady Talle turned around to see what all the fuss was about.

A woman stood on the buffet table. Her emerald silk skirts billowed around her legs, her blood-coloured hair was being shaken free from a long black wig and she was wielding a transluscent gentleman's rapier.

It was at this point that Aragon realised that his sword was missing.

"Talle," said the red-haired woman with a certain tone of menace in her voice. "I want a word with you."

"Kassa Daggersharp," said Lady Talle with a snakish smile. "How nice. Here we are. I am the Emperor, and you are the outlaw. Interesting, when you consider which of us was head prefect."

The crowd of nobles and underlings watched the scene entranced, all thinking this was the promised theatrical entertainment.

"Come a little closer, Talle," said Kassa Daggersharp dangerously. "You've been sending assassins after me, and I don't like that. If you don't come a little closer, maybe I'll come closer to you." The bunting which encircled the Parlour was draped above the buffet table. Kassa seized two handfuls and swung forward.

Daggar emerged from the alcove, running. "Not the chandelier, Kassa..." There was a sharp tinkling sound. Daggar's face went deliberately blank and he muttered something like, "Never seen her before in my life," before vanishing back into the thrilled crowd.

Kassa Daggersharp swung from the chandelier. A change seemed to have come over her. Her hair had a life of its own, writhing and twisting like a nest of attractively silky serpents. Her eyes flashed, her teeth glinted, her lips moistened and she wielded the sword like a natural. The blade sparkled with the freezing light of the ice-sprites and it glittered wildly as she swung it back and forth.

The crowd were so busy oohing and aahing at the amazing display of theatrics that no one noticed the little jester-poet who perched on the edge of a buffet table, scribbling furiously. His luck was in, and his work would be famous. This was a Pirate of Note.

A foreign potentate with a false beard strode out of an alcove, his face furious. "Kassa, stop this spectacle right now!" he ordered.

The Pirate Queen let go of the chandelier and dropped like a stone. Four enthusiastic fops broke her fall, and drew her to her feet. Moving as swiftly as silk, she darted towards the Lady Emperor. The Blackguards, all out of practice due to their recent stint as mummers, did not get there in time. Even Reed Cooper, pushing his way through an unhelpful crowd, couldn't make it in time.

Kassa Daggersharp pressed the transparent silver-steel blade against the throat of the Lady Emperor. She paused for a moment, flickers of thought disturbing her natural impulse to strike. *Pirates are ruthless, Pirates of Note doubly so. Witches don't kill, they just break things.*

"Just so you know," whispered Kassa Daggersharp, finally removing the sword from Lady Talle's throat. "Just so you know," she repeated softly. "I could have won right here and now."

The motley group left the garden party. Kassa took the opportunity to smash a crystal vase as she swaggered grandly away. The disguised potentate, who had not been recognised as Aragon Silversword, followed her. Daggar scuttled after them, hoping no one would notice he was a member of this group. The little jester-poet was still scribbling notes frantically as he also made his exit.

Surprisingly, no one thought to stop them.

Lady Talle stood very still, white-faced, outraged. "The performance," she hissed between perfectly clenched teeth. "Tell those damned mummers to start the theatrical performance now!"

The recently-restored mummers cowered behind the curtain of the little makeshift stage in a corner of the Parlour, darting worried glances at each other. They knew they had just witnessed an impossible act to follow.

-§-§-§-§-§-

"So that's what it's like," said Kassa Daggersharp. "To be a pirate, I mean. I really quite enjoyed it!"

"Well, don't do it again," said Aragon Silversword. "Just keep walking."

"It was wonderful," Kassa enthused, her eyes glowing eerily. "It felt so right."

"It felt bloody terrifying to me," Daggar grumbled, keeping his head down. "Where did you learn all that stuff?"

"I didn't," replied Kassa in stunned amazement. "It just came into my head. Isn't it wonderful? I've just made the most amazing discovery. I like being a pirate. I really, really, really want to be a pirate. Maybe I can work the whole witching thing into it as well. I have finally made up my mind!"

"We're happy for you," said Aragon. "Keep moving."

"But I was good, wasn't I?" she insisted, hoping for some word of encouragement.

Aragon stopped in the middle of the street, and turned to look straight into her eyes. "You were extraordinary," he told her.

Kassa was so pleased that she almost blushed. "Aragon, that is the nicest thing you have ever said to me."

"It wasn't a compliment," he growled, resuming a brisk walking pace.

"What do we do now?" broke in Tippett, eager for another ballad-worthy scene in the near future.

"Well," said Kassa thoughtfully, "I have decided that I enjoy crashing parties. So what we are going to do next is buy Aragon a horse."

"More money," groaned Daggar, who had spent most of the day watching Kassa spend his fortune.

Aragon looked at Kassa incredulously. "You are going to allow me to enter the tourney tomorrow, after everything you said on the subject?"

Kassa laughed in her melodic voice. "I was always going to let you enter, Silversword, but I can't let you take these things for granted."

-§-§-§-§-§-

The anti-climactic theatrical performance impressed nobody very much. The astoundingly original musical score drowned out most of the dialogue, and nobody seemed to notice the post-modern twist in the anti-historical costumes. It was supposed to be a play contest, but the enthusiastic ex-Blackguards of Dreadnought had been the only entrants. Still, they were presented with a gold cup full of Zibrian Delight at the end, and the audience clapped politely enough.

More than anything, the audience had enjoyed the intermission, which gave them an opportunity to gossip wildly. Many and varied subjects filled the air. There was the Glimmer, of course, and the interesting changes it had wrought during its brief but cataclysmic visitation. There was the surprising evidence that the Anglorachnis queen might be a witch, owing to her fondness for wearing a pointy headdress. Speculation ran riot about the non-attendance of Lordling Rorey who was rumoured to be adventuring somewhere with his warlock, hunting pirates or some such thing. Reed Cooper, the dashingly handsome ambassador with the fresh black eye, came under scrutiny by many of the prominent ladies of the court, particularly Baron Svenhilda of Axgaard who was the only female Lordling.

Surprisingly enough, the Lady Emperor herself barely qualified as a gossip subject, except when her intimacy with the Sultan of Zibria was speculated upon. Her role as the first female Emperor had ceased to become a novelty—it was old news. Lady Talle was such a smooth hostess that many people had forgotten that someone else had been Emperor barely a moon ago, and someone else two moons before that.

Despite everything, she had won. It would take more than an industrial-sized earthquake to dislodge Talle from her throne now. Where international espionage and grand politics had barely affected her position, trays of champagne cocktails and nibbly things on biscuits had succeeded beyond all expectation.

-§-§-§-§-§-

Kassa was sewing a banner for Aragon to carry into the tourney. It showed her own coat of arms: three drops of black blood on a field of poppies.

"I suppose you would not consider me carrying my own banner?" suggested Aragon dryly, not really expecting an answer.

Kassa obliged his expectations by completely ignoring him.

Tippett was doing the washing. He struggled under a huge basket filled with muddy clothes, blood-stained shirts and dirty underwear. He yelped and dropped it all over the deck when an insistent chirping came from within the bundle. "What is that?"

Kassa looked up, just in time to see the sacred bauble of Chiantrio leaping free of the bundle of dirty washing. It made a sound like, "Yipppeeeee!"

Kassa looked at Aragon. "Didn't you give that thing to me?"

"I may have done," said Aragon.

"Well?"

He sighed. He had preferred the days when he had been fully intending to murder her. This whole bond-servant routine did not suit him at all. "If you must know, it belonged to the Lady Emperor. It latched on to me for some reason. She never did tell me what it was for."

Kassa caught hold of the tiny trinket and tied it securely to a length of silver embroidery thread. Then she tucked it back into her bodice for safekeeping.

Daggar emerged from the undergrowth behind the ghost-ship, running hard. "Heeeellllpppp!" he wailed. Three large winged things glowing with a strange, glimmery light appeared to be chasing him.

"So the plague isn't completely buried," commented Aragon, watching Daggar run laps around the ship away from the winged things.

"What did you expect, a miracle?" said Kassa. "I'm only a witch. Anyway, rain wouldn't have affected the water magic so there's probably plenty of that waiting to come out of the woodwork."

As if they had heard her, several small glints burst out of a purple tree nearby. They headed straight for Daggar.

"Aaarrgghh!" he yelled accusingly. "Do something! Witch it!"

And Kassa did. She rolled her eyes and clicked her tongue and threw her spare needle in the direction of Daggar's supernatural pursuers. In the instant before it missed them completely, she sang a single note. The needle swung around, pointing due North, and sped off in that direction. As if compelled, the glints and the flying things swung around and followed the silvery point until they had all vanished over the horizon.

"You witched it!" said Daggar in astonishment.

"You owe me a needle," replied Kassa, and she continued to work on her banner.

"I suppose it didn't occur to you to do something lasting about those glints," suggested Aragon, "Rather than washing them away for someone else to deal with."

"That's rich, coming from someone who keeps urging me to walk away from the problem!" Kassa retorted. "I repeat, I'm only a witch! An untrained witch, who doesn't actually know how to do all this stuff."

Aragon looked faintly disturbed by this revelation. "You mean, all the magic you have been doing…"

"Yes," she said impatiently. "I have been making it up as I go along! And making quite a lot of mistakes, I might add. You may quote me," she added generously to Tippett.

Inside Kassa's bodice, the sacred bauble of Chiantrio burbled slightly and went back to sleep.

-§-§-§-§-§-

Elsewhere in the Skullcap Forest, Fredgic the warlock was bored, tired and hungry. "I really don't think there are any pirates," he mumbled drowsily as he trudged beside the golden carriage.

"Hmm, nonsense dear boy!" exclaimed Lordling Rorey, who was still as bright as a button despite the weeks of living on tinned cabbage and gathered berries. "I can practic'ly smell them, don't you know!"

"I think that's the goats, my Lord," said Fredgic wearily. "Perhaps if we are looking for pirates, we should try…the sea?"

"Hmm, stuff and rubbish!" announced the Lordling abrasively. "We'll find those piratical fellows if it's the last thing we do. Onward!"

Fredgic sighed and continued down the rocky path, followed by the smelly mutant mountain goats and the comfy golden carriage. All of the mummers and dancing bears had escaped by now, and the Lordling's pet jester had run away to find something more interesting to write epic-poetry about. Fredgic was alone with a mad Lordling and a mission. To find pirates.

"Here, pirey pirey pirates," he called dismally.

"Louder!" demanded the Lordling. "Hmm, and try to sound enticing, Fudgecake. Lure them out of their holes!"

"I don't think pirates live in holes, Lord."

"Hmm, what would you know, warlock? Just get me some pirates!"

It wouldn't be so bad, mused Fredgic as he trudged dismally onwards, if he wasn't completely and utterly certain that the Lordling had forgotten what he actually wanted the pirates for.

"Hmm, ha har my maties!" cried the Lordling in sudden triumph. "I see them! Over there!"

Fredgic turned with little enthusiasm in the direction in his Lordling's enthusiastic finger was gesturing. "I believe that is a gorgon, lord," he said patiently. "A woman with snakes for hair tending the wounds of a giant gargoyle with a sheep in his lap." It took perhaps three seconds for Fredgic's own observations to seep into his brain. He screamed with horror and dove headfirst into the golden carriage, just as the Lordling stepped out.

"Hmm, haven't you ever seen pirates before, man?" said the Lordling dismissively. "Fetch the net thing, eh?"

Fredgic threw his last clockwork net out of the window of the carriage and continued to cower under the plush velvet seat.

"Ho, there," said the Lordling amiably, approaching the couple who crouched beneath the polka-dotted elmworst tree. "Hmm, I don't suppose you'd be so obliging as to step into this clockwork net, my dear fellows?"

The woman, a hard-faced creature with a nest of vipers on her head and a red glint in her eyes, smiled nastily. "What do you want, old man?"

Lordling Rorey was quite put out, as he was hardly in his dotage. "Hmm, now look here, there's no call for that," he said in an offended tone of voice. "Are you pirates or what, wot?"

The massive gargoyle-man with the broken wing unfolded himself, putting the sheep to one side and standing to his full height. "Looking for pirates?" he growled.

The Lordling, who had no sense of personal danger, nodded happily. "Hmm, I say old fellow, if you are a pirate, how would you like to come back to Skullcap and join the old retinue, wot?"

The massive gargoyle smiled, thinly. "Honey?"

The woman glanced up at him with the closest thing she could manage to a tender look. Then she turned her flat, unblinking gaze back to the intruding Lordling. "Scrag him," she ordered her husband.

The gargoyle advanced menacingly on the Lordling. "First turned into stone gargoyle," he growled. "Then betrayed by bastard cabin boy. Ship sunk. Now turned into living gargoyle. Wife loses hair. Then flying boat stolen from under us. Fall. Break wing. Now you." He made history by becoming the first gargoyle ever to lift a solitary eyebrow. "Time to run away."

"This is when you make your exit, Lord!" came Fredgic's urgent muffled voice.

"Hmm, is it, dear boy?" said the Lordling vaguely, not quite sure what was going on. "If that's the way it's done." He backed away from the threatening figure of the gargoyle and clambered back into the carriage. "Onward!" he commanded the mountain goats.

The goats, knowing a sensible order when they heard one, beat a swift retreat. As the little golden carriage bounced away, the Lordling's voice could clearly be heard filtering through the trees. "Hmm, Fridgestick, but were they pirates or not?"

The warlock's response was not recorded for posterity.

Chapter 25
Hitting Things

At first light, the Imperial household was up and about, putting finishing touches on the tourney field. Banners had been ironed, pennants polished, and the whole lawn given a manicure. The knights started arriving shortly after sunrise. There were quite a few of them.

The chivalric companies initiated by Emperor Timregis still retained a certain vaguely honourable reputation. The Orders of the Unmentionable Garment, the Tangerine Gooseberry Bush and the Sharp Pointy Object were the three most reputable of these ex-knightly orders.

The various succeeding Emperors had attempted to create chivalric orders to replace Timregis' lost Companies, but their endeavours had been rather less successful. The Order of the Silver Gerbil had failed mainly because of a heraldic error which meant that the shields came back from the printers displaying a gerbil dessicated rather than a gerbil rampant.

Lady Talle's immediate predecessor, the Emperor Maarstigan, had initiated the Order of the Purple Beard but had been hard pressed to find anyone willing to join. At the time of his unfortunate but timely demise, the Order had consisted of three peasants, a small dog and the Court Jester (under duress).

Needless to say, most of the former knights who appeared at this particular Imperial Tourney were those known as Timregis's Mob. Although the names of their Companies still commanded prestige, the knights themselves had either gone to seed—hair and beards everywhere—or now looked far too reputable to be in this line of business. Many retired knights had taken up other trades such as accountancy, executive management or associate professorhood.

There were also the Spider-Knights provided by the visiting royals. They all wore identical tabards and shields displaying the coat of arms of Anglorachnis. None of them looked pleased to be there, probably because they had spent the last few days walking the length of the Empire to get to this tournament—in full battle dress. Luckily, none of them were expected to fight because they had not brought steeds with them. Only the King of Anglorachnis himself would compete as a Spider Knight.

Most of the local knights were known to each other, or at least recognisable by their coats of arms. Only one was anonymous. He carried a shield marked with three drops of black blood on a field of red and white poppies and his visor was always kept down. His horse, of course, was black.

His consort was a woman in a tightly-laced green dress, a blonde wig and a broad-brimmed hat. Her face seemed to be endlessly changing, as if she did not want anyone to recognise her. They were accompanied by a shifty-looking profit-scoundrel and a small jester who seemed to be writing some kind of poem.

Only the Lady Emperor, seated in the Imperial pavilion with her royal guests, knew who the strangers must be. She smiled a mysterious, secret smile. The time for unmasking was not yet.

-§-§-§-§-§-

Aragon was extremely uncomfortable in his dank jousting helm. There was no way to see out of it without tilting his head at an impossible angle. Despite this, he managed to get on his new horse and guide it towards where Kassa, disguised as a blonde, was seated on a picnic rug.

He inclined his head, quite an achievement in full plate armour, and reached a gauntlet down to her. "My lady consort," he said graciously in his best courtier's manner. "May I carry a token of yours into the battle this day?"

Out of the corner of his eye slot, he saw the glamour over her face shift suddenly as if she was disturbed. Kassa's familiar golden eyes glinted out of the stranger's face.

"Of course, my lord," she murmured, unclasping the silver thingummy shaped like a boat which she wore about her neck. Slowly, she looped the chain through his belt.

For once in his life, Aragon did not know what to say. She actually trusted him. A feeling of relief washed over him. He knew now what he had to do. Saluting his consort, Aragon Silversword turned his horse and rode towards the jousting area. Everything was clear to him now.

-§-§-§-§-§-

Queen Hwenhyfar watched intently as the armoured knights paraded before the Imperial Pavilion. Because of her husband's paranoia that she might find herself a Champion to have a torrid affair with, she had never before attended an actual tournament. The only reason she was attending now was because the King seemed bewitched by the Lady Emperor, and had not been able to contradict Talle's assumption that the Queen would be in attendance.

The King and Queen were the only real guests in Lady Talle's Imperial Pavilion, as all the Lordlings had got together and set up a game of strip poker in the Execution Tower which was underground somewhere in the East Wing. They had filched a significant number of ladies-in-waiting and most of the claret in the Imperial wine-cellars for this purpose. All the Lordlings had rather nasty memories of the sort of tournament Timregis used to hold, and they preferred not to be reminded of such hideous events as the Green Egg & Spoon Tourney or the Bewildered Hedgehog Derby.

Reed Cooper, the dark and dashing Mocklorn Ambassador, had been ordered to wait upon the Anglorachnis Queen and see to her every need. He fulfilled his duty by providing fizzy drinks, frozen sherbets and trays of cucumber sandwiches, all with gallant courtesy and much kissing of her slender, pale hand. When no one else was paying attention, he murmured an indecent proposal in her ear.

Queen Hwenhyfar gasped silently and turned the colour of a ripe strawberry.

-§-§-§-§-§-

"What is this place anyway?" Kassa asked, craning her neck to look around the huge walled courtyard which happily contained at least thirty mounted knights and several hundred assorted nobles, observers, consorts and hangers-on.

Daggar yawned, leaning back against a handy tree stump. "This is Dawn. Used to be the exercise enclosure for the Imperial concubines, though there are only a dozen or so left in the harem now, and I can't think what use our Talle will have for them."

Kassa looked at her cousin through narrowed eyes. "Just exactly how do you know so much about Imperial concubines?"

To his credit, Daggar did not blush. Neither did he answer the question. "Watch the tourney, Kassa."

-§-§-§-§-§-

The first part of the tournament was a joust. Time and again, one knight galloped towards another and attempted to push him off his horse with a long pointy stick. Those who fell while their opponent remained seated were eliminated.

Aragon waited his turn, and was eventually led to the starting enclosure. "There will be no biting, no scratching," announced the referee-herald in a booming voice. "No kicking the horse below the waist and no groin-shots with the lance unless absolutely justifiable. Lay on!"

Aragon tilted his head low and charged towards his opponent, twisting the lance sharply so that it would strike his opponent in a damagingly central area. Too late, he realised that his opponent had attempted the same move.

As he was hurled into mid air, Aragon recalled where he had seen his opponent's shield before. It belonged to Sir Spotty Harbinger, who had once tried to usurp Aragon's position as Imperial Champion by spreading a nasty rumour about him and the Palace dinner-lady.

Then the grass came up to meet him with a thud.

"Double toss!" announced the referee-herald. "At my Lady Emperor's command," he added.

Over in the Imperial pavilion, Lady Talle stood up and surveyed the two fallen knights. "Continue," she ordered gracefully.

Two small squires leaped forward to drag the horses out of the way. Both knights returned to the edge of the tourney field to swap their jousting helms for something more practical.

Aragon stood at the edge of the Daggersharp picnic rug, glaring at the fake blonde, the profit-scoundrel and the jester-poet. "Where is my foot-helm?" he demanded angrily.

They all looked at Daggar. "I sold it," he admitted.

Aragon just looked at him in shock. "You sold it?" He was almost lost for words. "Why?"

"I was bored," said Daggar defensively.

Aragon swung accusing eyes on Kassa, whom he blamed for this. She grinned amiably. "Don't worry, I have a spare for you." She rummaged in her handbag, producing a sturdy, reasonably attractive black steel helm.

Aragon took it from her, turning it over in his hands. There was something strange about it which he couldn't quite put his finger on. "It's not bewitched, is it?" he asked suspiciously.

"Aragon, you know how I feel about magic," said Kassa sternly.

"Good," he said, fastening the helm over his head with a resounding click.

"Of course it's bewitched," she added.

Aragon glared at her through the bars of his new helm. "Not funny, Kassa."

-§-§-§-§-§-

"My lady Emperor," murmured Griffin as the Nameless Knight and Sir Spotty Harbinger stalked towards each other, wooden swords in hand. "I presume you have some sort of programme in mind for this day's events?"

"Of course, boy," said Talle without moving her lips. "The King of Anglorachnis shall win the tournament and the honour of being my Champion. The happy relations between our two societies will thus be sealed. All the Mocklore knights have orders to lose gracefully to the Spider Shield."

Griffin frowned. "I presume that the King does intend to return to Anglorachnis?"

"Of course," she said scornfully. "I shall accept one of his knights as a proxy. The point is that while he holds the honour of being my Champion, relations between our two cultures must remain cordial!"

It made a vague sort of sense. "And what of the Nameless Knight, lady?" questioned Griffin. "Does he know that he must submit to the King?"

"He will learn, Griffin," murmured the Lady Emperor, her eyes fixed to the spectacle below. The Nameless Knight had just metaphorically removed Sir Spotty Harbinger's head with his wooden sword. "He will learn."

-§-§-§-§-§-

The day wore on. Lunch was served. The occasional limb was accidentally hacked off. The occasional consort went off with someone else while her knight was being flung off his horse. All was as it should be.

"So this is the good old days, ey?" said Daggar disapprovingly, chewing on a chicken wing. "Honour and chivalry and all that."

"Don't mock what you don't understand, Daggar," chided Kassa, biting into a cream-cheese wafer with pickled herring sprinkled on top.

Aragon returned, removing his helm and tossing down an exceptionally large jug of barley water in two gulps. "I have beaten everyone so far," he announced.

"So has the King of Anglorachnis," noted Kassa. "But of course, he does not have a witch working for him. Just a Lady Emperor."

Aragon dropped the empty barley-water jug. "Are you saying that the tourney is fixed?"

"It was fixed," said Daggar. "But you know how good Kassa is at breaking things."

Aragon glared at Kassa. "Once and for all, have you hexed my helm?"

Kassa batted her eyelids. "I can't imagine what you mean."

"Why?" he demanded. "Didn't you think I could do this on my own?"

"I don't know," she retorted. "Could you? Look, it's obvious by the way the knights are falling like flies as soon as they get near the King that she wants him to win. That means I have to go one better. I want my champion to beat hers, Aragon. You are going to win this tourney for me."

"Oh," he said flatly, turning to stalk away. "Am I, now?"

"Did you just win that argument?" Daggar questioned.

"I always win, Daggar," Kassa replied haughtily. "Even when I lose."

-§-§-§-§-§-

It came down to a bout between the Nameless Knight and King Durraldo of Anglorachnis, as everyone had guessed it would. The two opponents faced each other. There was no more jousting—just wooden swords, plain armour and multi-coloured shields.

"The winner of this, the final bout in the Championship tourney, shall serve as my own Lord Protector, Champion of the Lady Emperor of Mocklore," announced Talle, waving a silken scarf from the Royal Pavilion.

The King of Anglorachnis frowned slightly. "Is that right?" he asked. "I mean, I thought the prize was a trophy or a box of chocolates or something. I don't know if I could accept that kind of title…"

The purple-clad Ambassador of Anglorachnis tugged on one of the King's leather straps. "Do not fear, your Majesty," he whispered. "Should you happen to win, I am sure we can come to some arrangement."

This was the first anyone had heard about the prize. Aragon Silversword stood very still, considering the possibilities that it offered.

At the edge of the tourney field, Kassa Daggersharp stiffened with rising alarm.

"Didn't think of that, did you?" said Daggar casually.

Beside the Imperial Pavilion, the Nameless Knight and the King of Anglorachnis both assented to the conditions of the tournament.

"Best out of three, boys," cooed the Lady Emperor. "And do not forsake chivalry in your pursuit to win this day."

Both knights turned and dipped their wooden swords in reverence to the Lady Emperor. Then King Durraldo bowed in the direction of Queen Hwenhyfar, who jiggled her hankerchief nervously in response and then turned back to continue her intimate dialogue with Reed Cooper. The Nameless Knight turned to scan the crowd for his consort, almost wishing that she had kept her red hair so that he could find her more easily. Finally he spotted a particularly unfamiliar face at the edge of the field, and bowed to her for what he fully intended to be the last time.

The two knights saluted each other stiffly.

The Lady Emperor raised her silk scarf and allowed it to drift slowly through her fingers. As it slid to the ground, the two knights leaped towards each other.

Of course, neither of them were actually knights. King Durraldo had created the Company of Spider-Knights but had never been formally admitted to the Order. Aragon Silversword had belonged to the Order of the Unmentionable Garment, but murdering a patron Emperor was equivalent to a resignation. They leaped towards each other anyway, duelling with their wooden swords as if their lives depended upon it.

A low buzzing sound filed the arena, but it was so quiet that no one heard it. A small silver needle flew straight past the spectators and whirled around for a while until it accidentally embedded itself in the helm of the Nameless Knight.

Aragon Silversword did not notice the tiny clang. He had no way of knowing that an embroidery needle was sticking up out of his helm like a minature lightning rod. Neither did King Durraldo notice—he was much too busy.

Even the crowd did not really think anything was wrong until they saw what was following the needle.

A steady stream of glittering glints, nasty flying things and patches of wild magic swept across the tourney field, homing in on the Nameless Knight's helm.

"Oops," said Kassa Daggersharp.

King Durraldo and the Nameless Knight fought steadily on, ignoring the swirls of magical energy and nasty flying things which surrounded them.

The spectators were not so dedicated. When the first fop was transformed into a large rainbow trout, the screaming and rioting began. Tables were turned over, chairs were broken in half and three blonde ladies-in-waiting were transformed into mermaids.

Reed Cooper bravely flung Queen Hwenhyfar out of the way of a flying electric eel and dragged her to safety under the prize table, taking the opportunity to give her heaving bosom a tender squeeze.

The Queen of Anglorachnis gasped with mortification and slapped him hard on the face. Then, as if noticing for the first time that they were concealed from the world by a floor-length damask tablecloth, she threw herself upon him and stuck her tongue as far down his throat as was humanly possible.

The Glimmer had finally reached Dreadnought, even if it was by a roundabout path. Kassa Daggersharp was biting her lip, and trying to avoid Daggar's accusing glare. "Well," she said finally. "At least he might not win now."

"I thought you wanted him to win!" said Daggar exasperatedly.

"Yes," said Kassa. "Well. That was before I knew what the prize was."

Chapter 26
Losing Things

All around Lady Talle, everyone was screaming and trying to escape being turned into sea monsters by the viciously random water-glints. Ladies swooned and fops pretended to be brave while looking for things to hide behind. The local knights were too exhausted to do anything productive, while the Spider-Knights had never seen anything like this before and were reduced to staring openly.

The Lady Emperor was alone in the Imperial Pavilion. Queen Hwenhyfar had disappeared, as had Reed Cooper. Griffin had been swept away by a crowd of hysterical ladies-in-waiting. Talle forced her gaze to remain fixed upon the duel between the Nameless Knight and the King of Anglorachnis.

Suddenly a stray glint swept down, engulfing both combatants in a haze of blue light. When the haze faded, the swords in play were no longer making dull thunking sounds when they hit each other. They were going clang, clash, tink. Metal swords. Steel swords. Technically, the match was now null and void, but everyone was far too distracted to pay any attention to a minor detail like that.

The Lady Emperor leaned back, smiling snakishly. The stakes had been raised.

-§-§-§-§-§-

"Did you do this deliberately?" Daggar yelled.

"Of course, not!" Kassa retorted. "And to answer your next question, I don't know how to stop it either!"

Daggar nodded. "That's what I thought. I'll be over there, hiding behind those bushes."

"We'll meet up later," agreed Kassa absently.

Daggar smiled too brightly, and replied "Ey, of course we will." It was only as he loped off that he muttered, "Not if I get a head start, we won't."

Kassa craned her neck to see what was going on in the tourney field. She was about to look for something to climb up on for a better view when she became aware of a presence behind her. "Oh," she said guiltily. "It's you."

"Indeed It Is," replied Skeylles the Fishy Judge, Lord of the Underwater. He wore a long blue velvet cloak and carried opera glasses and a carton of popcorn.

Kassa tried to smile, but gave it up as a bad job. She swallowed hard instead. "What are you doing here?"

"Well, I Did Come Hoping To Watch The Tournament." He glared at her. "You Have Made A Right Mess Here, My Girl. I Still Haven't Forgiven You For Washing All Those Glints Into My Ocean."

She stared at him suspiciously. "Are you causing all this? To teach me a lesson?"

"Now, Would I?" boomed the voice ironically.

Kassa felt vaguely hopeful. "Could you take these water glints with you, then? Surely you could cancel out most of the other wild magic if you were armed with water glints—right?"

Skeylles looked very grim. "You Have A Very Simplistic View Of Life, Kassa. I Think This Goes Beyond The Boundaries of Godfather Duties."

"But you'll do it anyway, won't you?" she asked humbly.

His face looked like thunder. "I Don't Want To See You For At Least A Year After This."

She crossed her heart. "I promise. I won't ask you for anything else."

"Right," grumbled the Lord of the Underwater, not sounding as if he believed her. He vanished, and with him went the remaining glints, the lords and ladies who had been transformed into sea-creatures, and the giant pile of seaweed which had until recently been Aragon Silversword's tourney steed.

Kassa pushed her way to the edge of the crowd, which was much diminished now. Most of the remaining spectators were in a state of shock. "Fight well, my champion!" she cried unenthusiastically. *If you win now, I'll rip out your heart and eat it with a spoon.*

The Nameless Knight reacted to her voice, or perhaps to her unspoken thought, and his opponent took the opportunity to clout him in the groin. The Nameless Knight moved swiftly side, using his weight to knock the King of Anglorachnis flat on his back.

The victor lay his sword ceremonially at the throat of the vanquished. Then he looked at the sword more closely. "Who the hell gave us steel swords?" rasped Aragon.

King Durraldo shrugged, an awkward thing to do in armour.

All was quiet, which gave the Lady Emperor an opportunity to strut her stuff. She stood up, the elegant drapery of her gown falling around her in smooth curves. "You fought well, King Durraldo, and have done your good consort much honour this day."

Queen Hwenhyfar emerged from behind the prize table, looking slightly dishevelled. She absently kissed a hand to her husband and then sat down hurriedly on the throne provided. Reed Cooper tactfully waited a while longer before emerging himself.

King Durraldo bowed to the Lady Emperor and then trailed away to remove his armour. Talle turned then to the Nameless Knight. "Good sir, you have won this day the honour to serve your Emperor as Imperial Champion. Come forth, and bring your consort with you that she may share thine honour."

The Nameless Knight stalked into the crowd and took the hand of the woman in the blonde wig whose banner he had fought under. "Aragon, what are you doing?" she whispered.

"What you told me to do," he replied crisply, fastening his metal gauntlet around her wrist and pulling her in the direction of the Imperial Pavilion. "I won."

"That was before I knew what the prize was!" she hissed wildly. "I didn't want you to become her champion again!"

"Well now," he said calmly. "It is far too late to change your mind."

The Lady Emperor smiled benevolently as they knelt on the cushions by her feet. "Sir Knight, wilt thou not remove thy helm?" she asked, deliberately lapsing into archaic speech. "We are all friends here, and all the Empire must know the name of my champion."

Aragon hesitated for only a moment and then removed his helm, dropping it in Kassa's lap.

The Lady Emperor breathed out with relief, her suspicions confirmed. "Ahh, Sir Silversword. I am honoured that thou hast returned to me." She turned her head slightly. "And thy lady?" she questioned deliberately.

"Take it off, Kassa," said Aragon steadily, his grip around her wrist increasing.

She tried to pull free, but the metal gauntlet bit further into her skin. "Aragon, you're hurting me!"

"That has always been the plan," he replied in the coldest voice he could manage.

Kassa looked at him in horror, and the glamour which had disguised her features fell off her like a sheet of silk. She tossed her head and the wig slid to one side. Hair the colour of old blood cascaded down her back.

The Lady Emperor's hand lashed out, gripping Kassa's face tightly. "Ah, thou hast brought me a rare gift indeed, Sir Silversword."

"He has brought you nothing," snapped Kassa. "Take off your breastplate," she ordered Aragon.

For a moment, it looked as if he was about to refuse, but then he began undoing the buckles. He removed his gauntlets slowly and pulled off his breastplate, revealing a padded shirt underneath. Kassa lunged forward and grabbed at the collar, ripping the shirt open. "Do you see that mark, Talle?" she demanded, stabbing a finger at the brand mark. A spiral within a spiral burned over his heart. "Aragon Silversword belongs to me now!"

"The matter is still under discussion," said Aragon stiffly.

The Lady Emperor looked amused. "Indeed? Then you have a decision to make, my champion."

"He is not your champion," Kassa insisted.

"Is he not?" said the Lady Emperor with wide eyes. "Indeed." She looked harder at Kassa, her expression changing. "Are you the one responsible for this magical blight on my land?"

Kassa stared back at her. "Let's just say that pointless vandalism is a family trait," she said flatly.

"I see," said the Lady Emperor with a sparkle in her eyes. "Then I am afraid that I will have to sentence you to execution. For high treason," she added. "My champion, I take it you have no objections to carrying out my sentence?"

The mark over Aragon's heart was beginning to feel uncomfortably hot, but he paid it no mind. "With pleasure, my Lady Emperor," he said politely, picking up the sword he had unexpectedly been awarded during the tourney.

Kassa looked at him, stricken. "Don't even think it, Aragon," she warned.

He hefted the sword thoughtfully. "Oh, no? Kassa, if you don't start running, I'm going to cut you down in front of all these people." He lowered his voice to a more intimate tone. "Wouldn't you prefer some privacy?"

She glared at him, and took a deep breath to begin singing. His hand slammed over her mouth, making a spell impossible. "Don't even think it. I've had enough enchantments to last me a lifetime."

Kassa shot him a look which would have melted sand into glass. And then she turned on her heel, running as fast as she could in knee-high boots and a long silk dress.

Aragon paused for a moment to salute the Lady Emperor with a clipped bow, and then he ran after Kassa.

-§-§-§-§-§-

Behind a large shrubbery at the rear of the Imperial Pavilion, Tippett the jester-poet fidgeted restlessly. "Can we come out of hiding yet?" he asked.

"Not quite yet," said Daggar steadily.

"But I want to see what's going on! There can't be any gaps in the ballad…"

"All right then," sighed Daggar. "We'll follow them. But slowly, mind. Don't run—walk."

-§-§-§-§-§-

Kassa tore through the arched doorway in the wall and out towards the trees. She scraped wildy through the undergrowth, cursing herself for not considering this possibility. She had put too much trust in that bloody witchmark—she might have known that this magic stuff would fail her when she most needed it. She should have listened to Summer Songstel and got herself properly trained…

Aragon was close on her heels. Kassa ducked to avoid a low-hanging tree and tripped on a branch of brambles, landing in a puddle. She glared up at her pursuer, who smiled nastily.

"I should have listened to Daggar, much as I hate to say it!" she flung at him. "You really have been more trouble than you are worth!"

"Indeed?" Aragon said pleasantly, laying the tip of his sword to her throat. "Never mind, it will all be over soon."

She looked up at him with her wide golden eyes. "You can't kill me."

"Oh can't I?" he replied in a chilling tone, drawing his sword back to strike.

Of course he couldn't kill her. The brand over his heart was already burning hot, and he hated to think what would happen if he increased his betrayal any further. But he wasn't going to let her know that.

"Well?" Kassa insisted. "What are you waiting for?"

"Rip the hem off your dress," he said harshly.

"What's this, a plan to degrade me even further?"

"Just do it."

She scowled, but did as he had asked, ripping the length of her hem from her dress until it was one long strip of silk. "Now what?"

Aragon rolled up the sleeve of his shirt and drew the sword across his left arm, cutting into the flesh. Without a word, he held his bleeding arm out to Kassa. She bound it silently, winding the green bandage firmly around his self-inflicted wound. He pulled the shirt sleeve down to conceal the bandage, and turned to leave her. "If the Emperor ever discovers that I let you live, my head will be on the block. You might want to consider changing your name."

"So that's it?" she challenged. "You're just going to walk away from me?"

"Don't push me, Kassa," he threatened.

"You are my liegeman!" she burst out.

He turned slightly. "It was not my choice, and you know it. Witchmarks cannot work by trickery." And to prove it, he walked away.

No need to tell her of the burning pain in his chest as the brand exacted its revenge for his treachery. Aragon refused to look back as he walked through the trees. He told himself that it was to demonstrate how little he cared about her, refusing to accept the possibility that the sight of those golden eyes might diminish his resolve altogether...

Aragon Silversword continued to walk until he reached the arched doorway back into the tourney area, passing a nonchalant-looking Daggar and Tippett on the way.

Their deliberately casual expressions faded somewhat when they saw the blood on his sword, and they both ran past him at a surprising turn of speed.

Aragon kept walking through the tourney area, past the knights who were all packing up their armour, horses, squires and consorts. He did not stop until he reached the Imperial Pavilion, and knelt to lay his bloody sword at the feet of the Lady Emperor.

"Is she dead?" inquired Lady Talle, pronouncing the words delightedly.

Aragon met her gaze evenly. "As a doornail," he pronounced.

"Oh, my champion," breathed Lady Talle in true bloodthirsty fashion. "I shall reward you well for this day's work." She leaned forward eagerly. "Did she suffer?"

"I cannot help my exceptional sword skill, my lady," apologised Aragon. "The accused was perhaps executed more swiftly than you would have liked. I shall do better next time."

"See that you do," said Lady Talle with a little smile.

Aragon almost smiled himself. "While we are on the subject of rewards, my lady, I have another gift for you."

Lady Talle purred like a milk-fed kitten. "For me?"

-§-§-§-§-§-

Daggar burst through the trees. "Kassa, where are you?"

"Don't talk to me, Daggar, I'm in a bad mood," came the angry reply.

He barely restrained himself from throwing himself bodily into her arms. "I thought you were dead!"

"I think that was the general plan," she said grumpily. "Damn him to the Underworld and back!"

"What exactly happened?" asked Tippett, eager for details.

"Never mind that now," said Daggar. "Everything's all right. We've still got some ready cash and an escape route. Let's just go home while we still can."

"And where exactly is home?" asked Kassa in a strange voice.

Daggar shrugged. He hadn't thought about it much. "The ship, I suppose."

Kassa went very pale. She folded in on herself as if she had been punched in the stomach. If it wasn't so tragic, she might seriously have considered laughing at herself. "I gave him the ship!" she said incredulously. "Gods, I even gave him the ship!"

-§-§-§-§-§-

Lady Talle turned the silver thingummy around in her fingers. "A pretty trinket, my lord, but it is hardly appropriate to give me the favour you received from your consort this day."

"Allow me to demonstrate," said Aragon graciously. He took the silver thingummy from her and hurled it out into the centre of the tourney field, now empty. The flash of silver shimmered, and became a gleaming ghost-ship once again.

"Behold," said Aragon Silversword, "The *Splashdance* silver. Or, to be more precise, the *Silver Splashdance*."

Lady Talle was hardly able to speak. "You have done well, my champion," she said finally. "Indeed, I believe you may have just sealed my conquest of this Empire. How can I reward you?"

Chapter 27
Putting Things Back Together

Daggar hurried after her. "Can't you just witch it? Whistle it back like you did before?"

Kassa whirled around. "You don't understand! I gave it to him of my own free will. He didn't steal the damn thing. How can I whistle back something which technically belongs to him? What kind of witch do you think I am?"

"Is this a trick question?" asked Daggar hesitantly.

Kassa stalked away from him and he decided not to press her on the matter. They marched along the edge of the city towards the Skullcap forest. Well, Kassa marched. Tippett and Daggar followed nervously behind her, hoping she would find someone to take her anger out on soon.

Once they were well away from the city, Kassa let out a scream. A long, frustrated, ringing scream in a voice forged by the salt of the sea.

Daggar stood behind a large rock, and Tippett started taking surreptitious notes on his sleeve.

Kassa whirled around. "If you put any of this in my ballad, I'll nail you to a talking tree," she threatened.

Tippet's quill pen broke.

It was then that a giant clockwork net came spiralling down from the trees, tangling around the infuriated Kassa.

"Oh, oh," said Daggar.

"Gotchoo!" said a warlock, sneezing as he emerged from behind a fluorescent pink elderberry tree.

Several mounds of false shrubbery were flung aside to reveal a large golden carriage being pulled by several mutant goats. A rather flabby looking Lordling was hanging out of the window. "Hmm, well done, Forkbend," he called heartily. "Caught them red-handed, wot?"

Kassa stopped struggling with the clockwork net and stared at the newcomers. "What?" she said dangerously.

Tippett approached her bravely and helped her untangle her hair from the net. "It's my former master," he whispered. "He—he is hunting pirates, you see."

"Oh," said Kassa in a calm voice. She stood very still, considering her options. The pirate blood in her was urging her to grab a curvy sword, grow a beard and kill them all. The witch blood in her was making insidious suggestions about sleeping thorns and illusion songs. Kassa stifled both the inner pirate and the inner witch. She was going to handle this her way. She smiled at the Lordling and the warlock, and batted her eyelashes. "I'm not a pirate."

"You're not?" said Fredgic suspiciously.

"Of course not," she said in a wide-eyed voice. "I'm a lady."

"Hmm, no denying that!" agreed the Lordling wholeheartedly as he clambered out of his carriage. "Take the net off the lady, Frittchorn."

"But ladies can be pirates, your Lordship," protested Fredgic. "Think of Bessemund, Bloody Mary, Black Nell!"

"Hmm, true, true," mused the Lordling. "Tie her up, then."

"Don't be silly, your Lordship," said Kassa. "I'm nothing like a pirate. I have red hair, you know."

"Hmm, why so you do," said the Lordling, peering at her. "No denying it. Let her go, Frudgepup."

"And pirates don't have red hair," continued Kassa sweetly. "Especially lady pirates like Bold Brunhilde. They have fair hair, golden because of all the treasure they have stolen."

"I've never heard that before," said Fredgic suspiciously.

"Hmm, treasure," said the Lordling, pleased. "So who is this Bold Brunhilde, then?"

"Oh, I can show you where she is," said Kassa. "And her gang."

"I've never heard of a pirate called Bold Brunhilde," insisted Fredgic.

"I bet Tippett has," said Kassa confidently. "Go on, Tippett. I bet you have heard simply hundreds of ballads about Bold Brunhilde." She smiled at him.

Tippett smiled back hesitantly. He fetched his favourite lute, which was still in the Lordling's carriage. Suspecting that Kassa would kill him if he even considered wasting time by tuning it, he plucked awkwardly at the instrument, improvising lyrics about Bold Brunhilde—she was gold of hair and blue of eye, bold enough to steal sun from the sky, and so on. Within five minutes, the Lordling was convinced.

-§-§-§-§-§-

The Red Admiral clambered over the new boat, admiring it. "Marvellous, ingenious," he kept muttering happily, pleased with his new toy.

Lady Talle smiled. "You will notice, my lords, the ease with which the Blackguards and the mummers were returned to their rightful places."

"True enough," muttered the Captain, not mentioning that his two best sergeants refused to work unless they were in a pantomime horse costume, and that most of the newly-restored Blackguards now insisted on applause every time they apprehended someone.

The Chief Mummer also nodded reluctantly, but made a few hand signals which nobody felt brave enough to translate.

"The Royal Visit was, I trust, to your satisfaction," Lady Talle continued, looking pointedly at the purple-clad Anglorachnis Ambassador.

"Indeed, my Lady," he said jovially. "I've never seen the Queen so cheerful. She asked me to compliment you on your choice of ambassador." He shot a suspicious look at Reed Cooper.

"I believe I entertained her Highness to the best of my ability," replied Reed, straight-faced. He was wearing new Imperial livery with his collar turned up high to conceal the royal lipstick smudges. He had even bought a glamour spell from the Brewer's Pavilion to disguise the bruised eye given to him by Kassa Daggersharp. If it were not for the eyepatch and the earring, he would have almost looked respectable.

"And his Majesty was very pleased with the standard of fighters at the tournament," continued the Ambassador, nodding in the direction of the Imperial Champion.

Aragon Silversword, also garbed in new black and white livery, nodded briefly in return.

"So," said the Ambassador with glee, rubbing his palms together. "I think my pension is safe, my Lady Emperor. Consider me to be one of your most ardent supporters."

"Splendid," said Lady Talle sweetly. "And Master Lint, I hope you have nothing to complain about. After all, everyone was ordered to buy the souvenirs generated by the Royal Visit."

Tamb Lint regarded her flatly. "You really got no idea how the h'economy works, do ye?" he said in his greasy voice. "Luckily no one h'else does h'either. H'all the merchants reckon they were done right by, so I'm not making h'any complaints. Yet," he added darkly.

Lady Talle turned her attention to the member of the delegation who had always kept to the shadows. "And you, Chief Executive of Mercenaries? You never told me what you wanted in exchange for your support."

"We are mercenaries, my lady," replied the Hidden Leader. "There is no politics in what we do. If you ever have need of us, pay us and we will aid you. Of course, you will need to find us first."

Finally, Lady Talle turned to Leonardes of Skullcap. She was a tiny slip of a thing next to his massive bulk. "I trust you have no objection to the percentage you received from the silver found in the *Splashdance*."

"You'll do," said Leonardes shortly.

The delegation trooped out. The Red Admiral only agreed to leave if the Lady Emperor promised faithfully to deliver the ship to his harbour the next day.

When the leaders of Dreadnought were all gone, Lady Talle turned to face her retinue. Aragon and Reed both looked very smart in their new livery, although it was obvious that they were trying to keep as much distance between them as possible. Lady Talle didn't mind that at all. She approved of a little natural rivalry between colleagues. Griffin the urchin stood between the pirate and the champion, wearing an Imperial tabard big enough to cut into six urchin-sized robes.

"It looks as if I'm here to stay, boys," said Lady Talle in a silvery voice edged with pure pleasure. "I am the Emperor of Mocklore."

Three seconds after Lady Talle's exultant announcement, a large clockwork net appeared out of thin air and threw itself over her. No one noticed at the time, but it was guided into place by a tiny bauble on a piece of ribbon.

Reed and Aragon both reached for their swords, and realised that they had vanished. "Warlocks," said Reed in disgust. "I recognise that net!"

A large golden carriage towed by several mutant goats appeared in the large doorway, and a figure hopped out. He was youngish and rather flabby-looking, wearing the gaudiest gold lame tunic with jewelled cuffs that any of them had ever seen. "Hmm, he said cheerfully. "Finally captured you rascals, wot?"

"You fool!" screamed Lady Talle, completely enraged. "How dare you do this to me? I am the Emperor of Mocklore!"

"Hmm, impossible!" said the Lordling dismissively. "You're a girl, don't you know. Everyone knows that Emperors are boys. Anyway, I've met the Emperor, and he's nothing like you. Fredgecutters, have you heard anything about a new Emperor?"

"No," said Fredgic honestly. He never paid much attention to current affairs. As far as he was concerned, old Timregis was still Emperor.

Lordling Rorey decided to get back to the subject at hand. "Hmm, I know all about you, Bold Brunhilde."

"What?" shrieked Lady Talle, completely gobsmacked.

"Hmm, and the one with the eyepatch, he's a pirate too. And the dwarf, he's Ruthless Rodger, don't you know. It was all in the ballad."

Fredgic the warlock produced a large stick and herded Reed Cooper and Griffin the urchin towards the netted Lady Talle.

"This is preposterous!" she screamed.

"What about him?" said Reed suddenly, looking at Silversword.

"Hmm, he's not a pirate," said the Lordling dismissively. "He's a friend of the nice lady wench who told me all about you blighters. Now you're going to steal gold bullion for me, don't you know, and wear silk shirts and say 'Avast me hearties'. Take it away, Frucheface."

Aragon went to the window. Out in the courtyard, he thought he saw a familiar shadow. "The lengths that woman will go to to keep me near her," he murmured, wondering if he liked the idea. "Have a good trip, Talle," he volunteered cheerfully.

"Traitor!" Lady Talle screamed back as Fredgic tied her to Reed Cooper and Griffin with a length of white embroidery thread. "Craven, faithless apostate!"

Aragon walked towards her and gently removed the sacred bauble from the ribbon which tied it to the clockwork net. He put it in his pocket. "Well?" he said calmly. "What did you expect?"

The writhing, clockwork-netted mass of Lady Talle, Reed Cooper and Griffin the urchin vanished, along with the Lordling, Fredgic and the golden carriage. The mutant mountain goats remained, dolefully nibbling at the Lady Emperor's purple feathered chaise longue.

Left alone for the first time in weeks, Aragon Silversword opened the little door to the courtyard and went outside. "You can come out now," he said aloud.

"I wasn't hiding," said Kassa Daggersharp as she emerged from behind a potted tree. "I dislike crowds."

He almost smiled. "I know what you're thinking."

"No," she said softly, moving towards him. "You don't."

"Don't I?"

"I'm in charge, Aragon," she reminded him, very close now. "Never forget that."

"How could I forget?" he replied ironically.

"And I know what you are thinking," she continued.

"Oh, really?" Aragon was amused now.

"You are wondering why I didn't just pack you off to Skullcap with the Lady Emperor."

"That doesn't take a great stretch of imagination. I'm too useful to either of you. With me on her side, the Lady Emperor would be back in her Palace within a few hours. With those two bumbling around her, it could be weeks."

"And you think that's the only reason?" said Kassa.

His eyes held hers for a moment. "Of course not. You decided that if I wasn't around, you would miss me terribly. You've grown accustomed to my face."

She laughed. "Not even close. I just wanted my ship back."

"Oh, really?"

"Really." Her voice grew dangerous. "And you bear my mark, Silversword. Remember that. You took it of your own free will. You begged me to make you mine. And now you belong to me. I am not going to allow the Lady Emperor to benefit from my liegeman."

"Why are you so obsessed on the subject of liegemen?" he demanded impatiently. "What do you think you are, a princess?"

"I am the daughter of a Pirate King," snapped Kassa Daggersharp. "What do you think?"

"I think that you like me, Princess. It is the only possible interpretation of your actions."

She drew in a frustrated breath. "You have so much potential, Aragon! If you could just stop thinking about yourself for ten seconds, you could be so much more..."

"So much more dead," he concluded sharply.

"You might be a better person for it," she retorted.

Aragon raised an eyebrow. "If you want me, Kassa, my personality comes too. That's the deal."

"Who says I want you?" she snapped.

This time, he almost smiled. "You're so obvious."

Momentarily lost for words, Kassa Daggersharp turned on her heel and walked towards the *Silver Splashdance*. After a moment, Aragon Silversword followed her.

-§-§-§-§-§-

In the waters that surround the little island Empire of Mocklore, the magic still lurks as magic washed away by an unexpected rainstorm will do. Even the gods have little control over wild magic. It will be back.

Elsewhere in Mocklore, a giant gargoyle-man and a gorgon argue fiercely about whether their life together will be as mercenaries or as pirates. The fight continues until he throws a sheep at her and she tries to scratch his eyes out. Eventually they declare a mutual truce in order to cook dinner in peace. It could almost be happy ever after.

The sheep, of course, will run away at the earliest opportunity.

Elsewhere again, a royal carriage from a distant land trundles along the only road in Mocklore. The King of Anglorachnis wonders why his Queen looks so pleased with herself, and so damned attractive. He muses about how to ensure that the grim priestess-in-waiting will not be standing guard outside her door tonight...

Elsewhere again, the Lady Emperor of Mocklore is being forced to play croquet and Blind-Man's-Billiards with her pirate and her urchin while the Lordling of Skullcap lectures them on correct methods of piracy. In time, she too will return...

Deep in the multi-coloured forest which surrounds the deviously exotic Skullcap Mountains, a ghost of a pirate ship sails silently onwards. One of the crew is swabbing the deck and grumbling about how other people keep spending his money—he has obviously found out about the further ten per cent of his hoard that Lady Talle gave to the Profithood. Another member of the crew is writing epic-poetry, and hoping like anything that there will soon be enough material for a sequel…

A third member of the crew is seriously considering jumping ship, although for some reason he can never actually bring himself to do so. Instead, he watches the Captain and wonders just what she does to inspire them all to follow her—or at least to travel in the same direction.

Eventually, the sheep will meet up with them again, and then the crew will be complete.

The Captain is halfway up the rigging, hanging on to the mast for dear life. Her dark red hair blows wildly around her, obscuring the view that she climbed up there to see. Sometimes she sings sea-shanties, and sometimes she murmurs more enigmatic songs with vaguely disturbing melodies.

Eventually, she climbs down from the mast to discover that no one has done the washing up. This leads to a heated argument and much throwing of crockery.

They are travelling North, and she hasn't yet told them why, although they all have their suspicions. Their Captain is almost officially a Pirate of Note, but has not yet proved herself a Qualified Witch. There is also the morbid possibility that they are still, as far as they know, in the hands of Lady Luck. That particular curse will be hard to out-run.

If there is somewhere that the Captain wants to go, none of them really have any say in the matter. The strange thing is that not one of them has objected yet—except beneath their breath.

Some people are born to have ballads written about them, to cause major catastrophes, and to tell others what to do. That is the way of the world…

Author's Afterword for Splashdance Silver (2013)

When I was thirteen years old, I discovered the fantasy genre, and it blew my mind. Somewhere very close to my fourteenth birthday, I started writing my first novel. This book, let me tell you, had everything: war, epic, criminals, romance, angst, tragedy, doom and anti-heroes.

Over the next two years I wrote over 100,000 words of the Epic Fantasy to End All Epic Fantasies (number one of a projected twelve book series, I'm not even kidding), and at the same time I was reading fantasy novels by the metric tonne, gobbling them down without chewing.

Before I finished my first novel, I realised that it wasn't what I wanted to be writing at all. I had discovered Terry Pratchett and Esther Friesner and Robert Rankin, and I didn't want to be the writer who created the grand magical melodrama which made people cry, I wanted to be the writer who took a big sharp stick and started poking holes in the genre.

I laid my mighty Daggersharp tome aside and wrote some other things. I moved on. Then, on the first day of university, when I should have been in a cafe saying something hipsterish about Art and Philosophy (that's what we do at university, right?) I sat on a bench and started writing my new novel.

No epics here. This story was small and comedic and fluffy, and I loved it to bits. I took my favourite characters from the Angstodrama of Doom, and recast them in a piece of musical theatre with occasional explosions.

Mocklore happened, and by the time I got to the end of my (first) arts degree, I was a prize-winning, published author.

Splashdance Silver is my first novel, it feels like it happened a million years ago, and I can't tell you how hard it was to get over the idea that I shouldn't be showing it to people because OMG the author who wrote it, she was nineteen, what did she know?

But this is a new world we live in, where books don't die, and every year I hear from someone who has come upon *Splashdance* for the first time, and loved it. So maybe there's life in this flying sheep yet.

A first book is special, and this one changed my life. I have a soft spot for it, even if I had to physically restrain myself from rewriting ALL THE SENTENCES while proofing this edition, fifteen years after it was first published.

Welcome to Mocklore: come for the cranky pirate wenches; stay for the flying sheep.

Tansy Rayner Roberts
2013

Liquid Gold

A Mocklore Book

Tansy Rayner Roberts

For the body-building pagan sculptress who approves of witchy themes, low-cut bodices and goddesses.

For the historian-poet who wanted to read more about Sparrow (and is utterly convinced that he is the blueprint for Bigbeard).

Thanks for not being the kind of people who expect their daughter to a) get a sensible job, b) get married and c) avoid creativity like the plague.
[1998]

Yes, this one still works. Though I have to say the thing I'm most grateful about now is the quality grandparenting and babysitting you both manage to provide.
[2013]

CONTENTS

Chapter 1
Gold, Gold, the Mistress of Us All

The world was nothing special, but what world is when you get right down to it? There is nothing intriguing about a big round rock spinning through space. All those little creatures scampering around on its surface are what make a particular world interesting…

On this world was an island. It was an extraordinary place to live, if only for the number of times it had nearly exploded, sunk, and generally caused trouble for all concerned. This island was packed to the gills with witches, warlocks, merchants, minstrels, criminals and things which go bump in the night. To all intents and purposes, the island was also an Empire. The Mocklore Empire, a multi-coloured blot on the universal landscape. They had an Emperor and everything, even if she was of the female persuasion.

Below the surface of this cheerfully chaotic island (and simultaneously above the clouds, for various eldritch reasons) lurked the Underworld. From there, the dead watched the Mocklore Empire with hollow eyes, and thanked the various gods that they were well out of it.

At the edge of the island, skimming through the grass like a sterling silver styling comb, was a ship. A ghostly galleon, not quite there and yet somehow very real. It was silver, and its Captain's name was Kassa Daggersharp. Behind the ship, bobbing along on four stumpy little legs, trotted a sheep.

At that specific moment in time, a story began to weave its perilous web. A brewer made something. A green-eyed woman stole something. A ghostly ship full of pirates (more or less) bounced its way across a daffodil-encrusted meadow. And somewhere, a goddess laughed.

-§-§-§-§-§-

In one of the unworldly dimensions frequented by the gods, Lady Luck laughed unmercifully. She was the most elegant of goddess, with elaborate beige-blonde hair and hard eyes. "It can't be helped now, Destiny darling. You cursed them. Such a nasty, malicious curse. 'I leave you in the hands of Lady Luck,' you said. That means that they belong to me, lock stock and *destiny*."

Destiny, a green-haired girl goddess with translucent skin, made a far-from-elegant pout. "You're jealous because you only have the power to affect people's luck, whereas Fate and I work on much higher levels of manipulation."

"Not anymore," said Lady Luck sharply. It was a sore point. "You gave me a nice little bundle of destinies and I can play with them *how I like*." She smiled, and waved her manicured hand in the air. Images formed in the aether. Lady Luck examined each one critically, checking them for flaws. The profit-scoundrel, the jester…she lingered speculatively over the face of the traitor swordsman, but it was their leader who stood out from the rest, a proud, angry face surrounded by a cloud of hair the colour of old blood. "Miss High-And-Mighty Captain Daggersharp," mused the goddess. "You must miss dabbling in that cute, anst-ridden little life of hers."

"She could achieve some really interesting things…"

"Precisely my point," said Lady Luck. "They all could, if I chose to let them." She smiled a dazzlingly nasty smile.

Destiny pretended not to be bothered, but a tiny wrinkle creased her brow. "You can't randomly kill them off, you know. The framework of destiny is arranged at birth—you could only circumvent that if the cosmos was in total disarray."

Lady Luck clicked her tongue. "Well then," she said. "I'm going to have to improvise."

-§-§-§-§-§-

In the dim light of the Brewer's Pavilion, molten gold welled up out of the confines of the test tube, glowing in globules against the glass. A long droplet sank slowly from its rim down towards the canvas floor, elongating at an exceptionally leisurely pace. When it touched the ground, the droplet appeared to bounce, slowly being sucked up once more towards the residual mass in the narrow glass test tube. It was glorious. It was alien. It was liquid gold.

"Almost there," muttered the Brewmistress, her grandmotherly face creasing up into a raisin-like smile.

Mistress Opia was the matriarch of the Brewer's Pavilion, an unsightly structure which sat in the middle of the city of Dreadnought, monarch of the merchant's sector.

The Brewers of Dreadnought were legendary. They did not brew beer. Such a mundane task was beyond them; in any case, their predecessors had long ago perfected the ultimate beer recipe, selling the secret exclusively to various individuals for a wide variety of prices.

They all had their pet projects these days. Elder Grackling, who had been old and doddering since the age of seventeen, divided his time between trying to remember his long-lost warlock skills, and researching the theories behind portable rainclouds. Hobbs the gnome, whose highest ambition was to enter the Profithood, daily embarked on new schemes to make his fortune by means of various suspicious substances. The Soothsayer spent most working hours gazing into unsightly and unhealthy dimensions; that is, when she wasn't prophesying doom or making the tea. Even the adolescent apprentice, hired solely to do the sweeping and fetching, was secretly trying to animate a girlfriend he had built himself out of various spare odds and ends.

Mistress Opia herself, who had long ago discovered the secret of turning almost anything into gold, was now involved in the greatest brewing experiment of them all: turning gold into *time*.

"Liquid gold," she murmured to herself, gazing at the golden, globulous mass. "My, my."

It was almost ready for consumption—almost, but not quite. And then hers would be the greatest scientific reputation in history. She would be remembered as the Brewmistress who extracted and manipulated time. It was good. More than that—it was glorious.

She popped the liquid gold away, and went to lunch.

-§-§-§-§-§-

In Dreadnought, profit-scoundrels ruled the streets. By far the nastiest of these was Thumbs Skimmer. He was short, ugly, tough as nails and had personality problems which could maim at thirty paces. For some reason, he had the idea that he was the suave kind of gentleman crook who looked good in velvet doublets. At this exact moment, he caught up with the woman he had been trailing for several blocks, and slammed a meaty hand down on her arm, not able to quite reach her shoulder. "Oi," he snarled with the charm of a week-dead corpse. "What do you think you are doing, my fine lady-o?"

The woman turned. Thumbs couldn't help shuddering. There was something…something sinister about her. She wore a purple priestess robe which covered her almost entirely, but she didn't look like any priestess he had ever encountered. She should have been attractive enough, with that long tawny hair and those jade green eyes. But she wasn't pretty. A thin scar ran down her cheekbone, and she wore a chilling expression on her otherwise perfect face. "What did you say?" she rasped. The accent was strange, almost unrecognisable.

Thumbs puffed himself up, clenching his little fists around reassuring handfuls of his grubby velvet doublet.

"Now look here," he accused sternly. "You're no scoundrel!"

"I am so pleased you think so," said the green-eyed woman.

"I mean you're no *professional* scoundrel!" insisted Thumbs, losing his temper and forgetting to be either apprehensive or urbanely sophisticated. "You got no right to thieve around here!"

"Thieve?" she repeated, barely concealing her distaste. "What are you talking about?"

"You stole that sword from Smith the smith's smithy in Smithy Street just now!" yelled Thumbs, shaking a fist. "I saw you. And you're not a local profit-scoundrel! Leonardes is gonna want to have *words* with you!"

"This sword?" said the woman, regarding the steel weapon in her right hand and professing surprise. "I stole this sword?" In a flash of movement she had sliced the blade through the air with a nasty *snicking* sound and shoved Thumbs up against a handy brick wall. Her purple sleeves billowed in a sudden breeze along the alley. "Listen to me, you little man. I do not care about your human rules and regulations. I am in this city for one reason only, and then I will be gone."

Thumbs was terrified. "Who—who are you?" he managed to croak.

The woman tilted her head, ruffling her tawny blonde hair with a free hand. "You ask dangerous questions," she said. "Are you so tired of living?" Her eyes gleamed greenly in the shadows of the alley, and she lowered her sword. "My name is Sparrow."

As she released him and stalked off in the direction of the Brewer's Pavilion, Thumbs felt his knees dissolve under him with relief. She hadn't killed him. That was a good sign. "Hang on a minute," he said aloud. "What did she mean, *human* rules and regulations?"

-§-§-§-§-§-

Mistress Opia was pouring a steaming cup of lemonade for the Soothsayer. "Don't you see? Gold is the most malleable substance in the cosmos—why shouldn't it be used to control time?"

"Humph," said the Soothsayer, a garishly old woman wrapped in white rags and daubed with arcane symbols. "Beware the Eyes of Marshmallows," she added, stirring her hot lemonade with a biscuit.

Mistress Opia's lips thinned slightly. Biscuits were for eating, not for dunking in drinks. "And what is that supposed to mean?"

"I mean," said the Soothsayer with surprising clarity, "Don't meddle in what you don't understand."

"But I *do* understand it," insisted Mistress Opia, putting the teapot down with some force. "That's what I've been trying to tell you for the last half hour. I will be able to control time. Do you have any idea how valuable that will be? This goes beyond alchemical brewing. There is nothing I could not do!"

"Liquid gold," muttered the Soothsayer disparagingly. "Can't see any future in it. Now, *black*, black goes with everything…"

-§-§-§-§-§-

Getting into the Brewer's Pavilion was not the difficult part. Sparrow just walked through the canvas door and asked to see someone in charge. At first she got an adolescent apprentice who smiled in a hopeful sort of way and tried to look down her breastplate. "Not you," she said harshly. "Someone more senior."

Someone 'more senior' turned out to be Elder Grackling, who peered at her through crooked spectacles and talked about the weather for a shaky few minutes.

"Not you," snapped Sparrow. "Someone who is not completely useless." Out of the corner of her eye, she saw the ragged soothsayer in the corner start to haul her way out of a battered old rocking chair, but Mistress Opia came out of the darkroom just in time to avert *that* particular catastrophe.

Mistress Opia looked competent in a sturdy, matronly way. She was small, round and had a faintly distracted smile as if she had sniffed the chemicals once too often. She wore a starched white laboratory coat with flowers embroidered on the pockets, but nevertheless appeared what she was doing. "Can I help you?"

Sparrow pulled out a leather pouch, dropping it on the counter. "This is troll thunderdust," she announced.

The Brewmistress took a cautious step backwards. "We've never needed a regular supplier for this particular substance," she said casually. "There isn't much call for it around here, you know." Out of the corner of her eye, she saw Hobbs the gnome rubbing his hands together as he considered the possibilities of the retail value of thunderdust.

"You surprise me," said Sparrow. "Perhaps you would be more interested in a supplier of copha-dust, yes?" She pulled a second pouch out and tossed it on the counter.

Mistress Opia's eyes widened. "Now, that we can use!" Copha-dust was one of those valuable substances that had been inadvertently discovered by trolls banging rocks together. "We'll take as much as you can supply," she added, trying not to sound too eager. Copha-dust was as rare as hen's teeth—rarer, in fact, since the latest crop of Skullcap mutations had affected the local poultry farms in a *very* disturbing manner.

"Good," said Sparrow. "I also hear that you have an interest in the study of Time. Is that so?"

Mistress Opia was taken aback. Her eyes betrayed her, sliding automatically to the secret substances cupboard before she wrenched them back to focus on her customer. "Possibly..."

Unsmiling, Sparrow produced a third leather pouch. She pulled out a small gelatin capsule which contained a sinister orange-green powder. "When released into the air, this powder gives the impression of stopping time.

It freezes people within a limited area for up to an hour. Unless you take the antidote beforehand," she added as an afterthought.

Mistress Opia relaxed. It was a simple conjuring trick, nothing to threaten her own delicate research. "I don't think we're interested," she said politely. "But as for the copha-dust..." She broke off in mid-sentence.

Sparrow checked the capsule she had just cracked between her teeth. The orange powder had already dissipated into the immediate atmosphere. Mistress Opia, the old man, the gnome, the apprentice and the Soothsayer were all frozen rigid. Sparrow nodded in satisfaction.

She moved swiftly now, heading towards the cupboard to which Mistress Opia had indicated with her eyes. A few swift flicks opened the sophisticated lock.

The vial was warm to the touch. Sparrow took it down carefully, examining it from every angle. The golden liquid bubbled globulously. "Liquid gold," rasped Sparrow approvingly, in her native tongue. "How appropriate."

She wrapped the vial in leather, concealing it on her person. Then she turned to make her exit.

A uniformed Blackguard who had popped in to fetch some things for his mother barred her escape route. He stared at the frozen figures of Mistress Opia and her associates with a vague sort of horror. "I'm pretty sure this is a crime, you know," he accused.

Sparrow darted in his direction, bypassed his standard-issue cutlass and grabbed him by the tunic collar. Her kiss took him entirely by surprise. His eyes glazed over and closed. She released her hold on his tunic and was out into the street and away before the Blackguard's unconscious body even hit the ground.

In a nearby alley, she crooked her finger at a little bobbing bird and called it to her. It hopped on to her finger, extra friendly because of the copha-dust. For some reason, sparrows had a thing for chocolate. Sparrow scribbled a quick message on a scrap of parchment and tied it securely to the bird's leg. Under normal circumstances, using an ordinary bird to send a message across the breadth of the Empire would be a foolish endeavour, but Sparrow had come prepared. She slipped a tiny pellet out of her sleeve and stuck it firmly on to the bird's foot, where it began to glow.

The sparrow suddenly found itself compelled to fly north, and followed its inclinations. The homing pellets were another of those inadvertent troll-discoveries. It was amazing what came out when two rocks were smashed together in the Troll Triangle, and Sparrow had an unlimited supply of such products. Her sleep-inducing lipstick was another favourite.

And now there was no putting it off any longer. She unwrapped the vial, staring at the writhing, metallic contents. She closed her eyes, remembering her instructions, and poured a tiny measure of the liquid into her own mouth, swallowing quickly. It worked by willpower, and she had plenty of that. "Back," she whispered fiercely, willing the potion to work as she had been told it would. "*Back*, a week ago."

Her body was on fire for a split second, fast and slow. Suddenly the landscape was different, hardly at all, but in the right places. She expelled a breath, leaning tiredly against the alley wall. So, this was a week ago. After stretching her tired muscles, which felt as if she had been *running* for that week, she produced another scrap of parchment and wrote the other note. The one which her employer had dictated to her from the one he had himself already received, telling him of the liquid gold's existence. Time travel was already making her head hurt. She signed her professional name, Sparrow, with a flourish, and licked some more copha-dust on to her finger to coax another of her namesakes into carrying the message.

Sparrow watched the little bird fly, then tucked herself back into the folds of her priestess robe. Time to travel north herself. She had to make for that temple where, in a week's time, her armour would be waiting for her. The Brewers would have a fine time following a trail which had been laid before they were robbed.

The Sultan would be grateful. The Sultan had *better* be grateful.

-§-§-§-§-§-

The new Captain of the Dreadnought Blackguards, a bluff red-faced man with a handlebar moustache, strode efficiently through the Brewer's Pavilion. He paused by the side of the Blackguard who had been the first on the scene. "Ah," he said. "Young Hickory, isn't it?"

"McHagrty, sir," corrected the officer, standing to attention. His eyes were still slightly dazed, but he didn't appear to have sustained any permanent injuries.

"That's right," said the Captain. "Timmy McHagrty. Remember you well."

"That was my father, sir," said young McHagrty, saluting.

"Oh," said the Captain. "Let me see. Angus?"

"My brother, sir," said young McHagrty.

The Captain frowned, counting off on his finger. "Let me see. Tam McHagrty, Haymish McHagrty, Owen McHagrty, Roddy McHagrty, Sean McHagrty, Prissilla McHagrty..."

"Brothers, sir."

"What, all of them?"

"Yes, sir. Except for Prissilla, sir. She's my sister, sir."

The Captain gave him a long, slow look. "Finnley?" he said out of the corner of his mouth.

"Yes, sir," said Finnley McHagrty with a small smile of encouragement.

"Right," said the Captain, with a firm nod. "Knew I'd get it in the end. Now, then, let's see about this crime." He turned to the staff of the Brewer's Pavilion, all looking rather uncomfortable after their enforced paralysis. "Right. Can any of you describe what was stolen?"

Mistress Opia stepped forward, patting her tidy hair. "The thief stole a small vial containing of a yellow liquid which has the power to alter civilisation as we know it. I wouldn't worry yourself too much about getting involved. No one crosses a Brewer and gets away with it for long." She smiled her most grandmotherly smile.

"Glad to hear it, madam," said the Captain amiably. "Taking the law into your own hands, eh? Very sensible attitude. Saves time all round. Just to be on the safe side, take young Officer McHagrty with you." He glanced at the young Blackguard. "All right with you, boy?"

Officer Finnley McHagrty thought quickly. What if it wasn't all right? Could he get away with saying his grandmother was ill, or he had a dentist's appointment? "Glad to be of help, sir," his mouth said automatically. *Bugger*. It was spaghetti night at his Ma's tonight and he'd be in dead trouble for skipping it.

When the Captain had marched off in the direction of the nearest tavern, Mistress Opia looked the young Blackguard up and down. "You look like a good, strong lad who can carry things. Think you're up to aiding and abetting a spot of good old fashioned vigilante action, boy?"

"As long as someone else does the paperwork," said Officer McHagrty, saluting smartly.

Chapter 2
Death by Trinket

There was no warning, no dire portent of doom. Kassa Daggersharp did not wake up thinking, "Ah me, my last day of mortal life." As a matter of fact, she woke up with a sheep in her bed, but that was hardly her fault.

It was early. The sunrise had been fairly lacklustre and the morning light was dull, so Kassa was still asleep. Her wild blood-coloured hair spread out on the battered pillow, and her face was half covered by a patchwork bedspread.

Her wide golden eyes flew open. She stared blankly at the ceiling of her cabin. Something was wrong. The ship was moving. She could tell by the way the light from her porthole was making patterns of motion against her wall. The ship shouldn't be moving at all, not first thing in the morning. Not until she, its captain, was awake and fully dressed and in charge of the situation. Someone was undermining her authority...

Something licked her face.

There was a sheep in her bed.

Kassa screamed in outrage, pushing the woolly creature away from her. It baaed pitifully and regarded her with a soulful expression. She hit it between the eyes with her pillow.

Tippett was the first to respond to her scream. Ink-stained and breathless, the little jester-poet burst through her cabin door with his quill at the ready. He was her biographer, and didn't want to miss anything. "What is it?" he squeaked.

Daggar was next, a seedy profit-scoundrel with an unshaven face and wild eyes. "What's wrong? What's happening?" he babbled, already strapping on the life-belt he kept at the ready for occasions such as this. "Do we abandon ship?"

Aragon Silversword appeared at the door to Kassa's cabin, an almost-smile hovering over his mouth as he surveyed the scene with his clear grey eyes. "Something wrong, princess?"

Kassa was livid. "What did I say, Daggar? I said *no pets*!"

"Sorry," said Daggar shamefully. "I told him to stay in the cargo hold, but I think he likes you."

Kassa picked the sheep up bodily and flung it at Daggar. "Why is it on the ship at all?"

"This sheep," said Daggar with something approaching great dignity, "has followed us loyally for four months across mountain ranges, great gullies and a lake!"

"We left it behind at Axgaard!" Kassa snapped. "Don't tell me it caught up again!"

"Well," sniffed Daggar. "I think *some* people should be grateful instead of shouting all the time."

"Not every gang of pirates has a homing sheep for a mascot," commented Aragon Silversword.

"You stay out of this," Kassa flung at him. "And you!" she added to Daggar. "I want that sheep off the ship at the next port. Furthermore, you have all now seen me in my lilac nightgown, which means I am going to have to kill you. Unless you get out of my cabin in three seconds. Two...One."

The door swung closed behind them. Kassa was alone. She fell back onto her bed, scowling angrily to herself. "Mutiny," she muttered. "Bloody mutiny, that's what it is. They're all getting a bit too sure of themselves."

-§-§-§-§-§-

Ten minutes later, Captain Kassa Daggersharp was suitably garbed in her favourite pirating outfit—black suede bodice with bare midriff, scarlet silk skirts, too much silver jewellery and big black boots. Armed with the confident knowledge that she looked damn good, she emerged on deck. "Who gave the order to set sail?" she snapped without even a preliminary greeting.

Aragon Silversword leaned against the mast, not reacting to her tone of voice. If anything, he seemed amused. "If you are serious about going to Chiantrio, we needed to start at first light. Unless you feel that midnight is a suitable time to turn up on the shores of an unfamiliar land mass?" Technically, he was her lieutenant, her liegeman, her partner in crime. In truth, she didn't trust him as far as she could throw him. When it came to challenging her authority, he was a master at it.

Aragon Silversword had spent roughly nine years of his adult life as an Imperial champion, three years imprisoned as an Imperial traitor, and one year as a pirate, give or take the occasional moon. For some reason, it was the traitor bit which stuck in most people's memories.

He was tall and lean, with dark blond hair. He was never pleased to see anyone, and his eldritch-looking sword tended to scare most people away if his personality didn't get there first.

Aragon and Kassa had eventually come to a mutual understanding for their own mental wellbeing—she would resist flirting with him as much as was humanly possible, and in return he would challenge, duel, fight or just generally scare away anyone she wanted, as long as she asked nicely.

"You seem very sure of yourself," she accused.

"Well, now," said Aragon. "It isn't every day that a pirate like me gets to go witch-hunting."

Kassa glared at him. "I hadn't *decided* about Chiantrio!" She had been agonising for months whether she wanted to muddy her already complicated life by adding true witchcraft to her list of career options.

"You have now." His voice was crisp. "This ship has been sailing around in circles for months now, while we waited for you to make up your mind. We took a vote."

"A vote?" cried Kassa, outraged. "Since when did this crew get democratic?"

"We got tired of your delaying tactics," replied Aragon Silversword.

She looked wildly around, but the other crew members were nowhere to be seen. "And this democratic group promptly elected you to be the bearer of bad tidings?" she challenged.

Aragon almost smiled. "They didn't have the nerve to tell you, face to face."

"But you do."

"You don't scare me, Kassa. It is high time you went to Chiantrio and found out once and for all if you can be a Qualified Witch. Then maybe we can get back to..."

"Back to what?" she demanded. "An idle life of lawbreaking and outlawry? What have you got to do which is so much more worthwhile?"

"I have many ambitions," said Aragon coldly. "Most of them involve not being on this ship."

"Oh, you can leave at any time..."

"No, I can't." His grey eyes were suddenly very dark. "You know damn well I can't leave."

She had forced his oath of allegiance, while he happened to be incapacitated by a love spell. Maybe he wouldn't be quite so resentful about being physically bound to her for all time, if she hadn't actually branded him on the chest with her amateur witchmark. Still, it was too late to alter that now.

"You still hate me for it, don't you?" she demanded, her temper easing.

"I don't hate you," Aragon said calmly. "I don't hate anything. I merely prepare for the inevitable."

"And the inevitable is?"

"That one of your damn-fool expeditions will get you killed," he responded tonelessly. "And then I will be free."

Kassa's expression did not change. "It will be that easy?" she remarked, making it a question.

"Oh, yes," promised Aragon Silversword in tones of dry ice. "It will be that easy." he had betrayed her before. When the right opportunity came along, he could do it again.

-§-§-§-§-§-

Daggar Profit-scoundrel was mooching about in the cargo hold, trying to keep out of Kassa's way until she had calmed down a bit. "Witching," he grunted. "Never saw the use of it."

"It's a good way to weave supernatural elements into the story," said Tippett the jester-poet brightly, pausing in the act of composing a particularly deathless couplet. "Always good for pulling a crowd, the supernatural bits."

Daggar pulled a metal comb out of one of his many pockets and started to groom the sheep. "Never mind, Singespitter," he muttered. "She likes you really, I know she does. Go on, then," he said aloud to Tippett. "Read me some poem."

Tippett smiled shyly, adjusted his spectacles and struck an epic pose. "O!" he proclaimed.

"Indigestion?" suggested Daggar sympathetically.

"No," snapped the jester-poet. "O! It's proclaiming talk, it is. It means, hush up and listen."

"I'm listening," said Daggar in a hurt voice. "Go on, then."

Tippett struck another pose. "O!" he said loudly.

The door to the cargo hold opened. "You can both come out now," drawled Aragon Silversword. "She's forgiven you."

"That's our Kassa," said Daggar happily. "Quick to get angry and try to kill you, just as quick to forgive everything and make you a nice cup of tea."

"Go on," said Aragon in a humourless voice. "Ask her to make you a cup of tea. She probably won't cut off *all* your limbs."

"Isn't anyone going to listen to my poem?" asked Tippett plaintively, but the other two had already left. The little jester-poet's shoulders drooped somewhat. "Oh," he sighed.

Singespitter the sheep nudged him with a cold nose, inviting him to continue with the reading.

-§-§-§-§-§-

Later that day, it was Kassa's turn to prepare lunch which meant everyone was making do with dried meat and apples.

Daggar was greenishly seasick. "How far away is this island?" he groaned.

"You voted to go there," said Kassa sweetly, not willing to let any of them forget that in a hurry. She had said little all morning, too occupied with thinking about what would happen when she reached Chiantrio, and resenting that a major life decision had been taken out of her hands.

"I don't see why you can't get your Witchy Qualifications on dry land," Daggar grumbled.

"This is the smoothest ship in the world, Daggar," Kassa reminded him. "It goes *through* the waves, not over and under them. Crossing the ocean is no different to crossing a road or a meadow. This illness is all in your head."

"My stomach, too," he said thickly. "Anyway, you're a celebrity now, what with all that swashbuckling you've been doing lately, and having an Imperial price on your head, and saving the world from the Glimmer last year. People ask you for your autograph all the time, even when you're in the middle of robbing them of their valuables. Why can't this witch come to you?"

"Because that's not the way it works," said Kassa in exasperation. "The godmother witch assigned to me at my birth was Dame Crosselet, and she lives on Chiantrio. I can't just summon her to me, it would be bad manners."

"Not to mention that a message stating our whereabouts could be intercepted by the Lady Emperor," put in Aragon dryly. "She's managed to put quite a law-enforcing gang together in the year or so since she decided that Kassa is public enemy number one. Army, Navy, Blackguards...We would be dead or captured before this godmother witch could even hop on her broomstick."

"Exactly," said Kassa, glaring at Aragon for the interruption. "It's much safer this way, Daggar."

But Daggar wasn't listening. He was too busy emptying his lunch (and most of his breakfast) over the side.

-§-§-§-§-§-

Hours later, a tiny tropical island swam into view in the distance. "Land ho!" shouted Tippett, waving his humorous hat in enthusiasm.

"Bleugh!" replied Daggar, still hanging over the side of the ship and looking green.

"So that's Chiantrio," said Kassa Daggersharp, thoughtfully.

Half a dozen small islands might be vaguely orbiting Mocklore at any given time. Some were fixed to their spot in the ocean; other bobbed around a bit. Of all the most stable islands, Chiantrio was the largest and most colourful. North-west of Zibria (the most northerly city-state in Mocklore), the island was a paradise of sun, sand, colourful flowers and venomous snake pits. From a distance, it looked quite pretty.

Close up, it looked quite dangerous. And pretty.

As the *Silver Splashdance* slid its way through the shallows of the beach and up on to the sand, Kassa Daggersharp pulled on her most dramatic cloak and tidied her wild, blood-coloured hair. "I'll go ashore alone and see if I can find this Dame Crosselet person. Don't wait up."

Aragon raised an eyebrow coldly. "What are we supposed to do meanwhile? I suppose you would like us to do a spot of spring cleaning."

Kassa smiled brightly at him, batting her eyelids. "A marvellous idea. You should have this crate squeaky clean in no time." She blew him a kiss and swung herself overboard, making neat booted imprints on the sand.

Aragon glanced at Tippett and Daggar. "You heard the Captain." He went to fetch himself a deck chair, a foot stool and a very large drink.

In the cargo hold, a sturdy treasure chest began to rattle menacingly.

-§-§-§-§-§-

All the stories and legends about Chiantrio suggested that the isle was far too close for comfort to the OtherRealm—the moonlight dimension, the land of the fey—and that various supernatural creatures such as aelfs, faeries and wyrdings made this their first port of call when cruising the mortal dimension. Looking around the local village, Kassa believed the rumours. Nothing else explained the otherworldly beauty of the local people, or their extraordinary dress sense.

According to a girl with flowers in her hair and a coconut-shell brassiere, Dame Crosselet was to be found in the middle of the rainforest on the far side of the village. Kassa made her way through the spindly green trees and undergrowth, her mood descending a notch every time something dripped on her nose. By the time she reached the gingerbread cottage, she was just about ready to kill something.

It was a gingerbread cottage. A real, sticky, doughy cottage with sugar-glazed windows. As Kassa approached it, she noticed a swarm of flies hovering over the damp, sagging roof. A cloying scent of rotting cake filled the air. Mould was creeping up the walls.

"Hello?" Kassa called, trying to avoid breathing through her nose. "Is anyone there?"

"Don't want any," snapped a crackled old voice. A hunched woman emerged from the gingerbread cottage. If anything, she smelled even worse than her house did. "I've tole you people before," she added in a grumble. "I don't want to buy any of your newfangled crystal balls. I got better things to do than watch some Smug Family. Leave me alone, y'hear?"

"My name is Kassa Daggersharp," said Kassa patiently. "I've come for my training..."

"Bit late, aren't yer?" the old woman said with a sneer.

Kassa smiled faintly. "I couldn't make up my mind, you see. If I wanted to really be a witch." She frowned slightly. "You are Dame Crosselet, aren't you?"

"Reckon I am," said the old woman with a sniff. "You'd better come in. Don't eat the gingerbread, by the way," she added.

Kassa barely restrained a shudder. "I didn't intend to," she said with great conviction.

"Good, cos it's rat-poisoned," said Dame Crosslet.

Kassa stared at her in horror, the last of her childhood illusions falling away like so many autumn leaves. "You *poison* your gingerbread cottage?"

"Keeps out the cockroaches," said the old woman, sniffing again. "An' the fair folk. Slimy little buggers. Can yer cook?"

"I don't usually," said Kassa stiffly. "But under the circumstances I could make an exception." An apprentice witch had to start from the bottom and work her way up. It was traditional. Wasn't it?

"Good," said the old woman. "Come on, then. Yer can start by making me dinner."

-§-§-§-§-§-

It was their first holiday. For the first time in about fifteen moons (give or take a wax or a wane), Kassa was not there to bully her crew into attacking fat merchants or staging dramatic raids on the Lady Emperor's property. For the first time, the outlaws could relax.

"I say we take turns at being Captain," said Daggar lazily, sipping from a tall glass full of brightly-coloured bubbles with a paper umbrella.

"Good idea," said Aragon Silversword with his eyes closed and his feet up. "Why don't you put it to Kassa when she gets back? I'm sure she'll jump at the chance of taking a back seat while you turn this into a jewel-smuggling merchant vessel."

Daggar was a profit-scoundrel by nature, devoted to the gaining of wealth and prosperity by any means possible. Unfortunately, he was a bone-lazy coward by inclination, and could never quite bring himself to risk anything very much. Staying with Kassa meant that someone else made the decisions on a permanent basis. "Have you got any better ideas?" he said.

"Just the one," replied Aragon calmly. "We sail away. Right now."

Daggar's mouth dropped open. "Just leave her here? She'd kill us."

"If she ever caught us."

"But—I couldn't do that to Kassa," said Daggar with something like relief. "She's my cousin!"

"I can't leave," chimed in Tippett, sounding scared at the very idea. "She's my only chance to be a famous poet. I can't write epic poetry without a hero to follow around. Heroine," he corrected himself.

Aragon smiled thinly. "And Kassa thought she only had one sheep on board."

"What's with all this big talk anyway?" added Daggar. "You can't leave any more than we can. Kassa put that witchmark on you to keep you loyal. You can't leave her side, right?"

Aragon stiffened. "I am hardly likely to forget that." In his mind's eye he saw the small spiral-within-a-spiral that Kassa had branded into his chest. It was more than a symbol; he had tested its power too many times. If he deliberately put too much distance between himself and his redheaded captain, it filled his mind and body with unspeakable agony. "One of these days, I might just decide that the pain is worth it."

A chilly silence settled over the crew of the *Silver Splashdance.*

Aragon leaned back in his deckchair, forcing himself to relax. Being obliged to spend most of his time on this ship with this particular crew made his palms itch. The knowledge that he could not walk out at any time made it that much worse.

Deep in the bowels of the ghostly galleon, something went, *scrape scrape kchink.*

Aragon's hand moved swiftly to his transparent silver-steel rapier. "What was that sound?"

"It'll be Singespitter," muttered Daggar sleepily.

"No," said Tippett with a nervous twitch to his voice. He pointed at the sheep who was snoring peaceably on the sunny deck. Its fleece looked vaguely tanned, but no one thought that was worth worrying about.

"Quiet," ordered Aragon Silversword.

Scrape, scrape, kchink kchink.

"Why don't *you* go to investigate," suggested Daggar quickly.

"Why don't we all go?" squeaked Tippett.

"I'll go," said Aragon in disgust, rising to his feet in one swift motion. "If you hear my screams, don't hesitate to hide behind something."

-§-§-§-§-§-

Kassa chopped and sliced and sautéed and generally went about the ordinary, everyday business of putting a meal together. It had been a long time.

Dame Crosselet hovered around, sniffing loudly and getting in the way. The stench of rotting gingerbread overpowered any herbs or spices Kassa could get her hands on.

"Don't do this often, then?" snorted the crone.

"I live with three men and a sheep," said Kassa firmly, stirring the sauce and testing the potatoes. "If I cook one meal, none of them will ever lift a finger again."

"Humgh!" said the crone.

After the cooking of the meal (eaten noisily, but without comment) came the baking of new roof tiles, and after that came the sweeping of the floor. Kassa took about two and a half hours of concentrated domestic servitude before she lost her patience entirely. She faced down the crone, armed with a cobwebby broom, dusty hair and an implacable expression. "Just as a matter of interest, exactly how long am I going to have to behave like an unpaid skivvy before you admit me as an Apprentice Witch?"

The crone sniffed noisily and chewed on something which might have been tobacco, but was probably much more disgusting. "Who said anything about 'prenticing? I just needed some chores done. Not a witch, never said I was. Just cos I got a gingerbread house and I look like something someone stepped in, everyone always goes around making *assumptions* all over the place."

Kassa's mouth fell open. "But—you *are* Dame Crosselet?" she demanded.

"Course," grumbled the crone. "Dame Veedie Crosselet, esteemed baker of," she sniffed loudly, "comestibles."

"But I was looking for Dame *Veekie* Crosselet, the witch!" exclaimed Kassa. Her eyes narrowed suspiciously. "You knew that!"

"Tough," snarled the crone. "I knew 'er. Lived down the road a bit. No relation, if that's what you're thinkin'. Just a coincidence. Oh, an' she's dead."

Kassa felt faint. "But she can't be! She hasn't taught me to be a witch yet. Her name was set out for me at birth—no one else can officially initiate me into the Craft!"

"Hmm," said Dame Veedie, unimpressed. "Like I said. You took yer own sweet time about getting here. I remember her yappin' about it. You were due when you were sweet sixteen, thereabouts."

"But..." protested Kassa, and then realised that she had nothing to say. There really was no excuse. "I hadn't made up my mind," she finished lamely.

"Too late now, innit?" said Dame Veedie the baker, cackling. She spat deliberately into a tin cup. "Bog orf. I don't want you. Bloody young generation, all 'I want, I want!' No commitment. Well, you can't have what you want, missy. So there. Get lorst."

Kassa's beautiful golden eyes went very sharp and angry-looking. Her mouth reddened, and her eyebrows twitched. "I'll show you, crone!" she growled. "When I'm the best witch there's ever been, I'll come back and burn your rotten, smelly old gingerbread cottage to the ground!"

She stormed away, slamming the gingerbread door behind her.

Through a cloudy window of glazed sugar, Dame Veedie Crosselet watched Kassa stalk away. "*Smelly*?" she demanded in righteous indignation.

-§-§-§-§-§-

Aragon Silversword went down into the cargo hold. His whole body was on the alert, ready for anything. His transparent sword swept the empty space before him, and his cold grey eyes scanned the area for any anomaly.

In the dim light of the underbelly of the *Silver Splashdance*, something went *scrape scrape kchink kchink kchink*.

The noise was coming from the wooden sea chest in which Kassa kept all her spare jewellery. For someone who claimed to travel light, she had managed to acquire a huge quantity of spangles and baubles. No matter how many lobe-rings, toe-rings, bangles and bracelets she managed to wear at any given time, there was always enough left over to fill a good-sized sea chest. It was all in silver, her favourite metal—highest quality, of course.

A noise behind him warned Aragon. He spun and lunged, only just managing to prevent himself from skewering Daggar and Tippett together. "What do you want?" he demanded.

"We were just wondering what was going on," said Daggar, grinning uneasily.

"You may as well make yourself useful," said Aragon, lowering his sword. He indicated Kassa's sea chest. "Are you any good at locks? I think there's something alive in there."

Scrape, scrape, scrape. Kchink kchink kchink-chink.

Daggar automatically put his hands behind his back. "Me? Couldn't open a lock to save my life." He sounded almost believable.

Aragon raised his eyebrows slightly, and then glanced at Tippett. "What about you?"

The little jester-poet sighed. Somehow, the dirty jobs always made it down to him, the lowest on the pecking order. "It belongs to Kassa, doesn't it?" he said cautiously. "Won't it be booby-trapped?"

"Almost certainly," replied Aragon Silversword.

Tippett the jester took a deep breath and went forward to examine the sea chest, which had begun to shake wildly.

Scrape, scrape, kchink kchink, rattle-attle-attle.

-§-§-§-§-§-

On an alternate plane of reality Destiny was sulking, which meant that throughout the Empire, babies were being born who would grow up to be devastatingly normal: neither heroes, Emperors or damsels in distress.

"I *am* playing by the rules," chided Lady Luck, rattling her gemstone dice.

"Sabotage, that's what it is!" insisted her sister goddess, chewing a lock of rather ratty green hair.

"Oh, absolutely."

"Well, I like Kassa Daggersharp. She had all sorts of bright skeins to her future. I only lost my temper with her once..."

"And passed her along to me," said Lady Luck in her cool, aristocratic voice. "Now bite your tongue, watch and learn." She rolled the dice, which spun and danced and finally settled on a firm score of double-six.

"There!" said Destiny triumphantly. "You said you were playing by the rules. You *have* to give them good luck now, lots and lots of good luck!"

"Absolutely," agreed Lady Luck. "I don't cheat, my dear. Particularly not when I make up the rules. By an extraordinary stroke of luck, the lock they are so intrigued with will miraculously spring open, and the traitor, profit-scoundrel, jester and sheep will all survive the encounter with whatever is inside." And she smiled her nasty smile, flashing her bright white teeth triumphantly.

-§-§-§-§-§-

Tippett fell backwards as the lock sprang miraculously open. Something *zinged* out, bouncing off the walls and chittering in an angry burble.

"The sacred bauble of Chiantrio!" they all yelled in unison.

The bauble had been a prized possession of the Lady Emperor, before it had taken a fancy to Aragon Silversword and been passed hastily over to Kassa Daggersharp, who kept it in her bodice for a while. But time had passed and in the way of all cute new possessions, the bauble had found its way to the store of discarded spangles and abandoned glittering things. It didn't seem too pleased about it.

"Duck!" screeched Daggar, throwing himself flat on his face. The bauble skidded over his head, *zing*ing its way out of the cargo hold.

"When even the jewellery gets cabin fever, you know everyone's been working too hard," said Aragon caustically.

"Shouldn't we stop it?" suggested Tippett in a small voice.

"Good plan," agreed Daggar. "If you don't mind, I think I'll put some armour on first. That little blighter could put a hole in your head without blinking!"

Aragon lunged for the bauble and it *zipped* away from under his sword, bouncing madly off the silvery mast and finally *zinging* away from the ship.

"Good riddance!" Daggar shouted after it, breathing hard and clanking slightly from all the armour he had put on in a hurry—most of it was on backwards.

Then they saw who was standing at the edge of the beach path.

-§-§-§-§-§-

Kassa stalked back through the island paradise of Chiantrio with murder on her mind. Hobbling slightly, as her efforts to seriously wound a tree in her path had resulted in a broken boot-heel, she couldn't help noticing that something had changed.

The flower-bedecked women of Chiantrio were no longer lounging in the shade, looking attractive and nibbling on tropical fruit. The beautiful men of the island were no longer oiling their muscles and picking fights with each other.

Gathered together in the central oasis, they all wrapped their heads with translucent cloth, chanting loudly.

Kassa stopped a cloth-wrapped girl with a lantern and a ceremonial paw-paw. "What's going on?"

The girl looked at her with a hazy expression which suggested she had been smoking the paw-paw rather than just eating it. "Our sacred icon is returning," she said dreamily, swaying slightly. "It has returned to Chiantrio."

This didn't sound like it had anything to do with Kassa, so she let the girl go about her business and headed off down the beach path, muttering to herself. What with one thing and another, it had not been a good day.

The silver ghost-ship came into view, perched haphazardly on the sand. Kassa squinted against the dying sun. Her crew appeared to be dashing madly around on deck, even the usually cool and collected Aragon Silversword. They were all armed with swords, tennis rackets and what looked like giant butterfly nets. Odd.

Kassa opened her mouth, preparing to hail the ship and give them all a piece of her mind. Was this what they called spring cleaning? Suddenly, she saw something coming towards her at a super turn of speed. Something small. And everyone was shouting…

It could have been deliberate, some kind of punishment for inadvertently locking the sacred bauble in a chest of forgotten knick-knacks. Or it could have been an entirely random act. Either way, the sacred bauble zinged straight through Kassa Daggersharp's chest like hot butter as it sped towards its temple and the people waiting to worship it.

Kassa Daggersharp gasped, swayed and fell. Ignoring the immutable laws of physics, Aragon Silversword was there in time to catch her. He lowered her to the ground, very slowly.

Daggar and Tippett caught up, breathing hard. "Is she all right?" Daggar demanded anxiously.

Aragon was looking for a wound, some mark of the sacred bauble's passage, but he couldn't see anything. "You're fine," he assured her, ignoring the unexpected sensation of relief. "You're not hurt."

Kassa coughed, almost laughing at him. "Oh, it hurts," she assured him. "Trust me on this one."

"What can we do?" demanded Daggar, awaiting orders as always.

For no reason that he could immediately fathom, Aragon felt for Kassa's hand and gripped it firmly. "It's all right," he muttered. "We're here."

And this time Kassa Daggersharp really did laugh, the familiar throaty chuckle barely escaping her lips. "Is that supposed to make me feel better?" she challenged, and closed her eyes.

A very long time passed, and she didn't open them again.

"Well?" demanded Daggar hoarsely. "What's wrong?"

"She's dead," said Aragon shortly.

Daggar half-smiled, as if he couldn't believe it. "What?"

"Dead," Aragon repeated, clearly.

"Not—*dead* dead?" persisted Daggar.

"Dead," said Aragon for a third time, and to prove it he let go of Kassa and walked away across the sand.

Daggar looked down at the body of his cousin. "She won't like that," he predicted sombrely.

Chapter 3
Thunderdust

Sparrow was dreaming of gold. She ploughed waist-deep through the stuff, forcing her body onwards through the firm, globulous mass. It swamped around her, pulling her down and pushing her back. It clung to her skin, warm and supple. Golden waves crashed against her legs, golden arms reached up to catch hold of her.

Under the surface, everything was thick and liquid and amber. Sparrow swam, her hair surrounding her like a wide cloak. She saw fire in the gold, and snow, and pirates. She saw a red-haired woman, and took an instant dislike to her. In the final, frivolous moments before the gold filled her mouth and choked her lungs, Sparrow thought she heard a chorus of tiny laughing voices.

And then she woke up with her mouth full of dirt, a major disadvantage of sleeping on the ground. Still, she would sleep surrounded by stone tonight. Every step took her closer to familiar territory. Crossing the Skullcaps had been uncomfortable to say the least—that territory was so clogged up with residual magic that it was difficult even to sneeze without creating some strange and mysterious new species.

After checking that the leather-wrapped vial was still safely stowed in her boot, Sparrow started walking. She had caught up to her own time, but somehow the liquid gold was still a part of her. She couldn't stop thinking about it, resisting the urge to unwrap the vial and look at it again, even to taste it.

This was no different to any other kind of valuable cargo. She was not immune to greed. But she had the willpower to deal with this. Nothing would stop her handing it over to the Sultan, intact. After all, her reward would be well worth it. Freedom was priceless…

She didn't notice the dandelion-like flowers which sprung up wherever her feet trod. Neither did she notice the tiny spores which lifted with the breeze and swirled upwards, beyond the mortal sphere.

-§-§-§-§-§-

Aragon Silversword watched impassively as Daggar and Tippett brought Kassa's body, heavily bundled in blankets, on to the deck of the *Silver Splashdance*. "What *do* you think you are doing?"

"We're going to bury her at sea," said Daggar fiercely. "When we get out deep enough. Any objections?"

"Do what you like," replied Aragon Silversword, not sounding as if he cared one way or the other.

Daggar and Tippett exchanged glances. "You mean—you're not going to be Captain now?" said Tippett timidly.

This seemed to genuinely amuse Aragon. "Would you *want* me to?"

They both looked perplexed. Horrible though a life under the tyrannical hand of Aragon Silversword might be, it seemed a lot less trouble than being left to their own devices. "Well…" started Daggar.

Aragon cut him off with a dismissive gesture. "As soon as we reach the mainland, I'm on my own. You would only slow me down." He turned on his heel and went below decks, where he locked himself into the Captain's cabin.

Daggar trudged morosely to the wheel, and gave it a half-hearted spin. Sailing skills weren't really necessary for this ship, which pretty much did what it was told. "Go on, then," he ordered. "Open sea. Head back to Mocklore. Whatever."

The ghost-ship seemed to sigh, and glided away, over and through the shallow reef of the island.

Tippett the little jester was standing sadly by the railing, slurping lukewarm tea from a thermos flask. "I suppose I'll have to finish the ballad now."

"Not much point in stringing it out," agreed Daggar. He had a small flask of salt-whisky under his belt, but didn't fancy it much.

"What do you think happens—you know."

"After death?" replied Daggar. "Ah, the usual. Imps. Black robes. That sort of thing."

"My mum always told me that there were mermaids," said Tippett staunchly. "And butternut pancakes, and big monsters made out of jelly."

"Ah," said Daggar. "How old were you, exactly?"

"About six. An imaginative lady, my mum."

"She must have been." Daggar yawned, and stared up at the twinkling stars that were just starting to emerge in the evening sky. "I reckon that everyone ends up somewhere different. You know, somewhere suited for them."

Tippett thought that over carefully. "So there's an afterlife exactly suited for Kassa?"

"I'd say so." Daggar reflected on the subject a little longer. "Probably got crocodiles in it. And dress shops."

Tippett nodded. "At least there aren't any gods in the Underworld. All the legends agree on that. Kassa never really got on well with gods, did she?"

"Oh, I don't know. She's manipulated a few in her time." Daggar leaned heavily against the ship's wheel. "So if gods aren't allowed in the Underworld, who runs the place, then?"

Tippett dredged up a rare bit of humour as he slurped the last drops of tea from his flask. "Prob'ly Kassa, by now."

-§-§-§-§-§-

The little sisters of the Evangelical Turnip were an obscure order, devoted to one of the many gods who had been brushed under the carpet when a previous Emperor had decimalised the religious structure of Mocklore. The sisters were famous for their incredible cooking skills and high levels of gullibility, so that anyone in anything remotely resembling a priestly robe could claim endless hospitality and free meals without paying for the privilege.

It was late when Sparrow let herself into the temple, and made her way unchallenged to the little courtyard where she had arranged to have her armour hidden by one of the Sultan's lackeys. She pulled the leather satchel out from behind a clump of potted trees and checked the contents briefly. All was in order.

She had run out of time. The week had passed as she made her way north, and the Brewers would be coming after her soon.

A little sister in an embroidered cassock popped her head into the courtyard. "Ah, Sister Stranger. We are all going on a picnic, will you join us?"

Sparrow straightened. "Picnic?" she replied blankly. Just when she thought she understood the Mocklorn language, a new word always turned up to perplex her. Of course, the Sultan had taken to making up words on the spot in order to make her feel inferior, and so she was always suspicious about new additions to her vocabulary.

"Just for fun," explained the cassocked sister. We're going to take our lunch and eat it in the woods."

"Ah," said Sparrow, filing the strange custom in her head for future reference. "What if it rains?"

"That's half the fun!" declared the sister gaily. "It always rains!"

"I believe I will forego the fun," said Sparrow. "Will all the other sisters be going with you?"

"Oh, yes! Do come along if you change your mind." The little sister scurried away.

Sparrow pulled out her pouch of troll thunderdust and tossed it grimly from hand to hand. The strange customs of the little sisters made her plan so much easier to execute.

As she walked out of the courtyard, tiny bunches of yellow flowers began to push their way up from between the cobbles.

-§-§-§-§-§-

Sometime the next morning, the ghostly *Silver Splashdance* glided along an anonymous beach on the mainland of Mocklore.

Tippett was down in the hold, sniffing loudly as he completed his first significant work: *The Significant and Informative Ballad of Kassa Daggersharp, a Pirate Queen who almost destroyed Mocklore twice, came to Blows with the Lady Emperor (who she was at School with, apparently) and Rampaged around the Empire in a Ghost-Ship made of Silver before coming to an Unfortunate End for No Apparent Reason (and was quite Nice really, when you got to know her).*

He thought the title needed some work. It wasn't nearly elaborate enough for Big Time theatrics, but it would do for now. Tippett blew his nose loudly, and rewrote the last few couplets.

Up on deck, Aragon hauled his bag over the side. There wasn't much, just a spare cloak and a few odds and ends of treasure he had picked up on the various pirate rampages Kassa had dragged them through. He gave his sword a final polish, and called out for the ship to stop.

The *Silver Splashdance* slowed and halted in mid-glide. The translucent silver hull sank slowly into the sand. "This is where I get off," said Aragon Silversword.

"So who gets the ship?" Daggar asked in a miserable sort of voice, shoving his hands in deep, patched pockets.

"Keep it," said Aragon. "You never know when—" He stopped himself from whatever he had been about to say. "I don't need it. I don't need anything." He swung his legs over the railing and stepped down on to the sand. With one swift movement, he tossed his bag over a shoulder and walked away without looking back.

Daggar went to pack his own bags. It took longer than it had Aragon, as there were hundreds of valuable little items Daggar had squirrelled away, and most of them were really hard to find. Eventually, it was time for him to tip his own laden sack over the side of the *Silver Splashdance* and jump down to the sand. He clapped his hands in the way that Kassa had taught him, to turn the ghost-ship back into a silver charm which could be tied around the neck or put into a handy pocket.

A few moments later, he turned it back into a ship so that Tippett and Singespitter could get out.

Singespitter baaed pitifully, and Daggar made a last-minute decision to take the sheep with him. He picked up his treasure sack, the ghost-ship (changed back into a silver thingummy again) and the sheep. Then he walked dolefully off into the morning.

Tippett the jester sat cross-legged in the sand, finishing off his ballad with a few calligraphed swirls. He waggled the inky parchment around until it dried properly, and considered his next major life-decision.

Daggar's bootprints marched off in the opposite direction to those belonging to Aragon. Tippett considered very seriously which of them would make a better main character for his next ballad before, and then he too trotted away from the beach.

And that was that. More or less.

-§-§-§-§-§-

Sparrow moved lithely from room to room, scattering the thunderdust lightly across the floor. The stuff was safe enough, as long as it was kept dry and away from flame. Hopefully the Brewers would follow the trail here, and conclude she had been killed.

She tied a length of waxy string to the statue of the Turnip Goddess, which she had liberally sprinkled with the last of her thunderdust. She would be able to light the fuse from a great distance, and be on her way with no one the wiser.

It was a good plan. It probably would have worked, had she not forgotten about the Sacred Flame in the vestibule.

-§-§-§-§-§-

Daggar had never felt so despondent in his life. Much as he had fought against having to face untold dangers every day of the week (except Saturday, which was for housekeeping and shopping), piracy had given his life direction. A horribly inevitable direction, but direction nonetheless.

What he needed was a good old fashioned swindle to cheer himself up. Something magnificent and bold and just a bit cheeky. Something he could boast about to his grandchildren.

Grandchildren. That was a thought. He was going to have to get around to that someday too. The last serious relationship he'd contemplated was with a woman who regularly threatened to rip bits out of him and eat them slowly—she had eventually dumped him for her husband, who was over two feet taller than Daggar and had talons instead of hands.

Daggar shuddered. On the whole, Grand Larceny was safer than romance any day of the week. Right. Concentrate on the scam at hand.

Further inland, towards the mountains, he could see a cute little stone temple nestled within a grove of spindly trees. Everyone knew that priests were evil and corrupt and not averse to making a quick buck. Daggar strolled towards the little temple, whistling to himself and beginning to put the swindle together in his mind. Ah, yes. This was how it should be.

By the time Daggar neared the temple, he was puffing noisily and in desperate need of a cool drink and a sit down. He had forgotten how insidious these warm spring mornings could be; pleasantly cool one minute and sweatingly hot the next. Also, Singespitter was no lightweight. Daggar dropped the sheep to graze while he caught his breath and tried to figure out which deity this place of worship belonged to. Details like that were the key to a successful swindle.

Three minutes later, the temple exploded. Noisily.

Chapter 4
Black Goes With Everything

Death was a strange sensation. The living were still around, but they seemed insignificant. Kassa tried to keep track of their conversation, but the voices faded away before she could hear them properly. Their bodies seemed insubstantial, colourless. Before long, she could only see them as pastel shadows. She was alone.

Except for the imp. Somehow, whenever she had pictured death, Kassa hadn't expected imps. Oh, everyone knew that there was no actual God of the Underworld and the whole death business had to be organised by *someone*, but she certainly hadn't subscribed to the imp theory. Still, there it was. Undeniably a three-foot imp in a little black suit with a bow tie and a dead flower in its buttonhole.

"So that's it," Kassa said aloud. "That's all I get."

"That's what my chit says," said the imp of darkness, waggling a clipboard at her.

"I expected more time." Time, yes. But time to do what? She couldn't quite remember why it had seemed so important. A strange fuzz clouded her mind, preventing any kind of rational thought.

"That's life," said the imp with a certain degree of sympathy. "And death, o' course. Still, you got to laugh." To prove it, he giggled.

Kassa frowned as he led her towards a tunnel of the dark and winding variety. "Are there many imps in the Underworld?"

"Thousands!"

"Oh, that *will* be fun."

She forced herself to take one last look at the pale shadows of the living. "What about them?" The clouds in her brain were twisting her thoughts into insubstantial puffs of smoke, steering them in one direction only—towards the dark tunnel.

"Not your problem anymore," said the imp. "They'll be along sooner or later. Time just whizzes by down here. You play Ping Pong at all?"

"I don't think so," said Kassa Daggersharp, allowing herself to be led.

"You'll learn. Oh, and you can pick up a brochure at the front desk. Explains everything. Meaning of death, that sort of thing."

"Right," said Kassa with little interest.

"There isn't any, o' course."

Kassa narrowed her eyes. "Isn't any what?"

"Meaning of death. Don't think of it as the Afterlife. Think of it as a holiday camp for the terminally depressed." The imp giggled frantically.

Kassa wondered if it was possible to go quietly mad *after* death. "Do all the imps have your sense of humour?"

"Most of 'em. Chin up, my lady." The imp grinned suddenly, showing her the full measure of its three rows of sharp little white teeth. "Could be worse, you know."

They stepped into the tunnel, and a breeze of the mortal variety swirled around them, sweeping a substantial dose of tiny golden spores into the Realm of the Dead.

-§-§-§-§-§-

"This is the *Underworld*?" said Kassa incredulously, looking around her new quarters. The chamber was luscious, dripping with silk and flowers. A glistening hot spring bubbled up through the middle of the floor, and the bed...the bed was a dreamy concoction of puffed-white pillows and sugar-spun lace. Rose petals were scattered everywhere in various arcane patterns, and their intoxicating scent filled the room.

"Like it or lump it," said the imp. "Everyone gets the same."

Kassa weakly slapped a plump cushion. "And you really expect me to stay here for the rest of eternity?"

"*Course* not," said the imp. "This is just the waiting zone. The Underworld isn't actually the Afterlife, if you follow me."

"I don't think I am following you."

The imp sighed, and tried to explain it to her. "Look, we can't be expected to look after *everyone* down here. It's roomy, but not infinite, if you know what I mean. So this is where you dead fellers are supposed to hang around till you decide what to do next."

"Next?" said Kassa. "But I'm dead!"

"So?" said the imp. "Not the end of the world, is it? I can get you the reincarnation catalogue. It means wipin' out your memories and startin' again, so most people don't pick it straightaway. Generally takes a couple of weeks till they decide to go for that one. Course, there are other alternatives." He peered at her intently. "Don't play the harp, do you?"

"Just the harmonica. And the fiddle, on a good day."

"Well, that's *that* option out...there's always the Valholler suite upstairs, but they're a bit rowdy. Is anything wrong?"

"This all sounds a bit haphazard," Kassa declared, getting to her feet and preparing for action. "Who's in charge around here, anyway?"

The imp glanced furtively in every direction except directly at Kassa.

"The Boss," Kassa elaborated. "The Chief, the Big Pineapple. Whatever you call him. Or her." She spaced out the words carefully. "Take-me-to-your-leader."

The imp opened his mouth confidently, as if he was about to say something of great importance. Then he ran away.

-§-§-§-§-§-

Kassa lay on the luxurious bed, staring at the ceiling. She had never thought of death as being like a hotel with no people in it. She didn't feel dead, that was the problem. She was just bored. Her brain was full of fluff. Every time she tried to think about something seriously related to her old life, her mind slid away from the topic.

Just as she approached a state of total docility, a little orange person in a lime-green flared suit with sequins, platform shoes and small pink sunglasses fell in through the ceiling.

Kassa sat up, blinking. "Who the hell are you?"

He stood up and struck a pose. "I'm, like, your guardian sprite," he announced with a flourish, as if expecting applause.

"I don't think so," Kassa said darkly. "I already have a guardian sprite. She's an annoying blonde with a big mouth. Summer Songstrel."

"Dig it," agreed her new companion. "Right on. She's been, like, promoted. Y'know."

Kassa raised an eyebrow. "They *promoted* her?"

"Suuuure," said the little orange sprite, nodding with a vague smile. "To Personnel. She, like, assigned me to you. Babe."

"I knew she held a grudge," sighed Kassa. "And will you stop talking like that?"

"Sorry, I thought it sort of went with the outfit."

"Not even that outfit would go with that outfit. What's you name, ayway?"

"Vervain," said the sprite, looking dejected. "Vervain G. Merryweather. And what's wrong with my outfit?"

Kassa sighed and buried her face in her hands. After a moment, she became aware of Vervain's face pressed up close to hers. "By the way," he whispered. "Are you sure you're supposed to be dead? Because in my portfolio, it says you weren't due to kick the old bucket thing for another—"

"Look," said Kassa fiercely, "I'm here, aren't I? Shut up in a little grey cave in the middle of the Underworld, with nothing but the clothes I stand up in and a sprite with a stupid name! My body is back there on that *beach*!"

"Oh, yes," said Vervain, nodding thoughtfully. "The beach. Don't you think that's rather—"

Whatever he was about to say was swallowed hastily when the door to Kassa's room was flung open. There in the doorway stood a perfectly still and elegant girl. She was thin in a cheekboned, hobgoblinish sort of way, but that was as far as the resemblance went. Her hair was a smooth cascade of black, falling past her waist into nothingness. Her skin was a bright white, practically translucent, and every facial feature had been outlined in charcoal. All in all, she looked in serious need of a good square meal or three. She wore a skin-tight gown of dark velvet and a ribbon around her narrow throat.

"You wish to see the person in charge," she said in a surprisingly sensible voice.

"That's right," said Kassa, eyeing her suspiciously.

"Come on, then." The girl turned with an eerie grace, seeming to arrive from one pose to another without any ungainly movement in between. This was a person who glided rather than walked, and slid into conversations rather than just talking to people. "My name is Trixibelle Cream, daughter of the Watermelon clan, but my friends call me Ebony."

"Of course they do," said Kassa. "Lead on." She glanced back at Vervain, who was staring at the newcomer with blatant adoration. "Are you coming, or what?"

He scrambled to his feet and tugged at her arm insistently. "Do you think I could get away with that look?" he asked in a loud whisper. "I've always had a thing for velvet."

They followed the gliding Ebony through corridor after corridor. "Are you an imp?" Kassa couldn't help asking, although she found it highly unlikely.

Ebony sniffed disdainfully. "Do I look like a boy? I'm a *goth*."

"So imps are boys and goths are girls," said Kassa, her cloudy brain doing porridgy somersaults and threatening to escape from her completely at any given opportunity. "That makes a vague sort of sense. Do you ever..."

"Certainly not," said Ebony with a tinge of horror in her voice. "Horrible little creatures, imps. We may be biologically compatible, but a girl has to have *standards*." She smiled thinly. "Anyway, we prefer human meat."

Kassa couldn't reply to that comment in a normal tone of voice, so she followed the gliding goth in silence. A moment later, she paused to read a large notice which was tacked up on one of the winding stone walls:

FOR THE GENERAL HEALTH AND WELLBEING OF ALL—NO MAGIC, NO BALL GAMES, NO LOOKING OUT OF WINDOWS AND ABSOLUTELY NO PHILOSOPHY.

Kassa turned away from the notice to see Ebony staring at her. "They really mean it," said the goth girl. "If you're thinking about trying to magic your way out of here, forget it."

"I don't think I can do magic without my body," said Kassa. "I was never any good at it at the best of times. But thanks for the tip. Why is philosophy forbidden?"

"Let's just say that it is a redundant craft up here where anything and everything is possible," said Ebony. "It would only upset people if they indulged."

"You said 'up here'," Kassa challenged, trying to collect her thoughts, which were constantly bouncing away from her like horses on a carousel. "Isn't this the *Under*world?"

"Geographically speaking, we are absolutely everywhere, all at the same time," said Ebony with a thin charcoal smile. "Up *and* down. Now, if you want to see the Lord and Master I suggest we hurry. He goes for his Aerobics class at eleven."

Even in her present state of muddled thinking, that sounded very wrong to Kassa. "Aerobics?"

Tippett followed Aragon Silversword's footsteps as far as a small anonymous village, and a tavern with a rusty, faded sign. All thoughts of writing his next ballad immediately fled his little poet's brain. This was a tavern! A place of ale, hot pies and *merry music*.

Although he had never actually been into a tavern in his entire life, Tippett's romantic little mind exulted. He just knew that this was the place to launch his Daggersharp epic. He would be famous and rich and renowned (and Kassa's memory would be kept alive, he reminded himself guiltily) beyond his wildest dreams, which got pretty wild around midnight after a late night cheese sandwich.

Tippett took a deep breath, pushed open the swinging doors and went forth to meet his destiny.

Unfortunately, a rather nasty bar brawl broke out before he even got to declaim the first "O!" He spent the whole afternoon hiding under a table and hoping no one would hit him.

-§-§-§-§-§-

It was a magnificent chamber, tiled in black and white mosaics which portrayed the impossible in several easy steps. Kassa's eyes could hardly take in the elaborate images of staircases going nowhere and inside-out clockwork twisting in every direction. She squeezed her eyes shut.

"That's what I usually do," said a mournful voice. "Gets a bit much, doesn't it? Hang on."

There was a swishing sound. Kassa opened one eye, and then the other. The entire chamber was now swathed in black velvet curtains which mostly concealed the disturbing mosaics. And sitting on a jet-black throne was a tallish man, long-nosed and droopy of features. He was wearing…

"Great dress!" said Vervain enthusiastically.

"It's a robe, you little insect," snapped the long-nosed man. "It's supposed to symbolise grandeur and dignity."

"It's a very *nice* robe," said Kassa, for wont of something sensible to say. The robe was high-necked and full-skirted, made of black velvet. She couldn't help scanning the room to see if there was a robe-shaped hole in any of the curtains.

"It helps me look the part," the long-nosed man said, not sounding too pleased about it. "I'm forgetting my manners. How do you do, I'm the Dark One."

Something clicked in the back of Kassa's brain. "Hang on a minute," she said accusingly. "You're a god! You're not supposed to be here!"

"I assure you, I am," said the Dark One reproachfully.

"Oh, no you don't!" Kassa declared. "My brains may have turned to porridge since my unfortunate demise, but I know my Comparative Mythology and you, sir, are not supposed to be governing the Underworld." She frowned. "I'm not sure what it is you should be doing, but I do know that there are no gods in the Underworld. Everyone knows that!"

"That's what I tried to tell them," sighed the Dark One. "Nobody ever listens to me."

He explained, and Kassa tried to get her already-fuddled brain around the concept. "You're *temping*?"

"That's right," said the Dark One bitterly. "The King of the Imps had some vital mission, apparently. And who do they think of? Do they send in Amorata, or Wordern, or whatsisname, the Zibrian fellow who keep turning into a shower of gold and seducing women? No. The first one who springs to mind is Muggins here. Good old me. Just because I'm the Lord of Darkness, they assume I must know something about dead people! Not only that, but I can't vote in the God Council for as long as I'm allied with Underworld. Something about compromised neutrality. Hah!"

"So where is the King Imp now?" Kassa asked. Her mind was starting to clear a little, probably the influence of all the black velvet.

"Gone," said the Dark One. "I don't know where. I don't think he's coming back. Why should he bother? I'm stuck with it now. Lord of Darkness, Walker in Shadows, Slayer of the…oh, whatever it is I'm a Slayer of. I've got hundreds of titles like that, you know. All dark and dismal and thoroughly depressing."

Kassa nodded sympathetically and perched on the edge of his throne. "You know what? You don't sound like someone who's very happy with his self-image."

The Dark One laughed hollowly. "My self-image? How could anyone be happy with my self-image? I'm the Harbinger of Horribleness, the Despot of…"

"So change it!"

He broke off and stared at Kassa, his long nose twitching slightly. "Change what?"

"Listen," she said patiently, "All you need is a good propaganda agent. Trust me, I know. Look at the Lady Emperor. She started out as nothing but a calculating courtesan with no interests beyond boys and clothes. Now she rules Mocklore, and is halfway to being taken seriously. Propaganda. That's all it takes."

"You mean it could work for me?" said the Dark One enthusiastically. "I could have a—*new image*?"

"No problem," Kassa promised him. "First of all, we have to do something about your clothes." She leaned forward, whispering conspiratorially. "You know, just because you're called the Dark One, you don't have to wear black all the time."

"I don't?" said the Dark One, his eyes lighting up. It took him a moment to get the hang of it, but eventually he managed something approximating a smile. "I never thought of that!"

"Gods aren't used to new concepts," Kassa agreed sympathetically. "Skeylles—you know, the Fishy Judge, Lord of the Underwater—anyway, he's my godfather, and I've been trying to convince him of the benefits of wearing dolphin-friendly fishing nets for years now. He just can't wrap his head around the idea."

"I could wear—brown," said the Dark One hesitantly.

"Or blue," Kassa said encouragingly. "Even yellow, or crimson. The world is your book of samples. The image always starts with the clothes. Right, Vervain?"

The sprite leaped forward, eager to be of assistance. "Abso-lutely, your Dark Majesty," he babbled. "We'll get you kitted out in no time. Some nice suits, big lapels, bright colours, I can really see you in a lime green and pink ensemble. Then maybe for more casual events, we could get you a twin-set and pearls..."

"Is he serious?" the Dark One interjected with a worried frown.

"Mostly, but we'll work on it," Kassa promised. "We're going to have to work on that 'Dark Majesty' bit, though. You need a nice, unthreatening name."

"Like what?" asked the Dark One.

"Like..." Kassa picked a name at random. "Gerald! Or—Gervaise is very nice at this time of year. Something that's not ostentatious"

"I've always liked the sound of...Glorius the Third," the Dark One suggested tentatively.

"Cool!" Vervain chipped in.

"I can see you're both going to get on just famously," Kassa sighed.

The Dark One and Vervain fell into a deep discussion about the merits of vinyl as opposed to real leather, and whether it was suitable for men to wear silk (Vervain argued furiously that it was, but the Dark One remained unconvinced).

Eventually, Kassa took a deep breath and joined in the conversation. "As we're being so helpful, I was wondering if you could possibly show me if there were any back doors to this place." She smiled hopefully.

The Dark One regarded her suspiciously. "You're dead, aren't you? I can't just let you out. What would the neighbours say?"

Kassa made a face. "I don't actually believe that I'm dead. I certainly don't feel any different to when I was alive—my brain keeps turning into marshmallow, but I'm sure that will pass."

The Dark One sighed. "You'd better look out a window. Maybe that will sort you out." He gestured towards a particular expanse of black velvet. "Over there, fourth curtain from the left."

Kassa looked at him suspiciously. "I thought windows were against the rules."

"They're allowed by prescription."

"Oh. Fair enough." It took quite a while, but Kassa finally wrestled the black velvet out of the way and found herself staring through a panel of something which might in another reality have been called 'glass'.

The Mocklore Empire stretched out like a watercoloured map. The trouble was, it was several metres above her, hundreds of fathoms below her, right up close and a million miles away all at the same time. It was over to the left, under her feet, out of sight and, to complicate matters, everywhere else in a thousand different directions. Kassa struggled with the conflicting images which filled her head, pounding and pounding to make themselves understood.

The porridgy-marshmallow feeling lifted from her brain for an instant, and Kassa understood everything.

She turned to face Vervain and the Dark One, tears streaming out of her luminous golden eyes. "It's true," she said wildly. "I really am dead, aren't I?"

"Never mind," said the Dark One absently. "There, there. Come and explain what this Vervain chap means about pink lycra. It's all rather fascinating, but I can't make head nor tail of it."

-§-§-§-§-§-

It was evening now, and Aragon Silversword had spent the whole day on his own. There was no mad Emperor bursting into his room to demand opinions of his latest fruit salad sculpture, no smelly jailers making faces at him through the bars, no Lady Emperor breathing seductively down his neck, no Kassa bloody Daggersharp trying to mould him into some kind of hero.

There was no Kassa.

He hadn't taken it in yet. He was free, that much was certain. Free of the witchmark she had burned into his chest during a weak moment, sealing his 'loyalty' for all time. Free of her youthful expectations of the man he 'could be' if he started caring about anything other than himself—in other words, if he had a personality bypass.

Aragon sat on the thin, ordinary bed in the room above the tavern. His left hand slowly clenched and unclenched. He was free now, he told himself, free to do what he wanted, free to be his own man for a change. No one's champion, or liegeman. No one's slave.

But he wasn't free. Not in the least. Every time he closed his eyes, an image of golden eyes and tangled red hair filled his mind. "That bloody witchmark of yours," he said aloud in the grubby little room. "It won't even let me forget you now that you're dead." That wasn't in the rules. It wasn't fair. But then again, when had Kassa Daggersharp ever played fair?

"Talking to yourself," noted a voice from the window-ledge. "It's the first sign, you know. I'm not sure what it's a sign *of*, but it certainly can't be good for you."

Aragon stood very still. After a suitable pause, he flicked his eyes in the direction of the window. He wasn't surprised. Why should anything surprise him now? "Hello, Bounty."

His unexpected visitor smiled her sexy smile, and said nothing.

Chapter 5
The Priestess and the Profit-scoundrel

The explosion billowed and crashed and generally exploded. Bits of temple rained everywhere. The spindly trees bent and blistered. Daggar Profit-scoundrel hid himself under his many possessions and waited for the noise and the heat to go away.

Eventually, it did. And all was silent.

Daggar picked himself up, his ears still ringing, and looked around for Singespitter. As was usual in stressful situations, the sheep had sprouted purple wings and was currently flapping his way towards the nearest mountains.

The debris of the temple now cluttered the grassy area in a disorderly fashion. Daggar absently scooped up a piece of statue and picked off the burnt bits. It was a severed finger sculpted in bronze. He tucked it into one of his sacks and headed towards the biggest pile of rubble, peering this way and that in search of a handy bargain or three. If a swindle was out of the question (and he hadn't fully discarded the idea) he certainly wasn't averse to a bit of general profitmongery. There was some good stuff here, even if most of it was lying in pieces and steaming.

Wondering vaguely if it counted as desecration to rob a temple *after* it had been razed to the ground, Daggar tried to lever a nicely rounded statue off the still-smouldering pile of ex-temple without burning his fingers. It was then that he saw the hand.

A slender, female hand pushed its way up out of the rubble, moving tentatively around in the open air. Slowly the fingers felt their way across the top of the debris as if searching for an easy way out.

Due perhaps to his warped lifestyle, Daggar couldn't help thinking that this hand was the most alluring object he had seen in his life. A moment later, he pulled himself together and caught hold of the hand, calling some vague reassurances to whoever it was had been inside the temple when it blew up.

He began his rescue attempt, heaving the larger pieces of masonry and statue to one side (pocketing the smaller, more valuable bits). Finally, he uncovered a mass of tawny-blonde hair, and a young woman's face emerged from beneath the rubble. She was swearing. A long chain of obscenities issued forth from her attractive mouth, and didn't stop until her entire body (clad in a purple priestess's robe) was uncovered and pulled away from the hot stone remains of the destroyed temple.

What really impressed Daggar was that she didn't repeat any of the words.

Finally she fell silent, coughed weakly and sat up. Only then did Daggar realise how extraordinarily attractive she was, despite a harsh expression and a long scar on her face. He could have fallen into her jade-green eyes, and indeed was already hoping that such an opportunity would arise in the near future. He watched in something close to shock as she dragged her slender hands through her long crop of tawny-gold hair, and found himself wondering if the priestesses of this temple were a chaste order. He had heard that such oddities existed in the strange northern wastes of Mocklore.

"Well?" rasped the priestess finally in a strange accent, melodic but entirely unplaceable. "You are going to offer me a drink, yes?"

Daggar automatically drew his best salt-whisky flask from his belt and handed it to her, without shifting his gaze from her jade-green eyes.

She unscrewed the flask, sniffed suspiciously and then handed it back untasted. "Thank you, but I think I will prefer my own." To Daggar's amazement, she reached under her purple robes, drew out a similar flask and took a healthy gulp of the contents. Noticing his reaction, the woman offered him a taste.

Daggar took a cautious swallow from her flask, and gasped as the white-hot liquid clawed its way down his throat. He could still feel it burning as it passed various vital organs on its way down. "Whah—whah—" he choked wildly, waiting for the pain to stop. It didn't. Not for a long time.

"Troll-brandy," she said, not sounding particularly sympathetic. She took back her flask and swigged again before tucking it out of sight. "An acquired taste. Who are you?"

He tested his vocal cords for permanent damage. "Daggar," he managed to say.

"Daggar," she said thoughtfully. "A good name. I am Sparrow. We will travel together for a while, I think. You do not object?"

"I have to find my sheep," Daggar croaked.

She shook back her golden hair. "Very well. First we will find your sheep, and then we will travel together."

Daggar shrugged weakly, and agreed. What choice did he have?

-§-§-§-§-§-

Officer Finnley McHagrty stared at the flying carpet. "Are you sure this is safe?" The Blackguard's manual hadn't mentioned flying in the name of duty.

"We got it from the Hidden Army in exchange for half a barrel of invisible ink," replied Mistress Opia. "And *no one* attempts to palm shoddy goods off on to the Brewers."

A hard edge appeared momentarily in her sweet voice, but it vanished as quickly as it had arrived. "On you get, dear," she said briskly.

"But those things are lethal," McHagrty protested. Flying carpets had been officially classified the most dangerous life-form to have evolved in the Skullcap Mountains, and that was really saying something. This particular flying carpet was a tightly-woven rug the size of his ma's kitchen, sporting pin-striped motifs of the legendary Battle of the Eaglesbog Trenches (with Wildebeests). It lay innocently on the steps of the Brewer's Pavilion, rippling its fringe in a less-than-menacing way.

Mistress Opia loaded her big black bag on to the back of the carpet and climbed on, settling herself and looking at the carpet with a fixed smile as if daring it to do something she wouldn't approve of. "Now you," she said to Finnley. "Look sharp, we haven't got all day. And you, Hobbs. The rest of you can stay here."

The gnome looked outraged. "I can't go adventurin' now! I got stuff to do, profits to make…"

"You're not a profit-scoundrel yet," Mistress Opia reminded him. "But you are a Brewer, young gnome. Besides, did you really think I was going to leave you unsupervised with the cash register?"

Muttering under his breath, the gnome clambered on to the carpet.

"Oh, I say," said Elder Grackling suddenly in his wavery voice. "Can't I come too? I used to be a great explorer, you know."

"You've never been outside Dreadnought in your life," said Mistress Opia firmly. "The Soothsayer is tracking the thief in her Pool of Wonder and the boy has a lot of sweeping to do, so you have to look after the business for me, Dad. Be good." She turned, and fixed Officer Finnley with a sugary smile. "Well? Are you coming, lad?"

Finnley took a deep breath and stepped on to the carpet. To his amazement, it stayed still. Not even a flutter. "Well," he said in vague relief, "I suppose these things *can* be trained...*ahhahhhahahahhghghh*!"

The carpet, sensing the young Blackguard relax slightly, took off from a standing start, whizzing up and over the city of Dreadnought. It was only by clutching at Hobbs the gnome that young McHagrty managed to keep himself from falling off completely.

"She'll be heading for Zibria," stated Mistress Opia, hanging on to her travelling hat which was large, squat and floral in nature.

"How do you know that?" questioned Finnley, his heart sinking. They had to ride this deathtrap all the way to Zibria?

"Humph," she said. "I only know one person who is crazy enough to pull a stunt like this, and that's the Sultan of Zibria. He's been trying to get my attention for years. Hobbs, would you make the tea?"

The gnome, who had not ceased muttering mutinously during the entire trip, now muttered even more as he crawled over to Mistress Opia's big black bag and pulled out a kettle, teapot, several tins of things and a few handfuls of kindling.

Finnley, who had been busy staring with horror at the wildly colourful Skullcap Mountains below, now stared with equal horror as Hobbs the gnome prepared to light a small campfire in one corner of the flying carpet. "Are you sure that's a good idea?" he spluttered.

"You stick to your job, dear, and we'll stick to ours," said Mistress Opia with a click-clack as she pulled her knitting out of her bag and started in on it. "If you're very lucky, I might let you arrest the young lady when I'm finished with her." The flinty look behind her little horn-rimmed spectacles suggested that there would not be much left of the tawny-haired thief afterwards, grandmotherly smile or not.

-§-§-§-§-§-

"That's a sword!" accused Daggar.

"Indeed," said Sparrow. "It is a sword."

Daggar eyed her priestly garments. "Exactly *which* god do you serve?"

Sparrow gave him a hard look in response, and deliberately did not answer the question. "Which way did this sheep of yours run?"

"Fly," Daggar corrected dismally. "That way." He pointed.

"Ah," said Sparrow. "One of *those* sheep." She rummaged through the rubble for a moment and came up with a leather satchel. "Excuse me, while I go behind this tree."

Daggar modestly averted his eyes. There was a series of clinks and clanks. "What's that noise?" he demanded, not quite having the nerve to peek and see for himself.

"My garter belt," she replied dryly, emerging from behind the tree.

Daggar's eyes widened horribly. "You're in armour!" he accused wildly.

"Oh?" she replied, buckling her ornate black leather breastplate and shaking out her long tawny hair. "Am I really? What an extraordinary thing."

Daggar reassessed. She obviously was more dangerous than he had given her credit for. On the one hand, he was perversely attracted to dangerous women, and on the other hand, his survival instincts were telling him to start running. On the third hand, he needed help to track down Singespitter, who could be quite difficult when scared. "That way," he said weakly, pointing towards the trees. Singespitter was barely in sight.

"So," said Sparrow huskily as she and Daggar crept towards their target. "What is it that *you* do?"

Daggar shifted uncomfortably, turning up his collar to keep out the slimy spring drizzle which had descended upon them from the lone cloud in the sky. "I'm sort of a merchant, you see. A bit of this, bit of that…"

"A profit-scoundrel."

"Obviously, yes."

Sparrow did not look impressed. "I met one of your people in Dreadnought. He got very distressed about me stealing a sword without permission." She nodded at the skittish sheep up ahead. "You take it from the left, I will come at it from the right."

"His name's Singespitter," said Daggar, then brightened suddenly. "We're in the same line of business, then!"

"I hardly think so."

"But you said—"

"I steal when it is necessary. I have *not* made a career out of it."

Daggar hadn't realised there was a distinction. "So," he said as they closed in on the sheep. "What *do* you do? You're not a priestess," he added, just to let her know that he wasn't completely stupid.

"Usually I am a mercenary," said Sparrow. She glanced around. "Where have you gone?"

Daggar had vanished from sight. His voice emerged in a strangled little yelp from behind a clump of bushes. "Are you with the Hidden Army?"

"*What*? No, I am not."

"Are you sure? Because some of them would really like to skin me alive and caramelise my innards…"

"I will keep that in mind. There is no need to worry—at least, no more than you can obviously help. I am a free agent." She frowned. "At least, I will be when I have finished this job."

Daggar's dishevelled face slowly appeared from behind the bushes. "There are no free mercenaries in Mocklore," he said suspiciously.

Sparrow smiled thinly. "I intend to be the first." Without warning, her foot lashed out at the nearest tree.

Daggar screamed and ducked back behind the bushes. When he steeled himself to look up, it was to see that the tree had split perfectly and the two halves had fallen in such a way as to block Singespitter the sheep's escape route.

The sheep, his wings tucked out of sight, stood docilely while Sparrow grabbed it by the scruff of the neck. "Next time, I suggest you use a leash."

-§-§-§-§-§-

The Sultan of Zibria was not actually insane, although he *was* the only person who honestly believed that the streets of his city were paved with gold. Quite a bit of the city had been gilded once upon a time, but that was during his father's reign, and most of it had long since worn away.

Lord Marmaduc XV was a spindly young man with black hair, dramatic eyebrows and a habit of sneezing in the presence of beautiful young women. This combined with the fact that any woman daft enough to marry him would have to take the silly title of 'Sultana' meant that he had remained a bachelor.

The only girl whom he had ever formed a deep attachment to was his second cousin Talle (or Toadface to her friends), who had grown from a manipulative little girl with a cute mop of blonde hair into the devastatingly devious Lady Emperor of Mocklore.

Lord Marmaduc kept Talle's picture in his treasury (being noble, he never carried a wallet) and mooned droopily over it when he remembered to, which wasn't very often these days.

He was not supposed to be the Sultan. His father, Lord Marmaduc XIV and his mother, Lady Polynesie of Chiantrio, had produced two brilliantly talented princes. Rodrigo and Xerzes were powerful athletes, ingenious diplomats, talented artists, consummate politicians and handsome bastards. And then there was Marmie, the youngest, who wasn't really good at anything. He spent his childhood indoors, fiddling with his chemistry set and building model ships.

The old Sultan had made the mistake of sending all three of his boys off on a quest when they came of age. It doesn't really matter how brilliant your eldest sons are; the rule of Fate (and storytelling) is that the youngest will prevail. And so it was. Young Marmaduc hadn't actually succeeded in his quest, but Fate had seen to it that his brothers did much worse. Rodrigo was currently a marble statue in the Queen Mother's rock garden, and Xerzes lived above the stables, occasionally flying out and cawing at anyone who came into range.

So Marmaduc XV was the Sultan. He didn't mind really. It didn't matter how bad you were at your job as long as you had enough money to throw at every problem that came along, and the Sultan of Zibria had an awful lot of money (even if he wasn't exactly sure where most of it was).

He was not exactly insane. But some days he came quite close to it.

The very short High Priest of Raglah the Golden entered the Lordling's throne room with a swish of brocade and sequined silk. Raglah the Golden liked his priests to look good. "Eminence," he said loudly, barely preventing himself from tripping over his trailing silk hem, "I have a message from your mobile agent."

"Oh, really?" said Marmaduc, his eyes gleaming. Recent forays into espionage had excited him immensely. He now had three secret agents working within his information network: one in Dreadnought, one in Axgaard and one everywhere else. "Do tell."

The High Priest puffed himself up, obviously resenting being used as a messenger for common spies, but also not one to miss an opportunity. "All hail Raglah the Golden, Father of the Sun and Brother of the Night. To our mighty Lord all hail!"

"I'll write you a cheque for the temple," sighed Marmaduc. "What is the message?"

The High Priest deflated slightly and pulled a strip of parchment from his sleeve. "It reads, Eminence (ahem): *Got the gold. See you soon. Keep your side of the bargain.*"

"Is there anything else?" Marmaduc demanded greedily.

"There appears to be a signature of some kind scrawled at the bottom, Eminence," the High Priest admitted. "The message was winged to you by a sacred ibis, symbol of our mighty Overlord, Raglah the Golden, all glory to his Name."

The Sultan's eyes gleamed maniacally. "Not a *sparrow*?"

The High Priest sighed at this failure to solicit a second donation. "Quite possibly, Eminence, quite possibly."

"So," murmured Marmaduc, Sultan of Zibria, stroking his tapering black beard (which had never really grown in properly). "The little bird comes home to roost. We must prepare for her, priest. Have the dungeons been cleaned recently?"

-§-§-§-§-§-

"This is a stupid, dustsucking sheep," grumbled Sparrow as they walked past the recently-ruined temple. "It could not even run in the right direction. We have lost much valuable travelling time." She was wondering already why she had followed the impulse to take Daggar on as a travelling companion. True, it would make her less conspicuous than if she went on alone to Zibria, but was it worth it?

Singespitter the sheep was now sporting a strap of leather around his neck, attached to a length of rope which Daggar gripped firmly.

"Which is the right direction?" asked Daggar, whose mood had swung from being resigned to spending his time with this evidently dangerous woman, to being eager about the whole enterprise.

"We are going to Zibria," she said matter-of-factly.

Daggar perked up even more. "Zibria, eh? I've never been there. They say the streets are paved with gold."

"Really?" Sparrow replied in a disinterested tone. "In my language, the word for 'gold' is almost indistinguishable from the word meaning 'shit.'"

"Ah," said Daggar. "Still, a new city is always interesting. Things to see, lunches to do, profits to make." He rubbed his hands together. "Is that where you're from, then? Zibria?"

"No, I was born over there." Sparrow waved vaguely to the south, where a crown of rocky, orange mountains loomed. It wasn't home. It hadn't been home for a long time. But it was where her roots were. Someday she would go back…

"But," said Daggar. "That's the Troll Triangle, isn't it?" A nasty, evil-looking collection of plains and peaks inhabited by monstrous creatures, a landscape from which no human traveller ever emerged alive…

"Home sweet home," said Sparrow, the familiar phrase twisted by her remarkably alien accent. She glanced around quickly. "Where have you gone *this* time?"

Daggar's voice emerged, ghost-like, from behind a couple of trees. "You're not a troll," he babbled hopefully. "I've met female trolls, and you're not like them at all."

"No," said Sparrow exasperatedly. "I am not a troll. If you stop hiding behind things, I will promise not to hit you. Is it a deal?"

Daggar emerged. "So you're not a troll?" he said cautiously.

"I was raised by trolls. I am an honorary troll, you might say. This is why I am able drink their brandy without falling over. I was trained well. Now if you do not mind, it is nearly dark and I would like to make camp. Can you cope with that?"

"I think so," said Daggar bravely.

-§-§-§-§-§-

Something fell out of the sky, dropping like a stone through the layers of atmosphere. After a moment, Officer Finnley realised that it was him. "Aaahhh!"

"Oh, shush," said Mistress Opia. "Don't be silly, dear. We're just landing."

"Falling," he corrected wildly. "Falling!"

"Stop being so hysterical," she chided. "I'm sure we'll slow down sooner or later. Take a leaf out of Hobbs' book, he's not behaving like a big ninny."

Gripping on to the carpet fringe, Finnley risked a look at Hobbs. The gnome was indeed very calm, peering over the edge of the plummeting carpet with great interest. "Great view," he muttered finally. "Wonder how you could sell something like that…"

Exactly half a minute before they plunged to their deaths, the carpet twitched slightly and caught an updraught. It skimmed lightly across the grass and stopped, tumbling them all on to the ground.

Officer Finnley jumped up, brushing the dust off his uniform and resolving to go no further. Heroes in epic poetry didn't go through this kind of haphazard stress—all their adventures were carefully choreographed. "This is stupid!" he yelled. "We're on the other side of the Skullcaps. How do you expect this woman to have even *got* this far in a single day?"

"According to the Soothsayer's Pool of Wonder, the woman came this way several days ago," replied Mistress Opia.

Finnley just stared at her. "What's that got to do with anything? That was *before* the theft."

"She stole the extract of Time!" Mistress Opia declared, pushing her little horn-rimmed spectacles further up her nose and popping her knitting back into her big black bag. "She evidently used a drop or two to aid her escape, the silly mitten, going back where she came from before she even arrived in Dreadnought."

"Right," said Officer Finnley, his eyes as dazed as they had been by the lady thief's lipstick. This was his first solo investigation (actually his first investigation of any kind) and it was time he took charge of things. "Right. What we should do then is—"

"Hobbs," barked Mistress Opia. "Start sniffing."

"I beg your pardon?" said Officer Finnley, not sure if he had heard right.

"This is bloody undignified, this is," complained the gnome, getting down on all fours. "I should complain to my union."

"Don't be such a goose," said Mistress Opia. She waggled a stray knitting needle at him. "I need your superior sense of smell."

The gnome crawled around for a while, sniffing noisily. Eventually he got to his feet, brushed off his overalls and came back. "Right smelly forest, this," he commented.

"Well?" Mistress Opia commanded.

"She came this way," he confirmed. "The blonde.

Headin' north. Smells like she was headin' to go round the Troll Triangle and up to Zibria, but I could be wrong."

"Do you know the path she took?" Mistress Opia asked.

The gnome shrugged. "Reckon so, more or less. Somethin's not right, though. She smells sorta...decayed." He produced a handful of pale dandelions. "For some reason, these seem to be growin' wherever she's bin walking lately."

Mistress Opia nodded, her placid face unusually grim. "That's what she gets for using a potion without reading the instructions."

"What do you mean?" asked Officer Finnley, pulling out his notebook. "I thought you said that the substance was a perfectly distilled extract of Time."

"Perfectly distilled it may have been, but ready for consumption it most certainly was not," replied Mistress Opia, settling her floral hat more neatly on her head. "Back on the carpet, my dears. We have work to do."

Finnley and Hobbs resumed their places on the carpet, which flicked its fringe at them impatiently. Mistress Opia followed, settling herself. "Onwards," she said imperiously, and the carpet rose.

"So what will happen to the woman?" asked Officer Finnley. He had no reason to stick up for the tawny-haired thief, but couldn't help remembering that kiss which had sent him into oblivion. "It won't harm her, will it? Using the time essence?"

"It makes no difference," replied Mistress Opia, pulling her knitting out again and flicking her needles into action with a dazzling blur of clicks and purls. "She will not live long enough to regret taking Time without a prescription. Hobbs, get the canary."

Hobbs the gnome looked at Mistress Opia with undisguised horror. "Not the *canary*!"

"Oh, yes," said Mistress Opia with her sweet, grandmotherly smile. "If I've said it once, I've said it a thousand times, my dearies. No one steals from a Brewer and gets away with it."

-§-§-§-§-§-

Daggar emerged from sleep in the manner he usually did, bleary-eyed and still half-snoring. He pulled his heavy eyelids open to see a fully dressed (and armoured) Sparrow staring down at him. "What time is it?" he muttered.

"Past dawn," she said.

Daggar lifted his head and stared up at the sky. "Not by more than a minute!"

"Time we were moving."

Daggar pulled himself slowly to his feet and started lacing up his boots. "So who's following you, then?"

Sparrow raised an eyebrow. "If you think I am being followed, why are you not hiding behind something?"

He yawned, pulling a hand through his rumpled brown hair. "Maybe I'm running out of things to hide behind. Anyway, why else would you team up with me, except to cover your tracks? You want someone to think you vanished back there in that pile of ex-temple." He grinned suddenly. "It was you blew it up, wasn't it?"

Sparrow's mouth was a thin line. She obviously didn't like people guessing her secrets, which made Daggar resolve to do it more often. "If you know trolls, you know all about thunderdust," he elaborated. "My mad cousin Kassa used to come across that stuff all the time…" His voice trailed away, and he looked suddenly very glum.

"What's wrong?"

"Nothing. Anyway, that's why you want me around, isn't it? You're using me to cover your tracks."

"Possibly," she replied in a cool voice. "What is it you want, Daggar? Why are you so willing to go along with this?"

He grinned. "Maybe I felt like some amiable company. I've always had bad taste in travelling companions."

Sparrow shook her hair out of her face and picked up her leather satchel, hauling it over her shoulder. "So we go on to Zibria?"

"Zibria," Daggar agreed. "And then we can see about offloading whatever it is that you're keeping in the second secret compartment behind your breastplate." He smiled innocently at her and picked up Singespitter's leash, leading the way towards the network of canals which in turn led the way to Zibria.

Sparrow stared after him, her jade-green eyes nothing but narrow slits. And then she followed, catching him up easily with her long military stride.

They hiked for several hours—the north west lands of Mocklore were notorious for a lack of anything resembling a road, and the canal-paths were specifically designed to encourage people to travel by boat rather than on foot.

Daggar regarded his walking companion curiously. "Are you all right?"

"I am well," snapped Sparrow. Her stride had not faltered, but her face was looking decidedly yellowish.

"You look a bit peaky, is all," he continued.

Her teeth gritted, she opened her mouth as if to snarl a sharp rebuke at him, and promptly collapsed.

Daggar knelt beside her, and took the opportunity to take hold of her hand. He couldn't help noticing how unnaturally cool her skin was. "What exactly *is* it that you have under that breastplate of yours?" Something in the air seemed funny—not quite right. He couldn't help thinking back to the various magical explosions and misfortunes which he had witnessed in the last year or so. He touched Sparrow's armour briefly, and stared at the soft yellow dust which came off on his hand.

"That is none of your business," snapped Sparrow. "Help me up, or leave me here. Either way, I will answer no questions."

Daggar rocked back on his heels, staring at her. She returned his stare until, no longer quite able to meet his big brown eyes, she turned her head sharply aside, hiding her expression behind a veil of tawny-blonde hair.

No need to tell him that this wasn't the first time this had happened—or that she was just as worried about it. Why should she tell him anything? After a moment, Sparrow straightened her shoulders. "I will stand now," she said curtly. "I must be in Zibria by nightfall."

Daggar extended a hand in a vaguely courtly gesture which was interrupted when his other arm jerked high into the air. Singespitter's wings had unfolded, and only the leash attached to Daggar's wrist had stopped the sheep from flying off into the horizon again. "Oi!" Daggar yelped.

Sparrow drew her sword with a nasty *snick* sound, and pulled herself to her feet.

"He usually only does this at times of severe stress and/or imminent peril!" Daggar yelled at her above the noise of fluttering sheep wings.

"Then danger is coming." Sparrow had already guessed as much. She squinted into the distance. "Dust and *crag*-veins!"

Daggar steeled himself, and then looked. What he saw gave him no cause for alarm. "You mean the bird? That can't be it, Singespitter likes birds."

"Tell me it is a wren," said Sparrow in a voice of unnatural calm. "A small yellow pigeon, yes?"

"Don't be daft," said Daggar. "It's a canary."

Sparrow nodded slowly. "Then we are dead."

-§-§-§-§-§-

Officer Finnley was quite sure by now that they were all completely mad, himself included. "What makes you think this 'death canary' of yours has even half a chance of tracking the girl down?"

"If, as I suspect," replied Mistress Opia coldly, "the *girl*, as you so quaintly describe her, has used the liquid gold without correct safety precautions, she is now a walking time-explosion waiting to happen. She must be giving off vibrations that even an uneducated squirrel could distinguish. My highly trained death canary will be able to recognise, isolate and possibly even annihilate her. Meanwhile, the Soothsayer can track the canary in her Pool of Wonder and give us more explicit directions."

"Ah," said Officer Finnley, sure now that he had spotted the flaw in her plan. "How will she do that, then? We're miles from Dreadnought."

Mistress Opia smiled her sugary smile, and produced a small portable crystal ball from her large black bag. "As you can see, Officer McHagrty," she said calmly. "I have considered every possibility."

-§-§-§-§-§-

The canary zoomed in for the kill.

"Duck!" yelled Sparrow.

"It's just a bird," protested Daggar, throwing himself to the ground anyway. His whole personality was programmed to respond to non-existent threats, no matter what common sense had to say about it. "What harm can it—*ow*!"

The swooping canary neatly clipped his ear as it zipped past his head.

Sparrow lunged at the bird with her sword, gaining its attention. "Have you never heard of death canaries?"

"I refuse to admit that anything as dangerous as you imply could possibly exist without me knowing about it," replied Daggar loftily, throwing himself behind a bush as the canary came in for another swoop.

"They are a Zibrian invention. Assassins." She threw herself to the ground and rolled aside as the canary came at her. "As long as you keep moving, you have a chance. But the minute you stop—"

Singespitter the sheep had managed to slip his leash and was currently flapping his way out of the danger area.

"Can't we just wait for it to tire itself out?' yelled Daggar, dodging another aerial attack by the small bird.

"They do not get tired."

A jet of flame shot past Daggar's right ear, singing his collar and startling him half to death. "What the hell's that?"

"They also breathe fire!"

"Right," said Daggar in a very shaky voice. "I've had enough of this!" He pulled his second-best lucky dagger out from under his tunic and threw it at the approaching canary. As usual when he was absolutely terrified, his aim was true. The knife struck the canary in the centre, pinning it to the nearest tree.

Sparrow stood very still. "Thunderdust!" she gasped.

"A pretty good shot, even if I do say so myself," agreed Daggar proudly.

When Sparrow had finally got her breath back, she said, "You do not cut a death canary. Not under any circumstances!"

"Why not?" he demanded in a wounded voice.

The two halves of the dismembered canary fell to the ground. They began to buzz. Two sharp-beaked yellow canaries rose into the air, and a synchronised twin burst of flame streaked out in Daggar's direction.

"Not fair!" he howled, throwing himself behind yet another bush.

"I am sorry, Daggar," said Sparrow as she pulled an orange capsule out of a pouch on her belt and snapped it firmly between her teeth.

The buzzing sound stopped. The two death canaries hovered in mid air. So too did Singespitter the sheep, whose weight-to-wing ratio meant he couldn't fly very fast.

Sparrow barely paused. She scooped up her leather satchel, sheathed her sword and started walking.

"Aren't you forgetting something?" said Daggar.

Sparrow whirled around, surprise overwhelming her usual harsh expression. "Why are you not frozen?" she demanded.

"I don't know about that, but I do take antidotes to almost everything on a regular basis. You were just going to walk off and leave me!"

"Maybe."

"Now, why would you do a thing like that?" Daggar grabbed his sack and yanked the frozen Singespitter out of midair.

Sparrow glanced back at the canaries. "Let us move while we can." She began to stride, and Daggar soon caught up to her, despite the extra weight of the sheep in his arms.

"I thought you wanted to team up," he accused.

She shot an angry look sidelong at him. "The exploded temple did not stop them. Travelling with you did not stop them. An ordinary tracker might have been confused, but they are not using ordinary techniques. If even half of what I have heard about the Brewers is true, they will not give up on me easily. You will be safer if we part company."

"You mean you think you would make better time on your own," Daggar predicted, quite accurately as it turned out. "I thought..." he paused. "Hang on, did you say the *Brewers*?"

"Yes. I stole something from them, and they want it back."

"You'll never make it," said Daggar in a stunned voice. "I mean, the Brewers. They'll eat you alive and spit you out as chemical equations."

Sparrow stopped in her tracks, impatient. "All the more reason why you should go elsewhere! The canaries will not follow you."

"No fear," he said, shaking his head wildly. "I'm already connected with you. The Brewers will hunt me down, bite off my head and turn my kneecaps into frogs no matter what I do. If I stick with you, at least I have half a chance of you protecting me!"

Sparrow rolled her eyes, tiring of the discussion. She was a mercenary, not a diplomat. "Kiss me, Daggar."

He looked at her in astonishment. "What did you say?"

"Kiss me," she repeated. And then, because her suggestion had obviously left him in a state of shock, she kissed him.

Daggar's state of shock wore off, eventually. He even kissed her back, once he realised that she wasn't going to kill him for taking such a liberty. But then his eyes rolled back in his head, he dropped the frozen sheep and hit the ground snoring.

"So," said Sparrow softly. "You do not have an antidote to everything."

And she continued walking in her long confident stride, over the rough canal path towards the marble columns of Zibria.

Chapter 6
Chainmail, Ale and Deathless Prose

Zibria was a sprawling, haphazard city of pillars, temples, philosophers and scantily clad women. It was also the city where Aragon had spent a large portion of his misspent youth. He had not realised until this moment that this village was so close to the city, but it had to be if Bounty was here. Zibria was *her* territory, which was one of the main reasons he had not been back in a long time.

His unexpected visitor smiled her sexy smile, and said nothing. Framed against the yellowish window of the cheap tavern bedroom, she looked extraordinary. Hobgoblins were renowned for being the most obnoxiously attractive creatures in Mocklore, and Bounty Fenetre was more trouble than most. Unlike common or garden goblins (less than a foot high, hive mind, randomly destructive), hobgoblins were fiercely independent and dangerously self-aware. They were also entirely of human proportions.

Bounty's eyes were wide and deep. Her hair was a rather ratty brown colour, but tangled winsomely down her back. She wore chainmail. Not the usual bulky square-cut mail tunic that your average foot soldier might wear. Her chainmail was body-hugging, impossibly slinky as it slid its way from her curved shoulders down to mid-thigh.

Aragon regarded her slowly, his cool grey eyes taking in every detail. Finally, he spoke. "Doesn't it chafe?"

Bounty Fenetre struck a pose. "It looks good, and it stops me getting shot at." She smiled in sultry fashion, which showed her otherworldly cheekbones to their best advantage. "So, Silversword. Long time, no…" She allowed her eyes to drift deliberately towards the bed. "How have you been?"

Aragon stood up, tiring of her games already. "Go away."

Bounty pouted at his lack of open-armed welcome, and then promptly ignored it. She hitched up her slinky chainmail and sat on the bed, swinging her leather-booted legs in an annoying fashion. "I heard you became an outlaw." It would have been an accusation if not for her teasing voice.

"I heard *you* became a bounty hunter," he replied. "Finally decided to live up to your name?"

She chewed on a lock of ratty brown hair. "Something like that. So who was she?"

Aragon looked up sharply, his eyes giving nothing away. "Who?"

"The *woman*. The one who made you turn to a life of crime."

"I killed an Emperor. Didn't you hear?"

Bounty nodded with a gleam in her eye. "I heard you were still his champion at the time. You're the most famous traitor in the Empire." She dropped a slow wink. "I heard you did the same to the latest Emperor, our Lady Talle herself. Who would have thought a local bint would do so well for herself?" She laughed throatily. "I also heard you singlehandedly got her mistaken for a pirate and imprisoned by the Skullcap Lordling!"

Aragon was in no mood for laughing, and it showed in his face. Catching the sour mood, Bounty frowned curiously. "Did I say something wrong?"

In the following meaningful silence, the sound of a full-scale bar brawl drifted up the stairs.

"It's late," said Aragon curtly, moving across to where his rapier-belt lay slung across a chair. "You can leave any time you like."

"I could take you into custody," she pointed out, winding the nibbled lock of hair around her little finger. "Haven't you seen the posters? There's an Imperial price on your head. I'm quite good at my job, you know."

With a tiny *shikking* sound, Aragon drew his transparent silver-steel rapier and held it unwaveringly with the sharp end pointed directly at her throat. The hand which was not holding the sword was clenched into a tight fist. "Try," he invited.

Bounty licked her lips. "I thought you'd never ask."

Aragon paused. He gestured towards the door with his clenched fist. "Listen to that."

"There's nothing to hear," she said crossly. "Don't change the subject!"

But Aragon was already moving to the door. "The fighting's stopped," he told her, flinging the door wide open.

Bounty Fenetre jumped to her feet and followed him out to the landing. "The punch-ups don't *ever* stop till after midnight," she said disbelievingly.

In the bar below, the brawlers had paused in the act of brawling. Some still held chairs and broken limbs in mid-air. Everyone's attention was focused on the little jester who had finally got up the nerve to climb on a table and declaim his greatest work.

"O!" he declared in a theatrical voice which only squeaked occasionally.

"Sing, bright Goddess, of blood-red hair,
"A pirate bold, a Pirate Queen.
"Sing of those deeds which shook the world
"And chanced to change its colour scheme..."

There was something unrecognisable in Aragon Silversword's cold grey eyes as he listened to the exploits of Kassa Daggersharp unfolding in epic verse. He lowered his sword, and his other hand remained clenched tightly shut.

"So," said Bounty Fenetre at his elbow. "There *was* a woman."

"No," said Aragon shortly. "There wasn't. And anyway, she's dead."

To Bounty's open astonishment, he went back into his room, bolting the door behind him. She put her hands on her hips, expressing her indignation in one expelled, "Well!"

On the other side of the door, Aragon let his rapier fall to the floor. He prised open the fist which had remained clenched the whole time, wincing at the imprints left by his deeply-digging nails.

Lying on his reddened palm was a tiny object, a ring made of silver and steel, marked with a familiar symbol. A spiral within a spiral. It had fallen free when Daggar and Tippett solemnly tossed Kassa's body over the side of the ship. This ring was a symbol of Aragon's enslavement at her hands. She had used this, her witch ring, to brand her mark of loyalty into his chest, a magical ritual which prevented him from leaving her side as long as she lived.

He hated this ring. Detested all that it stood for. And he wasn't letting go of it.

-§-§-§-§-§-

Zibria was a pit. An exotic pit, but a pit nonetheless. The Gilded City was faded, peeling and falling apart. It was early evening, and the pillared streets were filled with flocking crowds, all selling, stealing and chattering at the top of their voices. It was much like Dreadnought on market day (which was every day except every other Sunday) only noisier and dirtier. Everyone wore less clothing, but that was about the only improvement.

There were more 'heroes' in Zibria than in the rest of the city-states of Mocklore put together. Every cheap drinking house or brothel had at least one lion-skinned muscle man on their door. It wasn't compulsory for a hero to have one divine parent, but it certainly was traditional, and no god put himself about as much as Raglah the Golden, the ferret-faced god of Zibria. His favourite method of visiting mortal women was as a shower of gold, although he rang the changes occasionally by taking the shape of an interesting farmyard animal.

Aragon made his way through the throng now, lost in his own thoughts. He had left the grimy tavern in the nameless village early that morning, via the kitchen so as to avoid both Tippett the jester-poet and the seductive Bounty Fenetre. His life was his own, now. Wasn't it?

Glancing at a plate glass window as he walked past, he caught sight of a familiar face, a glimpse of blood-red hair. It couldn't be, could it? He turned, scanning the market place. He was going out of his skull. She was dead—and yet there she was, a deep green cloak, a fall of hair, even the big black boots. Aragon started to move, pushing people out of the way, heading for the fleeing figure, who ducked into an alley. Finally, as he threw himself towards the mouth of the alley and caught sight of her, the woman turned.

She pushed back the dark green hood, the dark red hair, and it all dissolved away, leaving a beige-blonde goddess laughing at him until she, too, vanished into thin air.

Aragon stopped short, and someone crashed into the back of him, nearly knocking him to the ground. He had only time to see a flash of lion skin before he was lifted bodily into the air and pressed into the growling face of an angry hero. "You gotta watch where yer going, mate," snarled his assailant. "You know what happens when someone like you *inconveniences* someone like me?"

"You're not important," said Aragon Silversword tonelessly. "You're not even unique." Without even thinking about it, he had a knife at the hero's jugular and was tapping the blade thoughtfully back and forth. "Tell me quickly, is there a Temple of Luck in this city?"

The lion-skinned thug's eyes were startled. He opened his massive hand, letting Aragon (and the knife) fall harmlessly to the ground. "Yuh," he grunted. "End of the street. Green sign."

"Thank you," said Aragon, brushing his clothes absently and heading off in that direction.

He had seen that goddess before. He remembered lights, explosions, the last Glimmer to devastate Mocklore. They and their flimsy ghost-ship had been caught in the maelstrom, their only hope to throw themselves on the mercy of a god.

Kassa had chosen the Witch's Web, a construct formed of the three most dangerous goddesses ever to exist:

Fate, Destiny and the Other One, the one who was never summoned, no matter how desperate you were. Lady Luck.

Only when Aragon was inside the building did he realise his mistake. This wasn't a temple, it was a gaming house! Tables of people with money to burn were crammed in together, risking coins on the roll of a dice or the spin of a wheel. The women were wearing fur, the men were drinking from goblets with umbrellas in them, and the management were making an awful lot of money.

Aragon didn't want to be here. Firstly because it did not help him achieve his mission (which he was only just beginning to form in his mind) and secondly because it brought a vivid memory of Kassa flooding into his mind.

Just after they had gotten the better of the Lady Emperor and sailed off into the horizon in the *Silver Splashdance*, Kassa had decided that they needed some money. Daggar's hoard of treasure was being rapidly whittled down, and he had taken to weeping or collapsing with shock when any suggested using any more of it.

"A casino's the answer," said Kassa brightly. "Ship, home in on the nearest rich gaming house."

Obediently, the ghost-ship turned and headed towards the little sea-port of Skullcap, beyond the high-peaked mountains.

"Are you mad?" said Aragon acidly. "What good will that do?"

"I did say it was time I figured out this whole witch thing," she reminded him. "Let's see how much compulsion I can put on the Rolling Wheel, or a deck of cards. I'm a wicked Kraken's Curse player even without magic."

It had worked, rather more successfully than Kassa had hoped for. She had inadvertently chosen a gaming table which already had a witch at it, a sly old bat who cottoned on to what Kassa was doing and upped the ante.

Kassa won an unhealthy fortune—three times what she had expected to get away with. The witch across the table from her had smiled smugly to herself…

"We'll never get out of this alive," moaned Daggar.

"We could give it back," said Tippett hopefully.

Kassa wrapped her arms protectively around the calico money bag. "It's mine. I won it."

Aragon glared at her. "If we walk out that door, we're as good as dead."

"So protect me!" she flared. "That's what you're for!"

There was nothing in this musty Zibrian gaming house for Aragon Silversword. He turned to leave. *So*, he thought as he pushed open the heavy double doors. *That's what I was for.*

It had all been for nothing. Barely a farewell, and then a sea-burial. That was all. And something to do with Lady Luck, something he had not yet worked out in his mind.

A large heroic hand smacked down on Aragon's shoulder, barely shifting him out of his reverie.

"Silversword!" bellowed another lion-skinned hero, one Aragon remembered vaguely from his youthful adventures here in Zibria. "How are ya? What the hell are you doing here, mate?"

Cold grey eyes glinted in the lamplight. "I am here to discover the meaning of death," said Aragon Silversword in chilling tones. And he walked out into the night.

-§-§-§-§-§-

This was the Mystic District, well away from the ordinary thoroughfares and byways. Here was where you came to untangle myths, legends and unwelcome prophecies. There was also a fantastic souvlaki bar at the end of Newt Street, but that was incidental.

A very short soothsayer, wrapped in white rags and daubed in the holy symbols of her trade, emerged from a darkened alley and pointed a shaky finger at Aragon Silversword. "Beware!" she shrieked. "For you shall combat the Minestaurus before the glorious sun dips once more below the scabrous horizon!"

"How old are you?" Aragon demanded.

The soothsayer hesitated. "Nearly thirteen," she squeaked.

"They still start them young in Zibria, I see," he replied bitingly. "And am I really going to combat the Minestaurus tomorrow, whatever a Minestaurus is?"

The very young soothsayer chewed her adolescent lip. "Well," she said hesitantly. "I think someone is, but I don't know who. We've only got as far as gen'ral prophetic divinations in class, you see. We don't do specifics for another three months."

"So someone is going to combat something called a Minestaurus," said Aragon tiredly. "The chances that it might be me are…?"

"Unlikely," she admitted grudgingly.

Aragon raised a sardonic eyebrow. "Have you been telling *everyone* that they're going to combat the Minestaurus, just in case you get the right one?"

The soothsayer brightened. "How did you know?"

"Oh, go away," he said darkly. He wouldn't have let himself get into a stupid conversation like this a year ago. A year ago, he would have let the whole thing drop. *Admit it*, his subconscious said smugly. *She said she would change you, and fifteen moons in her company has done just that. You miss having her around!*

The minor soothsayer stuck out her tongue and ran away. Aragon continued onwards, stopping only when he saw the embossed doorway proclaiming that this was the dwelling of the Sacred Swami of Zibria. All questions answered daily, even the really hard ones about mathematics and philosophy.

You want her death to have meant something, Aragon's subconscious continued relentlessly. *You want to understand why you had to lose her, what made it possible for her to die before fulfilling any kind of destiny…*

"Enough!" Aragon said aloud. "I will go inside, ask my question, get my answer and get on with my life."

Ri-ight, said his subconscious, but not very loudly.

-§-§-§-§-§-

The Swami was taken by surprise. "I beg your pardon?" he said, peering over his bifocals. "Could you repeat that, young sir?"

Aragon took a deep breath. He should have been suspicious as soon as he found out that the legendary Swami of Zibria lived in a terrace house in the Mystic District rather than in a goat hut on an isolated mountainside somewhere. This was not at all what he had expected. The room was wrong, for a start. There should be more occult paraphernalia lying around, fewer comfy chairs and portraits of kittens. The Swami should not be wearing carpet slippers. That should be a goblet of eagle's blood or a bottle of dragon tears, not a blatant mug of cocoa congealing on the desk. Was that a plate of chocolate digestives over by the sideboard? Aragon had a nasty feeling that it was. "I wish to know the meaning of death," he said again.

The Swami, who despite the carpet slippers was decked out in swathes of brightly coloured silks and a beaded turban, looked uncomfortable. "Well," he said hesitantly. "Death is death, isn't it? What exactly do you want to know? My son," he added for effect, rather belatedly.

"I want to know what happens when someone dies," Aragon said patiently.

"Oh, said the Swami, relieved. "Is that all? I can do that one." He leaned back in his easy chair and put his feet up on a little embroidered footstool. "All righty, there are two schools of thought on how to solve this question of yours. In the profession, we call them the Easy Way and the Hard Way. You see, the Easy Way to find out what happens after death is to throw yourself off a cliff."

"Indeed," said Aragon stiffly.

"That's right," said the Swami cheerfully. "And the Hard Way is to spend twenty years travelling to distant climes, seeking out the wisest and most ancient of mortals and allowing them to share their time-honoured wisdoms with you. I can give you a list, if you like. And after twenty years of soul-searching and philosophy, *then* you throw yourself off a cliff."

Aragon stalked out, slamming the study door behind him.

The Swami's plaintive voice followed him. "I don't suppose you want to know the meaning of life? I can do you that one, no extra charge!"

-§-§-§-§-§-

Aragon walked away from the Mystic District, angry and confused. Only when he saw a priestess in a purple robe hurrying in his direction did he remember his earlier plan to get to the bottom of why Kassa had died. He could not remember if Lady Luck's colours included purple, but he hailed the priestess anyway. "Do you belong to Lady Luck?"

She halted in front of him, her jade green eyes surprisingly hard. "I'll belong to any god you want me to," she said in a cool, calculating voice.

It turned out that there was a Temple of Luck in the city, and the priestess gave Aragon a series of detailed instructions for finding it before hurrying off towards the Mystic District on business of her own.

Aragon had a suspicion that she was wearing armour under her holy robes. Dismissing the thought (and the obvious clanking sound) from his mind, he walked off in the direction of Lady Luck's Zibrian sanctum. Had he remained in that area much longer, Aragon would have noticed his old shipmate Daggar, who was busily tracking the purple-clad priestess and trying not to be spotted.

It was considered polite for deities to keep a fairly low profile in the cities they were not patron of, so the Temple of Lady Luck was actually a lean-to built on to the back of the same gaming house that Aragon Silversword had visited previously.

He purchased a bag of assorted praying accessories and gained entrance to the shabby little building. Inside, the temple was rather more spectacular. Gold tapestries and bunting hung from the walls and a hundred mirrors busily illuminated the central statue, a portrayal of Lady Luck in all her glory, sculpted in bronze and crowned with a garland of silver peacock feathers.

Aragon lit his stick of incense and wafted it haphazardly around. He opened a small bottle of sacred oil and poured a libation at the feet of the statue. "Now you listen to me," he said in a voice of icy calm. "I am going to find you, goddess, and when I do, you had better have some answers for me." He shook a handful of dried rose petals over the statue of the goddess and tossed the empty accessory bag aside. "She wasn't supposed to die, was she. *Was* she?"

Without waiting for an answer, he turned to stalk out of the temple, but the sound of laughter gave him pause. As he turned, slowly towards the altar, he saw a cloud of beige smoke coalesce into the goddess herself. Lady Luck posed dramatically for him. "So masterful! Such passion throbbing within the veins of such a cold fish."

Aragon regarded her with icy calm. "It was you, wasn't it? When we were in the Witch's Web, Destiny cursed Kassa to be in the hands of Lady Luck."

"Curse?" said Lady Luck in mock horror. "Some might say it was a blessing, to have the personal attention of such a goddess."

"You killed her!" he accused.

"Silly boy. Gods aren't allowed to kill mortals, it's a rule. Well, actually it's more of a subsection within the rules. Anyway, it doesn't happen."

"But Kassa died."

Lady Luck held up her hands in a mock attempt to pacify him. "Oh, I'm not saying that the rules can't be bent. If there happened to be a major glitch in the cosmos, an undestined death might slip through. But what does it really matter?" She shot a teasing look at him. "What do you care?"

Aragon opened his mouth as if to say something, and then turned his back and stormed out of the temple.

Lady Luck watching him go, admiring him openly. "Oh, this one is going to be fun."

There was a shimmer, and green-haired Destiny appeared in the temple. "Him as well?"

Lady Luck chuckled. "I can play with them all if I want to. You didn't object that time when I pumped their precious ship full of holes and sent the Daggersharp girl's entire crew into the Cellar Sea."

"Well, no," admitted Destiny plaintively. "But that was funny. This is just mean!"

"Life is mean, unkind and cruel," said Lady Luck. "Immortality doubly so." A flicker of light brightened her cool eyes for a moment. "And Destiny the cruelest of them all. Watch closely, sister my dear. The game is afoot."

Chapter 7
Take One Giggling Villain...

Sparrow the mercenary marched through the Mystic District, her tawny-blonde hair hidden from view by the deep hood of her purple robe. The role of a priestess would suit her for a little longer, at least until she made it safely to the Palace. Not that the Palace of Zibria was such a safe place these days. The whims of the Sultan were getting more and more perverse, and every loyal servant took life and sanity into their hands just by stepping over the royal threshold.

Then again, she wasn't a particularly loyal servant, so that was all right.

Hopefully, this was the last time she would have to face him. The liquid gold would be enough to buy back her freedom.

A diminutive soothsayer emerged from a little side street, pointing her finger unwaveringly at Sparrow. "Beware!" she shrieked in an eldritch voice, "For you shall battle the Minestaurus this day, and all for the sake of your own golden greed!"

"Go back to school," snapped Sparrow, not even breaking her stride.

The soothsayer, not used to being treated quite so harshly, burst into tears.

Sparrow kept marching at her soldier's pace until she had climbed the steps at the end of Cauldron Row. The steps coiled high, up and around until finally leading their way to the Golden Palace. "Take me to the Sultan," she said as she went inside. Two of the little liveried guards had to break into a trot in order to overtake her and pretend that they were leading her in the direction she was already heading.

One had to run full tilt in order to reach the big embossed doors and announce her presence before she had crossed fully into the chamber. "Miiiistress Sparrow, secret agent and royal mercenary-type person," he called desperately before tripping over his feet and landing in a heap on the gold tiles.

Sparrow stepped over him and continued marching, pausing only when she was face to face with the Sultan of Zibria. She did not prostrate herself as many of his servants did, but she did unbend enough to kneel at his feet. After all, it had been a long walk. "Eminence, I have returned from afar with the prize you charged me to seek out," she said, removing the vial from the second secret compartment behind her breastplate, and letting the leather wrapping fall away to display the contents.

"Excellent, Sparrow," murmured Lord Marmaduc of Zibria, tasting the words on his tongue. "You have done well."

"Indeed, Eminence," replied Sparrow, raising her jade-green eyes to meet his own small black ones. "I trust this has fully paid my debt to your service."

"Ah, that's right," said the Sultan, snapping his fingers as if her had forgotten something. "You wanted to leave, didn't you?" He shook his head. "So sad to lose such a fine agent. Where would you be today if I had not taken you in, a poor little refugee from Trollsville?"

Her eyes set hard. "The debt is discharged. You offered me my release if I brought you the liquid gold." She brandished the vial, and it gleamed in the lantern light.

"Indeed I did," agreed the Sultan with a nasty smile. "And you tasted it, of course. Otherwise you would not have returned to me in such good…time."

Sparrow hesitated. He was baiting her deliberately, setting her up for something. She was weary of these royal games. "As you instructed, Eminence."

"Indeed I did," mused the Sultan, stroking his straggly beard. "Very well, the debt is discharged." He waited a beat, just long enough to see the tension in her posture ease slightly. "Such a good servant you are, Sparrow, to give your life for my pleasures."

Sparrow stared up at him, thin-lipped. "You would order my execution as a reward for a successful mission, *Eminence*? Or is it just that your pride is hurt that I wish to leave your service?"

"I don't have to order anything, my dear," said the Sultan with a certain degree of malicious pleasure. "You are already dead. As dead as the proverbial dormouse with a doornail through its skull. You might say." He smiled pleasantly, and then he laughed out loud.

-§-§-§-§-§-

Daggar hurried through the streets of the Mystic District, only screeching to a halt when he saw a minor soothsayer by the pavement in Cauldron Row, sobbing and hiccupping noisily. Forgetting his mission for a moment, Daggar pulled out a giant handkerchief and sat on the pavement beside the child. "There, there," he said in a vaguely cheerful voice. "What's all this, then?"

"It's my *vocation*!" the young Soothsayer wailed. "I was doing my best, and this nasty lady shouted at me!"

"Never mind," said Daggar, passing over his handkerchief. "Have a good cry. This lady who yelled at you, was she about my height? Purple robe, armour, pretty green eyes?"

The minor soothsayer nodded, blew her nose and started sobbing even more loudly.

"Well, never mind," said Daggar cheerily. "I don't suppose you saw which way she went, did you?"

The child nodded twice, blew her nose again and then pointed up the street. "She followed the steps," she sniffed loudly. "Up to the Palace."

"Righty-ho," said Daggar, getting to his feet. "Keep the hanky. Hope you feel better, least said, soonest mended and all that."

As he hurried off in the direction of the Palace steps, the little soothsayer got to her feet, sniffed noisily and rearranged her white rags. Then she pointed a finger shakily in his direction. "Beware, scoundrel!" she cried in a voice of holy doom. "For thou shalt also combat the Minestaurus this day, yea verily, and for no reasons other than mindless lust and a misplaced sense of honour!"

Daggar glanced behind him and gave her the thumbs up sign. "Right, fine, see you later," he called cheerfully.

He hadn't heard. Either that, or he hadn't believed a word of it. No one took you seriously when you were thirteen. The little soothsayer made a face at his departing back, and felt a bit better.

-§-§-§-§-§-

Sparrow looked at the Sultan, incredulity, fear and anger fighting for ascendancy. This explained everything. The dizzy fits, the sallow complexion of her skin...the clumps of dandelions which grew wherever she trod; which even now were pushing their way up from under the richly embroidered carpets. All side-effects of taking the liquid gold—what was it, a drug, or a poison? She should have stolen the dustsucking instructions along with the vial.

"I apologise, my dear," said the Sultan of Zibria with a smarmy smile. "But it's worked out rather well for me, all things considered." He raised the vial and tipped it slightly, admiring the quality of the golden substance. "The value of this essence more than makes up for the loss of such a fine agent as yourself. And it leaves you free to do another little job for me."

Sparrow stood up straight, determined not to shake. "The last job I did for you cost me my life," she said coldly. "I do not think there is anything you can offer to outweigh that."

"Oh, but you are wrong," said Lord Marmaduc in his infuriatingly delighted voice. "It's a little cleaning up operation, you understand. With a certain amount of deadly danger, naturally. Normally I would not waste an agent of your calibre on such an undertaking, but under the circumstances I don't really have anything to lose, do I?"

"What is in it for me?" asked Sparrow bluntly.

"It's simple enough," said Lord Marmaduc. "If you do happen to succeed, I might see my way to giving you another precious drop of this." He lifted the vial of liquid gold, teasing it so that light gleamed off the yellow-stained glass. "Not enough to allow you to travel in time, but enough to stave off the withdrawal effects."

"Until the next time," Sparrow snorted. "I will not be your slave, *Eminence*, not even for my life."

His eyes took on a strange shimmering quality. "Consider, my dear, whether you have a choice."

Soldiers filtered into the sanctum, clothed in the golden livery of the Zibrian royal household. Two by two, they lined up at the back of the room. There were twenty of them, possibly more. Sparrow tried to focus her shaky vision on their bright-buttoned uniforms, but gave up. "I can take them," she muttered sullenly.

"In your present condition?" the Sultan replied with a tiny smirk. "I think not." And he gave her a quick kick in the centre of her breast plate. Hardly even a nudge, but to Sparrow's extreme embarrassment it was enough to knock her off her feet. She crumpled in a heap of armour and hair, with only enough energy to mutter one word in retaliation, "Bastard…" before lapsing into unconsciousness.

"Well now," said Lord Marmaduc in a thoughtful voice as he nudged the unconscious woman with the pointed toe of his elegant sandal. "I wonder who told her that."

-§-§-§-§-§-

Mistress Opia had knitted enough wool to cover a medium-sized sheep, and the flying carpet was fast approaching the city of Zibria.

Officer Finnley, bleary-eyed from motion sickness, raised his shaky vision to see their goal. "It doesn't look much like a golden city to me," he said bleakly. It was more white than gold, made up of marble pillars, greyish temples and pale cobblestones. Only one building, raised high on a hill, was remotely yellowish. It was surrounded by men in bright gold livery, and looked remarkably like a royal palace. Even the gilding here was faded, however, touched up with a paint which was more butter-coloured than gold.

"You can't believe everything the gossip minstrels tell you," said Mistress Opia, unreasonably cheerful. "It looked very pretty once upon a time." She clapped her hands. "Come on, carpet-my-lad, take us down to the Palace. I want words with that young popinjay, the Sultan." She removed a wicked-looking hatpin from the cabbage roses on her large floral hat, and tested the point thoughtfully.

-§-§-§-§-§-

Sparrow lifted her muzzy head as consciousness flooded back into her brain. She didn't know where she was.

Yes she did. She had seen these stone walls before, scrawled with threatening hieroglyphs, in the outer circle of the labyrinth under the Palace. She had joined a tour party once, interested in utilising the benefits of a secret passage into the royal quarters. But she had given it up as a bad job—the tour only went as far as the outer circle, and no one could give her any information on the inner mazes. It had seemed like too much work for little benefit.

But this was not the outer circle of the labyrinth. The hieroglyphs were older, dustier, and had not been touched up with paint. The floor tiles were chipped and faded with time. She had no way of knowing how deep into the labyrinth she was.

And only then did Sparrow recall the tiny soothsayer predicting that she would battle the Minestaurus. "Damn," she said explosively.

All the locals knew of the legend, or one of the many variations on a similar theme. Stories about the horned (and/or hairy and/or hoofed) man dwelling in the inner circles of the labyrinth were ten a penny in this neck of the woods. Every now and then, one of the many lion-skinned heroes of Zibria would stride in to make their reputation by slaying the beast, but none of them ever strode back out again.

A clean up job, with a little deadly danger thrown in for good measure. Huh. Sparrow leaned against one of the walls and closed her eyes. She could wait it out. According to the Sultan, who had revived her long enough to describe her condition in loving detail, her reactions to the time essence would overwhelm her again and again, drawing closer and closer together. Eventually, it would kill her. Either that, or she would starve first.

Starving didn't appeal. She hadn't even had breakfast yet. Sparrow stood up, forcing herself into a stiff-backed soldier's stance. At least if she came across this Minestaurus creature she could go down fighting. The passage stretched endlessly in two directions. One way might lead her to daylight, the other deeper into the labyrinth. She sniffed the air in both directions, and it was equally stale.

There was an odd sort of light down here, a pale phosphorescence. Some kind of fungus, perhaps. Sparrow didn't really care. She started walking, unsteadily at first until she regained her usual mercenary stride.

-§-§-§-§-§-

Halfway up the stairs spiralling to the Sultan's Palace, Daggar started huffing and puffing. He sat heavily down on one of the marble steps, wheezing and red in the face. "Got to get fitter," he muttered to himself in between wheezes. "Eat more vegetables, that sort of thing."

Singespitter, who had been straining against the leash all the way up, gave his 'master' a superior look.

"Oh, shut up," said Daggar when he finally had his breath back. "You're no picture of health yourself, you know."

Singespitter preened, well aware that he was a fine figure of a sheep no matter what anyone said.

"Right," said Daggar, his voice slightly hoarse. "I suppose we'd better go—hang on a minute."

He had seen the sign. Halfway up the hill, a little path led down and around, away from the stairs. All the sign with the arrow said was: *Ye Olde Labyrinth.*

"Let's have a look, then, shall we?" said Daggar, cheerful at this apparent detour.

Singespitter frowned. The trail of little dandelions quite obviously led up the steps.

"Well, I know you fancy her, but me slogging my guts out climbing these stairs isn't going to be much good if I have a heart attack, is it?" Daggar said reasonably. "We'll just have a little look-see to rest our legs and then we'll go on."

Singespitter's frown turned into a fully-fledged glare, and he almost growled menacingly.

"Just you remember who's the boss," Daggar threatened, tugging on the leash for good measure.

Singespitter did know who the boss was, and the sooner they caught up with her the better. He quite liked being around attractive young women, something which had never happened much when he was a human being. He had been very sulky after the *Splashdance* crew had so carelessly lost Kassa, but he missed Sparrow even more. It was something about that nice hay-colour of her hair…

"It's the blonde thing, isn't it?" Daggar accused, annoyed at Singespitter for dragging his toes into the gravel. "Like that tavern wench the other month, in Axgaard. The one with the braids. You had an unreasonable attachment to her, don't try to deny it…" His voice trailed off as he saw where the path had led them. Abruptly, Singepitter stopped straining against the leash, and trotted eagerly forward. Daggar almost fell over.

It was a plaza, tiled in mosaic fashion with the floor depicting scenes of gory battle, great nobility and furry animals chasing each other's tails. There was the mouth of the labyrinth, gaping open. Daggar almost expected to see blood dripping down from teeth above.

Around the entrance were several bronze plaques, obviously polished daily. "*The Fearsome Labyrinth*," Daggar read aloud. "*Wherein the hideous Minestaurus makes his bedde, and chews unwitting travellers by the hedde*. Gawd, even Tippett could make better poetry than that."

He read the other plaques, slowly taking in the various legends and history snippets pertaining to the Minestaurus and the labyrinth. "Here, Singespitter," he said, for wont of a human to talk to. "It says that if you go through the inner circles of the labyrinth and out the other side, it leads to a secret passage into the Palace. Bit of a turn up for the books, eh? Lucky we came."

Singespitter looked about as startled as was possible for a medium-sized sheep to get.

"Easy, isn't it?" Daggar continued. "We get through to the Palace this way, catch up with Sparrow and, well whatever comes next. No bother with those nasty-looking guards." He rummaged in a pocket and emerged triumphantly with a large ball of string. "You see? Easy. I'm surprised no one ever thought of this before now..."

If it had been possible for Singespitter the sheep to quirk his eyebrows sceptically—if, indeed, he had eyebrows—he most certainly would have been quirking them like mad. Instead, he resigned himself to following in his companion's rather muddled and foolhardy footsteps.

Singespitter hoped they would run into Sparrow as soon as possible. She would soon get them sorted. Now, there was a girl with a good head on her shoulders.

-§-§-§-§-§-

Sparrow was freaking out. She ran this way and that, not noticing specific directions or distances or even if she was crashing into walls, which she was. Bruised and bloody from throwing herself against hard surfaces, she was almost weeping. Almost, but not quite. Trolls don't cry, they don't know how.

She thought she heard a familiar, friendly voice bouncing its way around the echoing tunnels of the Labyrinth, and that just about finished her off. She dropped to the ground, arms wrapped around her knees, shuddering violently. She was alone and she was going to die here, and now she was hallucinating.

-§-§-§-§-§-

Mistress Opia walked into the Sultan's Palace in the same way that she walked everywhere—as if she owned the place. Hobbs the gnome scuttled along behind her, his eyes wide as he took in the expense of the various draperies and shiny bric a brac which littered the golden corridors.

Officer Finnley trailed along behind them, feeling like a third wheel on a two-wheeler chariot. He had hoped for adventure and excitement and all he had got was...well, adventure and excitement, but not the kind you read about in heroic epic. Nearly falling off a maddened flying carpet was exciting, yes, but it wasn't the sort of thing he had in mind.

The Brewers were mainly pretending that he wasn't there. Occasionally, Mistress Opia got his name wrong in her absent-minded way, as if she couldn't tell the difference between him and her apprentice dogsbody back home.

It wasn't right. He was a Blackguard. But Finnley was starting to realise that a Blackguard outside Dreadnought wasn't much use at all.

They reached the inner sanctum. The guards tried half-heartedly to stop them there, but Mistress Opia just walked on through. She came to a halt at the big shiny throne, regarding its occupant with sheer disdain. "I suppose you're quite pleased with yourself, young Marmaduc?" The grandmotherly tone had been replaced by something harder. And colder. "Just what do you think you are doing?"

Finnley turned his attention to the Sultan of Zibria, who was reclining on the golden throne, two stick-like legs dangling out from under his jewelled tunic. "I knew you'd come," the Sultan said airily. "I wanted you to come. I don't need any silly time-travelling potion, but I do need you. And if you don't agree to my terms, I'll have the liquid gold destroyed!"

For a moment, Finnley thought Mistress Opia was going to explode. Her face went all red, then all of a sudden her placid grandmotherly expression returned. "Better give it back to me, young man, before you do yourself an injury."

The Sultan of Zibria laughed. One of those laughs which conveys exactly how mad the villain is. He tipped back his head and giggled maniacally. "But then my mercenary girl would have died for nothing," he said in a pleased voice. "And wouldn't that be a terrible shame?"

Chapter 8
Dealing with Your Own Demise

Kassa had always been an expert when it came to throwing tantrums, hissy fits and general rages, and this was the culmination of her life's work. She screeched, wept, yelled, threatened, broke things and finally—to the fervent relief of the others in her immediate vicinity—stopped.

The Dark One peered at her from behind his throne. "Are you finished?" he asked nervously.

"Yes, thank you," replied Kassa in an unnaturally calm voice.

Vervain the sprite squeezed himself out of the only black ceramic urn which had not been trashed during Kassa's incontrollable rage. "All that velvet," he said sadly, looking at the clawed and ripped remains of the black curtains. Snatches of complicated mural showed through the ragged tears in the butchered fabric.

Kassa's eyes narrowed. "Duck," she advised her new guardian sprite.

Vervain whimpered and threw himself to one side as Kassa launched a small ebony statue at the remaining intact urn. As it exploded into little bits, Kassa took a deep breath and then exhaled. "Right," she said sensibly. "What do I do now?"

The Dark One raised his head from under his cloak. "Well," he said, trying to sound as if he wasn't scared stiff of her. "You could always reunite yourself with those of your family and friends who are currently available, that is, dead. Or you could try a quest—they're always popular in the first week. It helps you settle in, you see..."

"A quest in the Underworld?" Kassa said sceptically. "No, I think I'd better stick to the first choice. I have some unresolved issues with quite a few dead people." She glanced at Vervain. "Do you want to stick around here for a while, and keep working on his Dark Majesty's makeover?"

"Fine," stuttered Vervain, wide-eyed and shaking. "Whatever you want. Just call me if you need me. Or not," he added hastily. "Not is good."

Kassa sighed. She had been dead less than a day—if such units of time were recognised up here in the Underworld—and already she had alienated the Lord of Darkness and her own brand-new guardian sprite. Things were progressing as per usual.

Ebony the goth was waiting in the corridor. She glided onwards, her feet barely brushing the floor. Kassa Daggersharp followed her, her own hob-nailed boots making a satisfactory ringing sound as they struck the stone pathways. "All right," she said impatiently. "So where do they keep the dead people around here?"

"Where *don't* they?" replied Ebony. "What kind of dead person are you looking for? We have all sorts around here."

Kassa sighed. "Just take me to the cavern with the most rum in it."

-§-§-§-§-§-

She was a diminutive woman with naturally reddish-blonde hair (which she dyed black, even in the Underworld) and a substantial cleavage. She wore leather knickerbockers, a close-fitting blouse of the ruffled white variety, and an eyepatch. "Are you sure about this, Bigbeard?"

A huge sea-captain type with a bristling big beard and a single golden eye laughed heartily at her disapproval. "Don't be such a wet blanket, Nell! I learnt it off those imp fellas. Do it all the time, they do. Now come on, close your eyes and *throw*..."

Nellisand Witchdaughter—known to one and all as Black Nell—rolled her eyes at her husband's antics. "I think I preferred it when you just drank yourself into a stupor," she said, but followed his instructions and closed her eyes, tossing the small polished emerald high into the air. When it landed in one of the carefully chalked squares on the cave floor, she opened her eyes, sighed loudly and hop-skip-jumped her way through the interlacing pattern.

"See?" roared her husband cheerfully. "You just don't know a good thing when yer see it!"

"Oh, I agree," she flung back at him. "*Heart*-stoppingly entertaining. Is this really your idea of fun?"

His eyes lit up with an insinuating gleam. "What else did you have in mind, wench?"

Just as Nell hesitated between seducing her husband or throwing a brick at his head, she saw a familiar figure hovering in the cave entrance.

Kassa looked, for the first time in her life, completely at a loss. Her golden eyes flicked between Vicious Bigbeard Daggersharp and Black Nell, not quite able to cope with what she saw. "Dad," she said helplessly. "Mother?"

Black Nell Daggersharp put her hands on her hips and scowled ferociously at her only daughter. "What the hell do you think you are you doing here, young lady?"

Kassa folded her arms defensively. "If you really want to know, I'm dead." *So there*, her body language announced.

"You're bloody not," snapped her mother. "Don't lie to me, Kassa." She flung an angry glance at Bigbeard, who was absently rechalking his squares on the cave floor. "Bigbeard, tell her that she isn't due to die for..."

"Oh, let the wench be dead if she likes," said Vicious Bigbeard Daggersharp. "What ho, Kassa-girl. Come and play hop-skip-jump with me. Don't mind your mother, she's bein' difficult."

"Difficult?" shrieked Black Nell, white-faced. "I want you to tell your daughter to return to the land of the living, and all you say is that I'm being *difficult*?"

"Would you prefer bloody-minded?" he said mildly. He grinned at Kassa, showing off his missing teeth. "How did the pirating go, luv?"

"Oh, not bad," Kassa said weakly. "I'm getting the hang of it. Well, I was. Before I died, obviously."

"Jolly good. Kill anyone interestin', then?"

"Afraid not. I never really got around to it."

He shot a suspicious look at her. "Who did you marry?"

"No one, Dad. I didn't have time."

"Humph," he said disapprovingly. "Could be worse. Could o' been a McHagrty. Still got some sense, eh, girl?"

"How much worse do you want it to get?" demanded Black Nell scathingly. "Our daughter is dead, Daggersharp. Have you been listening to any of this?"

Kassa crouched down to Bigbeard's level, kissing him on the cheek. He patted her hand with a vague reassurance. "Never mind, wench. Your mother was pretty narked at me when I turned up too. She'll get used to it."

"Dad," Kassa whispered. "Do *you* think I'm supposed to be dead yet?"

He shrugged his massive shoulders. "Seems to me you'll end up here sooner or later. May as well stay now you're here. Save you the bother later on."

Kassa scowled darkly. "Oh, that's very comforting."

A shadow fell across the cave floor. A woman stood there, dressed head to toe in pale grey leather. Her silver hair stood up in a high arrangement involving feathers and the defiance of gravity. Beads and baubles were slung around her neck and hips like so many coils of rope, and her face was strikingly old. "Hmm," she said in a disapproving tone of voice. "Kassa Daggersharp. I presume. Better late than never. I suppose."

Kassa stood up, slowly regarding this stranger. "According to everyone else, I got here early."

"Not for me you didn't," snapped the grey-clad old woman, shaking her beads and feathers irritatedly. "You were due in Chiantrio on the dot of sixteen. And you never turned up. Still. Here you are." She stuck out a wrinkled hand bedecked in complicated charms made out of bone and twisted bits of metal. "Dame Veekie Crosselet. Godmother-witch." Her stone-coloured eyes moved up and down, regarding Kassa with intense and scornful interest. "Well," she said grudgingly. "I suppose you'll do."

The godmother-witch turned, and motioned Kassa to follow her. Kassa hesitated, looking back at her parents. She had only just found them again, and she had so much to tell them, to ask them…

"Go on, will you?" snapped her mother. "Family duty is one thing. Professional obligations are quite another. We're not going anywhere."

Still unsure, Kassa tossed a salute to her father who was still trying to even out his hopscotch squares, and tripped after the stern and forbidding witch. "So what do I do first? We can't use magic in the Underworld."

"Magic is easy enough," snapped her instructor. "Witch training is not about magic. You can pick that up on your own."

"Then what *are* you going to teach me? What am I going to do?"

"Study," said the witch succinctly, her long grey-clad legs making it hard to keep up with her. "Theories and practices. History. Moral philosophy. Dreamwork. Have you chosen a speciality?"

Kassa flinched at the stern question. "I'm a songwitch."

"Not until I say you are! First you will study. Then you will prepare for your quest."

Kassa stopped short, looking at the older witch in bemusement. "I have to complete a quest? How can I do that if I can't leave the Underworld?"

The Dame spun around to regard Kassa with unblinking grey eyes. Eyes which reminded Kassa of something, or someone… "Well now," said Dame Veekie in a voice of stainless steel. "Whoever said you couldn't leave the Underworld?"

All around them, almost invisible to mortal eye, microscopic filaments of golden pollen clung to the walls of the Underworld. Here in the realm of impossibilities and paradoxes, the tiny spores began to reproduce…

Chapter 9
Stitching up the Minestaurus

Daggar was beginning to worry. The string was nearly gone, and he was no closer to finding his way into the Palace than he had been before. If anything, he was further away. "Now, Singespitter, don't panic," he said bravely.

Singespitter sneered at him, lifting his stately nose into the air. Without hesitating, he began to trot along one of the tunnels. He could smell something. Something awfully familiar...

Daggar, not willing to be left alone in the darkness, hurried after the sheep. "Are you sure about this?" The string was taut in his hands. "Maybe we should head back and buy some extra string."

Singespitter trotted confidently on. Daggar sighed, and let go of the tight string, which snapped back into the shadows.

Finally, after weaving his way through a complex series of tunnels, Singespitter screeched to a halt. Up ahead, illuminated by the strange greenish glow of the tunnel walls, Sparrow crouched on the ground, curled into a ball. Last time Daggar had seen her she was armed to the teeth and garbed in stout black leather and with steel-plated legs. Now she was defenceless, clad only in a knee-length black shift and leggings with a few rust stains here and there.

"Sparrow!" Daggar called out in surprise, his voice bouncing off the walls.

She snapped to attention, her head shooting up and her eyes gazing blankly at him. "You," she said in a deadened voice. "What are you doing here?"

"Trying to cut corners, as per usual," he said cheerfully. "Seems to have paid off this time." He peered at her. "Gods, you look awful."

She shrugged weakly. "I am dying, it seems. The Sultan tricked me into drinking the extract of time that I stole from the Brewers. The liquid gold. Now he is playing mind-games, holding me to ransom for my next dose, to keep me alive a little longer." Her eyes lit up. "If you kill me now, it would solve everything."

"Are you kidding?" Daggar demanded, kneeling down beside her. "I wouldn't even know how to start! If this liquid gold stuff is what you need, then we can go into the Palace and get it. Easy enough. We can do that."

Sparrow looked at him in bemusement. "Why? You hardly know me."

"I know that I like you," he offered, drawing her to her feet.

"Nobody likes me," she mumbled drowsily, her alien accent slurring. "I am not a nice person."

"Probably," agreed Daggar. "But Singespitter likes you, and he's always had impeccable taste in women. Except for his blind spot when it comes to blondes," he added as an afterthought.

Sparrow almost laughed, pulling a shaky hand through her hair.

"Besides," said Daggar, sliding an arm under her shoulders to help her walk, "I can't go letting two gorgeous homicidal women die on me in the same week. It wouldn't be fair to the world."

"So how are we going to get into the Palace?" Sparrow did her best to pretend she was walking without assistance.

Daggar grimaced. "If you keep asking me difficult questions, we're never going to get anything done."

He kept his arm around her until Sparrow regained her strength and pushed him away. Now she strode ahead while

Daggar tried to keep up. Singespitter the sheep trotted between them, making it quite clear that his allegiance belonged entirely to Sparrow.

"Do you think this is the right way?" she asked, turning her head only slightly towards Daggar.

A mighty roar filled the cavernous corridors, coming from up ahead.

"That solves that question," said Daggar smartly, hooking his arm in Sparrow's and trying deftly to swing her in the opposite direction.

Sparrow shook him off easily. "Be reasonable. Do you think we can reach the secret passage into the Palace without going past the Minestaurus? The creature must be between us and the deepest part of the Labyrinth."

"I hate it when you're logical," Daggar grumbled. "Look at us. No armour, no weapons, you keep going yellow and falling over. How can we battle something that roars *that* loudly while we're armed with nothing but a sheep?"

"We will have to think of something," said Sparrow steadily. "The decision has been made for us already."

Up ahead, beyond a convenient bend in the corridor, a monstrous silhouette heralded the arrival of something large with horns and teeth...It roared again, before rounding the corner.

Daggar fainted.

-§-§-§-§-§-

Mistress Opia pushed her spectacles further up her nose and smiled nicely. "Now you listen to me, young Marmaduc. I'm the Brewmistress. You know that. I can call up all sorts of nasty things to deal with you. I could fill your bones with steam if I really wanted to. But I don't want to do that."

Officer Finnley was quite pleased to hear it. "Erm," he said nervously. "Would it help if I put him under arrest?"

"No thank you, dear," said Mistress Opia. "A good thought, but probably not altogether practical." She turned back to the Sultan, her mouth set. "Now then, young Sultan-my-lad. It's time you and I had a bit of a talk."

"What is there to talk about?" asked the Sultan delightedly. "You can come and work for me now, like you used to in the good old days when my father was Sultan. He told me you could turn anything into gold. Well, I want the Palace re-gilded for a start, and then the city. Every temple, every cobble, every roadhouse. It will look so pretty..."

Mistress Opia stared at him, open-mouthed. "You seriously expect me to come back here? And spend my days churning out metal for you to redecorate with? I'm the Brewmistress of *Dreadnought*. That's like expecting the Lady Emperor to come home and run her father's poultry farm!"

"But you're here now," purred the Sultan. "So what are you going to do about it?"

Mistress Opia's grandmotherly face took on a very dangerous expression.

Hobbs the gnome pulled urgently at Officer Finnley's sleeve, and the two of them crept back out of the firing line. "Can she really do that?" whispered Finnley. "The filling bones with steam thing?"

"You betcha," hissed back the gnome.

Finnley frowned. "I'm pretty sure that's illegal. I mean, there isn't anything in the rulebook specifically about filling bones with steam, but it doesn't sound very nice."

"Shut up, willya? I'm trying to listen."

Finnley sighed, and leaned up against a heavy amber curtain. He barely noticed when a small hand plucked at his sleeve and a tiny whisper said, "Sssst."

He pushed his head through the curtain opening and saw a quick blur of jangles and silk vanish behind a pillar. Curious, he followed. A girl barely as tall as his shoulder was waiting for him. She was wearing beads, mostly. With a few wisps of silk attached. "Who are you?" he asked.

"I'm a concubine," she said, rolling her eyes under heavily-painted lashes. "Don't you have those where you come from?"

"Well, yes," he admitted uncomfortably. "But I think they're kept indoors mostly."

She seemed to be waiting for something. "Well?" she demanded finally.

Finnley blushed. "Well what?"

"Anyway, you're one of those policemen, aren't you? The Blackguards of Dreadnought? I recognised your uniform." She sniffed with a certain amount of professional pride. "We're trained to recognise men in uniform. Didn't you come for the girl?"

This was more like it. Rescuing damsels and being heroic. "What girl?" Then an image struck him, a memory of the tawny-blonde thief kissing him into oblivion. "Oh, her. The one with the...armour. I think I'm supposed to arrest her." He frowned. "Actually, I have a suspicion that I'm expected to hold her down while Mistress Opia does something really nasty to her, but I think I'd better arrest her instead."

"You'll have to be quick," said the concubine. "That stuff she stole for the Sultan made her sick, and he threw her to the Minestaurus in the labyrinth." She snorted, in a particularly unladylike way. "Typical men!"

Finnley stared at her. Somehow, he had lost the thread of what they were talking about.

The concubine stamped her little sandalled foot angrily. "Well? Are you going to come and rescue her from the Minestaurus or not? *Then* you can arrest her. Well, what do you say?"

Put like that, he realised he didn't really have anything better to do.

-§-§-§-§-§-

Mistress Opia smiled her grandmotherly smile and rolled up her sleeves in a meaningful way. "It is apparent that you are not going to be sensible about this," she said calmly. "We'll just have to settle the matter with traditional methods."

"What are you going to do?" asked the Sultan of Zibria delightedly. "Box my ears? Send me to bed without supper? Smack my wrist and tell me not to be so naughty?" His voice dropped to an exultant whisper. "Stab me with a knitting needle?"

"No," said Mistress Opia steadily. "We're going to arm-wrestle."

This surprised Lord Marmaduc. He almost blinked. "I beg your pardon?"

"You heard," she said, rubbing her palms together in brisk fashion. "Best out of three, winner takes all." She looked at him over her glasses. Suddenly, she didn't seem grandmotherly any more.

The Sultan laughed merrily. "You forget, Mistress Opia. I've seen you arm-wrestle before. I know your strengths and your weaknesses." His hand slipped over a small knob on the side of his throne, and the ceiling opened up. Water gushed down over the Brewmistress, soaking her to the skin.

"Oi!" yelled Hobbs the gnome, suddenly taking an interest. He leaped forward to protect the Brewmistress, and was slammed to the ground by a pile of gold-clad guards.

Mistress Opia glared at the Sultan. "Clever boy. How did you know?"

"I've had my agents watching you, Brewmistress. You have been seen, turning things into gold without the aid of anything resembling potions or powders. And that can't be done without magic. What did you do, make a pact with the gods? Or a pact with the *moonlight dimension*?"

"You don't know what you're talking about," she hissed.

The Sultan raised an eyebrow expertly. "I know that water neutralises faery dust." He raised the vial of liquid gold, and examined it. "And I know that this is not a natural substance." He lifted the lid of the vial, releasing a cloud of golden fumes. "I hate to *think* what this is doing to the atmosphere. Still, all in a good cause, eh, Brewmistress?"

She snarled at him, all grandmotherly pretence wiped from her face. "You cannot make me work for you. No bonds will hold me!"

"It's true," he mused. "According to my agents, you can turn anything into molten gold, or gold dust. Well, almost everything." He snapped his fingers, and two gold-liveried guards leaped forward, snapping wooden handcuffs around the Brewmistress's wrists. She stared in horror.

The Sultan laughed. "Never had much luck with wood, though, did you? Apparently it's the one substance you can't transform. Maybe it's because it's so...natural." His tone became hard. "You will spin gold for me. You will gild my city. You will make Zibria great again."

"Zibria needs a half-decent Lordling," she spat. "Not a blackmailing brat!"

The Sultan laughed. "Well, at the very least you will amuse me. And if you don't amuse me, I'll destroy your liquid gold." He held up the vial teasingly. "It's your only sample, isn't it? And I doubt the moonlight dimension will be so accommodating a second time." He waved negligently with the other hand. "Take her away. We'll talk again another time."

-§-§-§-§-§-

Daggar stirred, mumbling to himself. "Danger...death... canary errghh."

"If you are awake," said Sparrow sharply, "have some tea."

Struggling with the misty consciousness that was tentatively making its way back into his head, Daggar opened one eye. He could see Sparrow's hair and just beyond that, Sparrow herself. She was sitting straight-backed on a plush green chair, balancing a cup of tea and a saucer full of biscuits.

Reassured, Daggar opened his other eye. And screamed.

Without even looking up, Sparrow reached out her free hand and clamped it over Daggar's mouth. "This is Magnus," she said evenly. "Do not be rude."

"It's the, it's the, it's the," babbled Daggar when she finally removed her hand.

"The Minestaurus," commented the third person in the room. "A *terrible* nickname. It's because of the resemblance to a bull, I know, and some old legend about me being nearly drowned in a soup cauldron. How are you feeling, by the way?"

"Oh," Daggar gulped. "Dandy." He looked around. Sparrow was perfectly relaxed, but that could mean anything. Singespitter the sheep was curled up in front of an open fire, growling contentedly to himself as he viciously attacked a plate of buttered crumpets. "Um," said Daggar. "I didn't expect you to be wearing a suit."

Magnus the Minestaurus plucked self-consciously at his cravat. "Well, you never know when visitors are going to drop in," he said in a pleasant voice. Other than the suit, he was almost as Daggar had expected. An eight-foot man with brown fur, neatly combed, a bull-like face and horns. But everything else…

"Um," said Daggar.

"Magnus will help us," said Sparrow patiently. "He knows the way into the Palace."

"Oh?" said Daggar, who had just been handed a cup of tea and jug of cream by the Minestaurus. "How nice."

She gave him a hard look. "You *are* still interested in breaking into the Palace and getting the liquid gold to save my life?"

"Sure," said Daggar vaguely. "Why not." He bit into a biscuit and discovered that it tasted good. He took another bite. "Nice place you've got here, Magnus."

It had been a cave once, but was now redecorated to within an inch of its life. Bookshelves lined the walls, stocked with hundreds of scrolls and parchments, and a few heavily-bound volumes. Daggar was lying on a particularly nice burgundy plush couch. The coffee table was polished pine, and a stylish mahogany hat-rack stood majestically in one corner.

"Thank you," said Magnus modestly. "The conservatory's really something to see," he added.

Sparrow set her empty teacup aside and stood up. "We must be going."

"Must we?" said Daggar in a dreamy voice. "I was just starting to get comfortable."

"Please excuse him," said Sparrow to Magnus, "I think he has reached his shock threshold."

"Happens to everyone," said Magnus cheerily. "Except me, of course. I'm unshockable." He turned and peered thoughtfully at the many bookshelves which lined the walls. "Now, which one was the secret passageway?"

Suddenly the wall swung to one side, scattering epic poetry and muffin recipes in every direction. Two people landed heavily on the tasteful carpet, coughing with the dust. One was small, female and garbed in a skimpy assortment of beads, sequins and silken wisps. The other was gangly, male and wearing the uniform of a Dreadnought Blackguard.

"Right," said Officer Finnley, getting to his feet. "I arrest…" He looked around the room. The only one of them all who looked remotely criminal was Sparrow, and that was because she had grabbed one of the ceremonial swords from over the fireplace as soon as she recognised his uniform. "Oh, hello again," he said apologetically. "We came to arrest you."

The concubine allowed the Minestaurus to help her to her feet. "It seemed like a good idea at the time." She adjusted her sequins.

"How do you do?" said the Minestaurus eagerly, diverting Finnley's attention. "I've always wanted to meet a Blackguard. Is it just like in the ballads? And a concubine too," he added, turning to greet Finnley's new companion. "Such a pleasant surprise, so many nice visitors."

At a creaking sound, Finnley's head jerked around. The bookshelves concealing the secret passage had just swung back into place. The tawny-blonde mercenary, her scruffy companion and their sheep were all nowhere to be seen.

"They've gone!" he said, outraged.

"And I hadn't even offered them any jam fancies," said the Minestaurus sadly.

-§-§-§-§-§-

Daggar and Sparrow ran up the secret staircase two or three steps at a time. For some reason, Singespitter the sheep had no problem keeping up with them. "You regained your senses in record time," Sparrow observed acidly.

"Those sequins do it every time," said Daggar. "What now?"

"Now we find the liquid gold and steal it back," she said, and glared at him. "You are not hiding behind anything yet."

"I know," he said with half a grin. "For once, *I've* got an escape route up my sleeve. Only just thought of it, but it's a doozy."

"Fine," she said, and slammed shoulder-first into the door at the top of the stairs, bursting it off its hinges.

"It wasn't necessarily locked," Daggar said darkly, picking splinters out of his beard and figuring it was time to shave. When the omnipresent stubble turned into beard, he knew he was letting himself go. On the other hand, he might look rather dashing in a beard. He would have to find a mirror to examine the effect.

The room they had crashed into just happened to be the Sultan's laboratory. Everything was white, except for the many multi-coloured liquids which bubbled in various glass structures.

"That was easy enough," said Sparrow, not even breathing hard. Her keen eyes sought out one vial among many. It stood out among the rest, its contents glowing goldly. Light from the overhead lamps hit it squarely, sending amber refractions out in every direction. "Almost too easy," she added.

The laboratory had eight doors circling its sterile white walls, and they all opened at the same time. Guards in golden livery poured into the room, filling it up line by line. The high-pitched giggle of the Sultan rose above the sound of marching feet. He stepped into the laboratory. "Do you like my playroom? And what about my ambush? It took a lot of reasoning out, so I hope you appreciate it."

Sparrow turned her mouth slightly towards Daggar's ear. "I hope this escape route of yours is still in play."

Daggar scrabbled under his jerkin for the ship-shaped charm he wore around his neck on a silver chain. In his clumsy haste, the clasp broke and the chain was flipped into the air, taking the tiny ship with it. It didn't travel very far. Only as far as the vial which Sparrow was holding gingerly between finger and thumb. Surprised by the sudden impact, her fingers twitched involuntarily. The vial dropped, shattering glass on the sterile white tiles and splashing the viscous liquid gold everywhere.

Golden light filled the laboratory. In the midst of the broken glass and essence of time, the broken piece of silver jewellery began to expand. Sparrow and Daggar both jumped backwards as the ghost-ship swelled into existence.

The Sultan stared, open-mouthed. His horror at the loss of his favourite bargaining tool was suddenly replaced with greed as he realised what was happening.

The *Silver Splashdance* was silver no longer. The giant ghost-ship pulsated with amber light, glowing golden against a bright white landscape of broken glass and liveried guards.

"Liquid gold," said Sparrow hoarsely.

Daggar gazed at the golden ship, his eyes wide with the realisation of what he had done. The first words out of his mouth bypassed his brain entirely. "Kassa's going to kill me!"

Chapter 10
Fishcakes and Philosophy

The various fortune-tellers of Entrail Row had offered Aragon Silversword very little as far as arcane knowledge went. He sat now on a park bench in Watchtower Square, staring at the pigeons and half-heartedly chewing on a fish cake. It was time to give up this mindless obsession. Time to get on with his life. If Lady Luck wanted Kassa dead, what could he do about it? Entering a butt-kicking contest with a god (or goddess) was one of his top ten list of things never to do to himself.

It was well past time he figured out some useful way to spend his life. And if the witchmark meant he couldn't forget Kassa, then he would have to live with it. Or not, as the case might be. He shoved the spiral ring deep into his belt pouch.

The bench creaked as someone else perched on the other end. Aragon glanced up disinterestedly and saw an old man with a bushy white beard and a furled umbrella. He went back to his fish cake.

A clear, bell-like voice interrupted Aragon's inner thoughts. "Young man, as Hypocritices once said, 'There are no tragedies but those we create for ourselves.' I think there's a message in that for all of us." The old man smiled, creasing his beard.

Aragon stared at the stranger with unfriendly eyes. "Is that your professional opinion?"

"It certainly is," said the old man, sticking out a cheerful hand. "Psittacus the philosopher, at your service. 'There is no art so wise as mine,' as the Bard was wont to say."

"Which bard?"

"Oh, any you choose to name, dear boy."

"I see," said Aragon darkly. "And you're here to solve all my problems, are you?"

"Certainly not," said the philosopher, horrified at the suggestion. "I don't have all year. Besides, I can see what your main problem is straight away. It's written all over your face."

"Tell me," said Aragon Silversword icily.

Psittacus the philosopher shared a conspiratorial smile, making himself comfortable on the rickety bench. "Well, it seems to me that you fell in love with a milkmaid at a very young age and soon after discovered that she was married to someone else, so you ran away to sea and returned only to discover that your entire village, milkmaid included, had been wiped out by the Green Plague." He waggled his eyebrows and bared his surprisingly even teeth in a delighted grin. "I'm right, aren't I?"

"No," said Aragon.

The grin faded slightly. "Oh," said Psittacus the philosopher, only slightly discouraged. After a moment of what appeared to be studious thought, he brightened. "Try this one, then. You were involved in a torrid love triangle with a Chiantrian exotic dancer and a Sparkling Nun, and..."

Aragon held up a hand to ward off the rest of the half-baked theory. "No."

"Oh." Psittacus looked dejected. "No vampire squirrels involved in the scenario, by any chance?"

"Not a single one."

"Oh."

Aragon leaned back into the park bench. "Do you really want to know?"

Psittacus leaned forward eagerly, his elbows balanced precariously on his knees. "If you wouldn't mind."

Aragon wondered if it would sound quite as stupid if he told someone else. He tried, and it did. "I was forced into the service of a Pirate Queen with minimal magic powers who put a witchmark on me to seal my so-called loyalty. She then got herself killed, leaving me marked for life. This magically-enforced loyalty has ensured that I can not only not put her out of my mind, but I have also developed an unhealthy obsession with the afterlife, and with getting my revenge on the goddess responsible for this whole mess."

He took a bite of his fish cake, which was cold.

"Oh, is that all?" said Psittacus the philosopher, slapping his thigh. "As Leodicranz the Unready once said, 'A problem shared is a problem doubled twice, divided by two and multiplied into submission.' Good thing you came to me when you did, we'll get you sorted out in no time at all!"

"Of course you will," said Aragon. He did not hold his breath.

Psittacus jumped to his feet, and to Aragon's immense disgust, led them straight to Entrail Row. "I've just come from here," Aragon protested. "They couldn't tell me anything."

Psittacus tapped his nose knowingly. "Ah, but you might not have known the right questions to ask," he suggested. "Leave this to me." And he barged right into one of the canvas-fronted scrying boutiques, snatched up a pack of fortune cards and started shuffling them quickly. "Self-serve, is it?" he asked the outraged gypsy behind the counter. "Won't be half a minute."

The gypsy stormed out, probably going to find six of her closest and largest friends to evict this interloper.

"Right," said Psittacus. "This young lady of yours. What's her date of birth?"

"I don't know," said Aragon.

Psittacus waggled his bushy eyebrows. "Approximate age?"

"Older than twenty," Aragon hazarded.

"Is that the best you can do?"

"Younger than thirty?"

"Remember her *name*, by any chance?"

Aragon Silversword gritted his teeth. "Kassa Daggersharp."

"Oh, *her*. Her fate's been written in the constellations for at least half an eternity." Psittacus gazed blankly at the fortune cards in his hand. "Hang on a mo. Dead, you say?"

"Dead," said Aragon evenly.

"Are you absolutely sure?"

"We buried her at sea." Aragon's voice was beyond frosty. Ice dripped from it.

"Well," grumbled Psittacus. He tossed the fortune cards into a corner. "Come on. These aren't going to do us much good, they haven't caught up to the cosmos yet. Someone's been buggering around with the space-time continuum. Your girl's just a symptom, I'd say. No one can die before their destiny's up, no matter how hard they try. We'll have to follow the problem to the source."

"Lady Luck," rasped Aragon Silversword.

"Oh?" replied Psittacus the philosopher. "Can't say I'm surprised." He looked slightly sick. "Planning to go toe to toe with Milady, are you? Brave lad."

"Actually, I had just decided to give it up as a bad job," admitted Aragon.

Psittacus looked outraged. "And let her win? Let her destroy the cosmos? Can't have that!" He frowned. "Even so, better let you know what you're up against. You'll have to be invisible."

"One of my life's ambitions," said Aragon dryly. Three minutes later, he couldn't help waving a hand in front of his face. As predicted, he couldn't see it.

"Of course you can't see it," said Psittacus irritably. "You're invisible. I did explain this."

"But if I'm invisible, how can I see anything at all? Surely I should be blind…"

Psittacus slapped a hand over Aragon's mouth. "You know that, and I know that," he hissed quietly, "But the cosmos hasn't caught up with us yet, so let's not give her any ideas, eh?"

"You haven't explained *why* we're invisible. Is there a reason for it, or are you just practising?"

"We, my boy, are about to trespass in the most exclusive club in Zibria—the Progressive Atheist's Committee."

Aragon hesitated. "We may be invisible, but are we lightning proof?"

Psittacus chuckled. "This way."

Unaware of the two invisible observers who had crept in at the back of the hall, the Progressive Atheist's Committee was brought to order.

"Now then," said the Chair, "Could you read the minutes from last meeting, Brother Garfunkl?"

A skinny, redheaded young man coughed and frantically swallowed his adam's apple. "At 2:51 of the clock, the meeting was brought to order and minutes were read. At 2:55 of the clock, Brother Francine denounced the almighty fiction of the concept that divine beings exist within our rational universe. At 2:56 of the clock, a large tidal wave unexpectedly emerged from the community privy and swallowed Brother Francine whole. At 3:01 of the clock, the meeting was closed due to an outbreak of irrational prayers and similar religious observances by Brothers Caramel and Ortman."

The Chair stared blackly at the two brothers in question, who stared apologetically at their boots.

The meeting was interrupted by a pale young woman who trudged in from a side door and cautiously took a chair. "Sorry I'm late, everybody," she said in a quiet voice. "I wasn't feeling very well."

The Chair turned his fierce expression on to the young woman, eyeing her waistline. "You are not *with child*, are you, Sister Maughan?"

"Well," she blushed suddenly, "I suppose I could be." She burst into tears. "Oh, I'm sorry, Chair, but he appeared in a shower of gold, and he had such a commanding presence and..." She subsided into mutinous sniffles.

"Does anyone else have anything to confess?" asked the Chair dangerously.

A small brother put his hand up. "Well, actually..."

"Yes, Brother Belfry?"

"I, well you see, I sort of maybe had a visitation last night," Brother Belfry muttered in an embarrassed tone.

"A visitation?" repeated the Chair ominously.

"Just a little one," said Brother Belfry in a squeak. "But you see, well have *you* heard the glorious word of Number Seven?"

"OUT!" roared the Chair.

Brother Belfry ran for it, clutching the hand of Sister Maughan who had decided to make a break at the same time.

The Chair folded his arms and regarded his three remaining committee members. "Does anyone *else* have anything to report?"

Feeling an invisible hand plucking at his invisible sleeve, Aragon quietly made his way out of the Zibrian community hall. In the sunlight, he watched his feet gradually became visible again, as did the rest of him. Psittacus the philosopher was also visible now, although his left hand and half of his beard remained missing for quite some time.

"Why did we leave halfway through?" asked Aragon curiously.

"Between you, me and the hedgehog, they're going to be struck by a divine fireball in about ten minutes," said Psittacus cheerfully. "The gods can cope with individual atheists, but they take it personally when they start forming committees. Anyway, you'd heard enough, hadn't you?"

"The lesson being that mortals should not pit themselves against the gods, I suppose," said Aragon dryly.

"Something like that," agreed Psittacus. "Still willing to go through with all this?"

Aragon was silent for a moment. "She wasn't supposed to die, was she?"

"No," said Psittacus the philosopher. "She wasn't. It's obviously a symbol that the cosmos is seriously ailing. Still, that's hardly your concern." He raised a bushy white eyebrow in a comical fashion. "Or is it?"

-§-§-§-§-§-

In one of the more tastefully decorated godly dimensions, Destiny wrinkled her nose. "When do the fireworks start?"

"I beg your pardon?" said Lady Luck haughtily.

"Well, you threatened to do all sorts of nasty things to Aragon Silversword, and it hasn't happened."

"Give it time," replied Lady Luck. "True mortal manipulation requires skill and subtlety—neither of which you possess, incidentally—and it takes *time* to unfurl every level of the plot in a truly dramatic fashion."

"I reckon you've lost your touch," said Destiny slyly.

"Stuff and nonsense!" But a worried expression hovered behind Lady Luck's superior smile. "Just because I can't actually locate him at this exact moment does not imply any kind of failure on my part. It is a momentary setback, nothing more."

-§-§-§-§-§-

"The thing about Lady Luck," confided Psittacus. "None of the gods like her much, but they're all scared stiff of her. When it comes to manipulation, she's the best there is. And you haven't a hope of doing what you *have* to do without assistance." He seemed to be deep in thought for a few moments. "It'll have to be Tmesis."

"Who?"

"She's the priestess of the lost gods, the mislaid divinities." Aragon still didn't seem to understand, so Psittacus spelled it out for him. "The ex-gods of Mocklore. From before the decimalisation. She'll help you reach the Underworld. None of the gods will risk it, but she doesn't have much to lose."

"Fine," said Aragon. "By the way, which one are you?"

Psittacus looked at him, a hint of a desperate smile taking over his heavily-bearded face. "Sorry, my boy? Didn't quite catch that."

"I think you know exactly what I mean," said Aragon in a hard voice. "Which—god—are—you?"

Psittacus sighed, and for a moment his face fell away to reveal another, younger but infinitely seedier face with blotchy eyes and lopsided stubble.

"Binx," said Aragon thoughtfully. "Patron god of Dreadnought…"

"Don't tell everybody," begged the Empire's most disreputable deity, quickly restoring his 'Psittacus' face. "If Milady finds out my involvement here, she'll make my eternity a living hell. Don't look at me like that, you don't have to live on the same plane of existence as her!"

"True," said Aragon acidly, "What I *would* like is to be on the same plane of existence as Kassa Daggersharp. Is that going to be possible?"

Psittacus tugged at his beard. "Not sure, old boy. Probably not. I mean, destiny is one thing, but once a mortal's dead that's supposed to be it. No going back. Mind you, if it's the cosmos at fault, and Lady Luck just took advantage of it, then there should be some way to unravel her handiwork. Loopholes are surprisingly common, if you know where to look. Anyway, if your priority is to find the dead lass, you'll have to travel to the Underworld. Gods aren't allowed there, except the Dark One, so only Tmesis the Forgotten Priestess can show you the way."

"Fine," said Aragon. "And where is she?"

Psittacus looked uncomfortable. "Ah. That's the thing, you see. I don't actually know…"

"*What*?"

"Come on!" The fake philosopher shuffled quickly down a marble-tiled avenue. "There's an amnesty on priests, you see. They're undetectable to any but their own gods. And as Tmesis' gods are officially Forgotten, they can't help you."

"So where now?" demanded Aragon. He wasn't going to let himself be dragged back and forth by a fake philosopher in the name of some indefinable goal—he had had enough of that sort of thing from Kassa.

"Well, there is another category who come under Tmesis' guiding hand, so to speak. The hemi-gods."

"Hemi-gods?"

"Certainly, old boy. This Decimalisation business is all very well, but gods are immortal. We don't all stay chaste. At least, not all of the time. Unplanned offspring are bound to turn up every now and then. The half mortals are usually all right—the boys slap on a lion skin and turn hero, while the girls get up to all sorts of interesting things. But if they don't have any mortal blood, the sprogs get stamped as hemi-gods and forgotten about. Not Forgotten, just forgotten. It means they could be gods if we had room for more than ten, which we don't."

"And you know one of these hemi-gods?" Aragon was discovering less and less sarcasm in his voice. He couldn't be getting used to this sort of life, could he?

"Hemi-goddess, as it happens." They were at the arched city walls now. Psittacus pushed Aragon out of the golden gates (foil-covered) and pressed a large red fruit into his hand. "This is her calling card. Good luck."

"Now wait a minute," said Aragon Silversword, but it was too late. The 'philosopher' had vanished. "I've just about had enough of this," he growled at the fruit, feeling stupid. It was round, an unfamiliar object with a red leathery skin. Aragon dropped it on the dusty ground where it bounced and lay still. He drew his sword and stabbed deeply down into the flesh of the fruit. As he pulled out the transparent blade, several pulpy seeds were clinging to it. Thoughtfully, Aragon picked off one seed, cracking it between his teeth.

The universe exploded for a little while.

-§-§-§-§-§-

Wordern the Sky-warrior, the god of thunder and lightning who was technically responsible for all the bearded and braided folk in Axgaard, had eight daughters. They were not gods, because the decimalisation of the religious structures of Mocklore had put an end to divine dynasties. They were not even demi-gods, because that wasn't allowed either.

On the other hand, they weren't mortal. Because they were girls, they weren't supposed to be heroes. So they hung around in their father's divine cloud mansion, braided their hair, rode around on flying horses while singing opera and generally made themselves available for the occasional odd job which was far too menial for any official god to bother with.

It was Pomegranate's turn to do the washing up. Her long braids were pinned to the ceiling to keep them out of the suds, and her slender arms were engulfed in long yellow rubber gloves. She sighed plaintively. Thursday was always a rotten day for washing up, because of the weekly banquet the night before. The sink was piled to the brim with eating axes, knives, tankards and gobbets of leftovers.

Everything smelled of beer—but then, everything in Axgaard always smelled of beer and Wordern the Sky-warrior liked his mansion in the clouds to reflect his favourite city in every way possible.

Pomegranate Wordernsdaughter gave another plaintive sigh and set to work.

Having successfully scoured the porridge stains from the last of the broadswords and stacked them neatly on the drying rack, she was removing her rubber gloves when a man fell out of the sky and crashed into her ornamental fountain, just outside the kitchen window.

Pomegranate hurried out, pulling the gloves off with her pearly white teeth as she did so. Halfway out the door, she had to trot back and unpin her lengthy braids from the ceiling.

He was handsome enough, she supposed, finally reaching the man. Hardly the tall dark stranger she had been promised in her sister Hvelga's fortune cards, but she wasn't going to turn her nose up at him. Even unconscious, he had a face of character. His dark blond hair was tied out of his face with a thread of leather. There was an age gap between them, but nothing insurmountable. Pomegranate regarded him critically. He was smeared from head to toe in the pulp of her least favourite fruit, the one she had been inadvertently named after.

The stranger groaned, and opened his eyes. "Thought you'd be…older," he groaned, one hand automatically twitching towards his fruit-stained sword.

"That's what everybody says," replied Pomegranate.

-§-§-§-§-§-

After his bath, in which he managed to get most of the pomegranate seeds out of his hair, Aragon Silversword descended back to the kitchen, where Wordern the Sky-warrior's eldest daughter was stamping cookies out with a star-shaped cutter. "Better now?" she asked without looking up.

He regarded her curiously. "Were you expecting me?"

Pomegranate clapped her hands together, dusting off the excess flour. "I was expecting someone. But not you." She sighed. "If you must know, I'm due to be kidnapped and carried off to marry some god."

"Oh," said Aragon. "Today?"

Pomegranate wiped a wisp of hair behind one ear, leaving a streaky mark of flour in her soft brown braids. "Sometime today, yes. You'll probably be here to witness it if you hang around much longer. Did you want something?"

"I was sent here to ask directions. I need to find the Priestess of Forgotten Gods."

"And hemi-goddesses," agreed Pomegranate cheerfully. "Nothing simpler." She crossed to the kitchen door. "See those mountains? Up behind the ornamental lake and the almost-ornamental albatross."

Aragon looked. At first he saw nothing but clouds, then somehow when he looked at them from a certain angle he *could* see finely-sculpted mountains. And the albatross.

"Tmesis lives up there," said Pomegranate. "It's a bit of a hike, I'm afraid."

"I'd better get started." Aragon hesitated, glancing back at the flour-streaked hemi-goddess. "Would you like me to wait? I could help you fight off your abductor..." Offering to rescue a damsel without being coerced? This was very unlike him. The sooner he removed Kassa's influence, the better.

"It's destiny," said Pomegranate sensibly. "No use trying to avoid it."

Aragon Silversword looked back at the cloud mountains in the distance. "Oh, I fully intend to," he said darkly. "Good luck."

"Good luck," echoed Pomegranate thoughtfully. "I think you'll need it more than me." And then she went back inside to finish stamping out her cookies.

-§-§-§-§-§-

Gant Peebles was a profit-scoundrel out of his depth. More precisely, out of his city. The only scoundrels who worked outside Dreadnought for any length of time were those who weren't much good—the fact that Gant Peebles was in Zibria, the city-state furthest from Dreadnought, should go some way to explaining his precise levels of ineptitude.

He had stolen the Eye of Obsidian. He hadn't meant to. It had been a straightforward mugging, with no dialogue and no complications. Only when he had scuttled away to examine his pouch of loot had he unfolded the linen bag and stared into the depths of the blackest pearl ever to claw its way out of the Cellar Sea. This rock was legendary.

It was worthless to him. No fence who would stoop to dealing with Gant Peebles would be able to perform the kind of lightning-gymnastic deal necessary to smuggle the pearl out of Mocklore. And no one who knew him would believe it was real.

He gulped miserably. The only thing to do was to throw the wretched thing away. If he was caught with it on his person...

"Well, well." It was a sultry voice, a voice worthy of the goddess Amorata herself. As it happened, it also belonged to a brunette. Bounty Fenetre the hobgoblin bounty-hunter stood with one hip slung against the brickwork of the alley. "Hello, hello," she drawled winsomely. "What do we have here? Twenty-two minutes from crime to capture—that's a record even I can be proud of."

The Eye of Obsidian slipped from Gant Peebles' shaking fingers and Bounty leaped forward in a flash of slinky chain-mail, catching up the precious rock before it hit the cobbles. She dangled the dark pearl from its thin chain and grinned at the terrified profit-scoundrel. "I could do all sorts of things to you," she said conversationally. "Things that would make your ears curl and your hair fall out. But I don't think you're worth it."

Quick as a wink, she pulled out a leather collar and snapped it around Gant Peebles' neck. She tugged impatiently on the leash, forcing him to put one foot in front of the other. "Come on. Let's get you arrested, shall we?"

After delivering Gant Peebles to the holding cells and collecting her fat reward from the client who had been desperate to have the dark pearl retrieved, Bounty Fenetre dropped into the local offices of the Zibrian secret police. "Anything for me today, Xandra?" she asked cheerfully as she slid her legs over the window ledge.

"I thought you were freelance," said the Commandant, a dark-skinned woman in a little spangled dress. "And we do have a door, you know."

"But your windows are so much cozier," teased Bounty. "Come on, give me a job. Something too complicated for your girls to handle. I haven't done anything interesting for at least fifteen minutes."

Xandra shrugged and pretended to consult her files. "An outlaw with an astounding Imperial price on his head has been seen moving around the city. We'd prefer that he was removed as quickly as possible—and that the Lady Emperor heard he was captured somewhere far from here.

We do have a low profile to maintain, after all." She raised a quirky eyebrow. "I don't want my agents involved, but if you capture him within Zibrian walls, we expect twenty percent of the Imperial bounty."

"Done," said Bounty, moistening her lips. "What's his name?"

"Aragon Silversword," said Commandant Xandra. "No known aliases. Think you can handle it?"

Bounty Fenetre widened her obnoxiously wonderful eyes. "Ohhh, I thought you'd never ask." She ran her fingers over her chainmail lovingly. "I've been putting this one off for far too long."

Chapter 11
Kpow

"Get that ship," ordered the Sultan of Zibria, his voice dripping with avarice. "Kill them and get me that *ship*!"

Something in Daggar's brain kicked into gear. "Get on board!" he shouted to Sparrow, pulling her towards the golden galleon which filled most of the sterile white room, its ghostly qualities allowing it to exist in the same space as the copious white benches and bubbling beakers, which were acting as obstacles for the golden-liveried guards.

"That thing?" said Sparrow sceptically.

"Just do it!" he shrieked, physically hurling Singespitter on to the deck and scrambling up after him. Shrugging, Sparrow followed suit.

"Stop them!" shouted the Sultan, just to make things difficult. "A pension to the man who stops them! I want them in the dungeon with the Brewmistress in five minutes or you all go without your supper!" The liveried guards were still scrambling awkwardly over benches and stools and test-tubes.

"Follow them!" shrieked the concubine who had come scrambling up the secret stairs with Officer Finnley in tow. She gave the young Blackguard a mighty shove towards the glowing ship as she ran, jumped and clung.

"*Up*!" commanded Daggar, his feet firmly on the deck and his hand on the wheel. The golden ghost-ship slowly rose towards the ceiling. Officer Finnley, trying to copy the concubine's actions, smacked hard into the seemingly translucent side of the ship, and slumped unconscious to the ground.

"The ship responds to voice signals?" demanded Sparrow.

"It always has," replied Daggar, still panicky.

"Good," she grated. "So does the liquid gold." Overwhelmed by a sudden wave of dizziness, Sparrow clung to the mast. "*Back*," she ordered the ship, forcing her will upon the liquid gold that had merged with it. It was a random command. She didn't really care where it went, as long as it was away from here.

And the golden ghost-ship went *KPOW*.

-§-§-§-§-§-

Many years previously, a shambling cart of strolling players sputtered its way along the track, pouring out the occasional burst of uncoordinated music. The dancing girls all clustered at the back of the cart, hanging their wet hair out to dry while a brightly-clad jester scampered along behind, picking up every hairpin and stray ribbon that they dropped.

Muzzlefud the playwright was chewing his quill and trying to squeeze some inspiration out of his exhausted brain. "I suppose," he said in a dull, hopeless voice. "We couldn't do something about pirates, could we?"

Bessemund Baker, an earthy girl with big hair, star-quality and too much facepaint, snorted loudly. "You mean like the Black Rogue, the Pirate Queen or the Great Sword-Swallowing Caper? We've done them all. There's nothing new and original to say about *pirates*."

"You're right," said Muzzlefud dismally. "All pirate stories are the same."

From somewhere, a booming voice proclaimed, "Stand and Deliver!"

The mummers' cart came to a clattering stop, mainly because the track ahead was lined with pirates. They were a fearsome, evil-looking lot, all black beards, eyepatches and pointy teeth. The leader of the pack was the nastiest of the lot, a huge bloke with a bristling big beard, startling yellow eyes and a ripped leather costume. He brandished his sword like he knew what to do with it. "What ho!" he roared threateningly. "Any of you chaps know anything about birthin' babies?"

Muzzlefud revolved his eyes frantically towards Bessemund, who stared at the pirates as if she didn't know quite what to make of them.

A powerful female hand pushed the bigbearded pirate aside, revealing a small woman with straggly dyed-black hair, a fierce expression and an alarming bulge under her dress. "You bastard, Bigbeard," she snarled. "You promised me a midwife months ago, but no, you just had to leave everything to the last minute!" She stared flatly at the travellers. "I'm not settling for second best. Let's just kill them and take their cart."

"Righty ho," said Vicious Bigbeard Daggersharp. "You heard her, lads! Let's scupper the land-sucking guttersnipes!"

The pirate band cheered raggedly and advanced.

"Brilliant," said Muzzlefud the playwright with a glint in his eye. "Pirates adventuring on roads. Highway... robbery! Why didn't I think of that before? Where's my quill?"

"Not *now*, Muzzlefud," said Bessemund thickly, snatching up a handy rolling pin and preparing for battle.

-§-§-§-§-§-

The Palace laboratory was far behind them now, or possibly ahead of them. Impossible lights and spiralling colours exploded around them in brilliant patterns of gold. Behind them, strands of alien amber light bled into the cosmos, warping it slightly.

Sparrow sat pressed against the side of the ship, her hair blowing wildly with the wind that came from everywhere and nowhere. Her hand was tightly curled around Singespitter's leather collar.

"Are you all right now?" Daggar asked.

She looked up at him with her pale eyes. "I do not feel right without my armour. The air itches."

"I mean, are you going to stop turning yellow and falling over now?" Daggar said with exaggerated patience.

"Oh, that." Sparrow's eyes went flinty. "For now." She pulled herself to her feet and gazed over his shoulder. "We have company."

"Right." Daggar turned and looked at the concubine who had scrambled uninvited on to their deck. "So who are you?"

She lifted a slender shoulder and unconsciously shimmied some of her sequins. "I'm Tione. Concubine and member of the secret police." She shrugged her other shoulder. A little more shimmying happened.

Daggar, very conscious of Sparrow beside him, did his best not to look remotely impressed. "You have secret police in Zibria? I've never heard that."

Tione rolled her heavily-kohled eyes. "I'm not even going to dignify that with a response." Daggar looked at her with big, baffled brown eyes, and she blew out a breath of impatience. "We're secret, all right?"

"You are an enforcer of the law," said Sparrow flatly. "What do you want with us?"

The concubine gave a tiny smile. "Adventure and excitement?" she suggested.

"Suits me," said Daggar, openly admiring her sequins.

Sparrow gave him a killer look. "Since when?"

"Look, I don't really know," the concubine admitted. "But when I heard the Sultan had thrown you to the Minestaurus, I just had to go after you. And when I saw the ship go all gold, I just had to jump aboard. I couldn't help myself." She smiled brightly. "Maybe it's destiny."

"Maybe," growled Sparrow.

The golden ship shimmered suddenly, and the swirling lights bled into a perfectly ordinary spring landscape:

the sky was sunny with the vague promise of rain, hail, blizzards and possible flying herrings. At the sight of all the fresh green grass, Singespitter baaed and attempted to climb over the side.

"Look at this," said Daggar, staring at the ship's wheel. A large amber crystal sat in its centre as if it had never been anywhere else. It glistened menacingly.

Sparrow leaned over his shoulder. "It was not there before?"

"Course it wasn't," said Daggar. "It would have clashed with the silver decor. Have we really gone back in time?"

Sparrow scowled, tapping one finger against the amber crystal. "This must be the way the liquid gold was *supposed* to be used—fixed to some kind of travelling vehicle. A cart would have done, or a flying carpet." She swore at herself, angrily. "Dusthead! I *swallowed* the gritting poison!"

"Is it out of your system now?" asked Daggar anxiously.

Sparrow shook her head. "I do not think it will be that easy."

"You can't spend the rest of your life yoyoing around in time," protested Daggar. "You'll get dizzy. Speaking of which, when do you think we are?"

Sparrow peered at the murky amber crystal, which suddenly cleared. She looked at the undulating image within its golden depths. "The Year of the Sculpted Concubine," she announced finally.

Daggar stared at the image in the crystal and his grin widened slightly. "Will you look at that?" he said slowly. "Sequins and all. Blimey," he added, after counting to himself for a moment. "I'm eight years old."

"Tall for your age," commented Sparrow. "And shaving already." She eyed his stubble. "I imagine."

He fingered his chin sheepishly. "Are you suggesting I need a shave?"

"The Year of the Sculpted Concubine was more than twenty years ago!" squealed Tione. "Have we really travelled in time? This is priceless!"

Sparrow glared at her. "Behave yourself or you will be walking home."

"Oi," said Daggar, elbowing her. "*I'm* the Captain of this ship!"

"You are?" challenged Sparrow.

"Well," he said weakly. "I'm related to her. Look, let's hop overboard and have a quick gander around the Year of the Sculpted Concubine. Then we'll see about getting home."

Sparrow nodded her assent. "I wonder if they sell armour anywhere around here." Her black linen shift and leggings were perfectly decent, but they wouldn't hold up well against a volley of arrows. She liked to be prepared for such possibilities.

The golden ship was hovering beside a grassy hillock which was covered in buttercups and gently buzzing bumblebees. The clouds were a long way off, birds were muttering to themselves in high tweety voices and the sounds of a battle were coming from the other side of the hill. Sparrow promptly started in that direction, single-minded in her quest for armour.

Daggar couldn't help noticing the trail of yellow flowers which followed in her wake. He had been seeing those a lot lately. "You look very familiar," he suggested as he turned to lift Tione down to the grass.

"That's original," the concubine sniffed loudly.

Daggar watched her trot up the hill after Sparrow, sequins glittering in the sun. "I'm sure I *know* her from somewhere," he mused, dragging Singespitter down and clapping his hands at the ship, turning it into a gold ship-shaped bauble which he stuck in his pocket. At least that still worked. "I suppose we'd better get after them before they do some damage," he muttered, taking hold of Singespitter's leash and yanking the sheep along with him.

-§-§-§-§-§-

On the crest of the hill, Sparrow stared down at a battle. The strolling players were defending themselves surprisingly well against the attack. Most of their prop swords were made of real metal because it didn't go all bendy when wet like cardboard did.

Sparrow noticed that one woman was standing aside from the fighting, offering nothing apart from the occasional sarcastic remark. Sparrow wandered down to her. "What is happening here?"

The pirate woman turned on her, gesturing angrily at the bulge under her dress. "A bloody farce, that's what!" She glared fiercely at Sparrow. "I don't suppose you know how to deliver babies?"

"Not noticeably," said Sparrow. "I could give you something to bite down on, if you think it would help." She stuck out a hand. "Sparrow. Mercenary."

The pirate woman grimaced and grasped Sparrow's hand with her own, shaking it briefly. A spiral ring of steel and silver glittered on her hand. "Black Nell. Pirate." A sudden look of panic came over her face, and she almost doubled up in pain. "Ohh...Bigbeard!" she screamed.

Vicious Bigbeard Daggersharp turned and waved cheerfully at his wife. Bessemund Baker took the opportunity to wallop him over the head with her rolling pin. His grin glazed over, and he slumped the grass. Of all the mummers, Bessemund was the most fearsome of them all, whacking various pirates with her improvised club and using a collection of nasty-looking hat pins as parrying weapons.

"Great," moaned Black Nell, staring at her unconscious husband. "Just what I need. Trust him to be no help whatsoever."

Almost tripping over her sequins, Tione caught up with Sparrow, just as Black Nell gasped with another contraction. "I do not suppose you can deliver babies?" asked Sparrow, not really expecting a positive answer.

Tione nodded breathlessly. "It's amazing what they teach you in the secret police," she said. "Well, actually it was at concubine school."

"Great," said Sparrow without too many traces of sarcasm in her voice. "So what do we do now?"

"Whatever it is, I suggest you start doing it soon," gasped Black Nell, grabbing on to Sparrow's arm for support.

"Oi!" screamed out Tione to those involved in the battle. "Stop being idiots and start boiling water!" Her shrill voice carried surprisingly well for a five-foot-nothing slip of a concubine.

"Such projection," marvelled Bessemund Baker, her rolling pin hovering in mid-air.

"Well?" demanded Tione. "Get on with it!"

The battle broke up as pirates and mummers alike tried to figure out how to boil water in the middle of nowhere. Tione the concubine turned her attention to Black Nell, fussing over her in a business-like way.

Daggar Profit-scoundrel had scrambled down to Sparrow's side, and was urgently tugging at her sleeve, eyes wide. "Sparrow, I know these people!" He stared around incredulously. "See him? That's my Uncle Bigbeard, Kassa's dad. He died last year. And that's my Aunty Nell. She died about ten years ago. This is my flipping family tree." He shook his head worriedly. "I don't think I can take this."

"Try," said Sparrow with little sympathy.

"That's Bessemund Baker," he hissed. "She became the most fearsome pirate to sail the seas. So this is how it happened!"

Tione was moving around like a miniature spangled whirlwind, ordering pirates and strolling players alike to fetch blankets, boiling water and other apparently vital substances.

One leather-clad pirate, lither and faster than the rest, stripped the cart of its blanket supply in record time and presented them to the frantic concubine-midwife with a flourish. "Cutlass Cooper at your service," he said with a diabolical grin, and their eyes met. Something held their gaze together for an earth-shattering minute, and then Tione wrenched herself away and went to tend the pirate queen who was still yelling obscenities at her unconscious husband.

"Did you see that?" said Daggar hoarsely. "Oh gods, I *thought* I recognised her!"

"Shut up," snapped Sparrow. "Go for a walk until all this is over."

"I think we've just witnessed a serious breach in the space-time continuum," said Daggar in a choked voice. "Either we caused it, or we just mended it."

"I do not care," Sparrow said angrily. "This is much too dangerous. Go and find that sheep of yours. I will get Tione and we will leave, immediately, before you say something you should not. Go!"

Muttering to himself, Daggar trudged back up the hill, looking for Singespitter the sheep. It was a shock, seeing people he remembered from his childhood. Halfway down the other side of the hill, he froze, having only just realised the implications of the bulge under Black Nell's dress. "Bloody hell. That's Kassa in there!"

He was so distracted by that thought that he didn't notice he was being ambushed until he had been thrown to the ground, bound tightly with gilded rope and tossed over someone else's shoulder.

-§-§-§-§-§-

Using the bright silken draperies from the cart, Tione had organised a makeshift pavilion—she gave the orders and various pirates, dancing girls and the occasional jester put the tent together.

Black Nell was inside, screaming blue murder and balancing awkwardly against a pile of ramshackle pillows, cushions and theatrical props.

Sparrow was still trying to convince Tione that they should leave.

"I don't care who he thinks he recognises, we must help this woman!" snapped Tione. "If you want to leave as soon as possible, help me."

"Why me?" said Sparrow in thinly-disguised horror. "I know nothing about babies."

"You're a warrior!" Tione insisted. "You must have some healing knowledge."

"External injuries, yes," snapped Sparrow. "If she stabs her husband or gouges her own eyes out, I can handle it. But do not ask me to get involved with childbirth."

Tione turned her wide eyes upwards, pleadingly. "Sparrow, I need your help. Please?"

-§-§-§-§-§-

Vicious Bigbeard Daggersharp regained consciousness slowly. Familiar screams echoed through the still afternoon. The large pirate opened one eye. It was the one behind the eyepatch, so it didn't do him much good. He opened his other eye and hauled himself to his feet. "What's going on, then?"

Cutlass Cooper sat perched on the end of the cart of the strolling players, swinging his long legs, twirling his moustache and watching the water-boiling attempts of the other pirates. So far, Bruised Cordwainer had burned his fingers, Turbot-face Gralhoun had come dangerously close to finding a kettle and Three-eyed Nadger had fallen into a nearby bear pit. All most entertaining.

"Come on matey, don't take all day about it," said Bigbeard impatiently. "Fill me in."

"Well," drawled Cutlass in his usual charming fashion. "So far, Nell has threatened to cut off just about every prominent part of your body except your ears."

A screeching voice emanated from the silken tent. "I'm going to pull off his ears and feed them to the bloody ship's cat!"

"I stand corrected," said Cutlass with every appearance of enjoyment.

Bigbeard sauntered over to the tent and stuck his head in. "Hullo, love. How's it going?"

A sharpened marionette came sailing out of the tent and missed him by inches. Black Nell was red-faced, panting and deliriously angry. "Damn it, Bigbeard, this is the last time I trust you to get things done!" she screeched. "I could have been in the Skullcap nursing home by now if we'd started moving when I told you to, with clean sheets and potions enough to knock me unconscious for a week!"

Sparrow, resenting the role of midwife's assistant, mopped the expectant mother's brow a little more roughly than was traditional and took a deep swallow of troll-brandy.

"I swear, Bigbeard," yelled Black Nell, "After this I'm getting my own ship. I won't be an unpaid deckhand any more!"

"Whatever you say, dear," said Bigbeard amiably. "Fancy a cup of tea?" He ducked back out of the tent before a fish-shaped cushion could hit him squarely between the eyes.

"All be over soon," said Tione comfortingly.

Nell refused to be comforted. "Don't you have any painkilling potions?" she begged.

The heat and the noise were getting to Sparrow. She wiped her own brow with her sleeve and then stood up. "I need some fresh air."

"It's all right for you," muttered the expectant mother.

Tione gave Sparrow a sharp look. "You *are* coming back, aren't you?"

"Of course," said Sparrow. She handed her flask of troll-brandy to Black Nell. "Try this."

The pirate woman took a swallow of the potent brew and her eyes flew open. "I can't feel anything," she choked. "Is my tongue still attached?"

Sparrow took this opportunity to make a break for it. Outside, she took a few big gulps of fresh cool air. She looked around for Daggar, and couldn't see him. One of the pirates offered her a flask of something as she walked past. She drained it unconsciously, strapping the empty flask to her own belt, which hung loosely around her hips now that she wasn't wearing armour.

She could see Singespitter up on the hill, his wings flapping madly. Something was wrong. Sparrow charged up the hill in a few long strides. "Where is he?" she demanded. "Where's Daggar?"

Obviously, the sheep could not speak. Sparrow scanned the hillside, and saw the crushed grass. Signs of a struggle. She examined the area minutely, and came up with a tiny golden button. She had seen these buttons before, on the livery of the Zibrian palace guards. "This is ridiculous! We will not do anything to warrant palace guards chasing us for another twenty-three years. Why would they take Daggar?"

Again, Singespitter said nothing, but capered around anxiously.

Sparrow nodded grimly. "Daggar has the liquid gold ship in his pocket, does he not? If we want to return to our own time, we must rescue him."

Singespitter nodded as eagerly as it was possible for a sheep to nod and rubbed himself up against her ankles.

Sparrow marched once more to the crest of the hill and looked around. There was the city, less than an hour's walk away. It glittered, more golden than she had ever seen it. And there, moving rapidly along the canal path, she could see several men in Zibrian livery, carrying something brown and sacklike. "They have him!"

Sparrow broke into a run, grabbing Singespitter's leash as she did so. "Come, there is no time to lose!"

Chapter 12
Matchmaking as a Last Resort

Kassa Daggersharp stormed into the Dark One's throne room, utterly livid. "Why didn't you tell me I could leave the Underworld if I went on a quest?" she yelled.

"You didn't ask," said the Dark One. "Am I going to have to hide behind my throne again? My knees aren't really up to the strain these days." He brushed a fine layer of yellow dust from his black throne.

Kassa glared at him, and then over his head, her eyes following the complex patterns of the disturbing mosaic as she turned her various frustrated thoughts over in her mind. "I saw my parents," she said finally.

"Ah," said the Dark One. "That explains your tempestuous mood. I met your parents once, and I was out of sorts for days. Not that time has any meaning here," he added hastily.

Kassa scowled. "I don't understand. Why are they still here? Is this all they want out of the afterlife? A cave, some booze and each other?"

The Dark One lifted his long-nosed face to gaze directly at her. "And why not? There are alternatives, for everyone. They could drink from the river Oblivion and forget their past life in order to be born again in the mortal sphere. That is always an option for every soul in the Underworld—except me, of course."

"So why don't they?" she demanded. "Why not start anew?"

"Perhaps they still have ties to the mortal world, to these lives," the Dark One suggested. "They may wish to stay together for a while longer. There are no guarantees with reincarnation."

"No," said Kassa definitely. "It wasn't like that. They weren't that wrapped up in each other. They had separate lives." She stared angrily at the long-nosed god. "They have no motive to want to spend their afterlives together!"

"Do they not?" inquired the Dark One gently. He tilted his head. "I bow to superior expertise."

Kassa shot him a killer look, but refrained from taking further action because of Vervain, who popped up out of nowhere to change the subject.

"Hey, Kassa!" he announced, blithely unaware of the frictions in the room. "Here I am, your ever loyal guardian sprite reporting for duty, come rain or shine!" He smiled edgily at her. "Are you in a better mood now?"

"Relax," Kassa sighed. "You're far too tense. I thought sprites were supposed to be thick-skinned."

"Not me," Vervain assured her, preening in his new black velvet robe. He was planning to put sequins on it. "I'm the sensitive type. Did someone say something about a quest?"

Kassa caught the Dark One's eye, and he smiled slightly. "It is not usual, but there is a loophole within the rules of the Underworld," he informed them.

She was instantly suspicious. "What kind of loophole?"

"When Dame Veekie wants something, nobody has the strength to argue," the Dark One said with a wry grin. "Least of all me."

Suddenly a thunderous sound resounded throughout the Underworld. Kassa, flung hard against one of the walls, felt it buckle and warp. "What is it?" she screamed.

Just as suddenly, the sound and shaking stopped. The Dark One mopped himself with his duster. "Just a few fluctuations in the cosmos. They affect us from time to time—that's the trouble with being slightly outside reality. Now, shouldn't you be going back to Dame Veekie?"

Only after Kassa had given him a hard look and left the chamber with Vervain at her heels did the Dark One allow himself to look worried. The 'fluctuations' had been happening a little too often lately.

-§-§-§-§-§-

The first stage of witch training involved concentrated study, and Kassa was not in the mood for it. "I feel sorry for the Dark One," she said aloud, ignoring the sheaves of parchments stretched out before her on the desk which detailed the important properties of various herbs, rocks and minor insect life as far as witchlore was concerned. She had always been interested in this sort of thing, but now she actually had an opportunity to study them the glamour had worn off. "He seems so lonely."

"He is a god," said Dame Veekie. "Don't impose your mortal-minded emotional baggage on him. He wouldn't know what to do with them."

"Even so," Kassa continued. "I wonder why he doesn't have a companion of some sort. You'd think there would be plenty to choose from with all these souls wandering around."

"Not allowed," replied the Dame sternly. "Gods can dally with mortals all they like. But not dead mortals."

"But live mortals can't visit the Underworld," Kassa protested. A horrible thought crossed her mind. "I *am* dead, aren't I? Everyone keeps saying I'm not..."

"Well, you weren't brought here to be the Dark One's concubine," said Dame Veekie humourlessly. "Trust me. Are you at all interested in these properties of herbs?"

Kassa wasn't listening. "What do you think, Vervain?"

"I think these scrolls are awfully dusty," said the orange sprite, polishing them with his sleeve. "You've already given him a new image."

"Every king needs a consort," Kassa shrugged, blowing a cloud of yellow dust from the nearest scroll. "What is this stuff? It gets everywhere." She laughed suddenly.

"That would be a quest, wouldn't it? To find a consort for the Harbinger of Horribleness."

"Perhaps," said Dame Veekie, unsmiling. "Now pay attention."

Kassa bowed her head to study, but bunked off at the earliest opportunity and went looking for an alternative accomplice, as Vervain had wandered off somewhere.

Ebony the goth girl listened to Kassa's half-baked plan with something like amusement. "Aren't you supposed to be doing your homework?"

"Never mind that now," said Kassa dismissively, shifting the huge stack of parchments awkwardly against her hip. "Is it possible?"

"I don't know. Don't gods usually make these decisions for themselves?"

Kassa waved her hand dismissively. "He can barely dress himself. Anyway, I'm good at this sort of thing. I'm a champion matchmaker."

Ebony looked unconvinced. "You're bored, aren't you?"

"Well, maybe," Kassa admitted. "I usually have a whole crewful of people to manipulate. Anyway, I need a quest as soon as humanly possible, so I can get back to the mortal realm."

"What if there isn't anything left there for you?" the goth girl challenged.

"There is," insisted Kassa. "If my head would stop being so fuzzy, I might remember what it was. Will you help me?"

Another titanic fluctuation hit the Underworld, and the corridor shuddered. A layer of fine golden dust drifted down from the ceiling. "It's getting worse," Ebony murmured.

Kassa ignored the disturbance. "Will you help me?"

"What do you want me to do?"

"If gods can't dally with mortals," mused Kassa, "what's the alternative? How about sprites?"

Ebony frowned. "Could be a grey area. After all, goths and imps are technically sprites, I think." Her darkly painted eyelids widened as she saw someone approaching over Kassa's shoulder. "Excuse me, I need to be somewhere else."

With an amazing turn of speed for one so slinky, Ebony the goth girl glided away.

Kassa spun around and the sudden movement dislodged the pile of herbal parchments from her arms. They slid to the floor in a resounding heap.

"Ah," said Dame Veekie icily, her grey starched-high hair standing more than usual. "Hard at work. I see."

Kassa briefly considered scrabbling around on the floor to gather all the parchments together, but dismissed the idea. She may not have much left, but she was holding on to her dignity. She gave the spilled pages a swishing kick with a long black leather boot, which scattered them even further. "That's what I think of your lists and regulations! I'm going on my quest." She stalked away down the rocky corridor.

Dame Veekie Crosselet smiled.

-§-§-§-§-§-

This time when Kassa Daggersharp stormed into the throne room, there was no one to intimidate. Frowning, she looked around the empty chamber. The black velvet curtains had been miraculously mended, concealing the dizzying mosaics from sight.

There was an embarrassed cough from the doorway. "Ahem."

Kassa turned around as the Dark One stepped into the room. He was wearing a rather swish pastel-peach suit with a spangly shirt underneath. Bobbing eagerly behind him was Vervain, carrying a full-length mirror. His orange skin clashed horribly with the Dark One's new attire; not that the suit wasn't doing a pretty good job of clashing with itself.

"Well?" inquired the Dark One, twirling around and sticking out his sleeves for inspection. "What do you think?"

"There's something to be said for basic black," Kassa muttered to herself.

A flicker of doubt crossed the Dark One's face. "What did you say?"

"I said it's a good start," she assured him, and then looked hard at Vervain. "Are you responsible for this?"

"All my own work," grinned the sprite proudly.

"Fabulous." Kassa moved aside so the Dark One could take his place on the black throne. "How are you feeling now?"

"Oh, much more confident," he assured her. "Wait until Amorata and the others see me in this!"

Kassa smiled. "That leads to my next question. I need a quest so I can get back to the real world for a few minutes, and I wondered if you wanted me to find you a consort." It was too much to hope that she might land anywhere near her crew, but it was worth a try. What were they doing now? What was *Aragon* doing now? Did he even miss her, or was he relishing his freedom?

The Dark One looked intrigued. "You want to get me a consort? Whatever for?"

"Well, if you had someone to rule the Underworld jointly with, you could take time off now and then. Holidays and such."

"Interesting idea," mused the Dark One. "I don't see why not."

"Right," said Kassa. "Come on, Vervain. Let's get out into the real world."

"Just as long as she's not dead," said the Dark One, preening his lapels in the mirror which had been propped up against his throne. "I can't abide dead people. No offence."

"None taken," said Kassa Daggersharp evenly. "Where do I start looking?"

"How would I know? Perhaps the library? Apparently it knows everything."

-§-§-§-§-§-

The library was hidden away on one of the uninhabited levels of the Underworld. Kassa waded through stacks of cardboard boxes and knee-high cobwebs spun by dead (and obviously confused) spiders. Eventually, she came to the shelves themselves. They lined the back wall of library, which went on…

Forever. There was no horizon in either direction, just a single wall of scrolls and papyrus stretching into infinity. Twice. Kassa stared, already exhausted by the magnitude of her task. "I don't suppose there's an index?" she said aloud.

A large scroll bucket whizzed out of nowhere, catching her a mighty whack across the temple. Knocked out by the blow, Kassa crumpled into a heap.

A few minutes later, she blearily opened her eyes to find a little grey face staring anxiously into her own. Kassa barely restrained a scream. "Who are you?"

"Library imp," said the creature sorrowfully. "Categoriser and organiser. Guardian of the tomes of knowledge, reader of the sacred texts. Holder of…"

Sensing that there wasn't going to be a pause, Kassa interrupted. "What hit me?" She regretted the question almost as soon as it came out.

"Index of Destiny," the library imp informed her. "Reference guide to all otherworldly knowledge. Composed by…"

"I get the picture! Can you find me any references to non-dead beings entering the Underworld?"

"There are ninety-eight thousand, two hundred and seventy-three texts which may be appropriate," droned the imp. "For cross referencing, please enter additional data. This can be implemented by…"

"I need information relevant to the here and now," said Kassa desperately.

"There is no time reference in the Underworld…"

"Here and now meaning, of course, the reign of the Dark One as king of the underworld! There was a pause.

"There are two thousand, three hundred and sixty…"

"Any texts directly related to the Dark One himself? Or me, Kassa Daggersharp." She spelled her name carefully for him.

Another pause.

A dusty scroll appeared in Kassa's lap. "Please enjoy your reading convenience. For further queries…"

"Thank you!" Kassa sang out.

The grey library imp vanished.

Kassa turned her attention to the scroll in her hands. *The Prophecies of Svelte, as dictated to the Sage of the Wandering Desert in the year of the Sculpted Concubine.* She couldn't resist a shiver at the sight of her own birth year. Surely it must be coincidence…

She unrolled the heavy book and began to read.

Four hours later, a headache started to form behind her eyes, but she continued to mechanically turn the pages.

-§-§-§-§-§-

Kassa burst into the throne room for the third time that day (not that daytime really mattered in the Underworld). The Dark One flinched. Vervain hid behind the new pot plants he had brought in to 'brighten up' the place.

"Look at this," said Kassa, brandishing the scroll. "There's a whole prophecy devoted to it! It explains everything, the earthquakes in the Underworld, the yellow dust everywhere."

The Dark One frowned. "Prophecies are not usually very helpful."

She waved the scroll. "It even has pictures! Apparently there some kind of unnatural time-distorting substance has been brought into the mortal world, and it is polluting the cosmos." She licked her finger and ran it over the back of the throne, staining her skin yellow with dust. "This is it. It's coming at us from the past, present and future. And if I don't fulfil my quest, it will tear the Underworld apart!"

"Good riddance," said the Dark One, seeming to cheer up at the thought.

Kassa glared at him. "I'm not sold on this place either, but can you imagine what will happen if it is destroyed?"

Suddenly considering the implications, the Dark One was aghast. "I could be struck off! If I let the dead invade the mortal world, there's no telling what all the other gods will do to me. They *never* liked me! I'll never, *ever* get my vote back!"

Kassa took a deep breath. "So I can go on my quest?"

He sighed heavily. "Yes, yes I suppose so. As long as you come right back. Does this suspiciously convenient prophecy tell you what to do?"

She nodded. "I have to find you a consort."

"Oh, not that again," the Dark One said dismissively. "I've totally gone off that idea now. I couldn't possibly share a bathroom. I was thinking, maybe a pet of some kind. Possibly a canary, or a kitty cat. Maybe even a snark."

Kassa stared him down, her hands firmly on her hips. "The book says a consort. I'm supposed to travel to Wordern's mansion in the clouds and bring back one of his daughters for you. Somehow, that's the one event which will prevent the Underworld from being destroyed."

"I remember them," sniffed the Dark One. "Lots of little girls in braids riding horses and singing. Horrible."

"I imagine they've grown up by now," Kassa assured him. "My quest is all here in muffled and obscure prophetic prose. Easy as sewing on a button."

"You won't even have to visit the mortal world to do it!" said the Dark One, clapping his hands.

"Oh," said Kassa. "Won't I?"

"Of course not. Quite unnecessary. Splendid, splendid."

"Indeed," said Dame Veekie Crosslet. She emerged from the shadows, resplendent in her pale grey ensemble of beads and feathers. "Well done. I'm sure you will choose to devote some time to your witch studies before undertaking such a venture."

"Not now," said Kassa impatiently. "No time. Maybe after the quest." She turned back to the Dark One, not catching the gleam which briefly appeared in Dame Veekie's grey eyes. "Do you know the way to Wordern's mansion?"

"Of course," the Dark One assured her. "I'll show you which door to take just as soon as you compliment me on my new suit." He leaned back on his throne, smiling confidently.

Kassa had been trying not to notice the garish combination of lavender and yellow pin-striped jacket over a blue-sequined shirt and flared green trousers. She smiled weakly, trying to muster a vague sort of enthusiasm. "I bet you're so glad to be out of all that tasteful black!" she managed.

Chapter 13
A Party of Paradoxes

Zibria glittered. It sparkled and shone. The Zibria of the past was gilded from head to foot. Bathed in sunlight, the gilded towers and temples were blindingly bright. Momentarily distracted from her mission, Sparrow stood and stared. So this was Zibria twenty-three years ago—a Zibria before decay set in.

She headed through the big gates and into the city. The streets were still not paved with gold, but enough drips of gilt and golden paint had fallen from the higher buildings to give that impression. The combination of bright white marble and pure gold was dazzling.

Sparrow had lost sight of the gold-liveried guards and their prisoner, but she had a fair idea where they were going. Anyway, she had to make a detour. There was no way she was heading into that Palace without buying herself some armour to replace that which the Sultan had confiscated.

It took her a while to find a blacksmith who would accept coins with a female (and unfamiliar) Emperor stamped on them, but Sparrow eventually found a sucker who didn't even look at the silver she handed over. She had to wait an hour or so for him to make some alterations to the pieces he had in the shop, but it was worth it to be properly kitted out in breast-plate and leather strapping again. She felt much more like herself.

Sparrow hoisted her new sword into the sheath on her back and led Singespitter up the Palace steps. "We can go in through the Labyrinth," she said to the sheep as they moved along the path around to the little entrance plaza.

"You mean the sewers," corrected an almost familiar voice.

Sparrow's head snapped around. She frowned. The dark, dashingly handsome Cutlass Cooper was standing behind her, posing dramatically in his black leather. She couldn't think why he might have followed her.

"Forgotten something?" inquired Tione, who stood beside Cooper, her arms folded over her spangled costume.

Sparrow shrugged. "I would have come back for you eventually. Probably. How did it go?"

"Mother and baby doing fine," said Tione, still sounding angry. "No thanks to you. What made you run off like that? We only caught up at all because you've been leaving a trail of dandelions wherever you go."

Sparrow looked down at her boots, which were surrounded by bright yellow dandelion-like objects. She made a conscious decision to ignore them. "Daggar has been kidnapped. As he holds the only chance we have of getting back to our own time, I thought I should rescue him. I will infiltrate the Palace through the Labyrinth."

"Sewers," said Cutlass Cooper again.

Sparrow frowned at him. "What is this 'sewers' you keep saying?"

Cutlass gestured along the path, and they all stepped through into the plaza. "It used to be a Labyrinth centuries ago, but now it's just used to process the Palace sewage. Which time did you say you were from?"

Sparrow looked, and her heart sank into her shoes. The mouth to the Labyrinth, which must have been restored to its former glory at some stage between now and her own time, was currently dripping with foul-smelling ooze.

"You're right, though," continued Cutlass relentlessly. "It's the only way to infiltrate the Palace. I've done it once or twice myself, before I signed up with Bigbeard. That's the good thing about pirating," he added. "No sewers."

Sparrow looked down at her new shiny leather boots, the ones she had bought to match her armour. "Oh, Daggar," she muttered, "I am going to kill you for this."

-§-§-§-§-§-

"Um," said Daggar as his captors cuffed him to the wall of the dungeon. "Not that I'm complaining, or doubting your ability to do your jobs, but is there a particular reason why you attacked me, kidnapped me and brought me here?"

One of the guards, with gravy stains soiling his otherwise pristine gold uniform, smiled nastily. This told Daggar two things: firstly, that this wasn't the sort of guard who would sympathise with his plight and instantly release him, and secondly that the state of dental hygiene would be much improved in the next twenty-three years.

"You're gonna be a snack," the other guard, an evil-looking skinhead, said with some relish. "Human sacrifice, isn't that what they said?"

"Yeah," said the gravy-stained guard. "That's what they said. Def'nitely. Human sacrifice." He leered.

Daggar winced as the last of the metal cuffs was clamped around his limbs. "Oh, joy," he squeaked.

-§-§-§-§-§-

Several unpleasant hours later, Sparrow and her 'rescue team' had discovered what in later years would be the lair of the Minestaurus. Tione had fainted twice from the smell, and Cutlass Cooper had taken to carrying her, not seeming to worry about the slime which covered his ornate black boots. Tione protested weakly about this particularly chauvinist action, but seemed to be enjoying it.

Singespitter the sheep had stayed outside. Not even an attractive blonde woman with a sword would Singespitter get his fleecy feet covered in effluent.

"This is it," said Sparrow now, stumbling into the cave. "There is a secret staircase which leads to the Palace." She felt the wall thoughtfully. "Somewhere around…here."

With a rumble, the cave wall slid outwards.

Tione struggled out of Cutlass's arms. "Let's go!" she said quickly. "The sooner the better."

They ran up the stairs two at a time, and the cave wall closed behind them.

The laboratory would not exist for many years. Instead, the secret stairway led to a nursery. Three little boys were napping in cribs of various sizes within a giant red playpen. Sparrow ran her hand along the wooden bars thoughtfully. "Rodrigo, Xerzes and…Marmaduc," she said to herself, looking down the thin, sallow little boy who was snoring peacefully beside his brothers. "Perhaps I should put a pillow over his face now and solve all our problems."

"Not all of them," said Tione. "What do we do now?"

Sparrow looked up. "This is your territory. Where do you think they will be keeping our profit-scoundrel?"

Tione bit her lip. "I think that sewers or no sewers, the dungeon is likely to be in the same place as it was in twenty years time."

"Twenty-three," said Sparrow. "But who's counting?"

Tione turned to lead the way, but Cutlass Cooper stopped her by placing a slinky leather-gloved hand on her arm. "Are you *really* from the future?"

"You'd better believe it," said Tione. Their eyes met again, locking together in a powerful gaze.

Sparrow thrust them apart, giving the concubine an extra shake for good measure. "Come, we have no time for this. Work to do!"

-§-§-§-§-§-

As soon as the grubby gold-clad guards had left the cell, Daggar started working on his cuffs. He had only got as far as prising the tiny pickpin out of his left sleeve when he heard the sound of a fight outside the cell doors. "What took you so long?" he yelled above the noise.

Sparrow shouldered her way into the cell. "We had to deliver a baby."

"*We?*" questioned Tione, sliding past Sparrow and heading for the prisoner.

Daggar smiled up at Sparrow. "You really smell terrible," he said.

She looked at him thoughtfully and smacked him over the forehead.

"Hey!" he protested.

Cutlass Cooper stood by the cell door, watching for incoming guards. Sparrow and Tione worked together on Daggar's cuffs, Tione with a beaded pin she had pulled out of her beaded bodice and Sparrow with the pickpin she snatched from Daggar's sleeve before he had a chance to tell her about it.

"So," said Daggar, managing a smile as he ignored the rough handling of his rescuers. "How's Black Nell?"

"She had a little girl," said Tione, freeing his left wrist with a click. "They're going to call her..."

"Kassa," Daggar completed. "I guessed."

Tione shrugged her sequins, setting to work on the left ankle-cuff. "The baby's hair is this funny dark red colour, but I think it will probably grow out blonde."

"I wouldn't count on it," said Daggar.

Cutlass backed into the cell, sword at the ready. "Are you finished?" he asked urgently. "Someone's coming."

A fearsome shadow fell against the dim light coming from the doorway. A horrific apparition rounded the corner into the cell, and immediately found a pirate's sword held to its throat. "Ah, there you are," the creature said to the still-imprisoned Daggar, seemingly unfazed by this violent attention.

Tione's scream was hastily swallowed. "It's you," she gasped in relief.

"Have we met?" asked the Minestaurus, stepping aside from the blade of Cutlass's sword and making a small half bow. I'm sorry about all this. It's my birthday, and the parents thought I might like a human sacrifice. I hadn't told them that I went vegetarian two years ago. Anyway, I'm Prince Magnus. Let's get you out of these shackles, and you can all join the party."

"Party," said Daggar faintly as Tione releaded the last cuff. "Cucumber sandwiches. Just what I need."

"*Prince* Magnus?" queried Sparrow with a frown.

-§-§-§-§-§-

The old Sultan of Zibria was mildly embarrassed to meet his new guests, who had been allowed the use of the Palace bathhouse before being presented to him. "Sorry about the mix-up," he said effusively. "It's so hard to know what to give an eighteen year-old monster for his birthday."

"So Magnus is your son," said Sparrow. "And heir?"

"Well," said the Sultan with a vague smile and a twitch of his tapering grey beard. "Not actually the heir. The Zibrians won't accept a monster as their Sultan, obviously. Anyway, my clever Queen managed to break the curse and produce some nice human babies, so that's all right."

Queen Polynesie smiled prettily and curtseyed.

Sparrow's mouth set in a flat line and she hooked her arm through that of the Minestaurus, dragging him to one side. "Magnus, this is all wrong," she hissed. "You should be the next Sultan, not that little psychopath in the nursery!"

Magnus the Minestaurus smiled politely at her. "Was it the debutante ball last autumn? I'm afraid I simply can't recall where we might have met…"

"Never mind that. Do you not want to be Sultan?"

"No, not really," he said after a moment's thought. "I'd much rather be a librarian. I was thinking of restoring the old Labyrinth—it's a sewer at the moment, you know—and installing my library there. What do you think?"

Sparrow gave up. Changing history was going to be harder than she thought. "I think it is a good idea, your Highness. Bound to be a success. Popular with the tourists."

"You know, I hadn't thought of that?" said Prince Magnus happily.

As the party progressed, Tione ended up dancing with the Sultan, trying to teach him the tango. "Is this a new dance?" he asked, puffing with the exertions.

"Quite new," she said airily, allowing him to get his breath back. Then she narrowed her eyes, her secret police skills kicking into action. "What's behind that tapestry? It keeps twitching..."

"No!" cried the Sultan in alarm, but before he could stop her Tione had swished the tapestry aside. She froze, her skin and clothes fading to a pale grey colour.

"What have you done to her?" yelled Cutlass Cooper, lunging forward with his sword flashing in true pirate style. Two guards grabbed him and held him out of harm's way, shielding his eyes and closing their own as they did so.

"Gosh," said Princess Medusa, who had been waiting in the alcove to make her entrance. She slipped on a pair of wire-rimmed sunglasses and smiled apologetically. "I wasn't ready."

Daggar tapped Tione thoughtfully on the head. She remained inert, a concubine-shaped stone statue. "I thought so," he said grimly.

Princess Medusa, garbed in an amazingly full-skirted pink crinoline-gown, sidestepped the struggling Cutlass Cooper who had been sensibly disarmed by the guards. She turned to Sparrow, offering a pink-gloved hand in greeting. "I'm terribly sorry, really I am. Were you very close?"

"Never mind that," said Sparrow quickly, taking Medusa's arm in what she hoped was a suitably girlish way. "Such a fascinating skill you have. How did you acquire it?"

"Fascinating skill?" choked Cutlass, outraged by Sparrow's attitude. Her hand slapped out and shut his mouth as she glided past, arm in arm with the Princess Medusa.

"I was born this way," sighed Medusa. "Daddy was cursed, you see. All his children were to be monsters. At least I *look* all right. Poor Magnus doesn't stand a chance in the real world."

"I do not know about that," said Sparrow. "I like the tall, dark and rugged type. Is the curse broken now?"

"I suppose it must be," said Medusa, straightening her sunglasses. "I've got three mortal brothers in the nursery, which sort of suggests they found a way around the curse, don't you think?"

"Undoubtedly," said Sparrow, casting a glance at Queen Polynesie, who looked as if butter wouldn't melt in her mouth.

Daggar moved towards Sparrow, smoothly disentangling her from the arm of Princess Medusa. "Just popping outside for a breath of fresh air," he announced brightly, pulling her towards the door.

No one at the Royal Party protested, except for the pirate Cutlass Cooper who still twisted and struggled in the firm hold of the Zibrian palace guards.

-§-§-§-§-§-

"Right," said Daggar in the corridor. "This is when we leave. Immediately. Where's Singespitter?"

Sparrow frowned. "We are not finished here."

"Oh yes we are," growled Daggar. "I'll make this simple. What happens next is, the Sultan sends the Tione-statue to Emperor Timregis as a gift, Cutlass Cooper breaks out of the Zibrian dungeon, follows and rescues her from old Timregis' private collection, somehow managing to break Medusa's spell. I don't remember all the details, but you get the drift. Somewhere along the way they fall in love, get married and before this year is out our Tione produces bouncing twin babies, one of whom grows up to betray my Uncle Bigbeard and shove a sword through his gullet. Meanwhile, Cutlass impresses the Emperor so much by his daring style and derring-do that he is named Imperial Champion and stays that way until some young bastard named Aragon Silversword comes along in ten years and takes his job. This is all family history, and I don't really want to go through it twice. We don't fit into the equation.

Tione belongs in this time, no matter which time she comes from originally. I think. Time travel's a bitch, and I think we should stop now before it becomes a habit. Everybody happy? Good."

There was a long pause as Sparrow thought about this. "Time to fetch the sheep?"

Daggar nodded tiredly. "Time to fetch the sheep."

Chapter 14
The Great Pomegranate Quest

Kassa dressed carefully for her quest, tossing aside her usual wench garb in favour of something more dignified. She had commandeered the slinkiest black dress owned by the goths, but it had taken some sewing and altering to get the outfit just right, none of the goth girls having a chest larger than size ten.

Finally it was finished, a clinging sulphurous gown which glowed blackly around Kassa's skin. She carved a hefty slit up one side, but somehow the fabric always swirled around in such a way that she never flashed any leg, even when she wanted to. She borrowed a length of the Dark One's black velvet collection, which she wrapped around her shoulders as a mantle. The glimmering blackness of the costume was offset with what jewellery she had been able to find: a thick gold torc for her throat and a dozen silently-jangling bangles hung heavy with gold coins.

She wrinkled her nose as she examined the effect. "I prefer silver."

"No silver in the Underworld," said the Dark One gloomily, watching her drape herself with bracelets. "Nor even a copper penny or a stainless steel fork. No one thinks to send me any different metal for a change, it's all gold torcs *this*, gold coins on the eyelids *that* and gold funeral vases the *other*."

Kassa turned slowly. "You take the funeral vases?"

The Dark One looked shifty. "Maybe."

Kassa regarded her new outfit critically in the full-length mirror for one last time, and then turned back with a satisfactory swish. "I'm ready to go."

"Now," the Dark One said sternly. "You do realise that you're not mortal anymore. You can't stay out in the real world for very long or you will fade into the scenery. Literally, I might add."

"But I'm not going to the real world, remember?" Kassa said between her teeth. "I'm going to the Cloud Dimension, whatever *that* is."

"Still and all," said the Dark One. "It's not the Underworld." He opened his hand to reveal a tiny black jewel which flew to her gold torc, firmly attaching itself to the centre of the metal collar. "If something goes wrong and you end up vanishing, your essence will attach itself to this, and we should be able to bring you back here."

Kassa stared at him. "What if I don't want to come back?"

"Then you will be a small, shiny black rock for the rest of eternity," he replied without blinking.

She scowled deeply. "Anything else you want to tell me?"

"Yes," said the Dark One. "Don't try to send any messages to your loved ones. It will only confuse them." He made a godly gesture, and a long, obsidian-black corridor opened up in the wall. "You might want to hurry," he added.

Kassa started running along the corridor. The goth dress clung to her ankles, warning her that this was *not* a dress to wear while running. She slowed to a swift walk, her eyes firmly fixed on the light at the end of the long tunnel. The light grew brighter and brighter…

The tunnel was spinning, or Kassa was spinning. Certainly one or the other. Possibly both. Patches of sky whirled through her dazed vision, and the last traces of the comfortable fog which had enveloped her senses for so long just whirled soundlessly into space.

She could think clearly now. She screamed. Then, because the noise she made was the only sound in the tunnel at all, she yelled for a while. The circle of light swam towards her at a sick-to-the-stomach speed until all she could see was light exploding behind her eyeballs. Then the light dimmed. Kassa could feel its warmth wash away from her, drifting away from her skin.

She opened her eyes, and her vision was awash with fluffy whiteness. She looked around, marvelling at the view. A landscape of cloud stretched in every direction, forming valleys and mountains and a squat, cozy-looking castle. In the distance, she could just make out the tiny shape of someone climbing the tallest of the purple-white mountains. "Poor fool," she muttered to herself. "All gods are bastards. You will just reach the top and those clouds will open up and dump you back at the foot, bet you anything." She thought about waiting around to see if her prophecy was fulfilled, but reflected that it might be a better idea to get on with the quest at hand.

Kassa arranged her black mantle in a suitably dignified manner and began walking towards the castle. After knocking in vain against the big front drawbridge, she wandered around to the ornamental garden in hope of finding a servant's entrance.

The kitchen door was open, and the smell of baking wafted out. Kassa sniffed hungrily and wondered how long it had been since she had eaten. Then she remembered that she didn't need to eat any more, because she was dead. What a depressing thought.

A young girl with excessively long brown braids and cookie dust on her nose was shaking a tea-towel out on to the steps. She stopped when she saw Kassa. "Oh," she said. "The Dark One's proxy, I assume. If I'd known you were coming, I'd have baked cookies." She put her hands on her hips, defiantly.

Taking from this remark that she wasn't going to be offered any of the freshly-baked products she could smell, Kassa responded by putting her own hands on her own hips. Her figure was rather more impressive, so this upstaged the younger girl's attempt to gain the upper hand. "I'm looking for Wordern's daughters," she announced.

This failed to invoke any reaction on the girl's face. "What do I look like, chopped liver? You'd better come in, I suppose. Wipe your feet."

Kassa followed her in. "Not you. I want one of the older ones. The eldest, if possible. It's traditional."

"I am the eldest," said Pomegranate, taking a warm cookie from the bench and sinking her little white teeth into it. "What you see is what you get."

Kassa stared at her. "But you don't look more than twelve years old!"

"Eleven and three quarters," replied Pomegranate evenly. "I'll get my coat."

"I can't do this," said Kassa in horror. "I can't send you to the Dark One, you're under-age!"

"Look," said Pomegranate, scooping the cookies into a foil bag. "I may not be suitable for arranged marriages and all that bedroom stuff that I'm supposed to be too young to know about, but I *am* ready to run the Underworld. It's my destiny, like it or not. You wouldn't deprive a girl of her destiny, would you?"

Kassa said nothing. Her eyes had that startled bunny look in them that suggested she wasn't going to be saying anything for a while.

Pomegranate sighed. "You can carry my suitcase." Nearly swallowed whole by an enormous fur coat, she led the way to the obsidian tunnel, her long braids trailing behind her in the cloud. "Well?" she said impatiently, turning to look at her abductor. Kassa still looked bemused. "Gods," Pomegranate muttered, shaking her head in disgust. "I don't know *what* he sees in you."

Kassa's attention returned vaguely. "Who?"

Pomegranate pointed to the shadowy figure still patiently trudging up the distant mountain. "Him. Poor sod. He'll get to the top and those bloody little cloud divinities will drop him right back down to ground level. It's their idea of a joke."

Kassa stared at the mountain, trying to spot something familiar in the distant shape. "Who is it?"

"Your feller," Pomegranate said patiently. "The sap who has been running around like a less-than-sane hatter trying to rescue you from the Underworld. Hah," she added gloomily, just for effect.

Kassa grabbed hold of the younger girl's furry sleeve. "Who is it? I don't know anyone who would do that for me...all the men in my life are cowards or traitors."

"Aragon Silversword," said Pomegranate with a smirk. Eleven-year-olds should never look that smug. "I kind of liked him. Though he's got rotten taste in women. Are we going through this tunnel or what?"

The tunnel opened wider, making a black and swallowing noise. Feeling the pressure as it began to suck them in, Kassa struggled to remain where she was. "Aragon," she breathed. "I have to..."

As she tried to break into a run, Pomegranate's surprisingly powerful arms gripped her. "Oh, no you don't. You've got an abduction to perpetrate. Time for the soppy romantic stuff later."

"But there is no other time," Kassa protested. "This is my only chance!"

Pomegranate held on tightly. "Too bad. I can't abduct myself, it's against the rules."

The tunnel sucked them both into the Underworld. Kassa struggled against its insistent pull. A tendril of grey-green vine wound around her waist, tugging her sharply into the darkness. She felt several of her bodice laces snap as she flew back, landing heavily in a bed of purple marigolds and sun-coloured foxgloves.

"So," said Pomegranate, trying to untwist her braids from a spiralling thorn bush. "This is the Underworld."

"No," said Kassa Daggersharp, wiping her own hair out of her eyes. "It isn't the Underworld."

Pomegranate frowned. "Then where are we?"

Kassa fumbled with the laces of her bodice, knotting them back together. "I don't know. But I have a nasty feeling about that mist."

A greyish mist hovered on the edges of the woodland scene, blocking any view there might have been. The mist was alive. Somehow that seemed obvious. Tiny sparkles of light glittered within its cloudy depths, like thousands of curious little eyes.

"This is the *OtherRealm*!" gasped Kassa in sudden realisation.

Pomegranate had painstakingly managed to unwind one braid from the thorn bush, only to discover that the other one had tangled itself up in the meantime. "Don't be ridiculous," she snapped. "Not even gods are safe in the OtherRealm. No one ever goes there."

"Witches do," said Kassa slowly. "The final stage of initiation. I think this is all my fault!"

"Well, I'd assumed that."

A hoarse, unreal cry sounded in the midst of the glowing mist. "So," said Pomegranate, finally wrenching her second braid free of the thorn bush. "This is the fair country. The kingdom of the lost. The land of the fey."

"All that and more," agreed Kassa. "Now, all we have to do..."

The mist pounced. It poured itself around them, snatching at their ankles and catching them up in its snarls. Pomegranate opened her mouth and the mist stuffed itself inside, gagging her. Kassa tried to lash out, but the ethereal white stuff only bound her tighter.

Pomegranate spat out the gag of mist. "They can't do this to me. I'm a *goddess*!"

"No, you're not," said Kassa. "You're a jumped-up glitch of existential angst who only escaped being turned into a puff of green smoke by having your classification changed before the decimalisation went into effect. Your life is halfway between dull and non-existent, which explains why you were so willing to follow me to the Underworld. Now shut up, and let me think."

"How do you know so much about me?" asked Pomegranate in a small voice.

"I've read your file. Much was prophesied in the year I was born."

"The Year of the Sculpted Concubine," sighed Pomegranate. "I came into being that year too."

Kassa blinked. "But you're–"

"I may look eleven and three quarters, but I'm actually twice that," said the hemi-goddess sourly. "It's still young by usual godly standards. My sisters and I came into being fully grown, but Wordern was getting on our nerves so we decided to go through childhood just to wind him up. Then the Decimalisation went into effect, and we were robbed of our godly powers." She wriggled awkwardly. "Each of us got one talent in compensation, and mine was an immunity to time. So I'm stuck looking like this forever. Great talent, eh? Still, it could be worse. My sister Octavy is immune to space. At least I have half a chance at a social life. Were you planning to get us out of this at any stage?"

"I might have half a chance if you stop wriggling!" Kassa drew in a deep breath, closing her eyes and opening her mind to the cosmos. She could feel the webbed substance within the mist that bound them together. Every time Pomegranate struggled, the mist squeezed in closer. "Stay *still*." After a moment, Kassa exhaled and opened her deep golden eyes, blinking awkwardly. "I can't use magic here. I might blow us up, or make things worse."

"If this is your initiation, why did they send you somewhere you couldn't use magic?" complained Pomegranate.

"A witch's ability isn't all about magic," said Kassa slowly. "It's about thinking like a witch. Do as you will, and harm none."

"So, what would a *witch* do in this situation?"

Kassa's palm was squished hard against the side of her right leg by the bindings of mist. She flexed her hand and dug her fingernails into a handful of the slinky fabric of her goth gown. There was a rending sound as the fabric tore. Kassa slid her hand into the tear, pressing her hand against her bare leg.

By twisting her head around, Pomegranate could just get a glimpse of what was going on behind her back. "You're going to use sex appeal?" she said dubiously.

"Better than that," said Kassa Daggersharp, her hand closing over the black leather sheath which was strapped to her thigh. "I'm going to use a knife."

As she drew and brandished her stainless steel knife, the mist bindings parted quickly, anxious to avoid contact with the cold iron. "Now, I don't want to hurt anyone or anything," Kassa warned. "But we're leaving."

Wiping the remains of the mist from her hands, Pomegranate ducked hastily as a flock of tiny-winged wyrdings screeched overhead, also trying to put distance between themselves and the woman with the knife. "If this is your initiation, should you be *trying* to escape?"

"If anyone wants me to gain my witchy qualifications, they can damn well make an appointment," flared Kassa. "I don't like surprises."

A web of spiderlight unfolded behind her, scooping Kassa up into its depths. Its razor-sharp edges clawed at her dress, shredding its skirt to ribbons. Struggling, she swept her knife around in a wide arc. The web fell in several limp pieces to the tangled forest floor.

A tear opened in the thick mist that encircled the woodland scene. A faery maiden clothed in sunshine and wild mistletoe made her appearance. "Welcome to reality, mortal kind," she drawled seductively, fluttering her eyelashes and wings simultaneously. "How may I elaborate upon your waking desires…" She paused, her eyes widening in horror. "Beard of the moon-mother, what *is* that?"

Kassa held up the knife. "Stainless steel. A surefire antidote to faery dust."

"Get that away from here," screeched the faery maiden, flapping her sunshine wings frantically. "Get out, you horrible, horrible mortals!" She burst into tears.

"Speaking of which," hissed Pomegranate. "How was it we were going to escape?"

"I was thinking of calling for help," replied Kassa.

She removed the gold torc from around her throat and fingered the tiny black stone that the Dark One had placed on it. "Hello? Can anyone hear me?"

"What are you doing?" interrupted Pomegranate.

"Shh. Attention, all imps. This is Kassa Daggersharp. Grave emergency. Contact the Dark…oh."

Pomegranate gasped. A tall, dark and rather beaky-nosed man in a bright pastel suit had materialised in front of Kassa and regarded her sternly. He held out a hand, and she let him take the golden torc. "It's not supposed to be used like that," he snapped.

"Sorry," said Kassa with an apologetic smile.

"What are you doing here, anyway?" he demanded. "You were supposed to come right back, not footle around in the moonlight dimension. Such frivolities are off limits to ex-mortals, and that means you."

"We got lost," said Kassa. "Can you take us back to the Underworld? I think my favourite knife is upsetting the OtherRealmers."

The Dark One looked suspiciously at the sobbing faery maiden. "I suppose I'd better. Unless it's something witchy, of course. I don't pretend to understand Dame Veekie's motives, and if she wanted you here…"

"By the way," said Kassa hastily. "Meet your new consort."

It was the Dark One, Pomegranate realised. Not what she had expected at all. She scooped her long braids over one shoulder and refused to curtsey.

"She's a child!" declared the Dark One.

"Possibly," said Kassa, "but she's the next best thing to a goddess. She's also *very* good at administration."

The Dark One brightened. He handed Kassa back the gold torc, and she put it around her throat again. At his command, the fair country vanished from around them, and the greyness of the Underworld swam into view.

After they had gone, the spiderlight web stopped feigning unconsciousness and scuttled away into the tangled faery wood.

-§-§-§-§-§-

Back in the familiar corridors of the Underworld, the Dark One spoke anxiously to Pomegranate. "Do you *really* like administration?"

"Doesn't everyone?" replied Pomegranate. "Where is the throne room? From what I've heard, I had better start repairing the damage to this dog's breakfast of an Underworld right away. Your whole system is tied up in knots. For a start," she added, gesturing at Kassa. "I suppose you do realise that she isn't supposed to be here…"

The Dark One hustled Pomegranate towards the throne room, and their voices trailed away. Kassa felt very tired. She sank down in a corner of the corridor, resting her chin on her hands and staring into empty air. So that was it. Her last chance to touch base with the real world was over almost as soon as it had started. She nudged the opposite wall glumly with her foot. Now she knew why so many people devoted so much energy to postponing death. All in all, it was quite an anti-climax.

An imp scuttled by, and Kassa's hand whipped out, catching it by the tails of its tuxedo. It gaped at her in horror. "Goths don't have red hair!"

"I'm not a goth, I just raided their wardrobe," Kassa growled. "Where do you imps go for fun around here? What is there to do? And don't fob me off. I am in serious need of entertainment."

"Well," stuttered the imp wildly, trying to break free from her iron grip. "There's always the tavern."

Kassa's eyes snapped to attention. She released the imp and stood up, wiping a thin layer of yellowish dust from her half-shredded slinky black dress. "There's a tavern in this godsforsaken place, and nobody thought to *tell* me?"

Chapter 15
The Year of the Greyest Winter

The mixed camp of mummers and pirates was in a state of high confusion when Daggar and Sparrow returned. Vicious Bigbeard kept swinging the new baby around in the air and forgetting where he left her, while Black Nell reclined on a couch made of second-best stage curtains and shouted abuse at him, or anyone else who came into her line of sight.

Around them, the mummers and the pirates had taken the birth of a healthy-lunged new baby pirate to be a good excuse for a party, and pooled their various supplies of food, drink, musical instruments and amusing balloons.

"Are we here for a reason?" asked Sparrow, surveying the chaotic scene.

"I never miss a good party," replied Daggar with a lopsided grin. "After all, they *are* celebrating the birth of my second favourite cousin." He extended his hand theatrically. "Shall we dance?"

Sparrow ignored the proffered hand and sat down on the grassy slope, crossing her arms stiffly in her new armour. "I will wait until you are finished," she said in a crisp voice.

Singespitter sat at her feet, looking up at Daggar with a highly superior expression on his sheepy face.

Daggar gave in. "All right, where shall we go next, then? We have the universe of time and space at our fingertips. Shall we visit the Hanging Gardens of Baboulsja or the

Lost Library of Philanthropia? How about a quick jaunt around the Siege of Catatonian Teatime?"

Sparrow gazed up at him, her face immobile. "If you do not object, I would like to do something about purging the poisonous liquid gold from my body."

"Oh," said Daggar, slightly deflated. "Well, we can do that. Who was it you said you stole it from?"

"The Brewmistress of Dreadnought."

"Right." Daggar looked slightly greenish. "I'd forgotten that. Where do you think she is now?"

Sparrow shrugged. "In the Sultan's dungeon, according to the Sultan."

"Right, then. If anyone can find a cure for you, it's got to be the one who created the liquid gold, right? She can help."

Sparrow eyed him darkly. "Faulty logic, Daggar. She is far more likely to do something hideous to me with a sharpened set of knitting needles."

"Do you have any better ideas?" he challenged, pulling the miniature ship out of his pocket. "Let's get going back to the present."

"And the matter of the knitting needles?"

Daggar gave her two thumbs up and an encouraging grin. "You're wearing armour. What have you got to worry about?"

-§-§-§-§-§-

Mistress Opia had never seen the inside of a dungeon before, unless you counted that time she had been called in to analyse the chemical properties of a new kind of sulphurous moss growing in the confinement cells under the Imperial Palace in Dreadnought. This was altogether different.

For a start, she was chained to the wall by wooden cuffs, with her large expanse of knitting placed tantalisingly just out of reach.

Hobbs the gnome and Officer Finnley were chained to the wall on either side of her, but she paid them little attention. During the long hours of her incarceration, she had devised seven hundred and thirty-two different diabolical escape plans, all of which depended on equipment she didn't have, skillful cell-mates she didn't have, and an unreasonable hope that her friendly neighbourly prison guards were more stupid than your average piece of cheese.

Every now and then, the Sultan of Zibria would cackle nastily down the speaking tube which ran from his inner sanctum down to the main dungeon. He had ordered its installation for precisely this purpose, and considered it to be money well spent. He also had a lever attached to his throne which would send a fresh torrent of water over Mistress Opia every half hour or so, preventing her from using her alchemical skills to escape.

The door to the cell was flung open. Sparrow, an imposing figure in her new (but old-fashioned) armour, gazed expressionlessly at the three of them. "First of all," she said in her strange, alien accent, "I wish you to give me your word you will not attempt to kill me."

"That's asking a lot," said Mistress Opia sharply. "Just pass me my knitting needles, there's a good girl."

Daggar, towing his sheep behind him, squeezed past Sparrow and grabbed the knitting, which he stuffed into one of his many belt pouches along with the two wickedly sharp needles. "None of that, madam. We're here to make you an offer you can't refuse."

"If you wish to converse in a civilised fashion," said Mistress Opia in her sternest voice, "I suggest you unchain me at once, young man. Chop chop."

Daggar made quick work of the cuffs, and Mistress Opia was set free. She stepped forward, and Sparrow was suddenly face to face with her.

"You," said Mistress Opia, almost unpleasantly.

"Me," said Sparrow the mercenary, in more chilling tones.

They eyeballed each other, like two lionesses after the same piece of meat. Mistress Opia's eyes swivelled towards the door, and Sparrow drew her sword, shoving the Brewmistress up against the wall. "Oh, no," she rasped.

"We will have a little talk first." She glared at Mistress Opia. "Do you not think a death canary was a *little* over the top?"

"Obviously not," replied Mistress Opia. She looked Sparrow up and down, slowly. "How did you escape?"

Sparrow grinned thinly and pulled one of her time-freezing capsules out of a pouch with her spare hand.

"Ingenious," Mistress Opia noted. "It won't work again. Their immune system is extraordinarily adaptable."

"Are you saying that those yellow fire-breathing guttersnipe bastard birds are still going to come after us?" demanded Daggar in a strangled voice.

Mistress Opia seemed amused. "More than one now? Oh dear me, you have been busy."

"Well," said Sparrow, shoving a little harder with the flat of her sword against Mistress Opia's throat. "You had better cancel their programming, had you not? I want to be sure they will not be waiting around the next corner for me."

"Dear me, I can't do that," said Mistress Opia, not quite sounding apologetic. "Until their specific mission has been fulfilled, they cannot be halted."

"I am *so* glad we have a time ship," said Daggar fervently.

"You really have quite the knack for avoiding imminent death, my dear," Mistress Opia continued, loudly. "I see the liquid gold within your system has done no significant damage yet—still, it's only a matter of Time."

"If you want to get out of this cell, you had better start thinking up ways to cure me," Sparrow growled.

"A cure for swallowing liquid gold?" Opia laughed, shaking her head. "You are a time explosion waiting to happen. Travelling through a correctly-generated chronometric field may cure your withdrawal cravings, but every time you step out of time, you risk meltdown. Can you imagine the damage your body could do to causality if it exploded during the critical moment of time-jump?" She made a *tsking* sound. "I think you had better chain me to the wall again, because I cannot help you in the least."

"She lies," Sparrow snapped. "We will take her with us. Daggar, call up the ship."

"Are you sure you know what you're doing?" Daggar asked dubiously.

Sparrow didn't dignify that with an answer, but fastened her hand firmly around Mistress Opia's wrist. "You know more than you say," she snarled. "Or you would not look so satisfied with yourself."

"Ouch!" shouted Daggar, who had stubbed his thumb on the rapidly-expanding ghost-ship. "What about her henchmen?"

Hobbs the gnome and Officer Finnley, both still chained to the wall, exchanged quick glances. "I quit," said Hobbs.

"I want to go home," said Officer Finnley.

"Bring them both," snapped Sparrow. She dragged Mistress Opia on to the translucent deck of the golden galleon. "Which way, forwards or backwards?"

Daggar, halfway between releasing Officer Finnley from his chains, looked at Sparrow in horror. "You can't risk time-travel. Didn't you hear what she just said?"

"I'm prepared to risk it if you are," said Sparrow evenly.

"Well, maybe I'm not!" he yelled back.

Finnley scrambled on board the translucent gold ship, helping the sheep up after him. Daggar started work on Hobbs' cuffs.

"I have just one thing to say," declared Sparrow hotly. "Canaries, Daggar. They are in this time zone. So let us be somewhere *else*."

As soon as he was released, Hobbs the gnome started running at a surprising speed, screeching out of the prison cell and away up the corridor. Not really caring, Daggar pulled himself up to the deck of the *Splashdance*. "Backwards or forwards?" he asked resignedly.

Sparrow shrugged. "We have already tried going backwards. Let us get ahead of ourselves for once."

"Forwards," agreed Daggar, not too happy about it.

And the golden ghost-ship went…*Kwoop*.

-§-§-§-§-§-

Hobbs ran like a scared wildebeest, ducking and dashing every which way. Crashing into the knees of a golden-robed somebody, he came to a halt. Slowly, fearfully, he stared upwards.

"Hello, little Brewer's lackey," said the Sultan of Zibria. "I have a job for you."

-§-§-§-§-§-

It was the greyest winter Mocklore had ever seen. Grimy snow packed up in drifts around what was left of the cities, sealing everyone in. Even the urchins, previously the most well-fed demographic in the Empire, were looking remarkably thin and pasty.

The Lord of the Green Manor, a swag of firewood hefted on his back, staggered through the snow to his front door. He tripped over the hall carpet and fell headlong, spilling the splintering logs in every direction.

A young woman exploded out of the kitchen, her long silk dress swamped in an oversized apron. "Oh, Tangent, you idiot! I just swept that carpet!"

The young Lord picked himself up. "I don't see you tromping about out there in all weathers."

"Well, I don't see you coming anywhere near the kitchen, except to feed your face," she snapped. "Don't you understand anything? The *Emperor* is coming, expecting hospitality. Would you rather I asked the Court to cook their own damn puddings when they come?"

"It's not just us, Ree," he said darkly, closing the door before the high winds could blow more snow on to the carpet. "All the manors are struggling this winter. They can't expect us to pretend this isn't happening."

"Oh no?" said his sister. "This is the Emperor, Tangent. One mistake even resembling an insult, and we're to the headman's axe, nobility or not. He's already confiscated four manors, two castles and a fortified village on his so-called grand tour. We're next."

-§-§-§-§-§-

"Where the hell are we?" Daggar choked, wiping a faceful of snow away with his sleeve.

Sparrow peered at the amber crystal set into the ship's wheel. "It shows a picture of—snow."

"Brilliant," he grumbled. "I could have worked that out all by myself."

"It does not matter what pictogram it shows," she flung back at him. "If this is the future, the name of the year will mean nothing to us." She stared hard at Mistress Opia. "Where exactly have you brought us?"

"Into the future of course," said Mistress Opia. "Twenty-three years, to be exact. You really must trust me."

"I would sooner trust a troll-hunter," Sparrow growled.

"I'll bite," said Daggar finally. "Why twenty-three years?"

"In order to successfully purge the liquid gold which the young woman ingested in such a foolhardy way, it is necessary to make a triangular chronometric oscillation," said Mistress Opia, as if that explained everything.

Sparrow blinked. "*What* did you say?"

Mistres Opia sighed. "You will need similar objects from two reference points at equal distances from your point of origin."

"So," said Sparrow slowly, wiping a handful of melted snow from her hair. "I have coins from the Year of the Sculpted Concubine, and from our own present. If I could get another from this time period, you could perform the purging ceremony?"

"Something like that," agreed Mistress Opia pleasantly. "Of course, if you would rather sail somewhere balmier, I wouldn't mind in the least."

"I would," said Sparrow harshly. "Daggar, let us go for a walk."

"But it's freezing," he complained.

"Tough. Bring the Blackguard too." Sparrow gave Officer Finnley a brief grimace which almost resembled a smile. "You can arrest the Brewmistress if she causes any trouble."

Finnley smiled very weakly in response, wishing that he had followed Hobbs' example and run like hell.

They all climbed off the boat and turned away to walk through the snow.

"Aren't you going to close up the ship?" Sparrow asked Daggar.

"Oh, sure." He clapped his hands in the requisite manner and then spun around, horrified. "I don't believe I just did that!"

"Did what?" Sparrow stared at him, and then into the bleak patch of dim snowiness around them. "Daggar, where's the ship?"

"Well," he said steadily. "It's about two inches long, and it's out in that." He gestured at the patch of grey snowiness. It was hard to see anything, let along a two-inch long piece of gold jewellery. It had vanished under the constant blanket of snow. "We have to find it." A horrible thought crossed his mind. "Singespitter's still in there! He'll go spare."

Sparrow grabbed his sleeve. "Daggar, we have to find shelter, and quickly. We could freeze to death rummaging around in that stuff."

"But it will be buried deep by morning!" he said in horror. "We'll never find it. What about my sheep?"

"Come on," she said urgently, pulling him away. "Get walking. Freezing to death is not a nice way to die. There are lights up ahead. There could be a house." She drew her sword and stuck it deeply into the snow at her feet. "We'll come back and find the ship when it stops snowing. Move it!"

They started trudging towards the dim lights up ahead, all shivering and trying not to think of what the consequences of losing the ghost-ship could be.

After all, there were worse things than being stuck twenty-three years in the future…were there not?

Chapter 16
Oracles Etc

"Gods!" said Lady Luck angrily, flinging her arms around dramatically. "Gods gods *gods* gods gods."

Destiny, flicking her way through the latest illustrated gossip-scroll, lifted her large eyes towards her elder sister. "Something wrong?"

"Someone's helping him," the goddess snapped, throwing an antique vase at the infinite mosaic floor. "I haven't been able to track him since he started nosing around in Zibria. Now he's vanished off the face of the… well, the island!"

"Perhaps he's gone interstate?"

"Don't be ridiculous," snapped Lady Luck. "No one goes interstate. It's a wasteland. A bland, colourless collection of primitive tribes…"

"They don't believe in us there," said Destiny with a humphing sigh. "We must be the only gods in the cosmos who are confined to one teeny tiny island."

"They would believe in me if I wanted them to," said Lady Luck dismissively. "Everyone believes in me. Some of them just don't know it yet."

"So where is he?" asked Destiny pointedly. "This Aragon Silversword of yours. How was it you were going to punish him? Or has it been so long since you started trying that you can't remember?"

This barbed comment had a devastating effect on Lady Luck. "I'll show you," she spat, and promptly vanished.

Destiny yawned, and picked up another gossip-scroll. A nearby cupboard opened and Fate, the gnarled and wizened third sister of the Witch's Web, climbed out. She shook out her legs and stretched her wrinkled arms over her head. "I thought she'd never leave," she said in a disgruntled voice. "No chance of tea and biscuits, I suppose?"

"Get them yourself," said Destiny.

-§-§-§-§-§-

Aragon waded through the murky cloud. It was too difficult to imagine himself walking blithely over the top of the stuff as if it were concrete, and likewise he was not keen on falling through to the world far below, so he pretended the cloud was deep grass and kept it at a steady ankle-height.

He couldn't see the finely-sculpted mountains anymore, just acres of drifting cloud in random shapes.

Then the vague mist faded, leaving him surrounded. High peaks of solid purplish cloud rose around him on all sides, forming cliffs and caves and ominous shadows. Aragon looked disparagingly up and up until he could see the top of the highest peak. "I don't suppose the Priestess of Forgotten Gods lives in a bungalow on the ground level?" he suggested aloud.

The only response was a low cackle which sounded through the cloudy mountains, echoing in a menacing refrain until it became too soft a sound to be heard at all.

"Yes, that's what I thought," said Aragon grimly. Setting his sights on a particularly narrow and rickety mountain path which swirled around the highest of the cloud mountains, he began to climb.

Just as he had reached the top of the highest cloud-mountain, it vanished under him. Someone's idea of a joke, he supposed.

Aragon fell onto the lower cloud layer with a muffled thud. For something so white and fluffy, this stuff packed quite a wallop when you fell on it from a great height.

There was a creaking sound, and a set of double doors opened in the foot of one of the mountains. A figure stood there, wrapped in robes of black and purple. "You were right," she told him in a voice which grated in harsh amusement. "About the bungalow."

-§-§-§-§-§-

Ten minutes later, Aragon was sitting in a cloud-shaped room holding a cup full of a strange hot pink liquid with leaves floating in it. He drew the line at drinking anything he didn't know the name of.

"Rosehip tea," said the Priestess of Forgotten Gods, reading his mind. "It's good for you."

"So is marriage, apparently, but you don't see me hobbling down the aisle," said Aragon in a cracked voice. He put the teacup down. "It appears that I need your help."

"Oh?" replied Tmesis harshly, beginning to unwrap the robes which bound her head, hands and face completely from sight.

"I have been told that this was the place to come," Aragon went on.

The wrappings fell away. Tmesis was a very dark woman with pale eyes and astoundingly smooth skin. She regarded Aragon patiently. "Perhaps it is."

"Purple," he said suddenly, noting the colour of her robes. "Is that the colour of reverence for forgotten gods?"

"Not exactly," replied Tmesis. "Purple and black are the only colours not assigned to any of the current legitimate holy orders, thus by default they belongs to the hidden gods. At least, I think that's right." She managed a smile which made her face appear even more distant. "We are all here by default. Even the troll-gods, who rejected our collective, are represented by the purple and the black. Have you seen such robes elsewhere?"

"Perhaps I have." Aragon could hardly remember. He dismissed it as unimportant. "I wish to travel to the Underworld."

Tmesis inclined her head gravely. "I thought as much. It will not be an easy journey."

"I did not expect it to be."

"It will require much sacrifice," she continued. "Do you believe your cause worthy of sacrifice, Aragon Silversword?"

"I believe my sanity is worth a great deal to me," said Aragon in a voice almost as harsh as her own.

"Well then," replied Tmesis, Priestess of Forgotten Gods. "By all means, let us do what we can to examine your sanity."

"Were you a goddess once?" Aragon couldn't help asking. "Are you one of the forgotten ones who were laid aside, because of the late Emperor's whim to decimalise Mocklore's deities?"

"Perhaps," said the smooth-skinned priestess, risking a tiny smile. "I no longer remember. Come, let us consult the crystals."

She produced several crystal balls from a velvet-draped chest and laid them in various strategic positions around the room. As they all began to glow softly, she spoke a long, winding prophecy in her harsh voice. When she had finished, there was a long pause.

"A golden *what*?" demanded Aragon Silversword finally.

"Frog," replied the smooth-skinned Priestess of Forgotten Gods, her face illuminated by the many glowing crystal balls. She frowned slightly. "At least, I'm almost certain that it's a frog. Possibly a log..."

"Could you check?" he said darkly.

The crystal balls seemed to be having a strange effect on Tmesis. She was losing track of the conversation. "Possibly a pond," she mused now. "What were you saying? Yes, of course I can check. Not a problem at all."

Aragon waited for a few seconds, watching Tmesis gaze in fascination at a blank white wall. "Will you do it soon, or shall I wait for you to forget a few more times?"

Tmesis shook her head and rose to her feet, lifting the china teapot to refill his already-brimming cup. "I'm sorry, what were we talking about?"

"Kassa Daggersharp," Aragon growled, putting out a hand to stop her from over-filling his teacup for the third time. "Rescuing from the Underworld. Some unidentified object which may or may *not* be golden."

"The bough, you mean?" she asked, replacing the teapot. "The silver bough?"

"It's silver now?" said Aragon, barely concealing his irritation.

"No, of course not," Tmesis said in a baffled tone of voice. "It's golden. A golden bough. Everyone knows that. What made you think it was silver?"

"Must have been something I read," he muttered. "And where is this bough?"

"At the mouth of the Underworld," said Tmesis as if it was obvious.

"Yes, and how do I find it?"

She frowned. "I've forgotten. Isn't that strange?"

Aragon scooped up all the glowing crystal balls, wrapped them in their thick cloths and dumped them back in the ceremonial chest. "Right," he said firmly. "Let's have a proper conversation, shall we?"

The intelligent glint returned to Tmesis's eyes. "You're not supposed to do that," she replied. "I am supposed to give you a vague interpretation of some irrelevant prophecy or other, and you are supposed to leave without the slightest idea about the quest you have to devote the rest of your life to."

"I prefer shortcuts."

"I had noticed. Tell me something first. Why do you wish to make this journey to the Underworld?"

"I don't know."

Tmesis clicked her tongue. "That means that you *do* know the true reason, but don't want to admit it, particularly to yourself."

"Oh, really?"

"Tell me, or I will not help you."

"I am compelled to rescue a person I do not like from death itself." He spoke in emotionless tones.

"Oh, a *witchmark*," said Tmesis, finally understanding. She sounded almost amused. "I thought they faded when one of the participants died."

"If it had faded," snarled Aragon, "would I be this obsessed? The only explanation is that it is lingering somehow. Trust Kassa to break the unwritten rules. Are you going to help me, or not?"

Tmesis leaned back in her padded armchair. "Do you have a pencil? This is what you have to do..."

-§-§-§-§-§-

Aragon returned to earth with a shudder, his feet slamming against the uneven cobblework of the Zibrian gateway. He stared at the marble pillars of the nearest temple as if seeing them for the first time. Then he turned his back on the city, staring out at the countryside. *The forest of the dead*, Tmesis had told him, *is anywhere you want it to be.*

And there it was. A sprawling collection of shades and ghostly branches, casting spidery shapes against the grass. A forest which had not been there before, and might not ever be there again. Aragon took one step towards it, and found himself slammed back against the walls of the city.

Something large and dense thudded into his stomach. Spinning away from the rebound of the solid blow, he saw a heavily-muscled man grinning nastily into his face, and felt another lay meaty hands on his shoulders. The two thugs tied his hands roughly behind his back and then threw him face-first into the dust of the road.

A pair of boots hovered in front of his face. He looked up, past the shiny buckles of the boots to the shapely calves beyond. Supporting himself on his elbows, his grey eyes took in the vision of slinky chainmail, straggly hair and hobgoblin smile. Behind him, one of the thugs behind kicked Aragon solidly in the kidneys, and he grunted in pain. "Hello, Bounty."

Bounty Fenetre glowed at him, nudging his bruised left shoulder with her boot. "Only doing my job. According to all the bounty bulletins, the Lady Emperor will pay good money to get you back in one or two pieces, and the Zibrian secret police want you turned in before you're found in their territory." She nodded firmly at her hired muscle. "Get him up. Don't break him yet." Her eyes flicked back to Aragon's dust-smeared face. "I'm feeling conversational."

The grizzled thugs hauled Aragon to his feet, dusted him off with a couple of well-placed slaps, and stood to attention. Their leather-strapped leotards bulged under excessive amounts of muscle and beer-fat.

Aragon looked past the bounty hunter and the thugs to focus on the shadowy forest of the dead. The spidery trees flickered and faded away, to be replaced by a cheerful green meadow. "No!" he muttered, twisting numbly at the ropes which bound his wrists. "Not now! You can't do this."

Bounty tipped her head to one side, nibbling a stray lock of hair. "I think I can, you know. I have a reputation to keep up." She smiled. "Besides, this gives us a chance to add new levels to our relationship, don't you think? We never did get around to playing with ropes."

Aragon's teeth drew back in a feral snarl. "You don't understand—I can get her back!"

Surprised by the passionate tones, Bounty nodded to her two hired thugs. "Head back to the Charterhouse and pick up your money. I can handle it from here."

They ambled off, grunting to each other. Bounty moved around Aragon, tugging hard on his tied wrists until he winced with pain. "Are you saying I should let you go free in the name of true love?" she suggested, her mouth very close to his ear.

"No," Aragon said harshly, staring straight ahead. "Not that."

Bounty nudged him in the ribs, her natural talent finding another of the bruises her thugs had inflicted on him. "Then what? Why should I bother to release you—this is my one chance to impress the Lady Emperor and get hired to her personal staff. I could do with a pension plan."

"Wait!" Aragon spoke haltingly, the words wrung painfully out of him. "You're right. I love her. That's why what I have to do is so important to me."

Bounty blinked, half a smile hovering over her perfectly-shaped lips. "I know you, Silversword," she accused. "Of old. You wouldn't admit to something like that unless it wasn't true." She shook her head incredulously. "Even now, you are lying to me."

"True," he admitted, finally meeting her gaze. Was he lying? He didn't know any more. All he knew was that he had some things to work out with Kassa Daggersharp, and he wouldn't have a chance to do so unless he got to that damn forest.

Bounty moved away, still staring at him like he had surprised hero in some way. After a long moment, she laughed. "Oh, one of these days, I'm going to figure out what goes on in that devious little mind of yours."

"Perhaps," Aragon replied, his eyes holding hers. "But not today."

"No," said Bounty ruefully, shaking her head. "Not today." She advanced towards him, pulling a wickedly sharp dagger from her belt…

Chapter 17
Tomorrow's Yore

Only the Emperor and his Court could travel through the Great Winter. His famous chariot, moulded from the remains of Mocklore's once-population of flying carpets, seated about sixty nobles. If they each brought suitable quantities of luggage and herald-serfs, which they usually did, there was barely room to house more than twenty-five.

The powerful city-states had long ago fallen apart due to war, famine, pestilence and some suspiciously specific natural disasters. Since the city of Dreadnought had vanished beneath the Astronomical Avalanche of the previous year, the Emperor's Court survived by travelling from manor to manor like parasites. When all the food, drink, fuel and minstrels had been consumed, the Court moved on. If the hospitality of their hosts was in any way lacking, they left several executions in their wake.

It said a great deal about the reign of this Emperor that the previous reign—that of Talle, the Lady Emperor—was secretly thought of as a Golden Age.

The Emperor was surrounded by fops, ministers, herald-serfs and glamorous noblewomen wearing peacock feathers and sequins, but he was entirely alone. He lived only to survive, and if possible to inflict misery on others. He now eased an arm out from under his heavy velvet mantle and tapped the nearest herald-serf on the head. "Where next?" he asked in the deliberately bored voice he had cultivated for years.

"Um," said the herald serf, consulting the brochure in his big book of files. "The Green Manor, close to the site of what used to be Zibria before it sank and exploded. The current Lord is one Tangent Cooper, age twenty. He inherited the title from his uncle, who was presented with the right to own a manor for, um…" He looked as embarrassed as a herald-serf could actually get. "For services to the previous Emperor."

The Emperor raised an eyebrow. "The Lady did leave the Empire in rather a mess, didn't she? Still, I don't suppose I can blame her for the weather." He laughed. It was a singularly unpleasant sound.

Everybody knew who was to blame for the weather.

-§-§-§-§-§-

Daggar grinned uneasily at his group gathered on the kitchen steps of the big, slightly snowbound house. A shabby profit-scoundrel, a grim blonde mercenary, a gangling young Blackguard and a suspiciously sweet old lady. Daggar figured they would be lucky if they didn't get the washing water thrown over them. He tapped hopefully on the kitchen window. "Look hungry and penitent, everyone," he whispered out of the corner of his mouth.

There was a long pause, then someone came to the kitchen door. As it cracked open, a young woman dwarfed by an enormous apron stared out at her visitors.

Daggar risked his most respectable smile. "Um, any chance of giving some weary travellers shelter from a snowstorm?" he asked.

The girl tilted her head, frowning speculatively. "Can you cook?"

Before any of them had a chance to respond, she hustled them into the big warm kitchen and introduced herself as Lady Reony, mistress of the manor. "We don't have any servants left, you see. We lost half of them to the factories, and the others all ran away when they heard the Emperor was coming."

"What's so scary about the Emperor?" said Daggar, frowning. "She's not exactly hard to please."

Lady Reony laughed out loud, a strangled sound. "*She*? Where have you been for the last ten years?"

Sparrow nudged Daggar sharply in the ribs, to remind him how far into the future they had travelled. He coughed. "Oh. So, being visited by the Emperor is a bad thing."

"It is when there's just two people to run the whole manor, with snow building up against the walls, no food and hardly any firewood."

"Can't you put him off, then?"

Lady Reony stared at him as if she were mad. "No one can avoid offering hospitality to the Emperor, whether noble or peasant—that would be high treason!"

"This Emperor sounds like a real hoot," muttered Daggar.

A deal was struck. The young Lord and Lady of the Manor were only too glad to take in the snowbound travellers, as long as they sang for their supper. Officer Finnley was promptly volunteered as head butler and bottle-washer, Mistress Opia was put in charge of the kitchen, Daggar was to play sergeant-at-arms and Lady Reony would take Sparrow up to her own chamber to prepare for her particular role.

"We were expecting to be clapped in irons as soon as the Court arrived," Reony confessed as she flung open her wardrobe doors. "Greyest winter or no greyest winter, the Emperor has had manors confiscated for less than not being able to provide a six-course banquet at a moment's notice. We simply can't manage without any staff at all."

"This Emperor of yours sounds like quite a charmer," said Sparrow. She regarded the wardrobe full of shiny dresses with some trepidation. "What exactly does a *chatelaine* do?"

"Runs the household, greets the guests and ensures that the Lady of the Manor looks like she does it all herself," said Reony with a grin. "Or, in your case, greeting the guests and keeping them vaguely entertained while the rest of us run around like headless chickens."

Sparrow pulled a face. "Why could I not be the sergeant-at-arms?"

"With all due respect to your friend Daggar," said Reony slyly, "I don't think he could get away with wearing this." She slid an extraordinary gown out from her wardrobe, holding it up for Sparrow's inspection.

Sparrow stared at it. "I cannot wear that!" she protested. "*You* are supposed to be the Lady of the Manor."

"Oh, I can't wear this one," Reony assured her. "I haven't the figure for it. Go on, try it on."

Sparrow stared at the shimmering garment. "How?" she said finally.

-§-§-§-§-§-

"You're not going to put anything nasty in the Imperial Soup, are you?" Daggar peered suspiciously at Mistress Opia. If it had been up to him, he certainly would not have put the Brewmistress in charge of the kitchen. "No turning the Court into lead?"

Mistress Opia just sniffed. "You object to roast duck?"

Daggar's stomach growled. "No objections," he said hastily. "Where did you get the duck from?"

Mistress Opia gave him a deadly look. "Never ask an alchemist where she gets her ingredients."

Lord Tangent stuck his head into the kitchen, his curly hair hanging in a wild mop over his eyes. "Everything going all right? Good of you chaps to help out. That butler fellow of yours just spotted the air-carriage, so they shouldn't be long now."

A large thudding sound echoed from outside. "Action stations!" cried Lord Tangent, sounding alarmed. "Quick, into the hall."

Daggar picked up the ceremonial sword he had been issued with and hurried into the entrance hall, taking up position next to Finnley who had traded his Blackguard uniform for something in royal blue velvet, with shiny buttons. He was holding a silver tray because apparently that was what butlers did.

"Right," said Lord Tangent. "I'd better pop upstairs so that Ree and I can make our grand entrance later. Good luck everyone." He ran up the stairs two at a time, but stopped short when he saw who was coming down.

Daggar saw what had caught Tangent's eye, and his mouth fell open.

Sparrow descended, clad in a shimmering gown of gold silk. The astounding golden bodice clung to her as if by magic, sweeping into a fall of shimmering fabric. Her tawny hair was piled in an extraordinary mass and pearls glistened from her throat and earlobes. She was scowling.

"Bloody hell," said Daggar.

Lord Tangent's reaction was a little more genteel. He stepped slowly up to the landing and took the lady's hand. "Our new chatelaine, I presume?" He brought her hand to his lips. "Charmed, absolutely charmed."

A loud banging sounded on the front door. Lord Tangent bowed swiftly to Sparrow, released her hand and vanished up the spiral staircase.

Sparrow, one hand gripping the banister with white knuckles, began to descend to the entrance hall below. "Open the door, Blackguard," she said between her teeth as she reached the newly-brushed hall carpet.

"You look," Daggar told her, "I mean, you really look—"

"I know," she said calmly. "Shut your mouth before your brains fall out. Officer, the door!"

Officer Finnley moved to pull the front door wide open. A herald in black and white livery marched in, shaking snow off his boots. He proceeded to tootle a short and triumphant melody on his long ceremonial trumpet. "His Imperial Majesty graces the Green Manor, to receive the hospitality of Lord Tangent Cooper!" he announced.

A parade of fops, noble ministers and women wearing peacock feathers crowded into the entrance hall. Daggar found himself shoved into a corner where he couldn't see anything but the backs of various cloaks. He heard Sparrow speak in a calm, rehearsed voice. "If your Imperial Majesty will follow me, I will show you to your rooms of residence so that you may refresh yourself and dress for dinner."

"I am adequately dressed and refreshed," came a harsh voice which Daggar could only presume belonged to the Emperor. "Lead us to your feasting hall."

Surprisingly obedient, Sparrow turned and led the way to the ballroom which Daggar had spent the afternoon hauling trestle tables into. The Court followed, rustling and muttering to themselves and scattering stray sequins wherever they walked. Behind them, four or five herald-serfs were bent double with huge quantities of travel chests, spare peacocks and the occasional lady-in-waiting strapped to their backs.

Daggar peeled himself off the hat stand, straightened out his ceremonial sword and stared after the departing crowd, frowning. "I know that voice," he muttered. "Don't I?" A moment later, he said, "Lord Tangent *Cooper*?"

-§-§-§-§-§-

Sparrow led the Emperor to the damask-draped high table and took his cloak from him, tossing it to a nearby herald. "Please make yourself comfortable," she said smoothly. "Drinks will be served immediately."

"Just as well," replied the Emperor.

Fires roared in the ballroom for the first time in years, burning up the wood that young Lord Tangent had spent so much time gathering. If they were sparing with the fuel, they might have enough to last a day or three, provided the Emperor allowed them to be sparing with the fuel.

As Finnley brought the hot mulled wine into the hall, Sparrow took the opportunity to examine Mocklore's future Emperor. He was in his late fifties, too thin for a man of that age, grey-haired with a face carved out of granite. He reminded Sparrow of an old troll she had known in her childhood, who always sat in the same shady corner of the same rocky plain, staring at the passers-by with a, sullen expression as if he blamed them all for his unhappy state.

The Emperor sipped from the steaming goblet and frowned, as if the taste was familiar to him.

"Our cook learned her recipes from the Brewers of Dreadnought, long ago," Sparrow said helpfully, and the Emperor appeared to nod, not really listening to her. He was lost in thoughts of his own.

Sparrow continued to stare, fascinated by this man. Was it the position that made his manner so cold—the pressures of running a dying Empire? Or was it something else?

Finnley finished making the rounds of the nobles and returned his tray to the kitchen. Daggar appeared at the double doors, looking quite respectable in his trim military uniform.

Sparrow nodded approvingly at him, and then realised that he was staring with a kind of wild-eyed horror. Not at her, not at the glamorous low-cut dress which had so unnerved him earlier. He was staring at the Emperor.

Daggar whispered something to the herald-serf who was hovering by the door and disappeared again.

"Our hosts, Lord Tangent and Lady Reony," announced the herald.

Sparrow was busily seething at Daggar's behaviour. He was supposed to escort the Lord and Lady to the Emperor, not run off when there was a job to do. She stepped back to allow Tangent and Reony to approach the Emperor with their aristocratic flatteries, then she withdrew to find out what Daggar was playing at.

He was pacing up and down the hall, muttering to himself and looking nervous. "What the crag are you up to?" Sparrow demanded. "We promised we would do this properly. Would you prefer to be freezing to death out in that blizzard?"

"I can't go in there," Daggar said hollowly. "The Emperor! It can't be, I can't believe it. It's too sick to be true."

Sparrow sniffed. "You do not believe all those stories Reony told us?"

"The executions, the confiscating of manors and castles, the neglect of his populace?" said Daggar quietly. "Oh, I believe it. I've met him before, you see. His name is—or *was*, Aragon Silversword."

Sparrow hesitated. "Your crewmate? The one who—"

"The one Kassa was going to turn into a hero," Daggar said bitterly. "Only trouble is, she left the job half-done. She went and died on us. Look at him, Sparrow. He used to just be a selfish bastard. Now he's a monster."

"So what do you want us to do about it?"

"If we had the ship, I'd have a simple answer. We could go back and change it. Stop this from happening."

"Is that what Kassa would do?" asked Sparrow sarcastically.

Daggar gave her a lopsided grin. "Yeah. And she'd make a right mess of it, and blow things up, and get everything topsy-turvy. But when she was in charge, everything always turned out fine. Even when things got blown up, and turned temporarily into pink dolphins. Nobody died. Nobody got executed for being late with the Emperor's dinner."

"So you want to change history?" said Sparrow.

"Future history," he corrected. "Will you help me?"

"It sounds like a case of chronological sabotage."

"Think you're up to it?"

"If you are." Sparrow stuck out her hand to seal the deal.

Daggar shook her hand firmly and then turned it over, giving her knuckles a quick kiss. Almost chivalrous.

Sparrow's eyes narrowed, but she didn't say anything.

The chief herald-serf burst out through the double doors. "His Imperial Majesty, Imperator Aragon I, wants his dinner," he said importantly.

Daggar released Sparrow's hand. "Do you hear that? The Emperor wants his dinner."

"Butler Finnley," Sparrow called to the kitchen. "The Emperor wants his dinner!"

They both stood well back, as Officer Finnley and Mistress Opia paraded into the ballroom, carrying steaming trays and tureens which smelled almost, but not entirely unlike sulphur.

Chapter 18
Blackmailing the Boatman

The knife cut deeply into the coarse rope, freeing Aragon's hands. He shook them loose, rubbing pins and needles out of his numbed fingers. "Thank you."

"Go on then," said Bounty Fenetre, slipping the knife back into her belt. "Before I change my mind. I'd like to meet her, you know."

Aragon looked at her, slightly startled. "Who?"

"The girl you're not in love with," Bounty said with a smirk. "I'd like to shake the hand of the woman who can make Aragon Silversword jump through hoops."

"My motives are purely selfish," Aragon told her.

"And personal," Bounty agreed. "I have no doubt of that. I'll see you again, Aragon."

He shaded his eyes against the sun, staring down into the valley. And there it was—not quite where it had been before, but there nevertheless—a shadowy, gnarled glimpse of a long dead forest. He glanced back at Bounty, and she was taken aback by the warmth in his smile. "No offense, but I hope not," grinned Aragon Silversword.

As he bounded off in the direction of the skeletal forest which only he could see, Bounty Fenetre shook her head slowly. "I'd like to see the woman who can make you smile like that," she murmured to herself. "Then again, maybe I have."

-§-§-§-§-§-

The forest of the dead clutched around Aragon like a shroud. Spindly branches plucked at his sleeves and a cloying smell arose mustily from the carpet of rotting leaves under his feet. "A golden twig," he muttered to himself, remembering the instructions of Tmesis. "Possibly silver, but almost certainly gold."

"Gold, you say?" teased a voice.

Aragon stiffened. "Lady Luck."

"The one and only." The goddess appeared beside him, dissolving out of thin air. "You don't really think you're going to succeed, do you?"

"Any reason why I shouldn't?" Ignoring her, he continued to walk. "You took advantage of a glitch in the cosmos to cause Kassa's death, apparently on a whim. I plan to rectify that."

"Well, aren't we the little upholder of justice," Lady Luck said sarcastically. "Why do you want to rescue her, even if it was possible? She used you, over and over again. She forced you into virtual servitude by means of trickery, and you *hated* her for it."

Aragon stopped. "I don't hate her."

"Then what do you feel?" sneered the goddess. "Love? You mortals are all the same. Petty, petty, petty. You're only obsessed with her because you can't have her. Even if you achieve the impossible and bring her back to the mortal world, you'll lose interest. And she certainly will, even assuming that she was interested in the first place. What's the point?"

A squawking sound filled the air above Aragon's head, and he looked up. A rain of feathers fell around him as a moth-eaten raven engaged a dove in what appeared to be a brutal fist-fight. Behind the squabbling birds, a twig was glowing. It wasn't exactly gold, not by any stretch of the imagination. It was certainly yellowish, but almost the colour of bronze. A bronzey yellowish twig. It would have to do.

"If your quest is righteous," said Aragon to himself, repeating the passage Tmesis had read him from one of her ancient scrolls, the one with the coffee stain in the centre. "It will come easily from the bough." He shoved away the squabbling birds, reached up and took hold of the bronze twig, giving it a swift tug which had no effect whatsoever. He pulled harder, and still it stuck fast to its branch. He pressed his other hand hard against the trunk and yanked the bronze twig down, his muscles straining with the effort.

Lady Luck laughed. "How righteous is your quest?"

"Are you doing this?" he snarled.

"*Would* I?"

The twig snapped free. Breathing hard, Aragon brandished it at her. "See?"

"Congratulations," Lady Luck said dryly. "You've won a twig."

"I don't believe you can come any further with me," he snapped. "Gods aren't allowed in the Underworld."

"The opinion is divided on the matter," she said snootily. "But I will leave you, for now." She lifted a single arm in the air, and began to fade from view. "I haven't finished with you yet, Aragon Silversword," her voice echoed, bouncing off the nearby trees in ghostly fashion. "Not by a long shot."

Aragon turned away, gazing at the twig in his hands. "What came next? Something about a river..."

There was a rushing, shuddering watery sound in the distance. It grew louder and louder, and Aragon only just stepped aside in time to avoid the river which forced its violent way through the dead forest. After a few minutes in which the river carved a fairly deep bed for itself in the forest floor, a small boat came trundling along. Its occupant, a shabby old man with a skeletal face and a lopsided pair of oars, sat up straight when he saw Aragon standing by the tree. "Oh naw," he groaned. "Nawt *ageen*."

"I want you to take me to the Underworld," said Aragon Silversword, giving the boatman a nasty look.

"Leyt me poot it this way," said the boatman with exaggerated patience. "*Naw*. Naw wey." He hefted his oars again, as if about to row away. Strangely, the powerful current seemed to have little effect on the now-stationary boat.

"You are the boatman," said Aragon icily. "Taking people to the Underworld is your job."

"Who tawld you aboot this route?" the boatman demanded. "Dawn't teell me. "Tme-bloody-sis. Too mooch *teeme* on her hands, that woon. Allus sending doon soom heero or oother." He folded his arms defiantly. Strangely, the oars he had been holding now hovered in mid air. "Geeve me woon good reason why I should leyt ye into t'Immortal realm."

"Because," suggested Aragon. "I have the bronzy-gold twig." He handed it over to the boatman, who made a great show of examining it.

"All reet," he said reluctantly, handing it back. "Hop un. But ee'l see me union aboot this. S'not reet, people hitching lifts awll over the pleece just caws o' that bloody brownze tweeg clause in me contract. Naw foony business, meend," he added with a cautionary wag of his finger.

"Funny business?" said Aragon disdainfully as he stepped into the boat and sat carefully on a pile of waterproof sacks. He didn't even like to guess what might be in them.

"Aye, lad. Every teem woon of you heeroes makes his weey intae t' Underworld, s'all *beatin'* up the three-heeded guard dawg, *seizin'* the pruttiest maid'n and awee yer gaw!"

"I promise if I meet a guard dog with three heads, I won't beat it up," said Aragon coldly.

The boatman raised an eyebrow. "And the maid'ns?"

"I'm not promising anything."

The boatman eyed him suspiciously, but shuffled his oars into place and pushed off from the shore of the newly-formed river. "Yee're nawt weerin' any lion-skun. Are ye sure ye're a heero?"

"I'm in disguise," Aragon said. "Doesn't this boat go any faster?"

As the river continued on its rushing path, the gloomy forest around the little boat faded away in favour of a darker and more menacing landscape. Mountains, valleys and various other less familiar land-masses formed ominous shapes against the horizon.

And that was another thing. The horizon was in entirely the wrong place.

The boatman leered at Aragon—obviously a man who enjoyed his work. "Git airseeck at all do ye?"

"Airsick?" replied Aragon, trying to sound as aloof and dignified as possible. "What has that got to do with anything? We're going to the Underworld. Isn't the Underworld underground?"

"*Een* a manner o' speykin," grinned the boatman.

The horizon turned upside-down, inside out. Aragon's stomach flipped around in circles and ended up somewhere around his ankles. Somewhere along the way he lost consciousness, which was quite a relief.

Aragon awoke to find himself face down at the foot of a vertical cliff; the river and the boatman nowhere to be seen. He looked up. He looked around. Apart from the small section of rock on which he was sitting, the landscape surrounding him was a featureless void. He didn't want to risk finding out if it *was* a featureless void. He stood up, and looked up again at the vertical cliff.

The bronze twig, still glowing, was stuck jauntily in his belt. He picked it out and stared at it, turning it over in his hands and trying to remember what Tmesis had told him about being stranded by a mad boatman in the middle of a void. She hadn't covered that part. Her implication had been that after getting aboard the boat, the rest would be easy. So much for the advice of the Priestess of Forgotten Gods.

Aragon flung the bronze twig away from him as hard as he could. It bounced off the cliff and lay still on the rocks, teetering on the edge of the void. And then…

A translucent spiral staircase grew out of the rock, twisting and turning its way up the vertical cliff. Aragon looked at the staircase, then at the twig, and turned his back on both of them. "If I climb up there," he said aloud,

"I'll get almost to the top and then the whole bloody thing will collapse under me and I'll end up at the foot again, possibly with multiple fractures. Life is so predictable."

He turned back, staring at the glittering staircase. He moved to pick up the bronze twig, sticking it back into his belt. "Then again, so am I. Predictable as anything."

Aragon Silversword began to climb the staircase.

-§-§-§-§-§-

The Underworld tavern bore the name, "Rusty Ballads," scrawled across the door in large golden lettering. It could have done with a new lick of paint, but then so could everything in the Underworld.

Kassa pushed open the door.

She had been to a great many taverns in her time, but this one took the biscuit. Kassa hadn't thought it was possible for any place to be so entirely devoid of atmosphere. Imps slouched in and out, hanging over small seedy tables or taking turns to jab a slow stick around the pool table.

Kassa took a deep breath and went up to the bar. "I want something with bubbles in it, please. Preferably a drink."

"Mineral water," grunted the imp behind the bar.

Kassa blinked. "I'm sorry—did you say mineral water?"

"Only thing we got with bubbles." The imp picked up a damp wash cloth and rubbed it half-heartedly over the bar. It only moved the grime around a bit.

"All right," she said calmly. "I'm willing to compromise. What do you serve which *doesn't* have bubbles in it?"

The imp snorted once into a spotted hanky which he then shoved back into his pocket. "Mineral water," he grunted.

Kassa waited. "And the difference between bubbled mineral water and non-bubbled mineral water is..." she invited.

"About a week."

Kassa's friendly smile had dissolved into something altogether less friendly. "I'll have a fresh mineral water *with* bubbles, please," she said.

The imp put a glass in front of her. It was bubbled water. Kassa regarded it with distaste, and then laughed at herself. "I'm in the Underworld and I'm worrying about the quality of the water?"

She took a mouthful, and tried tactfully not to spit it out again. It was almost entirely tasteless. She pushed the glass back along the counter. "Put a teaspoon of sea salt in it, and just maybe it will be drinkable."

By the time she reached her fourth salty mineral water, Kassa was becoming quite maudlin. "Gods but you've got a depressing place here," she muttered into her empty glass.

"Been working here all my life," said the bartender imp sadly.

She lifted her head and stared at him, her deep golden eyes slightly unable to focus. "How long's that?"

The imp, who was also on the mineral water (but without the salt), counted vaguely on his fingers. "When was the dawn of time?" he said finally. "Cos it was sometime before that. About four days before. Maybe less."

"How sad," said Kassa sympathetically. "That's so sad. Do you ever get a holiday?"

"Every other millennia," said the imp, on the verge of tears. "My cousin Stanley comes in, and I go tend his bar for a while. It's the one at the other end of the Underworld. The one that not even the imps use. I stand there behind the bar, and nobody ever comes in. That's my holiday. Compared to that, this place is Fun City."

Kassa took hold of the imp's shoulder in a comradely gesture. "You are the bravest imp I have ever met in my entire…death." She stared down at her empty glass. "There isn't a drop of alcohol in this water, is there?"

"Not an iota!" bawled the imp, big fat tears dribbling down his nose.

Kassa sighed. "Thought not." She turned on her stool, looking around the entire tavern, trying to spot something which might cheer her up. After a moment of concentrated searching, her arm lashed out and grabbed hold of the bartender imp by the collar, only just managing to avoid giving him a nasty scratch with her purple-painted fingernails. “Is that a piano over there?”

The imp followed her gaze to a large object covered with a grey floral dust sheet. “Could be,” he hazarded.

Kassa smiled an evil smile, her eyes lighting up for the first time since her death. “Well, then. Let’s get this party started!”

Chapter 19
The Other Silversword
(Imperator Aragon I)

The ballroom was thronged with dancing noblemen and glamorous women wearing peacock feathers. Sparrow, uncomfortable in her dreamlike golden gown, was dancing with the young and horribly handsome Lord Tangent.

"I say," he said cheerfully. "You're not like other girls."

"No," said Sparrow, forcing a friendly smile. "Ordinary girls do not hack people's heads off for a living."

It was to Lord Tangent's credit that he didn't even blink. "I say, do you really? Jolly good show."

Daggar hovered behind the hat-stand, doing his best to be inconspicuous. Ostensibly keeping a nervous eye on the Emperor, he couldn't help kept darting the occasional suspicious glance at Sparrow and her dancing partner. Not that he was jealous or anything. Of course not.

Lord Tangent suavely whispered something in Sparrow's ear. She smiled slightly, tilting her head up as if to hear him better. Then she slapped him soundly around the face and stalked off across the dance floor. She couldn't quite manage a full military stride in her clingy golden skirts, but it was an impressive march nonetheless.

Daggar tried not to grin too hard as she approached him. "Staying in character, are we?"

Sparrow scowled darkly. "I want my armour back. No one tries to seduce me when I am armoured."

Daggar looked ruefully down at his ceremonial plate and uniform. "So that's why no one will dance with me. Did the dashing young Lord Tangent insult your maidenly modesty? I could beat him up, if you like."

Sparrow glanced back at the wounded Lord Tangent, and then carefully looked Daggar up and down. "I do not think you could."

"True, true," he agreed amiably. "So, what do we do next?"

"We cannot risk searching for the ship until tomorrow. Let us hope Lady Reony is as generous with snowboots as she is with fancy dresses."

Daggar eyed her, not quite leering. "That *is* quite a dress."

"Oh, be quiet." Sparrow scanned the hall. "What is your friendly neighbourhood Emperor up to?"

Daggar nodded towards a corner of the hall, where the Imperator Aragon I was playing chess with Lady Reony, who was looking nervous. "He's behaving himself. No executions yet, in any case. Why don't you and I steal a platter of hors d'oeuvres and slink off for a while?"

Sparrow looked amused. "Is that an improper suggestion?"

Daggar thought about it. "Probably not," he said glumly.

-§-§-§-§-§-

Lady Reony Cooper had only just about figured out how the horse-shaped figures were supposed to move when the Emperor captured her last one. "I knew your uncle once," he said as he picked the ebony knight off the board and tossed it into the little velvet bag beside the chessboard. "The infamous Reed Cooper."

"I know," Reony said hesitantly. "He always spoke very highly of you."

The Emperor's chilly grey eyes flickered briefly, though there was little humour in his gaze. "Indeed? Then he became more of a hypocrite in his middle age than I."

Reony flashed a quick, worried smile, hoping that he was joking. "Perhaps," she admitted. "Is our hospitality to your liking, your Imperial Majesty?"

The Emperor waited for her to make her next move. "Perhaps," he mimicked.

-§-§-§-§-§-

Daggar was pouring drinks for himself and Sparrow at one of the buffet tables when she stumbled, and almost fell. He stuck out his arm to steady her, dropping the ladle back in the tureen of mulled wine with a splash. "You all right?"

Sparrow straightened up, staring in horror at the yellowish colour of her hands. For a moment, they seemed to age before her eyes. "I thought I had more time."

"You can't believe anything that Opia woman tells you," Daggar said authoritatively.

Sparrow opened her mouth as if to make a sarcastic retort, but giddiness overwhelmed her.

Daggar swung his arm around her waist. "Come on outside for some fresh air."

"I will not go outside," Sparrow protested as he steered her towards the corridor. "It is still snowing, we will freeze."

"The tower room, then. I found it when I was looking for somewhere to put on this fancy suit. This way."

"Your breastplate is on backwards," she noted as he pushed open a second set of double doors. Then she stared at the unfamiliar room in surprise.

The walls, several storeys higher than the rest of the manor put together, were lined with wide glass windows. Translucent spiral stairs lined the tower, leading up to an elegant balcony at the highest point. Even the ceiling was glass, and the softly-falling snow traced patterns everywhere.

Sparrow straightened up, breathing in the cool air of the glass-lined room. "I feel better now."

"Thought you might," grinned Daggar. "Feel up to a climb? It's a hell of a view."

Sparrow looked undecided. "We should go back to the party in case that Emperor friend of yours decides to execute everybody."

"It'll only take a minute," Daggar urged, grabbing her hand and heading for the steps. "Come on."

The view from the top of the glass tower was extraordinary—but puzzling. Sparrow turned around, trying to get her bearings. "We must be close to Zibria—the time trip never takes us far from where we left. But I cannot see it. That mountain is familiar, but that one is in the wrong place."

"Maybe it's the snow," suggested Daggar. "It makes things a funny shape sometimes..."

"It should not swallow cities," Sparrow said darkly. "Something is wrong. Mocklore cannot have changed this much in little more than twenty years!" She turned, staring in the opposite direction. "Daggar, there is a city."

"See, I told you it wouldn't have gone far," he said.

"Not Zibria. There is a city on the Troll Triangle."

Daggar turned, and peered out into the snowy landscape. He could just about catch a glimpse of the familiar orange-coloured rocks of the Troll Triangle in the distance, almost completely covered up by snow...and the spiky towers of what looked very much like a city. "I didn't think trolls had any interest in urban architecture," he said thoughtfully.

Sparrow's voice was icier than the snow-patterned glass. "We do not. *Trolls* do not, they would not. That city is the work of humans."

"Hang on," said Daggar, turning around again. "If that's the Troll Triangle, where the hell *is* Zibria?"

"That is what I asked!"

"An interesting question," said the Emperor. "If you don't mind me saying so."

Sparrow and Daggar both swivelled their eyes downwards. The Emperor of Mocklore stood at the foot of the glass stairs, looking up at them. Very slowly, he began to make his way up the stairs. "Hello, Daggar," he said almost conversationally. "I thought it was you."

"It's been a long time," said Daggar dubiously. "I could be…my son, for instance." So very convincing.

"Your son looks nothing like you," said the Emperor dismissively, as he reached their level at the top of the tower. He surveyed the glass balcony with some interest, peering at the intricate furniture and finally raising his eyes to examine the view through the wide windows. "Incidentally, why have you suddenly lost at least two decades in age?"

Daggar eyed him suspiciously. "What son? Are you telling me I have a…"

Sparrow digged him sharply in the ribs with her elbow. "Time travel," she said calmly. "Your Imperial Majesty."

A look of horror crossed the Emperor's face. "So it was true." He sat down on a flimsy glass chair, staring numbly at the snow-swirled scene outside. "I didn't believe you."

"So," said Daggar, taking a deep breath. "What happened to Mocklore?"

The Emperor shrugged a single shoulder. "Civil war. Lady Talle left quite a mess for her successor to clear up. The city states are a thing of the past. Everything is feudal now."

"What about the weather?" demanded Daggar. "This isn't normal. Neither are volcanoes or avalanches and whatever else has been going on around here. Speaking of which, what happened to Zibria?"

"It sank," said the Emperor calmly. "And then exploded."

Daggar's face was a picture of disbelief. "What happened?"

"The magic build-up was getting far too dangerous," said the Emperor, matter-of-factly. "There was a consignment of warlocks who seemed to know what they were talking about. I gave them a great deal of money to sort out the problem, back when I was first on the throne. They managed to tear most of Mocklore apart. The Skullcaps sank, and there's a whole new mountain where the Middens used to be. We lost Dreadnought last year." He stood up, straightening his Imperial tunic with a quick tug. "We get by."

"You get by," said Daggar in a strangled voice. "How many died of starvation this winter? How many did you murder for not having your soup hot enough, or not providing the right number of bread rolls? What would Kassa say if she could see you now?"

The Emperor's face hardened, and his eyes blazed bright grey. "Kassa died a long time ago."

Daggar looked at the man who had once been Aragon Silversword, professional traitor. "And when were you planning to get over it?" he demanded.

The Emperor was angry now. "You don't understand. I got her out of the Underworld. I rescued her, but it wasn't enough. I couldn't keep her in the mortal world. She slipped through my fingers." He looked suddenly very lost. "The cat ran away when I became Emperor. Even the cat ran away."

"He is mad, I think," hissed Sparrow.

Daggar nodded steadily, trying to understand. "Then what happened?"

The Emperor laughed bitterly. "I met you. You told me you had a time ship." His eyes flicked to Sparrow. "Her as well. You told me you could bring her back. But I didn't believe you." He unclenched a tightly folded hand, revealing a worn, twisted piece of metal. "I *refused* to believe you."

Daggar vaguely recognised the object in the Emperor's outstretched palm as Kassa's spiral ring, but it was heavily tarnished and warped as if it had been squeezed and held and examined for too many years.

Sparrow spoke now, her voice tightly controlled. "There is a city on the Troll Triangle. A *human* city."

The Emperor looked surprised. "Before the blizzards started, we were building my next capital there. It's almost finished."

She advanced on him, her jade-green eyes flashing. "What happened to the *trolls*?"

"They were wiped out over a decade ago. Too many of them had been leaving the Triangle, coming into human territory. It made some sort of sense at the time."

"Thunderdust," swore Sparrow. "You are lucky I do not have my sword with me."

Taking his life into his hands, Daggar stepped between the two of them. He stared up into the Emperor's face. "Listen to me, Silversword. I want to change this. We haven't met you yet. You haven't not believed me yet, not as far as we're concerned. If there's some way that time travel can bring Kassa back, we might still be able to change all this."

The Emperor's expression flickered slightly. "You would remove me from the throne?"

"I'd make bloody sure you never even got a sniff at the throne!" Daggar said explosively. "Look what you've done to the place. All this doesn't *have* to have happened."

The Emperor tugged again at his Imperial robes. "I could have you executed," he mused.

"Yeah," said Daggar. "I know."

The Emperor looked thoughtfully at Daggar and then at Sparrow, who looked as if she wanted to throttle somebody. He moved to the glass stairs, descending the translucent steps. His body held rigidly, he trod the slow spiral back to the ground level. "Do your worst, Daggar," said Aragon Silversword. "Do your worst."

Chapter 20
Rusty Ballads

The goth girls reclined in their recreation room, which was fully equipped with a swimming pool, a royal tennis court and a communal wardrobe.

The huge split-screen on the wall flickered into life, delivering a multiple image of a man climbing a staircase.

"One of *those*," said Flipfairy Cream in a bored voice as she streaked her long, black hair with silver glitter. "A hero come to rescue a dead maiden."

"Not another one," said Indigo Marshmallow, painting her mouth very carefully with her new inky lipstick. "That makes four in the last mortal moon. Bor-ring."

"I think it's romantic," said Peony Seashell, sticking her opal-studded tongue out at them all. "Why shouldn't he come and rescue her if he wants to?"

"Because it screws up the accounts something shocking, dingleberry," said Indigo scornfully. "You know how the Dark One feels about paperwork."

Ebony (née Trixibelle Cream) who had just come in from a lengthy corridor-gliding session, would never do anything so inelegant as to chew her lip, but she certainly considered it. "We should find out who he's after. Maybe it's something to do with the disturbances we've been having lately."

As if on cue, a shudder ran the length of the Underworld, and the walls of the recreation room seemed to buckle.

"Oh let me do it," squealed Peony. "Please, I've never got to use the mind probe before!"

Indigo opened the closest chest of drawer and pulled out a short sword in a hot-pink leather scabbard. "Do you know how to use it?"

Peony snatched it greedily. "Of course I do. I just point it at him." She drew the blade and pointed it dramatically at the screen. Immediately, a small machine in the corner began to make various *whir-clicking* noises, and a stream of thin paper issued forth.

Flipfairy Cream leaned over and tore off the readout, scanning it with a yawn. "The usual thoughts. Sore feet, slight headache, surprisingly homicidal tendencies about the bronze twig in his belt…hot damn." She let out a low whistle.

Everyone stared at her. "What is it?" Peony asked excitedly, dropping the mind-probing sword on to the nearest armchair.

Flipfairy Cream's dark eyes lifted to meet those of her cousin Ebony, who still hovered in the doorway. "Well?" requested Ebony, still maintaining her calm and elegant poise.

"He's after the Daggersharp woman," said Flipfairy in a tone of impending doom.

Ebony's face altered significantly. "*Shit.*"

There was a discreet cough from the corner, and a figure unfolded from the velvety armchair in which she had been lounging. "Don't sweat it, girls," said Honey Sugarglass, sweeping back her elegant fall of midnight hair and hiking up her little black dress to show off the proportions of her extraordinary legs. "Just leave this to the expert."

-§-§-§-§-§-

The spiral staircase finally came to an end, and Aragon staggered off on to the solid ground of the cliff top. Behind him, the staircase vanished with a soft 'pop'. "What do you know?" he said softly, looking back down over the edge. He had made it to the top without being dumped from a great height. Perhaps there was hope after all.

"Hello, Aragon," said a husky voice.

He looked up. A woman stood a little way away from him, wrapped in an impossibly clingy black dress. She looked almost ghostlike. Her wild, dark red hair flew around her, tangling in the wind and making blood-coloured patterns on her diaphanous dress. Her gold eyes bored into him, and she smiled a dazzlingly familiar smile with her extraordinarily well-shaped mouth.

Aragon got to his feet, staring at her.

She glided forward, into his arms. Well, not exactly into his arms, because his arms were remaining firmly at his side, but her own arms slid up and around his neck. "I've been waiting for you," she murmured, turning her face up for a kiss.

Aragon Silversword reached up and carefully peeled one of her arms from around his neck, then the other one. He briefly glanced at her hands before letting them fall.

She stared up at him, her golden eyes wide and impossibly hurt. "What's wrong?" she whispered, the ghost of a tear hovering at the edge of her thick eyelashes.

"I came here to find Kassa Daggersharp," Aragon said acidly. "You'll forgive me if I wait around for the real thing."

She stepped back, her lips thinning and darkening. The height and curves of Kassa Daggersharp receded, as did the wild red hair. A pale, slender goth girl with long dark hair glared at Aragon Silversword, crossing her arms. "How did you know?" breathed Honey Sugarglass, still using a fair facsimile of Kassa's voice.

Aragon favoured her with a thin smile. "The body language was wrong, the dialogue was wrong and the fingernails were the wrong shade of purple. Not to mention the fact that your Kassa Daggersharp was greeting a lover—and I was never that. Do you ever manage to fool anyone?"

Honey Sugarglass turned her black-lashed eyes up to stare at him with an expression of pure elegant petulance. "If you're not her sweetie, then what the glory gods are you doing here?" she demanded.

It was a good question. Aragon seriously considered devoting some time to answering it. But later. Much later. He pulled the bronze twig out of his belt and tapped the disgruntled goth girl on the nose with it. "Take me to your leader," he suggested with a quirk of his eyebrow.

She pouted, but led him onwards, into the cavernous stone walkways of the Underworld. "Well, now. Is this a special occasion, or do you put on this performance for all the guests you get through here?" asked Aragon.

"Technically we're not supposed to let anyone through here," Honey told him, snapping her chewing gum distractedly. "And as for your choice of maidens to rescue—well, we had to try and stop you."

"Any particular reason?"

"We have this prophecy thing," explained Honey. "The goth girls. We've never told anyone about it before but the thing is, it's always right. And it says that Kassa Daggersharp is inadvertently going to save the Underworld from total destruction. So we can't lose her, you see." She stopped, an apologetic look on her face. "Sorry."

"What—" Aragon started to say, but it was too late. The ground had already opened up and swallowed him. He was falling...

-§-§-§-§-§-

"It's very You," said Vervain the sprite, resting his bright orange chin on his bright orange hands.

The Dark One admired the canary-yellow suit in the full-length mirror. "It is, isn't it." He added a bright pink scarf and tossed it dramatically over one shoulder. "*Very* nice."

A loud knocking sound came at the door of the large dressing room, which was full of garbage bags stuffed to capacity with various garments in black velvet which were to be thrown out.

When gods change their image, they go all the way.

"Get that, will you?" said the Dark One casually, turning to check out his three-quarters profile.

Vervain snapped his fingers and the door swung open, tipping three agitated imps into the room.

"The Lady," gasped one imp, his little black suit in considerable disarray.

"Pomegranate," gasped the next imp, groping for his displaced toupée. "Has..."

"Taken over," choked the third imp, who was nearly flattened under the weight of the other two.

"Taken over the Underworld," they all chorused together.

"Of course, I told you," said the Dark One impatiently. "She is to be my entirely platonic consort—obey her orders as you would my own."

"She...she said," coughed the first imp, who had managed to scramble to his feet and was busily trying to tidy his buttonhole. "She said we have to obey *only* her, and you're not in power any more."

"She said you were a has-been," commented the one with the dodgy hairpiece. "And—she was going to streamline the operation and you didn't have any part in the new dynamic parameters!"

"That's what she said," the third imp agreed fervently. "She said that, all right."

The Dark One puffed himself up, his face blazing with anger. "Did she now?" he snarled. "Well, let's just see who is Lord of the Underworld, shall we? And find the Daggersharp woman," he added as he started to march down the nearest corridor. "This is all her fault."

-§-§-§-§-§-

The floor tiles were surprisingly soft. Aragon had fully expected to have his brains dashed out on them, considering the distance he had fallen. But then, this was the Underworld. If you weren't safe here, where would you be safe?

A steady, girlish voice spoke aloud. "Hello, Aragon." Pomegranate Wordernsdaughter sat on the throne. Her legs were slightly too short to reach the floor, and her long braids snaked in a puddle of hair beneath her dangling feet. "I didn't think to see you again quite so soon."

Aragon Silversword raised an eyebrow as he pulled himself to his feet and looked around, taking in the throne room. "Well, well. You have come up in the cosmos. And in such a short time."

Pomegranate smiled at him, her childish face looking surprisingly mature. She was a hemi-god, after all. "I owe it all to your ditzy girlfriend," she said, contempt evident in her voice. "She came along and abducted me, just at the right time. And now...I am in the position to offer you another favour, Silversword. The question is, do I want to?"

Before Aragon could respond to this, there was a great thump against the double doors. "Pomegranate, what is all this?" yelled the Dark One on the other side.

Pomegranate smiled beatifically. "You can't come in," she called out in a sing-song voice. "No one can enter the Lord's throne room if I don't want them to. *I'm* the Lord of Darkness now."

"But this is my Underworld!" the Dark One howled, beating on the doors with his fists.

"Not any more," Pomegranate called out in childish triumph. "You were running it into the ground. With proper administration, this place will be back on its feet in no time. You are *not* the one to do the job!" As if on cue, the Underground seemed to shake and ripple, as if in danger of being ripped apart. Looking up, Aragon saw a filmy layer of golden pollen-dust drift down from the ceiling.

Pomegranate smiled dangerously. "I'm the one who can do it," she repeated to herself. "Only me."

"Quite interesting," said Aragon. "A prepubescent hemi-goddess megalomaniac. I've never met one of those before."

"Tread carefully, Silversword," threatened Pomegranate. "Or I might change my mind about helping you." She stared at him for a moment, her eyes narrowing. "You can see the Daggersharp woman if you want. She should be easy enough to find. You may as well. Neither of you is going anywhere until my files are properly in order, and that could take several levels of eternity."

-§-§-§-§-§-

Kassa had succeeded where no one else had—she had cheered up Rusty Ballads. Seated at the piano, she bawled out the bawdiest song she could think of. The imps crowded around her and joined in the choruses enthusiastically. Some improvised jaunty hornpipes in the middle of the floor, and others were clapping and stamping in delight.

Even a few goth girls had crept into the previously all-imp tavern, drawn by the merry music and general happy noises.

The bartender imp was weeping for joy, blubbering into a bowl of peanuts like his heart was broken.

It was into this bedlam that Aragon Silversword entered by the side door. He stared at the happy crowd and at the woman in the centre of it all. He found a bar stool and sat down.

The bawdy song came to an end. Kassa instructed the nearest imp how to play piano chords so that she could sing a slow, throaty love ballad. Most of the imps stared at her, either sighing or desperately trying to memorise the words she sang and notes she played. Various combinations of imps and goths made shy attempts to lure each other out to the dance floor.

Aragon Silversword stayed on the sidelines, observing Kassa's strange effect on people. Somehow, wherever she was, a party broke out. Or a major explosion.

A thin, dark man in an outrageous suit stormed into the tavern, throwing imps right and left in an attempt to get close to Kassa. "What in the name of all that is holy are you doing?" he screeched. An orange sprite crashed in after the thin man, wringing its hands anxiously.

Kassa lifted her fingers slowly from the piano, turning around and offering the newcomer a friendly smile. "I'm cheering up your staff. They were all so miserable, I'm surprised you don't have a revolt on your hands."

"I *do* have a revolt on my hands!" insisted the Dark One angrily.

"Well," said Kassa calmly. "What did I just say?"

Aragon found himself smiling. Kassa Daggersharp was a world-class manipulator, and somehow it was a great deal more entertaining when her manipulations were not aimed at him.

"That hemi-goddess consort you brought me has taken over the running of the whole Underworld!" yelled the Dark One. "She has snatched the reins of power from my very hands!"

Kassa smiled blankly at him. "None of my business, of course, but wasn't that exactly what you wanted?"

The Dark One stared at her in total incomprehension.

"I mean," Kassa continued, widening her glorious golden eyes at him. "You loathe this job. You said yourself that you never wanted to be Lord of the Underworld—that you hated being typecast in such a way. That you longed for someone else to take the reins of power from your hands..."

The Dark One continued to stare. "I'm free," he muttered in astonishment.

Kassa clapped him on the back in comradely fashion. "That's right. So what you should do now is go pack a bag and vanish before she changes her mind. It's time for you to get on with your immortality, don't you think?" She smiled at him—that smile which Aragon remembered so well. The one which assured her victim that everything was all right, and he should trust her implicitly.

The Dark One continued to stare at her open-mouthed. Abruptly he sprang into action, kissed Kassa soundly and then tore out of the tavern at an astounding turn of speed.

The orange sprite turned to follow, but Kassa interrupted. "Ahem. Vervain. Aren't you supposed to be *my* guardian sprite?"

Vervain turned his little orange face towards her and then looked away to the Dark One's receding figure. He hunched his shoulders over and looked pleadingly at his mistress.

"Oh, go on," she sighed. "How will he cope without you to tell him what to wear? Just make sure they send me a half-decent replacement."

His eyes bright, Vervain shook her hand wildly and then ran after his new master. "Oh, Dark One! Don't forget to pack all those new shoes I ordered for you!"

Kassa sighed and turned back to the piano. The imps hungrily waited to see what she would play next.

Aragon took the opportunity to give a light cough.

Very slowly, Kassa turned around, and saw him sitting at the bar. Her face broke into the smile of a cat who knows where the mice are. She rose to her feet, walking at a steady, unhurried pace. Walking, Aragon noted, not gliding. This was the genuine article.

Behind her, the imps all complained at Kassa's departure, muttering mutinously to themselves. One of them attempted to bang out a few chords on the piano, but entirely failed to create any kind of melody.

Kassa slid on to the bar stool next to him. "Aragon Silversword," she said, widening those endless golden eyes of hers. "Not to sound pushy, but what took you so long?"

Chapter 21
Bodices and Snowdrifts

Finnley McHagrty had just about had it with slaving in the kitchen as Mistress Opia's dogsbody. "I'm a Blackguard, you know," he muttered into the sink of soapy water as he scrubbed at the first instalment of dirty pots. "Graduated first in my class. With Honours. All I wanted was to be a hero."

"A hero?" said Mistress Opia in one of her nastier grandmotherly voices. "You're dreaming, my lad. If you're a hero, I'm the wicked witch of the Western Skullcaps."

Finnley glared at the cauldron he was scouring. "You said it," he muttered. "Not me."

Lady Reony danced into the kitchen, beaming all over her face. "It's all going wonderfully!" she exclaimed. "Really it is. The Emperor almost *thanked* me for our hospitality!"

She flung her arms around a sudsy Finnley and gave him a kiss. "We couldn't have done it without you," she proclaimed. "Oh, and you, Mistress Opia!" She hugged the Brewmistress, who looked completely shocked, as if she had never been hugged before. "Your cooking was marvellous. It actually tasted like food, which is more than I could have managed on my own."

Reony then spun around to see Sparrow and Daggar, who had just entered the kitchen. "Oh, both of you!" She flung herself at Sparrow, hugging her madly. "Thank you so much, and you do look marvellous in that dress. You must keep it!"

Sparrow opened her mouth to say that she would rather die, but didn't get the chance. Reony had moved on to Daggar, whom she kissed with rampant enthusiasm. Finally she released him, returning to hug Finnley again. Daggar emerged from the kiss with a wide grin on his face which he directed at Sparrow. She raised an unimpressed eyebrow at him.

Having hugged Finnley and Mistress Opia all over again, Reony returned to Daggar. "If there's ever anything I can do for you," she gushed. "Please, don't hesitate…"

"Well, since you ask," said Daggar quickly, diverting her imminent embrace into something a little more arm's length than the lady seemed to have in mind. "Would you and that brother of yours have any snowboots you could lend us on the morrow?"

-§-§-§-§-§-

Balancing a flickering candlestick, Finnley led a herd of herald-serfs and peacock ladies to their various chambers for the night. One of them, a glamorous girl with purple hair and an inviting smile, hung back to talk with him. "I like butlers," she cooed. "What's your name, handsome?"

"Officer Finnley McHagrty," said Finnley automatically.

The girl frowned. "Officer?"

"Um," said Finnley, realising his blunder. "Ex-army?" he suggested.

"Ohhh." The girl widened her smile. "I like soldiers, too," she purred. "Would you like to come to my room?"

"Um," he said, lost for words. "Maybe?"

Sparrow appeared, wearing her clingy golden silk gown as if it were a suit of armour. "Finnley, I need you!"

"Oh," said Officer Finnley, snapping to attention. "Right. I'm coming." He smiled apologetically at the peacock girl. "Sorry. Maybe…"

"Forget it," the girl snitted, going into her room and slamming the door.

Finnley hurried in Sparrow's wake. "What exactly is it you want me to do?" he asked, skidding to a halt as Sparrow stopped outside her own room.

"I want you to stay out here on duty for the next couple of hours," she told him. "Make sure Lord Tangent of the sweaty palms does not get in this door. Understand?"

"Absolutely," said Finnley. Finally, he could feel useful doing something which didn't involve soap-suds. He stood to attention, sticking out his chest proudly. "You can rely on me."

"Good," said Sparrow. She hesitated. "Thanks."

Sparrow only just got inside her room before Lord Tangent came whistling around the corner with a bunch of rather droopy silk carnations in one hand. He paused when he saw Finnley. "Ah. This wouldn't be Mistress Sparrow's room by any chance?"

Finnley employed his most efficiently policeman-like voice. "Bog off," he said.

"Ah," said Lord Tangent. "Right. Thanks anyway." Looking rather cast down, he wandered off in the direction of the peacock ladies.

-§-§-§-§-§-

Sparrow moved towards the gratuitously luscious four-poster bed. She gave a few experimental tugs at the lacings on her bodice, and failed to notice any significant change in the silk's death-grip over her rib cage.

"Need a hand?" said a friendly voice.

Sparrow whirled around, and sighed in exasperation when she saw Daggar sitting in an over-stuffed armchair. "I have just put Officer Finnley on guard outside to *stop* unwelcome male visitors," she complained.

"Lord Tangent still pressing his suit, is he?" asked Daggar with mild interest.

"It is not his suit that I worry about," she grumbled. "It is his hands."

"And *do* you need a hand with that bodice?"

"I might take offence at that remark," Sparrow said tiredly. "If it was not for the fact that I have no idea how to get out of this monstrosity."

Daggar hopped to his feet and made a show of examining the laces holding the dress together. He pulled at one, and started unravelling the other. "I used to be quite good at this sort of thing, you know. In the good old days before I went pirating."

"Women's clothing?"

"The removal thereof," Daggar corrected, with a wink.

Sparrow looked curious. "How did you spend your time? Before you went adventuring. What does a profit-scoundrel do with his days?"

Daggar made a show of thinking about it. "Not a lot, really. Hence all the spare time devoted to learning about bodices." He moved around to the small of her back, working on the complex weavings of ribbons. "Cripes, bodice technology has made some advances since our time. I'm not absolutely sure how this thing is supposed to work." He pulled at one length of ribbon and Sparrow gasped as her waist was squeezed in another inch.

"Sorry," said Daggar cheerfully. "It must be the one on the left."

"Are you absolutely certain that you know what you are doing?" Sparrow growled. "I could do a lot of damage to you if I had sufficient provocation."

"Promises promises," said Daggar. "Hey, if I pull this bit, I can make your arms go up and down!"

-§-§-§-§-§-

Mistress Opia provided a hearty breakfast for the Manor "staff", which mostly consisted of egg. The breakfast, that is. Not the staff.

Sparrow bit into her single toasted soldier as Daggar balanced two boiled eggs and a pile of scrambled omelette on to his towering mound of toast. "Pass me a couple of poached and a couple of devilled, will you?" he said hopefully.

"I think I am going to be sick," said Sparrow, looking away as Daggar squelched various mustards, sauces and ketchups all over his assembled breakfast. She was wearing another borrowed dress, but this one was far more suited to everyday wear. It fitted quite nicely under her breastplate.

Lady Reony brought an armful of boots and protective clothing into the kitchen. "If you do find your carriage, you *will* still stay with us until the Emperor has moved on, won't you?" she asked anxiously. "I don't think we can manage without you."

Daggar looked sidelong at Sparrow. She had already had one relapse, which suggested that the liquid gold would be taking its toll on her body sooner rather than later.

Sparrow didn't even hesitate. "A deal's a deal," she said crisply, swallowing half a glass of juice. "Let's get going."

Lord Tangent, wrapped and muffled in various layers of wool and leather, joined them in the kitchen. "I'm ready when you are!" he said cheerfully. The only visible quarter of his face looked longingly at Sparrow. "It will give me a chance to tell you about my poetry," he told her happily.

-§-§-§-§-§-

It was snowing lightly as they trudged along the plains, searching for the sword Sparrow had left as a marker. Lord Tangent proved to be almost useful by providing a pocket compass. They walked slowly back to where Daggar thought the ship might be, waiting for the little needle to behave erratically. It turned out to have been a fairly unnecessary precaution, however. Yellow dandelions were even now pushing their way up through the heavy snowfall, and scattering yellow pollen everywhere, marking the path that Sparrow had trod on her way here.

"Are you sure you don't want to hear the rest of the poem?" asked Lord Tangent, smiling hopefully. He had been reciting his idea of romantic verse ever since they started off.

Sparrow glared at him. "No!"

"Hey," said Daggar, shaking the compass wildly. "It's started saying that west is north! I think."

Sparrow snatched the compass from him and lay it flat on the snowy ground. "You are right. The flowers also stop here. We must be close."

"And why exactly did you leave your sword to mark the spot?" asked Lord Tangent curiously. "Surely if you have a carriage out here, it would be more noticeable than a sword?"

"Do not ask," said Sparrow. "It is a very long story."

"Suffice to say," said Daggar, "the carriage in question is a ship about yay big at the moment." He held his finger and thumb a little way apart.

Lord Tangent hesitated. "If you say so, old boy."

There were only the three of them, shovels at the ready, on the snowy search. Mistress Opia had volunteered to stay behind as a hostage, and Lady Reony had confiscated Finnley for some urgent bottle-washing duties.

"Got it!" said Sparrow triumphantly, shoving mittened hands into a strangely-shaped snowbank and producing her sword. "It has not even rusted!"

"Right," said Daggar glumly. He stood where the sword had been. "So the ship's around here."

"Somewhere," agreed Sparrow. She handed him a shovel.

Daggar brightened somewhat. "I'm quite good with shovels."

It took close to three hours of concerted digging, shuffling and swearing before the tiny glitter of gold was uncovered. Daggar grabbed it happily, and Sparrow promptly took it off him and hid it in the bodice of the dress she wore beneath her armour. "I think we have conclusively proven that you are not to be trusted with important items," she said.

"I resent that!" said Daggar, who didn't. "Still, I can always steal it back…"

Sparrow gave him a sidelong look. "You think I am going to allow you near my bodice again? You almost strangled me last night."

As they approached the manor, a strange silence fell over them all. Sparrow's eyes flicked from window to window, trying to find some explanation for her sudden feeling of dread. She glanced at Lord Tangent. "What is wrong here?"

He looked puzzled. "I don't know. It shouldn't be this quiet."

Daggar, whose danger-detecting reflexes were kicking into overdrive, kept behind Sparrow as they approached the front doors. "I'm so glad you got your sword back," he said fervently.

The doors opened, and two herald-serfs stared blankly out at them.

"Let us through," commanded Lord Tangent importantly.

One of the heralds stepped to one side, and the other produced a single lock of hair, dangling it in front of him.

"That's Ree's!" announced Lord Tangent in horror, snatching it from the herald's outstretched hand.

"What is going on?" demanded Sparrow, fiercely.

The herald-serfs said nothing, silently motioning all three of them towards the Great Hall.

"I have a nasty feeling that Mistress Opia burned the breakfast," moaned Daggar quietly. "Either that, or something much more horrible has happened."

"No," said Sparrow evenly. "Horrible is what I do if that bastard Emperor has harmed anyone in this house."

The double doors to the Great Hall swung open.

"Ah, the wanderers return," said the Emperor of Mocklore. His tone might not have been quite so menacing were it not for the cages which hung from the ceiling, framing their view of him. Lady Reony, Mistress Opia and Finnley were all imprisoned behind the spidery steel bars.

"Practicing diplomacy, are we Aragon?" said Daggar in a strangled voice.

"I want the time ship," said the Emperor. "If anyone is going to change history, it is going to be me."

Sparrow offered a cool smile. "You don't trust us to get the job done?"

The Emperor seemed amused. "I intend to rescue Kassa and ensure that I still gain the throne of Mocklore. Can you guarantee to do the same?"

"It's one or the other," said Daggar steadily. "I don't think you can have both."

"Well," said the Emperor. "Let's just see about that, shall we?"

Chapter 22
Escape Plans and a Three-headed Hound

"Aragon Silversword," said Kassa Daggersharp. "Not to sound pushy, but what took you so long?"

The present-day Aragon rested his elbows on the counter and looked into her eyes. "I think I should warn you, I'm not dead."

Kassa absently tugged the ripped remains of her slinky black dress into some semblance of modesty. "That's all right. Neither am I. At least no one seems to think so. Except me, but apparently I have no say in the matter." She frowned for a moment. "Why are you here?"

He raised his eyebrows slowly. "Why do you think?"

Kassa laughed, looking sidelong at him from under her long lashes. "What happened to that rule we had about flirting games?"

When he spoke, his voice was deadly serious. "You died."

She sobered, staring at him. "So I did." Her eyes narrowed. "Have you come here to rescue me, like in the fairytales?"

"That's right, tell the universe," Aragon snapped.

Kassa couldn't help feeling terribly pleased with herself. "I don't know what to say."

Aragon stood up, grabbing her hand roughly. "Let's get this over with. According to the priestess I tortured, as long as you haven't eaten any substance of the Underworld, I can just walk out of here with you."

"You tortured a priestess?"

Aragon looked mildly embarrassed. "Well, not exactly torture. But I had tea with her."

Kassa pulled her hand away suddenly. "When you say I can't have eaten anything, does that include drinking?"

"Well, of course it does..." Aragon's voice trailed off as he realised the implication of her guilty expression. "Kassa, you didn't! You should know the songs better than anyone—you know the rules about rescuing people from the dead."

Kassa glanced back, along the polished counter to where her collection of empty glasses stood, salt still clinging to the rims. She smiled sadly. "Ah, well. It was a nice idea."

Aragon exhaled explosively. "I'm not putting up with this." He banged angrily on the counter. "Bartender!"

The bartending imp sidled over. "Yessir?" he said suspiciously.

Aragon indicated Kassa's empty glasses. "This water you served—it *was* water, wasn't it?" This question was directed back at Kassa.

Kassa gave him a complicated salute, and a half-curtsey. "Wench's honour."

"This water you served the lady," Aragon continued. "A natural product of the Underworld, was it?"

"Oh, yessir," said the imp proudly. "Best quality min'ral water there is."

Aragon raised an eyebrow. "Would I be right in thinking that this water came from one of your fine rivers?"

"Oh, yessir," said the imp. "Travelled miles, it has. Quality stuff, no question."

"I see," mused Aragon. "Travelled miles. Outside the Underworld, by any chance?"

"Well," said the imp dubiously. "A river's gotta start somewhere."

Aragon pounced on this. "So your water is *imported*."

"Well," said the imp slowly. "I suppose if you looks at it like that..."

"That's all I needed to know," said Aragon with some satisfaction. He glanced back to Kassa. "Unless there's anything else?"

"Salt," she whispered.

He turned back to the bartender. "Sea salt?"

"Best quality..." started the bartender.

"Right," said Aragon. "Also imported. Anything else, Kassa?"

She shook her head soundlessly.

"Right. Let's go."

"Wait!" Kassa said suddenly. "Aragon. Of all the people who might be affected by my death, I would have thought you were the least likely to object—not to mention the least likely to do something about it."

Aragon almost smiled, but it was an expression devoid of humour. "That only goes to show how much we have in common. Until recently, I thought the same thing."

-§-§-§-§-§-

The Dark One tapped enthusiastically on the door of the throne room for the last time. "Yoo hoo, Pomegranate?"

"I'm not coming out," came the surly reply.

"Oh, I don't want my job back," said the Dark One cheerfully. "I'm going on a holiday. I just wanted to wish you good luck."

The double doors opened a fraction, and Pomegranate stuck her snub nose through the crack suspiciously. "You wanted what?"

"I remembered that I never wanted to rule the Underworld," the Dark One beamed. "So I'm off for a bit of a holiday." He stuck out his hand. "All the best."

Still eyeing him with distrust, Pomegranate shook the hand. "You don't mind?"

"Oh, no. You're welcome to the grisly old dump." The Dark One straightened the collar of his dizzyingly apricot suit and winked at the hemi-goddess. "Don't let the goth girls use more than their monthly allowance of face paint, make sure the imps are properly groomed at all times, and don't forget to feed the three-headed guard dog."

Pomegranate looked faintly startled. "What three-headed guard dog?"

"Oh, it's around somewhere," the Dark One said airily.

"Wait," she protested. "What do three-headed guard dogs eat?"

"Heroes, usually," the Dark One tossed over his shoulder as he lifted his suitcases and turned to leave. "Don't worry, there's no shortage. Hardly a week goes by without some hero in a second-hand lion skin knock-knock-knocking on our doors and demanding to be allowed to rescue some cross-eyed maiden."

"Yes," said Pomegranate faintly. "We've got one in at the moment."

"Splendid," said the Dark One. "Well, you needn't worry, good old Roverspotfido will track him down in no time. Splendid beast. Amazing teeth. Byeee."

-§-§-§-§-§-

"Are you absolutely certain you know what you are doing?" asked Kassa.

Aragon glared at her. "I rescued you, didn't I?"

She looked around the dank, claustrophobic tunnel they had found themselves in. It was built for imp proportions rather than humans, and a funny smell wafted from somewhere. "I don't *feel* very rescued."

An eerie howling sound filled the tunnel. Kassa grabbed Aragon's arm. "What was that?"

He removed her hand, irritably. "I don't know—probably the three-headed guard dog. I was wondering when it would turn up."

"Three-headed guard dog? What three-headed guard dog? You never said anything about a three-headed guard dog!"

"You're the tavern wench," Aragon said, casually examining the ceiling. "Don't you know any ballads about the three-headed guard dog of the Underworld?"

"If I did, I might have elected to stay where I was!"

Aragon drew his sword and tapped thoughtfully at the ceiling. A fine film of yellow dust drifted down. "Dead, you mean?"

"Better dead than enduring your second rate rescue attempts!"

Aragon shoved the blade of his sword hard into the ceiling, dislodging a few tiles and several clumps of dirt and rock. When the minor rockfall had subsided, he gestured at the hole he had created. "You first."

Kassa folded her arms, glaring at him. "Just because you rescued me doesn't give you any right to order me around!"

Aragon rolled his eyes, stepped forward, and kissed her. It was a real, 24 carat, world class, thoroughly effective kiss, and it lasted for quite some time, mostly because she was kissing him back. When they separated, Kassa had a stunned look on her face. It rather suited her.

"Now," said Aragon, more gently than he meant to. "Will you please climb out of this tunnel?"

Kassa turned away and pulled herself through the hole in the low ceiling. As she scrambled up, the torn ribbons of her goth dress caught at various ragged edges ripping even further. She kept darting funny looks down at Aragon, not quite able to believe what had happened.

Aragon pulled himself up after her, and they looked around the forest clearing they had found themselves in. "I'm not sure we're out of the woods yet—" he started to say.

At the same time, Kassa demanded: "Did you just do what I think you just did?"

"Do we have to discuss that now? Rescuing first."

Nailed to a particularly sturdy tree was a sign, battered and mauled and spattered with gore. It read, CAVE CANEM. Beneath it was scrawled a translation: ['ware the dog(s?)!]

"That three-headed dog you were talking about," said Kassa. "Any more information?"

"Yes," said Aragon, moving to stand back to back with her, his sword at the ready and his eyes alert. "I promised that I wouldn't beat it up."

Kassa drew her stainless-steel knife from its sheath. "Oh, we'll try not to hurt it, shall we? Excellent plan."

A hideously echoing sound filled the glade, resounding off every tree, rock and blade of grass. It sounded like the screams of a thousand villagers, the songs of a thousand off-key vultures.

"It's yapping," said Kassa incredulously. "That three-headed dog of yours is yapping!"

The beast leaped into her field of vision, shrieking and slavering for meat.

Kassa breathed out. "Put your sword away, Aragon."

Aragon whirled around, staring at the curious three-headed beast. "What the hell is it?"

Kassa reached out her hand and the fearsome three-headed guard dog of the Underworld came to sniff her fingers in the hope of finding some doggy treat. A red collar around its neck displayed three metal tags, revealing that its name was, alternately, Rover, Spot and Fido. Kassa patted the nearest head awkwardly. "It's a Pomeranian. They, I should say."

"What does that mean?"

The dog, realising that no treats were to be forthcoming, began to yap in triplicate. "It means," said Kassa. "Small, fluffy, looks like a feather duster and yaps a lot. Only in this case, three heads as well. I don't think that's a usual feature of the species, but you never know."

Aragon finally relaxed, lowering his sword. "So its bark is worse than its bite?"

The smallest and most raggedy of the three fluffy Pomeranian heads stopped yapping for a moment, and stared up at Aragon with soulful brown eyes. Then it lunged towards his sword, neatly biting the blade in half.

"On the other hand," said Kassa quickly. "Leg it!"

Pomegranate, Lord of Darkness, opened her mind to the Underworld. Something was terribly wrong. Newcomer though she was, the thick layers of yellow dust and the near-constant earthquakes did not seem right. This was too hard for her to figure out by herself. She reached out her thoughts to her sister Octavy, whose talent was an immunity to space. The upshot of her talent was an ability to talk and hear over any distance. "Help me, sister."

She heard Octavy's instant reply. "What's wrong?"

"You tell me! Ask Sveta what's wrong with the Underworld, will you?" Sveta, the youngest of Wordern's daughters, had the ability to answer any question with uncanny accuracy.

A few moments passed, during which the worst ripple yet shook the Underworld to its very roots. "Hurry," begged Pomegranate.

Octavy's voice was clear in her ears. "She says it's best for Clarity to tell you."

Clarity, the second-youngest sister, never spoke, but was able to send perfect pictures into the minds of others.

An image filled Pomegranate's mind. She gasped, seeing the lines of the golden, globulous liquid, the pollen floating from the golden flowers left behind. She saw the exact implications, and reeled back from them. "No! We will be destroyed!"

"It's up to you," Octavy sent to her. "You are immune to time, and this substance eats time. You can save the Underworld, at least."

"But what about the rest of the cosmos?" Pomegranate demanded.

"Sveta says that it wears off eventually—the mortal world will probably survive it, but 'eventually' has no meaning in the Underworld. You are the one in danger. Be careful!"

Pomegranate gripped the arms of her throne in indecision. "What can I *do*?"

Chapter 23
A Sparrow Falls

"You bounder!" yelled Lord Tangent, red in the face.

"Surely you can do better than that," said the Emperor Aragon calmly. "I've been called far worse."

"We cannot take you back," Sparrow insisted. "It is impossible. You would be an anachronism."

"And what are you?" the Emperor replied.

"You can't argue with that," Daggar muttered, elbowing Sparrow in the breastplate. "Give it to him."

Sparrow was incredulous. "Are you serious?"

Daggar held out his hand to show her that he already had possession of the golden boat-shaped charm. He gave her an apologetic half-grin.

Sparrow's hand flew inside her breastplate and checked her bodice. Her jade-green eyes narrowed. "How the grit did you do that without me noticing?"

"I'm a profit-scoundrel," he said in a wounded voice. "I *told* you I was good."

"If you two have quite finished," said the Emperor Aragon. "Give me that ship or everybody in this room will die."

Sparrow lunged at Daggar, but not in time to stop him tossing the gold trinket to the Emperor. Sparrow seized Daggar by his lapels and shook him. "You are really starting to get on my tailfeathers! How do you think we are going to get back now?"

Daggar grinned and took the opportunity to peck her on the cheek in a friendly manner. He avoided her mouth, in case she still had some of that sleep-venom painted on her lips. "Trust me," he suggested.

Sparrow dropped him in disgust. "I would sooner trust a rattlesnake."

Emperor Aragon examined the little piece of gold and then tossed it into the air. The ghostly golden galleon unfolded into its proper dimensions, its lower half submerged into the floor.

"See you in the next future," said the Emperor, turning to make his way on to the ship. "With any luck it shall be rather more palatable to us all—"

A flying sheep hit him in the face. Singespitter, wings flapping ominously, had chosen to express his displeasure at being sealed up inside a dimensionally folded ship for several days by throwing his full weight at the first human-shaped person he saw. It was mere luck that the human in question happened to be the Imperator Aragon I.

The Emperor fell flat on his back, the weight of the sheep landing fully on his face. He did not move, which suggested he had been knocked out by the blow or had lost consciousness due to suffocation.

"*Good* sheep," said Daggar, picking himself up off the floor and grinning around at the room in general. "Best sheep in the world."

Sparrow turned and smacked him so hard on the back of his head that his eyeballs shuddered in their sockets.

"What was that for?" Daggar demanded when he recovered the means of speech.

"I will let you work that out for yourself!" Sparrow shoved a herald-serf out of the way and levered Finnley's cage open with her sword.

Lord Tangent joined her, eagerly working to release his sister. "May I gather from that exchange that no one else has a claim on your heart?" he asked hopefully.

"Not so as you would notice," replied Sparrow darkly.

As Lady Reony, Mistress Opia and Officer Finnley scrambled free, Lord Tangent took Sparrow's hand in his and kissed her palm, lingeringly. "Then may I dare to hope that I might find a place in your affections?"

"I don't think so," said Sparrow, patting his cheek. "But thank you for the thought." She glanced around. "Everybody on board? Daggar, grab the sheep."

Daggar hefted the growling Singespitter off the fallen Emperor. He nudged the Emperor Aragon with his toe. "We *will* try and fix things," he offered half-heartedly. "If it's any consolation, which it probably isn't." He hoisted himself and the winged sheep up on to the deck.

Lady Reony, after delivering a hefty kick to one of the herald-serfs who had imprisoned her, came over to wish them farewell. "Don't worry about him," she said, indicating the Emperor. "With luck, he won't even remember this." She reached up to Daggar, who was the closest to her, and drew him down for a farewell hug. "If you do get a chance to change things," she whispered as she did so. "Don't hesitate. We have nothing to lose."

Vaguely surprised, Daggar grinned down at her. "You're a smart cookie."

"I descend from a long line of them," she retorted. "Anyway, I've met you before. You're supposed to be in your fifties." She smiled slyly and winked at him. "Your son's pretty cute, though."

Daggar's eyes widened. "My son? What do you know about my son?"

"Time to go, Daggar," said Sparrow, appearing at his shoulder.

"Oh, I almost forgot," said Reony, ducking under the banquet table and pulling out a package. "I found this squished behind the washstand in your room. You mustn't forget it."

"Oh," said Sparrow, smiling uneasily as she received the packaged golden dress. "How could it have got behind there? Thank you."

Lord Tangent came forward again. "I don't suppose..."

"No," snapped Sparrow. Then she reconsidered, leaned down over the railing and kissed him full on the mouth. His eyeballs rolled back into his head, and he hit the ground heavily, snoring as he collapsed beside the fallen Emperor.

"Back to the present?" suggested Daggar.

"Back to the present," Sparrow agreed firmly. She moved to the ship's wheel and looked down at the foggy amber crystal. "*Back*," she willed firmly.

And the ship went...*kwoop*.

-§-§-§-§-§-

As the golden lights swirled around them, Sparrow felt the energy of time travel flood her veins. Daggar grabbed her suddenly, startling her. "We forgot to get a coin from the future! You know, for that purging thing."

Sparrow leaned against the rail. "What is your leg armour made from, Daggar?"

He looked down in surprise at the sergeant-at-arms uniform he still wore. "Steel, why?"

"Your armour is from the future, mine from the past. It should be easy enough to find a present equivalent in Zibria."

He relaxed. "You're so smart."

"I know."

As the golden lights faded, the *Splashdance* materialised inside the Palace of Zibria...and into the Sultan's trap.

Water cascaded from the ceiling, drenching the deck of the ship and all of its passengers. Mistress Opia spluttered, staring upwards. "Hobbs!"

The ex-Brewer gnome, poised on the ceiling beam from which an elegant sprinkler contraption had been fixed, shrugged apologetically. "The Sultan made me a better offer, Mistress. And wages. *You* never gave me wages."

Her grandmotherly face thunderous, Mistress Opia clawed her way over the side of the ship and towards the smirking Sultan. "What do you think you are doing?"

"I knew you would come back," he announced. "You just couldn't resist it. I've been preparing for you, Brewmistress."

"For the last time, I will not work for you!" she screeched.

"Oh, of course," said the Sultan theatrically, waving an arm. "Mistress Opia is too grand for us mere mortals now she had made a pact with the *other side*!"

"What pact?" demanded Sparrow harshly, pushing herself forward.

"There was no pact," said Mistress Opia dismissively. "The liquid gold was *my* invention."

"Hah!" said the Sultan.

"Tell me what pact!" Sparrow snapped.

"It really is none of your business," insisted Mistress Opia.

"None of my business!" cried Sparrow. "This feud between the two of you has nearly cost me my life, many times over!" She bent over, snatched up a handful of the dandelions that still grew underfoot. "It is not natural, this liquid gold! Is this natural?" Staring at the flowers closely for the first time, she noticed what she had never quite seen before. Tiny, almost microscopic little winged people crawled around on the petals, scattering pollen into the air. Sparrow screamed, and flung the flowers as far from her as she could. "*The moonlight dimension*!"

Mistress Opia was quite taken aback at her reaction, though the guilt was clear on her face.

The Sultan grinned evilly. "Did you know that our Sparrow here was a troll at heart, Brewmistress? We all know how trolls feel about the faery folk."

Sparrow was revolted. "How could you make such an alliance?" she demanded of Mistress Opia. "Are you so starved for power? What was the pact? What did you offer them?" Suddenly, she swung around to stare instead at the smug face of the Sultan. "More to the point, what did *you* offer them?"

The Sultan laughed at the stunned look on Mistress Opia's face. "You're not the only one to make a deal with the OtherRealm, my dear Brewsmistress. Did you really think you were unique? They offered you fame and power and liquid gold and asked for nothing in return. Did you not wonder about that? They already had their price, from *me*."

Daggar moved forward to stand beside Sparrow. "Her life? Was that the price? Is that why you made her drink the liquid gold?"

"Better," sneered the Sultan happily. He leaned over and plucked one of the many golden dandelions from between the floor tiles. "You have been spreading these little beauties through every time zone you visited, my dear Sparrow. Did you never wonder where the pollen was going?"

Sparrow stared at the tiny yellow spores which even now drifted away from the flowers and upwards, towards the ceiling. "Where?"

The Sultan laughed. "The Underworld, of course." He grinned merrily at Mistress Opia. "This substance of yours has finally given the OtherRealm a chance to infiltrate the one other place which is outside time itself. And my little mercenary helped you do it!"

Sparrow hit him, a good solid punch. She had been saving it up for some time. The Sultan fell hard, sprawling on the carpet. Sparrow glared at Mistress Opia. "You will purge me of the liquid gold, *now*!"

"I was not important," Mistress Opia said sullenly, hardly seeming to hear her. She was gripping a nearby tapestry, using it to wipe water from her hands. "Not relevant. It was all *him*." She looked up at Sparrow. "Do you know what they gave me? I could always turn almost everything into gold using Brewing skills. But they gave me the ability to do *this*." She flicked her hands, and Sparrow's armour exploded into gold dust.

Sparrow was blasted backwards through the air. Her body smashed heavily through the nearest window. The buzzing specks of gold held her immobile, the heel of one boot caught on the window edge. The rest of her body floated over a sheer drop down to the plaza below.

"No!" yelled Daggar, horrified, running to grab hold of her. He didn't reach her in time.

Mistress Opia waved her hand dismissively, and the cloud of golden specks deserted Sparrow, flocking instead to the Brewmistress.

Sparrow fell.

Chapter 24
How not to use Magic in the Underworld

Amorata, the brunette goddess of champagne flutes and erotic poetry, was having a lazy day in the sky dimension. She reclined on her hovering cloud-stitched doona and licked iced rose petals from her fingertips, humming a lustful little melody.

Somewhere, the sound of someone knocking on a non-existent door brought her back to earth with a jolt. She blinked, and the clouds wafted away to be replaced by a sturdy mahogany desk and an elegantly antique chair. In the same blink of the eye, the goddess clothed her body in a neatly tailored suit and perched tiny spectacles on the end of her perfect nose. Her wild chestnut hair wrapped itself up into a neat ensemble of pins, braids and tidy curls. "Come in," she said in a low, breathy voice.

An office door which had not existed until this very second, opened. A woman in an equally neat business suit wafted into the room. "Amorata, I need to talk to you," she said without ceremony, tossing a bunch of tulips down on to the immaculate desk.

"Ohhh," complained the brunette goddess of passionate thoughts and wishful thinking. "It's only *you*, Destiny." She exhaled, and the office wafted away like a dream. In the sky dimension once more, she took her place upon her cloud-stitched doona, absently examining the tulips for flaws. "What do you want?"

Destiny had joined her in the sky, the business suit melting away to reveal ankle-length green hair which slid around her body like a sari. "It's Milady."

"It's *always* Lady Luck," said Amorata. "Vengeance, thy name is goddess." She selected the most perfect tulip and bit into it, chewing hungrily. "Who is she after this time?"

"Kassa Daggersharp and Aragon Silversword," said Destiny, guiltily remembering that she had been responsible for handing their fates over to her sister.

This news made the sultry Amorata sit up and take notice. "Well, I'm not having that," she exclaimed. "I have *plans* for those two."

-§-§-§-§-§-

Lord Skeylles the Fishy Judge, Sea-God and Master of the Underwater, was in his bath. He wallowed happily in the large basin of seawater, splashing around and making funny shapes from the foamy bubbles. Several half-grown cats loitered on the marble tiling which surrounded the bath, sniffing disdainfully at the soapy smell.

The great doors of his bone-tiled hall were flung open, and a sultry brunette in a scarlet evening gown pushed her way past his lobster-shaped butler. "We need to talk, Skeylles," she announced, fanning herself with a handful of black ostrich feathers.

Skeylles sighed loudly and continued to soap his feet. "Really, Amorata. There *Is* A Time And Place For Everything."

Amorata practically screeched to a halt as she reached the bath. She stared challengingly down at him. "Do you know what Lady Luck has gone and done this time?"

Skeylles raised a godly eyebrow. "Milady Is Always Sticking Her Pearly Fingernails Into Some Mortal Or Other. Just Ignore Her."

Amorata perched gracefully on the edge of his bath and traced a heart in the bubbles. "Skeylles, she *killed* Kassa

Daggersharp. She actually arranged her death. Recently. On dry land. Now do you understand?"

The Fishy Judge went pale. "Towel," he boomed.

Amorata pushed several cats off the edge of the bath and produced a thick, fluffy towel out of nowhere. She held it out, politely averting her eyes as Skeylles wrapped it around his waist. "What *Is* The Point Of Organising the Future In Advance If People Like Milady Just Ignore The Filing System When It Suits Her?"

-§-§-§-§-§-

Raglah the Golden, ferret-faced god of Zibria and its environs, swooped down on a lovely young maiden as she sat alone by the river. He spread his wings wide, and displayed himself seductively, waiting for her to run into his feathery embrace.

She turned, and swatted him with her poetry scroll.

Raglah the Golden trotted away and hid under a bush. "All right," he quacked to himself. "A duck doesn't work. Maybe something bigger." His eyes lit up. "An emu! Hey, that could be sexy."

Just as he prepared to have another go at it, the ground opened up and a large lobster in a morning suit clambered out of the hole. He had a piece of parchment wedged into his claw.

Raglah the Golden pecked at the parchment and managed to unfold it with his ducky beak. He read silently for a moment and then gave a *squack* of alarm. He took to the air, the girl almost forgotten, his ducky wings flapping wildly.

-§-§-§-§-§-

The three-headed Pomeranian chased Aragon and Kassa around the skeletal meadow, three pairs of doggy nostrils flaring like mad. Eventually Aragon located the hole he had made and the two of them threw themselves back down into the relative safety of the tunnels.

Aragon furiously sheathed the broken remains of his rapier. "I *liked* that sword. Where am I going to get another like it?"

"So," said Kassa, trying to catch her breath. "Given that dogs are relatively good at digging, what do we do next?"

Aragon took a couple of lungfuls of the musty tunnel air. "That's it," he decided. "We'll just have to use magic." He looked meaningfully at Kassa.

Kassa stared back at him, her eyes panicky. "I can't use magic in the Underworld! It's the number one rule!"

"I don't imagine that escaping is particularly well-received either," said Aragon. "Since when were you one for keeping the rules? You always said witches were good at breaking things."

"I'm not an official witch yet," Kassa said. Then the colour drained from her face. "Dame Veekie. She's going to *kill* me. Aragon, you have to get me out of here now!"

"Me?" said Aragon mildly. "I'm not the magical one, Kassa. I got in here by myself...I think it's your turn."

"But you don't understand!" she said wildly. "I don't have any magic here! I wasn't very good at it under the best of circumstances but now I'm just a...well, not exactly a ghost, but I'm not connected to my body." She frowned. "At least, I don't think so. I don't even have any magical objects, and I don't stand a snowball's chance in a death canary of raising any kind of magic by myself!"

"So," said Aragon Silversword. "A magical object would help you?"

Kassa hesitated. "It might. The Underworld only really affects life. If we could find some inanimate object with magical properties..."

Aragon unfolded his palm. "Will this do?"

Kassa stared at his hand, and the sparkling silver-and-steel spiral ring which rested lightly in his grasp. She touched it, taking it from him and turning it over in her hands. "You kept it?" Her eyes softened, and she gave him a melting look. "I don't deserve you."

Aragon Silversword grimaced at the sentiment. "Oh, yes, you do." It was not meant as a compliment to either of them.

The ring, restored to Kassa's third finger, felt warm. She reached up and touched the golden torc around her neck, her fingers nimbly finding the tiny black jewel which the Dark One had placed there. "When I went on my quest, I was told that if I stayed too long away from the Underworld my spirit would fade, but this little black thing would catch it." She peeled off the black jewel and stuck it to the centre of her spiral ring.

Aragon was outraged. "Rescuing you isn't enough to keep you alive?"

Kassa smiled sadly. "It never is." She took his hand. "Shall we?"

Aragon took hold of her other hand, swinging her around to face him. "Like this?"

Her mouth twitched. "I keep expecting you to betray me again."

Aragon's grey eyes displayed no emotion. "What would be the point of that?"

Kassa gave him a glorious smile, and closed her eyes. After a moment, she began to sing.

-§-§-§-§-§-

There was a reason why magic was not allowed in the Underworld. The improbability level caused by the Realm of the Dead being simultaneously underground and above the clouds, coupled with the meaningless of time in such a space, meant that if magic was used it would expand into a disastrous implosion of magical density with nasty repercussions hard on its heels. But, of course, no one would be silly enough to use magic while in the Underworld.

The magic billowed. It poured out of the sky and up from under the earth, pouring purpleness everywhere. As the swirls passed, trees exploded into waterfalls of fairy dust, rabbits turned somersaults in the air, and frogs turned into printing presses. Out of the centre of the swirling magic, two figures exploded outwards, skidding along the Skullcaps and landing with an impossible splash in the Cellar Sea.

In a tavern somewhere on the border of Zibria, Bounty Fenetre swallowed a glassful of suspiciously clear liquid. She frowned, staring out at the brilliant colours through the window. After a moment they faded, leaving the sky its usual colour.

The bartender did a double take. "What was *that*?"

Bounty bared her teeth in something like a grin. "I'd say it was the work of a woman called Kassa Daggersharp." She tossed a coin in his direction. "Get me another. And have one yourself."

-§-§-§-§-§-

The magic shook the Underworld to its very core. Pomegranate clung to her new throne, preserving a semblance of dignity. Outside in the twisting and turning corridors, various imps ran about in a state of disarray.

Golden pollen swirled everywhere. Time had finally infested the Underworld. Pomegranate reached out her fingers, desperately trying to keep it all together by will alone.

She was ageing. A hemi-goddess with an immunity to time, here in a place supposedly outside time itself, and she could feel herself ageing. Her bones lengthened, her hair moved with a life of its own, and her gown was suddenly far too tight around the chest. Something ripped…

One imp plunged headfirst into the throne room, gibbering. "More witches and warlocks have escaped!" he cried. "Vicious Bigbeard Daggersharp and Black Nell have holed themselves up in G Block with some other disreputables an' they say they're establishing their own independent city state! Lots more people are joinin' them, some of the goths even!"

Pomegranate groaned, pulling herself to her feet and back into her throne, wrapping a torn length of velvet around her newly adult body. What more could go wrong?

"Hello, Pommy," boomed a rugged, bearded voice.

Still keeping a tight hold on her throne, Pomegranate whirled around. Her extra-long braids whirled with her, whipping around her waist in a tight grip. She struggled free of them, attempting to keep her composure. "Daddy, what are you doing here?"

Wordern the Sky God, nine-foot tall and almost as wide, strode into the throne room. "Nice place you've got here," he growled approvingly. "I like the madcap chaos. Very chic at this time of year. And you've grown up again. About time."

"What do you want?" his daughter asked, grating the words out from between her teeth.

"Old Fishguts told Raglah and Raggers told the Slimy One, he's calling himself Number Seven now by the way, and Slimy told Mavis and she told me."

"Told you what?" shrieked Pomegranate. Shattered remnants of the black and white mosaics fell all around them.

"Oh," said her father. "Kassa Daggersharp wasn't destined to die. Milady was messin' around. There's a major loophole due to be discovered any time now. You'd better double-check some of your entries for a while, in case she tries to pull anything else."

Pomegranate went white. "A god can't order the undestined death of a mortal! Do you have any idea what that does to the paperwork?"

Wordern shrugged. "Something's interfering with the cosmos. Gave her a window of opportunity." He frowned at her. "Haven't noticed any cosmological disasters, have you? Anything out of the ordinary?"

"Daddy," she shrieked exasperatedly as the ceiling collapsed around them.

"Oh," said Wordern the Sky-Warrior. He looked around. "Better leave you to it, then. And just you leave the Lady to us. We can handle her." He cracked his knuckles sharply, and a piece of falling masonry lodged itself in his beard.

-§-§-§-§-§-

Aragon's salty, sea-drenched clothes had dried in the sun. He stood now on the rocks along the beach, staring out to sea. Kassa, her hair wilder than usual and her black dress so tattered that it was held together by willpower alone, lay on her stomach by a rock pool, scrabbling around in the sand. "Look at this," she called.

Aragon turned to see Kassa pulling a bedraggled tuft of grey fur out from between the rocks. "It's a kitty," she said, snuggling it to her.

"What's it doing here?" he asked.

Kassa laughed. "What does that matter?" She cuddled the kitten some more.

"It will cost a fortune to feed."

"You have the soul of a merchant," she accused.

Aragon smiled thinly. "And you have the soul of a poet. Dangerous thing, poetry."

Kassa held the kitten close, picking sand from its fur. "Where do you think we are?"

"Somewhere along the West Coast. There's Chiantro, see?"

She peered out to sea. "Barely. Could we go there?"

"We don't have a ship any more."

Kassa glared sidelong at him. "Aragon Silversword, what have you done with my ship?"

"Daggar's probably sold it by now," he said humourlessly.

She laughed. "Oh, I miss Daggar. I wish I could see him again."

"He can't have gone far. We could look for him if you like."

Kassa made a face at him. "How much time do you think I have left? I wasted most of my ghostly quota abducting Pomegranate. I don't think I'm going to be around much longer."

"But I rescued you," Aragon said forcefully.

"And I told you it wasn't enough! I'm not real. My body...what did you do with my body?"

"They buried you at sea," he muttered.

"There you are then." She waved a hand. "My physical substance is out there, in the Cellar Sea. Even if you did manage to find it, do you really think I want to inhabit some bloated, half-rotted corpse?"

Aragon was staggered. "So all this was for nothing?"

"Oh, thank you very much!" She made herself comfortable on the rocks, spreading out the remains of her skirts for the kitten to settle on. "There must be a way, there's always a way. But you have to find it. In the meantime, of course, you could kiss me again."

Aragon gave her a stony look. "And why would I want to do that?"

Kassa leaned back on her elbows. "Incentive?"

"Incentive?" Aragon growled. "You put your mark on me, remember? That damned witchmark has been dragging me around by the nose for days, weeks—I don't even know how long it's been. It's the only explanation for my insane behaviour lately. You *do* remember putting your mark on me, I suppose?"

"In more ways than one, it would seem," Kassa said slyly.

"What's that supposed to mean?"

She tipped back her head, regarding him speculatively. "Take off your shirt."

"What game are you playing now?"

"I could fade into non-existence any minute and I am not going to miss the look on your face when you figure this one out! Show me your witchmark."

Aragon ripped open his shirt and displayed the spiral she had scorched into his skin, more than a year before. At least, that's what he thought he was doing.

Kassa admired him openly. "It's not there."

"What?" Aragon looked down. His chest was a blank canvas.

"Aragon, I died," Kass explained. "The witchmark I used to buy your allegiance…"

"To steal my allegiance," he said automatically.

"Borrowed," she corrected with a slow smile. "The

witchmark left you when I died. That's how they work. Until you die, or I die, or the world ends. Remember?"

Aragon's face was unmoving. "But why?"

"Why did you assume it was the witchmark driving you crazy? Why have you been running around like a madman, trying to bring me back to life? Why don't *you* tell *me*?" Kassa laughed delightedly, and stood up. She placed the kitten on her left boot, dusted sand from her tattered black dress and looked Aragon squarely in the eye. "We're wasting good kissing time here."

Thoughtfully, Aragon moved towards her. Kassa tensed suddenly. "You buried me at sea," she said.

"I said that," he said irritably.

"But I died on dry land!" Her eyes were bright and luminous. "Pirates don't die on dry land. It doesn't happen. There's the loophole, Aragon. Now you just have to figure out how to use it."

"So there is hope," he said ironically.

"Always," said Kassa Daggersharp.

Suddenly tempted, Aragon lunged for Kassa and caught her around the waist. She laughed at him again, and turned her face up to his. But he couldn't hold on to her. His hands drifted through her body like smoke, and he could see the beach through her skin. He tried to touch her face, but only blurred the image.

"Here we are again," whispered Kassa, just before she vanished. "Leaving it too late."

Her spiral ring clattered to the rocks. Aragon reached for it, but the kitten got there first. It nudged the ring with its face and then stared cross-eyed at the tiny black jewel which was now attached to the kitten's nose. Aragon picked up the animal, staring at it. Had its eyes been that colour before?

"Kassa?" he said aloud, looking into the little cat's dark golden eyes. Kassa's eyes.

The kitten mewed, and looked hungry.

"Kassa," said Aragon in a resigned voice. He put her spiral ring in a pouch and tucked the kitten into his belt. "Let's go, shall we?"

Chapter 25
Lady Luck

Time slowed. The descent, which should have been stomach-droppingly fast, stretched out in a seemingly endless ribbon of time.

Sparrow gazed at the spaces between her fingers, and past them to the wide blue sky. Frame by frame, she drifted towards the ground below. Falling. The Labyrinth plaza was below, wasn't it? She couldn't remember whether it was cobbled or concreted, but she assumed it was one or the other. Too much to hope for an ornamental lake.

She didn't have time to look down and see what awaited her, surely. Then again, she had all the time in the world.

The sheer side of the mountain rolled past. Sparrow arched her back and ran her eyes back up the wall of the Palace, counting the lines of windows, alternately arched, round and square panes of glass. Which was the window she had fallen from? She no longer remembered. But there—up there was the broken pane of glass, so far above her. Someone was leaning out. Was it Daggar?

So gradually that it took her a while to realise it, time sped up to a normal rate. Sparrow rolled as she dropped, and hit something warm and furry. She blinked. Not dead after all. That was all right, then. Her time-related illness was good for something.

She stared up into the face of her rescuer. "Magnus!" she cried, throwing her arms around the Minestaurus, surprising them both by hugging him hard. "You caught me!"

"Well if you go diving out of high windows, you must expect someone to catch you," replied Magnus in a perplexed voice. "It's a law of nature, surely."

It was Daggar's head sticking out of that window, yelling something. Sparrow waved once, to let him know she was all right, and the head ducked back in.

Magnus the Minestaurus set her down carefully, rubbing his chest where her armour had scraped him. "Glad to be of service," he said politely.

Sparrow gave him a sidelong look. "Magnus, why did you not tell us you were a prince? The *first-born* prince?"

"I assumed you knew," he said in surprise. "After all, we met quite a few years ago when I was still publicly acknowledged in that role."

"Yes," said Sparrow. "But last time when we met, I had not yet met you, if you see what I mean." She shook her head. "Try to forget I said that. Why did you not claim Zibria?"

"Because the people prefer to have a Sultan without horns and hooves," replied her mild-mannered friend. "I'm not eligible."

"It is that moustache-twirling torture-fanatic who is not eligible," Sparrow snapped. "Surely you must have realised he is illegitimate? He is not a monster, physically, therefore he can *not* be your father's son."

"Well, of course I know that," sighed Magnus. "Everyone knows that, there are ballads written about it, but what do you expect me to do? I don't want to be Sultan, and Marmaduc does seem to enjoy it."

Sparrow looked up at him, frowning. "You do not *want* to be Sultan?"

"Of course not," said Magnus patiently. "I have a thesis to write." He smiled absently, patted her on the head and wandered off. "Don't go falling out of any more high windows," he called behind him. "It really isn't safe."

Sparrow watched him go, shaking her head. Daggar came barrelling around the path into the plaza, his eyes wild, with Singespitter following close on his heels. "Are you okay?" he demanded.

"Fine," Sparrow said dismissively. "It is just the world spinning." She stamped on the ground, just to check it was still there.

"It's mayhem up there," Daggar panted. "Mistress Opia and the Sultan are throwing things at each other, and Officer Finnley and the gnome are hiding under a table."

"I think perhaps we should be somewhere else," said Sparrow. "Do you have the ship?"

Daggar patted a pocket reassuringly. "I'm sure there's something we're forgetting, though."

Sparrow snapped her fingers. "That lowdown, dustsucking Emperor bastard."

"Um," said Daggar. "Strictly speaking, Silversword isn't an Emperor yet, so please don't call him that if we see him. It will only give him ideas."

"We must stop him becoming Emperor, yes?" said Sparrow.

"Too right," said Daggar fervently. "From what he said about his motivations, our best chance is to rescue Kassa and get those two together."

Sparrow raised an eyebrow. "This Kassa is dead, in the Underworld?"

"Apparently so."

She leaned down and plucked up a handful of dandelions from under her feet, shaking them furiously. "The Underworld which I have destroyed, according to the Sultan."

"Never said it was going to be easy."

"We should begin by finding this Silversword person."

"Yes," agreed Daggar.

"And I shall beat him to within an inch of his life."

"Only if you've been good."

-§-§-§-§-§-

Aragon Silversword reached an apple orchard at the top of the hill, looking down at the pillars and avenues of Zibria. Now *there* was a city he was heartily sick of the sight of.

He would just call in to get some supplies and then—what? Where would he go next?

Perhaps he could head towards the land-bridge, and leave Mocklore altogether. Aragon was tired of madcap adventures. Perhaps outside the Empire he might have a chance to regain some dignity.

He reached up to pick an apple from the tree which towered above him.

"Are you sure about that?" asked a golden voice.

Aragon looked up. In the branches of the tree sat Lady Luck, combing her beige-blonde hair with an air of complete abandon. "I've had just about enough of you, too," he snarled.

"That attitude isn't going to get you anywhere!" she replied haughtily.

Aragon picked the half-grown kitten out from the larger of his belt pouches, and brandished it at her. "Do you see what you've done?"

"You rescued her from the Underworld!" said Lady Luck in surprise. "And turned her into a cat, how ingenious."

"It isn't her," he snapped. "The cat is just...carrying her."

"I'm sure that makes all the difference."

"Why are you doing all this?" he demanded. "Why kill Kassa off in the first place?"

Lady Luck shrugged lazily. "To prove a point, of course."

"*What* point?"

"I don't remember. Was it so very important?"

Aragon turned his back on her and started walking. "I don't care anymore. I'm not interested."

Lady Luck appeared in front of him, sticking out her lower lip. "Aren't you? How dull. I won't bother with you, then."

"Thanks," he said, continuing to walk.

She didn't follow this time. "Do you really want to know?" she called to his receding back.

Aragon whirled around. "I have had enough witch, sprite and god games to last me a lifetime," he growled. "If you wish to tell me, then tell me."

Lady Luck made an elegant shrug. "Because I could. The OtherRealm is challenging the Underworld, and they have both provided such delicious chaos and confusion that the cosmos didn't notice one teeny goddess sneaking an undestined death through." She laughed out loud. "We are more tangled in rules and regulations than you mortals. Why should I resist the *decadent* urge to do something naughty, if I knew I could get away with it?"

He stared at her. "You are *totally* immoral."

"I'm a goddess," Lady Luck said. "We're not like you. Why should we even *care* about you? We have our own games to play." She patted her beige-blonde hair into place, and vanished.

Aragon stuffed the kitten back into his pouch and headed for Zibria. He found a tavern, ordered lunch and sat at a table, not eating the food which had been put in front of him. For some reason, the staple ingredient in Zibrian cooking was the olive, which he had never found particularly appealing at the best of times. His platter was heaped with olive-stuffed bread, various vegetables of the dried and pickled variety, black olives, green olives, some puffy green-and-black rissoles and a single tentacle of some poor unsuspecting sea creature. He could only assume that it had been fried in olive oil.

The kitten was curled up at his feet, lapping from a saucer of goat's milk.

Aragon contemplated the future. It didn't look any more cheerful than it had an hour earlier, so he took a bite of fried tentacle. It tasted like salty rubber, but was strangely compelling. He took another bite and chewed, slowly.

Something white thudded into the window beside him. Very slowly, Aragon turned his head to look at it. It was a sheep. A very agitated sheep, waggling its face at his through the glass. Aragon turned back to his plate, selected a piece of pickled pepper, chewed and swallowed. Then he looked back up. The sheep was gone.

"Oh, so now I'm going mad," he said conversationally to himself. "Thank you, Kassa Daggersharp."

A moment later, the door to the tavern was flung open and Daggar Profit-scoundrel marched in, accompanied by his sheep and a dangerous woman in a black shift and leggings, the type usually worn under armour. "See!" Daggar announced to the room in general. "I *told* you that trainee soothsayer in the Mystic District knew what she was talking about."

"Oh," said Aragon Silversword. "It's you. I think I would have preferred insanity." He ate a piece of dried fish. At least, he assumed it was dried fish. The alternative was too unpleasant to contemplate.

Daggar joined him at the table, grinning all over his unshaven face. "Have you been to the Underworld yet?"

Aragon regarded him suspiciously. "How did you know about that?"

"I have my sources." Daggar's grin widened until it almost fell off his face. "Who would have picked you for being such a soft touch? Did you find her?"

"More or less," said Aragon icily. He bit down on a piece of pickled lettuce and spat it out hurriedly. "What do you want?"

"Well," said Daggar. "As far as I can make out, we can rescue Kassa!"

Aragon gave him a long, flat look. "Kassa is gone."

"Ah, but we have a timeship," said Daggar, tapping his nose confidently.

Aragon stood up, pushing his plate to one side. "Try not to be quite so stupid." He picked up his cat.

"No, really," Daggar said with great enthusiasm. "An honest to gods time-travelling ship! We can go anywhere. We can go back and stop Kassa being killed. Or something."

Aragon tossed a few coins on to his plate and picked up his cloak. "Goodbye, Daggar."

Daggar turned frantically to Sparrow. "He doesn't believe us."

"If you remember," said Sparrow coldly. "He did not believe us last time. His not believing us *created* that future. We have to show him the truth."

Aragon turned around and stared her in the eyes. "I don't know who you are, but you are correct. I prefer not to make a fool of myself when people are spouting fairy tales." He headed for the door, tucking the cat back into his belt.

Daggar stared glumly at the remains of Aragon's dinner. "So what do we do?"

Sparrow reached Aragon before he got to the door, and tapped him smartly on the shoulder.

He turned irritably. "What now?"

"I have wanted to do this for the next twenty-three years," said Sparrow, the troll-raised mercenary. And she laid him out with a single punch.

-§-§-§-§-§-

Aragon woke to the strong smell of salt and seagulls. He lifted his head and looked around with bleary eyes. "What's going on?"

"We kidnapped you," said Daggar cheerfully.

Aragon looked at the deckchair in which he had been dumped, trying to figure out why it was yellow. Then he saw the rest of the ship. "What have you done to the place?" he managed to say, staring at the glowing goldness of it all. "Kassa's going to kill you."

"With any luck, she will have the opportunity," Daggar told him. "If you suspend your disbelief for about a minute, I'll tell you how."

Aragon stood up carefully, testing his jaw. "That was quite a blow. Who's the girl?"

Sparrow, who was busily combing burrs out of Singespitter's wool, looked up with her narrow jade-green eyes.

Daggar stuck up a hand hastily. "Give him the benefit of the doubt just this once. He doesn't know you're secretly an evil, flesh-eating troll." He smiled weakly at Aragon. "Don't patronise her. It's not worth the pain."

Aragon regarded Sparrow thoughtfully and then turned his attention to more important questions. "Where are we going?"

"Where it all started," said Daggar. "Chiantrio. We still don't know exactly how and why Kassa died. If we're going to change the past, it's best to equip ourselves with all the information we can."

"A vaguely sensible plan," said Aragon. "Where's my kitten?"

-§-§-§-§-§-

Mistress Opia and the Sultan duelled ferociously, throwing objects and magic gold dust at each other. "For the last time," he gasped between breaths, avoiding a particularly devastating blast from the Brewmistress which set one of his favourite tapestries on fire. "Will you come and work for me?"

"Never!" she screamed.

"What have you got left?" he demanded. "The last evidence of your precious liquid gold is gone. You're never going to be the most famous Brewmistress. Why not win fame as the Brewer who gilded Zibria from head to foot?"

"I did that for a Sultan once!" she shrieked. "His heir let it fall to ruin. And I can always get *more* liquid gold!"

"Oh, really?" said the Sultan sceptically. "You think you can deal twice with the moonlight dimension?"

"I know I can!" She rolled across the floor, narrowly avoiding the large sideboard Officer Finnley and Hobbs the gnome were hiding under. Triumphantly, she snatched up a handful of the dandelion trail Sparrow had left behind her. "I promise you anything!" she screamed into the flowers. "Whatever your price, I will pay it! Only give me more liquid gold!"

A split second later, the Sultan stared at her and began to laugh. "You can't say they don't keep their promises!"

Mistress Opia glowed gold. The substance slid under her skin, behind her eyes, coursing through her veins. She stared at her own outstretched hands in horror.

It was then that the two death-canaries, following the tangled trail of dandelions and the scent of human mingled with liquid gold, flew in through the open doors. Mistress Opia leaped back out of their way, and crashed into the sideboard containing the cowering Blackguard and the gnome. The death-canaries, true to their orders, crashed into her.

The resulting explosion took out most of the West Wing. The Sultan himself only survived because he had the foresight to throw himself behind the most solid tapestry in the room. Of the various other guests, uninvited and otherwise, who had been in the room before the explosion, no trace was ever found.

Chapter 26
The Other Dame Crosselet

Busily throwing up over the rail, Daggar raised his sea-green face briefly to shout, "Land ho!"

Aragon came up from below, hurling an armful of glittering swords, knives and blunt instruments on to the deck in disgust. "Just look at this mess! This time-travelling essence of yours turned all our weapons, clothes and food supplies into gold, a singularly useless substance. What am I going to do for a sword?"

Daggar sat down on the deck with a thump. "Why do you need a new sword? What happened to the one you bought from the ice-sprites?"

Scowling, Aragon brought out the two pieces of his transparent silver-steel rapier. "A three-headed Pomeranian bit it in half."

Daggar fell about laughing.

Sparrow frowned. "Did you say not something about 'land ho'?"

"Yep, we should be halfway up the beach by now," replied Daggar, still chuckling. "Where did you find a three-headed Pomeranian?" he asked Aragon.

Sparrow looked over the side of the ship and commanded it to 'stop' just in time to prevent them from colliding with a palm tree. "Why exactly are we here?"

"This is where we find out exactly how the Sacred Bauble managed to kill Kassa without leaving a mark on her," said Aragon. "And if you're right about this time travel thing—"

"We showed you," Daggar insisted. "Twice, didn't we, Sparrow?"

"Admittedly the Cellar Sea looks much the same no matter what year you travel to," conceded Sparrow. "You will have to take our word for it that the gold swirly lights meant something."

"You've certainly changed the ship," Aragon agreed. "I'll just assume that you can't both be completely insane, shall I?"

"You half-believe us," said Sparrow. "And we got you here. It is a start."

"Not enough has been changed yet," warned Daggar. "I'm not going to relax until we've got Kassa back. She'll keep him on the straight and narrow."

Aragon looked from one to the other, suspicious. "Am I missing something?"

Sparrow gave him a long, hard look. "Let us say that if we do not rescue this redhead of yours, the future is going to be rather unpleasant."

"But on the bright side, you will get to inflict your miserable personality on as many people as possible," added Daggar. Sparrow kicked him sharply in the leg. "Oof."

Aragon's stony gaze flicked from one to the other and then he turned, vaulting over the side of the ship to the beach below.

"Be quiet, pebble-brain," snarled Sparrow to Daggar. "We do not want to make the future any worse than last time around."

"Fancy me being involved in an act of inter-dimensional sabotage!" chuckled Daggar. "Kassa would have been so proud."

"If we get this right, she can *still* be proud," said Sparrow. "Just what is so special about this Captain of yours, anyway?"

Daggar looked wistful. "I don't know. Maybe it's just that when she's around things seem to happen. Explosions, mostly. Bright colours and sparkly lights."

"She sounds a riot," said Sparrow dryly. Then, nodding towards Aragon Silversword, who was pacing the beach heavily and muttering to himself, she asked, "What does *he* see in her?"

Daggar jumped down on to the sand and reached up to give her a hand. "That's the big question, isn't it?"

Sparrow leaped down without assistance, landing neatly. "Do you think he has asked himself?"

Daggar grinned broadly. "Endlessly. Ooh, look. A native."

A stunning maiden clothed in two coconut shells, one garland of tropical flowers and various strategically placed fern fronds stood on the beach path, in the very position that Kassa had been when the sacred bauble hit her.

Aragon moved towards the maiden, and Sparrow and Daggar hurried after him, dragging Singespitter by a new rope from the ship's stores—like everything else in the ship, it was glowing and gold.

"Have you seen a white bauble about so big?" asked Aragon, holding his finger and thumb slightly apart. "Last seen, it was heading in that direction." He pointed over her shoulder.

The maiden smiled, shook her head slightly and batted her eyelashes.

"What language do they speak?" hissed Daggar.

Aragon stared steadily at the maiden. "Mocklorn," he said. "Like everyone else. They may have a different name for it, as the Anglorachnids do, but everybody in the world essentially speaks the same language."

"Except trolls," grated Sparrow.

"If you say so," said Aragon. He turned his piercing gaze back to the maiden and turned it up a notch.

Her wide, vapid eyes became more and more uncomfortable under the icy stare until finally she ducked her head and looked away.

"That's better," said Aragon calmly. "I think you'd better take us to your leader."

-§-§-§-§-§-

The Sacred Festival was finally coming to an end. The maidens of Chiantrio unhooked the decorations from the trees, the young men cleaned themselves up after the ceremonial bloodbashing duels, the matrons tidied up the sacrificial food leftovers and the older men buried the giant warthog carcass.

The Chief President Elect of the village was a large man with a hideous, bone-sharpened smile. He wore ferns and flowers like the other village men, but had topped off the ensemble with a silk cravat and white leather running shoes.

The distressed maiden ran to his side as soon as she entered the hut and bowed her head in shame. "I failed to act stupid enough, papa," she whispered.

The Chief patted her head. "Never mind, Leilorei. It is not important. Run and help your mother gut the pheasants for lunch."

The maiden nodded solemnly and made a speedy exit.

"Now, then, my friends," said the Chief President Elect. "How may I help you?"

"We want to know how Kassa Daggersharp died," said Aragon bluntly.

"Ah," said the Chief. "The young woman with the hair? I remember her well. But I'm afraid I cannot help you."

A spear carrier beside him snickered and whispered something to the Chief President Elect, who nodded and grinned nastily. "Jagh, garahrog ia!" he chuckled.

Sparrow's face went very flat and she pushed Aragon roughly aside. Then she leant down and shoved her face into that of the Chief. "Yagkh dorogh!" she snarled.

The Chief looked slightly taken aback. "It is unusual for a woman to be so fluent in our secret holy language," he choked. "Let alone a foreigner. I am impressed."

"Secret holy language?" snapped Sparrow.

The Chief turned his attention back to Aragon. "We did investigate the death of your…captain. The results revealed that the blame belongs in its entirety to the local witch, Dame Veedie."

The spear-carrier leaned over and whispered hurriedly in the Chief's ear.

"Ah," the Chief said slowly. "I am informed that she isn't exactly a witch but she does look like one. She also makes terrible gingerbread. You could probably find her house by smell alone—it is just beyond the village, along the breadcrumb path."

"Thank you for your assistance," said Aragon stiffly.

Daggar tugged on Sparrow's elbow. "Come on, let's go."

She gave him a wild look but followed him outside the hut, where she began swearing. Various complicated phrases, obscenities and dust-related blasphemies issued forth from her mouth as she stomped up and down in front of the hut.

Aragon regarded her with mild interest. "Does this happen often?"

"Only when something big happens," said Daggar. "Like a temple exploding on her head."

"Those bastards!" Sparrow said finally, descending into clarity. "Those grit-sucking, coconut-bashing…"

"Um," said Daggar. "Anything wrong? Only we've got this witch to visit…"

"Secret *holy* language," she sputtered. "Secret holy *language*?"

"What's wrong with them having a secret holy language?"

"It's my language," Sparrow said furiously. "Those sons of rock-toads are speaking Modern Troll."

-§-§-§-§-§-

The gingerbread house belonging to Dame Veedie Crosselet had degenerated into a whole new stage of putrefaction. The lemon-iced ceiling now sagged to such an extent that Dame Veedie could no longer live inside and so she had constructed a small shortbread lean-to beside the rotting pile of old dough. When Aragon approached, she was busy hanging out her washing on a thin line of liquorice, despite the fact that warm sunlight had melted the washing line enough to leave black sticky marks on all the damp clothes. Luckily all of the garments were so dark and mouldy-looking that the liquorice was unlikely to make a significant difference.

"Good morning," said Aragon politely.

Dame Veedie sniffed, wiped her arm across her nose and then wiped her arm on the nearest piece of washing. "What do you want, eh?"

"Kassa Daggersharp came here a few weeks ago. To complete her witchcraft training. I want to know what happened while she was here."

Dame Veedie stared unblinkingly at him. "Can yer cook?" she asked after a moment.

Aragon didn't turn a hair. "Almost certainly."

-§-§-§-§-§-

Daggar tried to keep up with Sparrow's furious stomping. "I just don't see what's got you so worked up," he said, trying to be patient. "What does it matter if some old codger on a tropical island speaks Troll?"

She whirled around to face him, her narrow green eyes blazing. "Trolls do not cross water. So how did these people get access to our native tongue? Not only that, but where do they get off using it as their secret holy language?" She paused, suddenly thoughtful. "Daggar, they have a sacred bauble and a holy language. What are you staring at?"

Daggar shook his head. His general attraction to angry women was a constant distraction. "Sorry, what were you saying?"

"They have a secret holy language and a sacred bauble," she repeated.

"So?"

"So?" she said incredulously. "*So*, what are these things sacred to? Who exactly is their god?"

Daggar realised that he had his mouth open. He shut it. "That's a very good question. Shall we find out?"

-§-§-§-§-§-

"Well, then," said Aragon as he whipped up an omelette over the outdoor campfire. The eggs came from Dame Veedie's rather pathetic-looking chocolate chip hen house, and her three miserable hens, who were obviously sick to death of chocolate chip cookie crumbs. "According to the villagers, you are entirely responsible for the death of Kassa Daggersharp."

"Oh, yeah?" said Dame Veedie, sniffing noisily. "Thadda be right. They're all jealous cause I banned them from my bakery, just before it mysteriously burnt to the ground."

Aragon flipped the omelette perfectly. "So what is the truth?"

"Well yer asked for it, yer know," snorted Dame Veedie. "Bringin' back that bauble of theirs. It always works out that way when people bring it back."

"Bring it back?" Aragon tipped the perfect omelette out on to a plate and handed it over to the Dame. "Does it leave the island often?"

"Course, it's traditional," she said as if it should have been obvious. "Ev'ry dozen years some beggar steals it, right, and when it gets brought back, someone always kicks the bucket. Kind of a sacrifice, see? To punish the villagers for lettin' it be stolen. Only it doesn't always work out that way, 'cos the bauble can't tell the difference between one human an' another. An' the people wot brings it back are usually closer to it than the villagers, geddit?"

"But how does the Sacred Bauble kill?" Aragon demanded. "We couldn't find any obvious cause of death."

"Ah, well, yer wouldn't," said Dame Veedie disparagingly. "S'not as if it goes an' sticks a knife in, izzit? Nah, what happens is, the bauble thingy wotsit goes sort of *transcendental* and it just zaps the soul off to the Underworld automatically, no mess or fuss. If more people could do that, the world'd be a better place, I reckon."

"So the body itself is undamaged," Aragon said slowly.

"Course. Now shut up and roast me some onions to go with this eggy thing. Then yer can slaughter a chicken for me tea."

The hens exchanged startled looks and started edging backwards, trying to hide behind each other.

-§-§-§-§-§-

Sparrow and Daggar met Aragon back on the beach. Quickly, he explained what he had learned from the hideously repulsive Dame Veedie Crosselet.

"So the Sacred Bauble zaps someone's soul away every twelve years?" repeated Sparrow. "Who would invent such a perverse ritual?"

Daggar nudged her. "We know the answer to that, remember?"

"What?" Aragon demanded.

"Well," said Daggar. "Sparrow started wondering about what the Sacred Bauble might actually be sacred to, and we had a look at their temple. Blow me if it isn't draped in beige."

Aragon's face lost what little colour it had. "Beige?"

"The deity in question's name is Lady Luck," interjected Sparrow. "Does that mean anything to you?"

Somewhere above them, a chime sounded, and an immaculate beige-blonde goddess appeared on the beach in a puff of rose petals. "I thought you'd never ask!" Lady Luck purred.

-§-§-§-§-§-

Officer Finnley's life flashed in front of his eyes. Most of it involved spaghetti, washing up and night patrol. Gold lights blazed in front of his face. He realised to his horror that he was travelling in time without the aid of a ship.

Mistress Opia was the vessel this time. She glowed gold, her eyes wide and startled. "Where are we?" she gasped.

A city swam up to meet them. Literally swam, as it was half underwater and the townspeople were wading about their everyday business. And then the city changed. Buildings rose and fell. Styles raced through fashion after fashion, and then warped backwards.

"I dunno," said Hobbs the gnome, who was hanging on to Mistress Opia's right leg for dear life. "Where *are* we?"

Finnley was gripping the Brewmistress's left leg, he realised. And they were travelling through time. Hadn't there been an explosion? He couldn't remember.

Mistress Opia cackled with laughter. "Time is at my beck and call!"

The scenery shifted in and out. Finnley kept seeing snatches of recognisable landscape, only to have his senses swamped by something utterly unfamiliar. He squeezed his eyes shut, and begged for it all to end.

When he opened his eyes, they were outside time.

Chapter 27
Gods, Politics and One of Those Kisses

Aragon looked the newcomer up and down slowly. "We've met before, Lady Luck."

Lady Luck tossed back her beautiful head and laughed her crystal-clear laugh. "You don't have to stand on ceremony with me, mortal man. You may call me Milady. Simply everyone does."

Aragon stared at her with his most unfriendly expression. "We're here to rescue Kassa Daggersharp," he said. "Are you going to stop us?"

"Yes, Milady," said Amorata, goddess of silk stockings and low-cut bodices, appearing beside her fellow deity. "*Are you going to stop them*?"

"Who are all those people?" hissed Sparrow, staring at the crowd who had suddenly materialised behind Lady Luck. Along with the sultry brunette woman in a string bikini, there was an insignificant-looking man with a chain of fish skulls around his neck, a waif-like girl with green hair, a very tall man in a golden ferret mask who kept metamorphosing into various forms of bird life, and many others.

"More gods," said Daggar. "Let's just slip away, shall we? Discretion is the better part of staying alive."

Aragon stared at the array of divinities. "Are you all in on this? Some godly conspiracy to eliminate one mortal woman?"

"You tread dangerously, mortal man," threatened Lady Luck.

"Does he?" said Amorata, frowning. "It seems to me that you are the one treading dangerously, Milady."

The Slimy One, a god who rarely climbed out of his hole, wagged an annoying finger. "You knew that the conflict between the OtherRealm and the Underworld was affecting the cosmos, and instead of warning us, you used it to exercise a whim!"

"To kill a mortal with a destiny like Kassa Daggersharp!" said Amorta, throwing up her hands. "What did you think you were doing?"

"May I speak?" suggested a deceptively mild voice. The crowd of bickering gods parted, and the Dark One stepped through, resplendent in a mint-green suit.

Lady Luck protested. "While he's associated with the Underworld, he doesn't get a vote!"

"True," agreed the Dark One. "But I've been set free of that particular obligation. Right, Wordern?"

Wordern the Sky-Warrior looked proud behind his big beard. "My girl's doing it now," he informed them all.

"So things are as they should be," said the Dark One. "No gods allied with the Underworld." He glanced at Lady Luck. "Shame the same can't be said for the OtherRealm."

"What?" she gasped.

"What?" demanded Amorata.

The Dark One shrugged. "Isn't it obvious? Who do you think brought the liquid gold into the mortal world in the first place? Faeries don't have that kind of brainpower, or they would have taken us over aeons ago."

The gods all stared at Lady Luck, who smiled desperately and tried to laugh it off. "So what if I did? It's all part of the game. I'm a goddess, for goodness' sake!"

"And Infinitely Replaceable," boomed Skeylles, the Fishy Judge.

Lady Luck regarded him suspiciously, trying to work out if he was joking. "You wouldn't!"

"It's been done before," threatened Raglah the Golden, transforming from a three-legged swan into his usual ferret-faced figure.

Amorata waved a golden hand dismissively. "When we hear the testimony of that ragtag bunch of pirates, we'll see about punishment."

Lady Luck smiled smugly. "What pirates?"

The gods all turned around, tripping over each other in their haste, and realised that the mortals they were discussing had all slipped away, taking their golden ghost-ship with them.

Amorata's eyes grew flinty as she turned her gaze back on Lady Luck. "Never mind. We've plenty here to be going on with."

"Look around you," the Dark One appealed to his fellow gods. "She has set up an unauthorised temple here on the landmass with the most connections to the OtherRealm. She has bribed the local populace by giving them a 'holy language' plagiarised from one of the godless races. She even used her own holy icon to perpetrate the death of Kassa Daggersharp. Charge her!"

Lady Luck looked bewildered. "What is the charge?"

"You are responsible for the impending destruction of the Underworld," said the Dark One flatly. "Even now, it teems with an infection of OtherRealmly substance."

Fix It," said Skeylles the Fishy Judge, passing sentence. "Or You Will Be Dealt With."

Lady Luck was aghast. "Fix it? After all the trouble I went to?"

As one, the gods of Mocklore stared coldly at her.

"And stay away from Kassa Daggersharp," added Amorata. "Some of us have quite a stake in her future activities."

Lady Luck stared at them all in astonishment. "Well!" she huffed. "Why didn't you *say* so?"

-§-§-§-§-§-

The golden *Splashdance* sidled away from the god-infested beach and around the coast of Chiantrio. "So there's nothing stopping us from just going back a week or so and stopping the sacred bauble," said Daggar with some satisfaction.

"Actually, there is rather a lot preventing us," said Aragon. "Even if we could stop that bauble—and we couldn't the first time—it would kill someone else. Quite likely one of us, as we would be closest to it."

Daggar had a horrible thought. "And if we got in its way, we wouldn't be able to avoid ourselves then seeing us now!"

"I think things are confusing enough as it is," agreed Aragon.

"Hang on a minute," said Daggar, trying to figure it all out. "Kassa only died because her soul was zapped by the bauble. Where did her soul go?"

"The Underworld, of course," said Aragon.

"And where is it now?" put in Sparrow.

Aragon's forehead creased. He pulled the silver spiral ring out from his belt pouch and looked at it. "There was a little black jewel attached to this ring. She said it would catch her soul."

"So where's the jewel now?" demanded Daggar.

Aragon almost smiled. "On the cat."

As one, they turned to stare at the little cat, and the tiny black dot on its nose. The cat mewed prettily and opened its wide golden eyes. "Right," said Daggar slowly. "We go back in time to just after Kassa was zapped, and we put her soul back!"

Aragon looked flatly at him. "If that is the case, whom will you bury at sea?"

Daggar's face fell. "Don't ask that question. I'm not up to it." He brightened suddenly. "Hang on, I've got it. When Tippett and I went back to collect the body, she was wrapped up in blankets. It could have been anything. I thought he'd done it, out of respect for the dead, you know, and he thought I'd done it."

Aragon raised an eyebrow. "Did that really happen?"

"It did now," Daggar said happily. "We should have about an hour between the time we left her and the time we came back, in order to resurrect Kassa and wrap something Kassa-shaped up in blankets."

"I don't believe I'm having this conversation," said Aragon tiredly. "What are we going to do, make her eat the cat?"

"Cross that bridge when we crash into it," said Sparrow. "Let's get going."

"I just thought of something," announced Daggar, poking a finger at the amber crystal which displayed which year it was. "We've only travelled in big jumps before. From one year to another. Can we really go back a week or so?"

Sparrow elbowed him aside, placing her hands on the crystal. "Do not think about it too hard. *Back*," she commanded fiercely. "*The day Kassa Daggersharp died*."

As the landscape filled with the flooding multi-coloured lights of time travel, she felt a familiar pressure against her chest. It was different this time. Sparrow had never experienced an attack during time travel. Her muscles tingled wildly, and as she stared at her clenching and unclenching hands she could see the yellowness spreading over her skin.

Daggar came to her side. "I thought time travel helped the symptoms," he said anxiously.

Sparrow raised her horrified eyes to his. "A timebomb waiting to happen," she rasped. "That's what the Brewmistress said."

"And you believe her?" he demanded. "I thought we'd proved once and for all that Mistress Opia was full of..."

Sparrow wasn't listening. Responding to the wild sensations under her skin, she clambered up on the rail and launched herself into the spiralling lights of the time void.

"No!" Daggar wrenched the rope from Singespitter the sheep's collar, shoved one end at Aragon and jumped after Sparrow, holding the other end of the rope.

Aragon stared at the rope in his hand, and then tied it securely to the railing. He exchanged glances with Singespitter and leaned over the rail to see what was going on. "I suppose this all makes sense to you," he said conversationally.

Singespitter, grooming the little cat with his tongue, said nothing. The cat looked properly disgusted.

As the time essence flooded her body, Sparrow fell slowly through the many layers of stars, sparkles and pretty lights. Her fingers moved slowly, drifting through the void. A warmth ran through her skin, tingling to the ends of her hair. She closed her eyes and tipped her head back, breathing in the liquid air.

Daggar swam wildly towards her, kicking his way though the swirling colours. The rope he held was elongating, itself twisted and manipulated by the time-stream. Daggar reached out with his free hand and grasped a handful of Sparrow's hair, pulling her towards him. As he grabbed her hand, he found himself holding the hand of a child, with spiky blonde hair and angry green eyes. She shouted at him, struggling and pummelling, spitting in his face.

As he bravely took a firm hold around her waist, he found himself holding an old woman with bleached-white hair and the same angry jade-green eyes. This old Sparrow didn't struggle as the child had, but stared at him in something like shock, her hands curled into his velvet doublet. As he watched, the creases and scars on her face slowly began to ebb away. Her hair shaded from grey to ash-blonde, and then to the bright tawny colour he knew.

Holding her firmly, Daggar tried to kick back towards the ship, but Sparrow choked in pain and resumed her wild struggling. He squeezed his eyes shut and held on for dear life.

They hit the grass hard, tumbling and rolling over each other. Pinning her to the ground, Daggar stared down at Sparrow. She in turn stared up at him, narrowing her eyes to slits.

"What was that?" he demanded, finally finding his voice. "Self-sacrifice?"

"Instinct," she shot back, glaring hard.

Aragon Silversword stepped down from the golden ship and walked past them, only glancing briefly in their direction. "I'm not even going to ask," he said.

Daggar rolled to one side and Sparrow sat up slowly. "I will not travel in time again," she said resolutely. "I will not risk it."

"Fair enough," said Daggar easily. "If this thing with Kassa works, we won't need the liquid gold again. What about your withdrawal effects?"

"I will have to manage." Sparrow looked back at him, her expression thoughtful. "I suppose I should thank you."

"If you two don't mind," cut in an acid voice. "We do have a job to do."

"We'll get to you in a minute," said Daggar, not wanting to lose the moment.

"Now," Aragon snapped. "I can see *Silver Splashdance* on the horizon."

Reluctantly, Daggar stood up and brushed the grass and twigs from his clothes. "You'd better close up the ship, then. Oh, and make sure Singespitter isn't trapped in there when you do. He really hates that."

-§-§-§-§-§-

"How much longer will we be hiding behind this shrubbery?" demanded Sparrow.

"As long as it takes," replied Aragon.

"You did not say we would be here all afternoon!"

"You didn't ask."

"I do not see why *I* should not get up and move about," she snapped. "It is not as if I have past versions of myself sunning themselves on that ship."

"Keep your head down," he ordered. "It won't be much longer."

Daggar, who had been scouting a few shrubberies away, hurried back. "She's coming!" he announced.

As Sparrow heard the sound of boots against the sandy path she lifted her head, curious to catch her first glimpse of Kassa Daggersharp. Instantly Aragon's hand came down on her head, forcing her face towards the ground.

Daggar's head shot up as he heard his own voice elsewhere, anxiously demanding, "Is she all right?"

"You're fine," assured the voice of Aragon Silversword. "You're not hurt."

The three crouched in the shrubbery heard a cough, and Kassa's voice say, "Oh, it hurts. Trust me on this one."

At the sound of his mistress's voice, Singespitter the sheep perked up and started scrabbling to go to her. It took the combined strength of Daggar, Aragon and Sparrow to keep the sheep still, and they only just heard the end of an the exchange between the other Aragon and Daggar.

"What?"

"Dead."

"Not—*dead* dead?"

"Dead."

"Oh. She won't like that."

After a long pause in which the three behind the bushes held their breath, they heard the slight crunching of people moving away.

"Incidentally," said Aragon as they stood up to stretch their legs. "You were correct. She didn't like it. She was most displeased about the whole thing."

"Can we move her yet?" asked Daggar. "She's still in line of sight from the ship."

"Do you have the substitute?" replied Aragon.

From behind another of the bushes, Daggar proudly produced a blanket-wrapped bundle. "I had to filch this from their *Splashdance* when they were looking the other way."

Aragon looked at him in horror. "Are you mad? Do you have any idea of the consequences if you should meet yourself?"

"No, and neither do you," replied Daggar amiably. "Don't sweat—I waited until we were all in the hold investigating that rattling sound, remember? I had to, all our blankets are that sparkly gold colour. Anyway, what do you think?" He held it up for inspection. "Is it lifelike enough?"

Aragon snatched the fake body bundle from him. "It isn't supposed to look lifelike. I'll make the switch."

"Oh, no you don't," said Sparrow, opening her arms to receive the bundle. "If I do it and one of you back on the ship happens to look in this direction, the worst they will see is some blonde stranger in armour stealing the body of their captain. An inconsistency, but not as much of a paradox as if one of them saw one of you. Right?"

"Right," said Daggar, who was convinced.

"If you say so," said Aragon, who wasn't.

"Right," said Sparrow. Grappling the unwieldy package, she climbed around the shrubbery and headed for the fallen body of Kassa Daggersharp. A few moments later she returned, Kassa's body by the boots. "Is she supposed to look like this?"

"What's wrong with her?" said Daggar, defensive of his second favourite cousin.

"She's not even wearing any armour," said Sparrow. "Good boots, though. How do we perform this resurrection?"

Daggar looked at the unmoving body and then back at Aragon. "Well?"

Aragon produced the ring. He flinched slightly as he took Kassa's hand. "She's still warm."

"Well, she *has* only just died," said Sparrow. "Thunderdust, will you get on with it?"

Aragon slid the spiral ring on to Kassa's finger and sat back. Nothing happened.

"Is it the right finger?" whispered Sparrow.

Aragon turned on her furiously. "Of course it's the right finger!"

"I was only asking!"

He looked down at Kassa's body. "Where's the cat?"

The little grey furball emerged from behind a shrub. It darted forward, nuzzling at Kassa Daggersharp's left boot. Its eyes slowly changed from amber to green.

"Aren't you supposed to kiss her?" suggested Daggar. "That's the way they do it in the ballads."

Aragon stared at him with considerable venom. "Turn your back," he commanded finally. "And you," he snapped, nodding at Sparrow.

Obediently, they turned their backs on him and Daggar even took the trouble to turn Singespitter's face away.

Aragon Silversword leaned over the body of Kassa Daggersharp and touched his mouth to hers. Just as he drew back, prepared to concede defeat, a pair of strong, warm arms slid around his neck. Kassa arched her neck, prolonging the kiss. Only then did she open her deep golden eyes.

"Aragon Silversword," she said, letting go of his neck and propping herself up on her elbows. "What took you so long *this* time?"

Chapter 28
Not Letting Sleeping Wenches Lie

The Underworld was dying. Pomegranate had done her best, but the liquid gold was winning. Indeed, if it wasn't for Pomegranate's particular immunity to time, the Underworld would already have been destroyed. Still, it was hard to see what difference that delay made right now. The liquid gold streamed everywhere, under the floor, through the corridor tunnels and in undetectable specks through the air. Pomegranate breathed it in. Everyone was breathing it in, even the dead mortals who weren't supposed to be breathing at all.

Throughout the Underworld, wraiths and spirits of the dead were changing. Child-ghosts suddenly shot through puberty and adolescence, causing no end of problems. Other ghosts reclaimed their youth. The ghosts of Vicious Bigbeard Daggersharp and Black Nell had reverted to their teens and were currently staging protest marches in the corridors.

Pomegranate felt as if she was being pulled apart. Bad enough that her newly-acquired business venture was exploding around her, but she also had to cope with suddenly being six-foot-one, with womanly hips and breasts. It was all far too much. None of her clothes fit!

In the midst of the chaos and collapsing ceilings, an immaculate beige-blonde goddess stepped into the breach. She waved a single hand irritably. "Come and be banished, then," she sighed.

Like flies to honey, the liquid gold swarmed to the newcomer. Pollen and dust, swirly light effects, every mote of it surrounded her, clinging to her skin, hair and gown.

The Underworld stabilised around them. Pomegranate stared in surprise at her saviour. "Who are you?"

"Just call me the cleaning lady," said Lady Luck bitterly, and vanished.

The liquid gold vanished with her, every trace of it gone forever from the Underworld. Unfortunately, the effects remained, but it was a tolerable price to pay for survival.

-§-§-§-§-§-

"What's wrong with you all?" said Kassa Daggersharp. "You look as if you've seen a ghost!" She extended her wrists to Aragon and he pulled her to her feet.

"It actually worked!" said Daggar in a stunned voice.

"Well, of course it worked," said Kassa, brushing her skirts down briskly with both hands. "Well done. Much better than being a cat, in any case." She glanced at Sparrow, her expression unreadable. "I don't believe we've met."

"That," said Sparrow evenly, "is a matter of opinion." She extended her hand in greeting. "Sparrow. Mercenary."

Kassa took the hand. "Kassa. Pirate. And now I really must change my clothes." She looked down at her black leather bodice and bright red skirts. "I've already discarded this outfit once, and I'm bloody sick of it." She stepped over the nearest shrubbery. "Where's the ship? Oh, there it is."

"No!" said Daggar and Aragon in unison, leaping to stop her.

"But the ship is back there," she protested as they both took hold of her elbows and steered her off the path, into the trees beyond. Sparrow followed them, with Singespitter close behind.

"That's not our version," said Aragon.

"We had to go back in time, you see," added Daggar.

"Well," said Kassa as they steered her towards a little beach cove well out of sight of both the village and the earlier version of the *Silver Splashdance*. "Where is my ship, then?"

"In Aragon's pocket, of course," said Daggar. "Silversword, do the honours. We'd better get Kassa out of here as quickly as possible."

"And what was that package lying on the path back there?" asked Kassa as Aragon threw the little ship-shaped charm into the air to turn it back into a full-sized pirate ship. "What did I miss while I was dead? And *what the blue-bearded blazes have you done to my ship?*"

"Uh oh," said Daggar guiltily, looking from the golden *Splashdance* to Kassa's livid face and then back again.

"You bastards," she said, sounding dazed. "My beautiful ship. I leave you alone for a few days and you redecorate my pride and joy." A look of absolute horror crossed her face. "My clothes!"

Aragon and Daggar exchanged looks. "Stop her," said Aragon.

They were too late. With three bounds Kassa was up on the deck and scrambling down the trapdoor into the hold. A few minutes later she emerged, much dishevelled, with an armful of her favourite garments. The fabrics were all in various shades of yellow, gold and amber, all glowing.

A feral growl issued from between Kassa's teeth and she started pelting Aragon and Daggar with golden bodices, skirts and boots. "You rats, you irresponsible, cold-blooded pieces of troll-dung!" Sand sprayed up as her feet hit the beach again and she advanced on the remaining members of her crew. "My silver jewellery is all *gold*! Do you know how long it took me to collect it all, how difficult it is to find decent quality silver? I'm going to tear you into little strips." Her voice rose up in one final wail. "My beautiful ship!"

"I suppose the fact that the new colour scheme is due to the fact that the ship can now travel in time and was directly responsible for your current 'alive' status will cut little ice?" said Aragon sardonically.

"No consolation," snapped Kassa. "Fix it!"

A sudden clap of pink lightning lit up the sky.

"Okay," said Daggar cautiously. "I think we should take that as a bad omen and get this ship moving. We can argue later."

"Count on it," said Kassa between her teeth.

The sky, which had up until this point been a rather nice late-evening blue with a few clouds dotted around, suddenly went grey. A solid scroll of blankness filled it from horizon to horizon.

"Speaking of bad omens," said Aragon. "I'm assuming the sky doesn't usually do that."

"Which god is it this time?" growled Sparrow.

"Not Lady Luck, for once," Daggar retorted. "Isn't grey the colour of Fate?"

"Will you all shut up about gods?" said Kassa frantically. "This isn't a god, this is witchwork."

Aragon shrugged. "Is that all?"

She turned on him. "Aside from myself, whom we all agree is pretty rotten at the whole witching thing, have you ever actually met a real witch?"

"Discounting the repulsive woman with the gingerbread house?" he said slowly.

"Who isn't actually a witch," interrupted Kassa.

"Then no." Aragon met her gaze evenly. "I have never actually met a real witch."

"Then keep your opinions to yourself. I say we batten down the hatches and hope for the best." Kassa climbed up into the golden *Splashdance* and disappeared down into the hold.

Daggar and Sparrow looked at each other. "Do you think we should...?" said Sparrow.

"She usually knows what she's talking about," said Daggar.

The two of them followed Kassa at double speed.

Aragon was left on the sand with Singespitter the sheep, who had only just caught up with them all, the grey kitten held firmly in his mouth. "You know," said Aragon conversationally. "I'm not witchmarked any more. I can leave any time I like."

Singespitter gave him a disdainful look, sprouted wings and flapped up on to the deck of the *Splashdance,* where he spat out the kitten.

"Just a thought," said Aragon, pulling himself up on to the deck.

The grey sky cracked open, making ominous rumbling noises. The trapdoor flew open and Kassa's head emerged. "Get down here, bone-brain," she said crossly.

Aragon raised an eyebrow. "What happened to that undying gratitude for rescuing you from the Underworld?"

"I got over it."

"Oh, really?"

Singespitter trotted over to Kassa and licked her face. "Euwghh!" She ducked out of sight. The sheep nosed open the trapdoor, pushed the kitten inside and crawled after it.

There was a splashing sound. Aragon turned around to see that a mermaid had taken up residence on the ship's rail. She was grey from head to scaly tail, and sported waist-length silver hair. "Have we met?" he asked. "Only I'm sure I would remember any acquaintance with a mermaid."

"We have not met," replied the mermaid coyly. "After all. You don't know any witches. Remember?"

Before Aragon could respond to this, her steel-grey tail flicked out, brushing his face. Aragon froze. His skin hardened, taking on a stone-like quality.

Kassa emerged from the trapdoor, brandishing what had once been a ruby-studded bronze umbrella, but was now glowingly gold all over. "You bitch!" she shouted.

"Witch," corrected Dame Veekie, restoring her usual appearance. "You should at least know that. *Initiate.*"

Sparrow was wedged behind Daggar, who was peering anxiously up through the trapdoor. "What is happening?" she hissed.

"It's a six-foot grey woman with feathers in her hair," reported Daggar. "She just turned Aragon into a statue."

"Get up there!" Sparrow ordered. "Are you a man or a mouse?'

"Do I seriously have to answer that question?" he replied loftily.

Sparrow jabbed him lightly with her elbow. "Move it!"

Daggar scrambled up on deck, with Sparrow hard on his heels. "Um," he said. "Everything all right, Kassa?"

Kassa ignored him, too busy shouting at Dame Veekie. "I never said I wasn't going to finish my initiation, I just had better things to do at the time! Like escaping from the Underworld, in case you've forgotten, and having my life restored and *why did you do that to Aragon?*"

"Incentive?" suggested Dame Veekie, unsmiling.

"You shouldn't even be here in this time period," Kassa continued. "I won't escape from the Underworld *or* the OtherRealm initiation for another week or more!"

"Time has no meaning in the Underworld," said Dame Veekie. "And this island contains many gateways to the OtherRealm. You will complete your initiation here. Or pay the consequences."

"What consequences?" interrupted Daggar, unwisely. Suddenly he doubled over, hair sprouting wildly from his clothes and face. His body shrunk in on itself, changing. A moment later, a small bear was making snuffly noises around the deck, looking confused.

Sparrow's narrow green eyes bored into Dame Veekie. "Stand aside, Mistress Daggersharp, while I carve this overgrown dustdevil into bite-size chunks."

"Will you stop metamorphosing my friends?" Kassa demanded of Dame Veekie. "Look, if I do the initiation right now, will you put everything back as it was?"

"Well," said Dame Veekie. "That all depends. On how well you complete your initiation."

"All right, I'm ready!" Kassa exclaimed. "Let's go."

"You may take a companion," Dame Veekie told her.

Kassa looked in dismay from the statue that was Aragon Silversword to the snuffling bear which had been Daggar. Her eye fell on Sparrow, the only human crew member left.

Sparrow sheathed her sword. "I will accompany you."

"But you don't even know me," Kassa protested.

"On the contrary," said Sparrow the mercenary. "I have known you since your birth. Besides, I have reasons of my own to visit the OtherRealm." She lifted a boot, and several stalks unfolded from between the boards of the deck to reveal bright yellow blooms.

The solid grey sky rumbled.

With a dramatic flourish, Dame Veekie produced a full-length mirror out of thin air. "Step inside. Witch-to-be."

Kassa eyed the mirror suspiciously. "I don't suppose there's any chance that you would prefer to go first?" she suggested half-heartedly to Sparrow.

"I was planning to guard your back," replied Sparrow. "Besides, this is your quest. I'm the sidekick."

Kassa frowned. "I'm not going to like having you around if you make a habit of being right." She held her nose and jumped headfirst at the mirror. It swallowed her up with a *shloopy* sound.

Sparrow sighed, wishing she had back her armour. Any armour. Still clad only in her black shift and leggings, she stepped cautiously towards the mirror.

Shloop.

-§-§-§-§-§-

Sparrow's fingers curled and clenched tightly over a jagged corner of rock. She had a reasonably firm grip, which was a good thing because that grip was all that supported her body. She glanced down, and a dizzying view of waves crashing over the rocks below swirled before her eyes until she forced her gaze upwards again and stared resolutely at the wall of rock from which she was hanging. The last thing she remembered was stepping through the mirror... to here? What was this place?

Kassa also clung to the cliff-face, her purple nail polish chipped from her frantic scrabbling to grasp a hand hold. She gritted her teeth in an expression of total concentration.

"Well," said Sparrow. "This is fun so far. What happens next?"

"Anything's possible," Kassa flung back. "This is the OtherRealm. The moonlight dimension, the land of the fey and all that. At least, I assume it's the OtherRealm. I don't remember any cliffs last time. What do you suggest we do?"

Sparrow scanned the rocks high above them. "I assume you have no climbing skills whatsoever."

"Good assumption," Kassa agreed. "Go with that."

"And may I also assume that the rules here are different to those of the real world?"

"I think we can take that for granted."

"Nothing seems to be happening here," Sparrow said thoughtfully. "I suggest we move along to the next stage of the test. We might find something a little more challenging, yes?"

Kassa swung her head slightly aside in order to glare fiercely at her new companion. "You want to jump, don't you!"

"Frankly," said Sparrow. "I do."

"Oh, all right," Kassa snapped. "But if we end up smashed on those rocks down there, I'm blaming you."

"Be my guest," said Sparrow. "On the count of three?"

"One," said Kassa.

"Two," contributed Sparrow.

They both pushed off from the cliff and let go at the same moment.

"You cheated!" yelled Kassa as the wind whistled through her hair. "You tried to go first!"

"So did you!" Sparrow retorted as they fell.

"We're going to die!"

"What is it like?'

"Surprisingly dull so far."

The rocks came up to meet them, and everything went temporarily purple.

Chapter 29
Faeryland With Teeth

"I've been *here* before," said Kassa, spitting out a mouthful of moss. The purple haze cleared, leaving them in the familiar mist-wreathed woodland clearing. "If only I knew what I was supposed to do."

Sparrow stared in disgust at her boots. "My people are raised to despise the moonlight creatures. They are everything we hate. They trick and tease and twist reality."

Kassa peered at the dandelions which emerged from under Sparrow's boots. "Does that happen everywhere you go?"

"It's part of the illness." Sparrow shrugged it off. "I swallowed liquid gold. If I do not travel in time regularly, I get sick. Every time I do travel in time, I risk destroying everything."

Kassa frowned. "The dandelions are a symptom?"

Sparrow stomped at the flowers, which refused to budge. "More of a metaphor, I think." A squeak came from beneath her boot. Sparrow lifted it, slowly. She stared. "What the grit are you?"

A rather squished silver faery emerged from beneath the leather sole. "It was a present," she said sulkily. "We always give presents to people we like, and your blood is such a pretty glittery gold colour. Everyone likes flowers."

"*I* do not," snapped Sparrow.

Kassa knelt down and held out her hand. The faery hopped into it, fluttering her silver wings and sniffing loudly. "Hello, little thing," said Kassa softly, trying not to startle it.

"Do not even talk to the evil wight," snapped Sparrow. "They have been following me around, scattering their poison everywhere I go."

The silver faery blinked. "What's poison?"

"Do you not know?" demanded Sparrow. "You made a deal with the Brewmistress to unleash your golden plague on the mortal world so that you could get a toehold in the Underworld. Did you *not*?"

The silver faery blinked. "What's an Underworld?"

Sparrow stared. "Are they all this stupid?"

Kassa shrugged. "I suppose so. What were you saying about the Underworld?"

"Do you not have a quest to be getting on with?" Sparrow complained.

"But this is far more interesting!"

Sparrow glared hard at the little faery, and flicked it with her finger. "If you are all this stupid, then who made the deals with Mistress Opia and the Sultan?"

"With who and who?" interrupted Kassa.

Sparrow rolled her eyes. "*Quest*?" she reminded in an unfriendly voice.

Kassa sighed. "This is stupid! Since when did witches go on quests, anyway?" Her eyes lit up. "Of course. Witches don't. No one makes a witch do anything she doesn't want to. This is all complete pigswill. As long as a witch harms no one, she can do what she pleases. I don't have to do any kind of quest!"

The little silver faery crossed her eyes. "Congratulations," she sniffed. "You're a witch!" She vanished.

Kassa grinned around proudly. "I'm a witch!"

"Congratulations," said Sparrow flatly, scrabbling in the grass for more flowers.

Kassa's face fell. "I forgot. You still need to be cured…"

"It does not matter," Sparrow insisted. "I can handle it myself."

Kassa crossed her arms, resolute. "You travel with Daggar. That means you travel with me."

"Do I get any say in the matter?"

"Of course not."

Sparrow grimaced. "No wonder Silversword turned out the way he did."

-§-§-§-§-§-

They hiked through the mists for what seemed like hours, dodging various slimy creatures and wing-flapping wyrdings; getting nowhere fast. "Time must be the key," mused Kassa.

"Took you that long to figure it out?" shot back Sparrow. "What *about* time?"

Kassa was frowning. "There is no time in the Underworld. Is there in the OtherRealm?"

Sparrow's temper was shortening rapidly. "I don't know, ask a faery." She stopped short. "Oh, these *gritsucking* flowers!" She yanked on one of the bright yellow blooms and it came away from the ground easily, bringing a full-sized faery maiden with it. The maiden's eyes widened in recognition as she saw Kassa. She hid behind a tree. "Please don't hit me."

"Have you been bullying faeries?" asked Sparrow, finally amused by something.

"We've met before," admitted Kassa.

The faery maiden lifted her face and wiped her nose on a sleeve made out of sunshine. "I only came to give the message."

"What message?" snarled Sparrow.

"The message from Mrs Suede!" said the faery maiden unhelpfully.

"What *message*?" Sparrow repeated, starting to believe that all the inhabitants of the OtherRealm were equally moronic. They certainly made her troll tribe look extra smart.

"Um," said the faery maiden, and then brightened. "Oh, yes. She wants to see you!"

All the lights went out. A sudden, uncompromising blackness blotted out everything visible. "Are you there?" whispered Kassa.

"Just about," replied Sparrow. "Where are we this time?"

There was a sneeze.

"Bless you," said both women automatically, and then froze.

"That wasn't you, was it?" Kassa asked.

"Or you," said Sparrow darkly.

Kassa took a deep breath. "So who was it?"

"You *had* to ask."

A spotlight appeared between them. It illuminated a very small figure, busily blowing her nose. She was female, dressed entirely in black leather and shorter than your average ale tankard. She tucked her hanky into her knee-high black boots and stared upwards, shielding her eyes from the spotlight. "I should be taller than this, you know. Still, can't complain. First go and all that. You try manifesting in a mostly illusionary landscape and see what shape you turn out."

"Who are you?" said Kassa in surprise. "And incidentally, where did you get that fabulous outfit?"

"Mrs Suede," the little person introduced herself. She clapped her hands together efficiently. "Shall we get started?"

"Can you help me?" Sparrow asked.

Mrs Suede crossed her eyes and vanished. A moment later she appeared again, perching on Sparrow's shoulder. The spotlight moved accordingly. "You know, I could murder a cup of tea," she said conversationally.

"Well, I'd like to oblige," said Kassa heavily. "But we're out at the moment."

"Hmm," said Mrs Suede, the disapproval obvious in her little voice. She peered into Sparrow's ear. "Is there any particular reason you are letting this poison continue in such a way?"

Sparrow laughed bitterly. "I wasn't aware that I had a choice."

Mrs Suede made a *tsk* sound. "There's always a choice. Particularly in the moonlight dimension." She tapped her boot. "The OtherRealm, as you mortals call it, is rather like being a witch. You can make anything happen, if you want to." She smiled thoughtfully. "We don't even have a stricture about harming none."

"Are you saying I could *will* the liquid gold away?" Sparrow demanded.

"Perhaps," said Mrs Suede with a gleam in her eye. "You never know until you try."

"What will happen when we get back to the real world?"

"That's assuming rather a lot, isn't it?" challenged Mrs Suede. "Get on with it, *do*." She hopped from Sparrow's shoulder to a nearby tree branch.

Kassa looked at Sparrow. "Looks like it's up to you after all."

"Just the way I like it," said Sparrow with a tight grin. She closed her eyes tight, clenched her hands into fists, and exploded into a million tiny pieces. Motes of gold streamed from her mouth and eye sockets, swirling around her whole body.

Kassa stepped back and whispered to Mrs Suede. "Did *you* make the deal with the Brewmistress and the Sultan?"

"No," said another voice, chill and melodic. Lady Luck stepped out of nowhere. With hardly a backwards glance, she waved her hand and made Mrs Suede vanish. "I did."

Sparrow hadn't seen the new arrival. She scrabbled at the grass, blinded by the piercing light. "Take it back!" she demanded wildly, trying to force the liquid gold away from her. "*Take it back!*"

"I suppose so," drawled Lady Luck, not sounding too pleased about it. She waved a hand at the gold cloud which surrounded the tawny-haired mercenary. "Return to me, if you must."

The golden motes swarmed towards the goddess, melding with her skin.

Sparrow yelled with shock as the liquid gold left her. She fell flat on the grass, feeling as if her skin had been peeled off her body. "The faeries were not to be blamed after all," she gasped.

"I should have thought that was obvious," sighed Lady Luck. She nodded a slight salute in the direction of Kassa

Daggersharp. "Next time, perhaps." She faded out of the OtherRealm, leaving Sparrow and Kassa alone.

Sparrow buried her head in her hands. "Did you get the number of that goddess?"

Kassa came over and helped her to her feet. "Are you cured?"

"I think so."

"Right." Kassa pushed up her sleeves in a business-like fashion. "Now it's my turn to do something stupid so we can get out of here. Do you believe in magic?"

"Not really," said Sparrow. It seemed a silly admission under the circumstances.

"Neither do I," laughed Kassa. "That's probably why I get it wrong all the time. Shall we go?"

"Yes."

Kassa clapped her hands, twice. "Dame Veekie!"

They were in darkness again. Somewhere, a candle was lit. Standing behind the circle of warm, waxy yellow light was the godmother-witch Dame Veekie Crosselet, large as life and twice as grey.

Kassa faced her bravely. "I will undertake my own initiation, when and if I choose. I am quite capable of witching without supervision, deciding for *myself* when I am suitably qualified to wreak havoc on the world of magic." She laughed. "It was a con job from the start. I should have known that the whole mentor-initiate thing was about as unwitchy as you get."

Dame Veekie regarded her coldly. "Is that your final word on the matter?"

Kassa put her hands on her hips, which made her feel much better. "It is."

"Well," said Dame Veekie Crosselet. "Congratulations. You're a witch. Or rather. You're not actually a witch. But you could be. If you wanted to. In other words. It's entirely up to you." She blinked.

-§-§-§-§-§-

"But where are we?" pleaded Officer Finnley.

"The OtherRealm," snapped Mistress Opia as they marched through the waist-high reeds of the swamp. "Stop asking questions."

"But how are we going to get home?"

"We're not," said Hobbs the gnome. "Not ever. And it's all her fault, as per usual!"

"Shut up!" snarled the Brewmistress. Her skin was still bright yellow and glowing. But try as hard as she might, she couldn't get the liquid gold to work any more. There was no time in the OtherRealm...and no time travel.

There was a polite cough, and a beige-blonde goddess appeared before them. "Another mess to tidy up," Lady Luck sighed. "You wouldn't *believe* what they threatened to do to me if I didn't obey them." She flicked a finger at Hobbs the gnome. "Go home." Then she flicked a similar finger at Officer Finnley. "Just go."

The two vanished.

Mistress Opia stared at Lady Luck. "It was you who gave me the liquid gold," she accused. "I thought you were..."

"I know, I know," sighed Lady Luck. "You thought I was a representative of the OtherRealm, whereas I was really using both you and them to further my own chaotic whims, blah blah." Her eyes narrowed. "You didn't know what you were getting into the first time around, and I've been ordered to fix it. But the second time...as far as I remember, you said that you didn't care what the price was, as long as you had another dose of liquid gold." The goddess eyed the gold-skinned Brewmistress up and down. "I don't think I actually *have* to do anything about this."

Lady Luck vanished.

Mistress Opia didn't. She stared slowly around her environment. The OtherRealm. The moonlight dimension. The land of the fey. She wondered vaguely if the Fair Folk had any need for a good Brewer, and suspected that it would take a lot of effort to sell them on the idea.

Still, life was all about challenges.

-§-§-§-§-§-

Sparrow swayed slightly and caught hold of the rail to steady herself. She snapped her head around, surveying their surroundings. It was the *Splashdance*. The liquid golden *Splashdance*, still glowing. All was as it should be.

Kassa shook her head slowly. "I could have avoided all that if I'd thought to declare independence from the beginning!"

"May I assume," broke in Aragon Silversword, human-fleshed again, "yet again we have been put through various forms of physical and mental aggravation in order to further *your* own benefit, Princess of Pirates?"

Kassa stared thoughtfully at him. "Do you know what this means?"

"I assume it means that we are all complete idiots for associating ourselves with you," he replied.

"Not that," she said, eyes shining. "It means I'm back in business. All systems go! I'm free." She kissed him suddenly, too quickly for him to protest. "I'm reneging on that no-flirting rule."

Aragon stepped out of range. "I'd guessed."

The newly-restored Daggar caught hold of Sparrow, swinging her up into the air. "Is it over?"

"Completely. No more liquid gold running around inside me." She struggled to get down. "Let me down, rockhead!"

He lowered her slowly, his eyes speculative. "I suppose you still have that sleepy potion on your mouth?"

She shrugged. "Actually, I used up the last on Lord Tangent."

Daggar grinned and leaned forward, but Sparrow quickly ducked the impending kiss. "No, thank you!" she said firmly. "I hardly think you would survive trollish mating rituals."

He shrugged, still amiable. "Worth a try. So you're cured now, and Kassa's alive. What about the future?"

Sparrow glanced at Aragon and Kassa, then back at Daggar. "Better check."

"Right." Daggar strode purposefully towards the ship's wheel. "'Scuse me, Kassa-girl."

Kassa broke off from teasing Aragon to stare at her cousin. "What do you think you're doing?"

Daggar put his hands on the amber crystal. "Unfinished business," he said.

Just as he opened his mouth to command the ship forward in time, something bright, yellow and loud crashed into their field of vision, landing with a splash into the sea.

"What was that?" cried Kassa.

Sparrow dived instantly into the water. A moment later she emerged, dragging the half-unconscious Officer Finnley with her.

"Where have you been?" Daggar demanded.

Finnley spat out a pitiful spout of water and collapsed exhaustedly on the deck.

Kassa glanced at Aragon. "Do you know who...?"

"Not a clue," he replied. "Did you know there were carnations growing under your feet?"

Kassa stared at her own boots, which were rapidly being lifted off the deck as a bunch of bright red and purple flowers sprouted out of the planks. "It's a present," she said. "I think it means the Fair Folk like me."

Chapter 30
Unfinished Business

The nourishing broth which Sparrow produced from various local roots and vegetables perked Officer Finnley up in no time. He lay half-conscious in one of the ship's hammocks, which had been strung up between two trees on the Chiantrian shore.

As Finnley took another mouthful of broth, the golden *Splashdance* reappeared on the beach. Daggar hopped down from the deck and came sauntering along the sand towards the hammock. "We took Kassa on a little jaunt through time, and she grudgingly admits that it might be useful to have access to time travel. She's still mad about the clothes, though." He sniffed heartily. "That soup smells good."

"For invalids only," said Sparrow, slapping his hand away as he reached for the bowl. "This tour of yours. Did it include the future?"

"Briefly."

"And did you…"

Daggar plucked a coin out of his pocket and showed it to her. "Undeniable proof that we changed history and Aragon Silversword will not be Emperor in twenty-three years time."

Sparrow took the coin from him and turned it over, looking at the Imperial head. "Oh," she said.

"Oh," Daggar agreed.

"Still," she said, handing it back. "It should be a better option, yes?"

Daggar put the coin back in a pocket. "Only time will tell. Are you coming?"

Sparrow blinked. "Coming where?"

"Aragon's been trying to convince Kassa that to make things right we have to go forward to where we were when you and I picked him up."

"No more time travel," she groaned.

"Either way, we're setting sail." Daggar glanced at Officer Finnley, who was snoring peacefully in the hammock. "Shall we bring him or leave him?"

"Which would you prefer?"

"Ah, bring him along. I'm sure he'll come in handy."

Together, they untied the rope hammock and began lugging Finnley towards the ship. "A Blackguard and a troll," said Sparrow disparagingly. "You really *do* pick your travelling companions."

"Between you and me," said Daggar, "I'm quite fond of trolls."

Sparrow grinned. "Between you and me…"

"Yes?" he said eagerly, leaning forward to catch whatever she might say.

"I cannot stand profit-scoundrels."

"Oh," he said, sounding disappointed.

As they crossed a patch of particularly bright moonlight, Sparrow stopped in her tracks. "Daggar, the hammock!"

"What about it?'

"It is rope."

"Well, of course it's rope…"

She waggled a handful in his face. "It is white rope."

They dumped Finnley and his hammock in the sand and tore towards the ship, where Kassa and Aragon were still arguing.

"I tell you, what does a week or two matter?" Kassa flung at him.

"Of course it doesn't matter to you, you haven't lived them!" insisted Aragon. "But *we* are overlapping ourselves. Do you have any idea how complicated that could make things?"

"Not if you go to different places," she snapped.

"That is completely irrational. We're nearly two weeks behind in time."

"*You* might be. Given the choice, I'd rather be two weeks younger than older. What is it, Daggar?"

Daggar stamped his boot on the deck and grinned cheerfully. "See for yourself. The liquid gold has worn off. Either that or Lady Luck finally got around to tidying up this particular loose end."

Kassa's eyes went saucer-shaped as she realised what he was telling her. She turned her head this way and that, taking it all in. "My ship!" She cuddled the nearest mast lovingly, relishing its translucent silver quality. "My beautiful ship!" Her eyes glazed over in delirious joy. "Gods, my clothes!" She scrambled down below decks in desperate search of a change of garb.

"Well," said Aragon sarcastically. "I suppose she won the argument, then. We get to repeat the next fortnight."

"No more time travel," said Daggar, grinning all over his unshaven face.

"No more time travel," agreed Sparrow, her own smile stretching from ear to ear.

For once, they were perfectly in agreement.

Aragon gave them both a disgusted look. "I don't understand you people. Do you have no conception of the opportunity we have lost here?"

"Just think," said Daggar slyly. "With power like that at your fingertips, you could have made yourself Emperor or something."

Sparrow stepped on his foot.

-§-§-§-§-§-

The *Silver Splashdance* set sail toward the easterly coast of Mocklore. Dressed in a purple leather bodice, swishing black skirts and half a ton of glittering silver, Kassa was at the wheel. Aragon was lost in his own thoughts. Daggar dealt out a hand of Kraken's Curse to Sparrow, Singespitter and the grey-furred kitten, explaining the rules as he laid out the cards. All was right with the world, and Officer Finnley looked worried.

Finally, Kassa whirled around and pointed a finger at him. "All right, who are you? I *know* I know you."

Embarrassed, he straightened his Blackguard uniform and shuffled forward. "Officer Finnley McHagrty, Dreadnought Blackguard," he mumbled.

Kassa snapped her fingers. "I used to babysit you! How's your ma?"

Finnley drew out his standard-issue cutlass and tested the point mournfully. "Just the same. I was sorry to hear about Bigbeard dying and that, um. Condolences."

Kassa moved towards the pile of assorted swords and other weapons that Aragon had dumped on the deck. "Yes, well he's quite settled in the Underworld. Plenty of rum, you know." She selected a rapier and flexed her hand thoughtfully. "Shall we get started?"

"Is it too much to ask what you two are doing?" put in Aragon, as Kassa and Finnley began to circle each other, swords drawn.

"He's a McHagrty," she said, as if it were obvious.

"She's a Daggersharp," agreed Finnley.

"There's a feud."

And the swords clashed together.

The duel was swift, and brief. Finnley may have passed with full marks at Blackguard school, but he was no match for a determined pirate wench in a purple bodice. She danced her rapier at a distance for a while until she got bored, then slammed him bodily against the mast and flipped him over the side of the ship.

Daggar applauded.

"I'll lower a rope!" Kassa called.

Finnley, who knew a good chance when he saw it, was already making strong swimming strokes towards the coastline. "I'll be right!" he called over his shoulder, splashing madly.

"Oi!" Kassa yelled after him. "I won! That means you owe me a year of service or your weight in sailcloth, right?"

Finnley just kept on determinedly swimming, putting

as much distance as possible between himself and the *Silver Splashdance*.

Kassa turned to face her crew, hands firmly planted on hips. "Well?" she demanded. "Isn't anyone going to fetch him for me?"

Her crew all suddenly found excuses to avoid eye contact with her.

Kassa glared at them all. "Is this what you call loyalty?"

There was a splash. Singespitter the sheep, paddling like mad, was in the water and heading towards the escaping Blackguard. As the crew all watched in amazement, the sheep overtook Officer Finnley and seized his collar between its jaws. Then, very slowly, it began tugging the Blackguard back to the ship.

Closing her mouth with a snap, Kassa turned to stare at Daggar. He grinned back at her, giving her his best and most winsome expression. "All right," she sighed. "The sheep can stay."

While everyone watched the rescue attempt, no one saw the little grey kitten move towards the stern. Slowly, it clambered up on the rail and dropped into the sea. It bobbed in the water for a few moments, and then vanished.

-§-§-§-§-§-

Morning came and went. Most of the crew were asleep, or nearly so. Singespitter watched over Officer Finnley in the hold, in case he made a break for it again. Kassa was still alert, steering the ship over and through the most dangerous rocky areas, just for entertainment's sake. Nothing could actually damage the *Silver Splashdance*, and it was fun to startle fishermen.

As she tired of playing eye-spy with herself and started counting trees, Kassa saw a sudden flash of light. A huge plume of black smoke rose upwards, dark against the bright blue sky.

Kassa nudged Daggar, the nearest sleeping crew member, with her boot. "Take a look at that."

He mumbled awake. "What whaaa danger?"

"No danger," Kassa assured him. "Just look at that smoke."

Daggar raised himself up slightly and stared into the distance. "Oh, that." He nudged Sparrow, who had been asleep on his shoulder. "Hey, troll woman. Up and at 'em."

She awoke instantly, her narrow green eyes focusing on him. "What is wrong?"

"Nothing's wrong," he assured her. "Look out there. The temple just exploded."

Sparrow lifted her head up and looked inland. Her face creased into a faint smile. "So it did. There we go again."

"Is there a story behind that?" asked Kassa curiously.

Daggar grinned, and yawned. "Save it for a rainy day. I'm starving. What's for breakfast?"

"Lunch," corrected Sparrow.

As they spread out the unappetising dregs of their supplies (liquid gold, it now appeared, had the side effect of making food soggy), a sudden thought occurred to Kassa. "What did you people do with Tippett?"

"Tippett who?" asked Daggar with his mouth full.

Aragon, now pretending never actually being asleep, prodded distastefully at a pile of what may or may not have been dried apple. "Last I saw, he was performing a certain epic poem in front of a tavern audience."

Kassa looked supremely flattered. "That epic he was writing about me?"

"I suppose so," drawled Aragon.

"When?" she demanded. "When is he performing it?"

Aragon thought about it. "Tonight, actually. In a tavern, halfway between here and Zibria."

"Right." Kassa stood up and headed for the helm. "This I want to see."

Daggar almost choked on his lunch. "Are you serious? We can't go inland—we'll cross paths with ourselves."

"How else do you suggest we get Tippett back?" Kassa turned the ship expertly towards the shore.

"Why bother?" insisted Daggar. "All he ever did was sit around and compose poetry about you."

"I like that in a man," she snapped. "Besides, I have a strong sense of responsibility for my crew."

"Since when?" challenged Aragon.

Kassa whirled around to face him. "Don't you start!"

"No, really Kassa," he said mildly. "At what point do we become responsible for ourselves? If you're going to make a habit of dying and leaving us in the lurch, surely you should encourage us to be more independent."

"Aragon, I can't help it if you took my death personally!"

They stared at each other in silence. Thick, meaningful silence.

"Um, Kassa-girl," said Daggar apologetically. "We're heading towards a certain recently-exploded temple."

She turned back to the helm, impatient. "So?"

"That's where I am!" he said frantically.

"Why didn't you say so?"

Daggar moaned. "Kassa, I can cope with another Sparrow and even a second Singespitter, but please don't make me meet myself."

She sent the ship careering in a more northerly direction across country. "How's that?"

"Fine," said Aragon, appearing at her elbow. "But slow the ship down to a crawl, otherwise you will overtake me."

Kassa smacked the side of the ship with her fist. "I hate time travel! It's so bloody constricting."

-§-§-§-§-§-

It was dark. Having parked the ship behind the stables, Kassa and Aragon crept on foot towards the tavern. Kassa peeped through the window, waving as she saw Tippett, but Aragon grabbed her hand and pulled her out of sight. "You can't go in there yet," he cautioned.

"Why not?" she protested.

"Because my past self is currently up on a balcony listening to your pet jester make his recital. Wait a few minutes."

"And then I can go in and get him?"

Aragon shrugged. "Let him finish first. It's a big moment in his little career."

Kassa looked at him in surprise. "Thoughtfulness, Aragon? Surely not."

"You never know," he replied, steering her away from the window.

"But I can't hear him," she complained, looking back at the jester poet who was busily declaiming his opus to a tavern full of yobs.

"There are some things a person shouldn't hear," said Aragon. "You'll just get conceited."

"Hmm." Kassa was barely able to make out his face in the shadows outside the tavern. "Aragon?"

"What?"

"You've got your arm around my waist."

"So I have."

Kassa smiled. "Planning to do anything about that?"

"You know, it's entirely possible?"

A voice cut into the cozy darkness. "Well, well. Aragon Silversword. I *do* hope I'm not interrupting anything."

Aragon broke away from Kassa, staring at the newcomer. "Bounty."

"Bounty," mimicked the hobgoblin bounty-hunter, striking a pose in the darkened doorway. "I have a nasty little suspicion that there are two of you in this tavern. Please say it isn't so. The concept of two Aragon Silverswords running around in the world is too much for any lass to cope with."

"It's temporary," he assured her. "A…side effect of time travel."

"Oh," she said, eyes dancing. "So if I bump into the other you in the next couple of days…"

"Weeks," he corrected. "Be gentle with me."

"As ever." Bounty's eye fell on Kassa, who was working hard to look neutral and in no way curious. "Well, now. This must be the legendary Kassa Daggersharp." She ran an appraising glance over the other woman, and then turned to Aragon. "The reports of her demise…"

"Greatly exaggerated," he agreed.

"I'll leave you to it then." Bounty tilted her face up expectantly to Aragon, and he kissed her on both cheeks. "Until I hear anything to the contrary, I'll assume you're in good hands." She smirked at them both, and sauntered away down the road, her hips swaying neatly back and forth.

Kassa frowned thoughtfully. "Who was that?"

"An old acquaintance," Aragon replied, watching Bounty disappear into the shadows.

"Should I be jealous?"

"Do you want to be?"

Kassa turned towards the tavern window. "He's finished. They're applauding, at least. Hate to think I'd come all this way to see him concussed by a flying tomato." She pushed open the heavy tavern door and yelled into its smoky atmosphere. "Tippett! Get your bony butt out here on the double!"

The little jester-poet pushed his spectacles up his nose and stared in her direction. "Kassa, is that you?"

She tapped her boot meaningfully. "Are you coming or what?"

Not one to be told twice, Tippett grabbed his piles of parchment and scurried out towards her. "Gosh," he said.

The three of them walked together to the stables and found the ship there, its mast casting a silvery shadow in the darkness. "Jump aboard and start introducing yourself to our new crew members," said Kassa.

"Right," said Tippett, heading obediently for the ship.

Aragon caught Kassa's sleeve as she attempted to follow Tippett. "You didn't answer my question."

"No," she said. "I didn't, did I?" She removed his hand from her sleeve, but held onto it, her fingers lacing into his. "Come on. We've got a horizon to sail into."

-§-§-§-§-§-

Skeylles the Fishy Judge, Lord of the Underwater, sat in his bath. He hummed loudly to himself as he scrubbed his back with a conch shell.

The lobster-shaped butler appeared in the entrance to the bone-tiled hall. His nose was firmly in the air, and his left claw held a small, bedraggled half-grown grey ball of fur. "Yours, I believe, milord," he said snootily.

"Ah," said Skeylles, pleased. He held out a hand, and the butler dropped the kitten into it as if he was pleased to divest himself of the creature. Skeylles tickled the kitten under the chin. "Everything Sorted Out?" he boomed.

The little cat stared back, a flicker of intelligence in its little eyes.

"Good," said Skeylles, settling back into his bath. "All Is As It Should Be." He dropped the little grey furball down with the other cats, who were busily swarming around the legs of his bath. "More Or Less," he added.

-§-§-§-§-§-

The horizon was still some way off. The silvery ghost-ship glided soundlessly over meadows and moors. Its crew were having a whale of a time, partying the night away. Tippett had found a harmonica somewhere and was noisily setting his Kassa Daggersharp epic to a jaunty tune. Daggar sang noisily along, while Sparrow taught him how to cheat at arm wrestling. Singespitter and Officer Finnley were sharing a bottle of rum they had found in the hold.

Aragon came up behind Kassa as she stood at the helm. "You've extended the crew rather successfully," he told her, not sounding as if he altogether approved.

"By another two, I should think," she added, pointing ahead.

Aragon followed her gaze and saw a fellow in a pastel pink suit hovering by the edge of a forest with a pile of luggage and a bright orange sprite. They were hopefully waggling their thumbs, a long-established gesture for hitch-hikers. "Kassa…" he said warningly.

"Oh, don't fuss," she smiled, pulling the ghost-ship to a slow stop. "They'll liven things up."

"You want things livened *up*?"

The hitch-hiking god and orange ex-guardian sprite were welcomed aboard with a raucous cheer and two mugs of bubbled wine. They joined the party.

Kassa shivered in the night air, and Aragon put his cloak around her. "I'm not sharing a cabin with them," he said.

She leaned her head back against his shoulder. Her hair smelled of sea-salt. "Actually, I was wondering if you would like to share one with me."

He gave her a quirky look. "The Captain's cabin?"

"Nothing but the best," she teased. As she turned to face him, her face sobered. "Aragon, I know what you're thinking."

"Now there's a surprise."

"You have a decision to make," she insisted. "You don't have the witchmark any more. You are not compelled to stay on this mad ship of mine. If you do…it will be because you want to. *Only* because you want to." She moved away from his arms. "I want to go say hello to the Dark One and Vervain. Think about it." She squeezed his hand briefly, and went to get herself some bubbled wine.

"Right," said Aragon Silversword, staring out at the dark landscape. He had filched a coin from Daggar for this very purpose. He flipped it over his fingers now, considering his options. "Heads I get off this ship and get a life of my own," he muttered. "Tails I do something I will probably regret."

He threw the coin, and watched it spiral up into the air. It fell smartly into his hand and he slapped it hard against his other arm. Very slowly, he lifted his hand and stared into the face of Kassa Daggersharp. It was quite a good likeness. Some years older, of course. He traced the lines of the coin thoughtfully, reading the date.

Then he opened his hand, and let the coin fall into the darkness. They were crossing marshland, weren't they? Hopefully the evidence would be gone for good. But he couldn't forget it. An omen, perhaps? It had been heads, after all.

The real Kassa came forward, grabbing his arm. Her smile was warm and inviting, full of life. "Come on. You're missing a great party."

"I hate parties," he reminded her, but let her draw him towards the others.

After all, he could pack his bags and get a life of his own at any time. It didn't have to be tonight. Or tomorrow, for that matter. He could wait until the day after that. Or the day after that.

Aragon Silverword didn't join in the laughing and singing with the pirate wench, the profit-scoundrel, the troll-raised mercenary, the sprite, the god, the Blackguard and the sheep. He still retained some standards, after all. He sat silently and watched Kassa Daggersharp enjoying herself, her dark red hair glinting in the silver light of their ship.

Kassa noticed him looking, and tilted her head speculatively in his direction. In answer to her unspoken question, Aragon Silversword leaned back against the mast of the *Silver Splashdance* and almost smiled.

ABOUT THE AUTHOR

Tansy Rayner Roberts was first published in 1998 with *Splashdance Silver*, the first of the Mocklore Chronicles. Since then, she has had nine more novels published (two under the name of Livia Day), travelled overseas, won a bunch of awards including a couple of shiny chrome rockets, gained a PhD in Classics, and had two children. She lives in a messy house with lots of bookshelves. Sometimes the Tasmanian landscape still looks like Mocklore to her, but she is yet to spot a flying sheep.

Tansy is the winner of the Hugo, Washington Small Press, Aurealis and Ditmar Awards, and a co-host on two all-female podcasts: Galactic Suburbia, talking about books and the SF publishing industry, and the Verity! podcast, talking about Doctor Who. She is also the co-editor of *Cranky Ladies of History*, with Tehani Wessely. Tansy's website can be found at http://tansyrr.com/ and you can follow her on Twitter at @tansyrr or listen to her podcasting her own fiction serials at Sheep Might Fly.

Look for our ebook-only collection and more FableCroft books at our website:

http://fablecroft.com.au/

The Rebirth of Rapunzel: A Mythic Biography of the Maiden in the Tower
by Kate Forsyth
Havenstar by Glenda Larke
Pratchett's Women by Tansy Rayner Roberts
50 Roman Mistresses by Tansy Rayner Roberts
The Bone Chime Song and Other Stories by Joanne Anderton
Guardian by Jo Anderton

The Mocklore Chronicles by Tansy Rayner Roberts
Splashdance Silver
Liquid Gold
Ink Black Magic

Isles of Glory trilogy by Glenda Larke
The Aware
Gilfeather
The Tainted

Worlds Next Door edited by Tehani Wessely
Australis Imaginarium edited by Tehani Wessely
After the Rain edited by Tehani Wessely
Epilogue edited by Tehani Wessely
One Small Step edited by Tehani Wessely
Phantazein edited by Tehani Wessely
Cranky Ladies of History
edited by Tansy Rayner Roberts & Tehani Wessely
Insert Title Here edited by Tehani Wessely
Focus 2014: highlights of Australian short fiction edited by Tehani Wessely
Focus 2013: highlights of Australian short fiction edited by Tehani Wessely
Focus 2012: highlights of Australian short fiction edited by Tehani Wessely
Canterbury 2100: Pilgrimages in a New World edited by Dirk Flinthart
Striking Fire by Dirk Flinthart
Path of Night by Dirk Flinthart
"Sanction" by Dirk Flinthart
"Flower and Weed" by Margo Lanagan
To Spin a Darker Stair
by Catherynne M Valente & Faith Mudge

Coming Soon:
In Your Face edited by Tehani Wessely
Bounty by Tansy Rayner Roberts

Ink Black Magic
by Tansy Rayner Roberts
ISBN: 978-0-9874000-0-0

Because sometimes, it takes cleavage and big skirts to save the world from those crazy teenagers.

Kassa Daggersharp has been a pirate, a witch, a menace to public safety, a villain, a hero and a legend. These days, she lectures first year students on the dangers of magic, at the Polyhedrotechnical in Cluft.

Egg Friefriedsson is Kassa's teenage cousin, a lapsed Axgaard warrior who would rather stay in his room and draw comics all day than hang out with his friends. If only comics had been invented.

Aragon Silversword is missing, presumed dead.

All the adventures are over. It's time to get on with being a grownup. But when Egg's drawings come to life, including an evil dark city full of villains and monsters, everyone starts to lose their grip on reality. Even the flying sheep.

Kassa and Egg are not sure who are the heroes and who are the villains anymore, but someone has to step up to save Mocklore, one last time.

...surprisingly layered...complex and ambitious...
— Jim C Hines

...fun fantasy adventure...that brings to mind Terry Prachett's Discworld...
— Carolyn Cushman, Locus

Shortlisted for the 2013 Aurealis Award for Best Fantasy Novel

Cranky Ladies of History
Edited by Tansy Rayner Roberts & Tehani Wessely
ISBN: 978-0-9922844-9-7

Warriors, pirates, murderers and queens…

Throughout history, women from all walks of life have had good reason to be cranky. Some of our most memorable historical figures were outspoken, dramatic, brave, feisty, rebellious and downright ornery.

Cranky Ladies of History is a celebration of 22 women who challenged conventional wisdom about appropriate female behaviour, from the ancient world all the way through to the twentieth century. Some of our protagonists are infamous and iconic, while others have been all but forgotten under the heavy weight of history.

Sometimes you have to break the rules before the rules break you.

Featuring work by Juliet Marillier, Garth Nix, Jane Yolen, Deborah Biancotti, Kirstyn McDermott and many more…

Cranky Ladies of History *is an important collection of fiction that gives voice to an extraordinary selection of women from a broad range of backgrounds, eras and cultures. I wouldn't hesitate to recommend it.*
—Book'd Out

Shortlisted for the 2016 Ditmar Award for Best Anthology

fablecroft.com.au

Striking Fire
by Dirk Flinthart
ISBN: 978-0-9807770-7-9

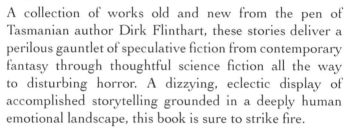

A lonely, overweight vampire tends a sleazy video store in inner-city Sydney…

A multi-billionaire sacrifices everything to become Earth's first ambassador to the stars…

A legendary time-travelling assassin finds himself pitted against the greatest detective that never was…

A young father goes to extraordinary lengths to save his child after a car accident…

A collection of works old and new from the pen of Tasmanian author Dirk Flinthart, these stories deliver a perilous gauntlet of speculative fiction from contemporary fantasy through thoughtful science fiction all the way to disturbing horror. A dizzying, eclectic display of accomplished storytelling grounded in a deeply human emotional landscape, this book is sure to strike fire.

Shortlisted for the 2015 Aurealis Award for Best Collection

fablecroft.com.au

One Small Step, an anthology of discoveries
edited by Tehani Wessely
ISBN: 978-0-9874000-0-0

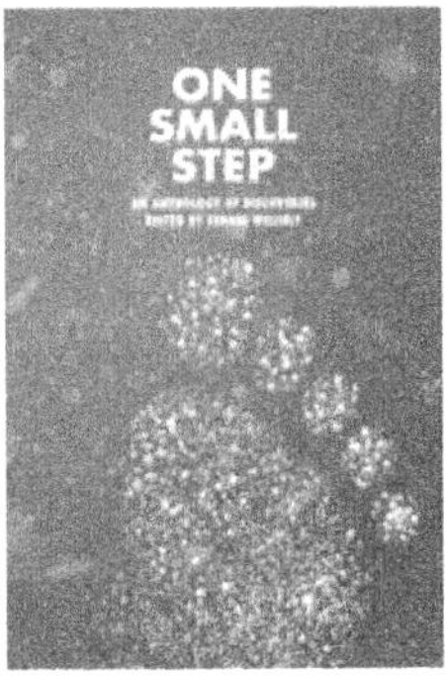

Sixteen stories of discovery from Australia's best writers. Each story in some way addresses the idea of discoveries, new beginnings, or literal or figurative "small steps", but each story takes you to places you far beyond the one small step you imagine...

Journey through worlds and explore the reaches of the universe with this collection.

CONTENTS

Foreword by Marianne de Pierres
"Sand and Seawater" by Joanne Anderton & Rabia Gale
"Indigo Gold" by Deborah Biancotti
"Firefly Epilogue" by Jodi Cleghorn
"The Ways of the Wyrding Women" by Rowena Cory Daniells
"The ships of Culwinna" by Thoraiya Dyer
"Shadows" by Kate Gordon
"By Blood and Incantation" by Lisa L. Hannett & Angela Slatter
"Ella and the Flame" by Kathleen Jennings
"Original" by Penny Love
"Always Greener" by Michelle Marquardt
"Morning Star" by DK Mok
"Winter's Heart"by Faith Mudge
"Cold White Daughter" by Tansy Rayner Roberts
"Baby Steps" by Barbara Robson
"Daughters of Battendown" by Cat Sparks
"Number 73 Glad Avenue" by Suzanne J Willis

Winner of the 2013 Aurealis Award for Best Anthology

fablecroft.com.au

Path of Night
by Dirk Flinthart
ISBN: 978-0-9807770-8-6

Michael Devlin is the first of a new breed. The way things are going, he may also be the last.

Being infected with an unknown disease is bad. Waking up on a slab in a morgue wearing nothing but a toe-tag is worse, even if it comes with a strange array of new abilities.

Medical student Michael Devlin is in trouble. With his flatmates murdered and an international cabal of legendary man-monsters on his trail, Devlin's got nowhere to hide. His only allies are a hot-tempered Sydney cop and a mysterious monster-hunter who may be setting Devlin up for the kill. If he's going to survive, Devlin will have to embrace his new powers and confront his hunters. But can he hold onto his humanity when he walks the *Path of Night*?

Dirk Flinthart is an Australian writer of speculative fiction who lives in northern Tasmania. Notable to date mostly for short stories, he is also the editor of the Canterbury 2100 anthology, from Agog press, and has the distinction of sharing a Ditmar award with Margo Lanagan, which he is quite proud of.

Path of Night *represents Flinthart's longest published work to date, and is planned as the first in a series of stories centering around Michael Devlin. The next one is well under way...*

...action driven, laced with humor...I am hoping that there will be a sequel. —Roger Ross (Amazon)

fablecroft.com.au

Guardian
by Jo Anderton
ISBN: 978-0-9922844-4-2

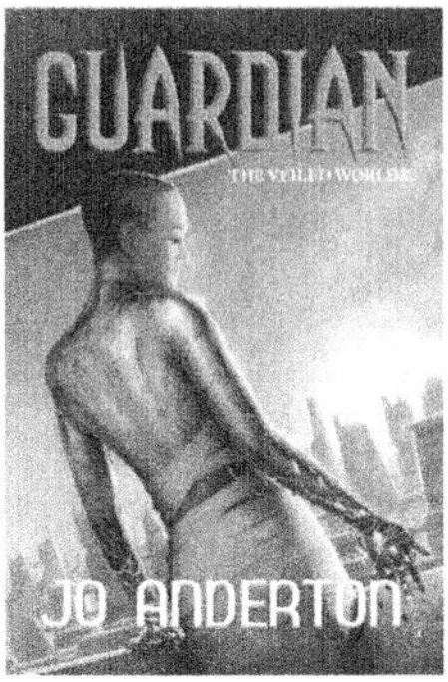

The grand city of Movoc-under-Keeper lies in ruins. The sinister puppet men have revealed their true nature, and their plan to tear down the veil between worlds. To have a chance of defeating them, Tanyana must do the impossible, and return to the world where they were created, on the other side of the veil. Her journey will force her into a terrible choice, and test just how much she is willing to sacrifice for the fate of two worlds.

Praise for The Veiled Worlds series:

"...a tremendously satisfying conclusion to an already celebrated series. ...Anderton is to be commended for her ability to create such rich and original settings."
—Alex Stephenson, Aurealis #72

"Refreshingly original..."—The Guardian

"Impressively combines far-future world-building, conspiracies, and a redemption quest..."
—Publishers' Weekly

"Anderton demonstrates a mastery of storytelling and world building"—Library Journal

Worlds Next Door
edited by Tehani Wessely
ISBN: 978-0-9807770-1-7

What you have here is not a book, but a key to worlds that exist under your bed, in your cupboard, in the dark of night when you're sure you're being watched. What you have is a passport to the worlds next door.

Containing 25 bite-sized stories for 9–13 year olds by Australian authors including Paul Collins, Michael Pryor, Pamela Freeman, Dirk Flinthart, Tansy Rayner Roberts and Jenny Blackford, *Worlds Next Door* is perfect for the budding reader.

"...a completely satisfying, wonderful collection..." — Aurealis Xpress

"There are so many excellent stories in this collection..." — Daniel Simpson

"...a fab little anthology..." — ASif!

"...a book that gives us tempting little slices of cleverness in the realm of magical writing..." — Kids' Book Review

"I love the diversity of this collection." — Kids' Book Capers

"An engaging collection of speculative fiction ... this is an excellent collection for both the library and the English faculty." — ReadPlus

fablecroft.com.au

Insert Title Here
edited by Tehani Wessely
ISBN: 978-0-9807770-0-0

On the [date redacted] of the [year redacted], [names redacted] of the [organisation redacted] discovered a hidden text that documented realities other than our own.

Dark, weird realities.

Within these pages they discovered monuments to a dying alien race, sentient islands caught like fish, a tree that grows pencils, a baby transformed into a hummingbird, and a steampunk Maori whaling crew.

They were afraid, as you should be afraid. They saw life, death and the space between; metamorphosis, terrible choices and bitter regrets.

[Names redacted] looked into the abyss, and what they saw within was nameless and terrible.

This is that book.

Enter if you dare.

<<Insert Title Here>>

...consistently astounding world-building. Story after story explores unfamiliar realms – and story after story succeeds in making those realms blindingly convincing. As the title suggests, the possibilities in these stories are endless...
—Joelene Pynnonen

...every single story is heart-breaking or grim or absurdly strange and wonderful, and all are incredibly read-able.
—Katharine Stubbs

fablecroft.com.au

Phantazein
edited by Tehani Wessely
ISBN: 978-0-9922844-9-7

You think you know all the fables that have ever been told. You think you can no longer be surprised by stories. Think again. With origins in myth, fairytales, folklore and pure imagination, the stories and poems in these pages draw on history that never was and worlds that will never be to create their own unique tales and traditions…

The next generation of storytellers is here.

Faith Mudge / Twelfth
Tansy Rayner Roberts / The love letters of swans
Thoraiya Dyer / Bahamut
Rabia Gale / The village of no women
Jenny Blackford / The Lady of Wild Things
Suzanne J. Willis / Rag and bone heart
Nicole Murphy / A Cold Day
Vida Cruz / How the Jungle Got Its Spirit Guardian
S.G. Larner / Kneaded
Charlotte Nash / The Ghost of Hephaestus
Cat Sparks / The Seventh Relic
Gitte Christensen / The nameless seamstress
Foz Meadows / Scales of Time (poem) reprint
Moni / Illustrations Scales of Time
Kathleen Jennings / Cover Art

…kudos to the writers who took long raked over material in a lot of cases and breathed life and originality in to them.
—Sean Wright

…there wasn't a story that disappointed…
— A Fantastical Librarian

…beautifully told with richly woven worlds and characters I want to know more about. —Welcome to My Library

Shortlisted for the 2014 Aurealis Award for Best Anthology and the 2014 Ditmar Award for Best Collection

fablecroft.com.au

CPSIA information can be obtained
at www.ICGtesting.com
Printed in the USA
BVOW09s1155210517
484763BV00001B/140/P
9 780994 469038